Sinister Street

by Compton MacKenzie

Chapter I: *The New World*

FROM a world of daisies as big as moons and of mountainous green hillocks Michael Fane came by some unrealized method of transport to the thin red house, that as yet for his mind could not claim an individual existence amid the uniformity of a long line of fellows. His arrival coincided with a confusion of furniture, with the tramp of men backwards and forwards from a cavernous vehicle very dry and dusty. He found himself continually being lifted out of the way of washstands and skeleton chests of drawers. He was invited to sit down and keep quiet, and almost in the same breath to walk about and avoid hindrance. Finally, Nurse led him up many resonant stairs to the night-nursery which at present consisted of two square cots that with japanned iron bars stood gauntly in a wilderness of oilcloth surrounded by four walls patterned with a prolific vegetation. Michael was dumped down upon a grey pillow and invited to see how well his sister Stella was behaving. Nurse's observation was true enough: Stella was rosily asleep in an undulation of blankets, and Michael, threatened by many whispers and bony finger-shakes, was not at all inclined to wake her up. Nurse retired in an aura of importance, and Michael set out to establish an intimacy with the various iron bars of his cage. For a grown-up person these would certainly have seemed much more alike than even the houses of Carlington Road, West Kensington: for Michael each bar possessed a personality. Minute scratches unnoticed by the heedless adult world lent variety of expression: slight irregularities infused certain groups with an air of deliberate consultation. From the four corners royal bars, crowned with brass, dominated their subjects. Passions, intrigues, rumours, ambitions, revenges were perceived by Michael to be seething below the rigid exterior of these iron bars: even military operations were sometimes discernible. This cot was guarded by a romantic population, with one or two of whose units Michael could willingly have dispensed: one bar in particular, set very much askew, seemed sly and malignant. Michael disliked being looked at by anybody or anything, and this bar had a persistent inquisitiveness which already worried him. 'Why does he look at me?' Michael would presently ask, and 'Nobody wants to look at such an ugly little boy,' Nurse would presently reply. So one more intolerable question would overshadow his peace of mind.

Meanwhile, far below, the tramp of men continued, until suddenly an immense roar filled the room. Some of the bars shivered and clinked, and Michael's heart nearly stopped. The roar died away only to be succeeded by another roar from the opposite direction. Stella woke up crying. Michael was too deeply frightened so to soothe himself, as he sat clutching the pointed ears of the grey pillow. Stella, feeling that the fretful tears of a sudden awakening were insufficient, set up a bellow of dismay. Michael was motionless, only aware of a gigantic heart that shook him horribly. At last the footsteps of Nurse could be heard, and over them, the quick 'tut-tut-tuts' that voiced her irritation.

"You naughty boy, to wake up your little sister."

"What was that noise?" asked Michael.

"Your own noise," said Nurse sharply.

"It wasn't. It was lions."

"And if it *was* lions, what next?" said Nurse. "Lions will always come, when little boys are naughty. Lions don't like naughty boys."

"Michael doesn't like lions."

He took refuge in the impersonal speech of earlier days, and with a grave obstinacy of demeanour resisted the unreasonableness of his nurse.

"What was that noise, Nanny? Do tell me."

"Why a train, of course. There's a molly-coddle. Tut-tut!"

"A train like we rode in from down in the country?"

"Yes, a train like we rode in from down in the country!" Nurse mimicked him in an outrageous falsetto.

"Not lions at all?"

"Not if you're a good boy."

"Nor bears—nor tigers—nor wolverines?"

The last was a dreadful importation of fancy from some zoological gift-book.

"Now that's enough," Nurse decided.

"Nor laughing hyenas?"

"Am I to speak to you again? As if there wasn't enough to do without children why-why-whying morning, noon and night."

Michael recognized finality of argument. The mention of morning, noon and night with their dreary suggestion of the infinite and unattainable plunged him into silence. Nurse, gratified by her victory and relieved to find that Stella was crooning happy mysteries to a rag doll, announced that she was prepared in return for the very best behaviour to push the two cots against the window. This done, she left the children to their first survey of London airs, to silent wonder amid the cheeping of countless sparrows.

Stella sat blinking at the light and the sailing clouds. She soon began to chant her saga. Primitive and immemorial sounds flowed from that dewy mouth; melodies and harmonies, akin to the day itself, voiced the progress of the clouds; and while she told her incommunicable delight there was actually no one to say 'Stella, will you stop that 'umming?' Michael could not compete with his sister in her interpretation of the clouds' courses. He had, indeed, tried once or twice; but Stella either stopped abruptly, leaving him to lag for a while with a lame tune of his own, or else she would burst into tears. Michael preferred an inspiration more immediately visual to Stella's incomprehensibly boundless observations. Michael would enjoy holding in his hand a bunch of blue cornflowers; Stella would tear them to pieces, not irritably, but absently in a seclusion of spacious visions. On this occasion Michael paid no attention to Stella's salutation of light; he was merely thankful she showed no sign of wishing to be amused by 'peep-bo,' or by the pulling of curious faces. Both these diversions were dangerous to Michael's peace of mind, because at some period of the entertainment he was bound, with disastrous results, to cross the line between Stella's joy and Stella's fear. Michael turned to look out of the window, finding the details of the view enthralling. He marked first of all the long row of poplar trees already fresh and vivid with young May's golden green. Those trees, waving with their youthfulness in the wind, extended as far as could be observed on either side. Three in every garden were planted close to the farthest wall. How beautiful they looked, and how the sparrows hopped from branch to branch. Michael let his eyes rove along the pleasant green line whose slightness and evenness caressed the vision, as velvet might have caressed a hand running lightly over the surface. Suddenly, with a sharp emotion of shame, Michael perceived that the middle tree opposite his own window was different from the rest. It was not the same shape; it carried little blobs such as hang from tablecloths and curtains; it scarcely showed a complete leaf. Here was a subject for speculation indeed; and the more Michael looked at the other trees, the more he grew ashamed for the loiterer. This problem would worry him interminably: he would return to it often and often. But the exquisite pleasure he had taken in the trim and equable row was gone; for as soon as the eye caressed it, there was this intolerably naked tree to affront all regularity.

After the trees, Michael examined the trellis that extended along the top of a stuccoed wall without interruption on either side. This trellis was a curiosity, for if he looked at it very hard, the lozenges of space came out from their frame and moved about in a blur—an odd business presumably inexplicable for evermore like everything else. Beyond the trellis was the railway; and while Michael was looking a signal shot down, a distant roar drew near, and a real train rumbled past which, beheld from Michael's window, looked like a toy train loaded with dolls, one of whom wore a red tam-o'-shanter. Michael longed to be sitting once again in that moving wonderland and to be looking out of the window, himself wearing just such another red tam-o'-shanter. Beyond the railway was surely a very extraordinary place indeed, with mountains of coal everywhere and black figures roaming about; and beyond this, far far away, was a very low line of houses with a church steeple against an enormous sky.

"Dinner-time! Tut-tut," said Nurse, suddenly bustling into the room to interrupt Stella's saga and Michael's growing dread of being left alone in that wilderness beyond the railway lines.

"Could I be left there?" he asked.

"Left where?"

"There." He pointed to the coal-yard.

"Don't point!" said Nurse.

"What is that place?"

"The place where coal comes from."

"Could I be left there?" he persisted.

"Not unless one of the coalmen came over the wall and carried you off and left you there, which he will do unless you're a good boy."

Michael caught his breath.

"Can coalmen climb?" he asked, choking at the thought.

"Climb like kittens," said Nurse.

A new bogey had been created, black and hairy with yellow cat's eyes and horrid prehensile arms.

Michael and Stella were now lifted out of the cots and dumped on to the cold oilcloth and marched into the adjacent bathroom, where their faces and hands were sponged with a new sponge that was not only rough in itself, but also had something that scratched buried in one of the pores. During this operation, Nurse blew violent breaths through her tightly closed lips. When it was over, Stella was lifted up into Nurse's arms; Michael was commanded to walk downstairs in front and not to let go of the banisters; then down they went, down and down and down—past three doors opening into furniture-heaped rooms, past a door with upper panels of coloured glass in a design of red and amber sparrows upon a crude blue vegetation—a beautiful door, Michael thought, as he went by. Down and down and down into the hall which was strewn with bits of straw and shavings and had another glass-panelled door very gaudy. Here the floor was patterned with terra-cotta, yellow, black and slate-blue tiles. Two more doors were passed, and a third door was reached, opening apparently on a box into which light was let through windows of such glass as is seen round the bottom of bird-cages. This final staircase was even in the fullest daylight very dim and eerie, and was permeated always with a smell of burnt grease and damp cloths. Half-way down Michael shrunk back against Nurse's petticoats, for in front of him yawned a terrible cavern exuding chill.

"What's that?" he gasped.

"Bless the boy, he'll have me over!" cried Nurse.

"Oh, Nanny, what is it—that hole? Michael doesn't like that hole."

"There's a milksop. Tut-tut! Frightened by a coal-cellar! Get on with you, do."

Michael, holding tightly to the banisters, achieved the ground and was hustled into the twilight of the morning-room. Stella was fitted into her high chair; the circular tray was brought over from behind and thumped into its place with a click: Michael was lifted up and thumped down into another high chair and pushed close up to the table so that his knees were chafed by the sharp edge and his thighs pinched by a loose strand of cane. Nurse, blowing as usual through closed lips, cut up his meat, and dinner was carried through in an atmosphere of greens and fat and warm, milk-and-water and threats of Gregory-powder, if every bit were not eaten.

Presently the tramping of furniture-men was renewed and the morning-room, was made darker still by the arrival of a second van which pulled up at right angles to the first. In the course of dinner, Cook entered. She was a fat masculine creature who always kept her arms folded beneath a coarse and spotted apron; and after Cook came Annie the housemaid, tall and thin and anæmic. These two watched the children eating, while they gossiped with Nurse.

"Isn't Mrs. Fane coming at all, then?" enquired Cook.

"For a few minutes—for a few minutes," said Nurse quickly, and Michael would not have been so very suspicious had he not observed the nodding of her head long after there was any need to nod it.

"Is mother going to stay with us?" he asked.

"Stay? Stay? Of course she'll stay. Stay for ever," asserted Nurse in her bustling voice.

"Funny not to be here when the furniture came," said Cook.

"Yes, wasn't it?" echoed Annie. "It *was* funny. That's what I thought. How funny, I thought."

"Not that I suppose things will be what you might call properly arranged just yet?" Cook speculated.

"Everything arranged. Everything arranged," Nurse snapped. "Nothing to arrange. Nothing to arrange."

And as if to stifle for ever any ability in Michael to ask questions, she proceeded to cram his mouth with a dessert-spoonful of rice pudding from her own plate, jarring his teeth with the spoon when she withdrew it.

Then Michael's lovely mother in vivid rose silk came into the room, and Cook squeezed herself backwards through the door very humbly and so quietly that Annie found herself alone before she realized the fact; so that in order to cover her confusion and assist her retreat she was compelled to snatch away Michael's plate of rice pudding before he had finished the last few clotted grains. Michael was grateful to Annie for this, and he regarded her from that moment as an ally. Thenceforth he would often seek her out in what she called 'her' pantry, there to nibble biscuits, while Annie dried cups and swung them from brass hooks.

"How cosy you all look," said mother. "Darling Stella, are you enjoying your rice pudding? And, darling Michael," she added, "I hope you're being very good."

"Oh, yes," said Nurse, "Good! Yes. He's very good. Oh, yes. Tut-tut! Tut-tut!"

After this exhalation of approval Nurse blew several breaths, leaned over him, pulled down his blue and white sailor-top, and elevated his chin with the back of her hand.

"There's no need to bother about the drawing-room or the dining-room or my bedroom or, in fact, any of the rooms except the night-nursery and the day-nursery. You're quite straight in here. I shall be back by the end of June."

Nurse shook her head very violently at this, and Michael felt tears of apprehension welling up into his eyes. Mrs. Fane paused a moment doubtfully; then she waved beautiful slim gloves and glided from the room. Michael listened to delicate footsteps on the stairs, and the tinkle of small ornaments. A bleak silence followed the banging of the front door.

"She's gone away. I know she's gone away," he moaned.

"Who's She?" demanded Nurse. "She's the cat's mother."

"Mother! Mother!" he wailed. "She always goes away from Michael."

"And no wonder," said Nurse. "Dear, dear! Yes—tut-tut!—but goodness gracious, she won't be gone long. She'll be back in June."

"What's June?" Michael asked.

"If you ask any more silly questions you'll go to bed, young man; but if you're a good boy, I'll tell you a story."

"A real story? A nice long story?" asked Michael.

"I'll tell you a story about Jack o' my Nory And now my story's begun. I'll tell you another about Jack and his brother And now my story's done."

Nurse twiddled her thumbs with a complacent look, as she smacked her palate upon the final line.

"That isn't a story," said Michael sullenly. "When will mother be back?"

"In June. That's enough," said Nurse.

Michael went to sleep that night, trying to materialize this mysterious June. It came to mean a distant warmth of orange light towards which he waited very slowly. He lay awake thinking of June in the luminousness of a night-light shielded from his direct vision by a basin. His hands were muffled in fingerless gloves to prevent thumb-sucking. Suddenly upon the quiet came a blaze of light. Had he reached June? His sleepy eyelids uncurled to the scented vision of his beautiful mother. But it was only gaslight playing and fluttering over the figure of anæmic Annie taking hairpin after hairpin from her hair. Yet there was a certain interest in watching Annie undress. Her actions were less familiar than those of Nurse. Her lips were softer to kiss. Then the vision of June, rising and falling with Annie's breath, recurred from distances unattainable, faded again into the blackness of the night, and after a while came back dazzling and golden. It was morning, and in a chirping of sparrows and depth of quiet sunlight Michael began to wonder why he was sleeping beside Annie in a big bed. It was an experience that stood for a long time in his memory as the first adventure of his life.

The adventure of Annie was a solitary occasion. By the following night the regular night-nursery was ready for occupation, and the pea-green vegetation of the walls was hidden by various furniture. Nurse's bed flanked by the two cots occupied much of its space. Round the fire was a nursery fender on which hung perpetually various cloths and clothes and blankets and sheers which, as it was summer at the time, might all have been dried much more easily out of doors. Pictures were hung upon the wall—pictures that with the progress of time became delightfully intimate experiences. They were mostly framed chromolithographs saved from the Christmas numbers of illustrated papers. There was Cherry Ripe—a delicious and demure girl in a white dress with a pink sash, for whom Michael began to feel a romantic affection. There was the picture of a little girl eating a slice of bread-and-butter on a doorstep, watched by a fox terrier and underneath inscribed 'Give me a piece, please.' Michael did not know whether to feel more sorry for the little girl or the dog; some sort of compassion, he thought, was demanded. It was a problem picture insoluble over many years of speculation. The night-nursery seemed always full of Nurse's clothes. Her petticoats were usually chequered or uniform red, preternaturally bright in contrast with the blackness of the exterior apparel. The latter of heavy serge or similar material was often sown with jet bugles which scratched Michael's face when he played 'Hide-Oh' among the folds of such obvious concealment. Apart from these petticoats and skirts, the most individual possession of Nurse's wardrobe was a moon-shaped bustle of faded crimson which Michael loved to swing from the bedpost whence out of use it was suspended. There was also in a top drawer, generally unattainable, a collection of caps threaded with many different velvet ribbons and often coquettish with lace flowers. Michael was glad when Nurse put on her best cap, a proceeding which took place just before tea. Her morning cap was so skimpy as scarcely to hide the unpleasant smoothness of her thin hair. In the amber summer afternoons or blue spring twilights, Nurse looked comparatively beautiful under the ample lace, with a softer apron and a face whose wrinkles were smoothed out by the consciousness of leisure and the pleasant brown teapot. Mostly, Michael was inclined to compare her with a monkey, so squab was her nose, so long her upper lip, and such a multitude of deep furrows twisted up her countenance. That Nurse was ever young, Michael could not bring himself to believe, and daguerreotypes framed in tin-foil which she produced as evidence of youth from a square box inlaid with mother-o'-pearl, never convinced him as a chromolithograph might have convinced him. At the same time the stories of her childhood, which Nurse was sometimes persuaded to tell, were very enthralling; moreover, by the fact of her obvious antiquity, they had the dimness and mystery of old fairy-tales.

On the whole Michael was happy in his pea-green nursery. He was well guarded by the iron soldiers of his cot. He liked the warmth and the smallness of the room; he liked to be able to climb from his cot on to Nurse's bed, from Nurse's bed into Stella's cot, and with this expanse of safe territory he felt sorry for the chilly and desolate and dangerous floor. Michael also liked the day-nursery. To begin with, it possessed a curious and romantic shape due to its nearness to the roof. The ceiling sloped on either side of the window almost to the floor. It was not a room that was square and obvious, for round the corner from the door was a fairly large alcove which was not destined to lose its romance for many years. The staircase that led up to the day-nursery was light and cheerful owing to the skylight in the roof. Yet this skylight Michael could have wished away. It was a vulnerable spot which made the day-nursery just a little uneasy at dusk—this and the cistern cupboard with its dark boomings and hammerings and clankings and utter inexplicableness. However, the day-nursery was a bright room, with a cosy atmosphere of its own. The pleasantest meal of the day was taken there, and in a black cupboard lived the golden syrup and the heraldic mugs and the dumpy teapot and the accessories of tea. What a much pleasanter cupboard this was than the smaller one in the night-nursery which revealed, when opened, slim and ugly ipecacuanha, loathsome Gregory-powder with wooden cap and squat cork, wicked envelopes of grey powders and slippery bottles of castor-oil. There, too, was the liver-coloured liquorice-powder, the vile rhubarb and the deceitful senna. In fact, apart from a bag of jaded acid-drops, there were only two pleasant inmates of this cupboard—the silvery and lucent syrup of squills and a round box of honey and borax. There were no pills because Nurse objected to pills. She was always telling Michael as he listened, sick at heart, to the stirring-up of the Gregory-powder with a muffled spoon, so different from the light-hearted tinkle and quick fizz of magnesia, to be thankful he was not on the verge of taking a pill. That she represented as something worthy of a struggle. Michael imagined the taking of a pill to be equivalent to swallowing a large painted ball full of a combination of all the nastiest medicines in the world. Even the omnipotent, omniscient Nanny could not take a pill.

There were other jolly cupboards in the day-nursery—one in particular pasted over with 'scraps' and varnished—a work of art that was always being added to for a treat. There was a patchwork hearthrug very comfortable to lie upon beside the cat and her two black kittens. There was Nanny's work-table in the window, gay with coloured silks and wools. There was a piano locked up until Michael's first lesson, but nevertheless wonderful on account of the smooth curve of the lid that allowed one moment's delicious balance and then an equally delicious slide on to the floor.

Certainly the day-nursery was the best room in the tall thin house, just as the morning-room was the worst. The morning-room was odious. In it were eaten breakfast and dinner, both nasty meals. Near it was the coal-cellar and the area-door with its grinning errand boys. The windows afforded foothold to strange cats that stared abominably with yellow eyes. Tramps and sweeps walked past the area-railings or looked in evilly. Horrid gipsies smirked through the window, and pedlars often tapped. The morning-room was utterly abominable, fit only for the boiled mutton and caper sauce and suet puddings that loaded its table.

The kitchen, although it was next to the morning-room, was a far pleasanter resort. So far as any ground-floor now could be considered safe, the kitchen was safe. It looked out upon its own fortified basement whose perforated iron staircase had a spiked door at the top, which could be securely shut. The kitchen contained a large number of objects of natural interest, among which was a shallow cupboard that included upon an attainable shelf jars of currants, sultanas, and rice much more edible in the raw state than cooked. There was the electric-bell case, recording with mysterious discs a far-off summons. There was the drawer in the kitchen table that contained, besides knives and forks, a rolling-pin, a tin-opener, a corkscrew, skewers and, most exciting of all, a club-shaped cage for whipping eggs. There was also a deep drawer in the dresser which held many revelations of the private history of Annie and Cook. Michael could easily have spent days in the kitchen without exhausting its treasures, and as for Cook, gross though she was and heavily though she smelt of onions and beer, her tales were infinitely superior to anything ever known in the way of narration.

Towards the end of June, Mrs. Fane came back. Her arrival was heralded by the purchase of several pots of marguerites and calceolarias—the latter to Michael a very objectionable flower because, detecting in it some resemblance to his dearly loved snapdragons, he pressed open the mouth of a flower and, finding inside a small insect, had to drop the whole pot in a shudder. This brought the punishment of not being allowed to watch from the steps for his mother's cab rounding the corner into Carlington Road, and made calceolarias for ever hateful. However, Mrs. Fane arrived in the richness of a midsummer twilight, and Michael forgot all about calceolarias in his happiness. All day long for many golden days he pattered up and down the house and in and out of all the rooms at his mother's heels. He held coils of picture-wire and hooks and hammers and nails and balls of wool and reels of silk and strands of art-muslin and spiders of cotton-wool and Japanese fans and plumes of pampas grass and all the petty utilities and beauties of house arrangement. By the end of July every room was finally arranged, and Michael and Stella with their mother, accompanied by Nurse and Annie, went down to the seaside to spend two wonderful months. Michael was often allowed to sit up an extra half-hour and even when he went to bed his mother would come to hear him say his prayers. She would sit by him, her lovely face flushed by the rose-red August sunsets that floated in through the open window on a sound of sea-waves. As it grew darker and, over the noise of happy people walking about in the cool evening, a distant band played music, his mother would lean over and kiss him good night. He would be loath to let her go, and just as she was closing the door quietly he would call her back and whisper 'One more kiss,' and because that good-night kiss was the most enchanting moment in his day, he would whisper as he held her to him very close, 'Only one more, but much, much, much the longest kiss in all the world.'

They were indeed two very wonderful months. In the morning Michael would sit beside his mother at breakfast, and for a great treat he would be given the segment she so cleverly cut off from the tip of her egg. And for another treat, he would be allowed to turn the finished egg upside down and present it to her as a second untouched, for which she would be very grateful and by whose sudden collapse before the tapping of the spoon, she would be just as tremendously surprized. After the egg would always come two delicious triangles of toast, each balancing a single strawberry from the pot of strawberry jam. After breakfast, Michael would walk round the heap of clinkers in the middle of the parched seaside garden while his mother read her letters, and very soon they would set out together to the beach, where in time they would meet Nurse and Stella with the perambulator and the camp-stools and the bag of greengages or William-pears. Sand castles were made and boats were sailed or rather were floated upside down in pools, and just as the morning was getting too good to last, they would have to go home to dinner, joining on to the procession of people returning up the cliffs. Michael would be armed with a spade, a boat with very wet sails, and sometimes with a pail full of sea-water and diminutive fish that died one by one in the course of the afternoon heat. After dinner Mrs. Fane would lie down for a while, and Michael would lie down for a great treat beside her and keep breathless and still, watching the shadows of light made by the bellying of the blind in the breeze. Bluebottles would drone, and once to his bodeful apprehension a large spider migrated to another corner of the ceiling. But he managed to restrain himself from waking his mother.

One afternoon Michael was astonished to see on the round table by the bed the large photograph in a silver frame of a man in knee-breeches with a sword—a prince evidently by his splendid dress and handsome face. He speculated during his mother's sleep upon this portrait, and the moment Annie had left the cup of tea which she brought in to wake his mother Michael asked who the man was.

"A friend of mine," said Mrs. Fane.

"A prince?"

"No, not a prince."

"He looks like a prince," said Michael sceptically.

"Does he, darling?"

"I think he does look like a prince. Is he good?"

"Very good."

"What's wrote on it?" Michael asked. "Oh, mother, when will I read writing?"

"When you're older."

"I wish I was older now. I want to read writing. What's wrote on it?"

"Always," his mother told him.

"Always?"

"Yes."

"Always what? Always good?"

"No, just plain 'always,'" said Mrs. Fane.

"What a funny writing. Who wrote it?"

"The man in the picture."

"Why?"

"To please mother."

"Shall I write 'always' when I can write?" he asked.

"Of course, darling."

"But what is that man for?"

"He's an old friend of mother's."

"I like him," said Michael confidently.

"Do you, darling?" said his mother, and then suddenly she kissed him.

That evening when Michael's prayers were concluded and he was lying very still in his bed, he waited for his mother's tale.

"Once upon a time," she began, "there was a very large and enormous forest——"

"No, don't tell about a forest," Michael interrupted. "Tell about that man in the picture."

Mrs. Fane was staring out of the window, and after a moment's hesitation she turned round.

"Because there *are* fairy-tales without a prince," said Michael apologetically.

"Well, once upon a time," said his mother, "there lived in an old old country house three sisters whose mother had died when they were quite small."

"Why did she die?"

"She was ill."

Michael sighed sympathetically.

"These three sisters," his mother went on, "lived with their father, an old clergyman."

"Was he kind to them?"

"According to his own ideas he was very kind. But the youngest sister always wanted to have her own way and one day when she was feeling very cross because her father had told her she was to go and stay with an aunt, who should come riding along a lane but——"

"That man," interrupted Michael, greatly excited.

"A rider on horseback. And he said good morning, and she said good morning, though she had no business to."

"Why hadn't she?"

"Because it isn't right for girls to speak to riders on horseback without being introduced. But the rider was very handsome and brave and after that they met very often, and then one day he said, 'Won't you ride away with me?' and she rode away with him and never saw her father or her sisters or the old house any more."

Mrs. Fane had turned her face to the sunset again.

"Is that all?" Michael asked.

"That's all."

"Was they happy ever afterwards?"

"Very happy—too happy."

"Are they happy now?"

"Very happy—too happy."

"Did they live in a castle?"

"Sometimes, and sometimes they lived in a beautiful ship and went sailing away to the most beautiful cities in the world."

"Can't Michael go with you?" he asked.

"Darling boy, it's a fairy-tale."

"Is it?" he said doubtfully.

The two wonderful months were over. One long day of packing up was the end of them, and when they got back to London there was more packing up, after a few days of which Mrs. Fane took Michael in her arms and kissed him good-bye and told him to be very good. Michael tried not to cry; but the tears were forced out by a huge lump in his throat when he saw a cab at the door, pointing the other way from London. He could not bear the heaped-up luggage and Nurse's promises of sitting up late that evening for a great treat. He did not want to sit up late, and when his mother whispered there was a surprize for him in the drawing-room, he did not care at all for a surprize. But nothing could make the minutes stay still. He was allowed to watch the cab going down the road, but he had no heart to wave his handkerchief in farewell, and when presently he went back with Nurse into the thin red house and was triumphantly led into the drawing-room, he was not raised to any particular happiness by the lancer's uniform, displayed on a large square of cardboard. He suffered himself to be dressed up and to have the scarlet breast-plate strapped around him and the plumed helmet to be pushed over his nose and the sabre-tache to be entangled with his legs; but there was no spirit of hope and adventure flaming in his breast—only an empty feeling and a desire to look out of the night-nursery window at the trains going by with happy people inside.

Chapter II: *Bittersweet*

HIS mother's absence made very sad for Michael the tall thin house in Carlington Road. He felt enclosed in the restraint from which his mother had flown like a bird. Time stretched before him in unimaginable reckonings. It was now the beginning of autumn, and the leaves of the lime trees, falling to lie stained and unlovely in sodden basements, moved Michael with a sense of the long winter before him, with the unending black nights and the dark wet dawns. From the window of the night-nursery he recognized for the first time the beauty of the unsymmetrical plane tree that now, when the poplars were mere swishing bundles of twigs, still defied the October winds with wide green leaves. Soon, however, by a damp frost the plane tree was conquered, and its blobs jigged to November gusts. Fogs began, and the morning-room was always gaslit, even for dinner at one o'clock. Stella was peevish, and games became impossible. The two black kittens were an entertainment and took part with Michael in numberless dramas of revenge and punishment, of remorse and exaggerated cherishing. These histrionic pastimes became infused with a terrible reality, when one day the favourite kitten jumped from Michael's arms over the banisters and fell on to the tiled floor of the hall, hurting herself internally so that she had to be poisoned. He stood by her grave in the blackened mould of the garden, and wished poignantly that he had never spoken harshly to her, had never banished her to a waste-paper basket prison for the length of a long foggy afternoon.

Christmas arrived with more uniforms, with a fishmonger's shop and a mechanical mackerel which when wound up would click in finny progress from one end of the bath to the other and back. It was wound up every Sunday afternoon for a treat, and was afterwards replaced in a high corner-cupboard that always attracted Michael's extreme curiosity and was the object of many vows to solve its secret, when he grew bigger. All these presents came from his mother together with half a dozen books. He received no other presents except from the household. Nurse gave him a china house, romantic when illuminated by a night-light; Annie shyly placed before him a crystal globe that when shaken gave a wonderful reproduction of a snow-storm falling upon a weather-worn tin figure with a green face, blue legs and an unpainted coat. Mrs. Frith the cook gave him a box of tops, none of which he or she or anyone else could spin. In addition to these presents Santa Claus allowed him on a still December night an orange, an apple, a monkey on a stick, five nuts (three of them bad) and a selection of angular sweets. As Michael with foresight had hung up two of Nurse's stockings as well as his own socks, he felt slightly resentful towards Santa Claus for the meagre response.

Christmas passed away in a week of extravagant rain, and a visit was paid to the pantomime of Valentine and Orson at the Surrey Theatre that reduced Michael to a state of collapse owing to the fight between the two protagonists, in which Orson's fingers were lacerated by the glittering sword of Valentine. Nurse vainly assured him the blood was so much red paint. He howled the louder and dreamed ghastly dreams for a month afterwards.

About this time Michael read many books in a strange assortment. Nurse had a collection of about a dozen in her trunk from which Michael was allowed to read three to himself. These were The Lamplighter, The Arabian Nights in a small paper-bound volume of diminutive print, and a Tale of the Black Rising in Jamaica which included an earthquake. In The Arabian Nights he read over and over again the stories of Aladdin, The Forty Thieves and Sinbad, owing to their familiarity through earlier narratives. On Sunday afternoons Nurse always read aloud from Baring-Gould's Lives of the Saints and Mrs. Gatti's Parables from Nature, and told the story of Father Machonochie's death in Argyll and of his faithful Skye terriers, whose portraits she piously possessed in Oxford frames. Michael's own books included at this period several zoological works, the Swiss Family Robinson, Holiday House, Struwwelpeter, Daddy Darwin's Dovecote, Jackanapes, The Battles of the British Army and an abbreviated version of Robinson Crusoe.

The winter and cold wet spring dragged by. Day by day life varied very little. In the morning after breakfast, if it was fairly fine, a visit would be paid to Kensington Gardens, a dull business; for the Round Pond was not visited, and indeed the Gardens were only penetrated as far as the Palace, with occasional promenades along the flower-walk for a treat. Treats were important factors in Michael's life. Apparently anything even mildly pleasant came under the category of treats. It was a treat to walk on the grass in the Gardens; it was a treat to help to push Stella's perambulator; it was a treat to have the sponge floating beside him in the bath, to hum, to laugh, to read, to stay up one minute after half-past six, to accompany Nurse on her marketing, and most of all to roll the slabs of unbaked dough down in the kitchen. The great principle of a treat was its rarity. As anything that had to be asked for became a treat automatically and as the mere fact of asking was made a reason for refusing to grant a treat, the sacred infrequency of the treat was secured. The result of this was that the visit to Kensington Gardens instead of being the jolly business it seemed to be for other children, became a tantalizing glimpse of an unattainable paradise. Michael would stand enraptured by the March winds, every impulse bidding him run and run eternally through the blowy spring weather; yet if he so much as climbed the lowest rung of the scaly part-railings, if he dallied one moment to watch a kite launched on the air, Nanny would haul him back to the perambulator's side. As for talking to other children, not even could the magic treat effect that. If Nurse was to be believed, conversation with strange children was the lowest depth to which human nature could sink. The enforced solitariness of his life bred in Michael a habit of contemplation. Much of his morning walk was passed in a dream, in which he seemed to be standing still while the world of houses and trees and railings and people swam by him unheeded. This method of existence led to several unpleasant shocks, as when he walked into a lamp-post and bruised his nose. Nanny used to jeer at him, calling him Little Johnny Head-in-air; but Michael was so much used to her derogatory opinions that he cared very little and made no attempt to cure himself of the habit, but even encouraged himself to put himself into these nihilistic trances.

It was probably owing to this habit that one morning Michael, looking round in Kensington Gardens, could discern no familiar figure. He was by himself in the middle of a broad gravel walk. Nurse and the perambulator had vanished. For a moment a sickening horror seized him. He would never see Carlington Road again; he would never see Stella or his mother; he would never go to the seaside; he was lost. Then he recalled to himself the knowledge of his name and address: he reassured himself by repeating both aloud, Charles Michael Saxby Fane, 64 Carlington Road, Kensington. A name and address he had often been warned was a talisman to enlist the service of policemen. His heart beat more gently again; his breathing became normal. He looked around him at the world seen for the first time with freedom's eyes. With waves of scent the beds of hyacinths impressed themselves upon his memory. He was free under a great gusty sky, free to climb railings, to pick up shells from the gravel walk, to lie on his back in the grass and brood upon the huge elm-trees that caught the clouds in their net. Michael wandered along to a drinking-fountain to which, access had often been forbidden. He drank four cups of water from the captive metal mug: he eyed curiously the many children who, as free as himself, ran up and down the steps of the fountain. He wished for barley-sugar that he might offer it to them and earn their approbation and company. He was particularly attracted to one group consisting of three funny little girls with splashed pinafores and holes in their stockings, and of two little boys with holes in their knickerbockers and half-peeled sticks. The group moved away from the fountain and Michael followed at a distance. The group turned somersaults over the highest railings and Michael watched it hungrily. The group strolled on, the girls nonchalant and enlaced, the boys still peeling their sticks with perseverance. Michael squeezed through the railings, and followed in the group's wake. The two boys finished peeling their sticks and pushed over in a heap the three little girls. There was laughter and shouting, and a confusion of pinafores and black stockings and hair and caps. Michael stood close to them, wide-eyed with admiration. Suddenly the group realized his propinquity and flocked together critically to eye him, Michael became self-conscious and turned away; he heard giggling and spluttering. He blushed with shame and began to run. In a moment he fell over a turret of grass and the group jeered openly. He picked himself up and fled towards the gate of the Gardens, anxious only to escape ridicule. He ran on with beating heart, with quickening breath and sobs that rose in his throat one after another like bubbles, breaking because he ran so fast. He was in Kensington High Street, among the thickening crowds of people. He seemed to hear pursuing shouts and mocking laughter. At last he saw a policeman whose tunic he clutched desperately.

"What's all this about?" demanded the constable.

"Please, my name is Charles Michael Saxby Fane and I live at 64 Carlington Road and I want to go home."

Michael burst into tears and the policeman bent over and led him by a convulsed hand to the police station. There he was seated in a wooden chair, while various policemen in various states of undress came and talked kindly to him, and in the end, riding on the shoulder of his original rescuer, he arrived at the tall thin house from whose windows Nurse was peering, anxious and monkey-like.

There seemed to be endless talk about his adventure. All day the affair was discussed, all day he was questioned and worried and scolded and threatened. Treats faded from possible granting for months to come. Restrictions and repressions assumed gigantic proportions, and it was not until Nanny went upstairs to put Stella to bed and left Michael in the kitchen with Mrs. Frith and Annie that his adventure came to seem a less terrible breach of natural law. Away from Nurse, the cook and the housemaid allowed a splendid laxity to gild their point of view.

"Well, what a fuss about nothing," said Mrs. Frith comfortably. "I declare. And what was *she* doing? That's what some people would like to know. You can't lose a child the same as you might lay down a thimble. I call it very careless."

"Yes. What a shame!" Annie agreed. "Supposing he'd been run over."

"He might of been run over a dozen times," said Mrs Frith. "It's all very fine to put all the blame on the poor child, but what was *she* doing?"

Then Mrs. Frith closed her right eye, tightened her mouth and very slowly nodded her head until the most of her pleated chin was buried in the bib of her apron.

"That's what I thought," said Annie mysteriously.

"What did you think, Annie?" Michael asked fretfully.

9

"She thought you hadn't no business to be so daring," said Mrs, Frith. "But there! Well! And I was daring myself. Very daring *I* was. Out and about. Hollering after boys. The slappings I've had. But I enjoyed myself. And if I sat down a bit tender, that's better than a sore heart, I used to think."

"I expect you enjoyed yourself," said Annie. "I was one of the quiet ones, I was. Any little trip, and I was sick."

"Couldn't bear the motion, I suppose?" Cook enquired.

"Oh, it wasn't the travelling as did it. It was the excitement. I was dreadfully sick in the crypt of St. Paul's Cathedral."

"What a grand place it is, though," said Mrs. Frith, nodding. "Oh, beautiful. So solemn. I've sat there with my late husband, eating nuts as peaceful as if we was in a real church. Beautiful. And that whispering gallery! The things you hear. Oh—well. I like a bit of fun, I do. I remember——"

Then Nurse came downstairs, and Michael was taken up to bed away from what he knew would be an enthralling conversation between Annie and Cook. It was hateful to be compelled to march up all those stairs farther and farther away from the cheerful voices in the basement.

August arrived without bringing Michael's mother, and he did not care for the days by the sea without her. Stella, to be sure, was beginning to show signs of one day being an intelligent companion, but Nurse under the influence of heat grew more repressive than ever, and the whole seaside ached with his mother's absence. Michael was not allowed to speak to strange children and was still dependent on rare treats to illuminate his dulness. The landlady's husband, Mr. Wagland, played the harmonium and made jokes with Nurse, while Mrs. Wagland sang hymns and whispered with Nurse. A gleam of variety came into Michael's life when Mr. Wagland told him he could catch birds by putting salt on their tails, and for many afternoons, always with a little foolscap of salt, Michael walked about the sunburnt-grass patch in front of the house, waiting for sparrows to perch and vainly flinging pinches of salt in the direction of their tails.

Church was more exciting by the seaside than at home, where every Sunday morning during the long sermon Michael subsided slowly from a wooden bench in the gallery on to a disembowelled hassock, or languished through the Litany with a taste of varnish in his mouth caused by an attempt to support his endurance by licking the back of the pew in front. Nurse told him of wonderful churches with music and incense and candles and scarlet and lace, but, for some reason of inexplicable contrariness, she took Michael to an old Calvinistic church with a fire-breathing vicar, a sniffling vicar's wife and a curate who sometimes clasped Michael's head with a damp hand that always felt as if it were still there when it had long been removed, like a cold linseed poultice. Now at the seaside, Michael went to a beautiful church and was so much excited by the various events that he pressed forward, peering on tiptoe. Luckily the two ladies in front of him were so devout and bobbed up and down so often that he was able to see most of what was happening. How he longed to be the little boy in scarlet who carried a sort of silver sauce-boat and helped to spoon what looked like brown sugar into the censer. Once during a procession, Michael stepped out into the aisle and tried to see what actually was carried in the boat. But the boat-boy put out his tongue very quickly, as he walked piously by, and glared at Michael very haughtily, being about the same size.

After submitting without pleasure to a farewell kiss from Mrs. Wagland, and after enduring much shame on account of Stella's behaviour in the crowded railway carriage, Michael came back to Carlington Road. During the space between arrival and bed-time he was gently happy in welcoming his toys and books, in marvelling at the quick growth of the black kitten and in a brief conversation with Mrs. Frith and Annie; but on the next morning which was wet with a wetness that offered no prospect of ever being dry, he was depressed by the thought of the long time before Christmas, by the foreboding of yellow days of fog and the fact that to-morrow was Sunday. He had been told to sit in the dining-room in order to be out of the way during the unpacking and, because he had been slow in choosing which book should accompany him, he had been called Mr. Particular and compelled to take the one book of all others that he now felt was most impossible even to open. So Michael sat in the bay-window and stared at the rainy street. How it rained, not ferociously as in a summer storm, when the surface of the road was blurred with raindrops and the water poured along the gutters, carrying twigs and paper and orange-peel towards the drain, and when there almost seemed a chance of a second flood, an event Michael did not fear, having made up his mind to float on an omnibus to the top of the Albert Hall which had once impressed him with its perfect security. Now it was raining with the dreary mediocrity of winter, dripping from the balcony above on to the sill below, trickling down the window-panes, lying in heavy puddles about the road, a long monotonous grey soak. He sighed as he looked out of the window at the piece of waste ground opposite, that was bordered in front by a tumble-down fence and surrounded on the three other sides by the backs of grey houses. A poor old woman was picking groundsel with a melancholy persistence, and the torn umbrella which wavered above her bent form made her look like a scarecrow. Presently round the corner a boy appeared walking very jauntily. He had neither coat nor waistcoat nor shoes nor stockings, his shirt was open in front, and a large piece of it stuck out behind through his breeches; but he did not seem to mind either the rain or his tattered clothes. He whistled as he walked along, with one hand stuck in his braces and with the other banging the wooden fence. He went by with tousled hair and dirty face, a glorious figure of freedom in the rain, Michael envied him passionately, this untrammelled fence-banging whistling spirit; and for a long time this boy walked before Michael's aspirations, leading them to his own merry tune. Michael would often think of this boy and wonder what he was doing and saying. He made up his mind in the beeswaxed dining-room that it was better to be a raggle-taggle wanderer than anything else. He watched the boy disappear round the farther corner, and wished that he could disappear in such company round corner after corner of the world beyond the grey house-backs.

The climax of this wet morning's despair was reached when a chimney-sweep came into sight, whooping and halloaing nearer and nearer. Of the many itinerant terrors that haunted polite roads, Michael dreaded sweeps most of all. So he hastily climbed down from the chair in the window and sat under the dining-room table until the sound had passed, shivering with apprehension lest it should stop by Number Sixty-four. It went by, however, without pausing, and Michael breathed more freely, but just as he was cautiously emerging from the table, there was an extra loud postman's knock which drove him back in a panic, so that when Nurse came fussing in to fetch him to wash his hands for dinner, he had to invent a plausible excuse for such a refuge. As he could not find one, he was told that for a punishment he could not be allowed to hear the message his mother had written at the end of what was evidently a very important letter, to judge by the many tut-tuts the reading of it provoked Nurse to click.

However, under the influence of tea Nanny softened, and the message was read just as the rain stopped and the sun glittered through the day-nursery window right across the room in a wide golden bar.

Como.

Darling Michael,

You are to go to kindergarten which you will enjoy. You will only go for the mornings and you will have to learn all sorts of jolly things—music and painting and writing. Then you'll be able to write to Mother. I'm sure you'll be good and work hard, so that when Mother comes home at Christmas, you'll be able to show her what a clever boy she has. You would like to be in this beautiful place. As I write I can see such lovely hills and fields and lakes and mountains. I hope darling Stella is learning to say all sorts of interesting things. I can't find any nice present to send you from here, so I've told Nanny that you and she can go and buy two canaries, one for you and one for Stella—a boy canary and a girl canary. Won't that be fun? Love and kisses from

Mother.

Michael sat in a dream when the letter was finished. It had raised so many subjects for discussion and was so wonderful that he could scarcely speak.

"Will mother really come home at Christmas?" he asked.

"You heard what I said."

"Christmas!" he sighed happily.

"Aren't you glad to go to school?" Nurse wanted to know.

"Yes, but I'd like Christmas to come," he said.

"Was there ever in this world anyone so hard to please?" Nurse apostrophized.

"When will we go to get these canaries, Nanny?"

"Plenty of time. Plenty of time."

"Soon, will we?"

"One more question and there'll be no canaries at all," said Nurse.

However, the sun shone so brightly, and the prospect of a visit to Hammersmith Broadway on a Saturday afternoon appealed so strongly to Nurse that she put on her bonnet and trotted off with Michael up Carlington Road, and stopped a red omnibus, and fussed her way into it, and held the tickets in her mouth while she put away her purse, and told Michael not to fidget with his legs and not to look round behind him at what was passing on that side of the road, until at last they arrived. The canary-shop was found, and two canaries and a bird-cage were bought, together with packets of seed and a bird's bath and a pennyworth of groundsel and plantains. Nurse told Michael to wait in the shop while the birds were being prepared for travelling, and while she herself went to the chemist to buy a remedy for the neuralgia which she prophesied was imminent. Michael talked to the canary-man and asked a lot of questions which the canary-man seemed very glad to answer; and finally Nurse, looking much better, came back from the chemist with a large bottle wrapped up in a newspaper. In the omnibus, going home, Michael never took his eyes from the cage, anxious to see how the birds bore the jolting. Sometimes they said 'sweet,' and then Michael would say 'sweet,' and a pleasant old lady opposite would say 'sweet,' and soon all the people inside the omnibus were saying 'sweet,' except Nurse, who was chewing her veil and making the most extraordinary faces.

It was very exciting to stand on tiptoe in the kitchen while Mrs. Frith cut the string and displayed the canaries in all the splendour of their cage.

"Beautiful things," said Mrs. Frith. "I'm that fond of birds."

"Don't they hop!" said Annie. "Not a bit frightened they don't seem, do they?"

"What are their names?" Mrs. Frith enquired.

Michael thought for a long time.

"What *are* their names, Mrs. Frith?" he asked at last.

"That's your business," said Cook.

"Why is it?" Michael wanted to know.

"Because they're your birds, stupid."

"One's Stella's."

"Well, Stella isn't old enough to choose for herself. Come along, what are you going to call them?"

"You call them," said Michael persuasively.

"Well, if they was mine I should call them——" Cook paused.

"What would you?" said Michael, more persuasively than ever.

"I'm blessed if I know. There, Annie, what does anyone call a canary?"

"Don't ask me, I'm sure. No," simpered Annie.

"I shouldn't call them nothing, I shouldn't," Mrs. Frith finally decided. "It isn't like dogs."

"What's the matter?" said Nurse, bustling into the kitchen. "Has one got out? Has one got out?"

"I was telling Master Michael here," said Cook, "as how I shouldn't call neither of them nothing. Not if I was he."

"Call what? Call what?" Nurse asked quickly.

"His new dicky-birds."

"Must have names. Yes. Yes. Must have names. Dick and Tom. Dick and Tom."

"But one's a girl," Michael objected.

"Can't be changed now. Must be Dick and Tom," Nurse settled, blowing rapidly as usual.

The decision worried Michael considerably, but as they both turned out to be hens and laid twenty-three eggs between them next spring, it ceased to bother him any more.

The Miss Marrows' School and Kindergarten, kept by Miss Marrow and Miss Caroline Marrow assisted by Miss Hewitt and Miss Hunt, struck Michael as a very solemn establishment indeed. Although its outward appearance was merely that of an ordinary house somewhat larger than others on account of its situation at the corner of Fairfax Terrace, it contained inside a variety of scholastic furniture that was bound to impress the novice.

At twenty minutes past nine on the first day of the autumn term, Nurse and Michael stood before a brass plate inscribed

The Misses Marrow
School and Kindergarten

while a bell still jangled with the news of their arrival. They were immediately shown into a very small and very stuffy room on the right of the front door—a gloomy little room, because blinds of coloured beads shut out the unscholastic world. This room was uncomfortably crowded with little girls taking off goloshes and unlacing long brown boots, with little boys squabbling over their indoor shoes, with little girls chatting and giggling and pushing and bumping, with little boys shouting and quarrelling and kicking and pulling. A huddled and heated knot of nurses and nursemaids tried to help their charges, while every minute more little boys and more little girls and more bigger girls pushed their way in and made the confusion worse. In the middle of the uproar Miss Marrow herself entered and the noise was instantly lulled.

"The new boys will wait in here and the new girls will *quietly* follow Helen Hungerford down the passage to Miss Caroline's room. Nurses need not wait any longer."

Then a bell vibrated shrilly. There was a general scamper as the nurses and the nursemaids and the old boys and the old girls hurried from the room, leaving Michael and two other boys, both about two years older than himself, to survey each other with suspicion. The other boys finding Michael beneath the dignity of their notice spoke to each other, or rather the larger of the two, a long-bodied boy with a big head and vacant mouth, said to the other, a fidgety boy with a pink face, a frog-like smile and very tight knickerbockers:

"I say, what's your name?"

The pink-faced boy gulped "Edward Ernest Arnott."

"What is it then?" asked the long-bodied boy.

"Arnott is my surname. Edward and Ernest," he gulped again, "are my Christian names."

"Mine's Vernon Brown. I say, what's your father?"

"A solicitor," said Edward. "What's yours?"

"A cricket—I mean a critic," said Vernon.

"What's that?"

This seemed to upset the long-bodied boy, who replied:

"Coo! Don't you know what a cricket is? I mean critic. You must be a kid."

Michael thought this was the most extraordinary conversation he had ever heard. Not even Mrs. Frith and Annie could be so incomprehensible.

"I don't believe you know yourself," said the pink-faced boy, deepening to crimson.

"Don't I? I bet I do."

"I bet you don't."

"I know better than you anyway."

"So do I than you."

Michael would have found a conversation between two fox-terriers more intelligible. It ended abruptly, however, with the entrance of Miss Marrow, who waved them all to follow her to the severity of her own room. Edward Arnott and Vernon Brown were despatched upstairs to take their places in the class above the Kindergarten for which Michael was destined and whither he followed Miss Marrow, wondering at the size and ugliness of her. Miss Marrow's base was a black bell, on which was set a black cushion, above which was Miss Marrow's round beetroot-coloured face. Miss Caroline was like a green curtain through the folds of which seemed to have burst a red face like her sister's but thinner. Miss Caroline was pleasanter than Miss Marrow and never shouted, perhaps because she was never without a cold in the head.

Michael was handed over to the care of Miss Hewitt, the Kindergarten mistress, who was very kind and very jolly. Michael enjoyed the Kindergarten. There he learned to write pothooks and hangers and very soon to write proper letters. He learned to sew alternate red and blue lines of wool upon a piece of cardboard. He learned to weave bookmarkers with shining slips of chocolate and yellow paper, and to pleat chequered mats of the same material: these, when term was over, appeared at the prize-giving, beautifully enhanced with paper frills cut by the clever Miss Hewitt. He learned to paint texts and to keep his pencil-box tidy and to play the treble of a very unmelodious duet with Miss Hunt, in whose bony fingers his own fingers would from time to time get entangled. He tried the treble without the bass accompaniment at home on Stella, but she cried and seemed as Annie, who was in charge, said 'to regular shudder.' Altogether Kindergarten was a pleasure to Michael, and he found the days went by more quickly, though still far too slowly.

About a week before Christmas his mother came back, and Michael was happy. All the rooms that were only used when she was at home changed from bare beeswaxed deserts to places of perfect comfort, so rosy were the lamp-shades, so sweet was the smell of flowers and so soft and lovely were his mother's scattered belongings. Christmas Day brought presents—a box of stone bricks, a rocking-horse, a doll's house for Stella, boxes of soldiers, a wooden battleship, and books—Hans Andersen and Grimm and the Old French Fairy-tales. As for the stockings that year, it was amazing how much managed to get into one stocking and how deliciously heavy it felt, as it was unhooked from the end of the cot and plumped down upon the bed in the gaslight of Christmas morning. There was only one sadness that hung over the festivities—the thought that his mother would be going away in two days. Boxing Day arrived and there were ominous open trunks and the scattered contents of drawers. To-morrow she was going. It was dreadful to think of. Michael was allowed the bitter joy of helping his mother to pack, and as he stood seriously holding various articles preparatory to their entombment, he talked of the summer and heard promises that mother would spend a long long time with Michael.

"Mother," he said suddenly, "what is my father?"

"What makes you ask that?"

"The boys at Miss Marrow's all ask me that. Have I got a father? Must boys have fathers? Oh, mother, do tell me," pleaded Michael.

Mrs. Fane seemed worried by this question.

"Your father was a gentleman," she said at last.

"What is a gentleman?"

"A good man, always thoughtful and considerate to others."

"Was that man in the photograph my father?"

"What photograph?" Mrs. Fane parried.

"By your bed at the seaside?"

"I don't remember," she said, "Anyway, your father's dead."

"Is he? Poor man!" said sympathetic Michael.

"And now run to Nanny and ask her if she remembers where mother put her large muff."

"Nanny," said Michael, when he had received Nurse's information, "why did my father die?"

"Die? Die? What questions. Tut-tut! Whatever next?" And Nurse blew very violently to show how deeply she disapproved of Michael's inquisitiveness.

That evening, just when Michael was going to bed, there came a knock at the door, and a tall fair man was shown into the drawing-room.

"How d'ye do, Mrs. Fane? I've come to ask you if you'll go to the theatre to-night. Saxby is coming on later."

"Oh, thank you very much, Mr. Prescott, but I really think I must stay in. You see," she said smilingly, "it's Michael's last night of me for a long time."

Michael stood gazing at Mr. Prescott, hating him with all his might and sighing relief at his mother's refusal to go out.

"Oh, Michael won't mind; will you, Michael?"

Nurse came in saying 'Bed-time! Tut-tut-tut! Bed-time!' and Michael's heart sank.

"There you are," said Mr. Prescott. "Here's Nurse to say it's bed-time. Now do come, Mrs. Fane."

"Oh, I really think I ought to stay."

"Now what nonsense. Saxby will be furiously disappointed. You must. Come along, Michael, be a brave chap and tell your mother she's got to go out; and here's something to square our account."

He pressed a little gold coin into Michael's unwilling hand.

"Would you mind very much, if I went?" his mother asked.

"No," said Michael tonelessly. The room was swimming round him in sickening waves of disappointment.

"Of course he won't," decided Mr. Prescott boisterously.

While he was being undressed, Nurse asked what he was holding. Michael showed the half-sovereign.

"Spoiling children," muttered Nanny. "That's for your money-box."

Michael did not care what it was for. He was listening for his mother's step. She came in, while he lay round-eyed in his cot, and leaned over to kiss him. He held her to him passionately; then he buried his face in the bedclothes and, while she rustled away from him, sobbed soundlessly for a long while.

In the morning he watched her go away until the warm summer-time and felt abandoned as he walked through the wintry rooms, where lately he and his mother had sat by the fire. As for the ten-shilling piece, he thought no more about it. Soon afterwards he fell ill with whooping-cough, he and Stella together, and the days dragged unendurably in the stuffy nursery away from school.

Chapter III: *Fears and Fantasies*

DURING whooping-cough Michael was sometimes allowed to sit in a room called the library, which was next to his mother's bedroom on the first floor and was therefore a dearly loved resort. Here he discovered the large volume of Don Quixote illustrated by Doré that influenced his whole life. He would pore over this work for hours, forgetting everything under a spell of chivalry. He read the tale seriously and thought it the saddest tale ever known. He wept over the knight's adventures, and big teardrops would spatter the page. He had not yet encountered much more than mild teasing at the Kindergarten, that with the unreasonableness of Nurse and his mother's absence made up the sum of the incomprehensible crosses which he had to bear. But even these were enough to make him sympathize with Don Quixote. He perceived that here was a man intent upon something—he could not understand exactly what—thwarted always by other people, thwarted and jeered at and even physically maltreated. Yet he was a man whose room was full of dragons and fairies, whose counterpane was the adventurous field of little knights-at-arms, whose curtains were ruffled by dwarfs, whose cupboards held enchanters. Michael loved the tall thin knight and envied Sancho Panza.

When whooping-cough was over, and Michael went back to Kindergarten, Nurse decided that he should sleep by himself in the room next to the night-nursery. She never explained to Michael her reasons for this step, and he supposed it to be because lately he had always woken up when she came to bed. This was not his fault, because Nurse always bumped into his cot as she came, into the room, shaking it so violently that no one could have stayed asleep. She used to look at him in a funny way with angry staring eyes, and when he sometimes spoke she would blow cheese-scented breath at him and turn away and bump into the washstand.

Everything in this new room was by Michael anticipated with dread. He would go to bed at half-past six: he would settle down in the wide white bed that stretched a long way on either side of him: the gas would be turned down: the door would be left ajar: Nurse's footsteps would gradually die away and he would be left alone.

The night was divided into two portions of equal horror. First of all he had to concentrate on closing his mouth when asleep, because Annie had told him a tale about a woman who slept with her mouth open, the result of which bad habit was that one night a mouse ran down it and choked her. Then he had to explore cautiously with his feet the ice-cold end of the bed, in case he should touch a nest of mice—another likely occurrence vouched for by Annie. Then outside, various sounds would frighten him. A dog would howl in the distance: cats would spit and wail, making Michael wonder whether they were coming through his window to claw his face. Presently, far up the street, newsboys would cry hoarsely the details of a murder or suicide. As they passed beneath his bedroom window their voices would swell to a paralyzing roar, and as the voices died away round the corner, Michael would be left shaking with fear. Once he was so frightened by a succession of these murder-shouts that he got out of bed and crept forth on to the landing, whence he peered down between the banisters into the quiet red light burning in the hall far below. While he was leaning over, a door banged suddenly on the top floor, and Michael fled barefooted down the stairs, until he reached the cold tiles of the front hall. Should he dare to descend still lower and disturb Nurse at her supper in the kitchen? Or were they all lying there, Cook and Annie and Nurse, with their throats cut? The door leading to the basement stairs was open, and he stole down over the oilcloth, past the yawning cellar, past the laundry-basket in the passage, past the cupboard under the stairs, to listen by the kitchen door. There was a murmur of voices, familiar yet unfamiliar: the kitchen door was ajar and he peered round stealthily. There was Nurse with a very red face in a heap on a chair, shaking her forefinger at Mrs. Frith, who with an equally red face was talking very indistinctly to Nurse; while between them, bolt upright and very pale, sat Annie nervously shaving from the cheese very thin segments which she ate from the knife's edge. They seemed to Michael, as he watched them, like people in a nightmare, so unreal and horrible were they: they frightened him more than ever, sitting there nodding at each other in the kitchen where the blackbeetles ran slyly in and out beneath the fender. Suddenly Annie saw Michael and waved him back; he turned at her gesture and withdrew from sight. While he stood shivering in the dark passage, Annie came out and, picking him up, carried him out of hearing.

"Whatever made you come downstairs?" she panted on the first-floor landing.

"I was frightened."

"You frightened *me*."

"Who are they murdering?"

"You've been having a bad dream," said Annie.

She led him upstairs again to his room and tucked him up, and at his earnest request turned the gas a trifle higher.

"Why did Nanny and Mrs. Frith look like that?" he asked.

"They're tired," said Annie.

"Why?"

"They have to work so hard to look after you."

Then she left him alone, and he fell asleep before they all came up to bed.

Generally speaking, the first part of the night, however bad the outside noises, was not so fearful as the second part. Mostly the second portion of the night was preceded by a bad dream in which Michael's nerves were so much shaken that he had no courage or common-sense left to grapple with the long hours in the ghastly stillness of his room. There was one dream in particular which he dreaded, and indeed it was the only one that repeated itself at regular intervals without any essential change. He would find himself alone in a long street in the middle of the night. Usually it would be shining with wet, but sometimes it would be dry and airless. This street stretched as far as one could see. It had on either side lamp-posts which burned with a steady staring illumination, long rows of lamp-posts that converged in the farthest distance. The houses all seemed empty, yet everyone was in some way a malignant personality. Down this street Michael would have to walk on and on. He would meet nobody, and the only living thing was a bony hound that pattered behind him at whatever pace he went, whether he ran or whether he loitered. He would in his dream be filled with a desire to enter one of these houses, and often he would mount the steps and knock a summons on the door—a knock that echoed all over the gloom within. While he knocked, the bony hound would howl in the shadows of the basement. Every house at which he knocked Michael would be more and more anxious to pass, more and more fearful to disturb. Yet however much he struggled against it, he would ultimately be compelled to knock his loud challenge. The street would now stretch for miles of lighted lamps before and behind him, and the knowledge would gradually be borne in upon Michael that sooner or later in one of these grey houses the door would open. He would hurry along, but however fast he travelled some house would draw him inexorably to its threshold, and he would wait in agony lest slowly the great door should swing back to a dim hall. The climax of the dream would now be reached. One house would simultaneously repel and draw him more than any of those left behind. He would struggle to go by, but he would find himself on the steps with legs that refused to carry him away. He would knock: very slowly the door would swing back and, convulsed and choking and warding off horror, Michael would wake in a frenzy of fear to his own real house of ghastly stillness, where no longer did even a belated luggage-train or jingling hansom assure him of life's continuity.

He did not always wake up suddenly: sometimes he would be aware that he was slowly waking and would struggle to keep asleep, lying for a long time without moving a muscle, in order to cheat himself into the belief that he was not awake. But gradually the strain would be too much and he would have to become conscious of the room. First of all he would turn on to his left side and view apprehensively the door ajar. This would seem to tremble, as he looked, to some invisible hand trying it. Then along the wall the wardrobe would creak, and every knot of its varnished surface would take on a fantastic countenance. He would wonder what was inside, and try to gain comfort and the sense of commonplace daytime existence by counting the cats swinging on a roundabout in one of Louis Wain's Christmas pictures. In the corner beyond the wardrobe was a large clothes-basket that crackled and snapped and must surely hold somebody inside, hidden as the Forty Thieves were hidden in the oil-jars. The fire-place, opposite the foot of the bed, seemed a centre for the noise of mice. How he hoped they would be content to play upon the hearth and not venture to leap over the fender and scuttle about the room. Then the door would begin to frighten him again, and Michael would turn very quietly on to his back, staring at the luminous ceiling where the gas-jet made a huge moon whose edges wavered perpetually. But the gas-jet itself became terrifying, when looked at too long, with its queer blue base and slim solemn shape, so melancholy, so desolate, so changeless. The ceiling would very soon become unendurable because various black marks would seem with intensest contemplation more and more like spiders and beetles. Michael would have to give up lying on his back and turn upon his right side. He would count each slat of the Venetian blinds and long passionately and sadly for the grey streaks to appear at the sides in proclamation of the approach of day. Without these grey streaks the windows were unbearable, so menacing were they with the unknown infinite night behind them. The curtains, too, would quiver, and even Michael's clothes, heaped upon a chair, would assume a worm-like vitality. The washstand made him feel oppressed, so silent and white were the jug and basin and soap-dish, so cold and chill were they. There was nothing to be done but to bury his head beneath the clothes and, trembling, try to believe in the reality of guardian angels. He would shut his eyes very tightly until the wheels of coloured lights thus evoked would circle and revolve, changing their colours in some mysterious way. These dissolving spots were a great consolation and passed the time for a little while, until the dread of fire began to come. He would fling back the clothes in a paroxysm and, heedless of any other danger, sit up with staring eyes and listening ears and keen nostrils, dreading and imagining and doubting. Surely he could hear a crackle; he could smell smoke. The house was on fire; yet not for anything could he have got out of bed to reassure himself. What might not be underneath, a burglar, a dead body, a murderer, a skeleton, a mad dog?

Underneath the clothes he would plunge, and then he would be sure that someone was coming into the room to smother him. He held his breath, waiting; with an effort he flung back the clothes again. There was nothing but the ghastly stillness and the solemn gaslight and the viewless blinds and the expectant door ajar. The bedposts would now take on a sort of humanity. They would look at him and wink and shiver. The wall-paper, normally a pattern of rosebuds and roses, began to move, to swim with unnatural life. The cistern upstairs began to clank; the bath began to drip. It must be blood—Nanny had been murdered. The blood was dripping slowly. Michael choked with horror. Somebody was tapping at the window-pane, yes, somebody was tapping. It was horrible this endless tapping. Cats must be coming in. The wardrobe creaked and rapped and groaned. Some of his clothes slid off the chair on to the floor with a soft plump; Michael tried to shriek his dismay; but his tongue was dry. Underneath him a knife was being pushed through the bed. A death-watch was ticking in the fastness of the wall at his head. A rat was gnawing his way into the room. Black-beetles were coming up the stairs.

Then along the edge of the Venetian blinds appeared a blue streak. It widened. It became more luminous. It turned from blue to grey. It turned from grey to dimmest silver. Hark! 'Cheep, cheep, cheep, cheep!' The sparrows were beginning. Their chorus rose. Their noise was cool as water to Michael's fever. An early cart rattled cheerfully down the road. It was morning.

Chapter IV: *Unending Childhood*

AFTER whooping-cough came chicken-pox, and it was settled that Michael should leave the Kindergarten where these illnesses were caught. A French governess was to teach him every morning and to walk with him every afternoon. Mrs. Fane wrote to Nurse to tell her of this decision and to announce that a Madame Flauve would on Monday next arrive at 64 Carlington Road to superintend the education of Michael. This news reached Nurse on the preceding Friday and threw her into an agitation. The whole house was turned upside down: curtains were changed; floors were beeswaxed; furniture was polished; pictures were dusted. All Saturday and Friday a great cleaning took place, and on Sunday every cushion was smoothed and patted; chairs were adjusted; mats were shaken; flowers were distributed, until in the evening Nurse and Cook and Annie, followed by Michael, marched over the house and examined their handiwork.

"Well, I hope we shall see something worth looking at," said Mrs. Frith. "I never worked so hard in all my natural."

"Oh, yes. Must get the place nice. Not going to have strange people come here and grumble," said Nurse.

"What is this Madame Flauve? Is she a lady?" Cook asked.

"Oh, yes. Yes. A lady. French. Very particular," Nurse replied.

Michael wondered what his governess would be like. He never remembered to have seen Nanny so reverently excited before.

"I've heard a lot about these French women," said Mrs. Frith. "A lot about them, I have. They live very gay, don't they?"

"Doesn't matter how they live. No. No. Must have everything at its best," Nurse insisted.

By the time the scouring of the house was done, Michael was prepared for the advent of a creature so lovely that he made up his mind the mere sight of her would fill him with joy. He had not settled exactly which princess she would most nearly resemble. As he turned over the pages of his fairy-books, he would fancy with every illustration that here was to be seen the image of his beautiful French governess. As he lay awake in his bed on a quiet Sunday evening, so pleasant was the imagination of her radiancy that fears and horrors were driven away by the power of her beauty's spell. The night acquired something of the peace and sanctity of Christmas Eve, when the air was hallowed by Santa Claus on his jovial pilgrimage. He had never felt so little oppressed by the night, so confident in the might of good.

On Monday morning Michael jigged through his dressing, jigged downstairs to breakfast, jigged through the meal itself and jigged upstairs to the dining-room to watch for the splendid arrival. He tambourinated upon the window-pane a gay little tune, jigging the while from foot to foot in an ecstasy of anticipation.

15

Nurse had decided that the morning-room was not a fit place for such a paragon to perform her duties. Nor did she feel that the day-nursery was worthy of her. So, even while Michael jigged at his vigil, Nurse was arming the dining-room table for an encounter with greatness. Inkpots were dusted and displayed; blotting-pads, including one poker—worked with a view of Antwerp Cathedral, were unfolded. Pens and pencils and pieces of india-rubber and pen-wipers and boxes of nibs and drawing-pins were lavishly scattered about the green tablecloth. Various blue exercise-books gleamed in the April sunlight and, to set the seal upon the whole business, a calendar of Great Thoughts was roughly divested of ninety-eight great thoughts at once, in order that for this rare female a correct announcement should celebrate the ninth of April, her famous date. At five minutes to ten Nurse and Michael were both in a state of excitement; Cook was saying that she had never regretted the inadequacy of the kitchen arrangements of Sixty-four until this moment; and Annie was bracing herself for the real effort, the opening of the door to Madame Flauve. The only calm person was Stella who, clasping a rubber doll with tight curly rubber hair and a stomachic squeak, chanted to herself the saga of Madame Flauve's arrival.

At two minutes past ten Michael said somebody was coming up the steps, and a ring confirmed his assertion. The door was opened. Madame Flauve was heard rubbing her boots on the SALVE of the mat, was heard putting away her umbrella in the peacock-blue china umbrella-stand, was heard enquiring for Mrs. Fane and was announced inaudibly by Annie.

Michael's heart sank when he beheld a fat young French-woman with a bilious complexion and little pig's eyes and a dowdy black mantle and a common black hat. As for Nurse, she sniffed quite audibly and muttered an insincere hope that Madame Flauve would find everything to her liking. The governess answered in the thick voice of one who is always swallowing jujubes that without a doubt she would find everything, and presently Nurse left the room with many a backward glance of contempt towards Madame Flauve.

When the lessons began (or rather before they began) a time-table was drawn up by Madame Flauve:

Monday	10—11 11—12 12—1	French Geography History	2.30 —4	Wa lk
Tuesday	10—11 11—12 12—1	Geography History French	2.30 —4	Wa lk
Wednesday	10—11 11—12 12—1	History Geography French	2.30 —4	Wa lk
Thursday	10—11 11—12 12—1	French History Geography	2.30 —4	Wa lk
Friday	10—11 11—12 12—1	Geography French History	2.30 —4	Wa lk

Michael, when he saw the programme of his work, felt much depressed. It seemed to lack variety and he was not very much cheered up to hear that at meals only French would be spoken. Those meals were dreadful. At first Nurse and Stella were present, but when Nanny found that Madame wanted to teach Stella the French for knife and fork, she declined to have dinner downstairs any longer, and Michael and Madame Flauve were left to dine tête-à-tête on dull food and a languishing conversation.

"Madam indeed," Nurse would sniff, when the governess had left after tea, "I never heard of such a thing in all my life. Madam! A fine Madam!"

"What an imperence," agreed Mrs. Frith. "Fancy, a ordinary volgar thing like that to go calling herself Madam, whatever shall we come to?"

"It does seem a cheek, don't it?" said Annie.

"I never!" Cook gasped. "I never! Madam! Well, I could almost laugh at the sauce of it. And all that cleaning as you might say for a person as isn't a scrap better than you and me."

"Oh, I've written to Mrs. Fane," said Nurse. "I said there must be some mistake been made. Oh, yes, a mistake—must be a mistake."

Michael did not much enjoy the walks with his governess. He was always taken to a second-hand furniture-shop in the Hammersmith Road, not a pleasant old furniture-shop with Toby mugs and stuffed birds and coins; but a barrack full of red washing-stands and white-handled chests of drawers. Madame Flauve informed him that she was engaged in furnishing at that moment, and would immediately show him a locket with the portrait of her husband inset. Michael could not gain any clear idea of what M. Flauve was like, since all that remained was a nebulous profile smothered by a very black moustache. Madame Flauve told him that M. Flauve was 'tout-à-fait charmant, mais charmant, mon petit. Il était si aimable, si gentil et d'un cœur très très bon.' Michael grew very tired of being jostled outside the furniture-shop every afternoon, while his governess grubbed around the ugly furniture and argued with the man about the prices. The only article she ever bought was a commode, which so violently embarrassed Michael that he blushed the whole way home. But Madame Flauve often made him blush and would comment upon subjects not generally mentioned except by Mrs. Frith, and even by her only in a spirit of hearty coarseness that did not make Michael feel ashamed like this Frenchwoman's suggestion of the nasty. He was on one occasion very much disgusted by her remarks on the inside of an egg that was slightly set. Yet while he was disgusted, his curiosity was stimulated by the information imparted, and he made further enquiries from Nurse that evening. Nanny was horrified, and said plainly that she considered this governess no better than a low beast and that she should write accordingly to Mrs. Fane.

After a month or two Michael was sent back to school in the morning, though the afternoon walks still continued for a time. When Michael returned to the Misses Marrow, he was promoted to the class above the Kindergarten and was set to learn the elements of Latin in a desultory and unpractical way, that is to say he was made to learn—

Nominative,	mensa,	a table
Vocative,	mensa,	O table
Accusative,	mensam,	a table

and the rest of the unintelligible rigmarole. He had no clear notion what Latin was, and so far as he could make out nobody else at the Miss Marrows' school had any clearer notion. Indeed, the only distinct addition to his knowledge of life was gained from Vernon Brown who with great ingenuity had hollowed out a cork and by the insertion of several pins in the front had made of it a miniature cage in which he kept a fly. All the other boys were much impressed by Vernon Brown's achievement, and very soon they all came to school with flies captive in excavated corks. Michael longed to be like these bigger boys and pined for a cage. One day Edward Arnott gave him one, and all the rest of that day Michael watched the fly trying to escape. When he showed it to Madame Flauve, she professed herself shocked by the cruelty of it and begged him to release the fly, asserting that she would find him a substitute which would deceive all the other boys. Michael agreed to release his captive and the long-imprisoned fly walked painfully out of his cell. Then Madame Flauve chipped off a little piece of coal and tied it round with one of her own hairs and showed Michael how by cunningly twisting this hair, the coal would gain the appearance of mobility. Michael was doubtful at first, but Madame's exaggerated encouragement led him to suppose that it was safe to practise the deception on his companions. So on the next day he proceeded to exhibit his 'fly.' But everybody knew it was coal and jeered at Michael and made him very unhappy and anxious never again to attempt to differentiate himself or his actions from the rest of mankind.

Michael's mother came home towards the end of July, and Madame Flauve vanished to her husband and house and furniture. Michael did not regret her. Mrs. Fane asked him many questions and particularly she wanted to know if he was perfectly happy. Michael said 'yes,' and his mother seemed satisfied. She was now very much taken up with Stella, who was a lovely little girl with grey eyes and light brown glinting hair. Michael did not exactly feel jealous of his sister, but he had an emotion of disappointment that no longer could he be alone with his mother in a fragrant intimacy from which the perpetually sleeping Stella was excluded. Now Stella no longer slept all the time, but, on the contrary, was very much awake and very eager to be entertained. Michael also felt a twinge of regret that Stella should be able out of her own self to entertain grown-up people. He wished that he could compose these wonderful, endless songs of hers. He could not but admit that they were wonderful, and exactly like real poetry. To be sure their subjects were ordinary enough. There was no magic in them. Stella would simply sing of getting up in the morning and of the morning bath and the towel and the bread and milk for breakfast. She would sing, too, of the ride in the perambulator and of the ladies who paid her compliments as she passed. It was a little galling to Michael that he, so long his mother's only companion, should have to share her love with such an insidious rival. Curious men with long hair came to the house, apparently just to see Stella; for they took no notice at all of Michael. These long-haired visitors would sit round in the drawing-room, while Stella played at the piano pieces that were not half so hummable as those which Michael had already learned to play in violent allegretto. Stella would sit upright in her starchiest frock and widest sash and play without any music a long and boring noise that made Michael feel very fidgety. He would endure it for a while and then he would have to go out of the room. The first time he had done this he had expected somehow that people would run after him to bring him back. But nobody moved. Everyone was intent upon Stella and her noise. They were all grunting and clearing their throats and making unintelligible exclamations. Michael was glad that they had begun to build houses in the waste ground opposite. It was better to watch men climbing up ladders and walking over planks and messing with lumps of mortar than to sit there among those guttural men in an atmosphere of Stella worship. He felt sometimes that he would like to pinch Stella's legs—they looked so sleek and well-behaved, as she sat there playing the piano. Michael was never invited to play on the drawing-room piano. He was only allowed to play up in the day-nursery, with merely the ambition of one day being able to reach the pedals to stir him on.

"Ach, Mrs. Vane," he heard these long-haired men declare. "Your daughter is wonderful. Ach! Ach! Ach! She is a genius. She will be the great bianist of the new generation. Ach! Ach! Ach!"

Michael began to feel that his love for his mother or her love for him did not matter. He began to feel that only what he himself thought and wanted did matter; and when she went away again he was sorry, but not so sorry as he used to be. One of these long-haired men now began to come every day to give Stella lessons on the drawing-room piano. He would give a very loud knock and hang up a wide-brimmed black hat in the hall and clear his throat and button up his coat very tightly and march into the drawing-room to wait for Stella to be brought down. Stella would come down the stairs with her grey eyes shining and her hair all fuzzy and her hands smelling of pink soap, while Nurse would blow very importantly and tell Michael not to peep round corners. Stella's music lessons were much grander than Michael's in the stuffy back-room of Miss Marrow's. Besides, Michael's music lessons were now particularly unpleasant, because Miss Hunt, his mistress, had grown two warts on her first finger during the summer holidays, which made him feel sick during their eternal duets.

The withdrawal of Madame Flauve from the superintendence of Michael's afternoon walks was apparently a great blow to Nurse. She had acquired a habit either of retiring to the night-nursery or of popping out of the back-door on secret errands. Stella in the charge of Annie was perfectly happy upstairs, and Nurse resented very strongly Michael's enquiries as to where she was going. Michael had no ulterior reasons for his questions. He was sincerely interested by these afternoon walks of Nurse, and speculated often upon her destination. She would always return very cheerful and would often bring him home small presents—a dark blue bird on a pin at boat-race time (for Nurse was staunchly Oxford), a penny packet of stamps most of which were duplicates inside, penny illustrated books of Cock Robin or Tom Thumb; and once she brought him home a Night Companion. This Night Companion was a club-headed stick, very powerful and warranted to secure the owner from a murderous attack. It was one of a row in the window of a neighbouring umbrella-shop, a long row of Night Companions that cost one shilling each. Michael liked his stick and took it to bed with him and was comforted, when he woke up, by the sight of its knotted head upon the bolster. He grew very intimate with the stick and endowed it with character and temperament and humanity. He would often stare at the still unpurchased Night Companions in the shop, trying to discover if any other of them were so beneficent and so pleasant a companion as his own. In time he took a fancy to another, and begged Nurse to be allowed to buy this for Stella. Nurse was gratified by his appreciation of her present and gave him leave to break into the ten-shilling piece to endow Stella with a Companion. Michael himself carried it home, wrapped in a flimsy brown paper and tied up as he thought unnecessarily with a flimsy string. Stella was told to take it to bed with her and did so, but by some accident grazed her forehead on the Night Companion's knotty head and cried so much that it was taken away from her. This was all the better for Michael who thenceforth had two Night Companions—one on either side of him to guard him from the door and the window.

Still, notwithstanding these presents, Nurse grew more and more irritable to find Michael watching her exits from and entrances into 64 Carlington Road. Once, she was so much annoyed to see Michael's face pressed against the pane of the morning-room window that she slid all the way down the area-steps and sent Michael to bed as a punishment for peeping. At last she decided that Michael must go for walks by himself and lest he should be lost or get into mischief, every walk must be in the same direction, along the same road to the same place and back. He was to walk up Carlington Road into the Hammersmith Road and along the Kensington Road as far as the Earl's Court Road. Here he was to stop and turn round and walk back to Carlington Road on his traces.

Michael detested this walk. He would stump up the area-steps, watched by Nurse, and he would walk steadily, looking neither to the right nor to the left according to orders, as far as 44 Carlington Road. Here in the morning-room window was a small aquarium, sadly mobile with half a dozen pale goldfish, that Michael would be compelled to watch for a few seconds before he turned round and acknowledged the fact that Nurse was flicking him on with her hand. Michael would proceed past the other houses until he came to 22 Carlington Road, where a break occurred, caused by a house entirely different from any of the others, at the side of which was a huge double door. This was sometimes open, and inside could be seen men hammering with chisels at enormous statues including representations of Queen Victoria and of a benignant lion. Next to this house was a post office, not an ordinary post office where stamps could be bought, but a harum-scarum place, full of postmen running up and down and emptying bags and hammering on letters and talking very loudly and very quickly. By this office Carlington Road made an abrupt rectangular turn past a tumble-down tarred fence, through whose interstices could be seen a shadowy garden full of very long pale grass and of trees with jet-black trunks. Beyond the trees was a tumble-down house with big bare windows glinting amongst the ivy. After this Carlington Road went on again with smaller houses of a deeper red brick than those in the part where Michael lived. They had no basements, and one could see into their dining-rooms, so close were they to the road. When 2 Carlington Road was reached a tall advertisement hoarding began, and for a hundred yards the walk became absolutely interesting. Then Carlington Mansions rose majestic, and Michael, who had been told that they were flats and had heard people wondering at this strange new method of existence, loitered for a moment in order to watch a man in a uniform, sitting on a wooden chair and reading a pink newspaper. He also read the names of people who were either out or in, and settled, when he was older, to live in a flat in the security of many other families and a man in a green uniform. The roar of the Hammersmith Road burst upon him, and dreams were over for a while, as he hurried along past eight shops, at none of which he would dare to look since he read in a book of a boy who had been taken off to the police station on a charge of theft, though he was actually as innocent as Michael himself and was merely interested by the contents of a shop window. The next turning to Carlington Road was a queer terrace, very quiet except that it overlooked the railway, very quiet and melancholy and somehow wicked. Nothing ever turned down here except an occasional dog or cat; no servants stood gossiping by area-gates, and at the end of it loomed the tumble-down house whose garden Michael had already seen near the post office. He used to think as he left Padua Terrace behind him that one day for a great adventure he would like to walk along under its elm-trees to discover if anyone did live in those dark houses; but he never managed to be brave enough to do so. Michael now crossed the railway bridge and looked at the advertisements: then followed a dull line of iron railings with rusty pineapples on top of each of them. These were bounded at each end by gates that were marked 'Private. No Thoroughfare,' and after the second gate came the first crossing. Michael had been told to be very careful of crossings, and he used to poise himself on the kerb for a moment to see if any carts were near. If none were even in sight, he used to run across as quickly as he could. There were three other crossings before Earl's Court Road was reached, and one of them was so wide that he was very glad indeed when it was put behind him. All the way, terrace after terrace of grim houses, set back from the high road behind shrubberies, had to be passed, and all the way Michael used to hum to himself for company and diversion and encouragement. The only interesting event was a pavement-artist, and he was very often not there. It was an exasperating and monotonous walk, and he hated it for the gloom it shed upon all his afternoons.

Sometimes Michael would arrive home before Nanny, and then he would have to endure a long cross-examination upon his route. The walk was not sufficiently interesting to invent tales about, and he resented Nurse's incredulous attitude and wrinkled obstinate face. Indeed, Michael began to resent Nurse altogether, and so far as he was able he avoided her. His scheme of things was logical: he had already a philosophy, and his conception of the wonder inherent in everything was evidently not unique, because the pictures in Don Quixote proved conclusively that what Michael thought, other people besides himself thought. He might be old-fashioned, as Nurse assured him he was; but if to be old-fashioned was to live in the world of Don Quixote, he certainly preferred it to the world in which Nanny lived. That seemed to him a circumscribed and close existence for which he had no sympathy. It was a world of poking about in medicine-cupboards, of blind unreasonableness, of stupidity and malice and blank ugliness. He would sit watching Nanny nibbling with her front teeth the capers of the caper sauce, and he would hate her. She interfered with him, with his day-dreams and toys and meals; and the only time when he wanted her presence was in the middle of the night, when she was either drinking her glass of ale in the kitchen or snoring heavily in the next room. Michael's only ambition was to live in his own world. This he would have shared with his mother, but her visits were now so rare that it was unwise to rely on her presence for happiness. He was learning to do without her: Nurse he had never yet learnt to endure. She charged ferociously into his fancies, shattering them with her fussy interference, just as she would snatch away his clay pipe, when the most perfect bubble was trembling on the edge of the bowl.

"Time for tea," she would mutter. "Time for bed," she would chatter. Always it was time for something unpleasant.

Mrs. Frith, on the other hand, was a person whose attractions grew with longer friendship, as Nurse's decreased even from the small quantity she originally possessed. As Michael month by month grew older, Mrs. Frith expanded towards him. She found him an attentive, even a breathless listener to her rollicking tales. Her life Michael plainly perceived to have been crammed with exciting adventures. In earliest youth she had been forced by cunning to outwit a brutal father with the frightening habit of coming home in the evening and taking off his belt to her and her brothers and her sisters. The house in which she lived had been full of hiding-places, and Mrs. Frith, picturing herself to Michael of less ample girth, described wonderfully how her father had actually routed for her with a broom-handle while her mother sat weeping into an apron. Then it appeared that it was the custom of small boys in the street of her youth to sell liquorice-water in exchange for pins.

"But was it nice?" asked Michael, remembering liquorice-powder.

"Lovely stuff," Mrs. Frith affirmed. "They used to go calling up and down, 'Fine liquorice-water! Fine liquorice-water! Bring out your pins and have a bottle of liquorice-water.'"

"And did you?" asked Michael.

"Did we? Of course we did—every pin in the place. There wasn't a pin in the whole street after those boys had gone by."

"What else did you do when you were little, Mrs, Frith?"

"What else? Why everything."

"Yes, but tell me what," Michael begged, clasping his knees and looking earnestly at Cook.

"Why once I went to a Sunday-school treat and got thrown off of a donkey and showed more than I meant and the boys all hollered after me going to Sunday-school and I used to stand behind a corner and dodge them. The saucy demons!"

These tales were endless, and Michael thought how jolly it would be to set out early one summer morning with Mrs. Frith and look for adventures like Don Quixote. This became a favourite day-dream, and he used to fancy Mrs. Frith tossed in a blanket like Sancho Panza. What company she would be, and it would be possible with two donkeys. He had seen women as fat as her riding on donkeys by the seaside.

One day Mrs. Frith told him she was thinking of getting married again, and on a Sunday afternoon Michael was introduced to her future husband, a certain Mr. Hopkins, who had a shining red head and an enormous coloured handkerchief into which he trumpeted continuously. Mr. Hopkins also had a daughter three or four years older than Michael—a wizened little girl called Flossie who spoke in a sort of hiss and wore very conspicuous underclothing of red flannelette. Michael and Flossie played together shyly under the admiring patronage of Mrs. Frith and Mr. Hopkins, and were just beginning to be friendly when Nurse came in and said:

"Can't be allowed. No, no. Never heard of such a thing. Tut-tut."

After this Nurse and Mrs. Frith did not seem to get on very well, and Mrs. Frith used to talk about 'people as gave theirselves airs which they had no business to of done.' She was kinder than ever to Michael and gave him as many sultanas as he wanted and told him all about the house into which she and Mr. Hopkins and Flossie would presently depart from Carlington Road.

"Are you going away?" Michael asked, aghast.

"Going to be married," said Mrs. Frith.

"But I don't want you to go."

"There, bless your heart, I've a good mind to stay. I believe you'll miss your poor old Mrs. Frith, eh, ducky?"

Everybody nice went away, Michael thought. It was extraordinary how only nasty food and nasty people were wholesome.

Mrs. Frith's departure was even more exciting than her stories. One afternoon Michael found her in the kitchen, dancing about with her skirts kilted above her knees. He was a little embarrassed at first, but very soon he had to laugh because she was evidently not behaving like this in order to show off, but because she enjoyed dancing about the kitchen.

"Why are you dancing, Mrs. Frith?" he asked.

"Happy as a lark, lovey," she answered in an odd voice. "Happy as a lark, for we won't go home till morning, we won't go home till morning," and singing, she twirled round and round until she sank into a wicker arm-chair. At this moment Annie came running downstairs with Nurse, and both of them glared at Mrs. Frith with shocked expressions.

"What ever are you doing, Cook?" said Nurse.

"That's all right, lovey. That's All Sir Garnet, and don't you make no mistake. Don't you—make no mistake."

Here Mrs. Frith gave a very loud hiccup and waved her arms and did not even say 'beg pardon' for the offensive noise.

"Michael," said Nurse, "go upstairs at once. Mrs. Frith, get up. You ignorant and vulgar woman. Get up."

"And you ought to be ashamed of yourself," said Cook to Nurse. "You old performing monkey, that's what you are."

"Annie," said Nurse, "fetch a policeman in, and go and get this woman's box."

"Woman!" said Mrs. Frith. "Woman yourself. Who's a woman? I'm not a woman. No, I'm not. And if I am a woman, you're not the one to say so. Ah, I know how many bottles have gone out of this house and come in—not by me."

"Hold your impudent tongue," said Nurse.

"I shall not hold my tongue, so now," retorted Mrs. Frith.

Michael had squeezed himself behind the kitchen door fascinated by this duel. It was like Alice in Wonderland, and every minute he expected to see Cook throwing plates at Nanny, who was certainly making faces exactly like the Duchess. The area door slammed, and Michael wondered what was going to happen. Presently there came the sound of a deep tread in the passage and a policeman entered.

"What's all this?" he said in a deep voice.

"Constable," said Nurse, "will you please remove this dreadful woman?"

"What's she been doing?" asked the policeman.

"She's drunk."

Mrs. Frith apparently overwhelmed by the enormity of the accusation tottered to her feet and seized a saucepan.

"None of that now," said the policeman roughly, as he caught her by the waist.

"Oh, I'm not afraid of a bluebottle," said Mrs. Frith haughtily. "Not of a bluebottle, I'm not."

"Are you going to charge her?" the policeman asked.

"No, no. Nothing but turn her out. The girl's packing her box. Give her the box and let her go."

"Not without my wages," said Mrs. Frith. "I'm not going to leave my wages behind. Certaintly I'm not."

Nurse fumbled in her purse, and at last produced some money.

"That's the easiest way," said the policeman. "Pay her the month and let her go. Come on, my lady."

He seized Mrs. Frith and began to walk her to the door as if she were a heavy sack. Michael began to cry. He did not want Mrs. Frith to be hurt and he felt frightened. In the passage she suddenly broke loose and, turning round, pushed Nurse into the laundry-basket and was so pleased with her successful effort that she almost ran out of the house and could presently be heard singing very cheerfully 'White wings, they never grow weary,' to the policeman. In the end her trunk was pushed down the front-door steps, and after more singing and arguing a four-wheeler arrived and Mrs. Frith vanished for ever from Carlington Road.

The effect of this scene on Nurse was to make her more repressive and secretive. She was also very severe on vulgarity; and all sorts of old words were wrapped up in new words, as when bread and dripping became bread and honey, because dripping was vulgar. The house grew much gloomier with Mrs. Frith's departure. The new cook whose name Michael never found out, because she remained the impersonal official, was very brusque and used to say: "Now then, young man, out of my kitchen or I'll tell Nurse. And don't hang about in the passage or in two-twos you'll be sorry you ever came downstairs."

It was autumn again, and the weather was dreary and wet. Michael suffered a severe shock one morning. It was too foggy to go to school and he was sitting alone in the window of the morning-room, staring at the impenetrable and fearful yellowness of the air. Suddenly he heard the cry, 'Remember, remember the Fifth of November, and gunpowder, treason and plot,' and, almost before he had time to realize it was the dreaded Guy Fawkes, a band of loud-voiced boys with blackened faces came surging down the area steps and held close to the window a nodding Guy. Michael shrieked with fear and ran from the room, only to be told by Nurse that she'd never heard such old-fashioned nonsense in all her life.

During that November the fogs were very bad and, as an epidemic term had compelled the Misses Marrow to close their school, Michael brooded at home in the gaslit rooms that shone dully in the street of footsteps. The long morning would drag its length out, and dinner would find no appetite in Michael. Stella seemed not to care to play and would mope with round eyes saddened by this eternal gloom. Dusk was merely marked by the drawing down of the blinds at the clock's hour without regard to the transit from day to night. Michael used to wonder if it were possible that this fog would last for ever, if for ever he would live in Carlington Road in this yellow twilight, if his mother had forgotten there ever was such a person as Michael Fane. But, at any rate, he would have to grow up. He could not always be the same size. That was a consolation. It was jolly to dream of being grown-up, to plan one's behaviour and think of freedom. The emancipation of being grown-up seemed to Michael to be a magnificent prospect. To begin with it was no longer possible to be naughty. He realized, indeed, that crimes were a temptation to some grown-ups, that people of a certain class committed murders and burglaries, but as he felt no inclination to do either, he looked forward to a life of unbroken virtue.

So far as he could ascertain, grown-up people were exempt from even the necessity to distinguish between good and evil. If Michael examined the Commandments one by one, this became obvious. *Thou shalt have none other gods than me.* Why should one want to have? One was enough. The Children of Israel must be different from Michael. He could not understand such peculiar people. *Make not to thyself any graven image.* The only difficulty about this commandment was its length for learning. Otherwise it did not seem to bear on present-day life. *Thou shalt not take the name of the Lord thy God in vain.* This was another vague injunction. Who wanted to? *Remember thou keep holy the Sabbath Day.* It was obviously a simple matter for grown-up people, who no longer enjoyed playing with toys, to keep this commandment. At present it was difficult to learn and difficult to keep. *Honour thy father and thy mother.* He loved his mother. He would always love her, even if she forgot him. He might not love her so much as formerly, but he would always love her. *Thou shalt do no murder.* Michael had no intention of doing murder. Since the Hangman in Punch and Judy he was cured of any inclination towards murder. *Thou shalt not commit adultery.* Why should he ever want to marry another man's wife? At present he could not imagine himself married to anybody. He supposed that as one result of growing up he would get married. But, forewarned, he would take care not to choose somebody else's wife. *Thou shalt not steal.* With perfect freedom to eat when and where and what one liked, why should one steal? *Thou shalt not bear false witness.* It would not be necessary to lie when grown up, because one could not then be punished. *Thou shalt not covet thy neighbour's ox.* He would covet nothing, for when he was grown up he would be able to obtain whatever he wanted.

This desire to be grown up sustained him through much, even through the long foggy nights which made his bedroom more fearfully still than before. The room would hardly seem any longer to exist in the murk which crept through it. The crocus-shaped jet of the gas burned in the vaporous midnight with an unholy flame somehow, thought Michael, as candles must look, when at the approach of ghosts they burn blue. How favourable to crime was fog, how cleverly the thief might steal over the coal-yard at the back of the house and with powerful tools compel the back-door to open. And the murderers, how they must rejoice in the impenetrable air as with long knives they stole out from distant streets in search of victims. Michael's nerves were so wrought upon by the unchanging gloom of these wintry days that even to be sent by Nurse to fetch her thimble or work-bag before tea was a racking experience.

"Now then, Michael, run downstairs like a good boy and fetch my needle and cotton which I left in the morning-room," Nurse would command. And in the gathering dusk Michael would practically slide downstairs until he reached the basement. Then, clutching the object of his errand, he would brace himself for the slower ascent. Suppose that when he reached the hall there were two skeletons sitting on the hall chest? Suppose that on the landing above a number of rats rushed out from the housemaid's closet to bite his legs and climb over him and gnaw his face? Suppose that from the landing outside his own room a masked burglar were stealing into his room to hide himself under the bed? Suppose that when he arrived back at the day-nursery, Stella and Nurse were lying with their heads chopped off, as he had once seen a family represented by a pink newspaper in the window of a little shop near Hammersmith Broadway? Michael used to reach his goal, white and shaking, and slam the door against the unseen follower who had dogged his footsteps from the coal-cellar. The cries of a London twilight used to oppress him. From the darkening streets and from the twinkling houses inexplicable sounds floated about the air. They had the sadness of church-bells, and like church-bells they could not be located exactly. Michael thought that London was the most melancholy city in the world. Even at Christmas-time, behind all the gaiety and gold of a main road lay the trackless streets that were lit, it seemed, merely by pin-points of gas, so far apart were the lamp-posts, such a small sad circle of pavement did they illuminate. The rest was shadows and glooms and whispers. Even in the jollity of the pantomime and comfortable smell of well-dressed people the thought of the journey home through the rainy evening brooded upon the gayest scene. The going home was sad indeed, as in the farthest corner of the jolting omnibus they jogged through the darkness. The painted board of places and fares used to depress Michael. He could not bear to think of the possibilities opened up by the unknown names beyond Piccadilly Circus. Once in a list of fares he read the word Whitechapel and shivered at the thought that an omnibus could from Whitechapel pass the corner of Carlington Road. This very omnibus had actually come from the place where murders were done. Murderers might at this moment be travelling in his company. Michael looked askance at the six nodding travellers who sat opposite, at the fumes of their breath, at their hands clasped round the handles of their umbrellas. There, for all he knew, sat Jack the Ripper. It happened that night that one of the travellers, an old gentleman with gold-rimmed eye-glasses, alighted at the corner and actually turned down Carlington Road. Michael was horrified and tugged at Nanny's arm to make her go faster.

"Whyever on earth are you dancing along like a bear for? Do you want to go somewhere, you fidgety boy?" said Nurse, pulling Michael to her side with a jerk.

"Oh, Nanny, there's a man following us, who got out of our bus."

"Well, why shouldn't he get out? Tut-tut. Other people besides you want to get out of buses. I shan't ever take you to the pantomime again, if you aren't careful."

"Well, I will be careful," said Michael, who, perceiving the lamp in their front hall, recovered from his fright and became anxious to propitiate Nanny.

"So I should think," muttered Nurse. "Tut-tut-tut-tut-tut." Michael thought she would never stop clicking her tongue.

About this time with the fogs and the rain and the loneliness and constant fear that surrounded him, Michael began to feel ill. He worried over his thin arms, comparing them with the sleek Stella's. His golden hair lost its lustre and became drab and dark and skimpy. His cheeks lost their rose-red, and black lines ringed his large and sombre blue eyes. He cared for little else but reading, and even reading tired him very much, so that once he actually fell asleep over the big Don Quixote. About two hundred pages were bent underneath the weight of his body, and the book was taken away from him as a punishment for his carelessness. It was placed out of his reach on top of the bookcase and Michael used to stand below and wish for it. No entreaties were well enough expressed to move Nurse; and Don Quixote remained high out of reach in the dust and shadows of the ceiling. Nurse grew more and more irrational in her behaviour and complained more and more of the neuralgia to which she declared she was a positive martyr. Annie went away into the country because she was ill and a withered housemaid took her place, while the tall thin house in Carlington Road became more grim every day.

Then a lucky event gave Michael a new interest. Miss Caroline Marrow began to teach him the elements of Botany, and recommended all the boys to procure window-boxes for themselves. Michael told Nurse about this; and, though she muttered and clicked and blew a great deal, one day a bandy-legged man actually came and fitted Michael's window-sills with two green window-boxes. He spent the whole of his spare time in prodding the sweet new mould, in levelling it and patting it, and filling in unhappy little crevices which had been overlooked. Then on a fine spring morning he paid a visit to the old woman who sold penny packets of seeds, and bought nasturtiums, mignonette, Virginia stocks and candytuft, twelve pansy roots and twelve daisy roots. Michael's flowers grew and flourished and he loved his window-boxes. He liked to turn towards his window at night now. Somehow those flowers were a protection. He liked to lie in bed during the sparrow-thronged mornings of spring and fancy how the birds must enjoy hopping about in his window-boxes. He was always careful to scatter plenty of crumbs, so that they should not be tempted to peck up his seeds or pull to pieces the pansy buds. He was disappointed that neither the daisies nor the pansies smelt sweet, and when the mignonette bloomed, he almost sniffed it away, so lovely was the perfume of it during the blue days of June. He had a set of gardening tools, so small and suitable to the size of his garden that rake and hoe and spade and fork were all originally fastened to one small square of cardboard.

But, best of all, when the pansies were still a-blowing and the Virginia stocks were fragrant, and when from his mother's window below he could see his nasturtium flowers, golden and red and even tortoiseshell against the light, his mother came home suddenly for a surprise, and the house woke up.

"But you're not looking well, darling," she said.

"Oh, yes, quite well. Quite well," muttered Nurse, "Quite well. Mustn't be a molly-coddle. No. No."

"I really must see about a nice governess for you," said Mrs. Fane. Nurse sniffed ominously.

Chapter V: *The First Fairy Princess*

MISS CARTHEW'S arrival widened very considerably Michael's view of life. Nurse's crabbed face and stunted figure had hitherto appropriately enough dominated such realities of existence as escaped from the glooms and shadows of his solitary childhood. Michael had for so long been familiar with ugliness that he was dangerously near to an eternal imprisonment in a maze of black fancies. He had come to take pleasure in the grotesque and the macabre, and even on the sunniest morning his imagination would turn to twilight and foggy eves, to basements and empty houses and loneliness and dust. Michael would read furtively the forbidden newspapers that Nurse occasionally left lying about. In these he would search for murders and crimes, and from their association with thrills of horror, the newspapers themselves had gradually acquired a definitely sinister personality. If at dusk Michael found a newspaper by Nurse's arm-chair, he would approach it with beating heart, and before he went over to read it where close to the window the light of day lingered, he would brood upon his own daring, as if some Bluebeard's revenge might follow.

When Michael's mother was at home, he was able to resume the cheerfulness of the last occasion on which her company had temporarily relieved his solitude; but always behind the firelit confidences, the scented good mornings and good nights, the gay shopping walks and all the joys which belonged to him and her, stood threatening and inevitable the normal existence with Nurse in which these rosy hours must be remembered as only hours, fugitive and insecure and rare. Now came Miss Carthew's brisk and lively presence to make many alterations in the life of 64 Carlington Road, Kensington.

Michael's introduction to his governess took place in the presence of his mother and, as he stood watching the two women in conversation, he was aware of a tight-throated feeling of pleasure. They were both so tall and slim and beautiful: they were both so straight and clean that they gave him the glad sensation of blinds pulled up to admit the sun.

"I think we're going to be rather good friends," said Miss Carthew.

Michael could only stare his agreement, but he managed to run before Miss Carthew in order to open the door politely, when she was going out. In bed that night he whispered to his mother how much he liked Miss Carthew and how glad he was that he could leave the Miss Marrows' for the company of Miss Carthew all day long.

"And all night?" he asked wistfully.

"No, not at present, darling," she answered. "Nanny will still look after you at night."

"Will she?" Michael questioned somewhat doubtfully.

After Mrs. Fane went away, there was a short interval before the new-comer assumed her duties. During this time Michael hummed incessantly and asked Nurse a thousand questions about Miss Carthew.

"Goodness gracious, what a fuss about a governess," commented Nanny. "Tut-tut. It might be the Queen of England. She'll be here quite soon enough for everyone, I dare say."

It fell out that Miss Carthew was to arrive on Valentine Day, and Michael with a delicious breathlessness thought how wonderful it would be to present her with a Valentine. He did not dare tell Nurse of his intention; but he hoped that by sending Valentines to every inmate of the house he might be allowed to include Miss Carthew. Nurse was agreeable to the notion of receiving a token, and in her company Michael set out to a neighbouring stationer's shop to make his purchases. A Valentine for Cook was bought, and one of precisely the same design for Gladys the withered housemaid, and a rather better one for Stella, and a better one still for Nurse.

"Come along now," said Nanny.

"Oh, but can't I get one for Miss Carthew? Do let me."

"Tut-tut-tut. What nonsense. I do declare. Whatever do you want to give her a Valentine for?" Nurse demanded, as she tried to hustle Michael from the shop.

"Oh, do let me, Nanny."

"Well, come along, and don't be all day choosing. Here, this will do," said Nurse, as she picked one from the penny tray.

But Michael had other ideas. He had noticed an exquisite Valentine of apple-green satin painted with the rosiest of Cupids, the most crimson of pierced hearts, a Valentine that was almost a sachet so thick was it, so daintily fringed with fretted silver-paper.

"That one," he declared, pointing.

"Now what have I told you about pointing?"

"That large one's a shilling," said the stationer.

"Come along, come along," grumbled Nurse. "Wasting good money."

"But I want to have that one," said Michael.

For the first time in his life he did not feel at all afraid of Nurse, so absolutely determined was he to present Miss Carthew with the Valentine of his own free choice.

"I will have that one," he added. "It's my money."

"You will, will you, you naughty boy? You won't, then. So now! You dare defy me. I never heard of such a thing. No, nothing more this morning, thank you," Nurse added, turning to the stationer. "The little boy has got all he wants. Say 'thank you' to the gentleman and 'good morning,'" Nurse commanded Michael.

"I won't," he declared. "I won't." Scowling so that his nose nearly vanished into his forehead, and beating back the tears that were surging to his eyes, Michael followed Nurse from the shop. As he walked home, he dug his nails wrathfully into the envelope of Valentines, and then suddenly he saw a drain in the gutter. He hastily stooped and pushed the packet between the bars of the grating, and let it fall beyond the chance of recovery. When they reached their house, Nurse told him to give her the cards, so that they might not be soiled before presentation.

"I've dropped them," said Michael sullenly.

"Dropped them? Dropped them? What do you mean—dropped them?"

"I threw them away," said Michael.

"On purpose?"

"Yes. I can do what I like with my own things."

"You ungrateful wicked boy," said Nurse, horrified by such a claim.

"I don't care if I am," Michael answered. "I wanted to give Miss Carthew a Valentine. Mother would have let me."

"Your mother isn't here. And when she isn't here, I'm your mother," said Nurse, looking more old and wrinkled and monkey-like than ever.

"How dare you say you're my mother?" gasped the outraged son. "You're not. You're not. Why, you're not a lady, so you couldn't ever be my mother."

Hereupon Nurse disconcerted Michael by bursting into tears, and he presently found himself almost petting her and declaring that he was very sorry for having been so unkind. He found a certain luxury in this penitence just as he used to enjoy a reconciliation with the black kittens. Perhaps it was this scene with Nurse that prompted him soon afterwards to the creation of another with his sister. The second scene was brought about by Stella's objection to the humming with which Michael was somewhat insistently celebrating the advent of Miss Carthew.

"Don't hum, Michael. Don't hum. Please don't hum," Stella begged very solemnly. "Please don't hum, because it makes my head hurt."

"I *will* hum, and every time you ask me not to hum, I'll hum more louder," said Michael.

Stella at once went to the piano in the day-nursery and began to play her most unmelodious tune. Michael ran to the cupboard and produced a drum which he banged defiantly. He banged it so violently that presently the drum, already worn very thin, burst. Michael was furious and immediately proceeded to twang an over-varnished zither. So furiously did he twang the zither that finally he caught one of his nails in a sharp string of the treble, and in great pain hurled the instrument across the room. Meanwhile, Stella continued to play, and when Michael commanded her to stop, answered annoyingly that she had been told to practise.

"Don't say pwactise, you silly. Say practise," Michael contemptuously exclaimed.

"Shan't," Stella answered with that cold and fat stolidity of demeanour and voice which disgusted Michael like the fat of cold mutton.

"I'm older than you," Michael asserted.

Stella made no observation, but continued to play, and Michael, now acutely irritated, rushed to the piano and slammed down the lid. Stella must have withdrawn her fingers in time, for there was no sign of any pinch or bruise upon them. However, she began to cry, while Michael addressed to her the oration which for a long time he had wished to utter.

"You are silly. You are a cry-baby. Fancy crying about nothing. I wouldn't. Everybody doesn't want to hear your stupid piano-playing. Boys at school think pianos are stupid. You always grumble about my humming. You are a cry-baby.

What are little boys made of?
Sugar and spice and all that's nice,
That's what little boys are made of.
What are little girls made of?
Slugs and snails and puppy-dogs' tails,
Ugh! that's what little girls are made of."

"They're not," Stella screamed. "They're not!" Michael's perversion of the original rhyme made her inarticulate with grief and rage. "They're not, you naughty boy!"

Michael, contented with his victory, left Stella to herself and her tears. As he hummed his way downstairs, he thought sensuously of the imminent reconciliation, and in about ten minutes, having found some barley-sugar buried against an empty day, Michael came back to Stella with peace-offerings and words of comfort.

Miss Carthew arrived on the next morning and the nervous excitement of waiting was lulled. Miss Carthew came through the rain of Valentine Day, and Michael hugged himself with the thought of her taking off her mackintosh and handing it to Gladys to be dried. With the removal of her wet outdoor clothes, Miss Carthew seemed to come nearer to Michael and, as they faced each other over the schoolroom table (for the day-nursery in one moment had become the schoolroom), Michael felt that he could bear not being grown up just for the pleasure of sitting opposite to his new governess.

It was not so much by these lessons that Michael's outlook was widened as by the conversations he enjoyed with Miss Carthew during their afternoon walks. She told him, so far as she could, everything that he desired to know. She never accused him of being old-fashioned or inquisitive, and indeed as good as made him feel that the more questions he asked the better she would like it. Miss Carthew had all the mental and imaginative charm of the late Mrs. Frith in combination with an outward attractiveness that made her more dearly beloved. Indeed Miss Carthew had numberless pleasant qualities. If she promised anything, the promise was always kept to the letter. If Michael did not know his lesson or omitted the performance of an ordained task, Miss Carthew was willing to hear the explanation of his failure and was never unreasonable in her judgment. One morning very soon after her arrival, Michael was unable to repeat satisfactorily the verse of the psalm Venite Adoremus set for him to learn.

"Why don't you know it, Michael?" Miss Carthew asked.

"I had to go to bed."

"But surely you had plenty of time before you went to bed?" Miss Carthew persisted.

"Nanny wanted to go out, and I went to bed early," Michael explained.

For a moment or two Miss Carthew considered the problem silently. Then she rang the bell and told withered Gladys that she wished to speak to Nurse. Presently Nurse came in, very aggressive and puckered.

"Did Michael have to go to bed very early last night?" Miss Carthew enquired.

"Oh, yes. Yes," Nurse blew out. "Early last night. Wednesday night. Yes. I had to go out. Yes."

"What time did he go to bed?" Miss Carthew went on.

"What time?" repeated Nurse. "Why the proper time, of course."

"Don't be insolent," said Miss Carthew very tranquilly.

Nurse blustered and wrinkled her nose and frowned and came very close to Miss Carthew and peered up into her face, blowing harder than ever.

"The arrangements can't be altered for governesses," said Nurse. "No. Tut-tut. Never heard of such a thing."

"The arrangements *will* be altered. In future Michael will go to bed at half-past seven. It's not good for him to go to bed earlier. Do you understand?"

"Do I understand? No, I don't understand," Nurse snapped.

"Very well," said Miss Carthew. "You need not wait, Nurse."

Nurse blinked and peered and fumed, but Miss Carthew paid so little attention that Michael felt himself blushing for her humiliation. However, he did not go to bed that night till half-past seven and at the end of the week could rattle off the Venite in two breaths. It was extraordinary how Nurse shrank into nothing at Miss Carthew's approach, like a witch in the presence of a good fairy.

The nights were still a trial to Michael, but gradually they became less terrible, as Miss Carthew's conversation gave him something better to meditate upon than the possibilities of disaster and crime. On the afternoon walks would be told stories of Miss Carthew's youth in the West Country, of cliffs and sea-birds and wrecks, of yachting cruises and swimming, of golden sands and magical coves and green islands. Miss Carthew's own father had been a captain in the Royal Navy and she had had one brother, a midshipman, who was drowned in trying to save the life of his friend. By all accounts the Carthews must have lived in as wonderful a house as was ever known. From the windows it was possible to look down into the very sea itself, and from the front door, all wreathed in roses, ran a winding path edged with white stones down to the foot of the cliff. Day and night great ships used to sail from the harbour, some outward bound with the crew singing in the cool airs of a summer morning, some homeward bound, battered by storms. Miss Carthew, when a little girl, had been the intimate friend of many coastguards, had been allowed to peep through their long telescopes, had actually seen a cannon fired at close quarters. Before her own eyes the lifeboat had plunged forth to rescue ships and with her own hands she had caught fish on quiet sunny mornings and on windless nights under the moon. Her most valuable possession, however, must have been that father who could sit for hours and never tell the same tale twice, but hold all who heard him entranced with a narrative of hostile Indians, of Chinese junks, of cannibals and wrecks and mutinies and bombardments. It was sad to hear that Captain Carthew was now dead: Michael would have been glad to make his acquaintance. It was sad to hear that the Carthews no longer lived in the West within the sound of waves and winds; but it was consoling to learn that they still lived in the depth of the country and that some time, perhaps during this very next summer, Michael should certainly pay Mrs. Carthew a visit. He would meet other Miss Carthews, one of whom was only fourteen and could obviously without ceremony be hailed immediately as Nancy. Of Joan and May, who were older, Michael spoke in terms of the familiar Christian name with embarrassment, and he was much perplexed in his own mind how he should address them, when actually they met.

"I wish you were going to take us away for our holidays to the seaside," Michael said.

"Perhaps I will another time," Miss Carthew replied. "But this year you and Stella are going with Nurse, because Stella isn't going to begin lessons with me till you go to school."

"Am I really going to school?"

"Yes, to St. James' Preparatory School," Miss Carthew assured him.

In consideration of Michael's swiftly approaching adventure, he was allowed to take in the Boy's Own Paper monthly, and as an even greater concession to age he was allowed to make friends with several boys in Carlington Road, some of whom were already scholars of St. James' Preparatory School and one of whom actually had a brother at St. James' School itself, that gigantic red building whose gates Michael himself would enter of right one day, however difficult at present this was to believe.

What with the prospect of going to school in the autumn and Miss Carthew's tales of freedom and naval life, Michael began to disapprove more than ever of Nurse's manners and appearance. He did not at all relish the notion of passing away the summer holidays in her society. To be sure, for the end of the time he had been invited by Mrs. Carthew's own thin writing to spend a week with her in Hampshire; but that was at least a month away, and meanwhile there was this month to be endured with Nurse at Mr. and Mrs. Wagland's lodgings, where the harmonium was played and conversation was carried on by whispers and the mysterious nods of three heads. However, the beginning of August arrived, and Miss Carthew said good-bye for a month. Wooden spades, still gritty with last year's sand, were produced from the farthest corners of cupboards: mouldy shrimping nets and dirtied buckets and canvas shoes lay about on the bed, and at last, huddled in paraphernalia, Nurse and Stella and Michael jogged along to the railway station, a miserable hour for Michael, who all the time was dreading many unfortunate events, as for the cabman to get down from his box and quarrel about the fare, or for the train to be full, or for Stella to be sick during the journey, or for him and her to lose Nurse, or for all of them to get into the wrong train, or for a railway accident to happen, or for any of the uncomfortable contingencies to which seaside travellers were liable.

During these holidays Michael grew more and more deeply ashamed of Nurse, and more and more acutely sensitive to her manners and appearance. He was afraid that people on the front would mistake him and Stella for her children. He grew hot with shame when he fancied that people looked at him. He used to loiter behind on their walks and pretend that he did not belong to Nurse, and hope sincerely that nobody would think of connecting him with such an ugly old woman. He had heard much talk of 'ladies and gentlemen' at the Kindergarten, and since then Miss Carthew had indirectly confirmed his supposition that it was a terrible thing not to be a gentleman and the son of a gentleman. He grew very critical of his own dress and wished that he were not compelled to wear a sailor-top that was slightly shabby. Once Mr. and Mrs. Wagland accompanied them to church on a Sunday morning, and Michael was horrified. People would inevitably think that he was the son of Mr. Wagland. What a terrible thing that would be. He loitered farther behind than ever, and would liked to have killed Mr. Wagland when he offered him the half of his hymn-book. This incident seemed to compromise him finally, to drag him down from the society of Miss Carthew to a degraded status of unutterable commonness. Mr. Wagland would persist in digging him with his elbow and urging him to sing up. Worse even, he once said quite audibly 'Spit it out, sonny.' Michael reeled with shame.

September arrived at last, and then Michael realized suddenly that he would have to make the journey to Hampshire alone. This seemed to him the most astonishing adventure of his life. He surveyed his existence from the earliest dawn of consciousness to the last blush caused by Nurse's abominable habits, and could see no parallel of daring. He was about to enter upon a direct relationship with the world of men. He would have to enquire of porters and guards; he would have to be polite without being prodded to ladies sitting opposite. No doubt they would ask questions of him and he would have to answer distinctly. And beyond this immediate encounter with reality was School. He had not grasped how near he was to the first morning. A feeling of hopelessness, of inability to grapple with the facts of life seized him. Growing old was a very desperate business after all. How remote he was getting from Nurse, how far away from the dingy solitude which had so long oppressed his spirit. Already she seemed unimportant and already he could almost laugh at the absurdity of being mistaken for a relation of hers. The world was opening her arms and calling to him.

On the day before he was to set out for Hampshire, he and Nurse and Stella and Mr. Wagland and Mrs. Wagland drove in a wagonette to picnic somewhere in the country behind the sea. It had been a dry August and the rolling chalk downs over which they walked were uniformly brown. The knapweed was stunted and the scabious blooms drooped towards the dusty pasture. Only the flamy ladies' slippers seemed appropriate to the miles of heat that flickered against the landscape. Michael ran off alone, sliding as he went where the drouth had singed the close-cropped grass. The rabbits ran to right and left of him, throwing distorted shadows on the long slopes, and once a field-mouse skipped anxiously across his path. On the rounded summit of the highest hill within reach he sat down near a clump of tremulous harebells. The sky was on every side of him, the largest sky ever imagined. Far away in front was the shining sea, above whose nebulous horizon ships hung motionless. Up here was the sound of summer airs, the faint lisp of wind in parched herbage, the twitter of desolate birds, and in some unseen vale below the bleating of a flock of sheep. Bumble-bees droned from flower to flower of the harebells and a church clock struck the hour of four. The world was opening her arms and calling to Michael. He felt up there in the silver weather as the ugly duckling must have felt when he saw himself to be a radiant swan. Michael almost believed, in this bewitching meditation, that he was in a story by Hans Christian Andersen. Always in those tales the people flew above the world whether in snow-time or in spring-time. It was really like flying to sit up here. For the first time Michael flung wide his arms to grasp the unattainable; and, as he presently charged down the hill-side in answer to distant holloas from the picnic party, he saw before him a flock of sheep manœuvring before his advance. Michael shouted and kept a swift course, remembering Don Quixote and laughing when he saw the flock break into units and gallop up the opposite slope.

"Tut-tut," clicked Nurse. "What a mess you do get yourself into, I'm sure. Can't you sit down and enjoy yourself quietly?"

"Did you see me make those silly old sheep run away, Nanny?" Michael asked.

"Yes, I did. And I should be ashamed to frighten poor animals so. You'll get the policeman on your tracks."

"I shouldn't care," said Michael boastfully. "He wouldn't be able to catch me."

"Wouldn't he?" said Nurse very knowingly, as she laid out the tea-cups on a red rug.

"Oh, Michael," Stella begged, "don't make a policeman come after you."

Michael was intoxicated by the thought of his future. He could not recognize the ability of any policeman to check his desires, and because it was impossible to voice in any other way the impulses and ambitions and hopes that were surging in his soul, he went on boasting.

"Ha, I'd like to see an old policeman run after me. I'd trip him up and roll him all down the hill, I would. I'd put his head in a rabbit hole. I would. I can run faster than a policeman, I can."

Michael was swaggering round and round the spread-out cups and saucers and plates.

"If you put your foot on those jam sandwiches, you'll go straight back to the carriage and wait there till we've finished tea. Do you hear?"

Michael considered for a moment the possibility that Nanny might execute this threat. He decided that she might and temporarily sobered down. But the air was in his veins and all tea-time he could not chatter fast enough to keep pace with the new power which was inspiring him with inexpressible energy. He talked of what he was going to do in Hampshire; he talked of what he was going to do on the journey; he talked of what he was going to do at school and when he was grown up. He arranged Stella's future and bragged and boasted and fidgeted and shouted, so that Nurse looked at him in amazement.

"Whatever's the matter with you?" she asked.

Just then a tortoiseshell butterfly came soaring past and Michael, swinging round on both his legs to watch the flight, swept half the tea-cups with him. For a moment he was abashed; but after a long sermon of reproof from Nurse he was much nearer to laughter than tears.

A gloomy reaction succeeded, as the party drove home through the grey evening that was falling sadly over the country-side. A chilly wind rustled in the hedgerows and blew the white dust in clouds behind the wagonette. Michael became his silent self again and was now filled with apprehensions. All that had seemed so easy to attain was now complicated by the unknown. He would have been glad of Miss Carthew's company. The green-shaded lamp and creaking harmonium of the seaside lodgings were a dismal end to all that loveliness of wind and silver so soon finished. Nevertheless it had made him very sleepy and he was secretly glad to get to bed.

The next day was a dream from which he woke to find himself clinging affectionately to Miss Carthew's arm and talking shyly to Nancy Carthew and a sidling spaniel alternately, as they walked from the still country station and packed themselves into a pony-chaise that was waiting outside behind a dun pony.

Chapter VI: *The Enchanted Palace*

THE dun pony ambled through the lanes to the village of Basingstead Minor where Mrs. Carthew and her four daughters lived in a house called Cobble Place. It stood close to the road and was two stories high, very trim and covered with cotoneaster. On either side of the door were two windows and above it in a level row five more windows: the roof was thatched. On the left of the house were double doors which led into the stable-yard, a large stable-yard overlooked by a number of irregular gables in the side of the house and continually fluttered by white fantail pigeons. Into the stable-yard the dun pony turned, where, clustered in the side entrance of Cobble Place under a clematis-wreathed porch, stood Mrs. Carthew and Miss May Carthew and Miss Joan Carthew, all smiling very pleasantly at Michael and all evidently very glad to see him safely arrived. Michael climbed out of the chaise and politely shook hands with Mrs. Carthew and said he was very well and had had a comfortable journey and would like some tea very much, although if Nancy thought it was best he was quite ready to see her donkey before doing anything else. However, Nancy was told that she must wait, and soon Michael was sitting at a large round table in a shady dining-room, eating hot buttered tea-cake and chocolate cake and macaroons, with bread-and-butter as an afterthought of duty. He enjoyed drinking his tea out of a thin teacup and he liked the silver and the satin tea-cosy and the yellow Persian cat purring on the hearthrug and the bullfinch flitting from perch to perch of his bright cage. He noticed with pleasure that the pictures on the wall were full of interest and detail, and was particularly impressed by two very long steel engravings of the Death of Nelson and the Meeting of Wellington and Blücher on the field of Waterloo. The only flaw in his pleasure was the difficulty of addressing Miss May Carthew and Miss Joan Carthew, and he wished that his own real Miss Carthew would suggest a solution. As for the bedroom to which he was taken after tea, Michael thought there never could have been such a jolly room before. It was just the right size, as snug as possible with its gay wall-paper and crackling chintzes and ribboned bed. The counterpane was patchwork and therefore held the promise of perpetual entertainment. The dressing-table was neatly set with china toilet articles whose individual importance Michael could not discover. One in particular like the antler of a stag stuck upright in a china tray he was very anxious to understand, and when he was told it was intended for rings to hang upon, he wished he had a dozen rings to adorn so neat a device.

After he had with Miss Carthew's help unpacked and put his clothes away, Michael joined Nancy in the stable-yard. He stroked the donkey and the dun-coloured pony and watched the fantail pigeons in snowy circles against the pale blue sky. He watched the gardener stirring up some strange stuff for the pig that grunted impatiently. He watched the pleasant Carthew cook shelling peas in the slanting sunlight by the kitchen door. The air was very peaceful, full of soft sounds of lowing cows, of ducks and hens and sheep. The air was spangled with glittering insects: over a red wall hung down the branch of a plum tree, loaded with creamy ovals of fruit, already rose-flushed with summer. Nancy said they must soon go into the garden.

"Is there a garden more than this?" Michael asked. His bedroom window had looked out on to the stable-yard.

"Through here," said Nancy. She led the way to a door set in the wall, which when open showed a green glowing oblong of light that made Michael catch his breath in wonder.

Then together he and Nancy sauntered through what was surely the loveliest garden in the world. Michael could scarcely bear to speak, so completely did it fulfil every faintest hope. All along the red walls were apples and pears and plums and peaches; all along the paths were masses of flowers, phloxes and early Michaelmas daisies and Japanese anemones and sunflowers and red-hot pokers and dahlias. The air was so golden and balmy that it seemed as though the sunlight must have been locked up in this garden for years. At the bottom of the vivid path was a stream with real fish swimming backwards and forwards, and beyond the stream, safely guarded and therefore perfectly beautiful, were cows stalking through a field beyond which was a dark wood beyond which was a high hill with a grey tower on the top of it. Some princess must have made this garden. He and Nancy turned and walked by the stream on which was actually moored a punt, a joy for to-morrow, since, explained Nancy, Maud had said they were not to go on the river this afternoon. How wonderful it was, Michael thought, to hear his dearest Miss Carthew called Maud. Never was spoken so sweet a name as Maud. He would say it to himself in bed that night, and in the morning he would wake with Maud calling to him from sleep. Then he and Nancy turned from the tempting stream and walked up a pleached alley of withies woven and interarched. Over them September roses bloomed with fawn and ivory and copper and salmon-pink buds and blossoms. At the end of the pleached alley was a mulberry tree with a seat round its trunk and a thick lawn that ran right up to the house itself. On the lawn Nancy and Michael played quoits and bowls and chased Ambrose the spaniel, until the sun sent still more slanting shadows across the garden and it was possible to feel that night was just behind the hill beyond the stream. The sun went down. The air grew chilly and Miss Carthew appeared from the door, beckoning to Michael. She sat with him in the dusky dining-room while he ate his bread and milk, and told him of her brother the midshipman, while he looked pensively at the picture of the Death of Nelson. Then Michael went to the drawing-room where all the sisters and Mrs. Carthew herself were sitting. He kissed everybody good night in turn, and Mrs. Carthew put on a pair of spectacles in order to follow his exit from the room with a kindly smile. Miss Carthew sat with him while he undressed, and when he was in bed, she told him another story and kissed him good night and blew out the candle, and before the sound of pleasant voices coming upstairs from the supper-table had ceased, Michael was fast asleep.

In the morning while he was lying watching the shadows on the ceiling, Nancy's freckled face appeared round the door.

"Hurry up and dress," she cried. "Fishing!"

Michael had never dressed so quickly before. In fact when he was ready, he had to wait for Nancy who had called him before she had dressed herself. Nancy and Michael lived a lifetime of delight in that golden hour of waiting for breakfast.

However, at Cobble Place every minute was a lifetime of delight to Michael. He forgot all about everything except being happy. His embarrassment with regard to the correct way of addressing May and Joan was terminated by being told to call them May and Joan. He was shown the treasures of their bedrooms, the butterfly collections, the sword of Captain Carthew, the dirk of their brother the midshipman, the birds' eggs, the fossils, the bones, the dried flowers, the photographs, the autographs, in fact everything that was most absorbing to look at. With Mrs. Carthew he took sedate walks into the village, and held the flowers while she decorated the altar in church, and sat with her while she talked to bed-ridden old women. With Nancy on one memorable day he crossed the river and disembarked on the other side and walked through the field of cows, through the meadowsweet and purple loosestrife and spearmint. Then they picked blackberries and dewberries by the edge of the wood and walked on beneath the trees without caring about trespassing or tramps or anything else. On the other side they came out at the foot of the high hill. Up they walked, up and up until they reached the grey tower at the top, and then, to Michael's amazement, Nancy produced the key of the tower and opened the door.

"Can we really go in?" asked Michael, staggered by the adventure.

"Of course. We can always get the key," said Nancy.

They walked up some winding stone steps that smelt very damp, and at the top they pushed open a trap-door and walked out on top of the tower. Michael leaned over the parapet and for the second time beheld the world. There was no sea, but there were woods and streams and spires and fields and villages and smoke from farms. There were blue distances on every side and great white clouds moving across the sky. The winds battled against the tower and sang in Michael's ears and ruffled his hair and crimsoned his cheeks. He could see the fantail pigeons of Cobble Place circling below. He could look down on the wood and the river they had just crossed. He could see the garden and his dearest Miss Carthew walking on the lawn.

"Oh, Nancy," he said, "it's glorious."

"Yes, it is rather decent," Nancy agreed.

"I suppose that's almost all of England you can see."

"Only four counties," said Nancy carelessly. "Berkshire and I forget the other three. We toboggan down this hill in winter. That's rather decent too."

"I'd like to come here every day," sighed Michael. "I'd like to have this tower for my very own. What castle is it called?"

"Grogg's Folly," said Nancy abruptly.

Michael wished the tower were not called Grogg's Folly, and very soon Nancy and he, shouting and laughing, were running at full speed down the hill towards Cobble Place, while the stalks of the plantains whipped his bare legs and larks flew up in alarm before his advance.

The time of his stay at Cobble Place was drawing to a close: the hour of his greatest adventure was near. It had been a visit of unspoiled enjoyment; and on his last night, Michael was allowed for a treat to stay up to supper, to sit at the round table rose-stained by the brooding lamp, while the rest of the room was a comfortable mystery in which the parlour-maid's cap and apron flitted whitely to and fro. Nor did Michael go to bed immediately after supper, for he actually sat grandly in the drawing-room, one of a semicircle round the autumnal fire of logs crackling and leaping with blue flames. He sat silent, listening to the pitter-pat of Mrs. Carthew's Patience and watching the halma board waiting for May to encounter Joan, while in a low voice Nancy read to him one of Fifty-two Stories of Adventure for Girls. Bed-time came at the end of the story and Michael was sad to say good night for the last time and sad to think, when he got into his ribboned bed, that to-morrow night he would be in Carlington Road among brass knobs and Venetian blinds and lamp-posts and sounds of London. Then came a great surprize that took away nearly all the regrets he felt at leaving Cobble Place, for Miss Carthew leaned over and whispered that she was coming to live at Sixty-four.

"Oh!" Michael gasped. "With us—with Stella and me?"

Miss Carthew nodded.

"I say!" Michael whispered. "And will Stella have lessons when I'm going to school?"

"Every morning," said Miss Carthew.

"I expect you'll find her rather bad at lessons," said Michael doubtfully.

He was almost afraid that Miss Carthew might leave in despair at Stella's ineptitude.

"Lots of people are stupid at first," said Miss Carthew.

Michael blushed: he remembered a certain morning when capes and promontories got inextricably mixed in his mind and when Miss Carthew seemed to grow quite tired of trying to explain the difference.

"Will you teach her the piano now?" he enquired.

"Oh dear, no. I'm not clever enough to do that."

"But you teach me."

"That's different. Stella will be a great pianist one day," said Miss Carthew earnestly.

"Will she?" asked Michael incredulously. "But I don't like her to play a bit—not a bit."

"You will one day. Great musicians think she is wonderful."

Michael gave up this problem. It was another instance of the chasm between youth and age. He supposed that one day he would like Stella's playing. One day, so he had been led to suppose, he would also like fat and cabbage and going to bed. At present such a condition of mind was incomprehensible. However, Stella and the piano mattered very little in comparison with the solid fact that Miss Carthew was going to live in Carlington Road.

On the next morning before they left, Michael and Mrs. Carthew walked round the garden together, while Mrs. Carthew talked to him of the new life on which he was shortly going to enter.

"Well, Michael," she said, "in a week, so my daughter tells me, you will be going to school."

"Yes," corroborated Michael.

"Dear me," Mrs. Carthew went on. "I'm glad I'm not going to school for the first time; you won't like it at all at first, and then you'll like it very much indeed, and then you'll either go on liking it very much or you'll hate it. If you go on liking it—I mean when you're quite old—sixteen or seventeen—you'll never do anything, but if you hate it then, you'll have a chance of doing something. I'm glad my daughter Maud is going to look after you. She's a good girl."

Michael thought how extraordinary it was to hear Miss Carthew spoken of in this manner and felt shy at the prospect of having to agree verbally with Mrs. Carthew.

"Take my advice—never ask questions. Be content to make a fool of yourself once or twice, but don't ask questions. Don't answer questions either. That's worse than asking. But after all, now I'm giving advice, and worst of anything is listening to other people's advice. So pick yourself some plums and get ready, for the chaise will soon be at the door."

Nurse was very grumpy when he and Miss Carthew arrived. She did not seem at all pleased by the idea of Miss Carthew living in the house, and muttered to herself all the time. Michael did no more lessons in the week that remained before the autumn term began; but he had to go with Miss Carthew to various outfitters and try on coats and suits and generally be equipped for school. The afternoons he spent in Carlington Road, trying to pick up information about St. James' Preparatory School from the boys already there. One of these boys was Rodber, the son of a doctor, and probably by his manner and age and appearance the most important boy in the school. At any rate Michael found it difficult to believe that there could exist a boy with more right to rule than this Rodber with his haughty eye and Eton suit and prominent ears and quick authoritative voice.

"Look here," said Rodber one evening, "can you borrow your mail-cart? I saw your sister being wheeled in one this morning. We've got three mail-carts and we want a fourth for trains."

Michael ran as fast as he could back to Sixty-four, rushed down the area steps, rang the bell half a dozen times and tapped continuously on the ground glass of the back door until Cook opened it.

"Whatever's the matter?" said Cook.

Michael did not stop to answer, but ran upstairs, until breathless he reached the schoolroom.

"Please, Miss Carthew, may we have Stella's mail-cart? Rodber wants it—for trains. Do let me. Rodber's the boy I told you about who's at school. Oh, do let us have the cart. Rodber's got three, but he wants ours. May I, Miss Carthew?"

She nodded.

Michael rushed downstairs in a helter-skelter of joy and presently, with Cook's assistance in getting it up the steps, Michael stood proudly by the mail-cart which was of the dogcart pattern, very light and swift when harnessed to a good runner. Rodber examined it critically.

"Yes, that's a fairly decent one," he decided.

Michael was greatly relieved by his approval.

"Look here," said Rodber, "I don't mind telling you, as you'll be a new kid, one or two tips about school. Look here, don't tell anybody your Christian name and don't be cocky."

"Oh, no, I won't," Michael earnestly promised.

"And don't, for goodness' sake, look like that when chaps speak to you, or you'll get your head smacked."

This was the sum of Rodber's advice, and presently Michael was stationed as signalman by the junction which was a pillar-box, while Rodber went off at express speed, bound for the next station which was a lamp-post. A signalman's life on the Carlington Road line was a lonely one, and it was also a very tiring one, when any obstruction caused the signals to be up. Michael's arm ached excruciatingly when Rodber's train got entangled with Garrod's train and Macalister's train had to be kept from running into them. Moreover, the signalman's life had none of the glories of controlling other people; a signalman on the Carlington Road line was dependent on the train for his behaviour. He was not allowed to interfere with the free running of any freight, but if the engine-driver insisted he had to let him go past, and if there was an accident, he was blamed. A signalman's life was lonely, tiring, humiliating and dangerous.

These few fine days of mid-September went quickly by and one evening Rodber said casually, almost cruelly it seemed to Michael:

"Well, see you to-morrow in the break, young Fane."

Michael wondered what on earth a 'break' was; he longed to ask Rodber, but he dared not display at the very beginning of his career what would evidently be a disgraceful ignorance, and so he said that he would see Rodber in the 'break' to-morrow. He asked Miss Carthew when he got home what a 'break' was, and she told him it was a large wagonette sometimes driven by four horses. Michael was very much puzzled, but thought school would be fun if large wagonettes were commonplace objects of school life, and dreamed that night of driving furiously with Rodber in a gigantic mail-cart along the Hammersmith Road.

At breakfast Miss Carthew asked Michael if he would like her to come with him. He thought for a moment, and wished that Rodber had invited him to accompany him that first morning.

"You know, it's for you to choose, Michael," said Miss Carthew.

"Well, I would like you to come," said Michael at last.

So at ten minutes past nine they set out. All sorts of boys were going to school along the Hammersmith Road, boys of every size carrying satchels or bags or loose bundles of books. Most of them wore the Jacobean cap, and Michael eyed them with awe; but many wore the cap of St. James' Preparatory School, and these Michael eyed with curiosity as well as awe. He spoke very little during the walk and felt all the way a sinking of the heart. When actually he reached the gate of Randell House, the less formal appellation of St. James' Preparatory School, he longed to turn back with Miss Carthew, as he thought with sentimental pangs of the pleasant schoolroom and of Stella sitting by Miss Carthew, learning to read through a sunlit morning.

"Don't come in with me," he whispered.

"Quite right," said Miss Carthew approvingly. "Much better without me."

"And don't wave, will you?" he begged. Then with an effort he joined the stream of boys walking confidently through the big gate.

In the entrance hall a ginger-haired foxy-faced man in a green uniform said sharply:

"New boy?"

Michael nodded.

"Stand on one side, please. Mr. Randell will see you presently."

Michael waited. He noticed with pride that the boy next to him had brought with him either his mother or his sister or his governess. Michael felt very superior and was glad he had resisted the temptation to ask Miss Carthew to come in with him. He noticed how curiously the other boys eyed this lady and fancied that they threw contemptuous glances at the boy who had introduced her. Michael was very glad indeed that he had let Miss Carthew turn back.

Chapter VII: *Randell House*

THE preliminaries of Michael's career at St. James' Preparatory School passed in a dream-like confusion of thought and action. First of all he waited anxiously in the Headmaster's study in an atmosphere of morocco-leather and large waste-paper baskets. Like every other room in which Michael had waited, whether of dentist or doctor, the outlook from the window was gloomy and the prospect within was depressing. He was glad when Mr. Randell led him and several other boys towards the First Form, where in a dream, peopled by the swinging legs of many boys, he learnt from a scarlet book that while Cornelia loved Julia, Julia returned Cornelia's affection. When this fact was established in both English and Latin, all the boys shuffled to their desks and the record of a great affection was set down largely and painfully.

1. Cornelia Juliam
   amat.

2. Julia Corneliam
   amat.

Blotted and smudged and sprawling though it ultimately appeared, Michael felt a great satisfaction in having dealt successfully with two nominatives, two accusatives and a verb. The first part of the morning passed away quickly in the history of this simple love. At eleven o'clock a shrill electric bell throbbed through the school, and Michael, almost before he knew what was happening, was carried in a torrent of boys towards the playground. Michael had never felt supreme loneliness, even at night, until he stood in the middle of that green prairie of recreation, distinguishing nobody, a very small creature in a throng of chattering giants. Some of these giants, who usually walked about arm in arm, approached him.

"Hullo, are you a new kid?"

Michael breathed his 'yes.'

"What's your name?"

With an effort Michael remembered Rodber's warning and replied simply:

"Fane."

"What's your Christian name?"

This was a terribly direct attack, and Michael was wondering whether it would be best to run quickly out of the playground, to keep silence or to surrender the information, when the quick and authoritative voice of Rodber flashed from behind him.

"Fish and find out, young Biden."

"Who are you calling young, young Rodber?"

"You," said Rodber. "So you'd jolly well better scoot off and leave this kid alone."

"Church said I was to collar all the new kids for his army," Biden explained.

"Did he? Well, this kid's in our army, so sucks! And you can tell young Church that Pearson and me are going to jolly well lam him at four o'clock," announced Rodber very fiercely.

"Why don't you tell him yourself?" asked Biden, whose teeth seemed to project farther and farther from his mouth as his indignation grew.

"All right, Toothy Biden," jeered Rodber. "We'll tell the whole of your rotten army at four o'clock, when we give you the biggest lamming you've ever had. Come on, young Fane," he went on, and Michael, somewhat perturbed by the prospect of being involved in these encounters, followed at his heels.

"Look here," said Rodber presently, "you'd better come and show yourself to Pearson. He's the captain of our army; and for goodness' sake look a bit cheerful."

Michael forced an uncomfortable grin such as photographers conjure.

Under the shade of a gigantic tree stood Pearson the leader, languidly eating a very small and very unripe pear.

"Hullo, Pinky," he drawled.

"I say, Pearson," said Rodber in a reverent voice, "I know this kid at home. He's awfully keen to be allowed to join your army."

Pearson scarcely glanced at Michael.

"All right. Swear him in. I've got a new oath written down in a book at home, but he can take the old one."

Pearson yawned and threw away the core of the pear.

"He's awfully glad he's going to join your army, Pearson. Aren't you, young Fane?"

"Yes, awfully glad," Michael echoed.

"It's the best army," said Pearson simply.

"Oh, easily," Rodber agreed. "I say, Pearson, that kid Biden said Church was going to lam you at four o'clock."

The offended Pearson swallowed a large piece of a second unripe pear and scowled.

"Did he? Tell the army to line up behind the lav. at four o'clock."

Rodber's eyes gleamed.

"I say, Pearson, I've got an awfully ripping plan. Supposing we ambush them."

"How?" enquired the commander.

"Why, supposing we put young Fane and two or three more new kids by the tuckshop door and tell them to run towards the haunted house, we could cop them simply rippingly."

"Give the orders before afternoon school," said Pearson curtly, and just then the bell for 'second hour' sounded.

"Wait for me at half-past twelve," Rodber shouted to Michael as he ran to get into school.

Michael grew quite feverish during 'second hour' and his brain whirled with the imagination of battles, so that the landing of Julius Cæsar seemed of minor importance. Tuckshops and haunted houses and doors and ambushes and the languid pale-faced Pearson occupied his thoughts fully enough. At a quarter-past twelve Mr. Whichelo the First Form master told Michael and the other new boys to go to the book-room and get their school caps, and at half-past twelve Michael waited outside on the yellow gravel for Rodber, splendidly proud of himself in a blue cap crested with a cockleshell worked in silver wire. He was longing to look at himself in the glass at home and to show Miss Carthew and Stella and Nanny and Cook and Gladys his school cap.

However, before he could go home Rodber took him round to where the tuckshop ambush would ensue at four o'clock. He showed him a door in a wall which led apparently into the narrow shady garden of an empty house next to the school. He explained how Michael was to hang about outside this door and when the Churchites demanded his presence, he told him that he was to run as hard as he could down the garden towards the house.

"We'll do the rest," said Rodber. "And now cut off home."

As soon as Michael was inside Number 64 he rushed upstairs to his bedroom and examined himself critically in the looking-glass. Really the new cap made a great difference. He seemed older somehow and more important. He wished that his arms and legs were not so thin, and he looked forward to the time when like Rodber he would wear Etons. However, his hair was now pleasantly and inconspicuously straight: he had already seen boys woefully teazed on account of their curls, and Michael congratulated himself that generally his dress and appearance conformed with the fashion of the younger boys' dress at Randell's. It would be terrible to excite notice. In fact, Michael supposed that to excite notice was the worst sin anybody could possibly commit. He hoped he would never excite notice. He would like to remain perfectly ordinary, and very slowly by an inconspicuous and gradual growth he would thus arrive in time at the dignity and honour enjoyed by Rodber, and perhaps even to the sacred majesty that clung to Pearson. Already he was going to take an active part in the adventures of school; and he felt sorry for the boys who without Rodber's influence would mildly go straight home at four o'clock.

Indeed, Michael set out for afternoon school in a somewhat elated frame of mind, and when he turned into the schoolyard, wearing the school cap, he felt bold enough to watch a game of Conquerors that was proceeding between two solemn-faced boys. He thought that to try to crack a chestnut hanging on a piece of string with another chestnut similarly suspended was a very enthralling pastime, and he was much upset when one of the solemn-faced antagonists suddenly grabbed his new school-cap and put it in his pocket and, without paying any attention to Michael, went on with the game as if nothing had happened. Michael had no idea how to grapple with the situation and felt inclined to cry.

"I say, give me my cap," he said at last.

The solemn-faced boys went on in silence with the game.

"I say, please give me my cap," Michael asked again.

No notice was taken of his appeal and Michael, looking round in despair, saw Rodber. He ran up to him.

"I say, Rodber, that boy over there has got my cap," he said.

"Well, don't come sneaking to me, you young ass. Go and smack his head."

"Am I to really?" asked Michael.

"Of course."

Michael was not prepared to withstand Rodber's advice, so he went up to the solemn-faced boy and hit him as hard as he could. The solemn-faced boy was so much surprized by this attack that he did not for a moment retaliate, and it was only his friend's gasp 'I say, what fearful cheek,' that restored him to a sense of what had happened.

In a moment Michael found himself lying on his back and almost smothered by the solemn-faced boy's whole body and presently suffering agony from the pressure of the solemn-faced boy's knees upon his arms pinioned cross-wise. Excited voices chattered about him from an increasing circle. He heard the solemn-faced boy telling his horrified auditors that a new kid had smacked his head. He heard various punishments strongly recommended, and at last with a sense of relief he heard the quick authoritative voice of the ubiquitous Rodber.

"Let him get up, young Plummer. A fight! A fight!"

Plummer got up, as he was told, and Michael in a circle of eager faces found himself confronted by Plummer.

"Go on," shouted Rodber. "I'm backing you, young Fane."

Michael lowered his head and charged desperately forward for the honour of Rodber; but a terrible pain in his nose and another in his arm and a third in his chin brought tears and blood together in such quantity that Michael would have liked to throw himself on to the grass and weep his life out, too weak to contend with solemn-faced boys who snatched caps.

Then over his misery he heard Rodber cry, 'That's enough. It's not fair. Give him back his cap.' The crowd broke up except for a few admirers of Rodber, who was telling Michael that he had done tolerably well for a new kid. Michael felt encouraged and ventured to point out that he had not really blabbed.

"You cocky young ass," said Rodber crushingly. "I suppose you mean 'blubbed.'"

Michael was overwhelmed by this rebuke and, wishing to hide his shame in a far corner of the field, turned away. But Rodber called him back and spoke pleasantly, so that Michael forgot the snub and wandered for the rest of the dinner-hour in Rodber's wake, with aching nose, but with a heart beating in admiration and affection.

Within a fortnight Michael had become a schoolboy, sharing in the general ambitions and factions and prejudices and ideals of schoolboyhood. He was a member of Pearson's victorious army; he supported the London Road Car Company against the London General Omnibus Company, the District Railway against the Metropolitan Railway; he was always ready to lam young boarders who were cheeky, and when an older boarder called him a 'day-bug' Michael was discreetly silent, merely registering a vow to take it out of the young boarders at the first opportunity. He also learnt to speak without blushing of the gym. and the lav. and arith. and hols. and 'Bobbie' Randell and 'my people' and 'my kiddy sister.' He was often first with the claimant 'ego,' when someone shouted 'quis?' over a broken pocket-knife found. He could shout 'fain I' to be rid of an obligation and 'bags I' to secure an advantage. He was a rigid upholder of the inviolableness of Christian names as postulated by Randellite convention. He laid out threepence a week in the purchase of sweets, usually at four ounces a penny; while during the beggary that succeeded he was one of the most persistent criers of 'donnez,' when richer boys emerged from the tuckshop, sucking gelatines and satin pralines and chocolate creams and raspberry noyau. As for the masters, he was always ready to hear scandalous rumours about their un-official lives, and he was one of the first to fly round the playground with the news that 'Squeaky' Mordaunt had distinctly muttered 'damn' beneath his breath, when Featherstone Minor trod on his toe towards the close of first hour. Soon also with one of the four hundred odd boys who made up the population of this very large private school, Michael formed a great friendship. He and Buckley were inseparable for sixteen whole weeks. During that time they exchanged the most intimate confidences. Buckley told Michael that his Christian names were Claude Arnold Eustace, and Michael told Buckley that he was called Charles Michael Saxby, and also that his mother was generally away from home, that his father was dead, that his governess was called Miss Carthew, that he had a sister who played the piano and that one day when he grew up he hoped to be an explorer and search for orchids in Borneo. Sometimes on Saturday or Wednesday half-holidays Buckley came to tea with Michael and sometimes Michael went to tea with Buckley, and observed how well Buckley kept in order his young brothers and kiddy sisters. Buckley lived close to Kensington Gardens and rode to school every morning on a London Road Car, which was the reason of Michael's keen partizanship of that company. In the eleven o'clock break between first and second hours, Michael and Buckley walked arm in arm round the field, and in the dinner-hour Michael and Buckley shared a rope on the Giant Stride and talked intimately on the top of the horizontal ladder in the outdoor gymnasium. During the Christmas holidays they haunted the banks of the Round Pond and fished for minnows and sailed capsizable yachts and cheeked keepers. Every night Michael thought of Buckley and every night Michael hoped that Buckley thought of him. Even in scholarship they were scarcely distinguishable; for when at the end of the autumn term Michael was top of the class in Divinity and English, Buckley headed the Latin list. As for Drawing they were bracketed equal at the very bottom of the form.

Then towards the middle of the Lent term Randell House was divided against itself; for one half of the school became Oxford and the other half Cambridge, in celebration of the boat-race which would be rowed at the end of March. When one morning Michael saw Buckley coming into school with a light blue swallow pinned to the left of his sailor-knot and when Buckley perceived attached to Michael's sailor-top a medal dependent from a dark blue ribbon, they eyed each other as strangers. This difference of opinion was irremediable. Neither romance nor sentiment could ever restore to Michael and Buckley their pristine cordiality, because Michael was now a despised Oxtail and Buckley was a loathed Cabbage-stalk.

They shouted to one another from the heart of massed factions mocking rhymes. Michael would chant:

"Oxford upstairs eating all the cakes; Cambridge downstairs licking up the plates."

To which Buckley would retort:

"Cambridge, rowing on and on for ever; Oxford in a matchbox floating down the river."

Snow fell in February, and great snow-ball fights took place between the Oxtails and the Cabbage-stalks in which the fortunes of both sides varied from day to day. During one of these fights Michael hit Buckley full in the eye with a snow-ball alleged to contain a stone, and the bitterness between them grew sharper. Then Oxford won the boat-race, and Buckley cut Michael publicly. Finally, owing to some alteration in the Buckley home, Buckley became a boarder, and was able with sneering voice to call Michael a beastly 'day-bug.' Such was the friendship of Michael and Buckley, which lasted for sixteen weeks and might not indeed have so much wounded Michael, when the rupture was made final, if Buckley had proved loyal to that friendship. Unfortunately for Michael's belief in human nature Buckley one day, stung perhaps by some trifling advantage gained by day-boys at the expense of boarders, divulged Michael's Christian names. He called out distinctly, "Ha! ha! Charles Michael Saxby Fane! Oh, what a name! Kiddy Michael Sacks-of-coals Fane!"

Michael regretted his intimacy with one who was not within the circle of Carlington Road. In future he would not seek friends outside Carlington Road and the six roads of the alliance. There all secrets must be kept, and all quarrels locally adjusted, for there Christian names were known and every household had its skeleton of nurse or governess.

Meanwhile, Mrs. Fane did not come home and Miss Carthew assumed more and more complete control of Number 64, until one day in spring Nurse suddenly told Michael that she was leaving next day. Somehow, Nurse had ceased to influence Michael's life one way or the other, and he could only feel vaguely uncomfortable over her departure. Nurse cried a good deal particularly at saying good-bye to Stella, whom she called her own girl whatever anybody might say. When Michael perceived Nurse's tears he tried hard to drag up from the depths of his nature a dutiful sentimentality. For the last time he kissed that puckered monkey-like face, and in a four-wheeler Nurse vanished without making any difference in the life of Sixty-four, save by a convenient shifting about of the upstair rooms. The old night-nursery was redecorated and became for many years Michael's bedroom. Miss Carthew slept in Michael's old big lonely front room, and Stella slept in a little dressing-room opening out of it. Down in the kitchen, whence withered Gladys and the impersonal cook had also vanished, Michael gleaned a certain amount of gossip and found that the immediate cause of Nurse's departure was due to Miss Carthew's discovery of her dead drunk in a kitchen chair. It seemed that Miss Carthew, slim and strong and beautiful, had had to carry the old woman up to her bedroom, while Michael lay sleeping, had had to undress and put her to bed and on the next day to contend with her asseverations that the collapse was due to violent neuralgia. It seemed also that for years the neighbourhood had known of Nurse's habits, had even seen her on two occasions upset Stella's perambulator. Indeed, so far as Michael could gather, he and Stella had lived until Miss Carthew's arrival in a state of considerable insecurity.

However, Nurse was now a goblin of the past, and the past could be easily forgotten. In these golden evenings of the summer-term, there was too much going forward in Carlington Road to let old glooms overshadow the gaiety of present life. As Mrs. Carthew had prophesied, Michael enjoyed being at school very much, and having already won a prize for being top of his class in Divinity and English at Christmas with every prospect of being top of his class again in the summer, he was anxious to achieve the still greater distinction of winning a prize in the school sports which were to be held in July. All the boys who lived in the Carlington Confederate Roads determined to win prizes, and Rodber was very much to the fore in training them all to do him credit. It was the fashion to choose colours in which to run, and Michael after a week's debate elected to appear in violet running-drawers and primrose-bordered vest. The twin Macalisters, contemporaries of Michael, ran in cerise and eau-de-nil, while the older Macalister wore ultramarine and mauve. Garrod chose dark green and Rodber looked dangerously swift in black and yellow. Every evening there was steady practice under Rodber, either in canvas shoes from lamp-post to lamp-post or, during the actual week before the sports, in spiked running-shoes on the grass-track, with corks to grip and a temperamental stop-watch to cause many disputes. It was a great humiliation for the Confederate Roads when Rodber himself failed to last the half-mile (under 14) on the day itself. However, the Macalister twins won the sack-race (under 11) and in the same class Michael won the hundred yards Consolation Race and an octagonal napkin-ring, so Carlington Road congratulated itself. In addition to athletic practice there were several good fights with 'cads' and a disagreeable Colonel had his dining-room window starred by a catapult. Other notable events included a gas explosion at Number 78, when the front door was blown across the street and flattened a passer-by against the opposite wall. There was a burglary at Number 33 and the housemaid at Number 56 fell backwards from the dining-room window-sill and bruised her back on the lid of the dustbin in the area.

With all these excitements to sustain the joy of life Michael was very happy and, when school broke up for the summer holidays, he had never yet looked forward so eagerly to the jolly weeks by the sea. Miss Carthew and Michael and Stella went to Folkestone that year, and Michael enjoyed himself enormously. Miss Carthew, provided that she was allowed a prior inspection, offered no opposition to friendship with strange children, and Michael joined an association for asking everybody on the Leas what the time was. The association would not have been disbanded all the holidays if one of the members had not asked the time from the same old gentleman twice in one minute. The old gentleman was so acutely irritated by this that he walked about the Leas warning people against the association, until it became impossible to find out the time, when one really wanted to know. Michael moved inland for a while after this and fell into Radnor Park pond, when he returned to the sea and got stung by a jelly-fish while he was paddling, and read Treasure Island in the depths of his own particular cave among the tamarisks of the Lower Sandgate Road.

After about a fortnight of complete rest a slight cloud was cast over the future by the announcement at breakfast one morning that he was to do a couple of hours' work at French every day with a French governess: remembering Madame Flauve, he felt depressed by the prospect. But Miss Carthew found a charming and youthful French governess at a girls' school, where about half a dozen girls were remaining during the holidays, and Michael did not mind so much. He rather liked the atmosphere of the girls' school, although when he returned to Randell's he gave a very contemptuous account of female education to his masculine peers. An incident happened at this girls' school which he never told, although it made a great impression on his imagination.

One afternoon he had been invited to take tea with the six girls and Mademoiselle, and after tea the weather being wet, they all played games in the recreation-room. One of the smaller girls happened to swing higher than decorum allowed, and caused Michael to blush and to turn his head quickly and look intently at houses opposite. He knew that the girl was unaware of the scandal she had created, and therefore blushed the deeper and hoped that the matter would pass off quietly. But very soon he heard a chatter of reproof, and the poor little girl was banished from the room in disgrace, while all the other girls discussed the shameful business from every point of view, calling upon Mademoiselle and Michael to endorse their censure. Michael felt very sorry for the poor little girl and wished very much that the others would let the matter drop, but the discussion went on endlessly and as, just before he went home, he happened to see the offending girl sitting by a window with tear-stained face, Michael felt more sorry than ever and wished that he dared to say a comforting word, to explain how well he understood it was all an accident. On the way home, he walked silently, meditating upon disgrace, and for the first time he realized something of human cruelty and the lust to humiliate and submerge deeper still the fallen. At the same time he himself experienced, in retrospect of the incident, a certain curious excitement, and did not know whether, after all, he had not taken pleasure in the little girl's shame, whether, after all, he would not have liked to go back and talk the whole matter out again. However, there was that exciting chapter in Treasure Island to finish and the September Boy's Own Paper to expect. On the next day Michael, walking with Miss Carthew on the Leas, met General Mace, and girls' schools with their curious excitements and blushes were entirely forgotten. General Mace, it appeared, was an old friend of Miss Carthew's father and was staying by himself at Folkestone. General Mace had fought in the Indian Mutiny and was exactly what a general should be, very tall with a white moustache fiercely curling and a rigid back that bent inwards like a bow and a magnificent ebony walking-stick and a gruff voice. General Mace seemed to take a fancy to Michael and actually invited him to go for a walk with him next day at ten o'clock.

"Sharp, mind," said the General as he saluted stiffly. "Ten o'clock to the minute."

Michael spent the rest of the day in asking questions of Miss Carthew about General Mace, and scarcely slept that night for fear he might be late. At nine o'clock, Michael set out from the lodgings and ran all the way to the General's house on the Leas, and walked about and fidgeted and fretted himself until the clock struck the first chime of ten, when he rang the bell and was shown upstairs and was standing on the General's hearthrug before the echo of the last chime had died away.

The General cleared his throat and after saluting Michael suggested a walk. Proudly Michael walked beside this tall old soldier up and down the Leas. He was told tales of the Mutiny; he learned the various ranks of the British Army from Lance-corporal to Field-marshal; he agreed at the General's suggestion to aim at a commission in the Bengal Cavalry, preferably in a regiment which wore an uniform of canary-yellow. Every morning Michael walked about Folkestone with General Mace, and one morning they turned into a toy-shop where Michael was told to choose two boxes of soldiers. Michael at first chose a box of Highlanders doubling fiercely with fixed bayonets and a stationary Highland Regimental Band, each individual of which had a different instrument and actually a music-stand as well. These two boxes together cost seven shillings, and Michael was just leaving the shop when he saw a small penny box containing twelve very tiny soldiers. Michael was in a quandary. For seven shillings he would be able to buy eighty-four penny boxes, that is to say one thousand and eight soldiers, whereas in the two boxes of Highlanders already selected there were only twelve with bayonets, twelve with instruments and twelve music-stands. It was really very difficult to decide, and General Mace declined to make any suggestion as to which would be the wiser choice, Michael was racked by indecision and after a long debate chose the original two boxes and played with his Highlanders for several years to come.

"Quite right," said the General when they reached the sunlight from the dusty little toy-shop. "Quite right. Quality before quantity, sir. I'm glad to see you have so much common sense."

Almost before the holidays seemed to have begun, the holidays were over. There was a short and melancholy day of packing up, and a farewell visit through the rain to General Mace. He and Michael sat for a while in his room, while they talked earnestly of the Indian Army and the glories of patriotism. Michael told tales, slightly exaggerated, of the exploits of Pearson's army and General Mace described the Relief of Lucknow. Michael felt that they were in profound sympathy: they both recognized the splendour of action. The rain stopped, and in a rich autumnal sunset they walked together for the last time over the golden puddles and spangled wetness of the Leas. Michael went through the ranks of the British Army without a single mistake, and promised faithfully to make the Bengal Lancers his aim through youth.

"Punctuality, obedience and quality before quantity," said the General, standing up as tall and thin as Don Quixote against the sunset glow. "Good-bye."

"Good-bye," said Michael.

They saluted each other ceremoniously, and parted. The next day Michael was in London, and after a depressing Sunday and an exciting Monday spent in buying a Norfolk suit and Eton collars, the new term began with all the excitements of 'moving up,' of a new form-master, of new boys, of seeing who would be in the Football Eleven and of looking forward to Christmas with its presents and pantomimes.

Chapter VIII: *Siamese Stamps*

IN the Upper Fourth class, under the tutorship of Mr. Macrae, Michael began to prosecute seriously the study of Greek, whose alphabet he had learnt the preceding term. He now abandoned the scarlet book of Elementary Latin for Henry's Latin Primer, which began with 'Balbus was building a wall,' and looked difficult in its mulberry-cloth binding. This term in the Upper Fourth was very trying to Michael. Troubles accumulated. Coincident with the appearance of Greek irregular verbs came the appearance of Avery, a new boy who at once, new boy though he was, assumed command of the Upper Fourth and made Michael the target for his volatile and stinging shafts. Misfortune having once directed her attention to Michael, pursued him for some time to come. Michael was already sufficiently in awe of Avery's talent for hurting his feelings, when from the Hebrides Mrs. Fane sent down Harris tweed for Michael's Norfolk suits. He begged Miss Carthew to let him continue in the inconspicuous dark blue serge which was the fashion at Randell's; but for once she was unsympathetic, and Michael had to wear the tweed. Avery, of course, was very witty at his expense and for a long time Michael was known as 'strawberry-bags,' until the joke palled. Michael had barely lived down the Harris tweed, when Avery discovered, while they were changing into football shorts, that Michael wore combinations instead of pants and vest. Combinations were held to be the depth of effeminacy, and Avery often enquired when Michael was going to appear in petticoats and stays. Michael spoke to Miss Carthew about these combinations which at the very moment of purchase he had feared, but Miss Carthew insisted that they were much healthier than the modish pants and vest, and Michael was not allowed to change the style of his underclothing. In desperation he tied some tape round his waist, but the observant Avery noticed this ruse, and Michael was more cruelly teazed than ever. Then one Monday morning the worst blow of all fell suddenly. The boys at Randell's had on Saturday morning to take down from dictation the form-list in a home-book, which had to be brought back on Monday morning signed by a parent, so that no boy should escape the vigilance of the paternal eye. Of course, Miss Carthew always signed Michael's home-book and so far no master had asked any questions. But Mr. Macrae said quite loudly on this Monday morning:

"Who is this Maud Carthew that signs your book, Fane?"

Michael felt the pricking of the form's ears and blushed hotly.

"My mother's away," he stammered.

"Oh," said Mr. Macrae bluntly, "and who is this person then?"

Michael nearly choked with shame.

"My governess—my sister's governess, I mean," he added, desperately trying to retrieve the situation.

"Oh, yes," said Mr. Macrae. "I see."

The form tittered, while the crimson Michael stumbled back to his desk. It was a long time before Avery grew tired of Miss Carthew or before the class wearied of crying 'Maudie' in an united falsetto whenever Michael ventured to speak. Mr. Macrae, too, made cruel use of his advantage, for whenever Michael tripped over an irregular verb, Mr. Macrae would address to the ceiling in his soft unpleasant voice sarcastic remarks about governesses, while every Monday morning he would make a point of putting on his glasses to examine Michael's home-book very carefully. The climax of Michael's discomfort was reached, when a snub-nosed boy called Jubb with a cockney accent asked him what his father was.

"He's dead," Michael answered.

"Yes, but what was he?" Jubb persisted.

"He was a gentleman," said Michael.

Avery happened to overhear this and was extremely witty over Michael's cockiness, so witty that Michael was goaded into retaliation, notwithstanding his fear of Avery's tongue.

"Well, what is your father?" he asked.

"My father's a duke, and I've got an uncle who's a millionaire, and my governess is a queen," said Avery.

Michael was silent: he could not contend with Avery. Altogether the Upper Fourth was a very unpleasant class; but next term Michael and half of the class were moved up to the Lower Fifth, and Avery left to go to a private school in Surrey, because he was ultimately

33

destined for Charterhouse, near which school his people had, as he said, taken a large house. Curiously enough the combination of half the Upper Fourth with the half of the Lower Fifth left behind made a rather pleasant class, one that Michael enjoyed as much as any other so far, particularly as he was beginning to find that he was clever enough to avoid doing as much school-work as hitherto he had done, without in any way permanently jeopardizing his position near the top of the form. To be sure Mr. Wagstaff, the cherub-faced master of the Lower Fifth, complained of his continually shifting position from one end of the class to the other; but Michael justified himself and incidentally somewhat annoyed Mr. Wagstaff by coming out head boy in the Christmas examinations. Meanwhile, if he found Greek irregular verbs and Latin gender rhymes tiresome, Michael read unceasingly at home, preferably books that encouraged the private schoolboy's instinct to take sides. Michael was for the Trojans against the Greeks, partly on account of the Greek verbs, but principally because he once had a straw hat inscribed H.M.S. Hector. He was also for the Lancastrians against the Yorkists, and, of course, for the Jacobites against the Hanoverians. Somewhat illogically, he was for the Americans against the English, because as Miss Carthew pointed out he was English himself and the English were beaten. She used to teaze Michael for nearly always choosing the beaten side. She also used to annoy him by her assertion that in taking the part of the Americans in the War of Independence, he showed that most of his other choices were only due to the books he read. She used to make him very angry by saying that he was at heart a Roundhead and a Whig, and even hinted that he would grow up a Radical. This last insinuation really annoyed him very much indeed, because at Randell House no boy could be anything but a Conservative without laying himself open to the suggestion that he was not a gentleman.

In time, after an absence of nearly two years, Mrs. Fane came home for a long time; but Michael did not feel any of those violent emotions of joy that once he used to feel when he saw her cab rounding the corner. He was shy of his mother, and she for her part seemed shy of him and told Miss Carthew that school had not improved Michael. She wondered, too, why he always seemed anxious to be playing with other boys.

"It's quite natural," Miss Carthew pointed out.

"Darling Michael. I suppose it is," Mrs. Fane agreed vaguely. "But he's so grubby and inky nowadays."

Michael maintained somewhat indignantly that all the boys at Randell's were like him, for he was proud that by being grubby and inky no boy could detect in him any inclination to differentiate himself from the mass. At Randell's, where there was one way only of thinking and behaving and speaking, it would have been grossly cocky to be brushed and clean. Michael resented his mother's attempt to dress him nicely and was almost rude when she suggested ideas for charming and becoming costumes.

"I do think boys are funny," she used to sigh.

"Well, mother," Michael would argue, "if I wore a suit like that, all the other boys would notice it."

"But I think it's nice to be noticed," Mrs. Fane would contend.

"I think it's beastly," Michael always said.

"I wish you wouldn't use that horrid word," his mother would say disapprovingly.

"All the boys do," was Michael's invariable last word.

Then, "Michael," Miss Carthew would say sharply, as she fixed him with that cold look which he so much dreaded. Michael would blush and turn away, abashed; while Stella's company would be demanded by his mother instead of his, and Stella would come into the room all lily-rosed beside her imp-like brother.

Stella was held by Michael to be affected, and he would often point out to her how little such behaviour would be tolerated at a boys' school. Stella's usual reply was to pout, a form of expression which came under the category of affectations, or she would cry, which was a degree worse and was considered to be as good as sneaking outright. Michael often said he hoped that school would improve Stella's character and behaviour; yet when she went to school, Michael thought that not only was she none the better for the experience, but he was even inclined to suggest that she was very much the worse. Tiresome little girl friends came to tea sometimes and altered Michael's arrangements; and when they came they used to giggle in corners and Stella used to show off detestably. Once Michael was so much vexed by a certain Dorothy that he kissed her spitefully, and a commotion ensued from the middle of which rose Miss Carthew, grey-eyed and august like Pallas Athene in The Heroes. It seemed to Michael that altogether too much importance was attached to this incident. He had merely kissed Dorothy in order to show his contempt for her behaviour. One would think from the lecture given by Miss Carthew that it was pleasant to kiss giggling little girls. Michael felt thoroughly injured by the imputation of gallantry, and sulked instead of giving reasons.

"I really think your mother is right," Miss Carthew said at last. "You are quite different from the old Michael."

"I didn't want to kiss her," he cried, exasperated.

"Doesn't that make it all the worse?" Miss Carthew suggested.

Michael shrugged his shoulders feeling powerless to contend with all this stupidity of opinion.

"Surely," said Miss Carthew at last, "Don Quixote or General Mace or Henry V wouldn't have kissed people against their will in order to be spiteful."

"They might," argued Michael; "if rotten little girls came to tea and made them angry."

"I will not have that word 'rotten' used in front of me," Miss Carthew said.

"Well, fat-headed then," Michael proposed as a euphemism.

"The truth is," Miss Carthew pointed out, "you were angry because you couldn't have the Macalisters to tea and you vented your anger on poor Stella and her friends. I call it mean and unchivalrous."

"Well, Stella goes to mother and asks for Dorothy to come to tea, when you told me I could have the Macalisters, and I don't see why I should always have to give way."

"Boys always give way to girls," generalized Miss Carthew.

"I don't believe they do nowadays," said Michael.

"I see it's hopeless to argue any more. I'm sorry you won't see you're in the wrong. It makes me feel disappointed."

Michael again shrugged his shoulders.

"I don't see how I can possibly ask your mother to let Nancy stay here next Christmas. I suppose you'll be trying to kiss her."

Michael really had to laugh at this.

"Why, I like Nancy awfully," he said. "And we both think kissing is fearful rot—I mean frightfully stupid. But I won't do it again, Miss Carthew. I'm sorry. I am really."

There was one great advantage in dealing with Miss Carthew. She was always ready to forgive at once, and, as Michael respected her enough to dislike annoying her, he found it perfectly easy to apologize and be friends—particularly as he had set his heart on Nancy's Christmas visit.

Carlington Road and the Confederate Roads were now under the control of Michael and his friends. Rodber had gone away to a public school: the elder Macalister and Garrod had both got bicycles which occupied all their time: Michael, the twin Macalisters and a boy called Norton were in a very strong position of authority. Norton had two young brothers and the Macalisters had one, so that there were three slaves in perpetual attendance. It became the fashion to forsake the school field for the more adventurous wasteland of the neighbourhood. At the end of Carlington Road itself still existed what was practically open country as far as it lasted. There were elm-trees and declivities and broken hedges and the excavated hollows of deserted gravel-pits. There was an attractive zigzag boundary fence which was sufficiently ruinous at certain intervals to let a boy through to wander in the allotments of railway workers. Bands of predatory 'cads' prowled about this wasteland, and many were the fierce fights at sundown between the cads and the Randellites. Caps were taken for scalps, and Miss Carthew was horrified to observe nailed to Michael's bedroom wall the filthiest cap she had ever seen.

Apart from the battles there were the luxurious camps, where cigarettes at five a penny were smoked to the last puff and were succeeded by the consumption of highly scented sweets to remove the traces of tobacco. These camps were mostly pitched in the gravelly hollows, where Michael and the Macalisters and Norton used to sit round a camp-fire on the warm evenings of summer, while silhouetted against the blue sky above stood the minor Macalister and the junior Nortons in ceaseless vigilance. The bait held out to these sentries, who sometimes mutinied, was their equipment with swords, guns, pistols, shields, bows, arrows and breastplates. So heavily and decoratively armed and sustained by the prospect of peppermint bull's-eyes, Dicky Macalister and the two Nortons were content for an hour to scan the horizon for marauding cads, while down below the older boys discussed life in all its ambiguity and complication. These symposiums in the gravel-pit tried to solve certain problems in a very speculative manner.

"There must be *some* secret about being married," said Michael one Saturday afternoon, when the sun blazed down upon the sentries and the last cigarette had been smoked.

"There *is*," Norton agreed,

"I can't make out about twins," Michael continued, looking critically at the Macalisters.

Siegfried Macalister, generally known as 'Smack' in distinction to his brother Hugh always called 'Mac,' felt bound to offer a suggestion.

"There's twenty minutes' difference between us. I heard my mater tell a visitor, and besides I'm the eldest."

Speculation was temporarily interrupted by a bout between Smack and Mac, because neither was allowed to claim priority. At the end of an indecisive round Michael struck in:

"But why are there twins? People don't like twins coming, because in Ally Sloper there's always a joke about twins."

"I know married people who haven't got any children at all," said Norton in order still more elaborately to complicate the point at issue.

"Yes, there you are," said Michael. "There's some secret about marriage."

"There's a book in my mater's room which I believe would tell us," hinted Smack.

"There's a good deal in the Bible," Norton observed. "Only it's difficult to find the places and then you can't tell for certain what they mean."

Then came a long whispering at the end of which the four boys shook their heads very wisely and said that they were sure that was it.

"Hullo!" Michael shouted, forgetting the debate. "Young Dicky's signalling."

"Indians," said Mac.

"Sioux or Apaches?" asked Smack anxiously.

"Neither. It's Arabs. Charge," shouted Norton.

All problems went to the winds in the glories of action, in the clash of stick on stick, in the rending of cad's collar and cad's belt, and in the final defeat of the Arabs with the loss of their caravan—a sugar-box on a pair of elliptical wheels.

In addition to the arduous military life led by Michael at this period, he was also in common with Smack and Mac and Norton a multiplex collector. At first the two principal collections were silkworms and silver-paper. Afterwards came postage stamps and coins and medals and autographs and birds' eggs and shells and fossils and bones and skins and butterflies and moths and portraits of famous cricketers. From the moment the first silkworm was brought home in a perforated cardboard-box to the moment when by some arrangement of vendible material the first bicycle was secured, the greater part of Michael's leisure was mysteriously occupied in swapping. This swapping would continue until the mere theory of swapping for swapping's sake as exemplified in a paper called The Exchange and Mart was enough. When this journal became the rage, the most delightful occupation of Michael and his friends was that of poring over the columns of this medium of barter in order to read of X.Y.Z. in Northumberland who was willing to exchange five Buff Orpingtons, a suit, a tennis racket and Cowper's Poems for a mechanical organ or a 5 ft. by 4 ft. greenhouse. All the romance of commerce was to be found in The Exchange and Mart together with practical hints on the moulting of canaries or red mange in collies. Cricket was in the same way made a mathematical abstraction of decimals and initials and averages and records. All sorts of periodicals were taken in—Cricket, The Cricketer,

Cricketing amongst many others. From an exact perusal of these, Michael and the Macalisters knew that Streatham could beat Hampstead and were convinced of the superiority of the Incogniti C.C. over the Stoics C.C. With the collections of cricketers' portraits some of these figures acquired a conceivable personality; but, for the most part, they remained L.M.N.O.P.Q. Smith representing 36·58 an innings and R.S.T.U.V.W. Brown costing 11·07 a wicket. That they wore moustaches, lived and loved like passionate humanity did not seem to matter compared with the arithmetical progression of their averages. When Michael and Norton (who was staying with him at St. Leonards) were given shillings and told to see the Hastings' Cricket Week from the bowling of the first ball to the drawing of the final stump, Michael and Norton were very much bored indeed, and deprecated the waste of time in watching real cricket, when they might have been better occupied in collating the weekly cricketing journals.

At Christmas Michael emerged from a successful autumn term with Stories from the Odyssey by Professor Church and a chestnut that was reputed to have conquered nine hundred and sixty-six other and softer chestnuts. That nine hundred and sixty-sixer of Michael's was a famous nut, and the final struggle between it (then a five hundred and forty-oner) and the four hundred and twenty-fourer it smashed was a contest long talked of in circles where Conquerors were played. Michael much regretted that the etiquette of the Lent term, which substituted peg-tops for Conquerors, should prevent his chestnut reaching four figures. He knew that next autumn term, if all fell out as planned, he would be at St. James' School itself, where Conquerors and tops and marbles were never even mentioned, save as vanities and toys of early youth. However, he swapped the nine hundred and sixty-sixer for seven white mice and a slow-worm in spirits of wine belonging to Norton; and he had the satisfaction of hearing later on that after a year in rejuvenating oil the nine hundred and sixty-sixer became a two thousand and thirty-threer before it fell down a drain, undefeated.

After Christmas Nancy Carthew came up from Hampshire to spend a fortnight at Carlington Road, and the holidays were spent in a fever of theatres and monuments and abbeys. Michael asked Nancy what she thought of Stella and her affectation, and was surprized by Nancy saying she thought Stella was an awfully jolly kid and 'no end good' at the piano. Michael in consideration of Nancy's encomium tried to take a fresh view of Stella and was able sincerely to admit that, compared with many other little girls of the neighbourhood, Stella was fairly pretty. He decided that it would be a good thing for Norton to marry her. He told Norton that there seemed no reason why he and Stella should not come together in affection, and Norton said that, if Michael thought he should, he was perfectly willing to marry Stella, when he was grown up. Michael thereupon swapped a box of somewhat bent dragoons for a ring, and presented this ring to Norton with the injunction that he should on no account tell Stella that he was engaged to her, in case it made her cocky. He also forbade Norton to kiss her (not that he supposed Norton wanted to kiss Stella), because Miss Carthew would be annoyed and might possibly close the area door to Norton for the future.

When Nancy went back to Hampshire, Michael felt lonely. The Macalisters and the Nortons had gone away on visits, and Carlington Road was dreary without them. Michael read a great deal and by reason of being at home he gradually became less grubby, as the holidays wore on. Also his hair grew long and waved over his forehead with golden lights and shadows and curled in bunches by his ears. A new Eton suit well became him, and his mother said how charming he looked. Michael deplored good looks in boys, but he managed to endure the possession of them during the little space that remained before the Lent term began. He took to frequenting the drawing-room again as of old and, being nowadays allowed to stay up till a quarter to nine, he used to spend a rosy half-hour after dinner sitting on a footstool in the firelight by his mother's knee. She used to stroke his hair and sigh sometimes, when she looked at him.

One afternoon just before term began Mrs. Fane told him to make himself as tidy as possible, because she wanted to take him out to pay a call. Michael was excited by this notion, especially when he heard that they were to travel by hansom, a form of vehicle which he greatly admired. The hansom bowled along the Kensington Road with Michael in his Eton suit and top-hat sitting beside his mother scented sweetly with delicious perfumes and very silky to the touch. They drove past Kensington Gardens all dripping with January rains, past Hyde Park and the Albert Memorial, past the barracks of the Household Cavalry, past Hyde Park Corner and the Duke of Wellington's house. They dashed along with a jingle and a rattle over the slow old omnibus route, and Michael felt very much distinguished as he turned round to look at the melancholy people crammed inside each omnibus they passed. When they came to Devonshire House, they turned round to the left and pulled up before a grand house in a square. Michael pressed the bell, and the door opened immediately, much more quickly than he had ever known a door open.

"Is his lordship in?" asked Mrs. Fane.

"His lordship is upstairs, ma'am," said the footman.

The hall seemed full of footmen, one of whom took Michael's hat and another of whom led the way up a wide soft staircase that smelt like the inside of the South Kensington Museum. All the way up, the walls were hung with enormous pictures of men in white wigs. Presently they stood in the largest room Michael had ever entered, a still white room full of golden furniture. Michael had barely recovered his breath from astonishment at the size of the room, when he saw another room round the corner, in which a man was sitting by a great fire. When the footman had left the room very quietly, this man got up and held Mrs. Fane's hand for nearly a minute. Then he looked at Michael, curiously, Michael thought, so curiously as to make him blush.

"And this is the boy?" the gentleman asked.

Michael thought his mother spoke very funnily, as if she were just going to cry, when she answered:

"Yes, this is Michael."

"My God, Valérie," said the man, "it makes it harder than ever."

Michael took the opportunity to look at this odd man and tried to think where he had seen him before. He was sure he had seen him somewhere. But every time just as he had almost remembered, a mist came over the picture he was trying to form, so that he could not remember.

"Well, Michael," said the gentleman, "you don't know who I am."

"Ah, don't, Charles," said Mrs. Fane.

"Well, he's not so wise as all that," laughed the gentleman.

Michael thought it was a funny laugh, more sad than cheerful.

"This is Lord Saxby," said Mrs. Fane.

"I say, my name is Saxby," Michael exclaimed.

"Nonsense," said Lord Saxby, "I don't believe it."

"It is really. Charles Michael Saxby Fane."

"Well, that's a very strange thing," said Lord Saxby.

"Yes, I think it's awfully funny," Michael agreed. "Because I never heard of anyone called Saxby. My name's Charles too. Only, of course, that's quite a common name. But nobody at our school knows I'm called Saxby except a boy called Buckley who's an awful beast. We don't tell our Christian names, you know. If a chap lets out his Christian name he gets most frightfully ragged by the other chaps. Chaps think you're an awfully silly ass if you let out your Christian name."

Michael was finding it very easy to talk.

"I must hear some more about this wonderful school," Lord Saxby declared.

Then followed a delightful conversation in which due justice was done to the Macalister twins and to Norton, and to the life they shared with Michael.

"By gad, Valérie, he ought to go to Eton, you know," declared Lord Saxby, turning to Michael's mother.

"No, no. I'm sure you were right, when you said St. James'," persisted Mrs. Fane.

"Perhaps I was," Lord Saxby sighed. "Well, Valérie—not again. It's too damnably tantalizing."

"I thought just once while he was still small," said Mrs. Fane softly. "Photographs are so unsatisfactory. And you haven't yet heard Stella play."

"Valérie, I couldn't. Look at this great barrack of a house. If you only knew how I long sometimes for—what a muddle it all is!"

Then a footman came in with tea, and Michael wondered what dinner was like in this house, if mere tea were so grand and silvery.

"I think I must drive you back in the phaeton," said Lord Saxby.

"No, no, Charles. No more rules must be broken."

"Yes, I suppose you're right. But don't—not again, please. I can't bear to think of the 'ifs.'"

Then Lord Saxby turned to Michael.

"Look here, young man, what do you want most?"

"Oh, boxes of soldiers and an unused set of Siamese," said Michael.

"Siamese what? Siamese cats?"

"No, you silly," laughed Michael, "Stamps, of course!"

"Oh, stamps," said Lord Saxby. "Right—and soldiers, eh? Good."

All the way back in the hansom Michael wished he had specified Artillery to Lord Saxby; but two days afterwards dozens of boxes of all kinds of soldiers arrived, and unused sets not merely of Siamese, but of North American Tercentenaries and Borneos and Labuans and many others.

"I say," Michael gasped, "he's a ripper, isn't he? What spiffing boxes! I say, he is a decent chap, isn't he? When are we going to see Lord Saxby again, mother?"

"Some day."

"I can have Norton to tea on Wednesday, can't I?" begged Michael. "He'll think my soldiers are awfully ripping."

"Darling Michael," said his mother.

"Mother, I will try and not be inky," said Michael in a burst of affectionate renunciation.

"Dearest boy," said his mother gently.

Chapter IX: *Holidays in France*

IN Michael's last term at St. James' Preparatory School, Mrs. Fane settled that he should for the holidays go to France with Mr. Vernon and Mr. Lodge, two masters who were accustomed each year to take a few boys away with them to the coast of Brittany. Five boys were going this summer—Michael and Hands and Hargreaves and Jubb and Rutherford; and all five of them bragged about their adventure for days before school broke up. Miss Carthew drove with Michael to Victoria Station and handed him over to Mr. Lodge who was walking about in a very thick and romantic overcoat. Mr. Lodge was a clean-shaven, large-faced and popular master, and Mr. Vernon was an equally popular master, deep-voiced, heavy-moustached, hook-nosed. In fact it was impossible to say which of the two one liked the better. Mr. Lodge at once produced two packets of Mazawattee tea which he told Michael to put in his pocket and say nothing about when he landed in France, and when Hands, Hargreaves, Rutherford and Jubb arrived, they were all given packets of tea by Mr. Lodge and told to say nothing about them when they landed in France. Mr. Vernon appeared, looking very business-like and shouting directions about the luggage to porters, while Mr. Lodge gathered the boys together and steered them through the barrier on to the platform and into the train for Newhaven. The steamer by which they were going to cross was not an ordinary packet-boat, but a cargo-boat carrying vegetable ivory. For Channel voyagers they were going to be a long while at sea, calling at Havre and afterwards rounding Cherbourg and Brest, before they reached St. Corentin, the port of their destination at the mouth of the Loire. It was rough weather all the way to Havre, and Michael was too ill to notice much the crew or the boat or any of the other boys. However, the excitement of disembarking at Havre about midnight put an end to sea-sickness, for it was very thrilling at such an hour to follow Mr. Lodge and Mr. Vernon through the gloomy wharves and under their dripping archways. When after this strange walk, they came to a wide square and saw cafés lighted up and chairs and tables in the open air before the doors, Michael felt that life was opening out on a vista of hitherto unimagined possibilities. They all sat down at midnight, wrapped up in their travelling coats and not at all too much tired to sip grenadine sucrée and to crunch Petit Beurre biscuits. Michael thought grenadine sucrée was just as nice as it looked and turned to Hands, a skull-headed boy who was sitting next to him:

"I say, this is awfully decent, isn't it?"

"Rather," squeaked Hands in his high voice. "Much nicer than Pineappleade."

After they had stayed there for a time, watching isolated passers-by slouch across the wind-blown square, Mr. Lodge announced they must hurry back to the boat and get a good night's sleep. Back they went between the damp walls of the shadowy wharves, plastered with unfamiliar advertizements, until they reached their boat and went to bed. In the morning when Michael woke up, the steamer was pitching and rolling: everything in the cabin was lying in a jumble on the floor, and Rutherford and Hargreaves were sitting up in their bunks wideawake. Rutherford was the oldest boy of the party and he was soon going in for his Navy examination; but he had been so sea-sick the day before that Michael felt that he was just as accessible as the others and was no longer afraid to talk to this hero without being spoken to first. Rutherford, having been so sick, felt bound to put on a few airs of grandeur; but he was pleasant enough and very full of information about many subjects which had long puzzled Michael. He spoke with authority on life and death and birth and love and marriage, so that when Michael emerged into the wind from the jumbled cabin, he felt that to dress beside Rutherford was an event not easily to be forgotten: but later on as he paced the foam-spattered deck, and meditated on the facts of existence so confidently revealed, he began to fear that the learned Rutherford was merely a retailer of unwarranted legends. Still he had propounded enough for Michael, when he returned to Carlington Road, to theorize upon and impart to the Macalisters; and anyway, without bothering about physiological problems, it was certainly splendid to walk about the deck in the wind and rain, and no longer to hate, but even to enjoy the motion of the boat. It was exhilarating to clamber right up into the bows among coils of rope and to see how the boat charged through the spuming water. Michael nearly made up his mind to be a sailor instead of a Bengal Lancer, and looked enviously at the ship's boy in his blue blouse. But presently he heard a savage voice, and one of the sailors so much admired kicked the ship's boy down the companion into the forecastle. Michael was horrified when, late in the grey and stormy afternoon, he heard cries of pain from somewhere down below. He ran to peer into the pit whence they came, and in the half-light he could see a rope's-end clotted with blood. This sight dismayed him, and he longed to ask Mr. Lodge or Mr. Vernon to interfere and save the poor ship's boy, but a feeling of shame compelled silence and, though he was sincerely shocked by the thought of the cruel scenes acted down there in the heart of the ship, he could not keep back a certain exultation and excitement similar to that which he had felt at Folkestone in the girls' school last summer.

Soon the steamer with its cargo of vegetable ivory and tortured ship's boy and brutal crew were all forgotten in the excitement of arriving at St. Corentin, of driving miles into the country until they reached the house where they were going to spend six weeks. It was an old house set far back from the high road and reached by a long drive between pollarded acacias. All round the house were great fig trees and pear trees and plum trees. The garden was rank with unpruned gooseberry and currant bushes, untidy with scrambling gourds and grape vines. It was a garden utterly unlike any garden that Michael had ever known. There seemed to be no flowers in this overwhelming vegetation which matted everything. It was like the garden of the Sleeping Beauty's palace. The crumbling walls were webbed with briars; their foundations were buried in thickets of docks and nettles, and the fruit trees that grew against them had long ago broken loose from any restraint. It was a garden that must surely take a very long time to explore, so vast was it, so trackless, so much did every corner demand a slow advance.

When the boys had unpacked and when they had been introduced to Mrs. Wylde, the mistress of the house, and when they had presented to her the packets of Mazawattee tea and when they themselves had eaten a deliciously novel dinner at the unusual hour of six, they all set out to explore the luxuriant wilderness behind the house. Mr. Vernon and Mr. Lodge shouted to them to eat only the ripe fruit and with this solitary injunction left them to their own amusements until bed-time. Rutherford, Hargreaves and Jubb at once set out to find ripe fruit, and as the first tree they came to was loaded with greengages, Rutherford, Hargreaves and Jubb postponed all exploration for the present. Michael and Hands, who was sleeping in his room and with whom he had already made friends, left the others behind them. As they walked farther from the house, they spoke in low tones, so silent was this old garden.

"I'm sure it's haunted," said Michael. "I never felt so funny, not exactly frightened, you know, but sort of frightened."

"It's still quite light," squeaked the hopeful Hands.

"Yes, but the sun's behind all these trees and you can't hear anything, but only us walking," whispered Michael.

However, they went on through a jungle of artichokes and through an orchard of gnarled apple trees past a mildewed summer-house, until they reached a serpentine path between privet bushes, strongly scented in the dampness all around.

"Shall we?" murmured Hands doubtfully.

"Yes. We can bunk back if we see anything," said Michael. "I like this."

They walked on following the zigzags of the path, but stopped dead as a blackbird shrilled and flapped into the bushes affrighted.

"By Jove, that beastly bird made me awfully funky," said Michael.

"Let's go back," said Hands. "Suppose we got murdered. People do in France."

"Rot," said Michael. "Not in a private garden, you cuckoo."

With mutual encouragement the two boys wandered on, until they found farther progress barred by a high hedge, impenetrable apparently and viewless to Michael and Hands who were not very tall.

"What sucks!" said Michael. "I hate turning back. I think it's rotten to turn back. Don't you? Hullo!" he cried. "Look here, Hands. Here's a regular sort of tunnel going down hill. It's quite steep."

In a moment Hands and Michael were half sliding, half climbing down a cliff. The lower they went, the faster they travelled and soon they were sliding all the way, because they had to guard their faces against the brambles that twined above them.

"Good Lord!" gasped Michael, as he bumped down a sheer ten-feet of loose earth. "I'm getting jolly bumped. Look out, Hands, you kicked my neck, you ass."

"I can't help it," gasped Hands. "I'm absolutely slipping, and if I try to catch hold, I scratch myself."

They were sliding so fast that the only thing to do was to laugh and give way. So, with shouts and laughter and bumps and jolts and the pushing of loose stones and earth before them, Michael and Hands came with a run to the bottom of the cliff and landed at last on soft sea-sand.

"By gum," said Michael, "we're right on the beach. What a rag!"

The two boys looked back to the scene of their descent. It was a high cliff covered with shrubs and brambles, apparently unassailable. Before them was the sea, pale blue and gold, and to the right and to the left were the flat lonely sands. They ran, shouting with excitement, towards the rippling tide. The sand-hoppers buzzed about their ankles: Hands tripped over a jelly-fish and fell into several others: sea-gulls swooped above them, crying continually.

"It's like Robinson Crusoe," Michael declared.

He was mad with the exhilaration of possession. He owned these sands.

"Oh, young Hands fell down on the sands," he cried, bursting into uncontrollable laughter at the absurdity of the rhyme. Then he found razor-shells and waved his arms triumphantly. He found, too, wine-stained shells and rosy shells and great purple mussels. He and Hands took off their shoes and stockings and ran through the limpid water that sparkled with gold and tempted them to wade for ever ankle deep. They reached a broken mass of rock which would obviously be surrounded by water at high tide; they clambered up to the summit and found there grass and rabbits' holes.

"It's a real island," said Michael. "It is! I say, Hands, this is our island. We discovered it. Bags I, we keep it."

"Don't let's get caught by the tide," suggested cautious Hands.

"All right, you funk," jeered Michael.

They came back to the level sands and wandered on towards the black point of cliff bounding the immediate view.

"I say, there's a cave. I bet you there's a cave," Michael called to his companion who was examining a dead fish.

"Wait a jiffy," shouted Hands; but Michael hurried on to the cave. He wanted to be the first to enter under its jagged arch. Already he could see the silver sand shimmering upon the threshold of the inner darkness. He walked in, awed by the secrecy of this sea-cavern, almost expectant of a mermaid or octopus in the deepest cranny. Suddenly he stopped. His heart beat furiously: his head swam: his legs quivered under him. Then he turned and ran towards the light.

"Good lummy!" said Hands, when Michael came up to him. "Whatever's the matter? You're simply frightfully white."

"Come away," said Michael. "I saw something beastly."

"What was it?"

"There's a man in there and a woman. Oh, it was beastly."

Michael dragged Hands by the arm, but not before they had left the cave far behind would he speak.

"What was it really?" asked Hands, when they stood at the bottom of the cliff.

"I couldn't possibly tell anybody ever," said Michael.

"You're making it up," scoffed Hands.

"No, I'm not," said Michael. "Look here, don't say anything to the others about that cave. Promise."

Hands promised silence; and he and Michael soon discovered a pathway up the cliff. When they reached the garden, it was a deeper green than ever in the falling twilight, and they did not care to linger far from the house. It was a relief to hear voices and to see Rutherford, Hargreaves and Jubb still eating plums. Presently they played games on a lawn with Mr. Vernon and Mr. Lodge, and soon, after reading sleepily for a while in the tumble-down room which was set apart for the boys' use, Michael and Hands went to bed and, after an exciting encounter with a bat, fell asleep.

The days in Brittany went by very swiftly. In the morning at eight o'clock there were great bowls of café au lait and rolls with honey and butter waiting in the dining-room for the boys, when they came back from bathing. All the other boys except Michael had come to France to improve their French; but he worked also at the first book of Ovid's Metamorphoses and at Lucian's Charon, because he was going in for a scholarship at St. James'. However, these classical subjects were put away at eleven o'clock, when déjeuner with all sorts of new and delicious dishes was served. After this there was nothing to do until six o'clock but enjoy oneself. Sometimes the boys made expeditions into St. Corentin, where they wondered at the number of dogs to each inhabitant and bought cakes and sweets at a pastrycook's and gas-filled balloons which they sent up in the market-place. Or they would stroll down to the quays and watch the shipping and practise their French on sailors looking more like pirates than ordinary sailors.

Once, while Michael was gazing into a shop window at some dusty foreign stamps in a brass tray, a Capuchin friar spoke to him in very good English and asked if he collected stamps. Michael said that he did, and the Capuchin invited him to come back to the convent and see his collection. Michael thought this was a splendid invitation and willingly accompanied the Capuchin whom, except for a sore on his lip, he liked very much. He thought the inside of the convent was rather like the inside of an aquarium, but he enjoyed the stamps very much. The friar gave him about a dozen of his duplicates, and Michael promised to write to him, when he got home, and to send him some of his own. Then they had tea in the friar's cell, and afterwards Michael set out to walk back to St. Antoine. It was not yet six o'clock when he reached the house, but there was a terrible fuss being made about his adventure. Telegrams had been despatched, the gendarmerie had been informed, and the British Vice-consul had been interviewed. Mr. Vernon asked in his deepest voice where the deuce he had been, and when Michael told him he had been taking tea with a monk, Mr. Vernon was more angry than ever.

"Don't do things like that. Good heavens, boy, you might have been kidnapped and turned into a Catholic, before you knew where you were. Hang it all, remember I'm responsible for your safety and never again get into conversation with a wandering monk."

Michael explained about the stamps, but Mr. Vernon said that was a very pretty excuse, and would by no means hear of Michael visiting the convent again. When Michael thought over this fuss, he could not understand what it had all been about. He could not imagine anything more harmless than this Capuchin friar with the sore on his lip. However, he never did see him again, except once in the distance, when he pointed him out to Mr. Vernon, who said he looked a dirty ruffian. Michael discovered that grown-up people always saw danger where there was no danger, but when, as on the occasion when Hands and he plainly perceived a ghost in the garden, there was every cause for real alarm, they merely laughed.

The weather grew warmer as August moved on, and Michael with Mr. Vernon and Mr. Lodge used sometimes to plunge into the depths of the country, there to construe Ovid and Lucian while the other boys worked at French with the Frenchman who came in from St. Corentin to teach them. Michael enjoyed these expeditions with Mr. Vernon and Mr. Lodge. They would sit down in the lush grass of a shady green lane, close to a pool where the bull-frogs croaked. Michael would construe the tale of Deucalion and Pyrrha to Mr. Lodge, while Mr. Vernon lay on his back and smoked a large pipe. Then a White Admiral butterfly would soar round the oak trees, and Ovid would be thrown behind them like Deucalion's stones; while Michael and Mr. Vernon and Mr. Lodge manœuvred and shouted and ran up and down, until the White Admiral was either safely bottled with the cyanide of potassium or soared away out of sight. When Ovid was finished for the day, Mr. Lodge used to light a big pipe and lie on his back, while Michael construed the Dialogue of Charon to Mr. Vernon. Then an Oak Eggar moth would fly with tumbling reckless flight beyond the pool, luring Michael and Mr. Lodge and Mr. Vernon to charge through in pursuit, not deterred by the vivid green slime of the wayside water as the ghosts were deterred by gloomy Styx. Indeed, as the hot August days went by, each one was marked by its butterflies more definitely than by anything else. Michael thought that France was a much better place for collecting them than England. Scarce Swallow-tails and Ordinary Swallow-tails haunted the cliffs majestically. Clouded Yellows were chased across the fields of clover. Purple Emperors and Camberwell Beauties and Bath Whites were all as frequent as Heath Browns at home. Once, they all went a long expedition to Bluebeard's Castle on the other side of the Loire, and, while they sat in a garden café, drinking their grenadine sucrée, hundreds of Silver-washed Fritillaries appeared over the tables. How the fat French bourgeois stared to see these mad English boys chasing butterflies in their sunny bee-haunted garden. But how lovely the Fritillaries looked, set upside down to show their powdered green and rosy wings washed by silver streaks. Perhaps the most exciting catch of all happened, close to the shutting in of a September dusk, in the avenue of pollarded acacias. Michael saw the moth first on the lowest bough of a tree. It was jet-black marked with thick creamy stripes. Neither he nor Hands had a net, and they trembled with excitement and chagrin. Michael threw a stone rather ineffectively and the moth changed its position, showing before it settled down on a higher branch underwings of glowing vermilion.

"Oh, what can it be?" Michael cried, dancing.

"It's frightfully rare," squeaked Hands.

"You watch it carefully, while I scoot for a net," commanded Michael.

He tore along up the darkening drive, careless of ghosts or travelling seamen bent on murder and robbery. He rushed into the hall and shouted, 'A terribly rare moth in the drive! Quick, my net!' and rushed back to the vigilant Hands. The others followed, and after every cunning of the hunter had been tried, the moth was at last secured and after a search through Kirby's Butterflies and Moths pronounced to be a Jersey Tiger, not so rare, after all, in fact very common abroad. But it was a glorious beast when set, richly black, barred and striped with damasked cream over a flame of orange-scarlet.

The six weeks were over. Michael had to leave in advance of the others, in order to enter for his scholarship examination at St. James'. Mr. Lodge took him to St. Malo and handed him over to the charge of Rutherford's older brother, who was already at St. James' and would see Michael safely to London. Michael could scarcely believe that this Rutherford was a boy, so tall was he, such a heavy black moustache had he and so pleasant was he to Michael. Michael thought with regret of the green and golden days in Brittany, as he waved to Mr. Lodge standing on the St. Malo jetty. He felt, as the steamer sailed across the glassy sea through a thick September haze, that he was coming back to greater adventures, that he was older and, as he paced beside Rutherford up and down the deck, that he was more important. But he thought with regret of Brittany and squeaky Hands and the warm days of butterflies. He hoped to return next year and see again the fig tree by his bedroom window and the level shore of the Loire estuary and the tangled tumble-down garden on the cliff's edge. He would always think of Mr. Lodge and Mr. Vernon, those very dearly loved schoolmasters. He would think of the ghostly Breton lanes at twilight and the glorious Sundays unspoilt by church or best clothes and of the bull-frogs in the emerald pools.

Michael disliked the examination very much indeed. He hated the way in which all the other competitors stared. He disliked the speed with which they wrote and the easy manners of some of them. However, he gained his scholarship mostly by age marks and was put in the Lower Third, the youngest boy in the class by two years, and became a Jacobean, turning every morning round the same gate, walking every morning up the same gravel path, running every morning up the same wide steps, meeting every morning the same smell of hot-water pipes and hearing every day the same shuffle of quick feet along the corridors past the same plaster cast of the Laocoön.

BOOK TWO
CLASSIC EDUCATION

"What is it then that thou hast got

   By drudging through that five-year task?

What knowledge or what art is thine?

   Set out thy stock, thy craft declare."

                         Ionica.

"Sic cum his, inter quos eram, voluntatum enuntianaarum signa conmunicavi; et vitae humanae procellosam societatem altius ingressus sum, pendens ex parentum auctoritate nutuque maiorum hominum."

ST. AUGUSTINE.

Chapter I: *The Jacobean*

MICHAEL found the Lower Third at St. James' a jolly class. He was so particularly young that he was called 'Baby,' but with enough obvious affection to make the dubious nickname a compliment. To be sure, Mr. Braxted would often cackle jokes in a raucous voice about his age, and if Michael made a false quantity he would grumble and say he was paid as a schoolmaster not as a wet-nurse. However, Mr. Braxted was such a dandy and wore such very sharply creased and tight trousers and was so well set up and groomed that the class was proud of his neat appearance, and would inform the Upper Third that Foxy Braxted did, at any rate, look a gentleman, a distinction which the Upper Third could scarcely claim for their own form-master.

Michael liked the greater freedom of a public school. There were no home-books to be signed by governesses: there was no longer any taboo upon the revelation of Christian names. Idiosyncrasies were overlooked in the vaster society of St. James'. The senior boys paid no attention to the juniors, but passed them by scornfully as if they were grubs not worth the trouble of squashing. There was no longer the same zest in the little scandals and petty spitefulness of a private school. There was much greater freedom in the choice of one's friends, and Michael no longer felt bound to restrict his intimacy to the twin Macalisters and Norton. Sometimes in the 'quarter' (as the break was now called) Michael would stand on the top of the steps that led down from the great red building into the school-ground. From this point he would survey the huge green field with its archipelago of countless boys. He would think how few of their names he knew and from what distances many of them travelled each morning to school. He could wander among them by himself and not one would turn a curious head. He was at liberty even to stare at a few great ones whom athletic prowess had endowed already with legendary divinity, so that among small boys tales were told of their daring and their immortality gradually woven into the folk-lore of St. James'. Sometimes a member of the first fifteen would speak to Michael on a matter of athletic business.

"What's your name?"

"Fane," Michael would answer, hoping the while that his contemporaries might be passing and see this colloquy between a man and a god.

"Oh, yes," the hero would carelessly continue, "I've got you down already. Mind you turn up to Little Side at 1.45 sharp."

Little Side was the football division that included the smallest third of the school. Sometimes the hero would ask another question, as:

"Do you know a kid called Smith P.L.?"

And Michael with happy blushes would be able to point out Smith P.L. to the great figure.

Michael played football on Little Side with great regularity, rushing home to dinner and rushing off again to change and be in the field by a quarter to two. He could run very fast and for that reason the lords of Little Side made him play forward, a position for which the slightness of his body made him particularly unsuited. One day, however, he managed to intercept a pass, to outwit a three-quarter, to dodge the full-back and to score a try, plumb between the posts. Luckily one of the heroes had strolled down from Pelion that afternoon to criticize Little Side and Michael was promoted from the scrum to play three-quarter back on the left wing, in which position he really enjoyed football very much indeed.

It fell out that year that the St. James' fifteen was the most invincible ever known in the school's history, and every Saturday afternoon, when there was a home match, Michael in rain or wind or pale autumnal sunlight would take up his position in the crowd of spectators to cheer and shout and urge St. James' to another glorious victory. Match after match that year earned immortal fame in the school records, sending the patriotic Jacobeans of every size and age home to a happy tea in the rainy twilight. Those were indeed afternoons of thunderous excitement. How everybody used to shout—School—Schoo-oo-ol—Schoo-ol! Play up—Schoo-oo-ool! James! Ja-a-a-mes! Oh, go low. Kick! Touch! Forward! Held! Off-side! Go in yourself! Schoo-ool!

How Michael's heart beat at the thud of the Dulford forwards in their last desperate rush towards the School 'twenty-five.' Down went the School halves, and over them like a torrent swept the Dulford pack. Down went the three-quarters in a plucky attempt to sit on the ball. Ah! There was an unanimous cry of agony, as everybody pressed against the boundary rope and craned towards the touch-line until the posts creaked before the strain. Not in vain had those gallant three-quarters been smeared with mud and bruised by the boots of the surging Dulford pack; for the ball had been kicked on too far and Cutty Jackson, the School back, had fielded it miraculously. He was going to punt. 'Kick!' yelled the despairing spectators. And Jackson, right under the disappointed groans of the Dulford forwards whose muscles cracked with the effort to fetch him down, kicked the ball high, high into the silvery November air. Up with that spinning greasy oval travelled the hopes of the onlookers, and, as it fell safely into touch, from all round the field rose like a rocket a huge sigh of relief that presently broke into volleys and pæans of exultation, as half-time sounded with St. James' a goal to the good. How Michael admired the exhausted players when they sucked the sliced lemons and lay about in the mud; how he envied Cutty Jackson, when the lithe and noble fellow leaned against the goalpost and surveyed his audience. 'Sidiness' could be easily forgiven after that never-to-be-forgotten kick into touch. Why, thought Michael, should not he himself be one day ranked as the peer of Cutty Jackson? Why should not he, six or seven years hence, penetrate the serried forces of Dulford and score a winning try, even as the referee's whistle was lifted to sound 'time'? Ambition woke in Michael, while he surveyed upon that muddy field the prostrate forms of the fifteen, like statues in a museum. Then play began and personal desires were merged in the great hope of victory for the School. Hardly now could the spectators shout, so tense was the struggle, so long was each full minute of action. Michael's brain swam with excitement. He saw the Dulford team as giants bull-necked and invulnerable. He saw the School halves shrinking, the School three-quarters shiver like grass and the School forwards crumple before the Dulford charges. They were beaten: the untarnished record was broken: Michael could have sobbed for his side. Swifter than swallows, the Dulford three-quarters flew down the now all too short field of play. They were in! Look! they were dancing in triumph. A try to Dulford! Disconsolately the School team lined up behind their disgraced goal. Jauntily the Dulford half walked away with the shapely leather. The onlookers held their breath, as the ball, evilly accurate, dangerously direct, was poised in position for the kick at goal. The signal was given: the School team made their rush: the ball rose in the air: hung for a moment motionless, hit a goalpost, quivered and fell back. One goal to a try—five points to three—and St. James' was leading. Then indeed did the School play up. Then indeed did every man in the team 'go low': and for the rest of the game to neither side did any advantage incline. Grunts and muttered oaths, the thud of feet, the smack of wet leather lasted continually. In the long line-ups for the throw in from touch, each man marked his man viciously: the sweat poured down from hanging jaws: vests were torn, knees were grimed with mud and elbows were blackened. The scrimmages were the tightest and neatest ever watched, and neither scrum could screw the other a foot. At last the shrill whistle of the referee proclaimed the end of an immortal contest. There were cheers for the victors by the vanquished, by the vanquished for their conquerors. The spectators melted away into the gathering mist and rain, a flotsam of black umbrellas. In a few moments the school-ground was desolate and silent. Michael, as he looked at the grass ploughed into mud by the severe struggle, thought what superb heroes were in his School team; and just as he was going home, content, he saw a blazer left on a post. It was Jackson's, and Michael, palpitating with the honour, ran as fast as he could to the changing-room through the echoing cloister beneath the school.

"I say, Jackson, you left this on the ground," he said shyly.

Jackson looked up from a conversation with the Dulford full-back.

"Oh, thanks very much," he murmured, and went on with his talk.

Michael would not have missed that small sentence for any dignity in the world.

During his first term at St. James', Michael went on with his study of the art of dancing, begun during the previous winter without much personal satisfaction and with a good deal of self-consciousness. These dancing lessons took place in the hall at Randell's, and Michael revisited his old school with a new confidence. He found himself promoted to stay beyond the hour of pupilage in order pleasantly to pass away a second hour by dancing formally with the sisters and cousins of other boys. He had often admired last year those select Jacobeans who, buttoning white gloves, stood in a supercilious group, while their juniors clumped through the Ladies' Chain uninspired by the swish of a single petticoat. Now he was of their sacred number. It was not surprizing that under the influence of the waltz and the Circassian circle and the schottische and the quadrille and the mazurka that Michael should fall in love. He was not anxious to fall in love: many times to other boys he had mocked at woman and dilated upon the folly of matrimony. He had often declared on his way to and from school that celibacy should be the ideal of every man. He used to say how little he could understand the habit of sitting in dark corners and kissing. Even Miss Carthew he grew accustomed to treat almost with rudeness, lest some lynx-eyed friend of his should detect in his relation with her a tendency towards the sentimental. However, Muriel in her salmon-coloured, accordion-pleated frock bowled Michael off his superior pedestal. He persuaded himself that this was indeed one of those unchangeable passions of which he read or rather did read now. This great new emotion was certainly Love, for Michael could honestly affirm that as soon as he saw Muriel sitting on a chair with long black legs outstretched before her, he loved her. No other girl existed, and when he moved towards her for the pleasure of the next dance, he felt his heart beating, his cheeks on fire. Muriel seemed to like him after a fashion. At any rate, she cordially supported him in a project of long-deferred revenge upon Mr. Macrae of the Upper Fourth at Randell's, and she kept 'cavé' while Michael tried the door of his empty class-room off the top gallery of the hall. It was unlocked, and Michael crept in and quickly threw the contents of Mr. Macrae's desk out of the window and wrote on the blackboard: 'Mr. Macrae is the silliest ass in England.' Then he and Muriel walked demurely back to join the tinkling mazurka down below and, though many enquiries were set on foot as to the perpetrator of the outrage, Michael was never found out.

Michael's passion for Muriel increased with every evening of her company, and he went so far as to make friends with a very unpopular boy who lived in her road, for the sake of holding this unpopular boy in close conversation by his threshold on the chance of seeing Muriel's grey muff in the twilight. Muriel was strangely cold for the heroine of such a romance, and indeed Michael only once saw her really vivacious, which was when he gave her a catapult. Yet sometimes she would make a clandestine appointment and talk to him for twenty minutes in a secluded terrace, so that he consoled himself with a belief in her untold affection. Michael read Don Quixote again on account of Dulcinea del Toboso, and he was greatly moved by the knight's apostrophes and declamations. He longed for a confidant and was half inclined to tell Stella about Muriel; but when he came to the point Stella was engrossed in a new number of Little Folks and Michael feared she was unworthy of such a trust. The zenith of his passion was attained at the Boarders' dance to which he and Muriel and even Stella were invited. Michael had been particularly told by Miss Carthew that he was to dance four times at least with Stella and never to allow her to be without a partner. He was in despair and felt, as he encountered the slippery floor with Stella hanging nervously on his arm, that round his neck had been tied a millstone of responsibility. There in a corner was Muriel exquisite in yellow silk, and in her hair a yellow bow. Boys flitted round her, like bees before a hive, and here was he powerless with this wretched sister.

"You wait here," said Michael. "I'll be back in half a jiffy."

"Oh, no," pouted Stella. "You're not to leave me alone, Michael. Miss Carthew said you were to look after me."

Michael groaned.

"Do you like ices?" he asked desperately. "You do, don't you?"

"No," said Stella. "They make my tooth ache."

Michael almost wept with chagrin. He had planned to swap with Stella for unlimited ices all her dances with him. Then he saw a friend whom he caught hold of, and with whom he whispered fiercely for a moment.

"I say, you might dance with my kiddy sister for a bit. She's awfully fond of ices, so you needn't really dance."

The friend said he preferred to remain independent at a dance.

"No, I say, do be a decent chap," begged Michael. "Just dance with her once and get another chap to dance with her after you've had your shot. Oh, do. Look here. What'll you swap for the whole of her programme?"

The friend considered the proposition in its commercial side.

"Look here," Michael began, and then, as he nervously half turned his head, he saw the crowd thickening about Muriel. He waved his arm violently in the hope that she would realize his plight and keep the rivals at arm's length. "Look here," he went on, "you know my bat with the whalebone splice?" This bat was Michael's most precious possession, and even as he bartered it for love, he smelt the fragrant linseed-oil of the steeped bandages which now preserved it for summer suns.

The friend's eyes twinkled greedily.

42

"I'll swap that bat," said Michael, "if you'll make sure my kiddy sister hasn't got a single empty place on her programme all the dance."

"All right," said the friend. And as he was led up to Stella, Michael whispered hurriedly, when the introduction had been decorously made:

"This chap's frightfully keen on you, Stella. He simply begged me to introduce him to you."

Then from the depths of Michael's soul a deep-seated cunning inspired him to add:

"I wouldn't at first, because he was awfully in love with another girl and I thought it hard cheese on her, because she's here to-night. But he said he'd go home if he didn't dance with you. So I had to."

Michael looked enquiringly at Stella, marked the smirk of satisfaction on her lips, then recklessly, almost sliding over the polished floor, he plunged through Muriel's suitors and proffered his programme. They danced together nearly all the evening, and alas, Muriel told him that she was going to boarding-school next term. It was a blow to Michael, and the dance programme with Muriel's name fourteen times repeated was many times looked at with sentimental pangs each night of next term before Michael went to bed a hundred miles away from Muriel at her boarding-school.

However, Muriel and her porcelain-blue eyes and the full bow of her lips and the slimness and girlishness of her were forgotten in the complexities of life at a great public school. Michael often looked back to that first term in the Lower Third as a period of Arcadian simplicity, a golden age. In his second term Michael after an inconspicuous position in the honest heart of the list was not moved up, for which he was very glad, as the man who took the Upper Third was by reputation a dull driver without any of the amenities by which Foxy Braxted seasoned scholastic life.

One morning, when the Lower Third had been pleasantly dissolved in laughter by Foxy's caustic jokes at the expense of a boy who had pronounced the Hebrides as a dissyllable, following a hazardous guess that the capital of New South Wales was New York, the door of the class-room opened abruptly and Dr. Brownjohn the Headmaster sailed in.

"Is there a boy called Fane in this class?" he demanded deeply.

The laughter had died away when the tip of Dr. Brownjohn's nose glistened round the edge of the door, and in the deadly silence Michael felt himself withering away.

"Oh, yes," said Mr. Braxted, cheerfully indicating Michael with his long forefinger.

"Tell him to pack up his books and go to Mr. Spivey in the Hall. I'll see him there," rumbled Dr. Brownjohn as, after transfixing the Lower Third with a glance of the most intense ferocity, he swung round and left the room, slamming the door behind him.

"You'd better take what you're doing to Mr. Spivey," said Mr. Braxted in his throatiest voice, "and tell him with my compliments you're an idle young rascal. You can get your books at one o'clock."

Michael gathered together pens and paper, and left his desk in the Lower Third.

"Good-bye, sir," he said as he went away, for he knew Foxy Braxted really rather liked him.

"Good-bye," cackled his late form-master.

The Lower Third followed his exit from their midst with an united grin of farewell, and Michael was presently interviewing Mr. Spivey in the Hall. He realized that he was now a member of that assorted Purgatory, the Special, doomed to work there for a term of days or weeks and after this period of intensive culture to be planted out in a higher form beyond the ordinary mechanics of promotion. Mostly in the Special class Michael worshipped the two gods εἰ and ἐάν, and his whole life was devoted to the mastery of Greek conditional sentences in their honour.

The Special form at St. James' never consisted of more than fourteen or fifteen boys, all of whom were taught individually, and none of whom knew when they would be called away. The Special was well called Purgatory. Every morning and every afternoon the inmates toiled away at their monotonous work, sitting far removed from one another in the great echoing hall, concentrated for the most part on εἰ and ἐάν. Every morning and every afternoon at a fatal moment the swinging doors of the lower end of the Hall would clash together, and the heavy tread of Dr. Brownjohn would be heard as he rolled up one of the two aisles between the long desks. Every morning and every afternoon Dr. Brownjohn would sit beside some boy to inspect his work; and every morning and every afternoon hearts would beat the faster, until Dr. Brownjohn had seized his victim, when the other boys would simultaneously work with an almost lustful concentration.

Dr. Brownjohn was to Michael the personification of majesty, dominion, ferocity and awe. He was huge of build, with a long grey beard to which adhered stale morsels of food and the acrid scent of strong cigars. His face was ploughed and fretted with indentations volcanic: scoriac torrents flowed from his eyes, his forehead was seared and cleft with frowning crevasses and wrinkled with chasms. His ordinary clothes were stained with soup and rank with tobacco smoke, but over them he wore a full and swishing gown of silk. When he spoke his voice rumbled in the titanic deeps of his body, or if he were angry, it burst forth in an appalling roar that shook the great hall. His method of approach was enough to frighten anyone, for he would swing along up the aisle and suddenly plunge into a seat beside the chosen boy, pushing him along the form with his black bulk. He would seize the boy's pen and after scratching his own head with the end of the holder would follow word by word the liturgy of εἰ and ἐάν, tapping the paper between the lines as he read each sentence, so that at the end of his examination the page was peppered with dots of ink. Dr. Brownjohn, although he had a voice like ten bulls, was himself very deaf and after bellowing in a paralyzing bass he would always finish a remark with an intoned 'um?' of tenor interrogation to exact assent or answer from his terrified pupil. When due reverence was absent from Michael's worship of εἰ and ἐάν Dr. Brownjohn would frown at him and roar and bellow and rumble and thunder and peal his execration and contempt. Then suddenly his fury would be relieved by this eruption, and he would affix his initials to the bottom of the page—S. C. B. standing for Samuel Constantine Brownjohn—after which endorsement he would pat Michael's head, rumble an unintelligible joke and plunge down beside another victim.

One of Michael's greatest trials was his inability to convince Miss Carthew how unutterably terrific Dr. Brownjohn really was. She insisted that Michael exaggerated his appearance and manners, and simply would not believe the stories Michael told of parents and guardians who had trembled with fear when confronted by the Old Man. In many ways Michael found Miss Carthew was very contentious nowadays, and very seldom did an evening pass without a hot argument between him and her. To be sure, she used to say it was Michael who had grown contradictory and self-assertive, but Michael could not see that he had radically altered since the first moment he saw Miss Carthew, now nearly four years ago.

Michael's purgatory in the Special continued for several weeks, and he grew bored by the monotony of his work that was only interrupted by the suspense of the Headmaster's invasions. Sometimes Dr. Brownjohn would make his dreadful descent early in the 'hour,' and then relieved from the necessity to work with such ardour, Michael would gaze up to the raftered roof of the hall and stare at the long lancet windows filled with the coats of arms in stained glass of famous bygone Jacobeans. He would wonder whether in those windows still unfilled a place would one day be found for his name and whether years and years hence, boys doing Greek conditional sentences would speculate upon the boyhood of Charles Michael Saxby Fane. Then Mr. Spivey would break into his dreams with some rather dismal joke, and Michael would make blushing amends to εἰ and ἐάν by writing as quickly as he could three complete conditional sentences in honour and praise of the twin gods. Mr. Spivey, the master in charge of the Special, was mild and good-humoured. No one could fail to like him, but he was not exhilarating; and Michael was greatly pleased when one morning Mr. Spivey informed him that he was to move into the Shell. Michael was glad to dodge the Upper Third, for he knew that life in the Shell under Mr. Neech would be an experience.

Chaps had often said to Michael, "Ah, wait till you get into old Neech's form."

"Is he decent?" Michael would enquire.

"Some chaps like him," the chaps in question would ambiguously reply.

When Mr. Spivey introduced Michael to the Shell, Mr. Neech was sitting in his chair with his feet on the desk and a bandana handkerchief over his face, apparently fast asleep. The inmates of the Shell were sitting, vigorously learning something that seemed to cause them great hardship; for every face was puzzled and from time to time sighs floated upon the class-room air.

Mr. Spivey coughed nervously to attract Mr. Neech's attention, and when Mr. Neech took no notice, he tapped nervously on the desk with Mr. Neech's ruler. Somewhere in the back row of desks a titter of mirth was faintly audible. Mr. Neech was presumably aroused with great suddenness by Mr. Spivey's tapping and swung his legs off the desk and, sitting bolt upright in his chair, glared at the intruders.

"Oh, the Headmaster has sent Fane from the Special," Mr. Spivey nervously explained.

Mr. Neech threw his eyes up to the ceiling and looked as if Michael's arrival were indeed the last straw.

"Twenty-six miserable boys are already having a detestable and stultifying education in this wretched class," lamented Mr. Neech. "And now comes a twenty-seventh. Very well. Very well. I'll stuff him with the abominable jargon and filthy humbug. I'll cram him with the undigested balderdash. Oh, you unhappy boy," Mr. Neech went on, directly addressing Michael. "You unfortunate imp and atom. Sit down, if you can find a desk. Sit down and fill your mind with the ditchwater I'm paid to teach you."

Mr. Spivey had by this time reached the door and with a nervous nod he abruptly vanished.

"Now then everybody," said Mr. Neech, closing his lips very tightly in a moment's pause and then breaking forth loudly. "You have had one quarter of an hour to learn the repetition you should all have learned last night. Begin, that mooncalf with a dirty collar, the boy Wilberforce, and if any stupid stoat or stockfish boggles over one word, I'll flay him. Begin! The boy Fane can sit still. The others stand up!" shouted Mr. Neech. "Now the boy Wilberforce!

Tityre tu patulæ recubans sub tegmine fagi—— Go on, you bladder of idiocy."

Michael watched the boy Wilberforce concentrate all his faculties upon not making a single mistake, and hoped that he would satisfy this alarming master. While Wilberforce spoke the lines of the Eclogue, panting between each hexameter, Mr. Neech strode up and down the room with his arms crossed behind him, wagging the tail of his gown. Sometimes he would strike his chin and, looking upwards, murmur to himself the lines with an expression of profound emotion. Wilberforce managed to get through, and another boy called Verney took up the Eclogue successfully, and so on through the class it was successfully sustained.

"You pockpuddings, you abysmal apes," Mr. Neech groaned at his class. "Why couldn't you have learned those lines at home? You idle young blackguards, you pestilent oafs, you fools of the first water, write them out. Write them out five times."

"Oh, sir," the Shell protested in unison.

"Oh, sir!" Mr. Neech mimicked. "Oh, sir! Well, I'll let you off this time, but next time, next time, my stars and garters, I'll flog any boy that makes a single mistake."

Mr. Neech was a dried-up, snuff-coloured man, with a long thin nose and stringy neck and dark piercing eyes. He always wore a frock-coat green with age and a very old top-hat and very shiny trousers. He read Spanish newspapers and second-hand-book catalogues all the way to school and was never seen to walk with either a master or a boy. His principal hatreds were Puseyism and actors; but as two legends were extant, in one of which he had been seen to get into a first-class railway carriage with a copy of the Church Times and in the other of which he had been seen smoking a big cigar in the stalls of the Alhambra Theatre, it was rather doubtful whether his two hatreds were as deeply felt as they were fervently expressed. He was reputed to have the largest library in England outside the British Museum and also to own seven dachshunds. He was a man who fell into ungovernable rages, when he would flog a boy savagely and, the flogging done, fling his cane out of the window in a fit of remorse. He would set impositions of unprecedented length, and revile himself for ruining the victim's handwriting. He would keep his class in for an hour and mutter at himself for a fool to keep himself in as well. Once, he locked a boy in at one o'clock, and the boy's mother wrote a long letter to complain that her son had been forced to go without his dinner. Legend said that Mr. Neech had been reprimanded by Dr. Brownjohn on account of this, which explained Mr. Neech's jibes at the four pages of complaint from the parents that were supposed inevitably to follow his mildest rebuke of the most malignant boy.

Michael enjoyed Mr. Neech's eccentricities after the drabness of the Special. He was lucky enough to be in Mr. Neech's good graces, because he was almost the only boy who could say in what novel of Dickens or Scott some famous character occurred. Mr. Neech had a conception of education quite apart from the mere instilling of declensions and genders and 'num' and 'nonne' and 'quin' and εἰ and ἐάν. He taught Geography and English History and English Literature, so far as the school curriculum allowed him. Divinity and English meant more to Mr. Neech than a mere hour of Greek Testament and a pedant's fiddling with the text of Lycidas. Michael had a dim appreciation of his excellence, even in the Shell: he identified him in some way with Tom Brown's Schooldays, with prints of Eton and Westminster, with Miss Carthew's tales of her brother on the Britannia. Michael recognized him as a character in those old calf-bound books he loved to read at home. Once Mr. Neech called a boy a dog-eared Rosinante, and Michael laughed aloud and when fiercely Mr. Neech challenged him, denying he had ever heard of Rosinante, Michael soon showed that he had read Don Quixote with some absorption. After that Mr. Neech put Michael in one of the favoured desks by the window and would talk to him, while he warmed his parchment-covered hands upon the hot-water pipes. Mr. Neech was probably the first person to impress Michael with the beauty of the past or rather to give him an impetus to arrange his own opinions. Mr. Neech, lamenting the old days long gone, thundering against modernity and denouncing the whole system of education that St. James' fostered, was almost the only schoolmaster with a positive personality whom Michael ever encountered. Michael had scarcely realized, until he reached the Shell, in what shadowy dates of history St. James' was already a famous school. Now in the vulgarity of its crimson brick, in the servility with which it truckled to bourgeois ideals, in the unimaginative utility it worshipped, Michael vaguely apprehended the loss of a soul. He would linger in the corridors, reading the lists of distinguished Jacobeans, and during Prayers he would with new interest speculate upon the lancet windows and their stained-glass heraldry, until vaguely in his heart grew a patriotism more profound than the mere joy of a football victory, a patriotism that submerged Hammersmith and Kensington and made him proud that he himself was veritably a Jacobean. He was still just as eager to see St. James' defeat Dulford at cricket, just as proud to read that St. James' had won more open scholarships at the Universities than some North-country grammar school; but at the same time he was consoled in the event of defeat by pride in the endurance of his school through so many years of English History.

It was about this time that Michael saw in a second-hand shop a print of the tower of St. Mary's College, Oxford. It was an old print and the people small as emmets, who thronged the base of that slim and lovely tower, were dressed in a bygone fashion that very much appealed to Michael. This print gave him the same thrill he experienced in listening to Mr. Neech's reminiscences or in reading Don Quixote or in poring over the inscriptions of famous Jacobeans. Michael had already taken it as an axiom that one day he would go to Oxford, and now he made up his mind he would go to St. Mary's College. At this moment people were hurrying past that tower, even as they hurried in this grey print and even as Michael himself would one day hurry. Meanwhile, he was enjoying the Shell and Mr. Neech's eccentricities and the prospect of winning the Junior Form Cricket Shield, a victory in which Michael would participate as scorer for the Shell.

Summer suns shone down upon the green playground of St. James' rippling with flannelled forms. The radiant air was filled with merry cries, with the sounds of bat and ball, with boyhood in action. In the great red mass of the school buildings the golden clock moved on through each day's breathless hour of cricket. The Junior Shield was won by the Shell, and the proud victors, after a desperate argument with Mr. Neech, actually persuaded him to take his place in the commemorative photograph. School broke up and the summer holidays began.

Chapter II: *The Quadruple Intrigue*

MICHAEL, although Stella was more of a tie than a companion, was shocked to hear that she would not accompany Miss Carthew and himself to Eastbourne for the summer holidays. He heard with a recurrence of the slight jealousy he had always felt of Stella that, though she was not yet eleven years old, she was going to Germany to live in a German family and study music. To Michael this step seemed a device to spoil Stella beyond the limits of toleration, and he thought with how many new affectations Stella would return to her native land. Moreover, why should Stella have all the excitement of going abroad and living abroad while her brother plodded to school in dull ordinary London? Michael felt very strongly that the balance of life was heavily weighted in favour of girls and he deplored the blindness of grown-up people unable to realize the greater attractiveness of boys. It was useless for Michael to protest, although he wasted an evening of Henty in arguing the point with Miss Carthew. Stella became primed with her own importance before she left England, and Michael tried to discourage her as much as he could by pointing out that in Germany her piano-playing would be laughed at and by warning her that her so evident inclination to show off would prejudice against her the bulk of Teutonic opinion. However, Michael's well-meant discouragement did not at all abash Stella, who under his most lugubrious prophecies trilled exasperatingly cheerful scales or ostentatiously folded unimportant articles of clothing with an exaggerated carefulness, the while she fussed with her hair and threw conceited glances over her shoulder into the mirror. Then, one day, the bonnet of a pink and yellow Fraulein bobbed from a cab-window, and, after a finale of affectation and condescension on the front-door steps for the benefit of passers-by, Stella set out for Germany and Michael turned back into the house with pessimistic fears for her future. The arrangements for Stella's transportation had caused some delay in Michael's holidays, and as a reward for having been forced to endure the sight of Stella going abroad, he was told that he might invite a friend to stay with him at Eastbourne during the remainder of the time. Such an unexpected benefaction made Michael incredulous at first.

"Anyone I like?" he said. "For the whole of the hols? Good Lord, how ripping."

Forthwith he set out to consider the personal advantages of all his friends in turn. The Macalisters as twins were ruled out; besides, of late the old intimacy was wearing thin, and Michael felt there were other chaps with more claim upon him. Norton was ruled out, because it would be the worst of bad form to invite him without the Macalisters and also because Norton was no longer on the Classical side of St. James'. Suddenly the idea of asking Merivale to stay with him occurred like an inspiration. Merivale was not at present a friend with anything like the pretensions of Norton or the Macalisters. Merivale could not be visualized in earliest Randell days, indeed he had been at a different private school, and it was only during this last summer term that he and Michael had taken to walking arm in arm during the 'quarter.' Merivale turned to the left when he came out of school and Michael turned to the right, so that they never met on their way nor walked home together afterwards. Nevertheless, in the course of the term, the friendship had grown, and once or twice Michael and Merivale had sat beneath the hawthorn trees, between them a stained bag of cherries in the long cool grass, while intermittently they clapped the boundary hits of a school match that was clicking drowsily its progress through the summer afternoon. Tentative confidences had been exchanged, and by reason of its slower advance towards intimacy the friendship of Michael and Merivale seemed built on a firmer basis than most of the sudden affinities of school life. Now, as Michael recalled the personality of Merivale with his vivid blue eyes and dull gold hair and his laugh and freckled nose and curiously attractive walk, he had a great desire for his company during the holidays. Miss Carthew was asked to write to Mrs. Merivale in order to give the matter the weight of authority; but Michael and Miss Carthew went off to Eastbourne before the answer arrived. The sea sparkled, a cool wind blew down from Beachy Head; the tamarisks on the front quivered; Eastbourne was wonderful, so wonderful that Michael could not believe in the probability of Merivale, and the more he thought about it, the more he felt sure that Mrs. Merivale would write a letter of polite refusal. However, as if they were all people in a book, everything happened according to Michael's most daringly optimistic hopes. Mrs. Merivale wrote a pleasant letter to Miss Carthew to say that her boy Alan was just now staying at Brighton with his uncle Captain Ross, that she had written to her brother who had written back to say that Alan and he would move on to Eastbourne, as it did not matter a bit to him where he spent the next week. Mrs. Merivale added that, if it were convenient, Alan might stay on with Michael when his uncle left. By the same post came a letter from Merivale himself to say that he and his uncle Kenneth were arriving next day, and that he jolly well hoped Fane was going to meet him at the railway station.

Michael, much excited, waited until the train steamed in with its blurred line of carriage windows, from one of which Merivale was actually leaning. Michael waved: Merivale waved: the train stopped: Merivale jumped out: a tall man with a very fair moustache and close-cropped fair hair alighted after Merivale and was introduced and shook hands and made several jokes and was on terms of equality before he and Merivale and Michael had got into the blue-lined fly that was to drive them to Captain Ross's hotel. During the few days of Captain Ross's stay, he and Michael and Merivale and Miss Carthew went sailing and climbed up Beachy Head and watched a cricket match in Devonshire Park and generally behaved like all the other summer visitors to Eastbourne. Michael noticed that Captain Ross was very polite to Miss Carthew and heard with interest that they both had many friends in common—soldiers and sailors and Royal Marines. Michael listened to a great deal of talk about 'when I was quartered there' and 'when he was stationed at Malta' and about Gunners and Sappers and the Service. He himself spoke of General Mace and was greatly flattered when Captain Ross said he knew him by reputation as a fine old soldier. Michael was rather disappointed that Captain Ross was not in the Bengal Lancers, but he concluded that next to being in the Bengal Lancers, it was best to be with him in the Kintail Highlanders (the Duke of Clarence's own Inverness-shire Buffs).

"Uncle Ken looks jolly ripping in a kilt," Merivale informed Miss Carthew, when on the last evening of Captain Ross's stay they were all sitting in the rubied light of the hotel table.

"Shut up, showman," said Captain Ross, banging his nephew on the head with a Viennese roll.

"Oh, I say, Uncle Kenneth, that loaf hurts most awfully," protested Merivale.

"Well, don't play Barnum," said the Captain as he twirled his little moustache. "It's not done, my lad."

When Captain Ross went away next morning, Miss Carthew at his earnest invitation accompanied the boys to see him off, and, as they walked out of the station, Merivale nudged Michael to whisper:

"I say, I believe my uncle's rather gone on Miss Carthew."

"Rot," said Michael. "Why, she'd be most frightfully annoyed. Besides, chaps' uncles don't get gone on——" Michael was going to add 'chaps' sisters' governesses,' but somehow he felt the remark was all wrong, and blushed the conclusion of the sentence.

The weather grew very hot, and Miss Carthew took to sitting in a canvas chair and reading books on the beach, so that Michael and Merivale were left free to do very much as they wanted which, as Michael pointed out, was rather decent of her.

"I say, Merivale," Michael began one day, as he and his friend, arm in arm, were examining the credentials of the front on a shimmering morning, "I say, did you notice that Miss Carthew called you Alan?"

"I know. She often does," replied Merivale.

"I say, Merivale," said Michael shyly, "supposing I call you Alan and you call me Michael—only during the hols, of course," he added hastily.

"I don't mind," Alan agreed.

"Because I suppose there couldn't be two chaps more friends than you and me," speculated Michael.

"I like you more than I do any other chap," said Alan simply.

"So I do you," said Michael. "And it's rather decent just to have one great friend who you call by his Christian name."

After this Michael and Alan became very intimate and neither held a secret from the other, as through the crowds of seaside folk they threaded their way along the promenade to whatever band of minstrels had secured their joint devotion. They greatly preferred the Pierrots to the Niggers, and very soon by a week's unbroken attendance at the three daily sessions, Michael and Alan knew the words and music of most of the repertory. Of the comic songs they liked best The Dandy Coloured Coon, although they admired almost equally a duet whose refrain was:

"We are a couple of barmy chaps, hush, not a word!

A little bit loose in our tiles, perhaps, hush, not a word!

We're lunatics, lunatics, everybody declares

We're a couple of fellows gone wrong in our bellows,

As mad as a pair of March hares."

Gradually, however, and more especially under the influence of Japanese lanterns and a moon-splashed sea, Michael and Alan avowed openly their fondness for the more serious songs sung by the Pierrettes. The words of one song in particular were by a reiteration of passionate utterance deeply printed on their memory:

"Two little girls in blue, lad,

Two little girls in blue,

They were sisters, we were brothers,

And learnt to love the two.

And one little girl in blue, lad,

Who won your father's heart,

Became your mother: I married the

other,

And now we have drifted apart."

This lyric seemed to Michael and Alan the most profoundly moving accumulation of words ever known. The sad words and poignant tune wrung their hearts with the tears always imminent in life. This lyric expressed for the two boys the incommunicable aspirations of their most sacred moments. As they leaned over the rail of the promenade and gazed down upon the pretty Pierrette whose tremolo made the night air vibrant with emotion, Michael and Alan were moved by a sense of fleeting time, by thoughts of old lovers and by an intense self-pity.

"It's frightfully decent, isn't it?" murmured Michael.

"Ripping," sighed Alan. "I wish I could give her more than a penny."

"So do I," echoed Michael. "It's beastly being without much tin."

Then 'Encore' they both shouted as the Pierrette receded from the crimson lantern-light into obscurity. Again she sang that song, so that when Michael and Alan looked solemnly up at the stars, they became blurred. They could not bear The Dandy Coloured Coon on such a night, and, seeing no chance of luring Pierrette once more into the lantern-light, they pushed their way through the crowd of listeners and walked arm in arm along the murmurous promenade.

"It's beastly rotten to go to bed at a quarter past nine," Michael declared.

"We can talk up in our room," suggested Alan.

"I vote we talk about the Pierrots," said Michael, affectionately clasping his chum's arm.

"Yes, I vote we do too," Alan agreed.

The next day the Pierrots were gone. Apparently they had had a quarrel with the Corporation and moved farther along the South Coast. Michael and Alan were dismayed, and in their disgust forsook the beach for the shrubberies of Devonshire Park where in gloomy by-ways, laurel-shaded, they spoke quietly of their loss.

"I wonder if we shall ever see that girl again," said Michael. "I'd know her anywhere. If I was grown up I'd know her. I swear I would."

"She was a clinker," Alan regretted.

"I don't suppose we shall ever see a girl half as pretty," Michael thought.

"Not by a long chalk," Alan agreed. "I don't suppose there is a girl anywhere in the world a quarter as pretty. I think that girl was simply fizzing."

They paced the mossy path in silence and suddenly round a corner came upon a bench on which were seated two girls in blue dresses. Michael and Alan found the coincidence so extraordinary that they stared hard, even when the two girls put their heads down and looked sidelong and giggled and thumped each other and giggled again.

"I say, are you laughing at us?" demanded Michael.

"Well, you looked at us first," said the fairer of the two girls.

In that moment Michael fell in love.

"Come away," whispered Alan. "They'll follow us if we don't."

"Do you think they're at all decent?" asked Michael. "Because if you do, I vote we talk to them. I say, Alan, do let's anyway, for a lark."

"Supposing anyone we know saw us?" queried Alan.

"Well, we could say *some*thing," Michael urged. He was on fire to prosecute this adventure and, lest Alan should still hold back, he took from his pocket a feverish bag of Satin Pralines and boldly offered them to the girl of his choice.

"I say, would you like some tuck?"

The girls giggled and sat closer together; but Michael still proffered the sweets and at last the girl whom he admired dipped her hand into the bag. As all the Satin Pralines were stuck together, she brought out half a dozen and was so much embarrassed that she dropped the bag, after which she giggled.

"It doesn't matter a bit," said Michael. "I can get some more. These are beastly squashed. I say, what's your name?"

So began the quadruple intrigue of Dora and Winnie and Michael and Alan.

Judged merely by their dress, one would have unhesitatingly set down Dora and Winnie as sisters; but they were unrelated and dressed alike merely to accentuate, as girl friends do, the unanimity of their minds. They were both of them older by a year or more than Michael and Alan; while in experience they were a generation ahead of either. The possession of this did not prevent them from giggling foolishly and from time to time looking at each other with an expression compounded of interrogation and shyness. Michael objected to this look, inasmuch as it implied their consciousness of a mental attitude in which neither he nor Alan had any part. He was inclined to be sulky whenever he noticed an exchange of glances, and very soon insisted upon a temporary separation by which he and Dora took one path, while Alan with Winnie pursued another.

Dora was a neatly made child, and Michael thought the many-pleated blue skirt that reached down to her knees and showed as she swung along a foam of frizzy white petticoats very lovely. He liked, too, the curve of her leg and the high buttoned boots and the big blue bow in her curly golden hair. He admired immensely her large shady hat trimmed with cornflowers and the string of bangles on her wrist and her general effect of being almost grown up and at the same time still obviously a little girl. As for Dora's face, Michael found it beautiful with the long-lashed blue eyes and rose-leaf complexion and cleft chin and pouting bow mouth. Michael congratulated himself upon securing the prettier of the two. Winnie with her grey eyes and ordinary hair and dark eyebrows and waxen skin was certainly not comparable to this exquisite doll of his own.

At first Michael was too shy to make any attempt to kiss Dora. Nevertheless the kissing of her ran in his mind from the beginning, and he would lie awake planning how the feat was to be accomplished. He was afraid that if suddenly he threw his arms round her, she might take offence and refuse to see him again. Finally he asked Alan's advice.

"I say, have you ever kissed Winnie?" he called from his bed.

Through the darkness came Alan's reply:

"Rather not. I say, have you?"

"Rather not." Then Michael added defiantly, "But I jolly well wish I had."

"She wouldn't let you, would she?"

"That's what I can't find out," Michael said despondently. "I've held her hand and all that sort of rot, and I've talked about how pretty I think she is, but it's beastly difficult. I say, you know, I don't believe I should ever be able to propose to a girl—you know—a girl you could marry—a lady. I'm tremendously gone on Dora and so are you on Winnie. But I don't think they're ladies, because Dora's got a sister who's in a pantomime and wears tights, so you see I couldn't propose to her. Besides, I should feel a most frightful fool going down on my knees in the path. Still I must kiss her somehow. Look here, Alan, if you promise faithfully you'll kiss Winnie to-morrow, when the clock strikes twelve, I'll kiss Dora. Will you? Be a decent chap and kiss Winnie, even if you aren't beastly keen, because I am. So will you, Alan?"

There was a minute's deliberation by Alan in the darkness, and then he said he would.

"I say, you are a clinker, Alan. Thanks most awfully."

Michael turned over and settled himself down to sleep, praying for the good luck to dream of his little girl in blue.

On the next morning Alan and Michael eyed each other bashfully across the breakfast table, conscious as they were of the guilty vow not yet fulfilled. Miss Carthew tried in vain to make them talk. They ate in silence, oppressed with resolutions. They saw Winnie and Dora in Devonshire Park at eleven o'clock, and presently went their different ways along the mazy paths. Michael talked of subjects most remote from love. He expounded to Dora the ranks of the British Army; he gave her tips on birds'-nesting; he told her of his ambition to join the Bengal Lancers and he boasted of the exploits of the St. James' Football Fifteen. Dora giggled the minutes away, and at five minutes to twelve they were on a seat, screened against humanity's intrusion. Michael listened with quickening pulses to the thump of tennis balls in the distance. At last he heard the first stroke of twelve and looked apprehensively towards Dora. Four more strokes sounded, but Michael still delayed. He wondered if Alan would keep his promise. He had heard no scream of dismay or startled giggle from the shrubbery. Then as the final stroke of midday crashed forth, he flung his arms round Dora, pressed her to him and in his confusion kissed very roughly the tilted tip of her nose.

"Oh, you cheek!" she gasped.

Then Michael kissed her lips, coldly though they were set against his love.

"I say, kiss me," he whispered, with a strange new excitement crimsoning his cheeks and rattling his heart so loudly that he wondered if Dora noticed anything.

"Shan't!" murmured Dora.

"Do."

"Oh, I couldn't," she said, wriggling herself free. "You have got a cheek. Fancy kissing anyone."

"Dora, I'm frightfully gone on you," affirmed Michael, choking with the emotional declaration. "Are you gone on me?"

"I like you all right," Dora confessed.

"Well then, do kiss me. You might. Oh, I say, do."

He leaned over and sought those unresponsive lips that, mutely cold, met his. He spent a long time trying to persuade her to give way, but Dora protested she could not understand why people kissed at all, so silly as it was.

"But it's not," Michael protested. "Or else everybody wouldn't want to do it."

However, it was useless to argue with Dora. She was willing to put her curly golden head on his shoulder, until he nearly exploded with sentiment; she seemed not to mind how often he pressed his lips to hers; but all the time she was passive, inert, drearily unresponsive. The deeper she seemed to shrink within herself and the colder she stayed, the more Michael felt inclined to hurt her, to shake her roughly, almost to draw blood from those soft lifeless lips. Once she murmured to him that he was hurting her, and Michael was in a quandary between an overwhelming softness of pity and an exultant desire to make her cry out sharply with pain. Yet as he saw that golden head upon his shoulder, the words and tune of 'Two little girls in blue' throbbed on the air, and with an aching fondness Michael felt his eyes fill with tears. Such love as his for Dora could never be expressed with the eloquence and passion it demanded.

Michael and Alan had tacitly agreed to postpone all discussion of their passionate adventure until the blackness of night and secret intimacy of their bedroom made the discussion of it possible.

"I say, I kissed Dora this morning," announced Michael.

"So did I Winnie," said Alan.

"She wouldn't kiss me, though," said Michael.

"Wouldn't she?" Alan echoed in surprise, "Winnie kissed me."

"She didn't!" exclaimed Michael.

"She did, I swear she did. She kissed me more than I kissed her. I felt an awful fool. I nearly got up and walked away. Only I didn't like to."

"Good Lord," apostrophized Michael. He was staggered by Alan's success and marvelled that Alan, who was admittedly less clever than himself, should conquer when he had failed. He could not understand the reason; but he supposed that Dora, being so obviously the prettier, was deservedly the more difficult to win. However, Michael felt disinclined to pursue the subject, because it was plain that Alan took no credit to himself for his success, and he wished still to be the leader in their friendship. He did not want Alan to feel superior in anything.

The next day Miss Carthew was laid up in bed with a sick headache, so that Michael and Alan were free to take Dora and Winnie upon the promenade without the risk of detection. Accordingly, when they met in Devonshire Park, Michael proposed this public walk. He was the more willing to go, because since Alan's revelation of Winnie, he took a certain pleasure in denying to her the attraction of Alan's company. Winnie was not very anxious for the walk, but Dora seemed highly pleased, and Dora, being the leader of the pair, Winnie had to give way. While they strolled up and down the promenade in a row, Dora pointed out to Michael and Alan in how many respects they both failed to conform to the standards of smartness, as she conceived them. For instance, neither of them carried a stick and neither of them wore a tie of any distinction. Dora called their attention to the perfectly dressed youths of the promenade with their high collars and butterfly ties and Wanghee canes and pointed boots and vivid waistcoats.

After the walk the boys discussed Dora's criticism and owned that she was right. They marshalled their money and bought made-up bow-ties of purple and pink that were twisted round the stud with elastic and held in position by a crescent of whalebone. They bought made-up white silk knotted ties sown with crimson fleurs-de-lys and impaled with a permanent brass horseshoe. They spent a long time in the morning plastering back their hair with soap and water, while in the ribbons of their straw hats they pinned inscribed medallions. Finally they purchased Wanghee canes and when they met their two little girls in blue, the latter both averred that Michael and Alan were much improved.

Miss Carthew remained ill for two or three days; so Michael and Alan were able to display themselves and their sweethearts all the length of the promenade. They took to noticing the cut of a coat as it went by and envied the pockets of the youths they met; they envied, too, the collars that surrounded the adolescent neck, and wished the time had come for them to wear 'chokers.' Sometimes, before they undressed, they would try to pin round their necks stiff sheets of note-paper in order to gauge, however slightly, the effect of high collars on their appearance.

The weather was now steadily fine and hot, and Michael begged Miss Carthew to let him and Alan buy two blazers and cricket belts. Somewhat to his surprise, she made no objection, and presently Michael and Alan appeared upon the front in white trousers, blue and yellow blazers and cherry-coloured silk belts fastened in front by a convenient metal snake. Dora thought they looked 'all right,' and, as Miss Carthew had succumbed again to her headache, Michael and Alan were free to swagger up and down on the melting asphalt of the promenade. Miss Carthew grew no better, and one day she told the boys that Nancy was coming down to look after them. Michael did not know whether he were really glad or not, because, fond as he was of Nancy, he was deeply in love with Dora and he had a feeling that Nancy would interfere with the intrigues. In the end, as it happened, Nancy arrived by some mistake on the day before she was expected and, setting forth to look for the boys, she walked straight into them arm in arm with Dora and Winnie. Michael was very much upset, and told the girls to scoot, a command which they obeyed by rushing across the road, giggling loudly, standing on the opposite curb and continuing to giggle.

"Hullo!" said Nancy, "who are your young friends in blue cashmere?"

Michael blushed and said quickly they were friends of Alan, but Alan would not accept the responsibility.

"Well, I don't admire your taste," said Nancy contemptuously. "No, and I don't admire your get-up," she went on. "Did you pick those canes up on the beach, what?"

"We bought them," said Michael, rather affronted.

"My goodness," said Nancy. "What dreadful-looking things. I say, Michael, you're in a fair way towards looking like a thorough young bounder. Don't you come to Cobble Place with that button on your hat. Well, don't let me disturb you. Cut off to the Camera Obscura with Gertie and Evangeline. I don't expect I'm smart enough for you two."

"We don't particularly want to go with those girls," said Michael, looking down at his boots, very red and biting his under-lip. Alan was blushing too and greatly abashed.

"Well," said the relentless Nancy, "it's a pity you don't black your faces, for I never saw two people look more like nigger minstrels. Where *did* you get that tie? No wonder my sister feels bad. That belt of yours, Michael, would give a South Sea Islander a headache. Go on, hurry off like good little boys," she jeered. "Flossie and Cissie are waiting for you."

Michael could not help admitting, as he suffered this persiflage from Nancy, that Dora and Winnie did look rather common, and he wished they would not stand, almost within earshot, giggling and prodding each other. Then suddenly Michael began to hate Dora and the quadruple intrigue was broken up.

"I say, Alan," he said, looking up again, "let's bung these sticks into the sea. They're rotten sticks."

Alan at once threw his as far as it would go and betted Michael he would not beat the distance. So Michael's stick followed its companion into oblivion. Nancy was great sport, after all, as both boys admitted, and when Michael grazed his finger very slightly on a barnacled rock, he bandaged it up with his silk tie. Very soon he discovered the cut was not at all serious, but he announced the tie was spoilt and dipped it casually into a rock pool, where it floated blatantly among the anemones and rose-plumed seaweed. Alan's tie vanished less obtrusively: no one noticed when or where. As for the buttons inscribed with mottoes they became insignificant units in the millions of pebbles on the beach.

Nancy was great sport and ready to do whatever the boys suggested in the way of rock-climbing and walking, provided they would give her due notice, so that she could get into a hockey skirt and thick shoes. They had fine blowy days with Nancy up on Beachy Head above

49

the sparkling blue water. They caught many blue butterflies, but never the famous Mazarin blue which legend in the butterfly-book said had once been taken near Eastbourne.

Michael and Alan, even in the dark privacy of their room, did not speak again of Dora and Winnie. Michael had an idea that Alan had always been ashamed of the business, and felt mean when he thought how he had openly told Nancy that they were his friends. Once or twice, when Michael was lying on his back, staring up at the sky over Beachy Head, the wind lisping round him sadly made him feel sentimental, but sentimental in a dominion where Dora and Winnie were unknown, where they would have been regarded as unpleasant intruders. Up here in the daisy's eye, the two little girls in blue seemed tawdry and took their place in the atmosphere of Michael's earlier childhood with Mrs. Frith's tales and Annie's love-letters. For Michael the whole affair now seemed like the half-remembered dreams which, however pleasant at the time, repelled him in the recollection of them. Moreover, he had experienced a sense of inequality in his passion for Dora. He gave all: she returned nothing. Looking back at her now under the sailing clouds, he thought her nose was ugly, her mouth flabby, her voice odious and her hair beastly. He blushed at the memory of the ridiculous names he had called her, at the contemplation of his enthusiastic praise of her beauty to Alan. He was glad that Alan had been involved, however unwillingly. Otherwise he was almost afraid he would have avoided Alan in future, unable to bear the injury to his pride. This sad sensation promoted by the wind in the grasses, by the movement of the clouds and the companionship of Alan and Nancy, was more thrilling than the Pierrette's tremolo in the lantern light. Michael's soul was flooded with a vast affection for Alan and for Nancy. He wished that they all could stay here in the wind for ever. It was depressing to think of the autumn rain and the dreary gaslit hours of afternoon school. And yet it was not depressing at all, for he and Alan might be able to achieve the same class. It would be difficult, for Michael knew that he himself must inevitably be moved up two forms, while Alan was only in the Upper Third now and could scarcely from being ninth in his class get beyond the Lower Fourth, even if he escaped the Shell. How Michael wished that Alan could go into the Special for a time, and how pleasant it would be suddenly to behold Alan's entrance into his class, so that, without unduly attracting attention, he could manage to secure a desk for Alan next to himself.

But when Michael and Alan (now again the austere Fane and Merivale) went back to school, Michael was in the Middle Fourth, and Alan just missed the double remove and inherited Michael's scrabbled desk in the Shell.

Chapter III: *Pastoral*

THE new term opened inauspiciously; for Miss Carthew fell ill again more seriously, and Michael's mother came back, seeming cross and worried. She settled that, as she could not stay at home for long, Michael must be a boarder for a year. Michael did not at all like this idea, and begged that Nancy might come and look after him. But Mrs. Fane told him not to make everything more difficult than it was already by grumbling and impossible suggestions. Michael was overcome by his mother's crossness and said no more. Mrs. Fane announced her intention of shutting up the house in Carlington Road and of coming back in the summer to live permanently at home, when Michael would be able to be a day-boy again. Mrs. Fane seemed injured all the time she had to spend in making arrangements for Michael to go to Mr. Wheeler's House. She wished that people would not get ill just when it was most inconvenient. She could not understand why everything happened at exactly the wrong moment, and she was altogether different from the tranquil and lovely lady whom Michael had hitherto known. However, the windows of Number 64 were covered with newspapers, the curtain-poles were stripped bare, the furniture stood heaped in the middle of rooms under billowy sheets, and Michael drove up with all his luggage to the gaunt boarding-house of Mr. Wheeler that overlooked the School ground.

Michael knew that the alteration in his status would make a great difference. Long ago he remembered how his friendship with Buckley had been finally severed by the breaking up of Buckley's home and the collapse of all Buckley's previous opinions. Michael now found himself in similar case. To be sure, there was not at St. James' the same icy river of prejudice between boarders and day-boys which divided them so irreparably at Randell's. Nevertheless, it was impossible for a boarder to preserve unspoilt a real intimacy with a day-boy. To begin with, all sorts of new rules about streets being in and out of bounds made it impossible to keep up those delightful walks home with boys who went in the same direction as oneself. There was no longer that hurried appeal to 'wait for me at five o'clock' as one passed a friend in the helter-skelter of reaching the class-room, when the five minutes' bell had stopped and the clock was already chiming three. It was not etiquette among the boarders of the four Houses to walk home with day-boys except in a large and amorphous company of both. It was impossible to go to tea with day-boys on Saturday afternoons without special leave both from the Housemaster and from the captain of the House. A boarder was tied down mercilessly to athletics, particularly to rowing, which was the pride of the Houses and was exalted by them above every other branch of sport. Michael, as a promising light-weight, had to swim, every Saturday, until he could pass the swimming test at the Paddington Baths, when he became a member of the rowing club, in order to cox the House four. It did not add to his satisfaction with life, when by his alleged bad steering Wheeler's House was beaten by Marlowe's House coxed by the objectionable Buckley, now on the Modern Side and, as a result of his capable handling of the ropes likely to be cox of the School Eight in the race against Dulford from Putney Bridge to Hammersmith. The Christmas holidays were a dismal business in Mr. Wheeler's empty barracks. To be sure, Mrs. Wheeler made herself as plumply agreeable as she could; but the boredom of it all was exasperating and was only sustained by reading every volume that Henty had ever written. Four weeks never dragged so endlessly, even in the glooms of Carlington Road under Nurse's rule. The Lent term with its persistent rowing practice on the muddy Thames was almost as bad as the holidays. Michael hated the barges that bore down upon him and the watermen who pulled across the bows of his boat. He hated the mudlarks by the river-side who jeered as he followed the crew into the School boathouse, and he loathed the walk home with the older boys who talked incessantly of their own affairs. Nor did the culminating disaster of the defeat by Marlowe's House mitigate his lot. When the Lent term was over, to his great disappointment, some domestic trouble made it impossible for Michael to spend the Easter holidays with Alan, so that instead of three weeks to weld again that friendship in April wanderings, in finding an early white-throat's nest in the front of May, and in all the long imagined delights of spring, Michael was left again with Mr. and Mrs. Wheeler to spend a month of rain at a bleak golf-resort, where he was only kept from an unvoiced misery by reading 'Brother takes the hand of brother' in Longfellow's Psalm of Life, melting thereat into a flood of tears that relieved his lonely oppression.

Even the summer term was a bondage with its incessant fagging for balls, while the lords of the House practised assiduously at the nets. He and Alan walked together sometimes during the 'quarter' and held on to the stray threads of their friendship that still resisted the exacting knife of the House's etiquette; but it became increasingly difficult under the stress of boarding-school existence. Indeed, it was only the knowledge that this summer term would end the miserable time and that Alan was catching up to Michael's class which supported the two friends through their exile. Michael was savagely jealous when he saw Alan leaving the School at five o'clock arm in arm with another boy. He used to sulk for a week afterwards, avoiding Alan in the 'quarter' and ostentatiously burying himself in a group of boarders. And if Alan would affectionately catch him up when he was alone, Michael would turn on him and with bitter taunts suggest that Alan's condescension was unnecessary. In School itself Michael was bored by his sojourn both in the Middle Fourth and in the Upper Fourth B. The Cicero and the Thucydides were vilely dull; all the dullest books of the Æneid were carefully chosen, while Mr. Marjoribanks and Mr. Gale were both very dull teachers. At the end of the summer examinations, Michael found himself at the bottom of the Upper Fourth B in Classics, in Drawing and in English. However, the knowledge that next term would now inevitably find him and Alan in the same class, meeting again as equals, as day-boys gloriously free, sustained him through a thunderous interview with Dr. Brownjohn. He emerged from the Doctor's study in a confusion of abusive epithets to find Alan loyally waiting for him by the great plaster cast of the Laocoön.

"Damn old Brownjohn," growled Michael. "I think he's the damnedest old beast that ever lived. I do hate him."

"Oh, bother him," cried Alan, dancing with excitement. "Look here, I say, at this telegram. It's just arrived. The porter was frightfully sick at having to give me a telegram. He is a sidy swine. What *do* you think? My uncle is going to marry Miss Carthew?"

"Get out," scoffed Michael, whose brain, overwhelmed by the pealing thunders of his late interview, refused to register any more shocks.

"No, really. Read this."

Michael took the piece of paper and read the news. But he was still under the influence of a bad year, and instead of dancing with Alan to the tune of his excitement, grumbled:

"Well, why didn't Miss Carthew send a telegram to me? I think she might have. I believe this is all bally rot."

Alan's face changed, changed indeed to an expression of such absolute disappointment that Michael was touched and, forgetting all that he had endured, thrust his arm into Alan's arm and murmured:

"By Jove, old Alan, it is rather decent, isn't it?"

When Michael reached the House, he found a letter from Miss Carthew, which consoled him for that bad year and made him still more penitent for his late ungraciousness towards Alan.

COBBLE PLACE,
July 27.

My dear old Michael,

You will be tremendously surprized to hear that I am going to marry Captain Ross. I fancy I can hear you say 'What rot, I don't believe it!' But I am, and of course you can understand how gloriously happy I feel, for you know how much you liked him. Poor old boy, I'm afraid you've had a horrid time all this year and I wish I hadn't been so stupid as to get ill, but never mind, it's over now and Captain Ross and I are coming up to London to fetch you and Alan down here to spend the whole of the holidays and make the wedding a great success. May, Joan and Nancy and my mother all send their very best love and Nancy says she's looking forward to your new ties (I don't know what obscure jest of hers this is) and also to hear of your engagement (silly girl!). I shall see you on Wednesday and you're going to have splendid holidays, I can promise you. Your mother writes to say that she is coming back to live at home in September, so there'll be no more boarding-school for you. Stella wrote to me from Germany and I hear from Frau Weingardt that everybody prophesies a triumphant career for her, so don't snub her when she comes back for her holidays in the autumn. Just be as nice as you can, and you can be very nice if you like. Will you? Now, dear old boy, my best love till we meet on Wednesday.

Your loving
Maud Carthew.

Then indeed Michael felt that life was the finest thing conceivable, and in a burst of affectionate duty wrote a long letter to Stella, giving with every detail an account of how Wheeler's beat Marlowe's at cricket, including the running-out of that beast Buckley by Michael amidst the plaudits of his House. Next morning Alan told him that his mother was frightfully keen for Michael to stay with them at Richmond, until his Uncle Ken and Miss Carthew arrived; and so Michael by special leave from Mr. Wheeler left the House a day or two before the others and had the exquisite pleasure of travelling up with Alan by the District Railway to Hammersmith Broadway for a few mornings, and of walking arm in arm with Alan through the School gates. Mrs. Merivale was as pretty as ever, almost as pretty as his own beautiful mother, and Mr. Merivale entertained Michael and Alan with his conjuring tricks and his phonograph and his ridiculous puns. Even when they reached the gate in a summer shower and ran past the sweet-smelling rose trees in the garden, Mr. Merivale shouted from the front door 'Hallo, here come the Weterans,' but when he had been severely punched for so disgraceful a joke, he was flatly impenitent and made half a dozen more puns immediately afterwards. In a day or two Miss Carthew and Captain Ross arrived, and after they had spent long mysterious days shopping in town, Michael and Alan and Miss Carthew and Captain Ross travelled down to Hampshire—the jolliest railway party that was ever known.

Nothing at Basingstead Minor seemed to have changed in five years, from the dun pony to the phloxes in the garden, from the fantail pigeons to the gardener who fed the pigs. Michael spent all the first few hours in rapid renewals of friendship with scenery and animals, dragging Alan at his heels and even suggesting about ten minutes before the gong would sound for dinner that they should bunk round and borrow the key of the tower on the hill. He and Alan slept up in the roof in a delightful impromptu of a room with uneven bare floor and sloping ceiling and above their beds a trap-door into an apple loft. There were at least half a dozen windows with every possible aspect to the neat high road and the stable-yard and the sun-dyed garden and the tall hills beyond. August was a blaze of blue and green and gold that year, but everybody at Cobble Place was busy getting ready for the wedding and Michael and Alan had the countryside to themselves. Their chief enterprize was the exploration of the sources of the stream in a canoe and a fixed endeavour to reach Basingstead Major by water. Early in the morning they would set out, well equipped with scarlet cushions and butterfly-nets and poison-bottles and sandwiches and stone bottles of ginger beer and various illustrated papers and Duke's Cameo cigarettes. Michael now paid fivepence for ten instead of a penny for five cigarettes: he also had a pipe of elegantly tenuous shape, which was knocked out so often that it looked quite old, although it was scarcely coloured at all by tobacco smoke. Nowadays he did not bother to chew highly scented sweets after smoking, because Captain Ross smoked so much that all the blame of suspicious odours could be laid on him.

Those were halcyon days on that swift Hampshire river. Michael and Alan would have to paddle hard all the morning scarcely making any progress against the stream. Every opportunity to moor the canoe was taken advantage of; and the number of Marsh Fritillaries that were sacrificed to justify a landing in rich water-meadows was enormous.

"Never mind," Michael used to say, "they'll do for swaps."

Through the dazzling weather the kingfishers with wings of blue fire would travel up and down the stream. The harvest was at its height and in unseen meadows sounded the throb of the reaper and binder, while close at hand above the splash and gurgle of the rhythmic paddles could be heard the munching of cattle. To left and right of the urgent boat darted the silver companies of dace, and deep in brown embayed pools swam the fat nebulous forms of chub. Sometimes the stream, narrowing where a large tree-trunk had fallen, gushed by their prow and called for every muscle to stand out, for every inch to be fought, for every blade of grass to be clutched before the canoe won a way through. Sometimes the stream widened to purling rapids and scarcely would even a canoe float upon the diamonded rivulets and tumbling pebbles and silting silver sand, so that Michael and Alan would have to disembark and drag the boat to deeper water. Quickly the morning went by, long before the source of the stream was found, long before even the village of Basingstead Major was reached. Some fathomless millpool would hold Michael and Alan with its hollow waterfall and overarching trees and gigantic pike. Here grew, dipping down to the water, sprays of dewberries, and here, remote even from twittering warblers and the distant harvest cries, Michael and Alan drowsed away the afternoon. They scarcely spoke, for they were too well contented with the languorous weather. Sometimes one of them would clothe a dream with a boy's slang, and that was all. Then, when the harvesters had long gone home and when the last cow was stalled, and when the rabbits were scampering by the edge of the sloping woodlands, Michael and Alan would unmoor their canoe and glide homeward with the stream. Through the deepening silence their boat would swing soundlessly past the purple loosestrife and the creamy meadowsweet, past the yellow loosestrife and scented rushes and the misted blue banks of cranesbill, past the figwort and the little yellow waterlilies, while always before their advance the voles plumped into the water one by one and in hawthorn bushes the wings of roosting birds fluttered. Around them on every side crept the mist in whose silver muteness they landed to gather white mushrooms. Home they would come drenched with dew, and arm in arm they would steal up the dusky garden to the rose-red lamps and twinkling golden candlelight of Cobble Place.

In the actual week before the wedding Michael and Alan were kept far too busy to explore streams. They ran from one end of Basingstead Minor to the other and back about a dozen times a day. They left instructions with various old ladies in the village at whose cottages guests were staying. They carried complicated floral messages from Mrs. Carthew to the Vicar and equally complicated floral replies from the Vicar to Mrs. Carthew. They were allowed to drive the aged dun pony to meet Mr. and Mrs. Merivale on the day before the wedding and had great jokes with Mr. Merivale because he would say that it was an underdone pony and because he would not believe that dun was spelt d-u-n. As for the wedding-day itself, it was for Michael and Alan one long message interrupted only by an argument with the cook with regard to the amount of rice they had a right to take.

Michael felt very shy at the reception and managed to avoid calling Miss Carthew Mrs. Ross; although Alan distinctly addressed her once with great boldness as Aunt Maud, for which he was violently punched in the ribs by Michael, as with stifled laughter they both rushed headlong from the room. However, they came back to hear old Major Carthew proposing the bride and bridegroom's health and plunged themselves into a corner with handkerchiefs stuffed into their mouths to listen to Captain Ross stammer an embarrassed reply. They were both much relieved when Mr. Merivale by a series of the most atrocious puns allowed their laughter to flow forth without restraint. All the guests went back to London later in the afternoon and Michael and Alan were left to the supervision of Nancy, who had promised to take them out for a day's shooting. They had a wonderful day over the flickering September stubble. Michael shot a lark by mistake and Alan wounded a land-rail; Nancy, however, redeemed the party's credit by bagging three brace of fat French partridges which, when eaten, tasted like pigeons, because the boys could not bear to wait for them to be hung even for two hours.

Michael had a conversation with Mrs. Carthew one afternoon, while they paced slowly and regularly the gay path beside the sunny red wall of the garden.

"Well, how do you like school now?" she asked. "Dear me, I must say you're greatly improved," she went on. "Really, when you came here five years ago, you were much too delicate-looking."

Michael kicked the gravel and tried to turn the trend of the conversation by admiring the plums on the wall, but Mrs. Carthew went on.

"Now you really look quite a boy. You and Alan both slouch abominably, and I cannot think why boys always walk on one side of their boots. I must say I do not like delicate boys. My own boy was always such a boy." Mrs. Carthew sighed and Michael looked very solemn.

"Well, do you like school?" she asked.

"I like holidays better," answered Michael.

"I'm delighted to hear it," Mrs. Carthew said decidedly.

"I thought last year was beastly," said Michael. "You see I was a boarder and that's rot, if you were a day-boy ever, at least I think so. Alan and me are in the same form next term. We're going to have a most frightful spree. We're going to do everything together. I expect school won't be half bad then."

"Your mother's going to be at home, isn't she?" Mrs. Carthew enquired.

"Yes. Rather," said Michael. "It will be awfully rum. She's always away, you know. I wonder why."

"I expect she likes travelling about," said Mrs. Carthew.

"Yes, I expect she does," Michael agreed. "But don't you think it's very rum that I haven't got any uncles or aunts or any relations? I do. I never meet people who say they knew my father like Alan does and like Miss—like Mrs. Ross does. Once I went with my mater to see an awfully decent chap called Lord Saxby and my name's Saxby. Do you think he's a relation? I asked the mater, but she said something about not asking silly questions."

"Humph!" said Mrs, Carthew, as she adjusted her spectacles to examine an espalier of favourite peaches. "I think you'll have to be very good to your mother," she continued after a minute's silence.

"Oh, rather," assented Michael vaguely.

"You must always remember that you have a particular responsibility, as you will be alone with her for a long time, and, no doubt, she has given up a great deal of what she most enjoys in order to stay with you. So don't think only of yourself."

"Oh, rather not," said Michael.

In his heart he felt while Mrs. Carthew was speaking a sense of remote anxiety. He could not understand why, as soon as he asked any direct questions, mystery enveloped his world. He had grown used to this in Miss Carthew's case, but Mrs. Carthew was just as unapproachable. He began to wonder if there really were some mystery about himself. He knew the habit among grown-up people of wrapping everything in a veil of uncertainty, but in his case it was so universally adopted that he began to be suspicious and determined to question his mother relentlessly, to lay conversational traps for her and thereby gain bit by bit the details of his situation. He was older now and had already heard such rumours of the real life of the world that a chimera of unpleasant possibilities was rapidly forming. Left alone, he began to speculate perpetually about himself, to brood over anxious guesses. Perhaps his father was in prison and not dead at all. Perhaps his father was in a lunatic asylum. Perhaps he himself had been a foundling laid on the doorstep long ago, belonging neither to his mother nor to anyone else. He racked his brain for light from the past to be shed upon his present perplexity, but he could recall no flaw in the care with which his ignorance had been cherished.

When Michael reached Carlington Road on a fine September afternoon and saw the window-boxes of crimson and white petunias and the sunlight streaming down upon the red-brick houses, he was glad to be home again in familiar Sixty-four. Inside it had all been re-papered and re-painted. Every room was much more beautiful and his mother was glad to see him. She took him round all the new rooms and hugged him close and was her slim and lovely self again. Actually, among many surprises, Michael was to have the old gloomy morning-room for himself and his friends. It looked altogether different now in the chequered sunlight of the plane tree. The walls had been papered with scenes from cow-boy life. There were new cupboards and shelves full of new books and an asbestos gas fire. There were some jolly chairs and a small desk which almost invited one to compose Iambics.

"Can I really have chaps to tea every Saturday?" Michael asked, stupefied with pleasure.

"Whenever you like, dearest boy."

"By Jove, how horribly decent," said Michael.

Chapter IV: *Boyhood's Glory*

WHEN at the beginning of term a melancholy senior boy, meeting Michael in one of the corridors during the actual excitement of the move, asked him what form he was going into and heard he was on the road to Caryll's, this boy sighed, and exclaimed:

"Lucky young devil."

"Why?" asked Michael, pushing his way through the diversely flowing streams of boys who carried household gods to new class-rooms.

"Why, haven't you ever heard old Caryll is the greatest topper that ever walked?"

"I've heard he's rather a decent sort."

"Chaps have said to me—chaps who've left, I mean," explained the lantern-jawed adviser, "that the year with Caryll is the best year of all your life."

Michael looked incredulous.

"You won't think so," prophesied Lantern-jaws gloomily. "Of course you won't." Then with a sigh, that was audible above the shuffling feet along the corridors, he turned to enter a mathematical class-room where Michael caught a glimpse of trigonometrical mysteries upon a blackboard, as he himself hurried by with his armful of books towards Caryll's class-room. He hoped Alan had bagged two desks next to each other in the back row; but unfortunately this scheme was upset by Mr. Caryll's proposal that the Upper Fourth A should for the present sit in alphabetical order. There was only one unit between Michael and Alan, a persevering and freckled Jew called Levy, whose life was made a burden to him in consequence of his interposition.

Mr. Caryll was an old clergyman reputed in school traditions to be verging on ninety. Michael scarcely thought he could be so old, when he saw him walking to school with rapid little steps and a back as straight and soldierly as General Mace's. Mr. Caryll had many idiosyncrasies, amongst others a rasping cough which punctuated all his sentences and a curious habit of combining three pairs of spectacles according to his distance from the object in view. Nobody ever discovered the exact range of these spectacles; but, to reckon broadly, three pairs at once were necessary for an exercise on the desk before him and for the antics of the back row of desks only one. Mr. Caryll was so deaf, that the loudest turmoil in the back row reached him in the form of a whisper that made him intensely suspicious of cribbing; but, as he could never remember where any boy was sitting, by the time he had put on or taken off one of his pairs of glasses, the noise had opportunity to subside and the authors were able to compose their countenances for the sharp scrutiny which followed. Mr. Caryll always expected every pupil to cheat and invented various stratagems to prevent this vice. In a temper he was apparently the most cynical of men, but as his temper never lasted long enough for him to focus his vision upon the suspected person, he was in practice the blandest and most amiable of old gentlemen. He could never resist even the most obvious joke, and his form pandered shamelessly to this fondness of his, so that, when he made a pun, they would rock with laughter, stamp their feet on the floor and bang the lids of their desks to express their appreciation. This hullabaloo, which reached Mr. Caryll in the guise of a mild titter, affording him the utmost satisfaction, could be heard even in distant class-rooms, and sometimes serious mathematical masters in the throes of algebra would send polite messages to beg Mr. Caryll kindly to keep his class more quiet.

53

Michael and Alan often enjoyed themselves boundlessly in Mr. Caryll's form. Sometimes they would deliberately misconstrue Cicero to beget a joke, as when Michael translated 'abjectique homines' by 'cast-off men' to afford Mr. Caryll the chance of saying, "Tut-tut. The great booby's thinking of his cast-off clothing." Michael and Alan used to ask for leave to light the gas on foggy afternoons, and with an imitation of Mr. Caryll's rasping cough they would manage to extinguish one by one a whole box of matches to the immense entertainment of the Upper Fourth A. They dug pens into the diligent Levy: they stuck the lid of his desk with a row of thin gelatine lozenges in order that, when after a struggle he managed to open it, the lid should fly up and hit him a blow on the chin. They loosed blackbeetles in the middle of Greek Testament and pretended to be very much afraid while Mr. Caryll stamped upon them one by one, deriding their cowardice. They threw paper darts and paper pellets with unerring aim: they put drawing-pins in the seat of a fat and industrious German called Wertheim: they filled up all the ink-pots in the form with blotting-paper and crossed every single nib. They played xylophonic tunes with penholders on the desk's edge and carved their initials inside: they wrote their names in ink and made the inscription permanent by rubbing it over with blotting-paper. They were seized with sudden and unaccountable fits of bleeding from the nose to gain a short exeat to stand in the fresh air by the Fives Courts. They built up ramparts of dictionaries in the forefront of their desks to play noughts and crosses without detection: they soaked with ink all the chalk for the blackboard and divested Levy of his boots which they passed round the form during 'rep': they made elaborate jointed rods with foolscap to prod otherwise unassailable boys at the other end of the room and when, during the argument which followed the mutual correction by desk-neighbours of Mr. Caryll's weekly examination paper, they observed an earnest group of questioners gathered round the master's dais, they would charge into them from behind so violently that the front row, generally consisting of the more eager and laborious boys, was precipitated against Mr. Caryll's chair to the confusion of labour and eagerness. Retribution followed very seldom in the shape of impots; and even they were soon done by means of an elaborate arrangement by which six pens lashed together did six times the work of one. Sometimes Michael or Alan would be invited to move their desks out close to Mr. Caryll's dais of authority for a week's disgrace; but even this punishment included as compensation a position facing the class and therefore the opportunity to play the buffoon for its benefit. Sometimes Michael or Alan would be ejected with vituperation from the class-room to spend an hour in the corridor without. Unfortunately they were never ejected together, and anyway it was an uneasy experience on account of Dr. Brownjohn's habit of swinging round a corner and demanding a reason for the discovery of a loiterer in the corridor. The first time he appeared, it was always possible by assuming an air of intentness and by walking towards him very quickly to convey the impression of one upon an urgent errand; but when Dr. Brownjohn loomed on his return journey, it was necessary to evade his savage glance by creeping round the great cast of the Antinous that fronted the corridor. On one of these occasions Michael in his nervousness shook the statue and an insecurely dependent fig-leaf fell with a crash on to the floor. Michael nearly flung himself over the well of the main staircase in horror, but deaf Dr. Brownjohn swung past into a gloom beyond, and presently Michael was relieved by the grinning face of a compatriot beckoning permission to re-enter the class-room. Safely inside, the fall of the fig-leaf was made out by Michael to be an act of deliberate daring on his part, and when at one o'clock the form rushed out to verify the boast, his position was tremendously enhanced. The news flew round the school, and several senior boys were observed in conversation with Michael, so that he was able to swagger considerably. Also he turned up his trousers a full two inches higher and parted his hair on the right-hand side, a mode which had long attracted his ambition.

Now, indeed, were Michael and Alan in the zenith of boyhood's glory. No longer did they creep diffidently down the corridors; no longer did they dread to run the gauntlet of a Modern class lined up on either side to await the form-master's appearance. If some louts in the Modern Fourth dared to push them from side to side, as they went by, Michael and Alan would begin to fight and would shout, 'You stinking Modern beasts! Classics to the rescue!' To their rescue would pour the heroes of the Upper Fourth A. Down went the Modern textbooks of Chemistry and Physics, and ignominiously were they hacked along the corridor. Doubled up by a swinging blow from a bag stood the leader of the Moderns, grunting and gasping in his windless agony. Back to the serenity of Virgilian airs went the Upper Fourth A, with Michael and Alan arm in arm amid their escort, and most dejectedly did the Modern cads gather up their scientific textbooks; but during the 'quarter' great was the battle waged on the 'gravel'—that haunt of thumb-biting, acrimonious and uneasy factions. Michael and Alan were not yet troubled with the fevers of adolescence. They were cool and clear and joyous as the mountain torrent: for them life was a crystal of laughter, many-faceted to adventure. Theirs was now that sexless interlude before the Eton collar gave way to the 'stick up' and before the Eton jacket, trim and jaunty, was discarded for an ill-fitting suit that imitated the dull garb of a man. No longer were Michael and Alan grubby and inky: no longer did they fill their pockets with an agglomeration of messes: no longer did their hair sprout in bistre sparseness, for now Michael and Alan were vain of the golden lights and chestnut shadows, not because girls mattered, but because like Narcissus they perceived themselves in the mirror of popular admiration. Now they affected very light trousers and very broad collars and shoes and unwrinkling socks and cuffs that gleamed very white. They looked back with detestation upon the excesses of costume induced by the quadruple intrigue, and they congratulated themselves that no one of importance had beheld their lapse.

Michael and Alan were lords of Little Side football and in their treatment of the underlings stretched the prerogatives of greatness to the limit. They swaggered on to the field of play, where in combination on the left wing they brought off feats of astonishing swiftness and agility. Michael used to watch Alan seeming very fair in his black vest and poised eagerly for the ball to swing out from the half-back. Alan would take the spinning pass and bound forward into the stink-stained Modern juniors or embryo subalterns of Army C. The clumsiest of them would receive Alan's delicate hand full in his face and, as with revengeful mutterings the enemy bore down upon him, Alan would pass the ball to Michael, who with all his speed would gallop along the touch-line and score a try in the corner. Members of Big Side marked Michael and Alan as the two most promising three-quarters for Middle Side next year, and when the bell sounded at twenty minutes to three, the members of Big Side would walk with Michael and Alan towards the changing room and encourage them by flattery and genial ragging. In the lavatory, Michael and Alan would souse with water all the kids in reach, and the kids would be duly grateful for so much acknowledgment of their existence from these stripling gods. In the changing room they would pleasantly fling the disordered clothes of trespassers near their sacred places on to the floor or kick the caps of Second-Form boys to the dusty tops of lockers, and then just as the clock was hard on three, they would saunter up the School steps and along the corridor to their class-room, where they would yawn their way through Cicero's prosy defence of Milo or his fourth denunciation of Catiline.

At home Michael much enjoyed his mother's company, although he was now in the cold dawn of affection for anything save Alan. He no longer was shocked by his mother's solicitude or demonstrativeness, fearful of offending against the rigid standards of the private school or the uncertain position of a new boy at a public school. He yielded gracefully to his mother's pleasure in his company out of a mixture of politeness and condescension; but he always felt that when he gave up for an hour the joys of the world for the cloister of domesticity, he was conferring a favour. At this period nothing troubled him at all save his position in the School and the necessity to spend every available minute with Alan. The uncertainty of his father's position which had from time to time troubled him was allayed by the zest of existence, and he never bothered to question his mother at all pertinaciously. In every way he was making a pleasant pause in his life to enjoy the new emotion of self-confidence, his distinction in football, his popularity with contemporaries and seniors and his passion for the absolute identification of Alan's behaviour with his and his own with Alan's. At home every circumstance fostered this attitude. Alone with his mother, Michael was singularly free to do as he liked, and he could always produce from the past precedents which she was unable to controvert for any whim he wished to establish as a custom. In any case, Mrs. Fane seemed to enjoy spoiling him, and Michael was no longer averse from her praise of his good looks and from the pleasure she expressed in the company of Alan and himself at a concert or matinée. Another reason for Michael's nonchalant happiness was his normality. Nowadays he looked at himself in the old wardrobe that once had power to terrify him with nocturnal creakings, and no longer did he deplore his thin arms and legs, no longer did he mark the diffidence of the sensitive small boy. Now he could at last congratulate himself upon his ability to hold his own with any of his equals whether with tongue or fist. Now, too, when he went to bed, he went to bed as serenely as a kitten, curling himself up to dream of sport with mice. Sometimes Alan on Friday night would accompany him to spend the week-end at Carlington Road, and when he did so, the neighbourhood was not allowed to be oblivious of the event. In the autumnal dusk Michael and he would practise drop-kicks and high punts in the middle of the street, until the ball had landed twice in two minutes on the same balcony to the great annoyance of the 'skivvy,' who was with debonair assurance invited to bung it down for a mere lordly 'thank you' from the offenders. Sometimes the ball would early in the afternoon strike a sun-flamed window, and with exquisite laughter Michael and Alan would retreat to Number 64, until the alarmed lady of the house was quietly within her own doors again. Another pleasant diversion with a football was to take drop-kicks from close quarters at the backs of errand-boys, especially on wet days when the ball left a spheroid of mud where it struck the body.

"Yah, you think yourselves—funny," the errand-boy would growl.

"We do. Oh, rather," Michael and Alan would reply and with smiling indifference defeat their target still more unutterably.

When dusk turned to night, Michael and Alan would wonder what to do and, after making themselves unbearable in the kitchen, they would sally out into the back-garden and execute some devilry at the expense of neighbours. They would walk along the boundary walks of the succeedant oblongs of garden that ran the whole length of the road; and it was a poor evening's sport which produced no fun anywhere. Sometimes they would detect, white in the darkness, a fox-terrier, whereat they would miaow and rustle the poplar trees and reduce the dog to a state of hysterical yapping which would be echoed in various keys by every dog within earshot. Sometimes they would observe a lighted kitchen with an unsuspicious cook hard at work upon the dinner, meditating perhaps upon a jelly or flavouring anxiously the soup. Then if the window were open Michael and Alan would take pot-shots at the dish with blobs of mould or creep down into the basement, if the window were shut, and groan and howl to the cook's pallid dismay and to the great detriment of her family's dinner. In other gardens they would fling explosive 'slap-bangs' against the wall of the house or fire a gunpowder train or throw gravel up to a lighted bath-room window. There was always some amusement to be gained at a neighbour's expense between six and seven o'clock, at which latter hour they would creep demurely home and dress for dinner, the only stipulation Mrs. Fane made with Michael in exchange for leave to ask Alan to stay with him.

At dinner in the orange glow of the dining-room, Michael and Alan would be completely charming and very conversational, as they told Mrs. Fane how they rotted old Caryll or ragged young Levy or scored two tries that afternoon. Mrs. Fane would seem to be much interested and make the most amusing mistakes and keep her son and her guest in an ecstatic risibility. After dinner they would sit for a while in the perfumed drawing-room, making themselves agreeable and useful by fetching Mrs. Fane's novel or blotting-pad or correspondence, or by pulling up an arm-chair or by extricating a footstool and drawing close the curtains. Then Michael and Alan would be inclined to fidget, until Michael announced it was time to go and swat. Mrs. Fane would smile exquisitely and say how glad she was they did not avoid their home work and remind them to come and say good night at ten o'clock sharp. Encouraged by Mrs. Fane's gracious dismissal, Michael and Alan would plunge into the basement and gain the sanctity of Michael's own room. They would elaborately lay the table for work, spreading out foolscap and notebooks and Cicero Pro Milone and Cicero In Catilinam and Thucydides IV and the green-backed Ion of Euripides. They would make exhaustive researches into the amount of work set to be shown up on Monday morning, and with a sigh they would seat themselves to begin. First of all the Greek Testament would be postponed until Sunday as a more appropriate day, and then Michael would feel an overpowering desire to smoke one cigarette before they began. This cigarette had to be smoked close to the open window, so that the smoke could be puffed outside into the raw autumnal air, while Alan kept 'cavé,' rushing to the door to listen at the slightest rumour of disturbance. When the cigarette was finished they would contemplate for a long time the work in front of them, and then Michael would say he thought it rather stupid to swat on Friday night with all Saturday and Sunday before them, and who did Alan think was the better Half-back—Rawson or Wilding? This question led to a long argument before Rawson was adjudged to be the better of the two. Then Alan would bet Michael he could not write down from memory the Nottinghamshire cricket team, and Michael would express his firm conviction that Alan could not possibly name the winners of the Oxford and Cambridge quarter-mile for the last three years. Finally they would both recur to the problem ever present, the best way to obtain two bicycles and, what was more important, the firm they would ultimately honour with their patronage. The respective merits of the Humber, the Rover, the Premier, the Quadrant, the Swift and the Sunbeam created a battleground for various opinions, and as for the tyres, it seemed impossible to decide between Palmers, Clinchers and Dunlops. In the middle of the discussion the clock in the passage would strike ten, at which Michael and Alan would yawn and dawdle their way upstairs. Perhaps the bicycle problem had a wearing effect, for Mrs. Fane would remark on their jaded appearance and hope they were not working too hard. Michael and Alan would look particularly conscious of their virtue and admit they had had a very tiring week, what with football and Cicero and Quadratic Equations; and so after affectionate good nights they would saunter up to bed. Upstairs, they would lean out of the bedroom window and watch the golden trains go by, and ponder the changing emeralds and rubies of the signal-box farther along the line: then after trying to soak a shadowy tomcat down below with water from the toilet-jug Michael and Alan would undress.

In the darkness Michael and Alan would lie side by side secure in a companionship of dreams. They murmured now their truly intimate thoughts: they spoke of their hopes and ambitions, of the Army with its glories of rank and adventure, of the Woods and Forests of India, of treasure on coral islands and fortunes in the cañons of the West. They spoke of the School Fifteen and of Alan's probable captaincy of it one day: they discussed the Upper Sixth with its legend of profound erudition: they wondered if it would be worth while for Michael to swat and be Captain of the School. They talked again of bicycles and decided to make an united effort to secure them this ensuing Christmas by compounding for one great gift any claims they possessed on birthday presents later in the year. They talked of love, and of the fools they had been to waste their enthusiasm on Dora and Winnie. They made up their minds to forswear the love of women with all its humiliations and disappointments and futilities. Through life each would be to the other enough. Girls would be for ever an intrusion between such deathless and endeared friends as they were. Michael pointed out how awkward it would be if he and Alan both loved the same girl and showed how it would ruin their twin lives and wreck their joint endeavour; while Alan agreed it would be mad to risk a separation for such froth of feminine attractiveness. The two of them vowed in the darkness to stick always together, so that whatever fate life held for either it should hold for both. They swore fidelity to their friendship in the silence and intimacy of the night; and when, rosy in the morning, they stood up straightly in the pale London sunlight, they did not regret the vows of the night, nor did they blush for their devotion, since the world conjured a long vista of them both arm in arm eternally, and in the immediate present all the adventurous charm of a Saturday's whole holiday.

If there was a First Fifteen match on the School ground, Michael and Alan honoured it with their attendance and liked nothing so well as to elbow their way through a mob of juniors in order to nod familiarly to a few members of the Fifteen. The School team that year was not so successful as its two predecessors, and Michael and Alan were often compelled to voice their disdain to the intense disgust of the juniors huddled about them. Sometimes they would hear an irreverent murmur of 'Hark at sidey Fane and sidey Merivale,' which would necessitate the punching of a number of heads to restore the disciplinary respect they demanded. On days when the School team was absent at Dulford or Tonbury or Haileybridge, Michael and Alan would scornfully glance at the Second Fifteen's desolate encounter with some other Second Fifteen, and vote that such second-rate football was bally rot. On such occasions the School ground used to seem too large and empty for cheerfulness, and the two friends would saunter round West Kensington on the chance of an adventure, ending up the afternoon by laying out money on sweets or on the fireworks now displayed in anticipation of the Fifth of November. Saturday evening would be spent in annoying the neighbours with squibs and Chinese crackers and jumping crackers and tourbillons and maroons and Roman candles and Bengal lights, while after dinner the elaborate preparations for home work would again be made with the same inadequate result.

On Sunday Michael and Alan used to brush their top-hats and button their gloves and tie their ties very carefully and, armed with sticks of sobriety and distinction, swagger to whatever church was fashionable among their friends. During the service they would wink to acquaintances and nudge each other and sing very loudly and clearly their favourite hymns, while through the dull hymns they would criticize their friends' female relations. So the week would fulfil its pleasant course until nine o'clock on Monday morning, when Michael and Alan would run all the way to school and in a fever of industry get through their home work with the united assistance of the rest of the Upper Fourth A, as one by one the diligent members arrived in Hall for a few minutes' gossip before Prayers. During Prayers, Michael and Alan would try to forecast by marking off the full stops what paragraph of Cicero they would each be called upon to construe; finally, when old Caryll named Merivale to take up the oration's thread, Michael would hold the crib on his knees and over Levy's laborious back whisper in the voice of a ghoul the meaning.

At Christmas, after interminable discussion and innumerable catalogues, the bicycles were bought, and in the Lent term with its lengthening twilights Michael and Alan devoted all their attention to bicycling, except in wet weather, when they played Fives, bagging the covered courts from small boys who had waited days for the chance of playing in them. Michael, during the Lent term, often rode back with Alan after School to spend the week-end at Richmond, and few delights were so rare as that of scorching over Barnes Common and down the Mortlake Road with its gardens all a-blow with spring flowers and, on the other bank of the river over Kew, the great spring skies keeping pace with their whirring wheels.

Yet best of all was the summer term, that glorious azure summer term of fourteen and a half, which fled by in a radiancy. Michael and Alan were still in the Upper Fourth A under Mr. Caryll: they still fooled away the hours of school, relying upon the charm of their joint personality to allay the extreme penalty of being sent up to the Headmaster for incorrigible knavery. They were Captain and Vice-Captain of the Classical Upper Fourth Second Eleven, preferring the glory of leadership to an ambiguous position in the tail of the First Eleven. Michael and Alan were in their element during that sunburnt hour of cricket before afternoon school. They wore white felt hats, and Michael in one of his now rare flights of imagination thought that Alan in his looked like Perseus in a Flaxman drawing. Many turned to look at the two friends, as enlaced they wandered across the 'gravel' on their way to change out of flannels, Michael nut-brown and Alan rose-bloomed like a peach.

At five o'clock they would eat a rowdy tea in the School Tuckshop to the accompaniment of flying pellets of bun, after which they would change again for amber hours of cricket, until the sun made the shadow of the stumps as long as telegraph poles, and the great golden clock face in the School buildings gleamed a late hour. They would part from each other with regret to ride off in opposite directions. Michael would linger on his journey home through the mellow streets of Kensington, writing with his bicycle wheels lazy parabolas and curves in the dust of each quiet road. Twilight was not far off, the murmurous twilight of a London evening with its trancéd lovers and winking stars and street-lamps and window-panes. More and more slowly Michael would glide along, loath to desert the dreaming populations of dusk. He would turn down unfrequented corners and sail by unfamiliar terraces, aware of nothing but the languors of effortless motion. Time, passing by in a sensuous oblivion, made Michael as much a part of the nightfall as the midges that spun incessantly about his progress. Then round a corner some night-breeze would blow freshly in his face: he would suddenly realize it was growing late and, pressing hard the pedals of his bicycle, he would dart home, swift as a bird that crosses against the dying glow of the sunset.

Michael's mother was always glad to see him and always glad when he sat with her on the balcony outside the drawing-room. If he had wanted to cross-examine her he would have found an easy witness, so tranquil and so benignant that year was every night of June in

London. But Michael had for the time put aside all speculation and drugged his imagination with animal exercise, allowing himself no time to think of anything but the present. He was dimly aware of trouble close at hand, when the terminal examinations should betray his idleness; but it was impossible to worry over what was now sheerly inevitable. This summer term was perfect, and why should one consider ultimate time? Even Stella's holiday from Germany had been postponed, as if there were a veritable conspiracy by circumstance to wave away the least element of disturbance. Next Saturday he and Alan were going to spend the day in Richmond Park; and when it came in its course what a day it was. The boys set out directly after breakfast and walked through the pungent bracken, chasing the deer and the dragonflies as if there were nothing to distinguish them. Down streamed the sun from the blue July heavens: but Michael and Alan clad in white went careless of the heat. They walked over the grass uphill and ran down through the cool dells of oak trees, down towards the glassy ponds to play 'ducks and drakes' in the flickering weather. They stood by the intersecting carriage-roads and mocked the perspiring travellers in their black garments. They cared for nothing but being alive in Richmond Park on a summer Saturday of London. At last, near a shadowy woodland where the grasses grew very tall, Michael and Alan, smothering the air with pollen, flung themselves down into the fragrancy and, while the bees droned about them, slept in the sun. Later in the afternoon the two friends sat on the Terrace among the old ladies and the old gentlemen, and the nurserymaids and the children's hoops. Down below, the Thames sparkled in a deep green prospect of England. An hour went by; the old ladies and the old gentlemen and the nurserymaids and the hoops faded away one by one under the darkling trees. Down below, the Thames threaded with shining curves a vast and elusive valley of azure. The Thames died away to a sheen of dusky silver: the azure deepened almost to indigo: lights flitted into ken one by one: there travelled up from the river a sound of singing, and somewhere in the houses behind a piano began to tinkle. Michael suddenly became aware that the end of the summer term was in sight. He shivered in the dewfall and put his arm round Alan's neck affectionately and intimately: only profound convention kept him from kissing his friend and by not doing so he felt vaguely that something was absent from this perfection of dusk. Something in Michael at that moment demanded emotional expression, and from afternoon school of yesterday recurred to his mind a note to some lines in the Sixth Æneid of Virgil. He remembered the lines, having by some accident learned his repetition for that day:

Huc omnis turba ad ripas effusa ruebat,

Matres atque viri defunctaque corpora vita

Magnanimum heroum, pueri innuptæque
puellæ,

Impositique rogis juvenes ante ora parentum;

Quam multa in silvis auctumni frigore primo

Lapsa cadunt folia, aut ad terram gurgite ab
alto

Quam multæ glomerantur aves ubi frigidus
annus

Trans pontum fugat et terris immittit apricis.

Compare, said the commentator, Milton, Paradise Lost, Book I.

Thick as autumnal leaves that strew the
brooks

In Vallombrosa.

As Michael mentally repeated the thunderous English line, a surge of melancholy caught him up to overwhelm his thoughts. In some way those words expressed what he was feeling at this moment, so that he could gain relief from the poignancy of his joy here in the darkness close to Alan with the unfathomable valley of the Thames beneath, by saying over and over again:

Thick as autumnal leaves that strew the
brooks

In Vallombrosa.

"Damn, damn, damn, damn," cried Alan suddenly. "Exams on Monday! Damn, damn, damn, damn."

"I must go home and swat to-night," said Michael.

"So must I," sighed Alan.

"Walk with me to the station," Michael asked.

"Oh, rather," replied Alan.

Soon Michael was jolting back to Kensington in a stuffy carriage of hot Richmond merrymakers, while all the time he sat in the corner, saying over and over again:

Thick as autumnal leaves that strew the
brooks

In Vallombrosa.

All Saturday night and all Sunday Michael worked breathlessly for those accursed examinations: but at the end of them he and Alan were bracketed equal, very near the tail of the Upper Fourth A. Dr. Brownjohn sent for each of them in turn, and each of them found the interview very trying.

"What do you mean by it?" roared the Headmaster to Michael. "What do you mean by it, you young blackguard? Um? Look at this list. Um? It's a contemptible position for a Scholar. Down here with a lump of rabbit's brains, you abominable little loafer. Um? If you aren't in the first five boys of the Lower Fifth next term, I'll kick you off the Foundation. What good are you to the School? Um? None at all."

As Dr. Brownjohn bellowed forth this statement, his mouth opened so wide that Michael instinctively shrank back as if from a crater in eruption.

"You don't come here to swagger about," growled the Headmaster. "You come here to be a credit to your school. You pestilent young jackanapes, do you suppose I haven't noticed your idleness? Um? I notice everything. Get out of my sight and take your hands out of your pockets, you insolent little lubber. Um?"

Michael left the Headmaster's room with an expression of tragic injury: in the corridor was a group of juniors.

"What the devil are you kids hanging about here for?" Michael demanded.

"All right, sidey Fane," they burbled. Michael dashed into the group and grabbed a handful of caps which he tossed into the dusty complications of the Laocoön. To their lamentations he responded by thrusting his hands deep down into his pockets and whistling 'Little Dolly Daydreams, pride of Idaho.' The summer term would be over in a few days, and Michael was sorry to say good-bye to Alan, who was going to Norway with his father and mother and would therefore not be available for the whole of the holidays. Indeed, he was leaving two days before School actually broke up. Michael was wretched without Alan and brooded over the miseries of life that so soon transcended the joys. On the last day of term, he was seized with an impulse to say good-bye to Mr. Caryll, an impulse which he could not understand and was inclined to deplore. However, it was too strong for his conventions, and he loitered behind in the confusion of merry departures.

"Good-bye, sir," he said shyly.

Mr. Caryll took off two pairs of spectacles and examined Michael through the remaining pair, rasping out the familiar cough as he did so.

"Now, you great booby, what do you want?" he asked.

"Good-bye, sir," Michael said, more loudly.

"Oh, good-bye," said Mr. Caryll. "You've been a very idle boy"—cough—cough—"and I"—cough—cough—"I don't think I ever knew such an idle boy before."

"I've had a ripping time in your class, sir," said Michael.

"What do you mean?"—cough—cough—"are you trying to be impudent?" exclaimed Mr. Caryll, hastily putting on a second pair of spectacles to cope with the situation.

"No, sir. I've enjoyed being in your class. I'm sorry I was so low down in the list. Good-bye, sir."

Mr. Caryll seemed to realize at last that Michael was being sincerely complimentary, so he took off all the pairs of spectacles and beamed at him with an expression of the most profound benignity.

"Oh, well"—cough—cough—"we can't all be top"—cough—cough—"but it's a pity you should be so very low down"—cough—cough—"you're a Scholar too, which makes it much worse. Never mind. Good boy at heart"—cough—cough—"better luck in your next form"—cough—cough. "Hope you'll enjoy yourself on your holidays."

"Good-bye, sir. Thanks awfully," said Michael. He turned away from the well-loved class-room of old Caryll that still echoed with the laughter of the Upper Fourth A.

"And don't work too hard"—cough—cough, was Mr. Caryll's last joke.

In the corridor Michael caught up the lantern-jawed boy who had prophesied this year's pleasure at the beginning of last autumn.

"Just been saying good-bye to old Christmas," Michael volunteered.

"He's a topper," said Lantern-jaws. "The best old boy that ever lived. I wish I was going to be in his form again next term."

"So do I," said Michael. "We had a clinking good time. So long. Hope you'll have decent holidays."

"So long," said the lantern-jawed boy lugubriously, dropping most of his mathematical books. "Same to you."

When Michael was at home, he took a new volume of Henty into the garden and began to read. Suddenly he found he was bored by Henty. This knowledge shocked him for the moment. Then he went indoors and put For Name and Fame, or Through Afghan Passes back on the shelf. He surveyed the row of Henty's books gleaming with olivine edges, and presently he procured brown paper and with Cook's assistance wrapped up the dozen odd volumes. At the top he placed a slip of paper on which was written 'Presented to the Boys' Library by C. M. S. Fane.' Michael was now in a perplexity for literary recreation, until he remembered Don Quixote. Soon he was deep in that huge volume, out of the dull world of London among the gorges and chasms and waterfalls of Castile. Boyhood's zenith had been attained: Michael's imagination was primed for strange emotions.

Chapter V: *Incense*

STELLA came back from Germany less foreign-looking than Michael expected, and he could take a certain amount of pleasure in her company at Bournemouth, For a time they were well matched, as they walked with their mother under the pines. Once, as they passed a bunch of old ladies on a seat, Stella said to Michael:

"Did you hear what those people said?"

Michael had not heard, so Stella whispered:

"They said 'What good-looking children!' Shall we turn back and walk by them again?"

"Whatever for?" Michael demanded.

"Oh, I don't know," said Stella, flapping the big violet bows in her chestnut hair. "Only I like to hear people talking about me. I think it's interesting. I always try to hear what they say when I'm playing."

"Mother," Michael appealed, "don't you think Stella ought not to be so horribly conceited? I do."

"Darling Stella," said Mrs. Fane, "I'm afraid people spoil her. It isn't her fault."

"It must be her fault," argued Michael.

Michael remembered Miss Carthew's admonition not to snub Stella, but he could not help feeling that Miss Carthew herself would have disapproved of this open vanity. He wished that Miss Carthew were not now Mrs. Ross and far away in Edinburgh. He felt almost a responsibility with regard to Stella, a highly moral sensation of knowing better the world and its pitfalls than she could. He feared for the effect of its lure upon Stella and her vanity, and was very anxious his sister should always comport herself with credit to her only brother. In his mother's attitude Michael seemed to discern a dangerous inclination not to trouble about Stella's habit of thought. He resolved, when he and Stella were alone together, to address his young sister seriously. Stella's nonchalance alarmed him more and more deeply as he began to look back at his own life and to survey his wasted years. Michael felt he must convince Stella that earnestness was her only chance.

"You're growing very fast, Michael," said his mother one morning. "Really I think you're getting too big for Etons."

Michael critically examined himself in his mother's toilet-glass and had to admit that his sleeves looked short and that his braces showed too easily under his waistcoat. The fact that he could no longer survey his reflection calmly and that he dreaded to see Stella admire herself showed him something was wrong.

"Perhaps I'd better get a new suit," he suggested.

In his blue serge suit, wearing what the shops called a Polo or Shakespeare collar, Michael felt more at ease, although the sleeves were now as much too long as lately his old sleeves were too short. The gravity of this new suit confirmed his impression that age was stealing upon him and made him the more inclined to lecture Stella. This desire of his seemed to irritate his mother, who would protest:

"Michael, do leave poor Stella alone. I can't think why you've suddenly altered. One would think you'd got the weight of the world on your shoulders."

"Like Atlas," commented Michael gloomily.

"I don't know who it's like," said Mrs. Fane. "But it's very disagreeable for everybody round you."

"Michael always thinks he knows about everything," Stella put in spitefully.

"Oh, shut up!" growled Michael.

He was beginning to feel that his mother admired Stella more than himself, and the old jealousy of her returned. He was often reproved for being untidy and, although he was no longer inky and grubby, he did actually find that his hair refused to grow neatly and that he was growing clumsy both in manners and appearance. Stella always remained cool and exasperatingly debonair under his rebukes, whereas he felt himself growing hot and awkward. The old self-consciousness had returned and with it two warts on his finger and an intermittent spot on his chin. Also a down was visible on his face that somehow blunted his profile and made him more prone than ever to deprecate the habit of admiring oneself in a looking-glass. He felt impelled to untie Stella's violet bows whenever he caught her posing before the mirror, and as the holidays advanced he and she grew less and less well matched. The old worrying speculation about his father returned together with a wish that his mother would not dress in such gay colours. Michael admired her slimness and tallness, but he wished that men would not turn round and stare at her as she passed them. He used to stare back at the men with a set frowning face and try to impress them with his distaste for their manners; but day by day he grew more miserable about his mother, and would often seek to dissuade her from what he considered a too conspicuous hat or vivid ribbon. She used to laugh and tell him that he was a regular old 'provincial.' The opportunity for perfect confidence between Michael and his mother seemed to have slipped by, and he found it impossible now to make her talk about his father. To be sure, she no longer tried to wave aside his enquiries; but she did worse by answering 'yes' or 'no' to his questions according to her mood, never seeming to care whether she contradicted a previous statement or not.

Once, Michael asked straight out whether his father was in prison and he was relieved when his mother rippled with laughter and told him he was a stupid boy. At the same time, since he had been positively assured his father was dead, Michael felt that laughter, however convincing it were, scarcely became a widow.

"I cannot think what has happened to you, Michael. You were perfectly charming all last term and never seemed to have a moment on your hands. Now you hang about the house on these lovely fine days and mope and grumble. I do wish you could enjoy yourself as you used to."

"Well, I've got no friends down here," Michael declared. "What is there to do? I'm sick of the band, and the niggers are rotten, and Stella always wants to hang about on the pier so that people can stare at her. I wish she'd go back to her glorious Germany where everything is so wonderful."

"Why don't you read? You used to love reading," suggested Mrs. Fane.

"Oh, read!" exclaimed Michael. "There's nothing to read. I hate Henty. Always the same!"

"Well, I don't know anything about Henty, but there's Scott and Dickens and——"

"I've read all them, mother," Michael interrupted petulantly.

"Well, why don't you ask Mrs. Rewins if you can borrow a book from her, or I'll ask her, as you don't like going downstairs."

Mrs. Rewins brought up an armful of books which Michael examined dismally one by one. However, after several gilded volumes of sermons and sentimental Sunday-school prizes, he came across a tattered Newgate Calendar and Roderick Random, both of which satisfied somewhat his new craving for excitement. When he had finished these books, Mrs. Rewins invited him to explore the cupboard in her warm kitchen, and here Michael found Peregrine Pickle, Tom Jones, a volume of Bentley's Miscellany containing the serial of Jack Sheppard by Harrison Ainsworth, and What Every Woman of Forty-five ought to Know. The last work upset him very much because he found it unintelligible in parts, and where it was intelligible extremely alarming. An instinct of shamefulness made him conceal this book in a drawer, but he became very anxious to find out exactly how old his mother was. She, however, was more elusive on this point than he had ever known her, and each elaborate trap failed, even the innocent production of the table for ascertaining anybody's age in a blue sixpenny Encyclopædia: still, the Encyclopædia was not without its entertainment, and the table of diseases at the end was very instructive. Among the books which Michael had mined down in Mrs. Rewins' kitchen was The Ingoldsby Legends illustrated by Cruikshank. These he found very enthralling, for though he was already acquainted with The Jackdaw of Rheims, he now discovered many other poems still more amusing, in many of which he came across with pleasure quotations that he remembered to have heard used with much effect by Mr. Neech in the Shell. The macabre and ghostly lays did not affect him so much as the legends of the saints. These he read earnestly as he read Don Quixote, discerning less of laughter than of Gothic adventure in their fantastic pages, while his brain was fired by the heraldic pomps and ecclesiastical glories.

About this time he happened to pay a visit to Christchurch Priory and by the vaulted airs of that sanctuary he was greatly thrilled. The gargoyles and brasses and effigies of dead knights called to him mysteriously, but the inappropriate juxtaposition of an early Victorian tomb shocked him with a sense of sacrilege. He could not bear to contemplate the nautical trousers of the boy commemorated. Yet, simultaneously with his outraged decorum, he was attracted to this tomb, as if he detected in that ingenuous boy posited among sad cherubs some kinship with himself.

In bed that night Michael read The Ingoldsby Legends in a fever of enjoyment, while the shadows waved about the ceiling and walls of the seaside room in the vexed candlelight. As yet the details of the poems did not gain their full effect, because many of the words and references were not understood. He felt that knowledge was necessary before he could properly enjoy the colour of these tales. Michael had always been inclined to crystallize in one strong figure of imagination his vague impressions. Two years ago he had identified Mr. Neech with old prints, with Tom Brown's Schooldays and with shelves of calf-bound books. Now in retrospect he, without being able to explain his reason to himself, identified Mr. Neech with that statue of the trousered boy in Christchurch Priory, and not merely Mr. Neech but even The Ingoldsby Legends as well. He felt that they were both all wrong in the sanctified glooms of the Middle Ages, and yet he rejoiced to behold them there, as if somehow they were a pledge of historic continuity. Without the existence of the trousered boy Michael would scarcely have believed in the reality of those stone ladies and carved knights. The candlelight fluttered and jigged in the seaside room, while Mr. Neech, The Ingoldsby Legends and the oratories of Christchurch became more and more hopelessly confused. Michael's excited brain was formulating visions of immense cathedrals beneath whose arches pattered continually the populations of old prints: the tower of St. Mary's College, Oxford, rose, slim and lovely, against the storm-wrack of a Doré sky: Don Quixote tilted with knights-at-arms risen from the dead. Michael himself was swept along in cavalcades towards the clouds with Ivanhoe, Richard Cœur de Lion, Roderick Random and half a dozen woodcut murderers from the Newgate Calendar. Then, just as the candlelight was gasping and shimmering blue in the bowl of the candlestick, he fell asleep.

In the sunshine of the next day Michael almost wondered whether like someone in The Ingoldsby Legends he had ridden with witches on a broomstick. All the cool security of boyhood had left him; he was in a turmoil of desire for an astounding experience. He almost asked himself what he wanted so dearly; and, as he pondered, out of the past in a vision came the picture of himself staring at the boy who walked beside the incense with a silver boat. What did the Lay of St. Alois say?

This with his chasuble, this with his rosary,

This with his incense-pot holding his nose
awry.

Michael felt a craving to go somewhere and smell that powerful odour again. He remembered how the boy had put out his tongue and he envied him such familiarity with pomps and glories.

"Are there any High Churches in Bournemouth?" he asked Mrs. Rewins. "Very high. Incense and all that, you know."

Mrs. Rewins informed him there was one church so high that some said it was practically 'Roming Catholic.'

"Where is it?" asked Michael, choking with excitement. Yet he had never before wanted to go to church. In the days of Nurse he had hated it. In the days of Miss Carthew he had only found it endurable if his friends were present. He had loathed the rustle of many women dressed in their best clothes. He had hated the throaty voices of smooth-faced clergymen. He had despised the sleek choir-boys smelling of yellow soap. Religion had been compounded of Collects, Greek Testament, Offertory Bags, varnish, qualms for the safety of one's top-hat, the pleasure of an extra large hassock, ambition to be grown up and bend over instead of kneeling down, the podgy feel of a Prayer Book, and a profound disapproval that only Eton and Winchester among public schools were mentioned in its diaphanous fumbling pages. Now religion should be an adventure. The feeling that he was embarking upon the unknown made Michael particularly reticent, and he was afraid to tell his mother that on Sunday morning he proposed to attend the service at St. Bartholomew's, lest she might suggest coming also. He did not want to be irritated by Stella's affectations and conceit, nor did he wish to notice various women turning round to study his mother's hat. In the end Michael did not go on Sunday to the church of his intention, because at the last moment he could not brace himself to mumble an excuse.

Late on the afternoon of the following day Michael walked through the gustiness of a swift-closing summer toward St. Bartholomew's, where it stood facing a stretch of sandy heather and twisted pine trees on the outskirts of Bournemouth. The sky was stained infrequently with the red of a lifeless sunset and, as Michael watched the desolation of summer's retreat, he listened sadly to the sibilant heather lisping against the flutes of the pines, while from time to time the wind drummed against the buttresses and boomed against the bulk of the church. Michael drew near the west door whose hinges and nails stood out unnaturally distinct in the last light of the sun. Abruptly on the blowy eve the church-bell began to ring, and from various roads Michael saw people approaching, their heads bent against the gale. At length he made up his mind to follow one of the groups through the churchyard and presently, while the gate rattled behind him in the wind, he reached the warm glooms within. As he took his seat and perceived the altar loaded with flowers, dazzling with lighted candles, he wondered why this should be so on a Monday night in August. The air was pungent with the smell of wax and the stale perfume of incense on stone. The congregation was scattered about in small groups and units, and the vaulted silence was continually broken by coughs and sighs and hollow footsteps. From the tower the bell rang in slow monotone, while the wind whistled and moaned and flapped and boomed as if, thought Michael, all the devils in hell were trying to break into the holy building. The windows were now scarcely luminous with the wan shadow of daylight and would indeed have been opaque as coal had the inside of the church been better lighted. But the few wavering gas-jets in the nave made all seem dark save where the chancel, empty and candle-lit, shone and sparkled in a radiance. Something in

Michael's attitude must have made a young man sitting behind lean over and ask if he wanted a Prayer Book. Michael turned quickly to see a lean and eager face.

"Yes, please. I left mine at home," he answered.

"Well, come and sit by me," said the young man.

Michael changed his place and the young man talked in a low whisper, while the bell rang its monotone upon the gusts which swept howling round the church.

"Solemn Evensong isn't until seven o'clock. It's our patronal festival, St. Bartholomew's Day—you know. We had a good Mass this morning. Every year we get more people. Do you live in Bournemouth?"

"No," whispered Michael. "I'm just here for the holidays."

"What a pity," said the stranger. "We do so want servers—you know—decent-looking servers. Our boys are so clumsy. It's not altogether their fault—the cassocks—you know—they're only in two sizes. They trip up. I'm the Ceremonarius, and I can tell you I have my work cut out. Of course I ought to have been helping to-night. But I wasn't sure I could get away from the Bank in time. I hope Wilson—that's our second thurifer—won't go wrong in the Magnificat. He usually does."

The bell stopped: there was a momentary hush for the battling wind to moan louder than ever: then the organ began to play and from the sacristy came the sound of a chanted Amen. Choristers appeared followed by two or three of the clergy, and when these had taken their places a second procession appeared, with boys in scarlet and lace and a tinkling censer and a priest in a robe of blood-red velvet patterned with dull gold.

"That's the new cope," whispered the stranger. "Fine work, isn't it?"

"Awfully decent," Michael whispered back.

"All I hope is the acolytes will remember to put out the candles immediately after the Third Collect. It's so important," said the stranger.

"I expect they will," whispered Michael encouragingly.

Then the Office began, and Michael, waiting for a spiritual experience, communed that night with the saints of God, as during the Magnificat his soul rose to divine glories on the fumes of the aspiring incense. There was a quality in the voices of the boys which expressed for him more beautifully than the full Sunday choir could have done, the pathos of human praise and the purity of his own surrender to Almighty God. The splendours of the Magnificat died away to a silence and one of the clergy stepped from his place to read the Second Lesson. As he came down the chancel steps Michael's new friend whispered:

"The censing of the altar was all right. It's really a good thing sometimes to be a spectator—you know—one sees more."

Michael nodded a vague assent. Already the voice of the lector was vibrating through the church.

In the end of the sabbath, as it began to dawn towards the first day of the week, came Mary Magdalene and the other Mary to see the sepulchre.

Michael thought to himself how he had come to St. Bartholomew's when Sunday was over. That was strange.

His countenance was like lightning and his raiment white as snow: and for fear of him the keepers did shake, and became as dead men.

"I wish that boy Wiggins wouldn't fidget with his zuchetto," Michael's friend observed.

And behold, he goeth before you into Galilee; there shall ye see him: lo, I have told you.

Michael felt an impulse to sob, as he mentally offered the best of himself to the worship of Christ, for the words of the lesson were striking on his soul like bells.

And when they saw him, they worshipped him: but some doubted.

"Now you see the other boy has started fidgeting with *his*," complained the young man.

And, lo, I am with you always, even unto the end of the world. Amen.

As the lector's retreating footsteps died away into the choir the words were burned on Michael's heart, and for the first time he sang the Nunc Dimittis with a sense of the privilege of personally addressing Almighty God. When the Creed was chanted Michael uttered his belief passionately, and while the Third Collect was being read between the exalted candles of the acolytes he wondered why never before had the words struck him with all their power against the fears and fevers of the night.

Lighten our darkness, we beseech thee, O Lord; and by thy great mercy defend us from all perils and dangers of this night, for the love of thy only Son, our Saviour, Jesus Christ. Amen.

The acolytes lowered their candles to extinguish them: then they darkened the altar while the hymn was being sung, and Michael's friend gave a sigh of relief.

"Perfectly all right," he whispered.

Michael himself was sorry to see the gradual extinction of the altar-lights; he had concentrated upon that radiance his new desire of adoration and a momentary chill fell upon him, as if the fiends without were gaining strength and fury. All dread and doubt was allayed when, after the murmured Grace of Our Lord, the congregation and the choir and the officiant knelt in a silent prayer. The wind still shrieked and thundered: the gas-jets waved uneasily above the huddled forms of the worshippers: but over all that incense-clouded gloom lay a spirit of tranquillity. Michael said the Our Father to himself and allowed his whole being to expand in a warmth of surrender. The purification of sincere prayer, voiced more by his attitude of mind than by any spoken word, made him infinitely at peace with life.

When the choir and clergy had filed out and the sacristan like an old rook came limping down the aisle to usher the congregation forth into the dark wind of Bartlemy-tide, Michael's friend said:

"Wait just a minute. I want to speak to Father Moneypenny for a moment, and then we can walk back together."

61

Michael nodded, and presently his friend came back from the sacristy with Father Moneypenny in cassock and biretta, looking like the photographs of clergymen that Michael remembered in Nurse's album long ago.

"So you enjoyed the Evensong?" enquired the priest. "Capital! You must come to Mass next Sunday. There will be a procession. By the way, Prout, perhaps your young friend would help us. We shall want extra torch-boys."

Mr. Prout agreed, and Michael, although he wondered what his mother would say, was greatly excited by the idea. They were standing now by the door of the church and as it opened a gust of wind burst in and whistled round the interior. Father Moneypenny shivered.

"What a night. The end of summer, I'm afraid."

He closed the door, and Michael and Mr. Prout forced their way through the gale over the wet gravel of the churchyard. The pine trees and the heather made a melancholy concert, and they were glad to reach the blown lamplight of the streets.

"Will you come round to my place?" Mr. Prout asked.

"Well, I ought to go back. My mater will be anxious," said Michael.

Mr. Prout thereupon invited him to come round to-morrow afternoon.

"I shall be back from the Bank about five. Good night. You've got my card? Bernard Prout, Esdraelon, Saxton Road. Good night. Pleased to have met you."

Mrs. Fane was surprized to hear of Michael's visit to St. Bartholomew's.

"You're getting so secretive, dearest boy. I'd no idea you were becoming interested in religion."

"Well, it is interesting," said Michael.

"Of course. I know it must be. So many people think of nothing else. And do you really want to march in the procession?"

"Yes, but don't you and Stella come," Michael said.

"Oh, I must, Michael. I'd love to see you in all those pretty clothes."

"Well, I *can* go round and see this chap Prout, can't I?" Michael asked.

"I suppose so," Mrs. Fane replied. "Of course, I don't know anything about him. Is he a gentleman?"

"Of course he's a gentleman," affirmed Michael warmly. "Besides I don't see it matters a bit whether he's a gentleman or not."

"No, of course it doesn't really, as it all has to do with religion," Mrs. Fane agreed. "Nothing is so mixed as religious society."

Saxton Road possessed no characteristic to distinguish it from many similar roads in Bournemouth. A few hydrangeas debated in sheltered corners whether they should be pink or blue, and the number of each house was subordinate to its title. The gate of Esdraelon clicked behind Michael's entrance just as the gate of Homeview or Ardagh or Glenside would have clicked. By the bay-window of the ground floor was planted a young passion-flower whose nursery label lisped against the brick-work, and whose tendrils were flattened beneath wads of nail-pierced flannel. Michael was directed upstairs to Mr. Prout's sitting-room on the first floor, where the owner was arranging the tea-cups.

"I'm so glad you were able to come," he said.

Michael looked round the room with interest, and while the tea-cake slowly cooled Mr. Prout discussed with enthusiasm his possessions.

"That's St. Bernardine of Sienna," he explained, pointing to a coloured statuette. "My patron, you know. Curious I should have been born on his day and be christened Bernard. I thought of changing my name to Bernardine, but it's so difficult at a Bank. Of course, I have a cult for St. Bernard too, but I never really can forgive him for opposing the Immaculate Conception. Father Moneypenny and I have great arguments on that point. I'm afraid he's a *little* bit wobbly. But absolutely sound on the Assumption. Oh, absolutely, I'm glad to say. In fact, I don't mind telling you that next year we intend to keep it as a Double of the First Class with Octave *which*, of course, it *is*. This rosary is made of olive-wood from the Garden of Gethsemane and I'm very anxious to get it blessed by the Pope. Some friends of mine are going to Rome next Easter with a Polytechnic tour, so I *may* be able to manage it. But it's difficult. The Cardinals—you know," said Mr. Prout vaguely. "They're inclined to be bitter against English Catholics. Of course, Vaughan made the mistake of his life in getting the Pope to pronounce against English Orders. I know a Roman priest told me he considered it a fatal move. However—you're waiting for your tea?"

Michael ate Mr. Prout's bread-and-butter and drank his tea, while the host hopped from trinket to trinket.

"This is a sacred amulet which belonged to one of the Macdonalds who fought at Prestonpans. I suppose you're a Jacobite? Of course, I belong to all the Legitimist Societies—the White Rose, the White Cockade, the White Carnation. Everyone. I wish I were a Scotchman, although my grandmother was a Miss Macmillan, so I've got Scotch blood. You *are* a Jacobite, aren't you?"

"Rather," said Michael as enthusiastically as his full mouth would allow him to declare.

"Of course, it's the only logical political attitude for an English Catholic to adopt," said Mr. Prout. "All this Erastianism—you know. Terrible. What's the Privy Council got to do with Vestments? Still the Episcopal appointments haven't been so bad lately. That's Lord Salisbury. Of course, we've had trouble with our Bishop. Oh, yes. He simply declines to listen to reason on the subject of Reservation for the Sick. Personally I advised Father Moneypenny not to pay any attention to him. I said the Guild of St. Wilfrid—that's our servers' guild, you know—was absolutely in favour of defiance, open defiance. But one of the churchwardens got round him. There's your Established Church. Money's what churchwardens think of—simply money. And has religion got anything to do with money? Nothing. 'Blessed are the poor.' You can't go against that, as I told Major Wilton—that's our people's warden—in the sacristy. He's a client of ours at the Bank, or I should have said a jolly sight more. I should have told him that in my opinion his attitude was simony—rank simony, and let it go at that. But I couldn't very well, and, of course, it doesn't look well for the Ceremonarius and the churchwarden to be bickering after Mass. By the way, will you help us next Sunday?"

"I'd like to," said Michael, "but I don't know anything about it."

"There'll be a rehearsal," said Mr. Prout. "And it's perfectly simple. You elevate your torch first of all at the Sanctus and then at the Consecration. And now, if you've finished your tea, I'll show you my oratory. Of course, you'll understand that I'm only in rooms here, but the landlady is a very pleasant woman. She let me plant that passion-flower in the garden. Perhaps you noticed it? The same with this oratory. It *was* a housemaid's cupboard, but it was very inconvenient—and there isn't a housemaid as a matter of fact—so I secured it. Come along."

Mr. Prout led the way on to the landing, at the end of which were two doors.

"We can't both kneel down, unless the door's open," said Mr. Prout. "But when I'm alone, I can *just* shut myself in."

He opened the oratory door as he spoke, and Michael was impressed by the appearance of it. The small window had been covered with a rice-paper design of Jesse's Rod.

"It's a bit 'Protty,'" whispered Mr. Prout. "But I thought it was better than plain squares of blue and red."

"Much better," Michael agreed.

A ledge nailed beneath the window supported two brass candlesticks and a crucifix. The reredos was an Arundel print of the Last Supper and on corner brackets on either side were statues of the Immaculate Conception and Our Lady of Victories. A miniature thurible hung on a nail and on another nail was a holy-water stoup which Michael at first thought was intended for soap. In front of the altar was a prie-dieu stacked with books of devotion. There were also blessed palms, very dusty, and a small sanctuary lamp suspended from the ceiling. Referring to this, Mr. Prout explained that really it came from the Turkish Exhibition at Earl's Court, but that he thought it would do as he had carefully exorcized it according to the use of Sarum.

"Shall we say Vespers?" suggested Mr. Prout. "You know—the Small Office of the Blessed Virgin. It won't take long. We can say Compline *too*, if you like."

"Just as you like," said Michael.

"You're sure you don't mind the door being left open? Because, you see, we can't both get in otherwise. In fact, I have to kneel sideways when I'm alone."

"Won't your landlady think it rather rum?" Michael asked.

"Good gracious, no. Why, when we have Vespers of St. Charles the Martyr, I have fellows kneeling all the way down the stairs, you know—members of the White Rose League. Bournemouth and South of England Branch."

Michael was handed a thin sky-blue book labelled *Office of the B.V.M.*

"Latin or English?" queried Mr. Prout.

"Whichever you like," said Michael.

"Well, Latin, if you don't mind. I'm anxious to learn Latin, and I find this is good practice."

"It doesn't look very good Latin," said Michael doubtfully.

"Doesn't it?" said Mr. Prout. "It ought to. It's the right version."

"I expect this is Hellenistic—I mean Romanistic—Latin," said Michael, who was proud of his momentary superiority in knowledge. "Greek Test is Hellenistic Greek."

"Do you know Greek?" asked Mr. Prout.

"A little."

Mr. Prout sighed.

When the Office was concluded, Michael promised he would attend a rehearsal of next Sunday's ceremony and, if he felt at ease, the Solemn High Mass itself. Mr. Prout, before Michael went away, lent him a book called Ritual Reason Why, and advised him to buy The Catholic Religion at One Shilling, and meanwhile to practise direct Invocation of the Saints.

At home Michael applied himself with ardour to the mastery of his religion. He wrestled with the liturgical colours; he tried to grasp the difference between Transubstantiation, Consubstantiation and the Real Presence; and he congratulated himself upon being under the immediate patronage of an Archangel. Also with Charles as his first name he felt he could fairly claim the protection of St. Charles the Martyr, though later on Mr. Prout suggested St. Charles Borromeo as a less ordinary patron. However, there was more than ritualism in Michael's new attitude, more than the passion to collect new rites and liturgies and ornaments as once he had collected the portraits of famous cricketers or silkworms or silver-paper. To be sure, it soon came to seem to him a terribly important matter whether according to the Roman sequence red were worn at Whitsuntide or whether according to Old English use white were the liturgical colour. Soon he would experience a shock of dismay on hearing that some reputed Catholic had taken the Ablutions at the wrong moment, just as once he had been irritated by ignorant people confusing Mr. W. W. Read of Surrey with Read (M.) of the same county. Beyond all this Michael sincerely tried to correct his morals and manners in the light of aspiration and faith. He experienced a revolt against impurity of any kind and was simultaneously seized with a determination to suffer Stella's conceit gladly. He really felt a deep-seated avarice for being good. He may not have distinguished between morality due to emotion and morality wrung out of intellectual assent: but he did know that the Magnificat's incense took him to a higher elation than Dora's curly head upon his shoulder, or even than Alan's bewitching company. Under the influence of faith, Michael found himself bursting with an affection for his mother such as he had not felt for a long time. Indeed Michael was in a state of love. He loved the candles on the altar, he loved his mother's beauty, he loved Stella, he loved the people on the beach and the August mornings and the zest for acquiring and devouring information upon every detail connected with the Catholic religion; and out of his love he gratified Mr. Prout by consenting to bear a torch at the Solemn High Mass on the Sunday within the octave of St. Bartholomew, Apostle and Martyr and Patron of St. Bartholomew's Church, Bournemouth.

Michael's first High Mass was an emotional experience deeper even than that windy Evensong. The church was full of people. The altar was brilliant with flowers and lights. The sacristy was crowded with boys in scarlet cassocks and slippers and zuchettos, quarrelling about their cottas and arguing about their heights. Everybody had a favourite banner which he wanted to escort and, to complicate matters still further, everybody had a favourite companion by whose side he wished to walk.

The procession was marshalled before the altar: the organ boomed through the church: the first thurifer started off, swinging his censer towards the clouded roof. After him went the cross of ebony and silver, while one by one at regular intervals between detachments of the choir the banners of the saints floated into action. Michael escorted the blue velvet banner of Our Lady, triumphant, crowned, a crescent moon beneath her feet and round about her stars and Cherubim. The procession was long enough to fill two aisles at once, and as Michael turned up the south aisle on the return to the chancel, he saw the pomp of the procession's rear—the second thurifer, Mr. Prout in a cotta bordered by lace two feet deep, the golden crucifix aloft, the acolytes with their golden candlesticks, the blood-red dalmatic and tunicle of the deacon and sub-deacon, and solemnly last of all the blood-red cope of the celebrant. Michael took no pleasure in being observed by the congregation; he was simply elated by the privilege of being able to express his desire to serve God, and during the Mass, when the Sanctus bell chimed forth, he raised his torch naturally to the pæan of the salutation. The service was long: the music was elaborate: it was back-breaking work to kneel on the chancel steps without support; but Michael welcomed the pain with pleasure. During the Elevation of the Host, as he bowed his head before the wonder of bread and wine made God, his brain reeled in an ecstasy of sublime worship. There was a silence save for the censer tinkling steadily and the low whispered words of the priest and the click of the broken wafer. The candles burned with a supernatural intensity: the boys who lately quarrelled over precedence were hushed as angels: the stillness became fearful; the cold steps burned into Michael's knees and the incense choked him. At last after an age of adoration, the plangent appeal of the Agnus Dei came with a melody that seemed the music of the sobbing world from which all tears had departed in a clarity of harmonious sound.

Before Michael left Bournemouth, Mr. Prout promised to come and see him in London, and Mr. Moneypenny said he would write to a priest who would be glad to prepare him for Confirmation. When Michael reached school again, he felt shy at meeting Alan who would talk about nothing but football and was dismayed to find Michael indifferent to the delights of playing three-quarter on Middle Side. Michael deplored Alan's failure to advance intellectually beyond mere football and the two of them temporarily lost touch with each other's ambitions. Michael now read nothing but ecclesiastical books and was greatly insulted by Mr. Viner's elementary questions. Mr. Viner was the priest to whom Mr. Moneypenny had written about Michael. He had invited him to tea and together they had settled that Michael should be confirmed early in the spring. Michael borrowed half a dozen books from Mr. Viner and returned home to make an attempt to convert the cook and the housemaid to the Catholic faith as a preliminary to converting his mother and Alan. In the end he did actually convert a boy in the Lower Fifth who for his strange beliefs suffered severely at the hands of his father, a Plymouth Brother. Michael wished that Stella had not gone back to Germany, for he felt that in her he would have had a splendid object on whom to practise his power of controversy. At Mr. Viner's house Michael met another Jacobean called Chator in whom he found a fellow-enthusiast. Chator knew of two other Jacobeans interested in Church matters, Martindale and Rigg, and the four of them founded a society called De Rebus Ecclesiasticis which met every Friday evening in Michael's room to discuss the Catholic Church in all her aspects. The discussions were often heated because Michael had violently Ultra-montane leanings, Chator was narrowly Sarum, Martindale tried to preserve a happy mean and Rigg always agreed with the last speaker. The Society De Rebus Ecclesiasticis was splendidly quixotic and gloriously unrelated to the dead present. To the quartette of members Archbishop Laud was a far more more vital proposition than Archbishop Temple, the society of cavaliers was more vividly realized than the Fabian Society. As was to be expected from Michael's preoccupation with the past, he became very anxious again about his parentage. He longed to hear that in some way he was connected with Jacobite heroes and the romantic Stuarts. Mrs. Fane was no longer able to put him off with contradictions and vagueness: Michael demanded his family tree. The hymn 'Faith of our Fathers' ringing through a Notting Dale mission-hall moved him to demand his birthright of family history.

"Well, I'll tell you, Michael," said his mother at last. "Your father ought to have been the Earl of Saxby—only—something went wrong—some certificate or something."

"An Earl?" cried Michael, staggered by the splendid news. "But—but, mother, we met Lord Saxby. Who was that?"

"He's a relation. Only, please don't tell people about this, because they wouldn't understand. It's all very muddled and difficult."

"My father ought to have been Lord Saxby? Why wasn't he? Mother, was he illegitimate?"

"Michael, how can you talk like that? Of course not."

Michael blushed because his mother blushed.

"I'm sorry, mother, I thought he might have been. People are. You read about them often enough."

Michael decided that as he must not tell Chator, Martindale and Rigg the truth, he would, at any rate, join himself on to the House of Saxby collaterally. To his disappointment, he discovered that the only reference in history to an Earl of Saxby made out that particular one to be a most pestilent Roundhead. So Michael gave up being the Legitimist Earl of Saxby, and settled instead to be descended through the indiscretion of an early king from the Stuarts. Michael grew more and more ecclesiastical as time went on. He joined several Jacobite societies, and accompanied Mr. Prout on the latter's London visit to a reception at Clifford's Inn Hall in honour of the Legitimist Emperor of Byzantium. Michael was very much impressed by kissing the hand of an Emperor, and even more deeply impressed by the Scottish piper who marched up and down during the light refreshment at one shilling a head afterwards. Mr. Prout, accompanied by Michael, Chator, Martindale and Rigg, spent the Sunday of his stay in town by attending early Mass in Kensington, High Mass in Holborn, Benediction in Shoreditch and Evensong in Paddington. He also joined several more guilds, confraternities and societies and presented Michael with one hair from the five hairs he possessed of a lock of Prince Charlie's hair (authentic) before he returned to Bournemouth. This single hair was a great responsibility to Michael, until he placed it in a silver locket to wear round his neck. During that year occurred what the papers called a Crisis in the Church, and Michael and his three friends took in every week The Church Times, The Church Review, The English Churchman, Church Bells, The Record and The Rock in order to play their part in the crisis. They attended Protestant meetings to boo and hiss from the gallery or to applaud violently gentlemen on their side who rose to ask the lecturer what they supposed to be irrefutable questions. In the spring Michael made his first Confession and was confirmed. The first Confession had more effect on his imagination than the Confirmation, which in retrospect seemed chiefly a sensation of disappointment that the Bishop in view of the crisis in the Church refused to wear the mitre temptingly laid out for him by Mr. Viner. The Confession, however, was a true test of Michael's depth. Mr. Viner was by no means a priest who only thought of candles and lace. He was a gaunt and humorous man, ready to drag out from his penitents their very souls.

64

Michael found that first Confession an immense strain upon his truthfulness and pluck, and he made up his mind never to commit another mortal sin, so deeply did he blush in the agony of revelation. Venial faults viewed in the aggregate became appalling, and the real sins, as one by one Michael compelled himself to admit them, stabbed his self-consciousness with daggers of shame. Michael had a sense of completeness which prevented him from making a bad Confession, from gliding over his sins and telling half-truths, and having embarked upon the duties of his religion he was not going to avoid them. The Confession seemed to last for ever. Beforehand, Michael had supposed there would be only one commandment whose detailed sins would make his heart beat with the difficulty of confessing them; but when he knelt in the empty church before the severe priest, every breach of the other commandments assumed a demoniac importance. Michael thought that never before could Father Viner have listened to such a narration of human depravity from a boy of fifteen, or even from a man full grown. He half expected to see the priest rise in the middle and leave his chair in disgust. Michael felt beads of sweat trickling from his forehead: the strain grew more terrible: the crucifix before him gave him no help: the book he held fell from his fingers. Then he heard the words of absolution, tranquil as evening bells. The inessentials of his passionate religion faded away in the strength and beauty of God's acceptation of his penitence. Outside in the April sunlight Michael could have danced his exultation, before he ran home winged with the ecstasy of a light heart.

Chapter VI: *Pax*

THE Lower Fifth only knew Michael during the Autumn term. After Christmas he moved up to the Middle Fifth, and, leaving behind him. many friends, including Alan, he found himself in an industrious society concentrated upon obtaining the Oxford and Cambridge Higher Certificate for proficiency in Greek, Latin, Mathematics and either Divinity, French or History. Removed from the temptations of a merry company, Michael worked very hard indeed and kept his brain fit by argument instead of football. The prevailing attitude of himself and his contemporaries towards the present was one of profound pessimism. The scholarship of St. James' was deteriorating; there was a dearth of great English poets; novelists were not so good as once they were in the days of Dickens; the new boys were obviously inferior to their prototypes in the past; the weather was growing worse year by year; the country was plunging into an abyss. In school Michael prophesied more loudly than any of his fellow Jeremiahs, and less and less did it seem worth while in these Certificate-stifled days to seek for romance or poetry or heroism or adventure. Yet as soon as the precincts of discipline and study were left behind, Michael could extract from life full draughts of all these virtues.

Without neglecting the Oxford and Cambridge Higher Certificate he devoured voraciously every scrap of information about Catholicism which it was possible to acquire. Books were bought in tawdry repositories—Catholic Belief, The Credentials of the Catholic Church, The Garden of the Soul, The Glories of Mary by S. Alphonso Liguori, Alban Butler's Lives of the Saints, The Clifton Tracts, and on his own side of the eternal controversy, Lee's Validity of English Orders, The Alcuin Club Transactions with many other volumes. Most of all he liked to pore upon the Tourist's Church Guide, which showed with asterisks and paragraph marks and sections and daggers what churches throughout the United Kingdom possessed the five points of Incense, Lights, Vestments, Mixed Chalice and Eastward Position. He found it absorbing to compare the progress of ritual through the years.

Michael, as once he had known the ranks of the British Army from Lance-corporal to Field Marshal, could tell the hierarchy from Sexton to Pope. He knew too, as once he knew the history and uniform of Dragoons, Hussars and Lancers, the history and uniform of the religious orders—Benedictines, Cistercians, Franciscans, Dominicans (how he loved the last in their black and white habit, *Domini canes*, watchdogs of the Lord), Carmelites, Præmonstratensians, Augustinians, Servites, Gilbertines, Carthusians, Redemptorists, Capuchins, Passionists, Jesuits, Oblates of St. Charles Borromeo and the Congregation of St. Philip Neri. Michael outvied Mr. Prout in ecclesiastical possessions, and his bedroom was nearly as full as the repository from which it was stocked. There were images of St. Michael (his own patron), St. Hugh of Lincoln (patron of schoolboys) and St. James of Compostella (patron of the school), together with Our Lady of Seven Dolours, Our Lady Star of the Sea and Our Lady of Lourdes, Our Lady of Perpetual Succour, Our Lady of Victories; there were eikons, scapulars, crucifixes, candlesticks, the Holy Child of Prague, rosaries, and indeed every variety of sacred bric-à-brac. Michael slept in an oriental atmosphere, because he had formed the habit of burning during his prayers cone-shaped pastilles in a saucer. The tenuous spiral of perfumed smoke carried up his emotional apostrophes through the prosaic ceiling of the old night-nursery past the stars, beyond the Thrones and Dominations and Seraphim to God. Michael's contest with the sins of youth had become much more thrilling since he had accepted the existence of a personal fiend, and in an ecstasy of temptation he would lie in bed and defy the Devil, calling upon his patron the Archangel to descend from heaven and battle with the powers of evil in that airy arena above the coal-wharf beyond the railway lines. But the Father of Lies had many tricks with which to circumvent Michael; he would conjure up sensuous images before his antagonist; succubi materialized as pretty housemaids, feminine devils put on tights and openwork stockings to encounter him from the pages of pink weekly papers, and sometimes Satan himself would sit at the foot of his bed in the darkness and tell him tales of how other boys enjoyed themselves, arguing that it was a pity to waste his opportunities and filling his thoughts with dissolute memories. Michael would leap from his bed and pray before his crucifix, and through the darkness angels and saints would rally to his aid, until Satan slunk off with his tail between his legs, personally humiliated.

At school the fever of the examination made Michael desperate with the best intentions. He almost learned the translations of Thucydides and Sophocles, of Horace and Cicero. He knew by heart a meanly written Roman History, and no passage in Corneille could hold an invincible word. Cricket was never played that summer by the Middle Fifth; it was more useful to wander in corners of the field, murmuring continually the tables of the Kings of Judah from Maclear's sad-hued abstract of Holy Scripture. In the end Michael passed in Greek and Latin, in French and Divinity and Roman History, even in Algebra and Euclid, but the arithmetical problems of a Stockbroker, a Paper-hanger and a Housewife made all the rest of his knowledge of no account, and Michael failed to see beside his name in the school list that printed bubble which would refer him to the tribe of those who had satisfied the examiners for the Oxford and Cambridge Higher Certificate. This failure depressed Michael, not because he felt implicated in any disgrace, but because he wished very earnestly that he had not wasted so many hours of fine weather in work. He made up his mind that the mistake should never be repeated, and for the rest of his time at St. James' he resisted all set books. If Demosthenes was held necessary, Michael would read Plato, and when Cicero was set, Michael would feel bound to read Livy.

Michael looked back on the year with dissatisfaction, and wondered if school was going to become more and more boring each new term for nine more terms. The prospect was unendurably grey, and Michael felt that life was not worth living. He talked over with Mr. Viner the flatness of existence on the evening after the result of the examination was known.

"I swotted like anything," said Michael gloomily. "And what's the good? I'm sick of everything."

The priest's eyes twinkled, as he plunged deeper into his wicker arm-chair and puffed clouds of smoke towards the comfortable shelves of books.

"You want a holiday," he remarked.

"A holiday?" echoed Michael fretfully. "What's the good of a holiday with my mater at some beastly seaside place?"

"Oh, come," said the priest, smiling. "You'll be able to probe the orthodoxy of the neighbouring clergy."

"Oh, no really, it's nothing to laugh at, Mr. Viner. You've no idea how beastly it is to dawdle about in a crowd of people, and then at the end go back to another term of school. I'm sick of everything. Will you lend me Lee's Dictionary of Ecclesiastical Terms?" added Michael in a voice that contained no accent of hope.

"I'll lend you anything you like, my dear boy," said the priest, "on one condition."

"What's that?"

"Why, that you'll admit life holds a few grains of consolation."

"But it doesn't," Michael declared.

"Wait a bit, I haven't finished. I was going to say—when I tell you that we are going to keep the Assumption this August."

Michael's eyes glittered for a moment with triumph.

"By Jove, how decent." Then they grew dull again. "And I shan't be here. The rotten thing is, too, that my mater wants to go abroad. Only she says she couldn't leave me alone. But of course she could really."

"Why not stay with a friend—the voluble Chator, for instance, or Martindale, that Solomon of schoolboys, or Rigg who in Medicean days would have been already a cardinal, so admirably does he incline to all parties?"

"I can't ask myself," said Michael. "Their people would think it rum. Besides, Chator's governor has gout, and I wouldn't care to be six weeks with the other two. Oh, I do hate not being grown up."

"What about your friend Alan Merivale? I thought him a very charming youth and refreshingly unpietistic."

"He doesn't know the difference between a chasuble and a black gown," said Michael.

"Which seems to me not to matter very much ultimately," put in Mr. Viner.

"No, of course it doesn't. But if one is keen on something and somebody else isn't, it isn't much fun," Michael explained. "Besides, he can't make me out nowadays."

"Surely the incomprehensible is one of the chief charms of faith and friendship."

"And anyway he's going abroad to Switzerland—and I couldn't possibly fish for an invitation. It is rotten. Everything's always the same."

"Except in the Church of England. There you have an almost blatant variety," suggested the priest.

"You never will be serious when I want you to be," grumbled Michael.

"Oh, yes I will, and to prove it," said Mr. Viner, "I'm going to make a suggestion of unparagoned earnestness."

"What?"

"Now just let me diagnose your mental condition. You are sick of everything—Thucydides, cabbage, cricket, school, schoolfellows, certificates and life."

"Well, you needn't rag me about it," Michael interrupted.

"In the Middle Ages gentlemen in your psychical perplexity betook themselves either to the Crusades or entered a monastery. Now, why shouldn't you for these summer holidays betake yourself to a monastery? I will write to the Lord Abbot, to your lady mother, and if you consent, to the voluble Chator's lady mother, humbly pointing out and ever praying, etc., etc."

"You're not ragging?" asked Michael suspiciously. "Besides, what sort of a monastery?"

"Oh, an Anglican monastery; but at the same time Benedictines of the most unimpeachable severity. In short, why shouldn't you and Mark Chator go to Clere Abbas on the Berkshire Downs?"

"Are they strict?" enquired Michael. "You know, saying the proper offices and all that, not the Day Hours of the English Church—that rotten Anglican thing."

"Strict!" cried Mr. Viner. "Why, they're so strict that St. Benedict himself, were he to abide again on earth, would seriously consider a revision of his rules as interpreted by Dom Cuthbert Manners, O.S.B., the Lord Abbot of Clere."

"It would be awfully ripping to go there," said Michael enthusiastically.

"Well then," said Mr. Viner, "it shall be arranged. Meanwhile confer with the voluble and sacerdotal Chator on the subject."

The disappointment of the ungranted certificate, the ineffable tedium of endless school, seaside lodgings and all the weighty ills of Michael's oppressed soul vanished on that wine-gold July noon when Michael and Chator stood untrammelled by anything more than bicycles and luggage upon the platform of the little station that dreamed its trains away at the foot of the Downs.

"By Jove, we're just like pilgrims," said Michael, as his gaze followed the aspiring white road which rippled upward to green summits quivering in the haze of summer. The two boys left their luggage to be fetched later by the Abbey marketing-cart, mounted their bicycles, waved a good-bye to the friendly porter beaming among the red roses of the little station and pressed energetically their obstinate pedals. After about half a mile's ascent they jumped from their machines and walked slowly upwards until the station and clustering hamlet lay breathless below them like a vision drowned deep in a crystal lake. As they went higher a breeze sighed in the sun-parched grasses, and the lines and curves of the road intoxicated them with naked beauty.

"I like harebells almost best of any flowers," said Michael. "Do you?"

"They're awfully like bells," observed Chator.

"I wouldn't care if they weren't," said Michael. "It's only in London I want things to be like other things."

Chator looked puzzled.

"I can't exactly explain what I mean," Michael went on.

"But they make me want to cry just because they aren't like anything. You won't understand what I mean if I explain ever so much. Nobody could. But when I see flowers on a lovely road like this, I get sort of frightened whether God won't grow tired of bothering about human beings. Because really, you know, Chator, there doesn't seem much good in our being on the earth at all."

"I think that's a heresy," pronounced Chator. "I don't know which one, but I'll ask Dom Cuthbert."

"I don't care if it is heresy. I believe it. Besides, religion must be finding out things for yourself that have been found out already."

"Finding out for yourself," echoed Chator with a look of alarm. "I say, you're an absolute Protestant."

"Oh, no I'm not," contradicted Michael. "I'm a Catholic."

"But you set yourself up above the Church."

"When did I?" demanded Michael.

"Just now."

"Because I said that harebells were ripping flowers?"

"You said a lot more than that," objected Chator.

"What did I say?" Michael parried.

"Well, I can't exactly remember what you said."

"Then what's the use of saying I'm a Protestant?" cried Michael in triumph. "I think I'll play footer again next term," he added inconsequently.

"I jolly well would," Chator agreed. "You ought to have played last football term."

"Except that I like thinking," said Michael. "Which is rotten in the middle of a game. It's jolly decent going to the monastery, isn't it? I could keep walking on this road for ever without getting tired."

"We can ride again now," said Chator.

"Well, don't scorch, because we'll miss all the decent flowers if you do," said Michael.

Then silently for awhile they breasted the slighter incline of the summit.

"Only six weeks of these ripping holidays," Michael sighed. "And then damned old school again."

"Hark!" shouted Chator suddenly. "I hear the Angelus."

Both boys dismounted and listened. Somewhere, indeed, a bell was chiming, but a bell of such quality that the sound of it through the summer was like a cuckoo's song in its unrelation to place. Michael and Chator murmured their salute of the Incarnation, and perhaps for the first time Michael half realized the mysterious condescension of God. Here, high up on these downs, the Word became imaginable, a silence of wind and sunlight.

"I say, Chator," Michael began.

"What?"

"Would you mind helping me mark this place where we are?"

"Why?"

"Look here, you won't think I'm pretending? but I believe I was converted at that moment."

Chator's well-known look of alarm that always followed one of Michael's doctrinal or liturgical announcements was more profound than it had ever been before.

"Converted?" he gasped. "What to?"

"Oh, not *to* anything," said Michael. "Only different from what I was just now, and I want to mark the place."

"Do you mean—put up a cross or something?"

"No, not a cross. Because, when I was converted, I felt a sudden feeling of being frightfully alive. I'd rather put a stone and plant harebells round it. We can dig with our spanners. I like stones. They're so frightfully old, and I'd like to think, if I was ever a long way from here, of my stone and the harebells looking at it—every year new harebells and the same old stone."

"Do you know what I think you are?" enquired Chator solemnly. "I think you're a mystic."

"I never can understand what a mystic was," said Michael.

"Nobody can," said Chator encouragingly. "But lots of them were made saints all the same. I don't think you ever will be, because you do put forward the most awfully dangerous doctrines. I do think you ought to be careful about that. I do really."

Chator was spluttering under the embarrassment of his own eloquence, and Michael, delicately amused, looked at him with a quizzical smile. Chator was older than Michael, and by reason of the apoplectic earnestness of his appearance and manner, and the natural goodness of him so sincerely, if awkwardly expressed, he had a certain influence which Michael admitted to himself, however much in the public eye he might affect to patronize Chator from his own intellectual eminence. Along the road of speculation, however, Michael would not allow

Chator's right to curb him, and he took a wilful pleasure in galloping ahead over the wildest, loftiest paths. To shock old Chator was Michael's delight; and he never failed to do so.

"You see," Chator spluttered, "it's not so much what you say now; nobody would pay any attention to you, and I know you don't mean half what you say; but later on you'll begin to believe in all these heretical ideas of your own. You'll end up by being an Agnostic. Oh, yes you will," he raged with torrential prophecies, as Michael leaned over the seat of his bicycle laughing consumedly. "You'll go on and on wondering this and that and improving the doctrines of the Church until you improve them right away."

"You are a funny old ass. You really are," gurgled Michael. "And what's so funny to me is that just when I had a moment of really believing you dash in with your warnings and nearly spoil it all. By Jove, did you see that Pale Clouded Yellow?" he shouted suddenly. "By Jove, I haven't seen one in England for an awful long time. I think I'll begin collecting butterflies again."

Disputes of doctrine were flung to the wind that sang in their ears as they mounted their bicycles and coasted swiftly from the bare green summits of the downs into a deep lane overshadowed by oak-trees. Soon they came to the Abbey gates, or rather to the place where the Abbey gates would one day rise in Gothic commemoration of the slow subscriptions of the faithful. At present the entrance was only marked by a stony road disappearing abruptly at the behest of a painted finger-post into verdurous solitudes. After wheeling their bicycles for about a quarter of a winding mile, the two boys came to a large open space in the wood and beheld Clere Abbey, a long low wooden building set as piously near to the overgrown foundations of old Clere Abbey as was possible.

"What a rotten shame," cried Michael, "that they can't build a decent Abbey. Never mind, I think it's going to be rather good sport here."

They walked up to the door that seemed too massive for the flimsy pile to which it gave entrance, and pealed the large bell that hung by the side. Michael was pleased to observe a grille through which peered the eyes of the monastic porter, inquisitive of the wayfarers. Then a bolt shot back, the door opened, and Michael and Chator entered the religious house.

"I'm Brother Ambrose," said the porter, a stubby man with a flat pock-marked face whose ugliness was redeemed by an expression of wonderful innocence. "Dom Cuthbert is expecting you in the Abbot's Parlour."

Michael and Chator followed Brother Ambrose through a pleasant book-lined hall into the paternal haunt where the Lord Abbot of Clere sat writing at a roll-top desk. He rose to greet the boys, who with reverence perceived him to be a tall dark angular man with glowing eyes that seemed very deeply set on either side of his great hooked nose. He could scarcely have been over thirty-five years of age, but he moved with a languid awkwardness that made him seem older. His voice was very remote and melodious as he welcomed them. Michael looked anxiously at Chator to see if he followed any precise ritual of salutation, but Dom Cuthbert solved the problem by shaking hands at once and motioning them to wicker chairs beside the empty hearth.

"Pleasant ride?" enquired Dom Cuthbert.

"Awfully decent," said Michael. "We heard the Angelus a long way off."

"A lovely bell," murmured Dom Cuthbert. "Tubular. It was given to us by the Duke of Birmingham. Come along, I'll show you the Abbey, if you're not too tired."

"Rather not," Michael and Chator declared.

The Abbot led the way into the book-lined hall.

"This is the library. You can read here as much as you like. The brethren sit here at recreation-time. This is the refectory," he went on, with distant chimings in his tone.

The two boys gazed respectfully at the bare trestle table and the raised reading-desk and the picture of St. Benedict.

"Of course we haven't much room yet," Dom Cuthbert continued. "In fact we have very little. People are very suspicious of monkery."

He smiled tolerantly, and his voice faded almost out of the refectory, as if it would soothe the harsh criticism of the world, hence infinitely remote.

"But one day"—from worldly adventure his voice came back renewed with hope—"one day, when we have some money, we shall build a real Abbey."

"This is awfully ripping though, isn't it?" observed Michael with sympathetic encouragement.

"I dare say the founder of the Order was never so well housed," agreed the Abbot.

Dom Cuthbert led them to the guest-chamber, from which opened three diminutive bedrooms.

"Your cells," the monk said. "But of course you'll feed in here," he added, indicating the small bare room in which they stood with so wide a sweep of his ample sleeve that the matchboarded ceiling soared into vast Gothic twilights and the walls were of stone. Michael was vaguely reminded of Mr. Prout and his inadequate oratory.

"The guest-brother is Dom Gilbert," continued the Abbot. "Come and see the cloisters."

They passed from the guest-room behind the main building and saw that another building formed there the second side of a quadrangle. The other two sides were still open to the hazel coppice that here encroached upon the Abbey. However, there was traceable the foundations of new buildings to complete the quadrangle, and a mass of crimson hollyhocks were shining with rubied chalices in the quiet sunlight. For all its incompleteness, this was a strangely beautiful corner of the green world.

"Are these the cloisters?" Michael asked.

"One day, one day," replied Dom Cuthbert. "A little rough at present, but before I die I'm sure there will be a mighty edifice in this wood to the glory of God and His saints."

"I'd like it best that way," said Michael. "Not all at once."

He felt an imaginative companionship with the aspirations of the Abbot.

"Now we'll visit the Chapel," said Dom Cuthbert. "We built the Chapel with our own hands of mud and stone and laths. You'll like the Chapel. Sometimes I feel quite sorry to think of leaving it for the great Abbey Church we shall one day build with the hands of workmen."

The Chapel was reached by a short cloister of primitive construction, and it was the simplest purest place of worship that Michael had ever seen. It seemed to have gathered beneath its small roof the whole of peace. On one side the hazel bushes grew so close that the windows opened on to the mysterious green heart of life. Two curtains worked with golden blazonries divided the quire from the congregation.

"This is where you'll sit," said Dom Cuthbert, pointing to two kneeling-chairs on either side of the opening into the quire. "Perhaps you'll say a prayer now for the Order. The prayers of children travel very swiftly to God."

Dom Cuthbert passed to the Abbot's stall to kneel, while Michael and Chator knelt on the chairs. When they had prayed for awhile, the Abbot took them into the sacristy and showed them the vestments and the sacred vessels of the altar, and from the sacristy door they passed into a straight woodland way.

"The Abbot's walk," said Dom Cuthbert, with a beautiful smile. "The brethren cut this wonderful path during their hours of recreation. I cannot envy any cloisters with this to walk in. How soft is the moss beneath our feet, and in Spring how loudly the birds sing here. The leaves come very early, too, and linger very late. It is a wonderful path. Now I must go and work. I have a lot of letters to write. Explore the woods and the downs and enjoy yourselves. You'll find the rules that the guests must observe pinned to the wall of the guest-room. Enjoy yourselves and be content."

The tall figure of the monk with its languid awkwardness of gait disappeared from the Abbot's walk, and the two boys, arm-in-arm, wandered off in the opposite direction.

"Everything was absolutely correct," burbled Chator. "Oh, yes, absolutely. Not at all Anglican. Perfectly correct. I'm glad. I'm really very glad. I was a bit afraid at first it might be Anglican. But it's not—oh, no, not at all."

In the guest-chamber they read the rules for guests, and discovered to their mortification that they were not expected to be present at Matins and Lauds.

"I was looking forward to getting up at two o'clock," said Michael. "Perhaps Dom Cuthbert will let us sometimes. It's really much easier to get up at two o'clock than five. Mass is at half-past five, and we must go to that."

Dom Gilbert, the guest-brother, came in with plates of bread and cheese while the boys were reading the rules, and they questioned him about going to Matins. He laughed and said they would have as much church as they wished without being quite such strict Benedictines as that. Michael was not sure whether he liked Dom Gilbert—he was such a very practical monk.

"If you go to Mass and Vespers and Compline every day," said Dom Gilbert, "you'll do very well. And please be punctual for your meals."

Michael and Chator looked injured.

"Breakfast after Mass. Bread and cheese at twelve. Cup of tea at five, if you're in. Supper at eight."

Dom Gilbert left them abruptly to eat their bread and cheese alone.

"He's rather a surly chap," grumbled Michael. "He doesn't seem to me the right one to have chosen for guest-brother at all. I had a lot I wanted to ask him. For one thing I don't know where the lav. is. I think he's a rotten guest-brother."

The afternoon passed in a walk along the wide ridge of the downs through the amber of this fine summer day. Several hares were seen and a kestrel, while Chator disposed very volubly of the claims of several Anglican clergymen to Catholicism. After tea in the hour of recreation they met the other monks, Dom Gregory the organist, Brother George and Brother William. It was not a very large monastery.

Chator found the Vespers somewhat trying to his curiosity, because owing to the interposition of the curtain he was unable to criticize the behaviour of the monks in quire. This made him very fidgety, and rather destroyed Michael's sense of peace. However, Chator restrained his ritualistic ardour very well at Compline, which in the dimness of the starlit night was a magical experience, as one by one with raised cowls the monks entered in black procession and silence absolute. Michael, where he knelt in the ante-chapel, was profoundly moved by the intimate responses and the severe Compline hymn. He liked, too, the swift departure to bed without chattering good-nights to spoil the solemnity of the last Office. Even Chator kept all conversation for the morning, and Michael felt he had never lain down upon a couch so truly sanctified, nor ever risen from one so pure as when Dom Gilbert knocked with a hammer on the door and, standing dark against the milk-white dawn, murmured 'Pax vobiscum.'

Chapter VII: *Cloven Hoofmarks*

IN the first fortnight of their stay at Clere Abbas Michael and Chator lived like vagabond hermits rejoicing in the freedom of fine weather. Mostly they went for long walks over the downs and through the woodlands of the southern slope. To the monks at recreation time they would recount their adventures with gamekeepers and contumacious farmers, their discoveries of flowers and birds and butterflies, their entertainment at remote cottage homes and the hospitalities of gipsy camps. To be sure they would often indulge in theological discussions, and sometimes, when caught by the azure-footed dusk in unfamiliar lanes, they would chant plainsong to the confusion of whatever ghostly pursuers, whether Dryads or mediæval fiends or early Victorian murderers, that seemed to dog their footsteps. So much nowadays did the unseen world mingle with the ordinary delights of youth.

"Funny thing," said Michael to Chator. "When I was a kid I used to be frightened at night—always. Then for a long time I wasn't frightened at all, and now again I have a queer feeling just after sunset, a sort of curious dampness inside me. Do you ever have it?"

"I only have it when you start me off," said Chator. "But it goes when we sing 'Te lucis ante terminum' or chant the Nicene Creed or anything holy."

"Yes, it goes with me," Michael agreed dubiously. "But if I drive it away it comes back in the middle of the night. I have all sorts of queer feelings. Sometimes I feel as if there wasn't any me at all, and I'm surprised to see a letter come addressed to me. But when I see a letter I've written, I'm still more surprised. Do you have that feeling? Then often I feel as if all we were doing or saying at a certain moment had been done or said before. Then at other times I have to hold on to a tree or hurt myself with something just to prove I'm there. And then sometimes I think nothing is impossible for me. I feel absolutely great, as if I were Shakespeare. Do you ever have that feeling?"

But Chator was either not sufficiently introspective so to resolve his moods, or else he was too simply set on his own naive religion for his personality to plunge haphazard into such spiritual currents uncharted.

The pleasantest time of the monastic week was Sunday afternoon, when Dom Cuthbert, very lank and pontifical, would lean back in the deepest wicker chair of the library to listen to various Thoughts culled by the brethren from their week's reading. The Thought he adjudged best was with a diamond pencil immortalized upon a window-pane, and the lucky discoverer derived as much satisfaction from the verdict as was compatible with Benedictine humility. Dom Cuthbert allowed Michael and Chator to share in these occasions, and he evidently enjoyed the variety of choice which displayed so nicely the characters of his flock.

One afternoon Michael chose for his excerpt Don Quixote's exclamation, "How these enchanters hate me, Sancho," with Sancho's reply, "O dismal and ill-minded enchanters."

The brethren laughed very loudly at this, for though they were English monks, and might have been considered eccentric by the Saxon world, their minds really ran on lines of sophisticated piety over platitudinous sleepers of thought. Michael blushed defiantly, and looked at Dom Cuthbert for comprehension.

"Hark at the idealist's complaint of disillusionment by the Prince of Darkness," said Dom Cuthbert, smiling.

"It's not a complaint," Michael contradicted. "It's just a remark. That's why I chose it. Besides, it gives me a satisfied feeling. Words often make me feel hungry."

The monks interrupted him with more laughter, and Michael, furiously self-conscious, left the library and went to sit alone in the stillest part of the hazel coppice.

But when he came back in the silent minutes before Vespers he read his sentence on the window-pane, and blinked half tearfully at the westering sun. He never had another Thought enshrined, because he was for ever after this trying to find sentences that would annoy Dom Gilbert, whom he suspected of leading the laughter. Visitors began to come to the Abbey now—and the two boys were much interested in the people who flitted past almost from day to day. Among them was Mr. Prout who kept up a duet of volubility with Chator from morning to night for nearly a week, at the end of which he returned to his Bournemouth bank. These discussions amused Michael most when he was able to break the rhythm of the battledores by knocking down whatever liturgical or theological shuttlecock was being used. He would put forward the most outrageous heresy as his own firm conviction, and scandalize and even alarm poor Mr. Prout, who did not at all relish dogmatic follow-my-leader and prayed for Michael's reckless soul almost as fervidly as for the confusion of the timid and malignant who annually objected to the forthcoming feast of the Assumption at St. Bartholomew's. Mr. Prout, however, was only one of a series of ritualistic young men who prattled continually of vestments and ceremonies and ornaments, until Michael began to resent their gossip and withdraw from their society into the woods, there to dream, staring up at the green and blue arch above him, of the past here in wind-stirred solitude so much the more real. Michael was a Catholic because Catholicism assured him of continuity and shrouded him with a sensuous austerity, but in these hours of revolt he found himself wishing for the old days with Alan. He was fond enough of Chator, but to Chator everything was so easy, and when one day a letter arrived to call him back to his family earlier than he expected, Michael was glad. The waning summer was stimulating his imagination with warm noons and gusty twilights; Chator's gossip broke the spell.

Michael went for solitary walks on the downs, where he loved to lie in hollows and watch the grasses fantastically large against the sky, and the bulky clouds with their slow bewitching motion. He never went to visit sentimentally the spot where stone and harebell commemorated his brief experience of faith's profundity, for he dreaded lest indifference should rob him of a perfect conception. He knew very well even already the dangerous chill familiarity of repetition. Those cloud-enchanted days of late summer made him listlessly aware of fleeting impulses, and simultaneously dignified with incommunicable richness the passivity and even emptiness of his condition. On the wide spaces of the downs he wandered luxuriously irresolute; his mind, when for a moment it goaded itself into an effort of concentration, faltered immediately, so that dead chivalries, gleaming down below in the rainy dusk of the valleys, suffered in the very instant of perception a transmutation into lamplit streets; and the wind's dull August booming made embattled drums and fanfares romantic no more than music heard in London on the way home from school. Everything came to seem impossible and intangible; Michael could not conceive that he ever was or ever would be in a class-room again, and almost immediately afterwards he would wonder whether he ever had been or ever would be anywhere else. He began to imagine himself grown up, but this was a nightmare thought, because he would either realize himself decrepit with his own young mind or outwardly the same as he was now with a mind hideously distorted by knowledge and sin. He could never achieve a consistent realization that would give him definite ambitions. He longed to make up his mind to aim at some profession, and the more he longed the more hopeless did it seem to try to fit any existing profession with the depressing idea of himself grown up. Then he would relax his whole being and let himself be once more bewitched into passivity by clouds and waving grasses.

Upon this mental state of Michael intruded one day a visitor to the Abbey. A young man with spectacles and a pear-shaped face, who wore grey flannel shirts that depressed Michael unendurably, made a determined effort to gain his confidence. The more shy that Michael became, the more earnestly did this young man press him with intimate questions about his physical well-being. For Michael it was a strange and odiously embarrassing experience. The young man, whose name was Garrod, spoke of his home in Hornsey and invited Michael to stay with him. Michael shuddered at the idea of staying in a strange suburb: strange suburbs had always seemed to him desolate, abominable and insecure. He always visualized a draughty and ill-lighted railway platform, a rickety and gloomy omnibus, countless Nonconformist chapels and infrequent policemen. Garrod spoke of his work on Sundays at a church that was daily gaining adherents, of a dissolute elder brother and an Agnostic father. Michael could have cried aloud his unwillingness to visit Garrod. But the young man was persistent; the young man was sure that Michael, from ignorance, was leading an unhealthy life. Garrod spoke of ignorance with ferocity: he trampled on it with polytechnic knowledge, and pelted it with all sorts of little books that afflicted Michael with nausea. Michael loathed Garrod, and resented his persistent instructions, his offers to solve lingering physical perplexities. For Michael Garrod defiled the country by his cockney complacency, his attacks upon public schools, his unpleasant interrogations. Michael longed for Alan that together they might rag this worm who wriggled so obscenely into the secret places of a boy's mind.

"Science is all the go nowadays," said Garrod. "And Science is what we want. Science and Religion. Some think they don't go together. Don't they? I think they do then."

"I hate science," said Michael. "Except for doctors, of course—I suppose they've got to have it," he added grudgingly. "At St. James' the Modern fellows are nearly always bounders."

"But don't you want to know what your body's made of?" demanded Garrod.

"I don't want to be told. I know quite enough for myself."

"Well, would you like to read——"

"No, I don't want to read anything," interrupted Michael.

"But have you read——"

"The only books I like," expostulated Michael, "are the books I find for myself."

"But you aren't properly educated."

"I'm at a public school," said Michael proudly.

"Yes, and public schools have got to go very soon."

"Who says so?" demanded Michael fiercely.

"We say so. The people."

"The people?" echoed Michael. "What people? Why, if public schools were done away with we shouldn't have any gentlemen."

"You're getting off of the point," said Garrod. "You don't understand what I'm driving at. You're a fellow I took a fancy to right off, as you might say. I don't want to see you ruin your health, for the want of the right word at the right moment. Oh, yes, I know."

"Look here," said Michael bluntly, "I don't want to be rude, but I don't want to talk about this any more. It makes me feel beastly."

"False modesty is the worst thing we've got to fight against," declared Garrod.

So the argument continued, while all the time the zealous young man would fling darts of information that however much Michael was unwilling to receive them generally stuck fast. Michael was relieved when Garrod passed on his way, and he vowed to himself never to run the risk of meeting him again.

The visit of Garrod opened for Michael a door to uneasy speculation. At his private school he had known the hostility of 'cads,' and later on he had been aware of the existence of 'bounders'; the cads were always easily defeated by force of arms, but this sudden attack upon his intimacy by a bounder was disquieting and difficult to deal with. He resented Garrod's iconoclasm, resented it furiously in retrospect, wishing that he had parried more icily his impudent thrusts; and he could almost have rejoiced in Garrod's reappearance that with disdain he might have wounded the fellow incurably. Yet he had a feeling that Garrod might have turned out proof against the worst weapons he knew how to use, and the memory of the 'blighter's' self-confidence was demoralizing to Michael's conception of superiority. The vision of a world populated by hostile Garrods rose up, and some of the simplicity of life vanished irredeemably, so that Michael took refuge in dreams of his own fashioning, where in a feudal world the dreamer rode at the head of mankind. Lying awake in the intense blackness of his cell, Michael troubled himself once more with his identity, wishing that he knew more about himself and his father, wishing that his mother were not growing more remote every day, wondering whether Stella over in Germany was encountering Garrods and praying hard with a sense of impotency in the darkness. He tried to make up his mind to consult Dom Cuthbert, but the lank, awkward monk, fond though he was of him, seemed unapproachable by daylight, and the idea of consulting him, still more of confessing to him, never crystallized.

These were still days bedewed with the approach of Autumn; milkwhite at morn and at noon breathless with a silver intensity that yearned upwards against an azure too ethereal, they floated sadly into night with humid, intangible draperies of mist. These were days that forbade Michael to walk afield, and that with haunting, autumnal birdsong held him in a trance. He would find himself at the day's end conscious of nothing but a remembrance of new stubble trodden mechanically with languors attendant, and it was only by a great effort that he brought himself to converse with the monks working among the harvest or for the Nativity of the Blessed Virgin to pick heavy white chrysanthemums from the stony garden of the Abbey.

Michael was the only guest staying in the Abbey on the vigil, and he sat almost in the entrance of the quire between the drawn curtains, not very much unlike the devout figure of some youthful donor in an old Italian picture, sombre against the blazing Vespers beyond. Michael was always hoping for a direct manifestation from above to reward the effort of faith, although he continually reproved himself for this desire and flouted his weakness. He used to gaze into the candles until they actually did seem to burn with angelic eyes that made his heart leap in expectation of the sign awaited; but soon fancy would betray him, and they would become candles again merely flickering.

On this September dusk there were crimson shadows of sunset deepening to purple in the corners of the chapel; the candles were very bright; the brethren in the stalls sang with austere fervour; the figure of Dom Cuthbert veiled from awkwardness by the heavy white cope moved before the altar during the censing of the Magnificat with a majesty that filled the small quire; the thurible tinkled its perfumed harmonies; and above the contentment of the ensuing hush blackbirds were heard in the garden or seen slipping to and fro like shadows across the windows.

Michael at this moment realized that there was a seventh monk in the quire, and wondered vaguely how he had failed to notice this new-comer before. Immediately after being made aware of his presence he caught the stranger's eye, and blushed so deeply that to cover his confusion he turned over the pages of a psalter. Curiosity made him look up again, but the new monk was devoutly wrapped in contemplation, nor did Michael catch his eye again during the Office. At supper he enquired about the new-comer of Dom Gilbert, who reproved him for inquisitiveness, but told him he was called Brother Aloysius. Again at Compline Michael caught his glance, and for a long time that night in the darkness he saw the eyes of Brother Aloysius gleaming very blue.

On the next day Michael, wandering by the edge of the hazel coppice, came upon Brother Aloysius with deep-stained mouth and hands gathering blackberries.

"Who are you?" asked the monk. "You gave me a very funny look at Vespers."

Michael thought this was an extremely unusual way for a monk, even a new monk, to speak, and hesitated a moment before he explained who he was.

"I suppose you can help me pick blackberries. I suppose that isn't against the rules."

"I often help the brothers," said Michael simply. "But I don't much care for picking blackberries. Still, I don't mind helping you."

Michael had an impulse to leave Brother Aloysius, but his self-consciousness prevented him from acting on it, and he kept the picker company in silence while the blackberries dropped lusciously into the basket.

"Feel my hand," said Brother Aloysius suddenly. "It's as hot as hell."

This time Michael stared in frank astonishment.

"Well, you needn't look so frightened," said the monk. "You don't look so very good yourself."

"Well, of course I'm not good," said Michael. "Only I think it's funny for a monk to swear. You don't mind my saying so, do you?"

"I don't mind. I don't mind anything," said Brother Aloysius.

Tension succeeded this statement, a tension that Michael longed to break; but he could do no more than continue to pick the blackberries.

"I suppose you wonder why I'm a monk?" demanded Brother Aloysius.

Michael looked at his questioner's pale face, at the uncomfortable eyes gleaming blue, at the full stained mouth and the long feverish hands dyed with purple juice.

"Why are you?" he asked.

"Well, I thought I'd try if anything could make me feel good, and then you looked at me in Chapel and set me off again."

"I set you off?" stammered Michael.

"Yes, you with your big girl's eyes, just like a girl I used to live with. Oh, you needn't look so proper. I expect you've often thought about girls. I did at your age. Three months with girls, three months with priests. Girls and priests—that's my life. When I was tired of women, I became religious, and when I was tired of Church, I took to women. It was a priest told me to come here to see if this would cure me, and now, damn you, you come into Chapel and stare and set me thinking of the Seven Sisters Road on that wet night I saw her last. That's where she lives, and you look exactly like her. God! you're the image of her. You might almost be her ghost incarnate."

Brother Aloysius caught hold of Michael's arm and spoke through clenched teeth. In Michael's struggle to free himself the basket of blackberries was upset, and they trod the spilt fruit into the grass. Michael broke away finally and gasped angrily:

"Look here, I'm not going to stay here. You're mad."

He ran from the monk into the depths of the wood, not stopping until he reached a silent glade. Here on the moss he sat panting, horrified. Yet when he came to compose the sentences in which he should tell Dom Cuthbert of his experience with the new monk, he found himself wishing that he had stayed to hear more. He actually enjoyed in retrospect the humiliation of the man, and his heart beat with the excitement of hearing more. Slowly he turned to seek again Brother Aloysius.

"You may as well tell me some more, now you've begun," said Michael.

For three or four days Michael was always in the company of Brother Aloysius, plying him with questions that sounded abominable to himself, when he remembered with what indignation he had rejected Garrod's offer of knowledge. Brother Aloysius spared no blushes, whether of fiery shame or furtive desire, and piece by piece Michael learned the fabric of vice. He was informed coldly of facts whose existence he had hitherto put down to his own most solitary and most intimate imaginations. Every vague evil that came wickedly before sleep was now made real with concrete examples; the vilest ideas, that hitherto he had considered peculiar to himself and perhaps a few more sadly tempted dreamers tossing through the vulnerable hours of the night, were commonplace to Brother Aloysius, whose soul was twisted, whose mind was debased to such an extent that he could boast of his delight in making the very priest writhe and wince in the Confessional.

Conversations with Brother Aloysius were sufficiently thrilling journeys, and Michael was always ready to follow his footsteps as one might follow a noctambulatory cat. The Seven Sisters Road was the scene of most of his adventures, if adventures they could be called, these dissolute pilgrimages. Michael came to know this street as one comes to know the street of a familiar dream. He walked along it in lavender sunrises watching the crenellated horizon of housetops; he sauntered through it slowly on dripping midnights, and on foggy November afternoons he speculated upon the windows with their aqueous sheen of incandescent gas. On summer dusks he pushed his way through the fetid population that thronged it, smelling the odour of stale fruit exposed for sale, and on sad grey Sabbaths he saw the ill-corseted servant girls treading down the heels of their ugly boots, and plush-clad children who continually dropped Sunday-school books in the mud.

And not only was Michael cognizant of the sordid street's exterior. He heard the creak of bells by blistered doors, he tripped over mats in narrow gloomy passages and felt his way up stale rickety stairs. Michael knew many rooms in this street of dreams: but they were all much alike with their muslin and patchouli, their aspidistras and yellowing photographs. The ribbed pianos tintinnabulated harshly with songs cut from the squalid sheets of Sunday papers: in unseen basements children whined, while on the mantelpiece garish vases rattled to the vibration of traffic.

Michael was also aware of the emotional crises that occur in the Seven Sisters Road, from the muttered curses of the old street-walkers with their crape bonnets cocked awry and their draggled musty skirts to Brother Aloysius himself shaken with excess of sin in colloquy with a ghostly voice upon a late winter dawn.

"A ghost?" he echoed incredulously.

"It's true. I heard a voice telling me to go back. And when I went back, there she was sitting in the arm-chair with the antimacassar round her shoulders because it was cold, and the carving-knife across her knees, waiting up to do for the fellow that was keeping her. I reckon it was God sent me back to save her."

Even Michael in his vicious mood could not tolerate this hysterical blasphemy, and he scoffed at the supernatural explanation. But Brother Aloysius did not care whether he was believed or not. He himself was sufficient audience to himself, ready to applaud and condemn with equal exaggeration of feeling.

After a week of self-revelation Brother Aloysius suddenly had spiritual qualms about his behaviour, and announced to Michael that he must go to Confession and free himself from the oppressive responsibility of his sin. Michael did not like the thought of Dom Cuthbert being aware of the way in which his last days at the monastery had been spent, and hoped that Brother Aloysius would confess in as general a manner as possible. Yet even so he feared that the perspicacious Abbot would guess the partner of his penitent, and, notwithstanding the sacred impersonality of the Confessional, regard Michael with an involuntary disgust. However, the confession, with all its attendant pangs of self-reproach, passed over, and Michael was unable to detect the slightest alteration in Dom Cuthbert's attitude towards him. But he avoided Brother Aloysius so carefully during the remainder of his stay, that it was impossible to test the Abbot's knowledge as directly as he could have wished.

The night before Michael was to leave the monastery, a great gale blew from the south-west and kept him wide awake hour after hour until the bell for Matins. He felt that on this his last night it would be in order for him to attend the Office. So he dressed quickly and hurried through the wind-swept corridor into the Chapel. Here, in a severity of long droning psalms, he tried to purge his mind of all it had acquired from the shamelessness of Brother Aloysius. He was so far successful that he could look Dom Cuthbert fearlessly in the face when he bade him good-bye next day, and as he coasted over the downs through the calm September sunlight, he to himself seemed like the country washed by the serene radiance of the tempest's aftermath.

Chapter VIII: *Mirrors*

MICHAEL somehow felt shy when he heard his mother's voice telling him to come into her room. He had run upstairs and knocked excitedly at her door before the shyness overwhelmed him, but it was too late not to enter, and he sat down to give her the account of his holidays. Rather dull it seemed, and robbed of all vitality by the barrier which both his mother and he hastened to erect between themselves.

"Well, dear, did you enjoy yourself at this Monastery?"

"Oh, rather."

"Is the—what do you call him?—the head monk a nice man?"

"Oh, yes, awfully decent."

"And your friend Chator, did he enjoy himself?"

"Oh, rather. Only he had to go before me. Did you enjoy yourself abroad, mother?"

"Very much, dear, thank you. We had lovely weather all the time."

"We had awfully ripping weather too."

"Have you got everything ready for school in the morning?"

"There's nothing much to get. I suppose I'll go into Cray's—the Upper Fifth. Do you want me now, mother?"

"No, dear, I have one or two letters to write."

"I think I'll go round and see if Chator's home yet. You don't mind?"

"Don't be late for dinner."

"Oh, no, rather not."

Going downstairs from his mother's room, Michael had half an impulse to turn back and confide in her the real account of his holidays. But on reflection he protested to himself that his mother looked upon him as immaculate, and he felt unwilling to disturb by such a revolutionary step the approved tranquillities of maternal ignorance.

Mr. Cray, his new form-master, was a man of distinct personality, and possessed a considerable amount of educative ability; but unfortunately for Michael the zest of classics had withered in his heart after his disappointment over the Oxford and Cambridge Certificate. Therefore Mr. Cray with his bright archæology and chatty scholarship bored Michael more profoundly than any of his masters so far had bored him. Mr. Cray resented this attitude very bitterly, being used to keenness in his form, and Michael's dreary indolence, which often came nearer to insolence, irritated him. As for the plodding, inky sycophants who fawned upon Mr. Cray's informativeness, Michael regarded them with horror and contempt. He sat surrounded by the butts and bugbears of his school-life. All the boys whose existence he had deplored seemed to have clambered arduously into the Upper Fifth just to enrage him with the sight of their industrious propinquity. There they sat with their scraggy wrists protruding from shrinking coat-sleeves, with ambitious noses glued to their books, with pens and pencils neatly disposed for demonstrative annotation, and nearly all of them conscious of having figured in the school-list with the printed bubble of the Oxford and Cambridge Higher Certificate beside their names. Contemplating them in the mass, Michael scarcely knew how he would endure another dusty year of school.

"And now we come to the question of the Homeric gate—the Homeric gate, Fane, when you can condescend to our level," said Mr. Cray severely.

"I'm listening, sir," said Michael wearily.

"Of course the earliest type of gate was without hinges—without hinges, Fane! Very much like your attention, Fane!"

Several sycophants giggled at this, and Michael, gazing very earnestly at Mr. Cray's benign but somewhat dirty bald head, took a bloody revenge upon those in reach of his javelin of quadruple penholders.

73

"For Monday," said Mr. Cray, when he had done with listening to the intelligent advice of his favourite pupils on the subject of gates ancient and modern, "for Monday the essay will be on Patriotism."

Michael groaned audibly.

"Isn't there an alternative subject, sir?" he gloomily enquired.

"Does Fane dislike abstractions?" said Mr. Cray. "Curious! Well, if Fane wishes for an alternative subject, of course Fane must be obeyed. The alternative subject will be An Examination into the Fundamental Doctrines of Hegelian Idealism. Does that suit Fane?"

"Very well indeed," said Michael, who had never heard of Hegel until that moment, but vowed to himself that somehow between this muggy Friday afternoon and next Monday morning he would conquer the fellow's opinions. As a matter of fact, the essay proved perfectly easy with the assistance of The Popular Encyclopedia, though Mr. Cray called it a piece of impudence and looked almost baleful when Michael showed it up.

From this atmosphere of complacent effort Michael withdrew one afternoon to consult Father Viner about his future. Underneath the desire for practical advice was a desire to talk about himself, and Michael was disappointed on arriving at Father Viner's rooms to hear that he was out. However, learning that there was a prospect of his speedy return, he came in at the landlady's suggestion to amuse himself with a book while he waited.

Wandering round the big bay-windowed room with its odour of tobacco and books, and casting a careless glance at Father Viner's desk, Michael caught sight of his own name in the middle of a neatly written letter on the top of a pile of others. He could not resist taking a longer glance to see the address and verify the allusion to himself, and with this longer glance curiosity conquered so completely the prejudice against prying into other people's correspondence that Michael, breathing nervously under the dread of interruption, took up the letter and read it right through. It was in his present mood of anxiety about himself very absorbing.

Clere Abbey,
Michael Mass.

PAX ✠

Dear Brother,

I have been intending to write to you about young Michael Fane ever since he left us, and your letter of enquiry has had the effect of bringing me up to the point.

I hardly know what to tell you. He's a curious youth, very lovable, and with enough brains to make one wish that he might have a vocation for the priesthood. At the same time I noticed while he was with us, especially after the admirable Chator departed, an overwhelming languor which I very much deplored.

He spent much of his time with a very bad hat indeed, whom I have just sent away from Clere. If you ever come across Mr. Henry Meats, be careful of him. Arbuthnot of St. Aidan's, Holloway, sent him to me. You know Arbuthnot's expansive (and for his friends expensive) Christianity. This last effort of his was a snorter, a soft, nasty, hysterical, little blob of vice. I ought to have seen through the fellow before I did. Heaven knows I get enough of the tag-rag of the Movement trying to be taken on at Clere. I suppose the monastic life will always make an imperishable appeal to the worst, and, thank God, some of the best. I mention this fellow to you because I'm afraid he and Michael may meet again, and I don't at all like the idea of their acquaintanceship progressing, especially as it was unluckily begun beneath a religious roof. So keep an eye on Mr. Henry Meats. He's really bad.

Another fellow I don't recommend for Michael is Percy Garrod. Not that I think there is much danger in that direction, for I fancy Michael was very cold with him. Percy is a decent, honest, hard-working, common ass, with a deep respect for the Pope and the Polytechnic. He's a trifle zealous, however, with bastard information about physical science, and not at all the person I should choose to lecture Michael on the complications of adolescence.

We are getting on fairly well at Clere, but it's hard work trying to make this country believe there is the slightest necessity for the contemplative life. I hope all goes well with you and your work.

Yours affectionately in Xt.,
Cuthbert Manners, O.S.B.

Poor Michael. His will be a difficult position one day. I feel on re-reading this letter that I've told you nothing you don't already know. But he's one of those elusive boys who have lived within themselves too much and too long.

Michael put this letter back where he had found it, and wondered how much of the contents would be discussed by Father Viner. He was glad that Brother Aloysius had vanished, because Brother Aloysius had become like a bad dream with which he was unwilling in the future to renew acquaintance. On his own character Dom Cuthbert had not succeeded in throwing very much light—at any rate not in this letter. Father Viner came in to interrupt Michael's meditations, and began at once to discuss the letter.

"The Lord Abbot of Clere thinks you're a dreamer," he began abruptly.

"Does he, Mr. Viner?" echoed Michael, who somehow could never bring himself to the point of addressing the priest as 'Father.' Shyness always overcame his will.

"What do you dream about, young Joseph?"

"Oh, I only think about a good many things, and wonder what I'm going to be and all that," Michael replied. "I don't want to go into the Indian Civil Service or anything with exams. I'm sick of exams. What I most want to do is to get away from school. I'm sick of school, and the fellows in the Upper Fifth are a greasy crowd of swats always sucking up to Cray."

"And who is the gentleman with the crustacean name that attracts these barnacles?"

"Cray? Oh, he's my form-master, and tries to be funny."

"So do I, Michael," confessed Mr. Viner.

"Oh, well, that's different. I'm not bound to listen to you, if I don't want to. But I have to listen to Cray for eighteen hours every week, and he hates me because I won't take notes for his beastly essays. I think I'll ask my mater if I can't leave school after this term."

"And then what would you do?"

"Oh, I don't know. I could settle when I'd left."

"What about Oxford?"

"Well, I could go to Oxford later on."

"I don't think you could quite so easily as you think. Anyway, you'd much better go to Oxford straight from school."

"Eight more terms before I leave. Phew!" Michael groaned. "It's such a terrible waste of time, and I know Oxford's ripping."

"Perhaps something will come along to interest you. And always, dear boy, don't forget you have your religion."

"Yes, I know," said Michael. "But at the Abbey I met some people who were supposed to be religious, and they were pretty good rotters."

The priest looked at him and seemed inclined to let Michael elaborate this topic, but almost immediately he dismissed it with a commonplace.

"Oh, well," Michael sighed, "I suppose something will happen soon to buck me up. I hope so. Perhaps the Kensitites will start making rows in churches again," he went on hopefully. "Will you lend me the Apocryphal Gospels? We're going to have a discussion about them at the De Rebus Ecclesiasticis."

"Oh, the society hasn't broken up?" enquired Mr. Viner.

"Rather not. Only everybody's changed rather. Chator's become frightfully Roman. He was Sarum last term, and he thinks I'm frightfully heretical, only of course I say a lot I don't mean just to rag him. I say, by the way, who wrote 'In a Garden'?"

"It sounds a very general title," commented Mr. Viner, with a smile.

"Well, it's some poem or other."

"Swinburne wrote a poem in the Second Series of Poems and Ballads called 'A Forsaken Garden.' Is that what you mean?"

"Perhaps. Is it a famous poem?"

"Yes, I should say it was distinctly."

"Well, that must be it. Cray tried to be funny about it to-day in form, and said to me, 'Good heavens, haven't you read "In a Garden"?' And I said I'd never heard of it. And then he said in his funny way to the class, 'I suppose you've all read it.' And none of them had, which made him look rather an ass. So he said we'd better read it by next week."

"I can lend you my Swinburne. Only take care of it," said Mr. Viner. "It's a wonderful poem."

In a coign of the cliff between lowland and highland,
At the sea-down's edge between windward and lee,
Walled round with rocks as an inland island,
The ghost of a garden fronts the sea.

"I say," exclaimed Michael eagerly, "I never knew Swinburne was a really great poet. And fancy, he's alive now."

"Alive, and living at Putney," said Mr. Viner.

"And yet he wrote what you've just said!"

"He wrote that, and many other things too. He wrote:

Before the beginning of years
There came to the making of man
Time, with a gift of tears;
Grief, with a glass that ran;
Pleasure, with pain for leaven,
Summer, with flowers that fell;
Remembrance fallen from heaven,
And madness risen from hell."

"Good Lord!" sighed Michael. "And he's in Putney at this very moment."

Michael went home clasping close the black volume, and in his room that night, while the gas jet flamed excitably in defiance of rule, he read almost right through the Second Series of Poems and Ballads. It was midnight when he turned down the gas and sank feverishly into bed. For a long while he was saying to himself isolated lines: *'The wet skies harden, the gates are barred on the summer side.' 'The rose-red acacia that mocks the rose.' 'Sleep, and if life was bitter to thee, brother.' 'For whom all winds are quiet as the sun, all waters as the shore.'*

In school on Monday morning Mr. Cray, to Michael's regret, did not allude to the command that his class should read 'In a Garden.' Michael was desperately anxious at once to tell him how much he had loved the poem and to remind him of the real title, 'A Forsaken Garden.' At last he could bear it no longer and went up flushed with enthusiasm to Mr. Cray's desk, nominally to enquire into an alleged mistake in his Latin Prose, but actually to inform Mr. Cray of his delight in Swinburne. When the grammatical blunder had been discussed, Michael said with as much nonchalance as he could assume:

"I read that poem, sir. I think it's ripping."

"What poem?" repeated Mr. Cray vaguely. "Oh, yes, 'Enoch Arden.'"

"'Enoch Arden,'" stammered Michael. "I thought you said 'In a Garden.' I read 'A Forsaken Garden' by Swinburne."

Mr. Cray put on his most patronizing manner.

"My poor Fane, have you never heard of Enoch Arden? Perhaps you've never even heard of Tennyson?"

"But Swinburne's good, isn't he, sir?"

"Swinburne is very well," said Mr. Cray. "Oh, yes, Swinburne will do, if you like rose-jam. But I don't recommend Swinburne for you, Fane."

Then Mr. Cray addressed his class:

"Did you all read 'Enoch Arden'?"

"Yes, sir," twittered the Upper Fifth.

"Fane, however, with that independence of judgment which distinguishes his Latin Prose from, let us say, the prose of Cicero, preferred to read 'A Forsaken Garden' by one Swinburne."

The Upper Fifth giggled dutifully.

"Perhaps Fane will recite to us his discovery," said Mr. Cray, scratching his scurfy head with the gnawed end of a penholder.

Michael blushed resentfully, and walked back to his desk.

"No?" said Mr. Cray with an affectation of great surprise.

Then he and the Upper Fifth, contented with their superiority, began to chew and rend some tough Greek particles which ultimately became digestible enough to be assimilated by the Upper Fifth; while Mr. Cray himself purred over his cubs, looking not very unlike a mangy old lioness.

"Eight more terms," groaned Michael to himself.

Mr. Cray was not so blind to his pupils' need for mild intellectual excitement, however much he might scorn the easy emotions of Swinburne. He really grew lyrical over Homeric difficulties, and even spoke enthusiastically of Mr. Mackail's translation of the Georgics; but always he managed to conceal the nobility of his theme beneath a mass of what he called 'minor points.' He would create his own rubbish heap and invite the Upper Fifth to scratch in it for pearls. One day a question arose as to the exact meaning of οὐλοχύται in Homer. Michael would have been perfectly content to believe that it meant 'whole barleycorns,' until Mr. Cray suggested that it might be equivalent to the Latin 'mola,' meaning 'grain coarsely ground.' An exhausting discussion followed, illustrated by examples from every sort of writer, all of which had to be taken down in notes in anticipation of a still more exhausting essay on the subject.

"The meal may be trite," said Mr. Cray, "but not the subject," he added, chuckling. "However, I have only touched the fringe of it: you will find the arguments fully set forth in Buttmann's Lexilogus. Who possesses that invaluable work?"

Nobody in the Upper Fifth possessed it, but all anxiously made a note of it, in order to acquire it over the counter of the Book Room downstairs.

"No use," said Mr. Cray. "Buttmann's Lexilogus is now out of print."

Michael pricked up at this. The phrase leant a curious flavour of Romance to the dull book.

"No doubt, however, you will be able to obtain it second-hand," added Mr. Cray.

The notion of tracking down Buttmann's Lexilogus possessed the Upper Fifth. Eagerly after school the diligent ones discussed ways and means. Parties were formed, almost one might say expeditions, to rescue the valuable work from oblivion. Michael stood contemptuously aside from the buzz of self-conscious effort round him, although he had made up his own mind to be one of the first to obtain the book. Levy, however, secured the first copy for fourpence in Farringdon Street, earning for his sharpness much praise. Another boy bought one for three shillings and sixpence in Paddington, the price one would expect to pay, if not a Levy; and there were rumours of a copy in Kensington High Street. To Michael the mart of London from earliest youth had been Hammersmith Broadway, and thither he hurried, hopeful of discovering Buttmann's dingy Lexilogus, for the purchase of which he had thoughtfully begged a sovereign from his mother. Michael did not greatly covet Buttmann, but he was sure that the surplus from three shillings and sixpence, possibly even from fourpence, would be very welcome.

He found at last in a turning off Hammersmith Broadway a wonderful bookshop, whose rooms upon rooms leading into one another were all lined and loaded with every kind of book. The proprietor soon found a copy of Buttmann, which he sold to Michael for half a crown, leaving him with fifteen shillings for himself, since he decided that it would be as well to return his mother at least half a crown from her sovereign. The purchase completed, Michael began to wander round the shop, taking down a book here, a book there, dipping into them from the top of a ladder, sniffing them, clapping their covers together to drive away the dust, and altogether thoroughly enjoying himself, while the daylight slowly faded and street-lamps came winking into ken outside. At last, just as the shop-boy was putting up the shutters, Michael discovered a volume bound in half-morocco of a crude gay blue, that proved on inspection to contain the complete poetical works of Algernon Charles Swinburne, for the sum of seventeen shillings and sixpence.

What was now left of his golden sovereign that should have bought so much beside Buttmann's brown and musty Lexilogus?

Michael approached the proprietor with the volume in his hand.

"How much?" he asked, with a queer choking sensation, a throbbing excitement, for he had never before even imagined the expenditure of seventeen shillings and sixpence on one book.

"What's this?" said the proprietor, putting on his spectacles. "Oh, yes, Swinburne—pirated American edition. Seventeen shillings and sixpence."

"Couldn't you take less?" asked Michael, with a vague hope that he might rescue a shilling for his mother, if not for cigarettes.

"Take less?" repeated the bookseller. "Good gracious, young man, do you know what you'd have to pay for Swinburne's stuff separate? Something like seven or eight pounds, and then they'd be all in different volumes. Whereas here you've got—lemme see—Atalanta in Calydon, Chastelard, Poems and Ballads, Songs before Sunrise, Bothwell, Tristram of Lyonesse, Songs of Two Nations, and heaven knows what not. I call seventeen shillings and sixpence very cheap for what you might almost call a man's life-work. Shall I wrap it up?"

"Yes, please," said Michael, gasping with the effect of the plunge.

But when that night he read

Swallow, my sister, O fair swift swallow,

he forgot all about the cost.

The more of Swinburne that Michael read, the more impatient he grew of school. The boredom of Mr. Cray's class became stupendous; and Michael, searching for some way to avoid it, decided to give up Classics and apply for admission to the History Sixth, which was a small association of boys who had drifted into this appendix for the purpose of defeating the ordinary rules of promotion. For instance, when the Captain of the School Eleven had not attained the privileged Sixth, he was often allowed to enter the History Sixth, in order that he might achieve the intellectual dignity which consorted with his athletic prowess.

Michael had for some time envied the leisure of the History Sixth, with its general air of slackness and its form-master, Mr. Kirkham, who, on account of holding many administrative positions important to the athletic life of the school, was so often absent from his class-room. He now racked his brains for an excuse to achieve the idle bliss of these charmed few. Finally he persuaded his mother to write to the Headmaster and apply for his admission, on the grounds of the greater utility of History in his future profession.

"But what are you going to be, Michael?" asked his mother.

"I don't know, but you can say I'm going to be a barrister or something."

"Is History better for a barrister?"

"I don't know, but you can easily say you think it is."

In the end his mother wrote to Dr. Brownjohn, and one grey November afternoon the Headmaster sailed into the class-room of the Upper Fifth, extricated Michael with a roar, and marched with him up and down the dusky corridor in a ferocious discussion of the proposal.

"Why do you want to give up your Classics?" bellowed Dr. Brownjohn.

In the echoing corridor Michael's voice sounded painfully weak against his monitor's.

"I don't want to give them up, sir. Only I would like to learn History as well," he explained.

"What's the good of History?" roared the Doctor.

"I thought I'd like to learn it," said Michael.

"You shouldn't think, you infamous young sluggard."

"And I could go on reading Classics, sir, I could really."

"Bah!" shouted Dr. Brownjohn. "Impudent nonsense, you young sloth. Why didn't you get your Certificate?"

"I failed in Arithmetic, sir."

"You'll fail in your whole life, boy," prophesied Dr. Brownjohn in bull-deep accents of reproach. "Aren't you ashamed of yourself?"

"No, sir," said Michael. "I don't think I am, because I worked jolly hard."

"Worked, you abominable little loafer? You've never worked in your life. You could be the finest scholar in the school, and you're merely a coruscation of slatternly, slipshod paste. Bah! What do you expect to do when you leave school? Um?"

"I want to go to Oxford."

"Then get the Balliol Scholarship."

"I don't want to be at Balliol," said Michael.

"Then get the major scholarship at Trinity, Cambridge."

"I don't intend to go to Cambridge," said Michael.

"Good heavens, boy," roared Dr. Brownjohn, "are you trying to arrange your own career?"

"No, sir," said Michael. "But I want to go to St. Mary's, Oxford."

"Then get a scholarship at St. Mary's."

"But I don't want to be a Scholar of any college. I want to go up as a Commoner."

The veins on Dr. Brownjohn's forehead swelled with wrath, astonishment and dismay.

"Get out of my sight," he thundered. "Get back into your class-room. I've done with you; I take no more interest in you. You're here to earn glory for your school, you're here to gain a scholarship, not to air your own opinions. Get out of my sight, you young scoundrel. How dare you argue with me? You shan't go into the History Sixth! You shall stew in your own obstinate juice in the Upper Fifth until I choose to move you out of it. Do you hear? Go back into your class-room. I'll write to your mother. She's an idiotic woman, and you're a slovenly, idle, good-for-nothing cub."

Overwhelmed with failure and very sensitive to the inquisitive glances of his classmates, Michael sat down in his own desk again as unobtrusively as he could.

Michael's peace of mind was not increased by the consciousness of Mr. Cray's knowledge of his appeal to withdraw from the Upper Fifth, and he became exposed to a large amount of sarcasm in allusion to his expressed inclination towards history. He was continually referred to as an authority on Constitutions; he was invited to bring forward comparisons from more modern times to help the elucidation of the Syracusan expedition or the Delian Confederacy.

All that Michael gained from Mr. Cray was a passion for second-hand books—the latest and most fervid of all his collecting hobbies.

One wintry evening in Elson's Bookshop at Hammersmith he was enjoying himself on the top of a ladder, when he became aware of an interested gaze directed at himself over the dull-gilt edges of a large and expensive work on Greek sculpture. The face that so regarded him was at once fascinating and repulsive. The glittering blue eyes full of laughter were immediately attractive, but something in the pointed ears and curled-back lips, something in the peculiarly white fingers faintly pencilled about the knuckles with fine black hairs, and after a moment something cruel in the bright blue eyes themselves restrained him from an answering smile.

"What is the book, Hyacinthus?" asked the stranger, and his voice was so winning and so melodious in the shadowy bookshop that Michael immediately fell into the easiest of conversations.

"Fond of books?" asked the stranger. "Oh, by the way, my name is Wilmot, Arthur Wilmot."

Something in Wilmot's manner made Michael suppose that he ought to be familiar with the name, and he tried to recall it.

"What's your name?" the stranger went on.

Michael told his name, and also his school, and before very long a good deal about himself.

"I live near you," said Mr. Wilmot. "We'll walk along presently. I'd like you to dine with me one night soon. When?"

"Oh, any time," said Michael, trying to speak as if invitations to dinner occurred to him three or four times a day.

"Here's my card," said the stranger. "You'd better show it to your mother—so that she'll know it's all right. I'm a writer, you know."

"Oh, yes," Michael vaguely agreed.

"I don't suppose you've seen any of my stuff. I don't publish much. Sometimes I read my poems to Interior people."

Michael looked puzzled.

"Interior is my name for the people who understand. So few do. I should say you'd be sympathetic. You look sympathetic. You remind me of those exquisite boys who in scarlet hose run delicately with beakers of wine or stand in groups about the corners of old Florentine pictures."

Michael tried to look severe, and yet, after the Upper Fifth, even so direct and embarrassing a compliment was slightly pleasant.

"Shall we go along? To-night the Hammersmith Road is full of mystery. But, first, shall I not buy you a book—some exquisite book full of strange perfumes and passionate courtly gestures? And so you are at school? How wonderful to be at school! How Sicilian! Strange youth, you should have been sung by Theocritus, or, better, been crowned with myrtle by some wonderful unknown Greek, some perfect blossom of the Anthology."

Michael laughed rather foolishly. There seemed nothing else to do.

"Won't you smoke? These Chian cigarettes in their diaphanous paper of mildest mauve would suit your oddly remote, your curiously shy glance. You had better not smoke so near to the savage confines of St. James' School? How ascetic! How stringent! What book shall I buy for you, O greatly to be envied dreamer of Sicilian dreams? Shall I buy you Mademoiselle de Maupin, so that all her rococo soul may dance with gilded limbs across your vision? Or shall I buy you A Rebours, and teach you to live? And yet I think neither would suit you perfectly. So here is a volume of Pater—Imaginary Portraits. You will like to read of Denys l'Auxerrois. One day I myself will write an imaginary portrait of you, wherein your secret, sidelong smile will reveal to the world the whole art of youth."

"But really—thanks very much," stammered Michael, who was beginning to suspect the stranger of madness—"it's awfully kind of you, but, really, I think I'd rather not."

"Do not be proud," said Mr. Wilmot. "Pride is for the pure in heart, and you are surely not pure in heart. Or are you? Are you indeed like one of those wonderful white statues of antiquity, unaware of the soul with all its maladies?"

In the end, so urgent was Mr. Wilmot, Michael accepted the volume of Pater, and walked with the stranger through the foggy night. Somehow the conversation was so destructive of all experience that, as Michael and his new friend went by the school-gates and perceived beyond the vast bulk of St. James' looming, Michael felt himself a stranger to it all, as if he never again would with a crowd of companions surge out from afternoon school. The stranger came as far as the corner of Carlington Road with Michael.

"I will write to your mother and ask her to let you dine with me one night next week. You interest me so much."

Mr. Wilmot waved a pontifical good-bye and vanished in the direction of Kensington.

At home Michael told his mother of the adventure. She looked a little doubtful at his account of Mr. Wilmot.

"Oh, he's all right, really, Mother. Only, you know, a little peculiar. But then he's a poet."

Next day came a letter from Mr. Wilmot.

205 Edwardes Square, W.
November.

Dear Mrs. Fane,

I must apologize for inviting your son to dinner so unceremoniously. But he made a great appeal to me, sitting on the top of a ladder in Elson's Bookshop. I have a library, in which he may enjoy himself whenever he likes. Meanwhile, may he come to dinner with me on Friday next? Mr. Johnstone, the Member for West Kensington, is coming with his nephew who may be dull without Michael. Michael tells me he thinks of becoming an ecclesiastical lawyer. In that case Johnstone will be particularly useful, and can give him some hints. He's a personal friend of old Dr. Brownjohn. With many apologies for my 'impertinence,'

Yours very truly,
Arthur Wilmot.

"This is a perfectly sensible letter," said Mrs. Fane.

"Perhaps I thought he was funnier than he really was. Does he say anything else except about me sitting on the top of a ladder?"

Somehow Michael was disappointed to hear that this was all.

Chapter IX: *The Yellow Age*

DINNER with Mr. Arthur Wilmot occupied most of Michael's thoughts for a week. He was mainly concerned about his costume, and he was strenuously importunate for a tail-coat. Mrs. Fane, however, was sure that a dinner-jacket would better become his youthfulness. Then arose the question of stick-up collars. Michael pointed out that very soon he would be sixteen, and that here was a fine opportunity to leave behind the Polo or Shakespeare collar.

"You're growing up so quickly, dearest boy," sighed his mother.

Michael was anxious to have one of the new double collars.

"But don't they look rather *outré*?" protested Mrs. Fane.

"Well, Abercrombie, the Secretary of the Fifteen, wears one," observed Michael.

"Have your own way, dear," said Mrs. Fane gently.

Two or three days before the dinner-party Michael braved everything and wore one of the new double collars to school. Its extravagant advent among the discreet neckwear of the Upper Fifth caused a sensation. Mr. Cray himself looked curiously once or twice at Michael, who assumed in consequence a particularly nonchalant air, and lounged over his desk even more than usual.

"Are you going on the stage, Fane?" enquired Mr. Cray finally, exasperated by Michael's indolent construing.

"Not that I know of," said Michael.

"I wasn't sure whether that collar was part of your get-up as an eccentric comedian."

The Upper Fifth released its well-worn laugh, and Michael scowled at his master.

However, he endured the sarcasm of the first two days and still wore the new collars, vowing to himself that presently he would make fresh attacks upon the convention of school attire, since apparently he was able thereby to irritate old Cray.

After all, the dinner-party was not so exciting as he had hoped from the sample of his new friend's conversation. To be sure he was able to smoke as much as he liked, and drink as much champagne as he knew how without warning headshakes; but Mr. Johnstone, the Member for West Kensington, was a moon-faced bore, and his nephew turned out to be a lank nonentity on the despised Modern side. Mr. Johnstone talked a good deal about the Catholic movement, which somehow during the last few weeks was ceasing to interest Michael so much as formerly. Michael himself ascribed this apostasy to his perusal, ladder-high, of Zola's novel Lourdes with its damaging assaults upon Christian credulity. The Member of Parliament seemed to Michael, after his psychical adventures of the past few months, curiously dull and antique, and he evidently considered Michael affected. However, he encouraged the idea of ecclesiastical law, and promised to talk to Dr. Brownjohn about Michael's release from the thraldom of Classics. As for the nephew, he seemed to be able to do nothing but stretch the muscles of his chicken-like neck and ask continually whether Michael was going to join the Field Club that some obscure Modern Lower Master was in travail with at the moment. He also invited Michael to join a bicycling club that apparently met at Surbiton every other Saturday afternoon. Mr. Wilmot contented himself with silence and the care of his guests' entertainment.

Finally the Member for West Kensington with his crudely jointed nephew departed into the fog, and Mr. Wilmot, with an exaggerated sigh, shut the front door.

"I must be going too," said Michael grudgingly.

"My dear boy, the evening has scarcely begun," objected Mr. Wilmot. "Come upstairs to my library, and tell me all about your opinions, and whether you do not think that everything is an affectation."

They went up together.

"Every year I redecorate this room," Mr. Wilmot explained. "Last year it was apple-green set out with cherry-red. Now I am become a mysterious peacock-blue, for lately I have felt terribly old. How well this uncertain tint suits your fresh languor."

Michael admired the dusky blue chamber with the plain mirrors of tarnished gilt, the gleaming books and exotic engravings, and the heterogeneous finery faintly effeminate. He buried himself in a deep embroidered chair, with an ebony box of cigarettes at his feet, while Mr. Wilmot, after a myriad mincing preliminaries, sought out various highly coloured bottles of liqueurs.

"This is a jolly ripping room," sighed Michael.

"It represents a year's moods," said Mr. Wilmot.

"And then will you change it?" asked Michael.

"Perhaps. The most subtly painted serpent casts ultimately its slough. Creme-de-Menthe?"

"Yes, please," said Michael, who would have accepted anything in his present receptive condition.

"And what do you think of life?" enquired Mr. Wilmot, taking his place on a divan opposite Michael. "Do you mind if I smoke my Jicky-scented hookah?" he added.

"Not at all," said Michael. "These cigarettes are jolly ripping. I think life at school is frightfully dull—except, of course, when one goes out. Only I don't often."

"Dull?" repeated Mr. Wilmot. "Listen to the amazing cruelty of youth, that finds even his adventurous Sicilian existence dull."

"Well, it is," said Michael. "I think I used to like it, but nowadays everything gets fearfully stale almost at once."

"Already your life has been lived?" queried Mr. Wilmot very anxiously.

"Well, not exactly," Michael replied, with a quick glance towards his host to make sure he was not joking. "I expect that when I leave school I shall get interested again. Only just lately I've given up everything. First I was keen on Footer, and then I got keen on Ragging, and then I got keen on Work even (this was confessed apologetically), and just lately I've been keen on the Church—only now I find that's pretty stale."

"The Church!" echoed Mr. Wilmot. "How wonderful! The dim Gothic glooms, the sombre hues of stained glass, the incense-wreathèd acolytes, the muttering priests, the bedizened banners and altars and images. Ah, elusive and particoloured vision that once was mine!"

"Then I got keen on Swinburne," said Michael.

"You advance along the well-worn path of the Interior and Elect," said Mr. Wilmot.

"I'm still keen on Swinburne, but he makes me feel hopeless. Sad and hopeless," said Michael.

"Under the weight of sin?" asked Mr. Wilmot.

"Not exactly—because he seems to have done everything and——"

"You'd like to?"

"Yes, I would," said Michael. "Only one can't live like a Roman Emperor at a public school. What I hate is the way everybody thinks you ought to be interested in things that aren't really interesting at all. What people can't understand about me is that I *could* be keener than anybody about things schoolmasters and that kind don't think right or at any rate important. I don't mean to say I want to be dissipated, but——"

"Dissipated?" echoed Mr. Wilmot, raising his eyebrows.

"Well, you know what I mean," blushed Michael.

"Dissipation is a condition of extreme old age. I might be dissipated, not you," said Mr. Wilmot. "Why not say wanton? How much more beautiful, how much more intense a word."

"But wanton sounds so beastly affected," said Michael. "As if it was taken out of the Bible. And you aren't so very old. Not more than thirty."

"I think what you're trying to say is that, under your present mode of life, you find self-expression impossible. Let me diagnose your symptoms."

Michael leaned forward eagerly at this proposal. Nothing was so entertaining to his egoism just now as diagnosis. Moreover, Mr. Wilmot seemed inclined to take him more seriously than Mr. Viner, or, indeed, any of his spiritual directors so far. Mr. Wilmot prepared himself for the lecture by lighting a very long cigarette wrapped in brittle fawn-coloured paper, whose spirals of smoke Michael followed upward to their ultimate evanescence, as if indeed they typified with their tenuous plumes and convolutions the intricate discourse that begot them.

"In a sense, my dear boy, your charm has waned—the faerie charm, that is, which wraps in heedless silver armour the perfect boyhood of man. You are at present a queer sort of mythical animal whom we for want of a better term call 'adolescent.' Intercourse with anything but your own self shocks both you and the world with a sense of extravagance, as if a centaur pursued a nymph or fought with a hero. The soul—or what we call the soul—is struggling in the bondage of your unformed body. Lately you had no soul, you were ethereal and cold, yet withal in some remote way passionate, like your own boy's voice. Now the silly sun is melting the snow, and what was a little while since crystalline clear virginity is beginning to trickle down towards a headlong course, carrying with it the soiled accumulation of the years to float insignificantly into the wide river of manhood. But I am really being almost intolerably allegorical—or is it metaphorical?"

"Still, I think I understand what you mean," Michael said encouragingly.

"Thrown back upon your own resources, it is not surprizing that you attempt to allay your own sense of your own incongruity by seeking for its analogy in the decorative excitements of religion or poetry. Love would supply the solution, but you are still too immature for love. And if you do fall in love, you will sigh for some ample and unattainable matron rather than the slim, shy girl that would better become your pastoral graces. At present you lack all sense of proportion. You are only aware of your awkwardness. Your corners have not yet been, as they say, knocked off. You are still somewhat proud of their Gothic angularity. You feel at home in the tropic dawns of Swinburne's poetry, in the ceremonious exaggerations of Mass, because neither of these conditions of thought and behaviour allow you to become depressed over your oddity, to see yourself crawling with bedraggled wings from the cocoon of mechanical education. The licentious ingenuity of Martial, Petronius and Apuleius with their nightmare comedies and obscene phantasmagoria, Lucian, that *boulevardier* of Olympic glades, all these could allow you to feel yourself more at home than does Virgil with his peaceful hexameters or the cold relentless narrations of Thucydides."

"Yes, that's all very well," objected Michael. "But other chaps seem to get on all right without being bored by ordinary things."

"Already spurning the gifts of Apollo, contemptuous of Artemis, ignorant of Bacchus and Aphrodite, you are bent low before Pallas Athene. Foolish child, do not pray for wisdom in this overwise thin-faced time of ours. Rather demand of the gods folly, and drive ever furiously your temperament like a chariot before you."

"I met an odd sort of chap the other day," Michael said thoughtfully. "A monk he was, as a matter of fact—who told me a skit of things— you know—about a bad life. It's funny, though I hate ugly things and common things, he gave me a feeling that I'd like to go right away from everything and live in one of those horrible streets that you pass in an omnibus when the main road is up. Perhaps you don't understand what I mean?"

Mr. Wilmot's eyes glittered through the haze of smoke.

"Why shouldn't I understand? Squalor is the Parthenope of the true Romantic. You'll find it in all the poets you love best—if not in their poetry, certainly in their lives. Even romantic critics are not without temptation. One day you shall read of Hazlitt and Sainte-Beuve. And now, dear boy, here is my library which holds as many secrets as the Spintrian books of Elephantis, long ago lost and purified by the sea. I am what the wise world would call about to corrupt your mind, and yet I believe that for one who like you must some day make trial of the uttermost corruption, I am prescribing more wisely than Chiron, that pig-headed or rather horse-bodied old prototype of all schoolmasters, who sent his hero pupils one after another into the world, proof against nothing but a few spear-thrusts. I offer you better than fencing-bouts and wrestling-matches. I offer you a good library. Read every day and all night, and when you are a man full grown, you will smile at the excesses of your contemporaries, at their divorces and disgraces. You will stand aloof like a second Aurelius, coining austere aphorisms and mocking the weakness of your unlearned fellows. Why are priests generally so inept in the confessional? Because they learn their knowledge of life from, a frowsy volume of Moral Theology that in the most utterly barbarous Latin emits an abstract of humanity's immeasurable vice. In the same way most young men encounter wickedness in some sudden shock of depravity from which they retire blushing and mumbling, 'Who'd have thought it!' ' Who'd have thought it!' they cry, and are immediately empanelled on a jury.

"Not so you, O more subtle youth, with the large deep eyes and secret sidelong smile.

"There on my shelves are all the ages. I have spoken to you of Petronius, of Lucian and Apuleius. There is Suetonius, with his incredibly improper tales that show how beastliness takes root and flowers from the deposited muck of a gossip's mind. There is Tacitus, ever willing to sacrifice decency to antithesis, and Ausonius, whose ribald verses are like monkish recreation; yet he had withal a pretty currency of honest silver Latin, Christian though he was. You must read your Latin authors well, for, since you must be decadent, it is better to decay from a good source. And neglect not the Middle Ages. You will glide most easily into them from the witches and robbers of Apuleius. You will read Boccaccio, whose tales are intaglios carved with exquisitely licentious and Lilliputian scenes. Neither forget Villon, whose light ladies seem ever to move elusively in close-cut gowns of cloth-of-gold and incredibly tall steeple-hats. But even with Villon the world becomes complicated, and you will soon reach the temperamental entanglements of the nineteenth century, for you may avoid the coarse, the beery and besotted obviousness of the Georgian age.

"But I like the eighteenth century almost best of all," protested Michael.

"Then cure yourself of that most lamentable and most démodé taste, or I shall presently believe that you read a page or two of Boswell's Life of Johnson every morning, while the water is running into your bath. You can never be a true decadent, treading delicately over the garnered perfection of the world's art, if you really admire and enjoy the eighteenth century."

Michael, however, looked very doubtful over his demanded apostasy.

"But, never mind," Mr. Wilmot went on. "When you have read Barbey d'Aurevilly and Baudelaire, Mallarmé, Verlaine, Catulle Mendès and Verhaeren, when the Parnassians and Symbolists have illuminated you, and you become an Interior person, when Aubrey Beardsley and Felicien Rops have printed their fierce debauchery upon your imagination, then you will be glad you have forsaken the eighteenth century. How crude is the actual number eighteen, how far from the passionate mystery of seventeen or the tired wisdom of nineteen! O wonderful nineteenth century, in whose grey humid dusk you and I are lucky enough to live!"

"But what about the twentieth century?" asked Michael.

Mr. Wilmot started.

"Listen, and I will tell you my intention. Two more years have yet to run before that garish and hideous date, prophetic of all that is bright and new and abominably raw. But I shall have fled, how I know not; haply mandragora will lure my weary mind to rest. I think I should like to die as La Gioconda was painted, listening to flute-players in a curtained alcove; or you, Michael, shall read to me some diabolic and funereal song of Baudelaire, so that I may fearfully pass away."

Michael, sitting in the dim room of peacock-blue made tremendously nocturnal by the heavy smoke of all the cigarettes, did not much care for the turn the conversation of Mr. Wilmot had taken. It had been interesting enough, while the discussion applied directly to himself; but all this vague effusion of learning meant very little to him. At the same time, there was an undeniable eccentricity in a member of the Upper Fifth sitting thus in fantastic communion with a figure completely outside the imagination of Mr. Cray or any of his inky groundlings. Michael began to feel a contemptuous pity for his fellows now buried in bedclothes, hot and heavy with Ciceronian sentences and pious preparation. He began to believe that if he wished to keep pace with this new friendship, he must acquire something of Mr. Wilmot's heightened air. And however mad he might seem, there stood the books, and there stood the cigarettes for Michael's pleasure. It was all very exciting, and it would not have been possible to say that before he met Wilmot.

The friendship progressed through the rest of the autumn-term, and Michael drifted farther away from the normal life of the school than even his incursion into Catholicism had taken him. That phase of his development had penetrated deeper than any other, and from time to time Michael knew bitter repentances and made grim resolutions. From time to time letters would arrive from Dom Cuthbert asking him down to Clere Abbey; Mr. Viner, too, would question him narrowly about his new set of friends, and Michael's replies never seemed perfectly satisfactory to the shrewd priest.

It was by his costume more than by anything else that Michael expressed at first his sense of emancipation. He took to coming to school in vivid bow-ties that raised Mr. Cray's most sarcastic comments.

"The sooner you go to the History Sixth, Fane, and take that loathsome ribbon with you, the better for us all. Where did you get it? Out of the housemaid's trunk, one would say, by its appearance."

"It happens to be a tie," said Michael with insolence in his tone.

"Oh, it happens to be a tie, does it? Well, it also happens to be an excellent rule of St. James' School that all boys, however clever, wear dark suits and black ties. There also happens to be an excellent cure for pretentious and flamboyant youths who disregard this rule. There happens to be a play by one Euripides called the Alcestis. I suggest you write me out the first two hundred lines of it."

Michael's next encounter was with Mr. Viner, on the occasion of his producing in the priest's pipe-seasoned sitting-room a handkerchief inordinately perfumed with an Eastern scent lately discovered by Wilmot.

"Good heavens, Michael, what Piccadilly breezes are you wafting into my respectable and sacerdotal apartment?"

"I rather like scent," explained Michael lamely.

"Well, I don't, so, for goodness' sake don't bring any more of it in here. Pah! Phew! It's worse than a Lenten address at a fashionable church. Really, you know, these people you're in with now are not at all good for you, Michael."

"They're more interesting than any of the chaps at school."

"Are they? There used to be a saying in my undergraduate days, 'Distrust a freshman that's always seen with third-year men.' No doubt the inference is often unjust, but still the proverb remains."

"Ah, but these people aren't at school with me," Michael observed.

"No, I wish they were. They might be licked into better shape, if they were," retorted the priest.

"I think you're awfully down on Wilmot just because I didn't meet him in some churchy set. If it comes to that, I met some much bigger rotters than him at Clere."

"My dear Michael," argued Father Viner, "the last place I should have been surprized to see Master Wilmot would be in a churchy set. Don't forget that if religion is a saving grace, religiosity is a constitutional weakness. Can't you understand that a priest like myself who has taken the average course, public-school, 'varsity, and theological college, meets a thundering lot of Wilmots by the way? My dear fellow, many of my best friends, many of the priests you've met in my rooms, were once upon a time every bit as decadent as the lilified Wilmot. They took it like scarlet fever or chicken-pox, and feel all the more secure now for having had it. Decadence, as our friend knows it, is only a new-fangled name for green-sickness. It's a healthy enough mental condition for the young, but it's confoundedly dangerous for the grown-up. The first pretty girl that looks his way cures it in a boy, if he's a normal decent boy. I shouldn't offer any objection to your behaviour, if you were being decadent with Mark Chator or Martindale or Rigg. Good heavens, the senior curate at the best East-end Mission, when he was at Oxford, used to walk down the High leading a lobster on a silver chain, and even that wasn't original, for he stole the poor little fantastic idea from some precious French poet. But that senior curate is a very fine fellow to-day. No, no, this fellow Wilmot and all his set are very bad company for you, and I do not like your being decadent with these half-baked fancy-cakes."

Michael, however, would not admit that Mr. Viner was right, and frequented the dangerous peacock-blue room in Edwardes Square more than ever. He took Chator there amongst others, and was immensely gratified to be solemnly warned at the end of the visit that he was playing with Hell-fire. This seemed to him an interesting and original pastime, and he hinted to solemn, simple, spluttering old Chator of more truly Satanic mysteries.

After Christmas Michael had his way and was moved into the History Sixth, mainly owing to the intervention of the Member for West Kensington. The History Sixth was presided over by Mr. Kirkham, whose nominal aim in life was the amelioration of Jacobean athletics. From the fact that he wore an M.C.C. ribbon round his straw hat, and an Oxford University Authentic tie, it is probable that the legend of his former skill at cricket was justified. In reality he was much more interested in Liberalism than anything else, and persistently read Blue Books, under-lining the dramatic moments of Royal Commissions and chewing his moustache through pages of dialogue hostile to his opinions. A rumour sped round the school that he had been invited to stand for Parliament, a rumour which Michael, on the strength of dining with the Member for West Kensington, flatly contradicted.

The History Sixth class-room was a pleasant place, the only class-room in the school that ever saw the sun. Its windows looked out on the great green expanse of the school ground, where during the deserted hours of work the solitary roller moved sedately and ancient women weeded the pitches.

There were only seven boys in the History Sixth. There was Strang, the Captain of the Eleven, who lounged through the dull Lent term and seemed, as he spread his bulk over the small desk, like a half-finished statue to which still adhered a fragment of uncarved stone. There was Terry, the Vice-Captain of the Fifteen and most dapper half-back that ever cursed forwards. He spent his time trying to persuade Strang to take an interest in Noughts and Crosses. There was beak-nosed Thomson who had gained an Exhibition at Selwyn College, Cambridge, and dark-eyed Mallock, whose father wrote columnar letters to The Times. Burnaby, who shocked Michael very much by prophesying that a certain H. G. Wells, now writing about Martian invasions, was the coming man, and Railton, a weedy and disconsolate recluse, made up with Michael himself the class-list.

There was an atmosphere of rest about the History Sixth, a leisured dignity that contrasted very delightfully with the spectacled industry of the Upper Fifth. To begin with, Mr, Kirkham was always ten minutes after every other master in entering his class-room. This habit allowed the members of his form to stroll gracefully along the corridors and watch one by one the cavernous doors of other class-rooms absorb their victims. Michael would often go out of his way to pass Mr. Cray's room, in order to see with a luxurious sense of relief the intellectual convicts of the Upper Fifth hurrying to their prison. Many other conventions of school-life were slackened in the History Sixth. A slight eccentricity of attire was not considered unbecoming in what was, at any rate in its own opinion, a faintly literary society. The room was always open between morning and afternoon school, and it was not an uncommon sight to see members of the form reading novels in tip-tilted chairs. Most of the home work was set a week in advance, which did away with the unpleasant necessity of speculating on the 'construe' or hurriedly cribbing with a hastily peppered variety of mistakes the composition of one's neighbour. Much of the work was simple reading, and as for the essays, by a legal fiction they were always written during the three hours devoted to Mathematics. Tradition forbade any member of the History Sixth to take Mathematics seriously, and Mr. Gaskell, the overworked Mathematical master, was not inclined to break this tradition. He used to write out a problem or two on the blackboard for the sake of appearances, and then settle down to the correction of his more serious pupils' work, while the History Sixth devoted themselves to their more serious work. One of the great social earthquakes that occasionally devastate all precedent occurred when Mr. Gaskell was away with influenza, and his substitute, an earnest young novice, tried to make Strang and Terry do a Quadratic Equation.

"But, sir, we never do Mathematics."

"Well, what are you here for?" asked the novice. "What am I here for?"

"We don't know," replied the History Sixth in unison; and the vendetta that followed the complaint of their behaviour to Mr. Kirkham made the novice's mastership a burden to him during Mr. Gaskell's illness. Enraged conservatism called for reprisals, until Mr. Kirkham pointed out with a felicity acquired from long perusal of Parliamentary humour, "You are Jacobeans, not Jacobins," and with this mild joke quenched the feud.

The effect of his transference to the History Sixth made Michael more decadent than ever, for the atmosphere of his new class encouraged him along the orchidaceous path pointed out by Arthur Wilmot. He was not now decadent from any feeling of opposition to established things, but he was decadent from conviction of the inherent rightness of such a state. At first the phase had manifested itself in outward signs, a little absurdly; now his actual point of view was veering into accord with the externals.

Sunday was a day at Edwardes Square from which Michael returned almost phosphorescent with decay. Sunday was the day on which Mr. Wilmot gathered from all over London specimens of corruption that fascinated Michael with their exotic and elaborate behaviour. Nothing seemed worth while in such an assembly except a novel affectation. Everything was a pose. It was a pose to be effeminate in speech and gesture; it was a pose to drink absinthe; it was a pose to worship the devil; it was a pose to buy attenuated volumes of verse at an unnatural price, for the sake of owning a sonnet that was left out in the ordinary edition; it was a pose to admire pictures that to Michael at first were more like wall-papers than pictures; it was really a pose to live at all. Conversation at these delicate entertainments was like the conversations overheard in the anterooms of private asylums. Everyone was very willowy in his movements, whether he were smoking or drinking or looking for a box of matches. Michael attempted to be willowy at school once, but gave it up on being asked if he had fleas.

One of the main charms at first of these Sunday afternoon gatherings was the way in which, one after another, every one of the guests would take Michael aside and explain how different he (the guest) was from all the rest of humanity. Michael was flattered, and used to become very intense and look very soul-searching, and interject sympathetic exclamations until he discovered that the confidant usually proceeded to another corner of the room to entrust someone else with his innermost heart. He became cynical after a while, especially when he found that the principal points of difference from the rest of the world were identical in every one of the numerous guests who sought his counsel and his sympathy.

However, he never became cynical enough to distrust the whole school of thought and admit that Father Viner's contempt was justifiable. If ever he had any doubts, he was consoled by assuring himself that at any rate these new friends were very artistic, and how important it was to be artistic no one could realize who was not at school.

Under the pressure of his insistent temperament, Michael found his collection of statuettes and ecclesiastical bric-à-brac very depressing. As a youth of the Florentine Renaissance he could not congratulate himself upon his room, which was much too much unlike either a Carpaccio interior or an Aubrey Beardsley bedroom. Between these two his ambition wavered.

One by one the statuettes were moved to the top of a wardrobe where for a while they huddled, a dusty and devoted crowd, until one by one they met martyrdom at the hands of the housemaid. In their place appeared Della Robbia reliefs and terra-cotta statuettes of this or that famous Greek youth. The muscular and tearful pictures of Guido Reni, the bland insipidities of Bouguereau soon followed the statuettes, meeting a comparable martyrdom by being hung in the servants' bedroom. The walls of Michael's room were papered with a brown paper, which was intended to be very artistic, but was really merely sad. It was lightened, however, by various daring pictures in black and red that after only a very short regard really did take shape as scenes of Montmartre. There were landscapes of the Sussex downs, with a slight atmosphere of Japan and landscapes of Japan that were not at all like Japan, but none the less beautiful for that. The books of devotion were banished to the company of superannuated Latin and Greek textbooks on the lower shelf of a cupboard in the morning-room, whose upper shelf was stacked with tinned fruits. Incense was still burnt, not as once to induce prayers to ascend, but to stupefy Michael with scent and warmth into an imitation of a drug-taker's listless paradise. This condition was accentuated by erecting over the head of his bed a canopy of faded green satin, which gave him acute æsthetic pleasure, until one night it collapsed upon him in the middle of the night. Every piece of upholstery in the room was covered with art linens that with the marching years had ousted the art muslins of Michael's childhood. He also covered with squares of the same material the gas brackets, pushing them back against the wall and relying for light upon candles only. Notwithstanding Wilmot's talk about literature, the influence of Wilmot's friends was too strong, and Michael could not resist the deckle-edges of negligible poets. As these were expensive, Michael's library lacked scope, and he himself, reflecting his pastime, came to believe in the bitterness and sweetness and bitter-sweetness of the plaintive sinners who printed so elegantly on such permanent paper the versification of their irregularity.

Irregularity was now being subjected to Michael's process of idealistic alchemy, and since his conception of irregularity was essentially romantic, and since he shrank from sentiment, he was able to save himself, when presently all this decoration fell to pieces, and revealed naked unpleasantness. Nothing in his present phase had yet moved him so actually as his brief encounter with Brother Aloysius. That glimpse of a fearful and vital underworld had been to him romantic without trappings; it was a glimpse into an underworld to which one day he might descend, since it asked no sighing for the vanished joys of the past, for the rose-gardens of Rome. He began to play with the idea of departing suddenly from his present life and entering the spectral reality of the Seven Sisters Road, treading whatever raffish raddled pavement knew the hollow steps of a city's prowlers. Going home on Sunday nights from the perfumed house in Edwardes Square and passing quickly and apprehensively figures that materialized in a circle of lamplight, he would contrast their existence with what remained in his senses of stale cigarette-smoke and self-conscious airs and attitudes. Yet the very picture he conjured of the possibility that haunted him made him the more anxious to substitute for the stark descent to hell the Sicilian or Satanic affectations of the luxurious mimes who postured against a background of art. Much of the talk at Edwardes Square concerned itself with the pastoral side of school-life, and Michael found himself being cross-questioned by elderly faun-like men who had a conception of an English public-school that was more Oriental than correct. Michael vainly tried to dispel these illusions, which made him resentful and for the moment crudely normal. He felt towards them much as he felt towards Garrod's attempt to cure his ignorance at Clere. These were excellent fellows from whom to accept a cigarette or sometimes even an invitation to lunch at a Soho restaurant, but when they presumed upon his condescension and dared to include in their tainted outlook himself as a personal factor, Michael shrivelled with a virginal disdain.

Unreasonably to the others, Michael did not object very much to Wilmot's oracular addresses on the delights of youth. He felt that so much of Wilmot was in the mere word, and he admired so frankly his embroideries of any subject, and above all he liked Wilmot so much personally, that he listened to him, and was even so far influenced by him as to try to read into the commonplace of a summer term all that Wilmot would suggest.

"O fortunate shepherd, to whom will you pipe to-morrow, or what slim and agile companion will you crown for his prowess? O lucky youth, able to drowse in the tempered sunlight that the elm-trees give, while your friend splendidly cool in his white flannels bats and bowls for your delight!"

"But I haven't got any particular friend that I can watch," objected Michael.

"One day you will terribly regret the privileges of your pastoral life."

"Do you really think I am not getting all I can out of school?" demanded Michael.

"I'm sure you're not," said Wilmot.

Michael began to trouble himself over Wilmot's warning, and also he began to look back with sentimental regret to what had really been his happiest time, his friendship with Alan. Pride kept him from approaching Alan with nothing to offer for nearly two years' indifference. There had been no quarrel. They had merely gradually drifted apart, yet it was with a deep pang of remorse that one day he realized in passing the dusty Upper Fifth that Alan was now wrestling with that imprisonment. Michael racked his brains to think of some way by which he and Alan might come together in their old amity, their perfect fellowship. He sought some way that would make it natural and inevitable, but no way presented itself. He could, so deep was his sudden regret, have stifled his own pride and deliberately invited Alan to be friends; he would even have risked a repulse; but with the renewal of his longing for the friendship came a renewal of the old sympathy and utter comprehension of Alan's most secret moods, and Michael realized that his old friend would be too shy to accept this strange, inexplicable revival, unless it were renewed, as it was begun, by careless, artless intercourse.

The immediate result of this looking back to an earlier period was to arouse in Michael an interest in boys younger than himself, and through his idealism to endow them with a conscious joy of life which he fell to envying. He had a desire to warn them of the enchantment under whose benign and dulcet influence they lived, to warn them that soon the lovely spell would be broken, and bid them make the most of their stripling time. Continually he was seeing boys in the lower forms whose friendship blooming like two flowers on a spray shed a fragrance so poignant that tears came springing to his eyes. He began to imagine himself very old, to feel that by some unkind gift of temperament he had nothing left to live for. It chanced that summer term the History Sixth learned for repetition the Odes of Keats, and in the Ode on a Grecian Urn Michael found the expression of his mood:

Fair youth, beneath the trees, thou canst not leave
*   Thy song, nor ever can those trees be bare;*
*   Bold Lover, never, never canst thou kiss,*
Though winning near the goal—yet, do not grieve;
*   She cannot fade, though thou hast not thy bliss,*
*   For ever wilt thou love, and she be fair!*

These lines were learnt in June, and for Michael they enshrined immortally his yearning. Never had the fugitive summer glided so fast, since never before had he sat in contemplation of its flight. Until this moment he had been one with the season's joy like a bird or a sunbeam, but now for the first time he had the opportunity of regarding the empty field during the hours of school, and of populating it with the merry ghosts of the year with Caryll. All through schooltime the mowing-machine hummed its low harmony of perishable minutes and wasted sunlight. The green field was scattered with the wickets of games in progress that stood luminously in golden trios, so brightly did the sunny weather enhance their wood. The scoring-board of the principal match stared like a stopped clock with the record of the last breathless run, and as if to mock the stillness from a distant corner came a sound of batting, where at the nets the two professionals practised idly. A bluebottle buzzed upon the window-pane; pigeons flapped from pinnacle to pinnacle of the chapel; sparrows cheeped on a persistent note; pens scratched paper; Mr. Kirkham turned a Blue Book's page at regular intervals.

*   Ah, happy, happy boughs! that cannot shed*
Your leaves, nor ever bid the Spring adieu;
*   And, happy melodist, unwearied*
For ever piping songs for ever new.

Thus for him would the trancèd scene for ever survive.

The History Sixth were for the purposes of cricket linked to the Classical Lower Sixth, but Michael did not play that term. Instead, a strayed reveller, he would move from game to game of the Junior School, hearing the shrill encouragement and pondering the rose-red agility of a Classical lower form, in triumph over minor Moderns. Michael was continually trying to perceive successors to himself and Alan, and he would often enter into shy colloquy with the juniors, who were awed by his solemn smile, and shuffled uneasily from leg to leg.

Two boys whom Michael finally determined should stand as types of Alan and him gradually emerged from the white throng of Lower School cricket. One of them was indeed very like Alan, and had the same freckled smile. With this pair Michael became intimate, as one becomes intimate with two puppies. He would pet and scold them, encourage them to be successful in their sport, and rebuke them for failure. They perhaps found him entertaining, and were certainly proud to be seen in conversation with him, for though Michael himself was not an athletic hero, he was the companion of heroes, and round him clung the shining mirage of their immortality.

Then one day, unknown to Michael, these two boys became involved in a scandal; the inquisition of a great public school pinned them down desperately struggling, miserably afraid; the rumour of their expulsion went callously round the gossiping ranks of their fellows.

Michael was informed of their disgrace by dark-eyed Mallock whose father wrote columnar letters to The Times. Michael said bitter things to the complacent Mallock and offered with serious want of dignity for a member of the leisurely and cultivated History Sixth, to punch Mallock's damned head.

Mallock said sneeringly that he supposed Michael sympathized with the little beasts. Michael replied that he merely sympathized with them because he was profoundly sure that it was a pack of lies.

"You'd better go and tell the Old Man that, because they say he's going to expel them to-day."

Michael turned pale with fury.

"I damned well will go, and when I come back I'll ram you upside down in the Tuck Shop butter-tub."

Mallock flushed under the ignominy of this threat, and muttered his conviction that Michael was talking through his hat. Just then Mr. Kirkham entered the class-room, and Michael immediately went up to him and asked if he might go and speak to the Headmaster.

Mr. Kirkham stared with amazement, and his voice, which always seemed to hesitate whether it should come out through his mouth or his nose, on this occasion never came out at all, but stayed in the roof of Mr. Kirkham's mouth.

"Can I, sir?" Michael repeated.

"I suppose you can," said Mr. Kirkham.

The class followed Michael's exit with wide eyes; even the phlegmatic Strang was so deeply moved that he sat upright in his chair and tapped his head to indicate midsummer madness.

Outside in the echoing corridor, where the plaster casts looked coldly down, Michael wrestled with his leaping heart, forcing it into tranquillity so that he could grapple with the situation he had created for himself. By the Laocoön he paused. Immediately beyond was the sombre doorway of the Head's room. As he paused on the threshold two ridiculous thoughts came to him—that Lessing's Laocoön was one of the set books for the English Literature prize, and that he would rather be struggling in the coils of that huge stone snake than standing thus invertebrate before this portentous door.

Then Michael tapped. There was no answer but a dull buzz of voices. Again Michael tapped and, beating down his heart, turned the handle that seemed as he held it to swell to pumpkin size in his grasp. Slowly he pushed the door before him, expecting to hear a bellowed summons to appear, and wondering whether he could escape unknown to his class-room if his nerve failed him even now. Then he heard the sound of tears, and indignation drove him onwards, drove him so urgently that actually he slammed the great door behind him, and made the intent company aware of his presence.

"What do *you* want?" shouted Dr. Brownjohn. "Can't you see I'm busy?"

"I want to speak to you, sir." The words actually seemed to come from his mouth winged with flames, such a volcano was Michael now.

"I'm busy. Go outside and wait," roared the Headmaster.

Michael paused to regard the scene—the two boys sobbing with painful regular intake of breath, oblivious of him; the witnesses, a sheepish crew; the school-porter waiting for his prey; old Mr. Caryll coughing nervously and apparently on the verge of tears himself; the odious Paul Pry of a Secretary nibbling his pen; and in the background other masters waiting with favourable or damning testimony.

The drama of gloating authority shook Michael to the very foundation of his being, and he came rapidly into the middle of the room, came right up to the Headmaster, until he felt engulfed in the black silk gown, and at last said slowly and with simple conviction:

"I think you're all making a mistake."

When he had spoken Michael could have kicked himself for not shouting furiously the torrid denunciations which had come surging up for utterance. Then he immediately began to talk again, to his own great surprise, calmly and very reasonably.

"I know these kids—these two boys, I mean—quite well. It's impossible for any of this to be true. I've seen them a lot this term—practically every day. Really, sir, you'll make a terrible mistake if you expel them. They're awfully decent little chaps. They are really, sir. Of course they're too frightened now to say anything for themselves. It's not fair for everybody to be set at them like this."

Michael looked despairingly at the masters assembled.

"And these other boys who've been brought in to tell what they know. Why, they're frightened too. They'd say anything. Why don't you, why don't you——"

Michael looked round in despair, stammered, broke down, and then to his own eternal chagrin burst into tears. He moved hastily over to the window, striving to pull himself together, seeing through an overpowering blur the great green field in the garish sunlight. Yet his tears, shameful to him, may have turned the scale, for one by one the masters came forward with eager testimony of good; and with every word of praise the tears rushed faster and faster to Michael's eyes. Then he heard old Caryll's rasping cough and broken benignant sentences, which with all their memories lulled his emotion to quietude again.

"Hope you'll bring it in non probatum, Headmaster"—cough—cough—"good boys both "—cough—cough—"sure it's a mistake—Fane's a good boy too—idle young rascal—but a good heart"—cough—cough—"had him under me for a year—know him well——"

Dr. Brownjohn, with a most voluminous wave, dismissed the matter. Everyone, even the Paul Pry of a Secretary, went out of the room, and as the door closed Michael heard Mr. Caryll addressing the victims.

"Now then, don't cry any more, you young boobies."

Michael's thoughts followed them upstairs to the jolly class-room, and he almost smiled at the imagination of Mr. Caryll's entrance and the multitudinous jokes that would demonstrate his relief at his pupils' rescue. Michael recovered from his dream to find the Headmaster speaking to him in his most rumbling bass.

"I don't know why I allowed you to interfere in this disgraceful affair, boy. Um?"

"No, sir," Michael agreed.

85

"But since you are here, I will take the opportunity of warning you that the company you keep is very vile."

Michael looked apprehensive.

"If you think nothing is known of your habits out of school, you are much mistaken. I will not have any boy at my school frequenting the house of that deboshed nincompoop Wilmot."

Dr. Brownjohn's voice was now so deep that it vibrated in the pit of Michael's stomach like the diapason of the school organ.

"Give up that detestable association of mental impostors and be a boy again. You have disappointed me during the whole of your career; but you're a winning boy. Um? Go back to your work."

Michael left the august room with resolves swaying in his brain, wondering what he could do to repay the Old Man. It was too late to take a very high place in the summer examinations. Yet somehow, so passionate was his gratitude, he managed to come out third.

Michael never told his mother about his adventure, but in the reaction against Wilmot and all that partook of decadence, and in his pleasure at having done something, however clumsily, he felt a great wish to include his mother in his emotion of universal love.

"Where are we going these holidays?" he asked.

"I thought perhaps you'd like to stay at your monastery again," said Mrs. Fane. "I was thinking of going abroad."

Michael's face fell, and his mother was solicitously penitent.

"My dearest boy, I never dreamed you would want to be with me. You've always gone out on Sundays."

"I know, I'm sorry, I won't again," Michael assured her.

"And I've made my arrangements now. I wish I'd known. But why shouldn't you go and see Stella? It seems a pity that you and she should grow up so much apart."

"Well, I will, if you like," said Michael.

"Dearest boy, what has happened to you? You are so agreeable," exclaimed Mrs. Fane.

In the end it was arranged that Michael should accompany Mr. Viner on his holiday in France, and afterwards stay with Stella with a family at Compiègne for the rest of the time. Michael went to see his mother off at Charing Cross before he joined Mr. Viner.

"Darling Michael," she murmured as the train began to move slowly forward. "You're looking so well and happy—just like you were two years ago. Just like——"

The rest of the comparison was lost in the noise of the speeding train.

Chapter X: *Stella*

MICHAEL spent a charming fortnight with Father Viner in Amiens, Chartres and Rouen. The early Masses to which they went along the cool, empty streets of the morning, and the shadowy, candle-lit Benedictions from which they came home through the deepening dusk gave to Michael at least a profound hope, if not the astonishing faith of his first religious experience. Sitting with the priest at the open window of their inn, while down below the footsteps of the wayfarers were pattering like leaves, Michael recaptured some of that emotion of universal love which with sacramental force had filled his heart during the wonder of transition from boyhood to adolescence. He did not wish to know more about these people than could be told by the sound of their progress so light, so casual, so essentially becoming to the sapphirine small world in which they hurried to and fro. The passion of hope overwhelmed Michael's imagination with a beauty that was perfectly expressed by the unseen busy populations of a city's waning twilight. Love, birth, death, greed, ambition, all humanity's stress of thought and effort, were merged in a murmurous contentment of footfalls and faint-heard voices. Michael supposed that somehow to God the universe must sound much as this tall street of Rouen sounded now to him at his inn window, and he realized for the first time how God must love the world. Later, the twilight and voices and footfalls would fade together into night, and through long star-scattered silences Michael would brood with a rapture that became more than hope, if less than faith with restless, fiery heart. Then clocks would strike sonorously; the golden window-panes would waver and expire; Mr. Viner would tap his pipe upon the sill; and Michael and he would follow their own great shadows up into bedrooms noisy in the night-wind and prophetic of sleep's immense freedom, until with the slanting beams of dawn Michael would wake and at Mass time seek to enchain with prayers indomitable dreams.

The gravity of Michael's demeanour suited the grey town in which he sojourned, and though Mr. Viner used to teaze him about his saintly exterior, the priest seemed to enjoy his company.

"But don't look so solemn when you meet your sister, or she'll think you're sighing for a niche in Chartres Cathedral, which for a young lady emancipated from Germany would be a most distressing thought."

"I'm enjoying myself," said Michael earnestly.

"My dear old chap, I'm not questioning that for a moment, and personally I find your attitude consorts very admirably with the mood in which these northern towns of France always throw me," said Mr. Viner.

The fortnight came to an end, and to commemorate this chastening interlude of a confidence and a calm whose impermanence Michael half dreaded, half desired, he bought a pair of old candlesticks for the Notting Dale Mission. Michael derived a tremendous consolation from this purchase, for he felt that, even if in the future he should be powerless to revive this healing time, its austere hours would be immortalized, mirrored somehow in the candlesticks' bases as durably as if engraved upon a Grecian urn. There was in this impulse nothing more sentimental than in his erection last year of the small cairn to celebrate a fleeting moment of faith on the Berkshire downs.

Stella was already settled in the bosom of the French family when Michael reached Compiègne, and as he drove towards the Pension he began for the first time to wonder what his sister would be like after these two years. He was inclined to suppose that she would be a problem, and he already felt qualms about the behaviour of her projected suddenly like this from Germany into an atmosphere of romance. For Michael, France always stood out as typically romantic to his fancy. Spain and Italy were not within his realization as yet, and Germany he conceived of as a series of towns filled with the noise of piano-scales and hoarse gutturals. He hoped that Stella was not even now plunged into a girlish love-affair with one of the idle young Frenchmen who haunted so amorously the sunshine of this gay land. He even began to rehearse, as his carriage jolted along the cobbled embankment of the Oise, a particularly scathing scene in which he coldly denounced the importunate lover, while Stella stood abashed by fraternal indignation. Then he reflected that after all Stella was only fifteen and, as he remembered her, too much wrapped up in a zest for public appreciation to be very susceptible of private admiration. Moreover, he knew that most of her time was occupied by piano-practice. An emotion of pride in his accomplished sister displaced the pessimism of his first thoughts. He took pleasure in the imagination of her swaying the whole Pension by her miraculous execution, and he began to build up the picture of his entrance upon the last crashing chords of a sonata, when after the applause had ceased he would modestly step forward as the brother of this paragon.

The carriage was now bowling comfortably along a wide tree-shaded avenue bordered on either side by stretches of greenery which were dappled with children and nursemaids and sedate little girls with bobbing pigtails. Michael wondered if Stella was making a discreet promenade with the ladies of the family, half hoped she was, that he might reach the Pension before her and gracefully welcome her, as she, somewhat flustered by being late for his arrival, hurried up the front-door steps. Then, just as he was wondering whether there would or would not be front-door steps to the Pension, the cab drew up by a house with a green verandah and front-garden geranium-dyed to right and left of a vivid gravel path. Michael perceived, with a certain disapproval, that the verandah sheltered various ladies in wicker chairs. He disliked the notion of carrying up his bag in the range of their cool criticism, nor did he relish the conversation that would have to be embarked upon with the neat maid already hurrying to meet him. But most contrary to his preconceived idea of arrival was the affectionate ambush laid for him by Stella just when he was trying to remember whether 'chambre' were masculine or feminine. Yet, even as he felt Stella's dewy lips on his, and her slim fingers round his neck, he reproached himself for his silly shyness, although he could only say:

"Hullo, look out for my collar."

Stella laughed ripplingly.

"Oh, Michael," she cried, "I'm most frightfully glad to see you, you darling old Michael."

Michael looked much alarmed at the amazing facility of her affectionate greeting, and vaguely thought how much easier existence must be to a girl who never seemed to be hampered by any feeling of what people within earshot would think of her. Yet almost immediately Stella herself relapsed into shyness at the prospect of introducing Michael to the family, and it was only the perfectly accomplished courtesy of Madame Regnier which saved Michael from summarily making up his mind that these holidays were going to be a most ghastly failure.

The business of unpacking composed his feelings slightly, and a tap at his door, followed by Stella's silvery demand to come in, gave him a thrill of companionship. He suddenly realized, too, that he and his sister had corresponded frequently during their absence, and that this queer shyness at meeting her in person was really absurd. Stella, wandering round the room with his ties on her arm, gave Michael real pleasure, and she for her part seemed highly delighted at the privilege of superintending his unpacking.

He noted with a sentimental fondness that she still hummed, and he was very much impressed by the flowers which she had arranged in the cool corners of the pleasant room. On her appearance, too, as she hung over the rail of his bed chatting to him gaily, he congratulated himself. He liked the big apple-green bows in her chestnut hair; he liked her slim white hands and large eyes; and he wondered if her smile were like his, and hoped it was, since it was certainly very subtle and attractive.

"What sort of people hang out in this place?" he asked.

"Oh, nice people," Stella assured him. "Madame Regnier is a darling, and she loves my playing, and Monsieur is fearfully nice, with a grey beard. We always play billiards in the evening, and drink cassis. It's lovely. There are three darling old ladies, widows I think. They sit and listen to me playing, and when I've finished pay me all sorts of compliments, which sound so pretty in French. One of them said I was 'ravissante.'"

"Are there any kids?" asked Michael.

Stella said there were no kids, and Michael sighed his relief.

"Do you practise much?"

"Oh, no, I'm having a holiday, I only practise three hours a day."

"How much?" asked Michael. "Good Lord, do you call that a holiday?"

"Why, you silly old thing, of course it is," rippled Stella.

Presently it was time for déjeuner, and they sat down to eat in a room, of shaded sunlight, watching the green jalousies that glowed like beryls, and listening to a canary's song. Michael was introduced to Madame Graves, Madame Lamarque and Madame Charpentier, the three old widows who lived at the Pension, and who all looked strangely alike, with their faces and hands of aged ivory and their ruffles and wristbands starched to the semblance of fretted white coral. They ate mincingly in contrast to M. Regnier who, guarded by a very large napkin, pitchforked his food into his mouth with noisy recklessness. Later in the mellow August afternoon Michael and he walked solemnly round the town together, and Michael wondered if he had ever before raised his hat so many times.

After dinner, when the coffee and cassis had been drunk, Madame Regnier invited Stella to play to them. Dusk was falling in the florid French drawing-room, but so rich was the approach of darkness that no lamps brooded with rosy orbs, and only a lighted candle on either side of Stella stabbed the gloom in which the listeners leaned quietly back against the tropic tapestries of their chairs, without trying to occupy themselves with books or crochet-work.

Michael sat by the scented window, watching the stars twinkle, it almost seemed, in tune with the vibrant melodies that Stella rang out. In the bewitching candlelight the keyboard trembled and shimmered like water to a low wind. Deep in the shadow the three old ladies sat in a waxen ecstasy, so still that Michael wondered whether they were alive. He did not know whose tunes they were that Stella played; he did not know what dreams they wove for the old ladies, whether of spangled opera-house or ball; he did not care, being content to watch the lissome hands that from time to time went dancing away on either side from the curve of Stella's straight back, whether to play with raindrops in the treble or marshal thunders from the bass. The candlelight sprayed her flowing chestnut hair with a golden mist that might have been an aureole over which the apple-green bows floated unsubstantial like amazing moths.

Michael continually tried to shape his ideas to the inspiration of the music, but every image that rose battling for expression lost itself in a peerless stupefaction.

Then suddenly Stella stopped playing, and the enchantment was dispelled by murmurous praise and entering lamplight. Stella, slim as a fountain, stood upright in the centre of the drawing-room and, like a fountain, swayed now this way, now that, to catch the compliments so dear to her. Michael wished the three old ladies would not appeal to him to endorse their so perfectly phrased enthusiasm, and grew very conscious of the gradual decline of 'oui' into 'wee' as he supported their laudation. He was glad when M. Regnier proposed a game of billiards, and glad to see that Stella could romp, romp so heartily indeed that once or twice he had to check a whispered rebuke.

But later on when he said good night to her outside his bedroom, he had an impulse to hug her close for the unimaginable artistry of this little sister.

Michael and Stella went out next day to explore the forest of Compiègne. They wandered away from the geometrical forest roads into high glades and noble chases; they speculated upon the whereabouts of the wild-boars that were hunted often, and therefore really did exist; they lay deep in the bracken utterly remote in the ardent emerald light, utterly quiet save for the thrum of insects rising and falling. In this intimate seclusion Michael found it easy enough to talk to Stella. Somehow her face, magnified by the proportions of the surrounding vegetation, scarcely seemed to belong to her, and Michael had a sensation of a fairy fellowship, as he felt himself being absorbed into her wide and strangely magical eyes. Seen like this they were as overwhelmingly beautiful as two flowers, holding mysteries of colour and form that could never be revealed save thus in an abandonment of contemplation.

"Why do you stare at me, Michael?" she asked.

"Because I think it's funny to realize that you and I are as nearly as it's possible to be the same person, and yet we're as different from each other as we are from the rest of people. I wonder, if you didn't know I was your brother, and I didn't know you were my sister, if we should have a sort of—what's the word?—intuition about it? For instance, you can play the piano, and I can't even understand the feeling of being able to play the piano. I wish we knew our father. It must be interesting to have a father and a mother, and see what part of one comes from each."

"I always think father and mother weren't married," said Stella.

Michael blushed hotly, taken utterly aback.

"I say, my dear girl, don't say things like that. That's a frightful thing to say."

"Why?"

"Why? Why, because people would be horrified to hear a little girl talking like that," Michael explained.

"Oh, I thought you meant they'd be shocked to think of people not being married."

"I say, really, you know, Stella, you ought to be careful. I wouldn't have thought you even knew that people sometimes—very seldom, though, mind—don't get married."

"You funny old boy," rippled Stella. "You must think I'm a sort of doll just wound up to play the piano. If I didn't know that much after going to Germany, why—oh, Michael, I do think you're funny."

"I was afraid these beastly foreigners would spoil you," muttered Michael.

"It's not the foreigners. It's myself."

"Stella!"

"Well, I'm fifteen and a half."

"I thought girls were innocent," said Michael with disillusion in his tone.

"Girls grow older quicker than boys."

"But I mean always innocent," persisted Michael. "I don't mean all girls, of course. But—well—a girl like you."

"Very innocent girls are usually very stupid girls," Stella asserted.

Michael made a resolution to watch his sister's behaviour when she came back to London next year to make her first public appearance at a concert. For the moment, feeling overmatched, he changed the trend of his reproof.

"Well, even if you do talk about people not being married, I think it's rotten to talk about mother like that."

"You stupid old thing, as if I should do it with anyone but you, and I only talked about her to you because you look so sort of cosy and confidential in these ferns."

"They're not ferns—they're bracken. If I thought such a thing was possible," declared Michael, "I believe I'd go mad. I don't think I could ever again speak to anybody I knew."

"Why not, if they didn't know?"

"How like a girl! Stella, you make me feel uncomfortable, you do really."

Stella stretched her full length in the luxurious greenery.

"Well, mother never seems unhappy."

"Exactly," said Michael eagerly. "Therefore, what you think can't possibly be true. If it were, she'd always look miserable."

"Well, then who *was* our father?"

"Don't ask me," said Michael gloomily. "I believe he's in prison—or perhaps he's in an asylum, or deformed."

Stella shuddered.

"Michael, what a perfectly horrible idea. Deformed!"

"Well, wouldn't you sooner he were deformed than that you were—than that—than the other idea?" Michael stammered.

"No, I wouldn't," Stella cried. "I'd much, much, much rather that mother was never married."

Michael tried to drag his mind towards the comprehension of this unnatural sentiment, but the longer he regarded it the worse it seemed, and with intense irony he observed to Stella:

"I suppose you'll be telling me next that you're in love."

"I'm not in love just at the moment," said Stella blandly.

"Do you mean to say you have been in love?"

"A good deal," she admitted.

Michael leaped to his feet, and looked down on her recumbent in the bracken.

"But only in a stupid schoolgirly way?" he gasped.

"Yes, I suppose it was," Stella paused. "But it was fearfully thrilling all the same—especially in duets."

"Duets?"

"I used to read ahead, and watch where our hands would come together, and then the notes used to get quite slippery with excitement."

"Look here," Michael demanded, drawing himself up, "are you trying to be funny?"

"No," Stella declared, rising to confront Michael. "He was one of my masters. He was only about thirty, and he was killed in Switzerland by an avalanche."

Michael was staggered by the confession of this shocking and precocious child, as one after another his chimeras rose up to leer at him triumphantly.

"And did he make love to you? Did he try to kiss you?" Michael choked out.

"Oh, no," said Stella. "That would have spoilt it all."

Michael sighed under a faint lightening of his load, and Stella came up to him engagingly to slip her arm into his.

"Don't be angry with me, Michael, because I have wanted so dreadfully to be great friends with you and tell you all my secrets. I want to tell you what I think about when I'm playing; and, Michael, you oughtn't to be angry with me, because you were simply just made to be told secrets. That's why I played so well last night. I was telling you a secret all the time."

"Do you know what it is, Stella?" said Michael, with a certain awe in his voice. "I believe our father is in an asylum, and I believe you and I are both mad—not raving mad, of course—but slightly mad."

"All geniuses are," said Stella earnestly.

"But we aren't geniuses."

"I am," murmured Stella in a strangely quiet little voice that sounded in Michael's ears like the song of a furtive melodious bird.

"Are you?" he whispered, half frightened by this assertion, delivered under huge overarching trees in the burning silence of the forest. "Who told you so?"

"I told myself so. And when I tell myself something very solemnly, I can't be anything but myself, and I must be speaking the truth."

"But even if you're a genius—and I suppose you might be—I'm not a genius. I'm clever, but I'm not a genius."

"No, but you're the nearest person to being me, and if you're not a genius, I think you can understand. Oh, Michael," Stella cried, clasping his arm to her heart, "you do understand, because you never laughed when I told you I was a genius. I've told lots of girl-friends, and they laugh and say I'm conceited."

"Well, you are," said Michael, feeling bound not to lose the opportunity of impressing Stella with disapproval as well as comprehension.

"I know I am. But I must be to go on being myself. Oh, you darling brother, you do understand me. I've longed for someone to understand me. Mother's only proud of me."

"I'm not at all proud of you," said Michael crushingly.

"I don't want you to be. If you were proud of me, you'd think I belonged to you, and I don't ever want to belong to anybody."

"I shouldn't think you ever would," said Michael encouragingly, as they paced the sensuous mossy path in a rapture of avowals. "I should think you'd frighten anybody except me. But why do you fall in love, then?"

"Oh, because I want to make people die with despair."

"Great Scott, you are an unearthly kid."

"Oh, I'm glad I'm unearthly," said Stella. "I'd like to be a sort of Undine. I think I am. I don't think I've got a soul, because when I play I go rushing out into the darkness to look for my soul, and the better I play the nearer I get."

Michael stopped beneath an oak-tree and surveyed this extraordinary sister of his.

"Well, I always thought I was a mystic, but, good Lord, you're fifty times as much of a mystic as I am," he exclaimed with depressed conviction.

Suddenly Stella gave a loud scream.

"What on earth are you yelling at?" said Michael.

"Oh, Michael, look—a most enormous animal. Oh, look, oh, let me get up a tree. Oh, help me up. Push me up this tree."

"It's a wild-boar," declared Michael in a tone of astonished interest.

Stella screamed louder than ever and clung to Michael, sobbing. The boar, however, went on its way, routing among the herbage.

"Well, you may be a genius," said Michael, "but you're an awful little funk."

"But I was frightened."

"Wild-boars aren't dangerous except when they're being hunted," Michael asserted positively.

Stella soon became calm under the influence of her brother's equanimity. Arm-in-arm they sauntered back towards Compiègne, and so for a month of serene weather they sauntered every day, and every day Michael pondered more and more deeply the mystery of woman. He was sorry to say good-bye to Stella when she went back to Germany, and longed for the breathless hour of her first concert, wishful that all his life he might stand between her and the world, the blundering wild-boar of a world.

Chapter XI: *Action and Reaction*

ALMOST before the confusion of a new term had subsided, Michael put his name down to play football again, and it was something in the nature of an occasion when in the first sweltering Middle-side game he scored six tries. Already his contemporaries had forgotten that he was once a fleet and promising three-quarter, so that his resurrection was regarded as an authentic apparition, startling in its unexpectedness. Michael was the only person not much surprised when he was invited by Abercrombie to play as substitute for one of the Seniors absent from a Big-side trial. Yet even Michael was surprised when in the opening match between Classics and Moderns he read his name on the notice-board as sixteenth man; and when, through the continued illness of the first choice, he actually found himself walking on to the field between the black lines of spectators, he was greatly content. Yet the finest thrill of all came when in the line-out he found himself on the left wing with Alan, with Alan not very unlike the old Alan even now in the coveted Tyrian vest of the Classical First Fifteen.

Into that game Michael poured all he felt of savage detestation for everything that the Modern side stood for. Not an opponent was collared that did not in his falling agony take on the likeness of Percy Garrod; not a Modern half-back was hurled into touch who was not in Michael's imagination insolent with damnably destructive theories of life. It was exhilarating, it was superb, it was ineffable, the joy of seeing Alan hand off a Modern bounder and swing the ball out low to him crouching vigilant upon the left. It was intoxicating, it was divine to catch the ball, and with zigzag leap and plunge to tear wildly on towards the Modern goal, to hear the Classical lower boys shriek their high-voiced thrilling exhortations, to hear the maledictions of the enemy ricochetting from a force of speed that spun its own stability. Back went the ball to Alan, shouting with flushed face on his right, just as one of the Modern three-quarters, with iron grip round Michael's faltering knees, fetched him crashing down.

"Good pass," cried the delighted Classical boys, and "Well run, sir, well run, sir!" they roared as Alan whizzed the ball along to the dapper, the elusive, the incomparable Terry. "Go in, yourself," they prayed, as Terry like a chamois bounded straight at the despairing full-back, then with a gasp that triumphed over the vibrant hush, checked himself, and in one peerless spring breasted the shoulders of the back to come thudding down upon the turf with a glorious try.

Now the game swayed desperately, and with Alan ever beside him Michael lived through every heroic fight of man. They were at Thermopylae, stemming the Persian charges with hack and thrust and sweeping cut; they were at Platea with Aristides and Pausanias, vowing death rather than subjugation; the body of Terry beneath a weight of Modern forwards, crying, "Let me up, you stinkers!" was fought for as long ago beneath the walls of Troy the battle raged about the body of Patroclus. And when the game was over, when the Moderns had been defeated for the first time in four resentful years of scientific domination, when the Classical Fifteen proudly strode from the field, immortal in muddied Tyrian, it was easy enough to walk across the gravel arm-in-arm with Alan and, while still the noise of the contest and the cries of the onlookers echoed in their ears, it was easy to span the icy floes of two drifting years in one moment of careless, artless intercourse.

"You'll get your Second Fifteen colours," said Alan confidently.

"Not this year," Michael thought.

"You'll get your Third Fifteen cap for a snip."

"Yes, I ought to get that," Michael agreed.

"Well, that's damned good, considering you haven't played for two years," Alan vowed.

And as he spoke Michael wondered if Alan had ever wished for his company in the many stressful games from which he had been absent.

Michael now became one of that group of happy immortals in the entrance-hall, whose attitudes of noble ease graced the hot-water pipes below the 'board' on which the news of the school fluctuated daily. This society, to which nothing gave admission but a profound sense of one's own right to enter it, varied from time to time only in details. As a whole composition it was immutable, as permanent, as decorative and as appropriate as the frieze of the Parthenon. From twenty minutes past nine until twenty-seven minutes past nine, from twenty-five minutes past eleven until twenty-eight minutes past eleven, from ten minutes to three until two minutes to three the heroes of the school met in a large familiarity whose Olympian laughter awed the fearful small boy that flitted uneasily past and chilled the slouching senior that rashly paused to examine the notices in assertion of an unearned right. Even masters entering through the swinging doors seemed glad to pass beyond the range of the heroes' patronizing contemplation.

Michael found a pedestal here, and soon idealized the heedless stupidity of these immortals into a Lacedemonian rigour which seemed to him very fine. He accepted their unimaginative standards, their coarseness, their brutality as virtues, and in them he saw the consummation of all that England should cherish. He successfully destroyed a legend that he was clever, and though at first he found it difficult to combat the suspicion of æsthetic proclivities and religious eccentricity, even of poetic ambitions which overshadowed his first welcome, he was at last able to get these condoned as a blemish upon an otherwise diverting personality with a tongue nimble enough to make heroes guffaw. Moreover, he was a friend of Alan, who with his slim disdain and perfectly stoic bearing was irreproachable, and since Michael frankly admired his new friends, and since he imparted just enough fantasy to their stolid fellowship to lend it a faint distinction, he was very soon allowed to preserve a flavour of oddity, and became in time arbiter of whatever elegance they could claim. Michael on his side was most anxious to conform to every prejudice of the Olympians, esteeming their stolidity far above his own natural demeanour, envious too of their profoundly ordinary point of view and their commonplace expression of it.

Upon this assembly descended the news of war with the Transvaal, and for three months at least Michael shared in the febrile elation and arrogance and complacent outlook of the average Englishman. The Olympians recalled from early schooldays the forms of heroes who were even now gazetted to regiments on their way to the front, and who but a little while ago had lounged against these very hot-water pipes. Sandhurst and Woolwich candidates lamented their ill-luck in being born too young, and consoled themselves with proclaiming that after all the war was so easy that scarcely were they missing anything at all. Then came the first low rumble of defeat, the first tremulous breath of doubt.

Word went round that meetings were being held to stop the war, and wrathfully the heroes mounted a London Road Car omnibus, snatched the Union Jack from its socket, and surged into Hammersmith Town Hall to yell and hoot at the farouche Irishmen and dirty Socialists who were mouthing their hatred of the war and exulting in the unlucky capture of two regiments. The School Cadet Corps could not accept the mass of recruits that demanded to be enrolled. Drums were bought by subscription, and in the armoury down under the School tattoo and rataplan voiced the martial spirit of St. James'.

One day Alan brought back the news that his Uncle Kenneth was ordered to the front, that he would sail from Southampton in a few days. Leave was granted Alan to go and say good-bye, and in the patriotic fervour that now burned even in the hearts of schoolmasters, Michael was accorded leave to accompany him.

They travelled down to Southampton on a wet, windy November day, proud to think as they sat opposite one another in the gloomy railway-carriage that in some way since this summons they were both more intimately connected with the war.

In a dreary Southampton hotel they met Mrs. Ross, and Michael thought that she was very beautiful and very brave waiting in the chilly fly-blown dining-room of the hotel. Three years of marriage scarcely seemed to have altered his dear Miss Carthew; yet there was a dignity, a carven stillness that Michael had never associated with the figure of his governess, or perhaps it was that now he was older, more capable of appreciating the noble lines of this woman.

It gave Michael a sentimental pang to watch Mrs. Ross presiding over their lunch as she had in the past presided over so many lunches. They spoke hardly at all of Captain Ross's departure, but they talked of Nancy, and how well she was doing as secretary to Lord Perham, of Mrs. Carthew, still among the roses and plums of Cobble Place, and of a hundred jolly bygone events. Mrs. Ross was greatly interested to hear of Stella, and greatly amused by Michael's arrangement of her future.

Then Captain Ross came in, and after a few jokes, which fell very flat in the bleak dining-room—perhaps because the two boys were in awe of this soldier going away to the wars, or perhaps because they knew that there was indeed nothing to joke about—said:

"The regiment comes in by the 2.45. We shall embark at once. What's the time now?"

Everyone, even the mournful waiter, stared up at the wall. It was two o'clock.

"Half an hour before I need go down to the station," said Captain Ross, and then he began to whistle very quietly. The wind was getting more boisterous, and the rain rattled on the windows as if, without, a menacing hand flung gravel for a signal.

"Can you two boys amuse yourselves for a little while?" asked Captain Ross.

"Oh, rather," said Michael and Alan.

"I've just one or two things I wanted to say to you, dear," said Captain Ross, turning to his wife. They left the dining-room together. Michael and Alan sat silently at the table, crumbling bread and making patterns in the salt-cellar. They could hear the gaunt clock ticking away on the stained wall above them. From time to time far-off bugles sounded above the tossing wind. So they sat for twenty solemn minutes. Then the husband and wife came back. The bill was paid; the door of the hotel swung back; the porter said 'Good luck, sir,' very solemnly, and in a minute they were walking down the street towards the railway-station through the wind and rain.

"I'll see you on the dock in a moment," said Captain Ross. "You'd better take a cab down and wait under cover."

Thence onwards for an hour or more all was noise, excitement and bustle in contrast to the brooding, ominous calm of the dingy hotel. Regiments were marching down to the docks; bands were playing; there were drums and bugles, shouts of command, clatter of horses, the occasional rumble of a gun-carriage, enquiries, the sobbing of children and women, oaths, the hooting of sirens, a steam-engine's whistle, and at last, above everything else, was heard the wail of approaching pipes.

Nearer and nearer swirled the maddening, gladdening, heart-rending tune they played; the Kintail Highlanders were coming; they swung into view; they halted, company after company of them; there were shouts of command very close; suddenly Michael found his hand clenched and saw Captain Ross's grey eyes smiling good-bye; Alan's sleeve seemed to have a loose thread that wanted biting off; the sirens of the great transport trumpeted angrily and, resounding through the sinking hearts of those who were not going, robbed them of whatever pluck was left. Everywhere in view sister, mother, and wife were held for a moment by those they loved. The last man was aboard; the gangway was hauled up; the screw pounded the water; the ship began to glide away from the dock with slow, sickening inevitableness. Upon the air danced handkerchiefs, feeble fluttering envoys of the passionate farewells they flung to the wind. Spellbound, intolerably powerless, the watchers on shore waved and waved; smaller grew the faces leaning over the rail; smaller and smaller, until at last they were unrecognizable to those left behind; and now the handkerchiefs were waved in a new fever of energy as if with the fading of the faces there had fallen upon the assembly a fresh communal grief, a grief that, no longer regarding personal heartbreaks, frantically pursued the great graceful ship herself whose prow was straining for the open sea. Still, though now scarcely even were human forms discernible upon the decks, the handkerchiefs jigged on for horribly mechanic gestures, as if those who waved them were become automatons through sorrow.

Glad of the musty peace of a railway-carriage after the tears and confusion of the docks, Michael and Alan and Mrs. Ross spoke very little on the journey back to London.

"Aren't you going to stay the night with us at Richmond?" Alan asked.

"No, I must get down to Cobble Place. My large son has already gone there with his nurse."

"Your son?" exclaimed Michael. "Oh, of course, I forgot."

So Alan and he put Mrs. Ross into her train and rode back together on an omnibus, proud citizens of an Empire whose inspiration they had lately beheld in action.

Next morning the Olympians on their frieze were considerably impressed by Michael's account of the stirring scene at Southampton.

"Oh, the war will be over almost at once. We're not taking any risks. We're sending out enough men to conquer more than the Transvaal," said the heroes wisely.

But soon there came the news of fresh defeats, and when in the middle of January school reassembled there were actually figures missing from the familiar composition itself. Actually contemporary heroes had left, had enlisted in the Volunteers and Yeomanry, were even now waiting for orders and meantime self-consciously wandering round the school-grounds in militant khaki. Sandhurst and Woolwich candidates passed with incredible ease; boys were coming to school in mourning; Old Jacobeans died bravely, and their deaths were recorded in the school magazine; one Old Jacobean gained the Victoria Cross, and everyone walked from prayers very proudly upon that day.

Michael was still conventionally patriotic, but sometimes with the progress of the war a doubt would creep into his mind whether this increasing blazonry of a country's emotion were so fine as once he had thought it, whether England were losing some of her self-control under reverses, and, worst of all, whether in her victories she were becoming blatant. He remembered how he had been sickened by the accounts of American hysteria during the war with Spain, whose weaker cause, true to his earliest inclinations, he had been compelled to champion. And now when the tide was turning in England's favour, when every other boy came to school wearing a khaki tie quartered with blue or red and some of them even came tricked out with Union Jack waistcoats, when the wearing of a British general's head on a button and the hissing of Kruger's name at a pantomime were signs of high emotion, when many wastrels of his acquaintance had uniforms, and when the patriotism of their friends consisted of making these undignified supernumeraries drunk, Michael began to wonder whether war conducted by a democracy had ever been much more than a circus for the populace.

And when one bleak morning in early spring he read in a fatal column that Captain Kenneth Ross had been killed in action, his smouldering resentment blazed out, and as he hurried to school with sickened heart and eyes in a mist of welling tears, he could have cursed everyone of the rosetted patriots for whose vainglory such a death paid the price. Alan, as he expected, was not at school, and Michael spent a restless, miserable morning. He hated the idea of discussing the news with his friends of the hot-water pipes, and when one by one the unimaginative, flaccid comments flowed easily forth upon an event that was too great for them even to hear, much less to speak of, Michael's rage burst forth:

"For God's sake, you asses, don't talk so much. I'm sick of this war. I'm sick of reading that a lot of decent chaps have died for nothing, because it is for nothing, if this country is never again going to be able to stand defeat or victory. War isn't anything to admire in itself. All the good of war is what it makes of the people who fight, and what it makes of the people who stay at home."

The Olympians roared with laughter, and congratulated Michael on his humorous oration.

"Can't you see that I'm serious? that it is important to be gentlemen?" Michael shouted.

"Who says we aren't gentlemen?" demanded a very vapid, but slightly bellicose hero.

"Nobody says *you* aren't a gentleman, you ass; at least nobody says you eat peas with a knife, but, my God, if you think it's decent to wear that damned awful button in your coat when fellows are being killed every day for you, for your pleasure, for your profit, for your existence, all I can say is I don't."

Michael felt that the climax of this speech was somewhat weak, and he relapsed into silence, biting his nails with the unexpressed rage of limp words.

"You might as well say that the School oughtn't to cheer at a football match," said Abercrombie the Captain.

"I would say so, if I thought that all the cheerers never expected and never even intended to play themselves. That's why professional football is so rotten."

"You were damned glad to get your Third Fifteen cap," Abercrombie pointed out gruffly.

The laugh that followed this rebuke from the mightiest of the immortals goaded Michael into much more than he had intended to say when he began his unlucky tirade.

"Oh, was I?" he sneered. "That's just where you're quite wrong, because, as a matter of fact, I don't intend to play football any more, if School Footer is simply to be a show for a lot of wasters. I'm not going to exert myself like an acrobat in a circus, if it all means nothing."

The heroes regarded Michael with surprize and distaste; they shrank from him coldly as if his unreasonable outburst in some way involved their honour. They laughed uncomfortably, each one hiding himself behind another's shoulders, as if they mocked a madman. The bell for school rang, and the heroes left him. Michael, still enraged, went back to his class-room. Then he wondered if Alan would hate him for having made his uncle's death an occasion for this breach of a school's code of manners. He supposed sadly that Alan would not understand any more than the others what he felt. He cursed himself for having let these ordinary, obvious, fat-headed fools impose upon his imagination, as to lead him to consider them worthy of his respect. He had wasted three months in this society; he had thought he was happy and had congratulated himself upon at last finding school endurable. School was a prison, such as it always had been. He was seventeen and a schoolboy. It was ignominious. At one o'clock he waited for nobody, but walked quickly home to lunch, still fuming with the loss of his self-control and, as he looked back on the scene, of his dignity.

His mother came down to lunch with signs of a morning's tears, and Michael looked at her in astonishment. He had not supposed that she would be much affected by the death of Captain Ross, and he enquired if she had been writing to Mrs. Ross.

"No, dear," said Mrs. Fane. "Why should I have written to Mrs. Ross this morning?"

"Didn't you see in the paper?" Michael asked.

"See what?"

"That Captain Ross was killed in action."

"Oh, no," gasped his mother, white and shuddering. "Oh, Michael, how horrible, and on the same day."

"The same day as what?"

Mrs. Fane looked at her son for a moment very intently, as if she were minded to tell him something. Then the parlour-maid came into the room, and she seemed to change her mind, and finally said in perfectly controlled accents:

"The same day as the announcement is made that—that your old friend Lord Saxby has raised a troop of horse—Saxby's horse. He is going to Africa almost at once."

"Another gentleman going to be killed for the sake of these rowdy swine at home!" said Michael savagely.

"Michael! What do you mean? Don't you admire a man for—for trying to do something for his country?"

"It depends on the country," Michael answered, "If you think it's worth while doing anything for what England is now, I don't. I wouldn't raise a finger, if London were to be invaded to-morrow."

"I don't understand you, dearest boy. You're talking rather like a Radical, and rather like old Conservative gentlemen I remember as a girl. It's such a strange mixture. I don't think you quite understand what you're saying."

"I understand perfectly what I'm saving," Michael contradicted.

"Well, then I don't think you ought to talk like that. I don't think it's kind or considerate to me and, after you've just heard about Captain Ross's death, I think it's irreverent. And I thought you attached so much importance to reverence," Mrs. Fane added in a complaining tone.

Michael was vexed by his mother's failure to understand his point of view, and became harder and more perverse every minute.

"Lord Saxby would be shocked to hear you talking like this, shocked and horrified," she went on.

"I'm very sorry for hurting Lord Saxby's feelings," said Michael with elaborate sarcasm. "But really I don't see that it matters much to him what I think."

"He wants to see you before he sails," said Mrs, Fane.

"To see me? Why?" gasped Michael. "Why on earth should he want to see me?"

"Well, he's—he's in a way the head of our family."

"He's not taken much interest in me up to the present. It's rather odd he should want to see me now when he's going away."

"Michael, don't be so bitter and horrid. Lord Saxby's so kind, and he—and he—might never come back."

"Dearest mother," said Michael, "I think you're a little unreasonable. Why should I go and meet a man now, and perhaps grow to like him—and then say good-bye to him, perhaps for ever?"

"Michael, do not talk like that. You are selfish and brutal. You've grown up to be perfectly heartless, although you can be charming. I think you'd better not see Lord Saxby. He'd be ashamed of you."

Michael rose in irritation.

"My dear mother, what on earth business is it of Lord Saxby's how I behave? I don't understand what you mean by being ashamed of me. I have lived all these years, and I've seen Lord Saxby once. He sent me some Siamese stamps and some soldiers. I dare say he's a splendid chap. I know I liked him terrifically, when I was a kid, and if he's killed I shall be sorry—I shall be more than sorry—I shall be angry, furious that for the sake of these insufferable rowdies another decent chap is going to risk his life."

Mrs. Fane put out her hand to stop Michael's flowing tirade, but he paid no attention, talking away less to her than to himself. Indeed, long before he had finished, she made no pretence of listening, but merely sat crying quietly.

"I've been thinking a good deal lately about this war," Michael declared. "I'm beginning to doubt whether it's a just war, whether we didn't simply set out on it for brag and money. I'm not sure that I want to see the Boers conquered. They're a small independent nation, and they have old-fashioned ideas and they're narrow-minded Bible-worshippers, but there's something noble about them, something much nobler than there is in these rotten adventurers who go out to fight them. Of course, I don't mean by that people like Captain Ross or Lord Saxby. They're gentlemen. They go either because it's their duty or because they think it's their duty. And they're the ones that get killed. You don't hear of these swaggerers in khaki being killed. I haven't heard yet of many of them even going to the front at all. Oh, mother, I am fed up with the rotten core of everything that looks so fine on the outside."

Mrs. Fane was now crying loud enough to make Michael stop in sudden embarrassment.

"I say, mother, don't cry. I expect I've been talking nonsense," he softly told her.

"I don't know where you get these views. I was always so proud of you. I thought you were charming and mysterious, and you're simply vulgar!"

"Vulgar?" echoed Michael in dismay.

Mrs. Fane nodded vehemently.

"Oh, well, if I'm vulgar, I'll go."

Michael hurried to the door.

"Where are you going?" asked his mother in alarm.

"Oh, Lord, only to school. That's what makes a scene like this so funny. After I've worked myself up and made you angry——"

"Not angry, dear. Only grieved," interrupted his mother.

"You were more than grieved when you said I was vulgar. At least I hope you were. But, after it's all over, I go trotting off like a good little boy to school—to school—to school. Oh, mother, what is the good of expecting me to believe in the finest fellows in the world being killed, while I'm still at school? What's the good of making me more wretched, more discontented, more alive to my own futile existence by asking me now, when he's going away, to make friends with Lord Saxby? Oh, darling mother, can't you realize that I'm no longer a little boy who wants to clap his hands at the sight of a red coat? Let me kiss you, mother, I'm sorry I was vulgar, but I've minded so dreadfully about Captain Ross, and it's all for nothing."

Mrs. Fane let herself be petted by her son, but she did not again ask Michael to see Lord Saxby before he went away to the war.

Alan was still absent at afternoon school, and Michael, disdaining his place in the heroic group, passed quickly into the class-room and read in Alison of Salamanca and Albuera and of the storming of Badajoz, wondering what had happened to his country since those famous dates. He supposed that then was the nation's zenith, for from what he could make out of the Crimean War, that had been as little creditable to England as this miserable business of the present.

In the afternoon Michael thought he would walk over to Notting Dale and see Mr. Viner—perhaps he would understand some of his indignation—and this evening when all was quiet he must write to Mrs. Ross. On his way down the Kensington Road he met Wilmot, whom he had not seen since the summer, for luckily about the time of the row Wilmot had been going abroad and was only lately back. He recognized Wilmot's fanciful walk from a distance, and nearly crossed over to the opposite pavement to avoid meeting him; but on second thoughts decided he would like to hear a fresh opinion of the war.

"Why, here's a delightful meeting," said Wilmot, "I have been wondering why you didn't come round to see me. You got my cards?"

"Oh, yes, rather," said Michael.

"I have been in Greece and Italy. I wish you had been with me. I thought of you, as I sat in the ruined rose-gardens of Paestum. You've no idea how well those columns of honey-coloured Travertine would become you, Michael. But I'm so glad to see that you have not yet clothed yourself in khaki. This toy war is so utterly absurd. I feel as if I were living in a Christmas bazaar. How dreadfully these puttees and haversacks debase even the most beautiful figures. What is a haversack? It sounds so Lenten, so eloquent of mortification. I have discovered some charming Cyprian cigarettes. Do come and let me watch you enjoy them. How young you look, and yet how old!"

"I'm feeling very fit," said Michael loftily.

"How abruptly informative you are! What has happened to you?"

"I'm thinking about this war."

"Good gracious," cried Wilmot in mincing amazement. "What an odd subject. Soon you will be telling me that by moonlight you brood upon the Albert Memorial. But perhaps your mind is full of trophies. Perhaps you are picturing to yourself in Piccadilly a second column of Trajan displacing the amorous and acrobatic Cupid who now presides over the painted throng. Come with me some evening to the Long Bar at the Criterion, and while the Maori-like barmaids titter in their *dévergondage*, we will select the victorious site and picture to ourselves the Boer commanders chained like hairy Scythians to the chariot of whatever absurd general chooses to accept the triumph awarded to him by our legislative *bourgeoisie*."

"I think I must be getting on," said Michael.

"How urgent! You speak like Phaeton or Icarus, and pray remember the calamities that befell them. But seriously, when are you coming to see me?"

"Oh, I'm rather busy," said Michael briefly.

Wilmot looked at him curiously with his glittering eyes for a moment. Then he spoke again:

"Farewell, Narcissus. Have you learnt that I was but a shallow pool in which to watch your reflection? Did I flatter you too much or not enough? Who shall say? But you know I'm always your friend, and when this love-affair is done, I shall always be interested to hear the legend of it told movingly when and where you will, but perhaps best of all in October when the full moon lies like a huge apricot upon the chimneys of the town. Farewell, Narcissus. Does she display your graces very clearly?"

"I'm not in love with anybody, if that's what you mean," said Michael.

"No? But you are on the margin of a strange pool, and soon you will be peeping over the bulrushes to stare at yourself again."

Then Mr. Wilmot, making his pontifical and undulatory adieu, passed on.

"Silly ass!" said Michael to himself. "And he always thinks he knows everything."

Michael turned out of the noisy main road into the sylvan urbanity of Holland Walk. A haze of tender diaphanous green clung to the boles of the smirched elms, softening the sooty decay that made their antiquity so grotesque and so dishonourable. Michael sat down for a while on a bench, inhaling the immemorial perfume of a London spring and listening to the loud courtship of the blackbirds in the ragged shrubberies that lined the railings of Holland Park. He was not made any the more content with himself by this effluence of revivified effort that impregnated the air around him. He was out of harmony with every impulse of the season, and felt just as tightly fettered now as long ago he used to feel on waits by this same line of blackened trees with Nurse to quell his lightest step towards freedom. Where was Nurse now? The pungent odour of privet blown along a dying wind of March was quick with old memories of forbidden hiding-places, and he looked up, half expectant of her mummified shape peering after his straying steps round the gnarled and blackened trunk of the nearest elm. Michael rose quickly and went on his way towards Notting Dale. This Holland Walk had always been a haunted spot, not at all a place to hearten one, especially where at the top it converged to a silent passage between wooden palings whose twinkling interstices and exudations of green slime had always been queerly sinister. Even now Michael was glad when he could hear again the noise of traffic in the Bayswater Road. As he walked on towards Mr. Viner's house he gave rein to fanciful moralizings upon these two great roads on either side of the Park that ran a parallel course, but never met. How foreign it all seemed on this side with unfamiliar green omnibuses instead of red, with never even a well-known beggar or pavement-artist. The very sky had an alien look, seeming vaster somehow than the circumscribed clouds of Kensington. Perhaps after all the people of this intolerably surprising city were not so much to be blamed for their behaviour during a period of war. They had nothing to hold them together, to teach them to endure and enjoy, to suffer and rejoice in company. These great main roads sweeping West and East with multitudinous chimney-pots between were symbolic of the whole muddle of existence.

"But what do I want?" Michael asked himself so loudly that an errand-boy stayed his whistling and stared after him until he turned the corner.

"I don't know," he muttered in the face of a fussy little woman, who jumped aside to let him pass.

Soon he was deep in one of Mr. Viner's arm-chairs and, without waiting even to produce one of the attenuated pipes he still affected, exclaimed with desolating conviction:

"I'm absolutely sick of everything!"

"What, again?" said the priest, smiling.

"It's this war."

"You're not thinking of enlisting in the Imperial Yeomanry?"

"Oh, no, but a friend of mine—Alan Merivale's uncle—has been killed. It seems all wrong."

"My dear old chap," said Mr. Viner earnestly, "I'm sorry for you."

"Oh, it isn't me you've got to pity," Michael cried. "I'd be glad of his death. It's the finest death a fellow can have. But there's nothing fine about it, when one sees these gibbering blockheads shouting and yelling about nothing. I don't know what's the matter with England."

"Is England any worse than the rest of the world?" asked Mr. Viner.

"All this wearing of buttons and khaki ties!" Michael groaned.

"But that's the only way the man in the street can show his devotion. You don't object to ritualism, do you? You cross yourself and bow down. The church has colours and lights and incense. Do all these dishonour Our Lord's death?"

"That's different," said Michael. "And anyway I don't know that the comparison is much good to me now. I think I've lost my faith. I am sorry to shock you, Mr. Viner."

"You don't shock me at all, my dear boy."

"Don't I?" said Michael in slightly disappointed tones.

"You forget that a priest is more difficult to shock than anyone on earth."

"I like the way you take yourself as a typical priest. Very few of them are like you."

"Come, that's rather a stupid remark, I think," said Mr. Viner coldly.

"Is it? I'm sorry. It doesn't seem to worry you very much that I've lost my faith," Michael went on in an aggrieved voice.

"No, because I don't think you have. I've got a high enough opinion of you to believe that if you really had lost your faith, you wouldn't plunge comfortably down into one of my arm-chairs and give me the information in the same sort of tone you'd tell me you'd forgotten to bring back a book I'd lent you."

"I know you always find it very difficult to take me seriously," Michael grumbled. "I suppose that's the right method with people like me."

"I thought you'd come up to talk about the South African War. If I'd known the war was so near home, I shouldn't have been so frivolous," said the priest. His eyes were so merry in the leaping firelight that Michael was compelled against his will to smile.

"Of course, you make me laugh at the time and I forget how serious I meant to be when I arrived, and it's not until I'm at home again that I realize I'm no nearer to what I wanted to say than when I came up," protested Michael.

"I'm not the unsympathetic boor you'd make me out," Mr. Viner said.

"Oh, I perfectly understand that all this heart-searching becomes a nuisance. But honestly, Mr. Viner, I think I've done nothing long enough."

"Then you do want to enlist?" said the priest quickly.

"Why must 'doing' mean only one thing nowadays? Surely South Africa hasn't got a monopoly of whatever's being done," Michael argued. "No, I don't want to enlist," he went on. "And I don't want to go into a monastery, and I'm not sure that I really even want to go to church again."

"Give up going for a bit," advised the priest.

Michael jumped up from the chair and walked over to the bay-window, through which came a discordant sound of children playing in the street outside.

"It's impossible to be serious with you. I suppose you're fed up with people like me," Michael complained. "I know I'm moody and irritating, but I've got a lot to grumble about. I don't seem to have any natural inclination for any profession. I'm not a musical genius like my young sister. That's pretty galling, you know, really. After all, girls can get along better than boys without any special gifts, and she simply shines compared with me. I have no father. I've no idea who I was, where I came from, what I'm going to be. I keep on trying to be optimistic and think everything is good and beautiful, and then almost at once it turns out bad and ugly."

"Has your religion really turned out bad and ugly?" asked the priest gently.

"Not right through, but here and there, yes."

"The religion itself or the people who profess it?" Mr. Viner persisted.

"Doesn't it amount to the same thing ultimately?" Michael parried. "But leave out religion for the moment, and consider this war. The only justification for such a war is the moral effect it has on the nations engaged. Now, I ask you, do you sincerely believe there has been a trace of any purifying influence since we started waving Union Jacks last September? It's no good; we simply have not got it in us to stand defeat or victory. At any rate, if the Boers win, it will mean the preservation of something. Whereas if we win, we shall just destroy everything."

"Michael, what do you think is the important thing for this country at this moment?" Mr. Viner asked.

"Well, I suppose I still think it is that the people—the great mass of the nation, that is—should be happier and better. No, I don't think that's it at all. I think the important thing is that the people should be able to use the power that's coming to them in bigger lumps every day. I'd like to think it wasn't, I'd like to believe that democracy always will be as it always has been—a self-made failure. But against my own will I can't help believing that this time democracy is going to carry everything before it. And this war is going to hurry it on. Of course it is. The masses will learn their power. They'll learn that generals can make fools of themselves, that officers can be done without, that professional soldiers can be cowards, but that simply by paying we can still win. And where's the money coming from? Why, from the class that tried to be clever and bluff the people out of their power by staging this war. Well, do you mean to tell me that it's good for a democracy, this sudden realization of their omnipotence? Look here, you think I'm an excitable young fool, but I tell you I've been pitching my ideals at a blank wall like so many empty bottles and——"

"Were they empty?" asked Mr. Viner. "Are you sure they were empty? May they not have been cruses of ointment the more precious for being broken?"

"Well, I wish I could keep one for myself," Michael said.

"My dear boy, you'll never be able to do that. You'll always be too prodigal of your ideals. I should have no qualms about your future, whatever you did meanwhile. And, do you know, I don't think I have many qualms about this England of ours, however badly she behaves sometimes. I'm glad you recognize that the people are coming into their own. I wish that *you* were glad, but you will be one day. The Catholic religion must be a popular religion. The Sabbath was made for man, you know. Catholicism is God's method of throwing bottles at a blank wall—but not empty bottles, Michael. On the whole, I would sooner that now you were a reactionary than a Dantonist. Your present attitude of mind at any rate gives you the opportunity of going forward, instead of going back; there will be plenty of ideals to take the places of those you destroy, however priceless. And the tragedy of age is not having any more bottles to throw."

During these words that came soothingly from Mr. Viner's firm lips Michael had settled himself down again in the arm-chair and lighted his pipe.

"Come, now," said the priest, "you and I have muddled through our discussion long enough, let's gossip for a change. What's Mark Chator doing?"

"I haven't seen much of him this term. He's still going to take orders. I find old Chator's eternal simplicity and goodness rather wearing. Life's pretty easy for him. I wish I could get as much out of it as easily," Michael answered.

"Well, I can't make any comment on that last remark of yours without plunging into platitudes that would make you terribly contemptuous of my struggles to avoid them. But don't despise the Chators of this world."

"Oh, I don't. I envy them. Well, I must go. Thanks awfully for putting up with me again."

Michael picked up his cap and hurried home. When he reached Carlington Road, he was inclined to tell his mother that, if she liked, he would go and visit Lord Saxby before he sailed; but when it came to the point he felt too shy to reopen the subject, and decided to let the proposal drop.

He was surprized to find that it was much easier to write to Mrs. Ross about her husband than he thought it would be. Whether this long and stormy day (he could scarcely believe that he had only read the news about Captain Ross that morning) had purged him of all complexities of emotion, he did not know; but certainly the letter was easy enough.

64 CARLINGTON ROAD.

My dear Mrs. Ross,

I can't tell you the sadness of to-day. I've thought about you most tremendously, and I think you must be gloriously proud of him. I felt angry at first, but now I feel all right. You've always been so stunning to me, and I've never thanked you. I do want to see you soon. I shall never forget saying good-bye to Captain Ross. Mother asked me to go and say good-bye to Lord Saxby. I don't suppose you ever met him. He's a sort of cousin of ours. But I did not want to spoil the memory of that day at Southampton. I haven't seen poor old Alan yet. He'll be in despair. I'm longing to see him to-morrow. This is a rotten letter, but I can't write down what I feel. I wish Stella had known Captain Ross. She would have been able to express her feelings.

With all my love,
Your affectionate
Michael.

In bed that night Michael thought what a beast he had made of himself that day, and flung the blankets feverishly away from his burnt-out self. Figures of well-loved people kept trooping through the darkness, and he longed to converse with them, inspired by the limitless eloquence of the night-time. All that he would say to Mr. Viner, to Mrs. Ross, to Alan, even to good old Chator, splashed the dark with fiery sentences. He longed to be with Stella in a cool woodland. He almost got up to go down and pour his soul out upon his mother's breast; but the fever of fatigue mocked his impulse and he fell tossing into sleep.

Chapter XII: *Alan*

MICHAEL left the house early next day that he might make sure of seeing Alan for a moment before Prayers. A snowy aggregation of cumulus sustained the empyrean upon the volume of its mighty curve and swell. The road before him stretched shining in a radiant drench of azure puddles. It was a full-bosomed morning of immense peace.

Michael rather dreaded to see Alan appear in oppressive black, and felt that anything like a costume would embarrass their meeting. But just before the second bell he came quickly up the steps dressed in his ordinary clothes, and Michael in the surging corridor gripped his arm for a moment, saying he would wait for him in the 'quarter.'

"Is your mater fearfully cut up?" he asked when they had met and were strolling together along the 'gravel.'

"I think she was," said Alan. "She's going up to Cobble Place this morning to see Aunt Maud."

"I wrote to her last night," said Michael.

"I spent nearly all yesterday in writing to her," said Alan. "I couldn't think of anything to say. Could you?"

"No, I couldn't think of very much," Michael agreed. "It seemed so unnecessary."

"I know," Alan said. "I'd really rather have come to school."

"I wish you had. I made an awful fool of myself in the morning. I got in a wax with Abercrombie and the chaps, and said I'd never play football again."

"Whatever for?"

"Oh, because I didn't think they appreciated what it meant for a chap like your Uncle Kenneth to be killed."

"Do you mean they said something rotten?" asked Alan, flushing.

"I don't think you would have thought it rotten. In fact, I think the whole row was my fault. But they seemed to take everything for granted. That's what made me so wild."

"Look here, we can't start a conversation like this just before school. Are you going home to dinner?" Alan asked.

"No, I'll have dinner down in the Tuck," said Michael, "and we can go for a walk afterwards, if you like. It's the first really decent day we've had this year."

So after a lunch of buns, cheese-cakes, fruit pastilles, and vanilla biscuits, eaten in the noisy half-light of the Tuckshop, accompanied by the usual storm of pellets, Michael and Alan set out to grapple with the situation Michael had by his own hasty behaviour created.

"The chaps seem rather sick with you," observed Alan, as they strolled arm-in-arm across the school-ground not yet populous with games.

"Well, they are such a set of sheep," Michael urged in justification of himself.

"I thought you rather liked them."

"I did at first. I do still in a way. I do when nothing matters; but that horrible line in the paper did matter most awfully, and I couldn't stick their bleating. You see, you're different. You just say nothing. That's all right. But these fools tried to say something and couldn't. I always did hate people who *tried* very obviously. That's why I like you. You're so casual and you always seem to fit."

"I don't talk, because I know if I opened my mouth I should make an ass of myself," said Alan.

"There you are, that's what I say. That's why it's possible to talk to you. You see I'm a bit mad."

"Shut up, you ass," commanded Alan, smiling.

"Oh, not very mad. And I'm not complaining. But I *am* a little bit mad. I always have been."

"Why? You haven't got a clot on your brain, have you?"

"Oh, Great Scott, no! It's purely mental, my madness."

"Well, I think you're talking tosh," said Alan firmly. "If you go on thinking you're mad, you will be mad, and then you'll be sorry. So shut up trying to horrify me, because if you really were mad I should bar you," he added coolly.

"All right," said Michael, a little subdued, as he always was, by Alan's tranquil snubs. "All right. I'm not mad, but I'm excitable."

"Well, you shouldn't be," said Alan.

"I can't help my character, can I?" Michael demanded.

"You're not a girl," Alan pointed out.

"Men have very strong emotions often," Michael argued.

"They may have them, but they don't show them. Just lately you've been holding forth about the rotten way in which everybody gets hysterical over this war. And now you're getting hysterical over yourself, which is much worse."

"Damn you, Alan, if I didn't like you so much I shouldn't listen to you," said Michael, fiercely pausing.

"Well, if I didn't like you, I shouldn't talk," answered Alan simply.

As they walked on again in silence for a while, Michael continually tried to get a perspective view of his friend, puzzling over his self-assurance, which was never offensive, and wondering how a person so much less clever than himself could possibly make him feel so humble. Alan was good-looking and well-dressed; he was essentially debonair; he was certainly in appearance the most attractive boy in the school. It always gave Michael the most acute thrill of admiration to see Alan swinging himself along so lithe and so graceful. It made him want to go up and pat Alan's shoulder and say, "You fine and lovely creature, go on walking for ever." But mere good looks were not enough to explain the influence which Alan wielded, an influence which had steadily increased during the period of their greatest devotion to each other, and had never really ceased during the period of their comparative estrangement. Yet, if Michael looked back on their joint behaviour, it had always been he who apparently led and Alan who followed.

"Do you know, old chap," said Michael suddenly, "you're a great responsibility to me."

"Thanks very much and all that," Alan answered, with a mocking bow.

"Have you ever imagined yourself the owner of some frightfully famous statue?" Michael went on earnestly.

"Why, have you?" Alan countered, with his familiar look of embarrassed persiflage.

Michael, however, kept tight hold of the thread that was guiding him through the labyrinth that led to the arcana of Alan's disposition.

"You've the same sort of responsibility," he asserted. "I always feel that if I were the owner of the Venus of Milo, though I could move her about all over the place and set her up wherever I liked, I should be responsible to her in some way. I should feel she was looking at me, and if I put her in a wrong position, I should feel ashamed of myself and half afraid of the statue."

"Are you trying to prove you're mad?" Alan enquired.

"Do be serious," Michael begged, "and tell me if you think you understand what I mean. Alan, you used to discuss everything with me when we were kids, why won't you discuss yourself now?"

Alan looked up at the sky for a moment, blinking in the sun, perhaps to hide the tremor of feeling that touched for one instant the corners of his mouth. Then he said:

"Do you remember years ago, when we were at Eastbourne and you met Uncle Kenneth for the first time, he told me at dinner not to be a showman? I've always remembered that remark of his, and I think it applies to one showing off oneself as much as to showing off other people. I think that's why I'm different from you."

Michael glanced up at this.

"You can be damned rude when you like," he murmured.

"Well, you asked me."

"So I'm a showman?" said Michael.

"Oh, for Heaven's sake don't begin to worry over it. It doesn't make any odds to me what you are. I don't think it ever would," he added simply, and in this avowal was all that Michael craved for. Under a sudden chill presentiment that before long he would test this friend of his to the last red throb of his proud heart, Michael took comfort from this declaration and asked no more for comprehension or sympathy. Those were shifting sands of feeling compared with this rock-hewn permanence of Alan. He remembered the stones upon the Berkshire downs, the stolid, unperceiving, eternal stones. Comparable to them alone stood Alan.

They had turned out of the gates of the school-ground by now, and were strolling heedless of direction through the streets of West Kensington that to Michael seemed all at once strangely alluring with their display of a sedate and cosy life. He could not recall that he had ever before been so sensitive to the atmosphere of sunlit security which was radiated by these windows with their visions of rosy babies bobbing and laughing, of demure and saucy maids, of polished bird-cages and pots of daffodils. The white steps were in tune with the billowy clouds, and the scarlet pillar-box at the corner had a friendly, human smile. It was a doll's-house world, whose dainty offer of intimate citizenship refreshed Michael's imagination like a child's picture-book.

He began to reflect that the opinions of Abercrombie and his friends round the hot-water pipes were wrought out in such surroundings as these, and he arrived gradually at a sort of compassion for them, picturing the lives of small effort that would inevitably be their portion. He perceived that they would bear the burden of existence in the future, struggling to preserve their gentility against the envy of the class beneath them and the contempt of those above. These gay little houses, half of whose charm lay in their similarity, were as near as they would ever come to any paradise of being. Michael had experienced many spasms of love for his fellow-men, and now in one of these outbursts he suddenly realized himself in sympathy with mediocrity.

"Rather jolly round here," said Alan. "I suppose a tremendous lot of chaps from the school live about here. Funny thing, if you come to think of it. Practically everybody at St. James' slides into a little house like this. A few go into the Army; a few go to the 'Varsity. But this is really the School."

Alan indicated an empty perambulator standing outside one of the houses. "Funny thing if the kid that's waiting for should be Captain of the School in another eighteen years. I wouldn't be surprised."

Alan had just expressed so much of what Michael himself was thinking that he felt entitled to put the direct question which a moment ago he had been shy of asking.

"Do you feel as if you belonged to all this?"

"No," said Alan very coolly.

"Nor do I," Michael echoed.

"And that's why it was rotten of you to give yourself away to Abercrombie and the other chaps," Alan went on severely.

"Yes, I think it was," Michael agreed.

Then they retraced their steps unconsciously, wandering along silently in the sunlight towards the school. Michael did not want to converse because he was too much elated by this walk, and the satisfying way in which Alan had lived up to his ideal of him. He began to weave a fine romance of himself and Alan going through life together in a lofty self-sufficiency from which they would condescend to every aspect of humanity. He was not sure whether Alan would condescend so far and so widely as himself, and he was not sure whether he wanted him to, whether it would not always be a relief to be aware of Alan as a cold supernal sanctuary from the vulgar struggles in which he foresaw his own frequent immersion. Meanwhile he must make it easy for Alan by apologizing to Abercrombie and the rest for his ridiculous passion of yesterday. He did not wish to imperil Alan's superb aloofness by involving him in the acrimonious and undignified defence of a friend. There should be no more outbreaks. So much Michael vowed to his loyalty. However, the apology must be made quickly—if possible, this afternoon before school—and as they entered the school-ground again, Michael looked up at the clock, and said:

"Do you mind if I bunk on? I've something I must do before the bell goes."

Alan shook his head.

To Abercrombie and the other immortals Michael came up quickly and breathlessly.

"I say, you chaps, I'm sorry I made such an ass of myself yesterday; I felt chippy over that friend of mine being killed."

"That's all right, old bangabout," said Abercrombie cordially, and the chorus guffawed their forgiveness. They did more. They called him 'Bangs' thereafter, commemorating, as schoolboys use, with an affectionate nickname their esteem.

The next day a letter came for Michael from Mrs. Ross, and impressed with all the clarity of writing much of what he had dimly reached out for in his friendship with Alan. He read the letter first hurriedly on his way to school in the morning; but he read it a second and third time along those serene and intimate streets where he and Alan had walked the day before.

Cobble Place,
March, 1900.

My dearest Michael,

You and Alan are the only people to whom I can bear to write to-day. I am grieving most for my young son, because he will have to grow up without his father's splendid example always before him. I won't write of my own sorrow. I could not.

My husband, as you know, was very devoted to you and Alan, and he had been quite worried (and so had I) that you and he seemed to have grown away from one another. It was a moment of true delight to him, when he read a long letter from dear old Alan describing his gladness at playing football again with you. Alan expresses himself much less eloquently than you do, but he is as deeply fond of you as I know you are of him. His letters are full of you and your cleverness and popularity; and I pray that all your lives you will pull together for the good. Kenneth used always to admire you both so much for your ability to 'cope with a situation.' He was shot, as you know, leading his men (who adored him) into action. Ah, how I wish he could lead his own little son into action. You and Alan will have that responsibility now.

It is sweet of you to thank me for being so 'stunning' to you. It wasn't very difficult. But you know how high my hopes have always been and always will be for you, and I know that you will never disappoint me. There may come times which with your restless, sensitive temperament you will find very hard to bear. Always remember that you have a friend in me. I have suffered very much, and suffering makes the heart yearn to comfort others. Be very chivalrous always, and remember that of all your ideals your mother should be the highest. I hope that you'll be able to come and stay with us soon after Easter. God bless you, dear boy, and thank you very much for your expression of the sorrow I know you share with me.

Your loving
Maud Ross.

I wonder if you remember how you used to love Don Quixote as a child. Will you always be a Don Quixote, however much people may laugh? It really means just being a gentleman.

Chapter XIII: *Sentiment*

BACK once more upon his pedestal in the frieze, Michael devoted himself to enjoying, while still they were important to his life, the conversation and opinions of the immortals. He gave up worrying about the war and yielded himself entirely either to the blandishments of his seniority in the school or of dreams about himself at Oxford, now within sight of attainment. Four more terms of school would set him free, and he had ambitions to get into the Fifteen in his last year. He would then be able to look back with satisfaction to the accomplishment of something. He actually threw himself into the rowdiest vanguard of Mafeking's celebrators, and accepted the occasion as an excuse to make a noise without being compelled to make the noise alone. These Bacchanalia of patriotism were very amusing, and perhaps it was a good thing for the populace to be merry; moreover, since he now had Alan to idealize, he could afford to let his high thoughts of England's duty and England's honour become a little less stringent.

He spent much time with Alan in discussing Oxford and in building up a most elaborate and logical scheme of their life at the University. He was anxious that Alan should leave the classical Lower Sixth, into which he had climbed somewhat hardly, and come to join him in the leisure of the History Sixth. He spoke of Strang whose Captaincy of Cricket shed such lustre on the form, of Terry whose Captaincy of Football next year would shed an equal lustre. But Alan, having found the journey to the Lower Sixth so arduous, was disinclined to be cheated of the intellectual eminence of the Upper Sixth which had been his Valhalla so long.

Michael and Alan had been looking forward to a visit to Cobble Place during the Easter holidays; but Mrs. Fane was much upset by the idea of being left alone, and Michael had to decline the invitation, which was a great disappointment. In the end he and his mother went to Bournemouth, staying rather grandly at one of the large hotels, and Michael was able to look up some old friends, including Father Moneypenny of St. Bartholomew's, Mrs. Rewins, their landlady of three years back, and Mr. Prout.

The passion-flower at Esdraelon had grown considerably, but that was the only thing which showed any signs of expansion, unless Mr. Prout's engagement to be married could be accepted as evidence of expansion. Michael thought it had a contrary effect, and whether from that cause or from his own increased age he found poor Prout sadly dull. It was depressing to hear that unpleasantness was expected at the Easter vestry that year; Michael could not recall any year in which that had not been the case. It was depressing to learn that the People's Churchwarden was still opposed to the Assumption. It was most depressing of all to be informed that Prout saw no prospect of being married for at least five years. Michael, having failed with Prout, tried to recapture the emotion of his first religious experience at St. Bartholomew's. But the church that had once seemed so inspiring now struck him as dingily and poorly designed, without any of the mystery which once had made it beautiful. He wondered if everything that formerly had appealed to his imagination were going to turn out dross, and he made an expedition to Christchurch Priory to test this idea. Here he was relieved to find himself able to recapture the perfect thrill of his first visit, and he spent a rich day wandering between the grey church and the watery meadows near by, about whose plashy levels the green rushes were springing up in the fleecy April weather.

Michael concluded that all impermanent emotions of beauty proved that it was merely the emotion which had created an illusion of beauty, and he was glad to have discovered for himself a touchstone for his æsthetic judgments in the future. He would have liked to see Alan in the cloistral glooms of the Priory, and thought how he would have enhanced with his own eternity of classic shape the knights and ladies praying there. Michael sympathized with the trousered boy whom Flaxman, contrary to every canon, might almost be said to have perpetrated. He felt slightly muddled between classic and romantic art, and could not make up his mind whether Flaxman's attempt or the mediæval sculptor's achievement were worthier of admiration. He tried to apply his own test, and came to the conclusion that Flaxman was really all wrong. He decided that he only liked the trousered boy because the figure gave him sentimental pleasure, and he was sure that true classical art was not sentimental. Finally he got himself in a complete muddle, sitting among these hollow chantries and pondering art's evaluations; so he left the Priory behind him, and went dreamily through the water-meadows under the spell of a simple beauty that needed no analysis. Oxford would be like this, he thought; a place of bells and singing streams and towers against the horizon.

He waited by a stile, watching the sky of which sunset had made a tranced archipelago set in a tideless sea. The purple islands stood out more and more distinct against the sheeted gold that lapped their indentations; then in a few moments the gold went out to primrose, the purple isles were grey as mice, and by an imperceptible breath of time became merged in a luminous green that held the young moon led downwards through the west by one great sulphur star.

This speculation of the sky made Michael late for dinner, and gave his mother an opportunity to complain of his daylong desertion of her.

"I rather wish we hadn't come to Bournemouth," said Michael. "I think it's a bad place for us to choose to come together. I remember last time we stayed here you were always criticizing me."

"I suppose Bournemouth must have a bad effect on you, dearest boy," said Mrs. Fane in her most gentle, most discouraging voice.

Michael laughed a little bitterly.

"You're wonderful at always being able to put me in the wrong," he said.

"You're sometimes not very polite, are you, nowadays? But I dare say you'll grow out of this curious manner you've lately adopted towards me."

"Was I rude?" asked Michael, quickly penitent.

"I think you were rather rude, dear," said Mrs. Fane. "Of course, I don't want you never to have an opinion of your own, and I quite realize that school has a disastrous effect on manners, but you didn't apologize very gracefully for being late for dinner, did you, dear?"

"I'm sorry. I won't ever be again," said Michael shortly.

Mrs. Fane sighed, and the meal progressed in silence. Michael, however, could never bear to sulk, and he braced himself to be pleasant.

"You ought to come over to Christchurch, mother. Shall we drive over one day?"

"Well, I'm not very fond of looking at churches," said Mrs. Fane. "But if you want to go, let us. I always like you to do everything you want."

Michael sighed at the ingenuity of his mother's method, and changed the subject to their fellow-guests.

"That's rather a pretty girl, don't you think?"

"Where, dear?" asked Mrs. Fane, putting up her lorgnette and staring hard at the wife of a clergyman sitting across the room from their table.

"No, no, mother," said Michael, beaming with pleasure at the delightful vagueness of his mother which only distressed him when it shrouded his own sensations. "The next table—the girl in pink."

"Yes, decidedly," said Mrs. Fane. "But dreadfully common. I can't think why those sort of people come to nice hotels. I suppose they read about them in railway guides."

"I don't think she's very common," said Michael.

"Well, dear, you're not quite at the best age for judging, are you?"

"Hang it, mother, I'm seventeen."

"It's terrible to think of," said Mrs. Fane. "And only such a little while ago you were the dearest baby boy. Then Stella must be sixteen," she went on. "I think it's time she came back from the Continent."

"What about her first concert?"

"Oh, I must think a lot before I settle when that is to be."

"But Stella is counting on it being very soon."

"Dear children, you're both rather impetuous," said Mrs. Fane, deprecating with the softness of her implied rebuke the quality, and in Michael at any rate for the moment quenching all ardour.

"I wonder if it's wise to let a girl be a professional musician," she continued. "Dear me, children are a great responsibility, especially when one is alone."

Here was an opportunity for Michael to revive the subject of his father, but he had now lost the cruel frankness of childhood and shrank from the directness of the personal encounter such a topic would involve. He was seized with one of his fits of shy sensitiveness, and he became suddenly so deeply embarrassed that he could scarcely even bring himself to address his mother as 'you.' He felt that he must go away by himself until he had shaken off this uncomfortable sensation. He actually felt a kind of immodesty in saying 'you' to his mother, as if in saying so much he was trespassing on the forbidden confines of her individuality. It would not endure for more than an hour or so, this fear of approach, this hyperæsthesia of contact and communication. Yet not for anything could he kiss her good night and, mumbling a few bearish excuses, he vanished as soon as dinner was over, vowing that he would cure himself of this mood by walking through the pine trees and blowy darkness of the cliffs.

As he passed through the hotel lounge, he saw the good-looking girl, whom his mother had stigmatized as common, waiting there wrapped up in a feathery cloak. He decided that he would sit down and observe her until the sister came down. He wished he knew this girl, since it would be pleasant after dinner to stroll out either upon the pier or to listen to the music in the Winter Garden in such attractive company. Michael fancied that the girl, as she walked slowly up and down the lounge, was conscious of his glances, and he felt an adventurous excitement at his heart. It would be a daring and delightful novelty to speak to her. Then the sister came down, and the two girls went out through the swinging doors of the hotel, leaving Michael depressed and lonely. Was it a trick of the lamplight, or did he really perceive her head turn outside to regard him for a moment?

During his walk along the cliffs Michael played with this idea. By the time he went to bed his mind was full of this girl, and it was certainly thrilling to come down to breakfast next morning and see what blouse she was wearing. Mrs. Fane always had breakfast in her room, so Michael was free to watch this new interest over the cricket matches in The Sportsman. He grew almost jealous of the plates and forks and cups which existed so intimately upon her table, and he derived a sentimental pleasure from the thought that nothing was more likely than that to-morrow there would be an exchange of cups between his table and hers. He conceived the idea of chipping a piece out of his own cup and watching every morning on which table it would be laid, until it reached her.

At lunch Michael, as nonchalantly as he could speak, asked his mother whether she did not think the pretty girl dressed rather well.

"Very provincial," Mrs. Fane judged.

"But prettily, I think," persisted Michael. "And she wears a different dress every day."

"Do you want to know her?" asked Mrs. Fane.

"Oh, mother, of course not," said Michael, blushing hotly.

"I dare say they're very pleasant people," Mrs. Fane remarked. "I'll speak to them after lunch, and tell them how anxious you are to make their acquaintance."

"I say, mother," Michael protested. "Oh, no, don't, mother. I really don't want to know them."

Mrs. Fane smiled at him, and told him not to be a foolish boy. After lunch, in her own gracious and distinguished manner which Michael always admired, Mrs. Fane spoke to the two sisters and presently beckoned to Michael who crossed the room, feeling rather as if he were going in to bat first for his side.

"I don't think I know your name," said Mrs. Fane to the elder sister.

"McDonnell—Norah McDonnell, and this is my sister Kathleen."

"Scotch?" asked Mrs. Fane vaguely and pleasantly.

"No, Irish," contradicted the younger sister. "At least by extraction. McDonnell is an Irish name. But we live in Burton-on-Trent. Father and mother are coming down later on."

She spoke with the jerky speech of the Midlands, and Michael rather wished she did not come from Burton-on-Trent, not on his own account, but because his mother would be able to point out to him how right she had been about their provincialism.

"Are you going anywhere this evening?" Michael managed to ask at last.

"I suppose we shall go on the pier. We usually go on the pier. Eh, but it's rather dull in Bournemouth. I like Llandudno better. Llandudno's fine," said the elder Miss McDonnell with fervour.

Mrs. Fane came to the rescue of an awkward conversation by asking the Miss McDonnells if they would take pity on her son and invite him to accompany them. And so it was arranged.

"Happy, Michael?" asked his mother when the ladies, with many smiles, had withdrawn to their rooms.

"Yes. I'm all right," said Michael. "Only I rather wish you hadn't asked them so obviously. It made me feel rather a fool."

"Dearest boy, they were delighted at the idea of your company. They seem quite nice people too. Only, as I said, very provincial. Older, too, than I thought at first."

Michael asked how old his mother thought they were, and she supposed them to be about twenty-seven and thirty. Michael was inclined to protest against this high estimate, but since he had spoken to the Miss McDonnells, he felt that after all his mother might be right.

In the evening his new friends came down to dinner much enwrapped in feathers, and Michael thought that Kathleen looked very beautiful in the crimson lamplight of the dinner-table.

"How smart you are, Michael, to-night!" said Mrs. Fane.

"Oh, well, I thought as I'd got my dinner-jacket down here I might as well put it on. I say, mother, I think I'll get a tail-coat. Couldn't I have one made here?"

"Isn't that collar rather tight?" asked Mrs. Fane anxiously. "And it seems dreadfully tall."

"I like tall collars with evening dress," said Michael severely.

"You know best, dear, but you look perfectly miserable."

"It's only because my chin is a bit sore after shaving."

"Do you have to shave often?" enquired Mrs. Fane, tenderly horrified.

"Rather often," said Michael. "About once a week now."

"She has pretty hands, your lady love," said Mrs. Fane, suddenly looking across to the McDonnells' table.

"I say, mother, for goodness' sake mind. She'll hear you," whispered Michael.

"Oh, Michael dear, don't be so foolishly self-conscious."

After dinner Michael retired to his room, and came down again smoking a cigarette.

Mrs. Fane made a little *moue* of surprise.

"I say, mother, don't keep on calling attention to everything I do. You know I've smoked for ages."

"Yes, but not so very publicly, dear boy."

"Well, you don't mind, do you? I must begin some time," said Michael.

"Michael, don't be cross with me. You're so deliciously amusing, and so much too nice for those absurd women," Mrs. Fane laughed.

Just then the Miss McDonnells appeared on the staircase, and Michael frowned at his mother not to say any more about them.

It was a fairly successful evening. The elder Miss McDonnell bored Michael rather with a long account of why her father had left Ireland, and what a blow it had been to him to open a large hotel in Burton-on-Trent. He was also somewhat fatigued by the catalogue of Mr. McDonnell's virtues, of his wit and courage and good looks and shrewdness.

101

"He has a really old-fashioned sense of humour," said Miss McDonnell. "But then, of course, he's Irish. He's accounted quite the cleverest man in Burton, but then, being Irish, that's not to be wondered at."

Michael wished she would not say 'wondered' as if it were 'wandered,' and indeed he was beginning to think that Miss McDonnell was a great trial, when he suddenly discovered that by letting his arm hang very loosely from his shoulder it was possible without the slightest hint of intention occasionally to touch Kathleen's hand as they walked along. The careful calculation that this proceeding demanded occupied his mind so fully that he was able to give mechanical assents to Miss McDonnell's praise of her father, and apparently at the same time impress her with his own intelligence.

As the evening progressed Michael slightly increased the number of times he tapped Kathleen's hand with his, and after about an hour's promenade of the pier he was doing a steady three taps a minute. He now began to speculate whether Kathleen was aware of these taps, and from time to time he would glance round at her over his shoulder, hopeful of catching her eyes.

"Are you admiring my sister's brooch?" asked Miss McDonnell. "Eh, I think it's grand. Don't you?"

Kathleen giggled lightly at this, and asked her sister how she could, and then Michael with a boldness that on reflection made him catch his breath at the imagination of it, said that while he was admiring Miss Kathleen's brooch he was admiring her eyes still more.

"Oh, Mr. Fane. How can you!" exclaimed Kathleen.

"Well, he's got good taste, I'm sure," said Miss McDonnell. "But, there, after all, what can you expect from an Irish girl? All Irish girls have fine eyes."

When Michael went to bed he felt that on the whole he had acquitted himself that first evening with considerable success, and as he fell asleep he dreamed triumphantly of a daring to-morrow.

It was an April day, whose deeps of azure sky made the diverse foliage of spring burn in one ardent green. Such a day spread out before his windows set Michael on fire for its commemoration, and he made up his mind to propose a long bicycling expedition to the two Miss McDonnells. He wished that it were not necessary to invite the elder sister, but not even this April morning could embolden him so far as to ask Kathleen alone. Mrs. Fane smilingly approved of his proposal, but suggested that on such a warm day it would be wiser not to start until after lunch. So it was arranged, and Michael thoroughly enjoyed the consciousness of escorting these girls out of Bournemouth on their trim bicycles. Indeed, he enjoyed his position so much that he continually looked in the shop-windows, as they rode past, to observe the effect and was so much charmed by the result that he crossed in front of Miss McDonnell, and upset her and her bicycle in the middle of the town.

"Eh, that's a nuisance," said Miss McDonnell, surveying bent handlebars and inner tyre swelling like a toy balloon along the rim. "That was quite a mishap," she added, shaking the dust from her skirt.

Michael was in despair over his clumsiness, especially when Miss Kathleen McDonnell remarked that there went the ride she'd been looking forward to all day.

"Well, you two go on an I'll walk back," Miss McDonnell offered.

"Oh, but I can easily hire another machine," said Michael.

"No. I'll go back. I've grazed my knee a bit badly."

Michael was so much perturbed to hear this that without thinking he anxiously asked to be allowed to look, and wished that the drain by which he was standing would swallow him up when he realized by Kathleen's giggling what he had said.

"It's all right," said Miss McDonnell kindly. "There's no need to worry. I hope you'll have a pleasant ride."

"I say, it's really awfully ripping of you to be so jolly good-tempered about it," Michael exclaimed. "Are you sure I can't do anything?"

"No, you can just put my bicycle in the shop along there, and I'll take the tram back. Mind and enjoy yourselves, and don't be late."

The equable Miss McDonnell then left her sister and Michael to their own devices.

They rode along in alert silence until they left Branksome behind them and came into hedgerows, where an insect earned Michael's cordial gratitude by invading his eye. He jumped off his bicycle immediately and called for Kathleen's aid, and as he stood in the quiet lane with the girl's face close to his and her hand brushing his cheeks, Michael felt himself to be indeed a favourite of fortune.

"There it is, Mr. Fane," said Miss Kathleen McDonnell. And, though he tried to be sceptical for a while of the insect's discovery, he was bound to admit the evidence of the handkerchief.

"Thanks awfully," said Michael. "And I say, I wish you wouldn't call me Mr. Fane. You know my Christian name."

"Oh, but I'd feel shy to call you Michael," said Miss McDonnell.

"Not if I called you Kathleen," Michael suggested, and felt inclined to shake his own hand in congratulation of his own magnificent daring.

"Well, I must say one thing. You don't waste much time. I think you're a bit of a flirt, you know," said Kathleen.

"A flirt," Michael echoed. "Oh, I say, do you really think so?"

"I'm afraid I do," murmured Kathleen. "Shall we go on again?"

They rode along in renewed silence for several miles, and then they suddenly came upon Poole Harbour lying below them, washed in the tremulous golden airs of the afternoon.

"I say, how ripping!" cried Michael, leaping from his machine and flinging it away from him against a bank of vivid grass. "We must sit down here for a bit."

"It is pretty," said Kathleen. "It's almost like a picture."

"I'm glad you're fond of beautiful things," said Michael earnestly.

"Well, one can't help it, can one?" sighed Kathleen.

"Some people can," said Michael darkly. "There's rather a good place to sit over there," he added, pointing to a broken gate that marked the entrance to an oak wood, and he faintly touched the sleeve of Kathleen's blouse to guide her towards the chosen spot.

Then they sat leaning against the gate, she idly plucking sun-faded primroses, he brooding upon the nearness of her hand. In such universal placidity it could not be wrong to hold that hand wasting itself amid small energies. Without looking into her eyes, without turning his gaze from the great tranquil water before him, Michael took her hand in his so lightly that save for the pulsing of his heart he scarcely knew he held it. So he sat breathless, enduring pins and needles, tolerating the uncertain pilgrimage of ants rather than move an inch and break the yielding spell which made her his.

"Are you holding my hand?" she asked, after they had sat a long while pensively.

"I suppose I am," said Michael. Then he turned and with full-blooded cheeks and swimming eyes met unabashed Kathleen's demure and faintly mocking glance.

"Do you think you ought to?" she enquired.

"I haven't thought anything about that," said Michael. "I simply thought I wanted to."

"You're rather old for your age," she went on, with an inflection of teazing surprize in her soft voice. "How old are you?"

"Seventeen," said Michael simply.

"Goodness!" cried Kathleen, withdrawing her hand suddenly. "And I wonder how old you think I am?"

"I suppose you're about twenty-five."

Kathleen got up and said in a brisk voice that destroyed all Michael's bravery, "Come, let's be getting back. Norah will be thinking I'm lost."

Just when they were nearing the outskirts of Branksome, Kathleen dismounted suddenly and said:

"I suppose you'll be surprized when I tell you I'm engaged to be married?"

"Are you?" faltered Michael; and the road swam before him.

"At least I'm only engaged secretly, because my fiancé is poor. He's coming down soon. I'd like you to meet him."

"I should like to meet him very much," said Michael politely.

"You won't tell anybody what I've told you?"

"Good Lord, no. Perhaps I might be of some use," said Michael. "You know, in arranging meetings."

"Eh, you're a nice boy," exclaimed Kathleen suddenly.

And Michael was not perfectly sure whether he thought himself a hero or a martyr.

Mrs. Fane was very much diverted by Michael's account of Miss McDonnell's accident, and teazed him gaily about Kathleen. Michael would assume an expression of mystery, as if indeed he had been entrusted with the dark secrets of a young woman's mind; but the more mysterious he looked the more his mother laughed. In his own heart he cultivated assiduously his devotion, and regretted most poignantly that each new blouse and each chosen evening-dress was not for him. He used to watch Kathleen at dinner, and depress himself with the imagination of her spirit roaming out over the broad Midlands to meet her lover. He never made the effort to conjure up the lover, but preferred to picture him and Kathleen gathering like vague shapes upon the immeasurable territories of the soul.

Then one morning Kathleen took him aside after breakfast to question his steadfastness.

"Were you in earnest about what you said?" she asked.

"Of course I was," Michael affirmed.

"He's come down. He's staying in rooms. Why don't you ask me to go out for a bicycle ride?"

"Well, will you?" Michael dutifully invited.

"I'm so excited," said Kathleen, fluttering off to tell her sister of this engagement to go riding with Michael.

In about half an hour they stood outside the small red-brick house which cabined the bold spirit of Michael's depressed fancies.

"You'll come in and say 'how do you do'?" suggested Kathleen.

"I suppose I'd better," Michael agreed.

They entered together the little efflorescent parlour of the house.

"This is my fiancé—Mr. Walter Trimble," Kathleen proudly announced.

"Pleased to meet you," said Mr. Trimble. "Kath tells me you're on to do us a good turn."

Michael looked at Mr. Trimble, resolutely anxious to find in him the creator of Kathleen's noble destiny. He saw a thick-set young man in a splendidly fitting, but ill-cut blue serge suit; he saw a dark moustache of silky luxuriance growing amid regular features; in fact, he saw someone that might have stepped from one of the grandiose frames of that efflorescent little room. But he was Kathleen's choice, and Michael refused to let himself feel at all disappointed.

"I think it's bad luck not to be able to marry, if one wants to," said Michael deeply.

"You're right," Mr. Trimble agreed. "That's why I want Kath here to marry me first and tell her dad afterwards."

"I only wish I dared," sighed Kathleen. "Well, if we're going to have our walk, we'd better be getting along. Will I meet you by the side-gate into the Winter Garden at a quarter to one?"

"Right-o," said Michael.

"I wonder if you'd lend Mr. Trimble your bicycle?"

"Of course," said Michael.

103

"Because we could get out of the town a bit," suggested Kathleen. "And that's always pleasanter."

Michael spent a dull morning in wandering about Bournemouth, while Kathleen and her Trimble probably rode along the same road he and she had gone a few days back. He tried to console himself with thoughts of self-sacrifice, and he took a morbid delight in the imagination of the pleasure he had made possible for others. But undeniably his own morning was dreary, and not even could Swinburne's canorous Triumph of Time do much more than echo somewhat sadly through the resonant emptiness of his self-constructed prison, whose windows opened on to a sentimental if circumscribed view of unattainable sweetness.

Michael sat on a bench in a sophisticated pine-grove and, having lighted a cigarette, put out the match with his sighing exhalation of *'O love, my love, and no love for me.'* It was wonderful to Michael how perfectly Swinburne expressed his despair. *'O love, my love, had you loved but me.'* And why had she not loved him? Why did she prefer Trimble? Did Trimble ever read Swinburne? Could Trimble sit like this smoking calmly a cigarette and breathing out deathless lines of love's despair? Michael began to feel a little sorry for Kathleen, almost as sorry for her as he felt for himself. Soon the Easter holidays would be over, and he would go back to school. He began to wonder whether he would wear the marks of suffering on his countenance, and whether his friends would eye him curiously, asking themselves in whispers what man this was that came among them with so sad and noble an expression of resignation. As Michael thought of Trimble and Kathleen meeting in Burton-on-Trent and daily growing nearer to each other in love, he became certain that his grief would indeed be manifest. He pictured himself sitting in the sunlit serene class-room of the History Sixth, a listless figure of despair, an object of wondering, whispering compassion. And so his life would lose itself in a monotone of discontent. Grey distances of time presented themselves to him with a terrible menace of loneliness; the future was worse than ever, a barren waste whose horizon would never darken to the silhouette of Kathleen coming towards him with open arms. Never would he hold her hand again; never would he touch those lips at all; never would he even know what dresses she wore in summer. *'O love, my love, and no love for me.'*

When Michael met Kathleen by the side-gate of the Winter Gardens, and received his bicycle back from Trimble, he suddenly wondered whether Kathleen had told her betrothed that another had held her hand. Michael rather hoped she had, and that the news of it had made Trimble jealous. Trimble, however, seemed particularly pleased with himself, and invited Michael to spend the afternoon with him, which Michael promised to do, if his mother did not want his company.

"Well, did you have a decent morning?" Michael enquired of Kathleen, as together they rode towards their hotel.

"Oh, we had a grand time; we sat down where you and me sat the other day."

Michael nearly mounted the pavement at this news, and looked very gloomy.

"What's the matter?" Kathleen pursued. "You're not put out, are you?"

"Oh, no, not at all," said Michael sardonically. "All the same, I think you might have turned off and gone another road. I sat and thought of you all the morning. But I don't mind really," he added, remembering that at any rate for Kathleen he must remain that chivalrous and selfless being which had been created by the loan of a bicycle. "I'm glad you enjoyed yourself. I always want you to be happy. All my life I shall want that."

Michael was surprized to find how much more eloquent he was in the throes of disappointment than he had ever been through the prompting of passion. He wished that the hotel were not already in sight, for he felt that he could easily say much more about his renunciation, and indeed he made up his mind to do so at the first opportunity. In the afternoon he told his mother he was going to pay a visit to Father Moneypenny. He did not tell her about Trimble, because he feared her teazing; although he tried to deceive himself that the lie was due to his loyalty to Kathleen.

"What shall we do?" asked Trimble. "Shall we toddle round to the Shades and have a drink?"

"Just as you like," Michael said.

"Well, I'm on for a drink. It's easier to talk down at the Shades than in here."

Michael wondered why, but he accepted a cigar, and with Trimble sought the speech-compelling Shades.

"It's like this," Trimble began, when they were seated on the worn leather of the corner lounge. "I took a fancy to you right off. Eh, I'm from the North, and I may be a bit blunt, but by gum I liked you, and that's how it is. Yes. I'm going to talk to you the same as I might to my own brother, only I haven't got one."

Michael looked a little apprehensive of the sack of confidences that would presently be emptied over his head, and, seeking perhaps to turn Trimble from his intention, asked him to guess his age.

"Well, I suppose you're anything from twenty-two to twenty-three."

Michael choked over his lemon-and-dash before he announced grimly that he was seventeen.

"Get out," said Trimble sceptically. "You're more than that. Seventeen? Eh, I wouldn't have thought it. Never mind, I said I was going to tell you. And by gum I will, if you say next you haven't been weaned."

Michael resented the freedom of this expression and knitted his eyebrows in momentary distaste.

"It's like this," Mr. Trimble began again, "I made up my mind to-day that Kath's the lass for me. Now am I right? That's what I want to ask you. Am I right?"

"I suppose if you're in love with her and she's in love with you, yes," said Michael.

"Well, she is. Now you wouldn't think she was passionate, would you? You'd say she was a bit of ice, wouldn't you? Well, by gum, I tell you, lad, she's a furnace. Would you believe that?" Mr. Trimble leaned back triumphantly.

Michael did not know what comment to make on this information, and took another sip of his lemon-and-dash.

"Well, now what I say is—and I'm not a chap who's flung round a great deal with the girls—what I say is," Trimble went on, banging the marble table before him, "it's not fair on a lass to play around like this, and so I've made up my mind to marry her. Am I right? By gum, lad, I know I'm right."

"I think you are," said Michael solemnly. "And I think you're awfully lucky."

"Lucky?" echoed Trimble, "I'm lucky enough, if it wasn't for her domned old father. The lass is fine, but him—well, if I was to tell you what he is, you'd say I was using language. So it's like this. I want Kath to marry me down here. I'll get the license. I've saved up a hundred pounds. I'm earning two hundred a year now. Am I right?"

"Perfectly right," said Michael earnestly, who, now that Trimble was showing himself to possess real fervour of soul, was ready to support him, even at the cost of his own suffering. He envied Trimble his freedom from the trammels of education, which for such a long while would prevent himself from taking such a step as marriage by license. Indeed, Michael scarcely thought he ever would take such a step now, since it was unlikely that anyone with Kathleen's attraction would lure him on to such a deed.

Trimble's determination certainly went a long way to excuse the failings of his outer person in Michael's eyes, and indeed, as he pledged him a stirrup-cup of lemon-and-dash, Trimble and Young Lochinvar were not seriously distinct in Michael's imaginative anticipation of the exploit.

So all day and every day for ten days Michael presumably spent his time with Kathleen, notwithstanding Mrs. Fane's tenderly malicious teazing, notwithstanding the elder Miss McDonnell's growing chill, and notwithstanding several very pointed questions from the interfering old spinsters and knitters in the sun of the hotel-gardens. That actually he spent his time alone in watching slow-handed clocks creep on towards a quarter to one or a quarter to five or a quarter to seven, filled Michael daily more full with the spiritual rewards of his sacrifice. He had never known before the luxury of grief, and he had no idea what a variety of becoming attitudes could be wrought of sadness, and not merely attitudes, but veritable dramas. One of the most heroically poignant of these was founded on the moment when Kathleen should ask him to be godfather to her first-born. "No, no," Michael would exclaim. "Don't ask me to do that. I have suffered enough." And Kathleen would remorsefully and silently steal from the dusky room a-flicker with sad firelight, leaving Michael a prey to his own noble thoughts. There was another drama scarcely less moving, in which the first-born died, and Michael, on hearing the news, took the night express to Burton in order to speak words of hope above the little duplicate of Trimble now for ever still in his cradle. Sometimes in the more expansive moments of Michael's celibacy Trimble and Kathleen would lose all their money, and Michael, again taking the night express to Burton-on-Trent, would offer to adopt about half a dozen duplicates of Trimble.

Finally the morning of the marriage arrived, and Michael, feeling that this was an excellent opportunity to have the first of his dramas staged in reality, declined to be present. His refusal was a little less dramatic than he had intended, because Kathleen was too much excited by her own reckless behaviour to act up. While Michael waited for the ceremony's conclusion, he began a poem called 'Renunciation.' Unfortunately the marriage service was very much faster than his Muse, and he never got farther than half the opening line, 'If I renounce.' Michael, however, ascribed his failure to a little girl who would persist in bouncing a tennis ball near his seat in the gardens.

The wedding was only concluded just in time, because Mr. and Mrs. McDonnell arrived on the following day and Michael's expeditions with Kathleen were immediately forbidden. Possibly the equable Miss McDonnell had been faintly alarmed for her sister's good name. At any rate she had certainly been annoyed by her continuous neglect.

Michael, however, had a long interview with Trimble, and managed to warn Kathleen that her husband was going to present himself after dinner. Trimble and he had thought this was more likely to suit Mr. McDonnell's digestion than an after-breakfast confession. Michael expressed himself perfectly willing to take all the blame, and privately made up his mind that if Mr. McDonnell tried to be 'too funny,' he would summon his mother to 'polish him off' with the vision of her manifest superiority.

Somewhat to Michael's chagrin his share in the matter was overlooked by Mr. McDonnell, and the oration he had prepared to quell the long-lipped Irish father was never delivered. Whatever scenes of domestic strife occurred, occurred without Michael's assistance, and he was not a little dismayed to be told by Kathleen in the morning that all had passed off well, but that in the circumstances her father had thought they had better leave Bournemouth at once.

"You're going?" stammered Michael.

"Yes. We must be getting back. It's all been so sudden, and Walter's coming into the business, and eh, I'm as happy as the day is long." Michael watched them all depart, and after a few brave good-byes and three flutters from Kathleen's handkerchief turned sadly back into the large, unfriendly hotel. He knew the number of Kathleen's room, and in an access of despair that was, however, not so overwhelming as to preclude all self-consciousness, he wandered down the corridor and peeped into the late haunt of his love. The floor was littered with tissue paper, broken cardboard-boxes, empty toilet-bottles, and all the disarray of departure. Michael caught his breath at the sudden revelation of this abandoned room's appeal. Here was the end of Kathleen's maidenhood; here still lingered the allurement of her presence; but Trimble could never see this last virginal abode, this elusive shrine that Michael wished he could hire for sentimental meditations. Along the corridor came the sound of a dustpan. He looked round hastily for one souvenir of Kathleen, and perceived still moist from her last quick ablution a piece of soap. He seized it quickly and surrendered the room to the destructive personality of the housemaid.

"Well, dear," asked Mrs. Fane at lunch, "did your lady love give you anything to commemorate your help? Darling Michael, you must have made a most delicious knight-errant."

"Oh, no, she didn't give me anything," said Michael. "Why should she?"

Then he blushed, thinking of the soap that was even now enshrined in a drawer and scenting his handkerchiefs and ties. He wondered if Alan would understand the imperishable effluence from that slim cenotaph of soap.

Chapter XIV: *Arabesque*

IN the air of the Easter holidays that year there must have been something unusually amorous even for April, for when Michael came back to school he found that most of his friends and contemporaries had been wounded by love's darts. Alan, to be sure, returned unscathed, but as he had been resting in the comparatively cloistral seclusion of Cobble Place, Michael did not count his whole heart much honour to anything except his lack of opportunity. Everybody else had come back in possession of girls; some even had acquired photographs. There was talk of gloves and handkerchiefs, of flowers and fans, but nobody, as far as Michael could cautiously ascertain, had thought of soap; and he congratulated himself upon his relic. Also, apparently, all his friends in their pursuit of Eastertide nymphs had been successful, and he began to take credit to himself for being unlucky. His refusal (to this already had come Kathleen's suddenly withdrawn hand) gave him a peculiar interest, and those of his friends in whom he confided looked at him with awe, and listened respectfully to his legend of despair.

Beneath the hawthorns on the golden afternoons and lingering topaz eves of May, Michael would wait for Alan to finish his game of cricket, and between lazily applauded strokes and catches he would tell the tale of Kathleen to his fellows:

"I asked her to wait for me. Of course she was older than me. I said I was ready to marry her when I was twenty-one, but there was another chap, a decent fellow, devilish handsome, too. He was frightfully rich, and so she agreed to elope with him. I helped them no end. I told her father he simply must not attempt to interfere. But, of course, I was frightfully cut up—oh, absolutely knocked out. We're all of us unlucky in love in our family. My sister was in love with an Austrian who was killed by an avalanche. I don't suppose I shall ever be in love again. They say you never really fall in love more than once in your life. I feel a good deal older this term. I suppose I look ... oh, well hit indeed—run it out, and again, sir, and again ...!"

So Michael would break off the tale of his love, until one of his listeners would seek to learn more of passion's frets and fevers.

"But, Bangs, what about the day she eloped? What did you do?"

"I wrote poetry," Michael would answer.

"Great Scott, that's a bit of a swat, isn't it?"

"Yes, it's a bit difficult," Michael would agree. "Only, of course, I only write *vers libre*. No rhymes or anything."

And then an argument would arise as to whether poetry without rhymes could fairly be called poetry at all. This argument, or another like it, would last until the cricket stopped, when Michael and his fellows would stroll into the pavilion and examine the scoring-book or criticize the conduct of the game.

It was a pleasant time, that summer term, and life moved on very equably for Michael, notwithstanding his Eastertide heartbreak. Alan caused him a little trouble by his indifference to anything but cricket, and one Sunday, when May had deepened into June, Michael took him to task for his attitude. Alan had asked Michael over to Richmond for the week-end, and the two of them had punted down the river towards Kew. They had moored their boat under a weeping willow about the time when the bells for church, begin to chime across the level water-meadows.

"Alan, aren't you ever going to fall in love?" Michael began.

"Why should I?" Alan countered in his usual way.

"I don't know. I think it's time you did," said Michael. "You've no idea how much older it makes you feel. And I suppose you don't want to remain a kid for ever. Because, you know, old chap, you are an awful kid beside me."

"Thanks very much," said Alan. "I believe you're exactly one month older, as a matter of fact."

"Yes, in actual time," said Michael earnestly. "But in experience I'm years older than you."

"That must be why you're such a rotten field," commented Alan. "After forty the joints get stiff."

"Oh, chuck being funny," said Michael severely. "I'm in earnest. Now you know as well as I do that last term and the term before I was miserable. Well, look at me now. I'm absolutely happy."

"I thought you were so frightfully depressed," said Alan, twinkling. "I thought you'd had an unlucky love affair. It seems to take you differently from the way it takes most people."

"Oh, of course, I *was* miserable," Michael explained. "But now I'm happy in her happiness. That's love."

Alan burst out laughing, and Michael observed that if he intended to receive his confidences in such a flippant way, he would in future take care to be more secretive.

"I'm showing you what a lot I care about you," Michael went on in tones of deepest injury, "by telling you about myself. I think it's rather rotten of you to laugh."

"But you've told everybody," Alan pointed out.

Michael took another tack, and explained to Alan that he wanted the spur of his companionship in everything.

"It would be so ripping if we were both in love," he sighed. "Honestly, Alan, don't you feel I'm much more developed since last term? I say, you played awfully well yesterday against Dulford Second. If you go on improving at the rate you are now, I don't see why you shouldn't get your Blue at Oxford. By Jove, you know, in eighteen months we shall be at Oxford. Are you keen?"

"Frightfully keen," said Alan. "Especially if I haven't got to be in love all the time."

"I'm not going to argue with you any more," Michael announced. "But you're making a jolly big mistake. Still, of course, I do understand about your cricket, and I dare say love might make you a bit boss-eyed. Perhaps when footer begins again next term, I shall get over this perpetual longing I have for Kathleen. You've no idea how awful I felt when she said she loved Trimble. He was rather a bounder too, but of course I had to help them. I say, Alan, do you remember Dora and Winnie?"

"Rather," said Alan, smiling. "We made pretty good asses of ourselves over them. Do you remember how fed up Nancy got?"

So, very easily the conversation drifted into reminiscences of earlier days, until the sky was quilted with rose-tipped pearly clouds. Then they swung a Japanese lantern in the prow and worked up-stream towards Richmond clustering dark against the west, while an ivory moon shimmered on the dying azure of the day behind.

Throughout June the image of Kathleen became gradually fainter and fainter with each materialization that Michael evoked. Then one evening before dinner he found that the maid had forgotten to put a fresh cake of soap in the dish. It was a question of ringing the bell or of callously using Kathleen's commemorative tablet. Michael went to his drawer and, as he slowly washed his hands, he washed from his mind the few insignificant outlines of Kathleen that were printed there. The soap was Trèfle Incarnat, and somewhat cynically Michael relished the savour of it, and even made up his mind to buy a full fat cake when this one should be finished. Kathleen, however, even in the fragrant moment of her annihilation, had her revenge, for Michael experienced a return of the old restlessness and discontent that was not mitigated by Alan's increasing preoccupation with cricket. He did not complain of this, for he respected the quest of School Colours, and was proud for Alan. At the same time something must be done to while away these warm summer evenings until at Basingstead Minor, where his mother had delightfully agreed to take a cottage for the summer, he and Alan could revive old days at Cobble Place.

One evening Michael went out about nine o'clock to post a letter and, finding the evening velvety and calm, strolled on through the enticing streets of twilight. The violet shadows in which the white caps and aprons of gossiping maids took on a moth-like immaterial beauty, the gliding, enraptured lovers, the scent of freshly watered flower-boxes, the stars winking between the chimney-pots, and all the drowsy alertness of a fine London dusk drew him on to turn each new corner as it arrived, until he saw the sky stained with dull gold from the reflection of the lively crater of the Earl's Court Exhibition, and heard over the vague intervening noises music that was sometimes clearly melodious, sometimes a mere confusion of spasmodic sound.

Michael suddenly thought he would like to spend his evening at the Exhibition, and wondered to himself why he had never thought of going there casually like this, why always he had considered it necessary to devote a hot afternoon and flurried evening to its exploitation. By the entrance he met a fellow-Jacobean, one Drake, whose accentuated mannishness, however disagreeable in the proximity of the school, might be valuable at the Exhibition. Michael therefore accepted his boisterous greeting pleasantly enough, and they passed through the turnstiles together.

"I'll introduce you to a smart girl, if you like," Drake offered, as they paused undecided between the attractions of two portions of the Exhibition. "She sells Turkish Delight by the Cave of the Four Winds. Very O.T., my boy," Drake went on.

"Do you mean——" Michael began.

"What? Rather," said Drake. "I've been home to her place."

"No joking?" Michael asked.

"Yes," affirmed Drake with a triumphant inhalation of sibilant breath.

"Rather lucky, wasn't it?" Michael asked. "I mean to say, it was rather lucky to meet her."

"She might take you home," suggested Drake, examining Michael critically.

"But I mightn't like her," Michael expostulated.

"Good Lord," exclaimed Drake, struck by a point of view that was obviously dismaying in its novelty, "you don't mean to say you'd bother about that, if you could?"

"Well, I rather think I should," Michael admitted. "I think I'd want to be in love."

"You are an extraordinary chap," said Drake. "Now if I were dead nuts on a girl, the last thing I'd think of would be that."

They walked along silently, each one pondering the other's incomprehensibleness, until they came to the stall presided over by Miss Mabel Bannerman, who in Michael's opinion bore a curious resemblance to the Turkish Delight she sold. With the knowledge of her he had obtained from Drake, Michael regarded Miss Bannerman very much as he would have looked at an animal in the Zoological Gardens with whose habits he had formed a previous acquaintanceship through a book of natural history. He tried to perceive beyond her sachet-like hands and watery blue eyes and spongy hair and full-blown breast the fascination which had made her man's common property. Then he looked at Drake, and came to the conclusion that the problem was not worth the difficulty of solution.

"I think I'll be getting back," said Michael awkwardly.

"Why, it's not ten," gasped Drake. "Don't be an ass. Mabel gets out at eleven, and we can take her home. Can't we, Mabel?"

"Sauce!" Mabel archly snapped.

This savoury monosyllable disposed of Michael's hesitation, and, as the personality of Mabel cloyed him with a sudden nausea like her own Turkish Delight, he left her to Drake without another word and went home to bed.

The night was hot and drew Michael from vain attempts at sleep to the open window where, as he sat thinking, a strange visionary survey of the evening, a survey that he himself could scarcely account for, was conjured up. He had not been aware at the time of much more than Drake and the Turkish Delight stall. Now he realized that he too craved for a Mabel, not a peony of a woman who could be flaunted like a vulgar button-hole, but a more shy, a more subtle creature, yet conquerable. Then, as Michael stared out over the housetops at the brooding pavilion of sky which enclosed the hectic city, he began to recall the numberless glances, the countless attitudes, all the sensuous phantasmagoria of the Exhibition's population. He remembered a slim hand, a slanting eye, lips translucent in a burst of light. He caught at scents that, always fugitive, were now utterly incommunicable; he trembled at the remembrance of some contact in a crowd that had been at once divinely intimate and unendurably remote. The illusion of all the city's sleepers calling to him became more and more vivid under each stifling breath of the night. Somewhere beneath that sable diadem of chimney-tops she lay, that lovely girl of his desire. He would not picture her too clearly lest he should destroy the charm of this amazing omnipotence of longing. He would be content to enfold the imagination of her, and at dawn let her slip from his arms like a cloud. He would sit all the night time at his window, aware of kisses. Was this the emotion that prompted poets to their verses? Michael broke his trance to search for paper and pencil, and wrote ecstatically.

In the morning, when he read what he had written, he hastily tore it up, and made up his mind that the Earl's Court Exhibition would feed his fire more satisfactorily than bad verses. Half a guinea would buy a season-ticket, and July should be a pageant of sensations.

Every night Michael went to Earl's Court, and here a hundred brilliant but evanescent flames were kindled in his heart, just as in the Exhibition gardens every night for three hours the fairy-lamps spangled the edge of the paths in threads of many-tinted lights. Michael always went alone, because he did not desire any but his own discoveries to reward his excited speculation. At first he merely enjoyed the sensation of the slow stream of people that continually went up and down, or strolled backwards and forwards, or circled round the bandstand that was set out like a great gaudy coronet upon the parterres of lobelias and geraniums and calceolarias that with nightfall came to seem brocaded cushions.

107

It was a time profitable with a thousand reflections, this crowded hour of the promenade. There was always the mesmeric sighing of silk skirts and the ceaseless murmur of conversation; there was the noise of the band and the tapping of canes; there was, in fact, a regularity of sound that was as infinitely soothing as breaking waves or a wind-ruffled wood. There were the sudden provocative glances which flashed as impersonally as precious stones, and yet lanced forth a thrill that no faceted gem could give. There were hands whose white knuckles, as they rippled over Michael's hands in some momentary pressure of the throng, gave him a sense of being an instrument upon which a chord had been clearly struck. There were strands of hair that floated against his cheeks with a strange, but exquisitely elusive intimacy of communication. It was all very intoxicating and very sensuous; but the spell crept over him as imperceptibly as if he were merely yielding himself to the influence of a beautiful landscape, as if he were lotus-eating in a solitude created by numbers.

Michael, however, was not content to dream away in a crowd these passionate nights of July; and after a while he set out to find adventures in the great bazaar of the Exhibition, wandering through the golden corridors and arcades with a queer sense of suppressed expectancy. So many fantastic trades were carried on here, that it was natural to endow the girls behind the counters with a more romantic life than that of ordinary and anæmic shop-assistants. Even Miss Mabel Bannerman amid her Turkish Delight came to seem less crude in such surroundings, and Michael once or twice had thoughts of prosecuting his acquaintanceship; for as yet he had not been able to bring himself to converse with any of the numerous girls, so much more attractive than Mabel, who were haunting him with their suggestion of a strange potentiality.

Michael wandered on past the palmists who went in and out of their tapestried tents; past the physiognomists and phrenologists and graphologists; past the vendors of scents and silver; past the languid women who spread out their golden rugs from Samarcand; past the Oriental shops fuming with odorous pastilles, where lamps encrusted in deep-hued jewels of glass glimmered richly; past that slant-eyed cigarette-seller with the crimson fez crowning her dark hair.

July was nearing its end; the holidays were in sight; and still Michael had got no farther with his ambitions; still at the last moment he would pass on and neglect some perfect opportunity for speech. He used to rail at his cowardice, and repeat to himself all his academic knowledge of frail womanhood. He even took the trouble to consult the Ars Amatoria, and was so much impressed by Ovid's prescription for behaviour at a circus that he determined to follow his advice. To put his theory into practice, Michael selected a booth where seals performed for humanity at sixpence a head. But all his resolutions ended in sitting mildly amused by the entertainment in a condition of absolute decorum.

School broke up with the usual explosion of self-congratulatory rhetoric from which Michael, owing to his Exhibition ticket, failed to emerge with any calf-bound souvenir of intellectual achievement. He minded this less than his own pusillanimous behaviour on the brink of experience. It made him desperate to think that in two days he would be at Basingstead with his mother and Alan and Mrs. Ross, utterly remote even from the pretence of temptation.

"Dearest Michael, you really must get your things together," expostulated Mrs. Fane, when he announced his intention of going round to the Exhibition as usual on the night before they were to leave town.

"Well, mother, I can pack when I come in, and I do want to get all I can out of this 'season.' You see it will be absolutely wasted for August and half September."

"Michael," said Mrs. Fane suddenly, "you're not keeping anything from me?"

"Good gracious, no. What makes you ask?" Michael demanded, blushing.

"I was afraid that perhaps some horrid girl might have got hold of you," said Mrs. Fane.

"Why, would you mind very much?" asked Michael, with a curious hopefulness that his mother would pursue the subject, as if by so doing she would give him an opportunity of regarding himself and his behaviour objectively.

"I don't know that I should mind very much," said Mrs. Fane, "if I thought you were quite certain not to do anything foolish." Then she seemed to correct the laxity of her point of view, and substituted, "anything that you might regret."

"What could I regret?" asked Michael, seeking to drive his mother on to the rocks of frankness.

"Surely you know what better than I can tell you. Don't you?" The note of interrogation caught the wind, and Mrs. Fane sailed off on the starboard tack.

"But as long as you're not keeping anything from me," she went on, "I don't mind. So go out, dear child, and enjoy yourself by all means. But don't be very late."

"I never am," said Michael quickly, and a little resentfully as he thought of his very decorous homecomings.

"I know you're not. You're really a very dear fellow," his mother murmured, now safe in port.

So at nine o'clock as usual Michael passed through the turnstiles and began his feverish progress across the Exhibition grounds, trying as he had never tried before to screw himself up to the pitch of the experience he craved.

He was standing by one of the entrances to the Court of Marvels, struggling with his self-consciousness and egging himself on to be bold on this his last night, when he heard himself accosted as Mr. Michael Fane. He looked round and saw a man whom he instantly recognized, but for the moment could not name.

"It is Mr. Michael Fane?" the stranger asked. "You don't remember me? I met you at Clere Abbey."

"Brother Aloysius!" Michael exclaimed, and as he uttered the high-sounding religious appellation he almost laughed at the incongruity of it in connection with this slightly overdressed and dissolute-looking person he so entitled.

"Well, not exactly, old chap. At least not in this get-up. Meats is my name."

"Oh, yes," said Michael vaguely. There seemed no other comment on such a name, and Mr. Meats himself appeared sensitive to the implication of uncertainty, for he made haste to put Michael at ease by commenting on its oddity.

"I suppose you're thinking it's a damned funny exchange for Brother Aloysius. But a fellow can't help his name, and that's a fact."

"You've left the Abbey then?" enquired Michael.

"Oh Lord, yes. Soon after you went. It was no place for me. Manners, O.S.B., gave me the push pretty quick. And I don't blame him. Well, what are you doing? Have a drink? Or have you got to meet your best girl? My, you've grown since I saw you last. Quite the Johnny nowadays. But I spotted you all right. Something about your eyes that would be very hard to forget."

Michael thought that if it came to unforgettable eyes, the eyes of Mr. Meats would stand as much chance of perpetual remembrance as any, since their unholy light would surely set any heart beating with the breathless imagination of sheer wickedness.

"Yes, I have got funny eyes, haven't I?" said Meats in complacent realization of Michael's thoughts. And as he spoke he seemed consciously to exercise their vile charm, so that his irises kindled slowly with lambent blue flames.

"Come on, let's have this drink," urged Meats, and he led the way to a scattered group of green tables. They sat down, and Michael ordered a lemon-squash.

"Very good drink too," commented Meats. "I think I'll have the same, Rosie," he said to the girl who served them.

"Do you know that girl?" Michael asked.

"Used to. About three years ago. She's gone off though," said Meats indifferently.

Michael, to hide his astonishment at the contemptuous suggestion of damaged goods, enquired what Meats had been doing since he left the Monastery.

"Want to know?" asked Meats.

Michael assured him that he did.

"You're rather interested in me, aren't you? Well, I can tell you a few things and that's a fact. I don't suppose that there's anybody in London who could tell you more. But you might be shocked."

"Oh, shut up!" scoffed Michael, blushing with indignation.

Then began the shameless narration of the late Brother Aloysius, whom various attainments had enabled to gain an equal profit from religion and vice. Sometimes as Michael listened to the adventures he was reminded of Benvenuto Cellini or Casanova, but almost immediately the comparison would be shattered by a sudden sanctimonious blasphemy which he found nauseating. Moreover, he disliked the sly procurer that continually leered through the man's personality.

"You seem to have done a lot of dirty work for other people," Michael bluntly observed at last.

"My dear old chap," replied Meats, "of course I have. You see, in this world there are lots of people who can always square their own consciences, if the worst of what they want to do is done for them behind the scenes as it were. You never yet heard a man confess that he ruined a girl. Now, did you? Why, I've heard the most shocking out-and-outers anyone could wish to meet brag that they've done everything, and then turn up their eyes and thank God they've always respected real purity. Well, I never respected anything or anybody. And why should I? I never had a chance. Who was my mother? A servant. Who was my father? A minister, a Nonconformist minister in Wales. And what did the old tyke do? Why, he took the case to court and swore my mother was out for blackmail. So she went to prison, and he came smirking home behind the village band; and all the old women in the place hung out Union Jacks to show they believed in him. And then his wife gave a party."

Michael looked horrified and felt horrified at this revelation of vileness, and yet, all the time he was listening, through some grotesquery of his nerves he was aware of thinking to himself the jingle of Little Bo-peep.

"Ah, that's touched you up, hasn't it?" said Meats, eagerly leaning forward. "But wait a bit. What did my mother do when she came out? Went on the streets. Do you hear? On the streets, and mark you, she was a servant, a common village servant, none of your flash Empire goods. Oh, no, she never knew what it was like to go up the river on a Sunday afternoon. And she drank. Well, of course she drank. Gin was as near as she ever got to paradise. And where was I brought up? Not among the buttercups, my friend, you may lay on that. No, I was down underneath, underneath, underneath where a chap like you will never go because you're a gentleman. And so, though, of course, you're never likely to ruin a girl, you'll always have your fun. Why shouldn't you? Being a nicely brought-up young gentleman, it's your birthright."

"But how on earth did you ever become a monk?" asked Michael, anxious to divert the conversation away from himself.

"Well, it does sound a bit improbable, I must say. I was recommended there by a priest—a nice chap called Arbuthnot who'd believe a chimney-sweep was a miller. But Manners was very sharp on to me, and I was very sharp on to Manners. Picking blackberries and emptying slops! What a game! I came with a character and left without one. Probationer was what they called me. Silly mug was what I called myself."

"You seem to know a lot of priests," said Michael.

"Oh, I've been in with parsons since I was at Sunday-school. Well, don't look so surprised. You don't suppose my mother wanted me hanging round all the afternoon! Now I very soon found out that one can always get round a High Church slum parson, and very often a Catholic priest by turning over a new leaf and confessing. It gets them every time, and being by nature generous, it gets their pockets. That's why I gave up Dissenters and fashionable Vicars. Dissenters want more than they give, and fashionable Vicars are too clever. That's why they become fashionable Vicars, I suppose," said Meats pensively.

"But you couldn't go on taking in even priests for ever," Michael objected.

"Ah, now I'll tell you something. I do feel religious sometimes," Meats declared solemnly. "And I do really want to lead a new life. But it doesn't last. It's like love. Never mind, perhaps I'll be lucky enough to die when I'm working off a religious stretch. I give you my word, Fane, that often in these fits I've felt like committing suicide just to cheat the devil. Would you believe that?"

"I don't think you're as bad as you make out," said Michael sententiously.

"Oh, yes, I am," smiled the other. "I'm rotten bad. But I reckon the first man I meet in hell will be my father, and if it's possible to hurt anyone down there more than they're being hurt already, I'll do it. But look here, I shall get the hump with this blooming conversation you've started me off on. Come along, drink up and have another, and tell us something about yourself."

"Oh, there's nothing to tell," Michael sighed. "My existence is pretty dull after yours."

"I suppose it is," said Meats, as if struck by a new thought. "Everything has its compensations, as they say."

"Frightfully dull," Michael vowed. "Why, here am I still at school! You know I wouldn't half mind going down underneath, as you call it, for a while. I believe I'd like it."

"If you knew you could get up again all right," commented Meats.

"Oh, of course," Michael answered. "I don't suppose Æneas would have cared much about going down to hell, if he hadn't been sure he could come up again quite safely."

"Well, I don't know your friend with the Jewish name," said Meats. "But I'll lay he didn't come out much wiser than he went in if he knew he could get out all right by pressing a button and taking the first lift up."

"Oh, well, I was only speaking figuratively," Michael explained.

"So was I. The same here, and many of them, old chap," retorted Meats enigmatically.

"Ah, you don't think I'm in earnest. You think I'm fooling," Michael complained.

"Oh, yes, I think you'd like to take a peep without letting go of Nurse's apron," sneered Meats.

"Well, perhaps one day you'll see me underneath," Michael almost threatened.

"No offence, old chap," said Meats cordially. "It's no good my giving you an address because it won't last, but London isn't very big, and we'll run up against one another again, that's a cert. Now I've got to toddle off and meet a girl."

"Have you?" asked Michael, and his enquiry was tinged with a faint longing that the other noticed at once.

"Jealous?" enquired Meats. "Why, look at all the girls round about you. It's up to you not to feel lonely."

"I know," said Michael fretfully. "But how the deuce can I tell whether they want me to talk to them?"

Meats laughed shrilly.

"What are you afraid of? Leading some innocent lamb astray?"

Again to Michael occurred the ridiculous rhyme of Bo-peep. So insistent was it that he could scarcely refrain from humming it aloud.

"Of course I'm not afraid of that," he protested. "But how am I to tell they won't think me a brute?"

"What would it matter if they did?" asked Meats.

"Well, I should feel a fool."

"Oh, dear. You're very young, aren't you?"

"It's nothing to do with being young," Michael asserted. "I simply don't want to be a cad."

"Somebody else is to be the cad first and then it's all right, eh?" chuckled Meats. "But it's a shame to teaze a nice chap like you. I dare say Daisy'll have a friend with her."

"Is Daisy the girl you're going to see?"

"You've guessed my secret," said Meats. "Come on, I'll introduce you."

As Michael rose to follow Meats, he felt that he was like Faust with Mephistopheles. But Faust had asked for his youth back again. Michael only demanded the courage not to waste youth while it was his to enjoy. He felt that his situation was essentially different from the other, and he hesitated no longer.

The next half-hour passed in a whirl. Michael was conscious of a slim brunette in black and scarlet, and of a fairy-like figure by her side in a dress of shimmering blue; he was conscious too of a voice insinuating, softly metallic, and of fingers that touched his wrist as lightly as silk. There were whispers and laughters and sudden sweeping embarrassments. There was a horrible sense of publicity, of curious mocking eyes that watched his progress. There was an overwhelming knowledge of money burning in his pocket, of money hard and round and powerful. There were hot waves of remorse and the thought of his heart hammering him on to be brave. A cabman leaned over from his box like a gargoyle. A key clicked.

Then, it seemed a century afterwards, Carlington Road stretched dim, austere, forbidding to Michael's ingress. A policeman's deep salutation sounded portentously reproachful. The bloom of dawn was on the windows. The flames in the street-lamps were pale as primroses. At his own house Michael saw the red and amber sparrows in their crude blue vegetation horribly garish against the lighted entrance-hall. The Salve printed funereally upon the mat was the utterance of blackest irony. He hastily turned down the gas, and the stairs caught a chill unreality from the creeping dawn. The balustrade stuck to his parched hands; the stairs creaked grotesquely to his breathless ascent. His mother stood like a ghost in her doorway.

"Michael, how dreadfully late you are."

"Am I?" said Michael. "I suppose it is rather late. I met a fellow I know."

He spoke petulantly to conceal his agitation, and his one thought was to avoid kissing her before he went up to his own room.

"It's all right about my packing," he murmured hastily. "In the morning I shall have time. I'm sorry I woke you. Good night."

He had passed; and he looked back compassionately, as she faded in her rosy and indefinite loveliness away to her room.

Then, with the patterns of foulard ties crawling like insects before his strained eyes, with collars coiling and uncoiling like mainsprings, with all his clothes in one large intolerable muddle, Michael pressed the cold sheets to his forehead and tried to imagine that to-morrow he would be in the country.

Chapter XV: Grey Eyes

AS Michael sat opposite to his mother in the railway-carriage on the following morning, he found it hard indeed to realize that an ocean did not stretch between them. He did not feel ashamed; he had no tremors for the straightforward regard; he had no uneasy sensation that possibly even now his mother was perplexing herself on account of his action. He simply felt that he had suffered a profound change and that his action of yesterday called for a readjustment of his entire standpoint. Or rather, he felt that having since yesterday travelled so far and lived so violently, he could now only meet his mother as a friend from whom one has been long parted and whose mental progress during many years must be gradually apprehended.

"Why do you look at me with such a puzzled expression, Michael?" asked Mrs. Fane. "Is my hat crooked?"

Michael assured her that nothing was the matter with her hat.

"Do you want to ask me something?" persisted Mrs. Fane.

Michael shook his head and smiled, wondering whether he did really wish to ask her a question, whether he would be relieved to know what attitude she would adopt towards his adventure. With so stirring a word did he enhance what otherwise would have seemed base. His mother evidently was aware of a tension in this ridiculously circumscribed railway-carriage. Would it be released if he were to inform her frankly of what had happened, or would such, an admission be an indiscretion from which their relationship would never recover? After all she was his mother, and there must positively exist in her inmost self the power of understanding what he had done. Some part of the impulse which had actuated his behaviour would surely find a root in the heart of the handsome woman who travelled with such becoming repose on the seat opposite to him. He forgot to bother about himself in this sudden new pleasure of observation that seemed to endow him with undreamed-of opportunities of distraction and, what was more important, with a stable sense of his own individuality. How young his mother looked! Until now he had taken her youth for granted, but she must be nearly forty. It was scarcely credible that this tall slim creature with the proud, upcurving mouth and lustrous grey eyes was his own mother. He thought of his friends' homes that were presided over by dumpy women in black silk with greying hair. Even Alan's mother, astonishingly pretty though she was, seemed in the picture he conjured of her to look faded beside his own.

And while he was pondering his mother's beauty, the train reached the station at which they must alight for Basingstead. There was Alan in white flannels on the platform, there too was Mrs. Ross; and as she greeted his mother Michael's thoughts went back to the day he saw these two come together at Carlington Road, and by their gracious encounter drive away the shadow of Nurse.

"I vote we walk," said Alan. "Mrs. Fane and Aunt Maud can drive in the pony-chaise, and then your luggage can all come up at once in the cart."

So it was arranged, and as Michael watched his mother and Mrs. Ross drive off, he was strangely reminded of a picture that he had once dearly loved, a picture by Flaxman of Hera and Athene driving down from Olympus to help the Greeks. Λευκώλενος Ἥρη—that was his mother, and γλαυκῶπις Ἀθήνη—that was Mrs. Ross. He could actually remember the line in the Iliad that told of the gates of heaven, where the Hours keep watch, opening for the goddesses' descent—αὐτόμαται δέ πύλαι μύκοον οὐρανοι ἁς ἐχον Ὧραι. At the same time for all his high quotations, Michael could not help smiling at the dolefully senescent dun pony being compared to the golden steeds of Hera or at the pleasant old porter who hastened to throw open the white gate of the station-drive serving as a substitute for the Hours.

The country air was still sweet between the hazel hedgerows, although the grass was drouthy and the scabious blooms were already grey with dust. Nothing for Michael could have been more charged with immemorial perfume than this long walk at July's end. It held the very quintessence of holiday airs through all the marching years of boyhood. It was haunted by the memory of all the glad anticipations of six weeks' freedom that time after time had succeeded the turmoil of breaking up for the August holidays. The yellow amoret swinging from the tallest shoot of the hedge was the companion of how many summer walks. The acrid smell of nettles by the roadside was prophetic of how many pastoral days. The butterflies, brown and white and tortoiseshell, that danced away to right and left over the green bushes, to what winding paths did they not summon. And surely Alan gave a final grace to this first walk of the holidays. Surely he crystallized all hopes, all memories, all delights of the past in a perfection of present joy.

Yet Michael, as he walked beside him, could only think of Alan as a beautiful inanimate object for whom perception did not exist. Inanimate, however, was scarcely the word to describe one who was so very definitely alive: Michael racked his invention to discover a suitable label for Alan, but he could not find the word. With a shock of misgiving he asked himself whether he had outgrown their friendship, and partly to test, but chiefly to allay his dread, he took Alan's arm with a gesture of almost fierce possession. He was relieved to find that Alan's touch was still primed with consolation, that companionship with him still soothed the turbulence of his own spirit reaching out to grasp what could never be expressed in words, and therefore could never be grasped. Michael was seized with a longing to urge Alan to grow up more quickly, to make haste lest he should be left behind by his adventurous friend. Michael remembered how he used to dread being moved up, hating to leave Alan in a class below him, how he had deliberately dallied to allow Alan to overtake him. But idleness in school-work was not the same as idleness in experience of life, and unless Alan would quickly grow up, he knew that he must soon leave him irremediably behind. It was distressing to reflect that Alan would be shocked by the confidence which he longed to impose upon him, and it was disquieting to realize that these last summer holidays of school, however complete with the quiet contentment of familiar pleasures, would for himself grow slowly irksome with deferred excitement.

But as the green miles slowly unfolded themselves, as the dauntless yellow amoret still swung from a lissome stem, as Alan spoke of the river and the grey tower on the hill, Michael saw the fretful colours of the Exhibition grow dim; and when dreaming in the haze of the slumberous afternoon they perceived the village and heard the mysterious murmur of human tranquillity, Michael's heart overflowed with gratitude for the sight of Alan by his side. Then the church-clock that struck a timeless hour sounded for him one of those moments whose significance would resist eternally whatever lying experience should endeavour to assail the truth which had made of one flashing scene a revelation.

Michael was ineffably refreshed by his vision of the imperishable substance of human friendship, and he could not but jeer at himself now for having a little while back put Alan into the domain of objects inanimate.

"There's your cottage," said Alan. "It's practically next door to Cobble Place. Rather decent, eh?"

Michael could not say how decent he thought it, nor how decent he thought Alan.

"I vote we go up the river after tea," he suggested.

"Rather," said Alan. "I expect you'll come round to tea with us. Don't be long unpacking."

"I shan't, you bet," said Michael.

Nor was he, and after a few minutes he and his mother were sitting in the drawing-room at Cobble Place, eating a tea that must have been very nearly the same as an unforgettable tea of nine years ago. Mrs. Carthew did not seem quite so old; nor indeed did anybody, and as for Joan and May Carthew, they were still girls. Yet even when he and Alan had stayed down here for the wedding only four years ago, Michael had always been conscious of everybody's age. And now he was curiously aware of everybody's youth. He supposed vaguely that all this change of outlook was due to his own remarkable precocity and rapid advance; but nevertheless he still ate with all the heartiness of childhood.

After tea Mrs. Ross with much tact took up Michael by himself to see her son and, spared the necessity of comment, Michael solemnly regarded the fair-haired boy of two who was squeaking an india-rubber horse for his mother's benefit.

"O you attractive son of mine," Mrs. Ross sighed in a whisper.

"He's an awfully sporting kid," Michael said.

Then he suddenly remembered that he had not seen Mrs. Ross since her husband was killed. Yet from this chintz-hung room whose casements were flooded with the amber of the westering sun, how far off seemed fatal Africa. He remembered also that to this very same gay room he had long ago gone with Miss Carthew after tea, that here in a ribboned bed he had first heard the news of her coming to live at 64 Carlington Road.

"We must have a long talk together soon," said Mrs. Ross, seeming to divine his thoughts. "But I expect you're anxious to revive old memories and visit old haunts with Alan. I'm going to stay here and talk to Kenneth while Nurse has her tea."

Michael lingered for a moment in the doorway to watch the two. Then he said abruptly, breathlessly:

"Mrs. Ross, I think painters and sculptors are lucky fellows. I'd like to paint you now. I wish one could understand the way people look, when one's young. But I'm just beginning to realize how lucky I was when you came to us. And yet I used to be ashamed of having a governess. Still, I believe I did appreciate you, even when I was eight."

Then he fled, and to cover his retreat sang out loudly for Alan all the way downstairs.

"I say, Aunt Enid wants to talk to you," said Alan.

"Aunt Enid?" Michael echoed.

"Mrs. Carthew," Alan explained.

"I vote we go for a walk afterwards, don't you?" Michael suggested.

"Rather," said Alan. "I'll shout for you, when I think you've jawed long enough."

Michael found Mrs. Carthew in her sun-coloured garden, cutting down the withering lupins whose silky seed-pods were strewn all about the paths.

"Can you spare ten minutes for an old friend?" asked Mrs. Carthew.

Michael thought how tremendously wise she looked, and lest he should be held to be staring unduly, he bent down to sweep together the shimmering seed-pods, while Mrs. Carthew snipped away, talking in sentences that matched the quick snickasnack of her weapon.

"I must say you've grown up into an attractive youth. Let me see, you must be seventeen and a half. I suppose you think yourself a man now? Dear me, these lupins should have been cut back a fortnight ago. And now I have destroyed a hollyhock. Tut-tut, I'm getting very blind. What did you think of Maud's son? A healthy rosy child, and not at all amenable to discipline, I'm glad to say. Well, are you enjoying school?"

The old lady paused with her scissors gaping, and looked shrewdly at Michael.

"I'm getting rather fed up with it," Michael admitted. "It goes on for such a long time. It wasn't so bad this term, though."

Then he remembered that whatever pleasures had mitigated the exasperation of school last term were decidedly unscholastic, and he blushed.

"I simply loathed it for a time," he added.

"Alan informs me he acquired his first eleven cap this term and will be in the first fifteen as Lord Treasurer or something," Mrs. Carthew went on. "Naturally he must enjoy this shower of honours. Alan is decidedly typical of the better class of unthinking young Englishman. He is pleasant to look at—a little colt-like perhaps, but that will soon wear off. My own dear boy was very like him, and Maud's dear husband was much the same. You, I'm afraid, think too much, Michael."

"Oh, no, I don't think very much," said Michael, disclaiming philosophy, and greatly afraid that Mrs. Carthew was supposing him a prig.

"You needn't be ashamed of thinking," she said. "After all, the amount you think now won't seriously disorganize the world. But you seem to me old for your age, much older than Alan for instance, and though your conversation with me at any rate is not mature, nevertheless you convey somehow an impression of maturity that I cannot quite account for."

Michael could not understand why, when for the first time he was confronted with somebody who gave his precocity its due, he was unable to discuss it eagerly and voluminously, why he should half resent being considered older than Alan.

"Don't look so cross with me," Mrs. Carthew commanded. "I am an old woman, and I have a perfect right to say what I please to you. Besides, you and I have had many conversations, and I take a great interest in you. What are you going to be?"

"Well, that's what I can't find out," said Michael desperately. "I know what I'm not going to be, and that's all."

"That's a good deal, I think," said Mrs. Carthew. "Pray tell me what professions you have condemned."

"I'm not going into the Army. I'm not going into the Civil Service. I'm not going to be a doctor or a lawyer."

"Or a parson?" asked Mrs. Carthew, crunching through so many lupin stalks at once that they fell with a rattle on to the path.

"Well, I have thought about being a parson," Michael slowly granted. "But I don't think parsons ought to marry."

"Good gracious," exclaimed Mrs. Carthew, "you're surely not engaged?"

"Oh, no," said Michael; but he felt extremely flattered by the imputation. "Still, I might want to be."

"Then you're in love," decided Mrs. Carthew. "No wonder you look so careworn. I suppose she's nearly thirty and has promised to wait until you come of age. I can picture her. If I had my stick with me I could draw her on the gravel. A melon stuck on a bell-glass, I'll be bound."

"I'm not in love, and if I were in love," said Michael with dignity, "I certainly shouldn't be in love with anyone like that. But I could be in love at any moment, and so I don't think I shall be a parson."

"You've got plenty of time," said Mrs, Carthew. "Alan says you're going to Oxford next year."

Michael's heart leapt—next year had never before seemed so imminent.

"I suppose you'll say that I'm an ignorant and foolish old woman, if I attempt to give you advice about Oxford; but I gave you advice once about school, and I'll do the same again. To begin with, I think you'll find having been to St. James' a handicap. I have an old friend, the wife of a don, who assures me that many of the boys who go up from your school suffer at Oxford from their selfish incubation by Dr. Brownjohn. They're fit for killing too soon. In fact, they have been forced."

"Ah, but I saw that for myself," said Michael. "I had a row with Brownjohn about my future."

"How delighted I am to hear that!" said Mrs. Carthew. "I think that I'll cut back the delphiniums also. Then you're not going in for a scholarship?"

"No," said Michael. "I don't want to be hampered, and I think my mother's got plenty of money. But Alan's going to get a scholarship."

"Yes, that is unfortunately necessary," said Mrs. Carthew. "Still, Alan is sufficiently typical of the public-school spirit—an odious expression yet always unavoidable—to carry off the burden. If you were poor, I should advise you to buy overcoats. Three smart overcoats are an equipment for a poor man. But I needn't dwell on social ruses in your case. Remember that going to Oxford is like going to school. Be normal and inconspicuous at first; and when you have established yourself as an utterly undistinguished young creature, you can career into whatever absurdities of thought, action or attire you will. In your first year establish your sanity; in your second year display your charm; and in your third year do whatever you like. Now there is Alan calling, and we'll leave the paths strewn with these cut stalks as a Memento Mori to the gardener. What a charming woman your mother is. She has that exquisite vagueness which when allied with good breeding is perfectly irresistible, at any rate to a practical and worldly old woman like me. But then I've had an immense amount of time in which to tidy up. Pleasant hours to you down here. It's delightful to hear about the place the sound of boys laughing and shouting."

Michael left Mrs. Carthew, rather undecided as to what exactly she thought of him or Alan or anybody else. As he walked over the lawn that went sloping down to the stream, he experienced a revulsion from the interest he took in listening to what people thought about him, and he now began to feel an almost morbid sensitiveness to the opinion of others. This destroyed some of the peace which he had sought and cherished down here in the country. He began to wonder if that wise old lady had been laughing at him, whether all she said had been an implied criticism of his attitude towards existence. Her praise must have been grave irony; her endorsement of his behaviour had been disguised reproof. She really admired Alan, and had only been trying as gently as possible to make him come into line with her nephew. He himself must seem to her eccentric, undignified, a flamboyant sort of creature whom she pitied and whose errors she wished to remedy. Michael was mortified by his retrospect of the conversation, and felt inclined when he saw Alan to make an excuse and retire from his society, until his self-esteem had recovered from the rebuke that had lately been inflicted. Indeed, it called for a great effort on Michael's part to embark in the canoe with his paragon and sit face to face without betraying the wound that was damaging his own sense of personality.

"You had a very long jaw with Aunt Enid," said Alan. "I thought you were never coming. She polished me off in about three minutes."

Michael looked darkly at Alan for a moment before he asked with ungracious accentuation what on earth Alan and Mrs. Carthew had talked about.

"She was rather down on me," said Alan. "I think she must have thought I was putting on side about getting my Eleven."

Michael was greatly relieved to hear this, and his brow cleared as he enquired what was wrong.

"Well, I can't remember her exact words," Alan went on. "But she said I must be careful not to grow up into a strong silent Englishman, because their day was done. She practically told me I was rather an ass, and pretended to be fearfully surprised when she heard I was going to try for a scholarship at Oxford. She was squashing slugs all the time she was talking, and I could do nothing but look a bigger fool than ever and count the slugs. I ventured to remark once that most people thought it was a good thing to be keen on games, and she said half the world was composed of fools which accounted for the preponderance—I mean preponderance—of pink on the map. She said it always looked like an advertizement of successful fox-hunting. And when I carefully pointed out that I'd never all my life had a chance to hunt, she said 'More's the pity,' I couldn't make out what she was driving at; so, feeling rather a worm, I shot off as soon as I could. What did she say to you?"

"Oh, nothing much," said Michael triumphantly. "She's a rum old girl, but rather decent."

"She's too clever for me," said Alan, shaking his head. "It's like batting to a pro."

Then from the complexities of feminine judgment, the conversation glided easily like the canoe towards a discussion of the umpire's decision last term in giving Alan out l.b.w. to a ball that pitched at least two feet away from the off stump.

"It was rotten," said Alan fervidly.

113

"It was putrid," Michael agreed.

To avoid the difficulty of a first night in a strange cottage, Mrs. Fane and Michael had supper at Cobble Place; and after a jolly evening spent in looking for pencils to play games that nobody could ever recollect in all their rich perfection of potential incidents, Michael and Mrs. Fane walked with leisurely paces back to Woodbine Cottage through a sweet-savoured moonless night.

Michael enjoyed the intimate good night beneath so small a roof, and wished that Stella were with them. He lay awake, reading from each in turn of the tower of books he had erected by his bedside to fortify himself against sleeplessness. It was a queer enough mixture— Swinburne, Keats, Matthew Arnold, Robinson Crusoe, Half-hours with the Mystics, Tom Brown's Schooldays, Daudet's Sappho, the second volume of The Savoy, The Green Carnation, Holy Living and Dying; and as each time he changed his mind and took another volume, on the gabled ceiling the monstrous shadow that was himself filled him with a dreadful uncertainty. After an hour or so, he went to sit by the low window, leaning out and seeming to hear the dark world revolve in its course. Stars shook themselves clear from great rustling trees, and were in time enmeshed by others. The waning moon came up behind a rounded hill. A breeze fluttered down the dusty road, and was silent.

Michael fell to wondering whether he could ever bring himself in tune with these slow progressions of nature, whether he could renounce after one haggard spell of experience the mazy stir of transitory emotions that danced always beyond this dream. An Half-hour with St. John of the Cross made him ask himself whether this were the dark night of the soul through which he was passing. But he had never travelled yet, nor was he travelling now. He was simply sitting quiescent, allowing himself to be passed. These calm and stately figures of humanity whom he admired in their seclusion had only reached it after long strife. Mrs. Carthew had lost a husband and a son, had seen her daughter leave her house as a governess. Joan and May had for many years sunk their hopes in tending their mother. Nancy was away earning money, and would be entitled to retire here one day. Mrs. Ross had endured himself and Stella for several years, had married and lost her husband, and had borne a child. All these had won their timeless repose and their serene uncloying ease. They were not fossils, but perdurable images of stone. And his mother, she was—he stopped his reverie. Of his mother he knew nothing. Outside the dust stirred in the road fretfully; a malaise was in the night air. Michael shivered and went back to bed, and as he turned to blow out his candle he saw above him huge and menacing his own shadow. A cock crowed.

"Silly ass," muttered Michael, "he thinks it's already morning," and turning over after a dreamless sleep he found it was morning. So he rose and dressed himself serenely for a long sunburnt day.

On his way up the road to call for Alan he met the postman, who in answer to his enquiries handed him a letter from South Africa stamped all over with mysterious official abbreviations. He took it up to his mother curiously.

At lunch he asked her about the news from the war.

"Yes, dear, I had a letter," she murmured.

"From Lord Saxby, I suppose?"

"Yes, dear."

"Anything interesting?" Michael persisted.

"Oh, no, it's only about marches and not being able to wash properly."

"I thought it might be interesting," Michael speculated.

"No, dear. It wouldn't interest you," said Mrs. Fane in her tone of gentle discouragement.

"I don't want to be inquisitive," said Michael resentfully.

"No, dear, I'm sure you don't," his mother softly agreed.

The holidays ran their pastoral course of sun and rain, of clouds and winds, until the last week arrived with September in her most majestic mood of flawless halcyon. These were days that more than any hitherto enhanced for Michael the reverence he felt for the household of Cobble Place. These were days when Mrs. Carthew stepped wisely along her flowery enclosure, pondering the plums and peaches on the warm walls that in a transcendency of mellow sunlight almost took on the texture of living sunburnt flesh. These were days when Joan and May Carthew went down the village street with great bunches of Michaelmas daisies, of phloxes and Japanese anemones, or sat beneath the mulberry tree, sewing in the bee-drowsed air.

At the foot of the hill beyond the stream was a straggling wind-frayed apple-orchard, fresh pasturage for lambs in spring, and now in September a jolly haunt for the young son of Mrs. Ross. Here one afternoon, when Alan was away at Basingstead Major playing the last cricket match of the year, Michael plunged down in the grass beside her.

They sat for a while in silence, and Mrs. Ross seemed to Michael to be waiting for him to speak first, as if by her own attitude of mute expectation she could lure him on to express himself more openly than by direct question and shy answer. He felt the air pregnant with confidences, and kept urging himself on to begin the statement and revelation of his character, sure that whatever he desired to ask must be asked now while he was perhaps for the last time liable to this grave woman's influence, conscious of the security of goodness, envious of the maternity of peace. This grey-eyed woman seemed to sit above him like a proud eagle, careless of homage, never to be caught, never to be tamed, a figure for worship and inspiration. Michael wondered why all the women who awed him had grey eyes. Blue eyes fired his senses, striking sparks and kindling answering flames from his own blue eyes. Brown eyes left him indifferent. But grey eyes absorbed his very being, whether they were lustrous and violet-shaded like his mother's and Stella's, or whether, like Mrs. Ross's, they were soft as grey sea-water that in a moment could change to the iron-bound rocks they were so near.

Still Michael did not speak, but watched Mrs. Ross solemnly hand back to the rosy child sitting beside her in the grass the fallen apples that he would always fling from him exuberantly, panting the while at laughter's highest pitch.

"I wonder if I ever laughed like that," said Michael.

"You were a very serious little boy, when I first knew you," Mrs. Ross told him.

"I must have been rather depressing," Michael sighed.

"No, indeed you were not, dear Michael," she answered. "You had much too much personality."

"Have I now?" Michael asked sharply.

"Yes, of course you have."

"Well, what gives it to me?"

"Surely personality is something that is born with one. Personality can't be made," said Mrs. Ross.

"You don't think experience has got anything to do with it?" Michael pressed.

"I think experience makes the setting, and according to the experience the personality is perfected or debased, but nothing can destroy personality, not even death," she murmured, far away for a moment from this orchard.

"Which would you say had the stronger personality—Alan or I?" asked Michael.

"I should say you had," said Mrs. Ross. "Or at any rate you have a personality that will affect a larger number of people, either favourably or unfavourably."

"But Alan influences me more than I influence him," Michael argued.

"That may be," Mrs. Ross admitted. "Though I think your influence over Alan is very strong in this way. I think Alan is always very eager to see you at your best, and probably as your friendship goes on he will be more solicitous for you than for himself. I should say that he would be likely to sink himself in you. I wonder if you realize what a passionately loyal soul he is."

Michael flushed with pleasure at this appreciation of his friend, and his ambition went flying over to Basingstead Major to inspire Alan to bat his best. Then he burst forth in praise of him; he spoke of his changelessness, his freedom from moods, his candour and toleration and modesty.

"But the terrible thing is," said Michael suddenly, "that I always feel that without noticing it I shall one day leave Alan behind."

"But when you turn back, you'll find him just the same, don't forget; and you may be glad that he did not come with you. You may be glad that from his slowness you can find an indication of the road that I'm sure you yourself will one day try to take. Alan will travel by it all his life. You'll travel by it ultimately. Alan will never really appreciate its beauty. You will. That will be your recompense for what you suffer before you find it."

Mrs. Ross, as if to conceal emotion, turned quickly to romp with her son. Then she looked at Michael:

"And haven't you already once or twice left Alan behind?"

Suddenly to Michael her grey eyes seemed accusing.

"Yes, I suppose I have," he granted. "But isn't that the reason why my personality affects more people than his? You said just now that experience was only the setting, but I'm sure in my case it's more than a mere setting."

And even as he spoke all his experience seemed to cloud his brow, knitting and lining it with perplexed wrinkles.

"Mrs. Ross, you won't think me very rude if I say you always remind me of Pallas Athene? You always have, you know. At first it was just a vague outward resemblance, because you're tall and sort of cool-looking, and I really think your nose is rather Greek, if you don't mind my saying so."

"Oh, Michael," Mrs. Ross smiled. "I think you're even more unalterable than Alan. I seem to see you as a little boy again, when you talk like that."

Michael, however, was too keen on the scent of his comparison to be put off by smiles, and he went on eagerly:

"Now I realize that you actually are like Athene. You're one of those people who seem to have sprung into the world fully armed. I can't imagine that you were ever young."

Mrs. Ross laughed outright at this.

"Wait a minute," cried Michael. "Or ever old for that matter. And you know all about me. No, you needn't shake your head like that. Because you do."

Young Kenneth was so much roused by Michael's triumphant asseverations that he began to shout and kick in delighted tune and fling the apples from him with a vigour that he had never yet reached.

"You know," Michael continued breathlessly, while the boy on the grass gurgled his endorsement of every word. "You know that I'm old for my age, that I've already done things that other chaps at school only whisper about."

He stopped suddenly, for the grey eyes had become like rocks, and though the baby still panted ecstatically, there fell a chill.

"I'm very sorry to hear it," said Mrs. Ross.

"Well, why did you lead me on to confide in you?" said Michael sullenly. "I thought you would sympathize."

"Michael, I apologize," she said, melting. "I didn't mean to hurt your feelings. I dare say—ah, Michael, you see how easily all my shining armour falls to pieces."

"Another broken bottle," Michael muttered.

He got up abruptly and, though there were tears in his eyes, she could not win him back.

"Dear old boy, do tell me. Don't make the mistake of going back into yourself, because I failed you for a moment."

Mrs. Ross held out her hand, but Michael walked away.

"You don't understand," he turned to say. "You couldn't understand. And I don't want you to be able to understand. You mustn't think I'm sulking, or being rude, and really I'd rather you didn't understand. That boy of yours won't ever want you to understand. I don't think he'll ever do anything that isn't perfectly comprehensible."

"Michael," said Mrs. Ross, "don't be so bitter. You'll be sorry soon."

"Soon?" asked Michael fiercely. "Soon? Why soon? What's going to happen to make me sorry soon? Something is going to happen. I know. I feel it."

He fled through the wind-frayed orchard up the hill-side. With his back against the tower called Grogg's Folly he looked over four counties and vowed he would go heedless of everything that stood between him and experience. He would deny himself nothing; he would prove to the hilt everything.

"I must know," he wrung out of himself. "Everything that has happened must have happened for some reason. I will believe that. I can't believe in God, until I can believe in myself. And how can I believe in myself yet?"

The four counties under September's munificence mocked him with their calm.

"I know that all these people at Cobble Place are all right," he groaned. "I know that, just as I know Virgil is a great poet. But I never knew Virgil was great until I read Swinburne. Oh, I want to be calm and splendid and proud of myself, but I want to understand life while I'm alive. I want to believe in immortality, but in case I never can be convinced of it, I want to be convinced of something. Everything seems to be tumbling down nowadays. What's so absurd is that nobody can understand anybody else, let alone the universe. Mrs. Ross can understand why I like Alan, but she can't understand why I want love. Viner can understand why I get depressed, but he can't understand why I can't be cured immediately. Wilmot could understand why I wanted to read his rotten books, but he can't understand why the South African War upset me. And so on with everybody. I'm determined to understand everybody," Michael vowed, "even if I can't have faith," he sighed to the four counties.

Chapter XVI: *Blue Eyes*

MICHAEL managed to avoid during the rest of the week any reference, direct or indirect, to his interrupted conversation with Mrs. Ross, though he fancied a reproachfulness in her manner towards him, especially at the moment of saying good-bye. He was not therefore much surprised to receive a letter from her soon after he was back in Carlington Road.

Cobble Place,
September 18th.

My dear Michael,

I have blamed myself entirely for what happened the other day. I should have been honoured by your confidence, and I cannot think why a wretched old-fashioned priggishness should have shown itself just when I least wished it would. I confess I was shocked for a moment, and perhaps I horridly imagined more than you meant to imply. If I had paused to think, I should have known that your desire to confide in me was alone enough to prove that you were fully conscious of the effect of anything you may have done. And after all in any sin—forgive me if I'm using too strong a word under a misapprehension—it is the effect which counts most deeply.

I'm inclined to think that in all you do through life, you will chiefly have to think of the effect of it on other people. I believe that you yourself are one of those characters that never radically deteriorate. This is rather a dangerous statement to make to anyone so young as you are. But I'm sure you are wise enough not to use it in justification of any wrong impulse. Do always remember, my dear boy, that however unscathed you feel yourself to be, you must never assume that to be the case with anyone else. I am really dreadfully distressed to think that by my own want of sympathy on a crucial occasion I have had to try to put into a letter what could only have been hammered out in a long talk. And we did hammer out something the other day. Or am I too optimistic? Write to me some time and reassure me a little, for I'm truly worried about you, and so indignant with my stupid self. Best love from us all,

Your affectionate
Maud Ross.

Michael merely pondered this letter coldly. He was still under the influence of the disappointment, and when he answered Mrs. Ross he answered her without regard to any wound he might inflict.

64 Carlington Road,
Sunday.

Dear Mrs. Ross,

Please don't bother any more about it. I ought to have known better. I don't think it was such a very crucial occasion. The weather is frightfully hot, and I don't feel much like playing footer this term. I'm reading Dante, not in Italian, of course. London is as near the Inferno as anything, I should think. It's horribly hot. Excuse this short letter, but I've nothing to say.

Yours affectionately,
Michael.

Mrs. Ross made one more brief attempt to recapture him, but Michael put her off with the most superficial gossip of school-life, and she did not try again. He meant to play football, notwithstanding the hot weather, but finding that his boots were worn out, he continually put off buying another pair and let himself drift into October before he began. Then he hurt his leg, and had to stop for a while. This spoiled his faint chance for the First Fifteen, and in the end he gave up football altogether without much regret.

Games were a great impediment after all, when October's thin blue skies and sheen of pearl-soft airs led him on to dream along the autumnal streets. Sometimes he would wander by himself through the groves of Hyde Park and Kensington Gardens, or on some secluded green chair he would sit reading Verlaine, while continuously about him the slow leaves of the great planes swooped and fluttered down ambiguously like silent birds.

One Saturday afternoon he was sitting thus, when through the silver fog that on every side wrought the ultimate dissolution of the view Michael saw the slim figure of a girl walking among the trees. His mind was gay with Verlaine's delicate and fantastic songs, and this slim girl, as she moved wraith-like over the ground marbled with fallen leaves, seemed to express the cadence of the verse which had been sighing across the printed page.

The girl with downcast glance walked on, seeming to follow her path softly as one might follow through embroidery a thread of silk, and as she drew nearer to Michael out of the fog's enchantment she lost none of her indefinite charm; but she seemed still exquisite and silver-dewed. There was no one else in sight, and now already Michael could hear the lisping of her steps; then a breath of air among the tree-tops more remote sent floating, swaying, fluttering about her a flight of leaves. She paused, startled by the sudden shower, and at that moment the down-going autumnal sun glanced wanly through the glades and lighted her gossamer-gold hair with kindred gleams. The girl resumed her dreaming progress, and Michael now frankly stared in a rapture. She was dressed in deepest green box-cloth, and the heavy folds that clung to that lissome form made her ankles behind great pompons of black silk seem astonishingly slender. One hand was masked by a small muff of astrakhan; the other curled behind to gather close her skirt. Her hair tied back with a black bow sprayed her tall neck with its beaten gold. She came along downcast until she was within a few feet of Michael; then she looked at him. He smiled, and her mouth when she answered him with answering smile was like a flower whose petals have been faintly stirred. Indeed, it was scarcely a smile, scarcely more than a tremor, but her eyes deepened suddenly, and Michael drawn into their dusky blue exclaimed simply:

"I say, I've been watching you for a long time."

"I don't think you ought to talk to me like this in Kensington Gardens. Why, there's not a soul in sight. And I oughtn't to let you talk."

Her voice was low with a provocative indolence of tone, and while she spoke her lips scarcely moved, so that their shape was never for an instant lost, and the words seemed to escape like unwilling fugitives.

"What are you reading?" she idly asked, tapping Michael's book with her muff.

"Verlaine."

"French?"

He nodded, and she pouted in delicious disapproval of his learned choice.

"Fancy reading French unless you've got to."

"But I enjoy these poems," Michael declared. "As a matter of fact you're just like them. At least you were when I saw you first in the distance. Now you're more real somehow."

Her gaze had wandered during his comparison and Michael, a little hurt by her inattention, asked if she were expecting somebody.

"Oh, no. I just came out for a walk. I get a headache if I stay in all the afternoon. Now I must go on. Good-bye."

She scattered with a light kick the little heap of leaves that during their conversation she had been amassing, and with a half-mocking wave of her muff prepared to leave him.

"I say, don't tear off," Michael begged. "Where do you live?"

"Oh, a long way from here," she said.

"But where?"

"West Kensington."

"So do I," cried Michael, thinking to himself that all the gods of luck and love were fighting on his side this afternoon. "We'll walk home together."

"Shall we?" murmured the girl, poised on bent toes as if she were minded to flee from him in a breath.

"Oh, we must," vowed Michael.

"But I mustn't dawdle," she protested.

"Of course not," he affirmed with almost an inflexion of puritanical rigour.

"You're leaving your book, stupid," she laughed, as he rose to take his place by her side.

"I wouldn't have minded, because all that's in that book is in you," he declared. "I think I'll leave it behind for a lark."

She ran back lightly and opened it to see whether his name were on the front page.

"Michael Fane," she murmured. "What does 'ex libris' mean?" Yet even as she asked the question her concentration failed, and she seemed not to hear his answer.

"You didn't really want to know, you funny girl," said Michael.

"Know what?" she echoed, blinking round at him over her shoulder as they walked on.

"The meaning of 'ex libris.'"

"But I found out your name," she challenged. "And you don't know mine."

"What is it?" Michael dutifully asked.

"I don't think I'll tell you."

"Ah, do."

"Well, then, it's Lily—and I've got a sister called Doris."

"How old are you?"

"How old do you think?"

"Seventeen?" Michael hazarded.

She nodded. It was on the tip of his tongue to claim kinship on the score of their similar years, but discretion defeated honesty, and he said aloofly, gazing up at the sky:

"I'm nineteen and a half."

She told him more as they mingled with the crowds in Kensington High Street, that her mother was Mrs. Haden, who recited in public sometimes, that her sister Doris wanted to go on the stage, and that they lived in Trelawny Road.

"I know Trelawny Road," Michael interjected, and in the gathering crowds she was perforce closer to him, so that he was fain to guide her gently past the glittering shops, immensely conscious of the texture of her dress. They emerged into wider, emptier pavements, and the wind came chilly down from Camden Hill, so that she held her muff against her cheek, framing its faint rose. Twilight drew them closer, and Michael wishful of an even less frequented pavement suggested they should cross the road by Holland Park. A moment she paused while a scarlet omnibus clattered past, then she ran swiftly to where the trees overhung the railings. It was exhilarating to follow her over the wooden road that answered to his footsteps like castanets, and as he caught up with her to fondle her bent arm. Their walk died away to a saunter, while the street-lamps beamed upon them with longer intervals of dark between each succeeding lampshine. More slowly still they moved towards West Kensington and parting. Her arm was twined round his like ivy, and their two hands came together like leaves. At last the turning she must take appeared on the other side of the road, and again she ran and again he caught her arm. But this time it was still warm with long contact and divinely familiar, since but for a moment had it been relinquished. The dim side-street enfolded them, and no dismaying passers-by startled their intercourse.

"But soon it will be Trelawny Road," she whispered.

"Then kiss me quickly," said Michael. "Lily, you must."

It was in the midmost gloom between two lamps that they kissed first.

"Lily, once again."

"No, no," she whispered.

"But you're mine," he called exultantly. "You are. You know you are."

"Perhaps," she whispered, but even as his arms drew her towards him, she slipped from his embrace, laughed very low and sweet, bounded forward, waved her muff, ran swiftly to the next lamp-post, paused and blew him kisses, then vanished round the corner of her road.

But a long time ago they had said they would meet to-morrow, and as Michael stood in a maze all the clocks in the world ding-donged in his ears the hour of their tryst.

There was only one thing to do for the expression of his joy, and that was to run as hard as he could. So he ran, and when he saw two coal-holes, he would jump from one to the other, rejoicing in the ring of their metal covers. And all the time out of breath he kept saying, "I'm in love, in love, in love."

Every passer-by into whose eyes he looked seemed to have the most beautiful expression; every poor man seemed to demand that he should stay awhile from his own joy to comfort him. The lamp-posts bloomed like tropic flowers, swaying and nodding languorously. Every house took on a look of the most unutterable completeness; the horses galloped like Arabian barbs; policemen expanded like beneficent genii; errand boys whistled like nightingales; all familiarity was enchanted, and seven-leagued boots took him forward as easily as if he travelled a world subdued to the effortless transitions of sleep. Carlington Road stretched before him bright, kindly, beckoning to his ingress. Against the lighted entrance-hall of Number 64 Michael saw the red and amber sparrows like humming-birds, ruby-throated, topaz-winged. The parlour-maid's cap and apron were of snow, and the banisters of sandalwood.

Michael went to bed early that he might meet her in dreams, but still for a long time he sat by his window peering at the tawny moon, while at intervals trains went quickly past sparkling and swift as lighted fuses. The scent of the leaves lying in the gardens all along Carlington Road was vital with the airs from which she had been evoked that afternoon, and his only regret was that his bedroom looked out on precisely the opposite direction from that where now she was sleeping. Then he himself became envious of sleep, and undressed quickly like one who stands hot-footed by a lake's edge, eager for the water's cool.

Michael met Lily next day by the dusky corner of a street whose gradual loss of outline he had watched occur through a patient hour. It was not that Lily was late, but that Michael was so early. Yet in his present mood of elation he could enjoy communion even with bricks and mortar. He used every guileful ruse to cheat time of his determined moment. He would walk along with closed eyes for ten paces and with open eyes for ten paces, the convention with himself, almost the wager, being that Lily should appear while his eyes were closed. It would have been truly disappointing had she swung round the corner while his eyes were open. But as it still lacked half an hour of her appointment, there was not much fear of that. Then, as really her time drew near, a tenser game was played, by which Lily was to appear when his left foot was advanced. This match between odd and even lasted until in all its straightness of perfect division six o'clock was inscribed upon his watch. No other hour could so well have suited her form.

Now began the best game of all, since it was played less with himself than with fortune. Michael went to the next turning, and, hiding himself from the view of Trelawny Road, only allowed himself to peep at each decade. At a hundred and sixty-three he said "She's in sight," one hundred and sixty-four, "She's coming." The century was eliminated, too cumbersome for his fiery enumeration. Sixty-five, "I know she is." Sixty-six, sixty-seven, sixty-eight, sixty-nine! One hundred and seventy was said slowly with an exquisite dragging deliberation. Then Michael could look, and there she was with muff signalling through the azure mists of twilight.

"I say, I told mother about you," murmured Lily. "And she said, 'Why didn't you ask him to come in to tea?' But of course she doesn't know I'm meeting you this evening. I'm supposed to be going to church."

Michael's heart leaped at the thought that soon he would be able to see her in her own home among her own belongings, so that in future no conjured picture of her would be incomplete.

"Rather decent of your mother," he said.

"Oh, well, she's got to be very easy-going and all that, though of course she doesn't like us to get talked about. What shall we do now?"

"Walk about, I suppose," said Michael. "Unless we get on top of a bus and ride somewhere? Why not ride up to Hammersmith Broadway and then walk along the towing-path?"

They found a seat full in the frore wind's face, but yet the ride was all too short, and almost by the time Michael had finished securing the waterproof rug in which they sat incapable of movement, so tightly were they braced in, it was time to undo it again and dismount. While the church bells were ringing, they crossed Hammersmith Suspension Bridge ethereal in the creeping river-mist and faintly motionable like a ship at anchor. Then they wandered by the river that lapped the dead reeds and gurgled along the base of the shelving clay bank. The wind drearily stirred the osier-beds, and from time to time the dull tread of indefinite passing forms was heard upon the sodden path. Michael could feel the humid fog lying upon Lily's sleeve, and when he drew her cheek to his own it was bedewed with the falling night. But when their lips met, the moisture and October chill were all consumed, and like a burning rose she flamed upon his vision. Words to express his adoration tumbled around him like nightmare speech, evasive, mocking, grotesquely inadequate.

"There are no words to say how much I love to hold you, Lily," he complained. "It's like holding a flower. And even in the dark I can see your eyes."

"I can't see yours," she murmured, and therefore nestled closer, "I like you to kiss me," she sighed.

"Oh, why do you?" Michael asked. "Why me?"

"You're nice," she less than whispered.

"Lily, I do love you."

And Michael bit his lip at the close of "love" for the sweet pain of making the foolish word more powerful, more long.

"What a funny husky voice," she murmured in her own deep indolent tones.

"Do you like me to call you 'darling' or 'dearest' best?" he asked.

"Both."

"Ah, but which do you like best?"

To Michael the two words were like melodies which he had lately learned to play. Indeed, they seemed to him his own melodies never played before, and he was eager for Lily to pronounce judgment.

"Why do you ask questions?" she wondered.

"Say 'dearest' to me," Michael begged.

"No, no," she blushed against his heart.

"But say which you like best," he urged. "Darling or dearest?"

"Well, darling," she pouted.

"You've said it," cried Michael rapturously. "Now you can say it of your own accord. Oh, Lily, say it when you kiss me."

"But supposing I never kiss you ever again?" asked Lily, pulling away from his arms. "And besides we must go back."

"Well, we needn't hurry."

"Not if you come at once," she agreed.

One more kiss, one more gliding dreaming walk, one more pause to bid the river farewell from the towering bridge, one more wrestle with the waterproof-rug, one more slow lingering and then suddenly swift escaping finger, one more wave of the muff, one last aerial salutation, and she was gone till Wednesday.

Michael was left alone between the tall thin houses of Kensington, but beneath his feet he seemed to feel the world swing round through space; and all the tall thin houses, all the fluted lamp-posts, all the clustering chimney-pots reeled about him in the ecstasy of his aroused existence.

Chapter XVII: Lily

WHEN Michael came into the dining-room after he had left Lily, his mother said: "Dearest boy, what have you been doing? Your eyes are shining like stars."

Here was the opportunity to tell her about Lily, but Michael could not avail himself of it. These last two days seemed as yet too incomplete for revelation. Somehow he felt that he was creating a work of art, and that to tell his mother of conception or progress would be to spoil the perfection of his impulse. There was only one person on earth to whom he could confide this cataclysmic experience, and that was Alan. He and Alan had dreamed enough together in the past to make him unashamed to announce at last his foothold on reality. But supposing Alan were to laugh, as he had laughed over the absurdity of Kathleen? Such a reception of his news would ruin their friendship; and yet if their friendship could not endure the tale of true love, was it not already ruined? He must tell Alan, at whatever cost. And where should he tell him? Such a secret must not be lightly entrusted. Time and place must come harmoniously, befalling with that rare felicity which salutes the inevitable hours of a human life.

"Mother," said Michael, "would you mind if I stayed the night over at Richmond?"

"To-night?" Mrs. Fane echoed in astonishment.

"Well, perhaps not to-night," conceded Michael unwillingly. "But to-morrow night?"

"To-morrow night by all means," Mrs. Fane agreed.

"Nothing has happened?" she asked anxiously. "You seem so flushed and strange."

"I'm just the same as usual," Michael declared. "It's hot in this room. I think I'll take a short walk."

"But you've been out all the afternoon," Mrs. Fane protested.

"Oh, well, I've nothing to do at home."

"You're not feverish?"

"No, no, mother," Michael affirmed, disengaging his parched hand from her solicitous touch. "But you know I often feel restless."

She released him, tenderly smiling; and for one moment he nearly threw himself down beside her, covetous of childhood's petting. But the impulse spent itself before he acted upon it, and soon he was wandering towards Trelawny Road. How empty the corner of it looked, how stark and melancholy soared the grey houses guarding its consecrated entrance, how solitary shone the lamp-posts, and how sadly echoed the footsteps of people going home. Yet only three hours ago they had met on this very flagstone that must almost have palpitated to the pressure of her shoes.

Michael walked on until he stood opposite her house. There was a light in the bay-window by the front door; perhaps she would come out to post a letter. O breathless thought! Surely he heard the sound of a turning handle. Ah, why had he not begged her to draw aside the blind at a fixed time that he could be cured of his longing by the vision of her darling form against the pane? How bitter was the irony of her sitting behind that brooding window-pane, unconscious of him. Two days must crawl past before she would meet him again, before he would touch her hand, look actually into her eyes, watch every quiver and curve of her mouth. Places would be enriched with the sight of her, while he ached with the torment of love. School must drag through ten intolerable hours; he must chatter with people unaware of her; and she must live two days apart from his life, two days whose irresponsible minutes and loveless occupations made him burn with jealousy of time itself.

Suddenly the door of Lily's house opened, and Michael felt the blood course through his body, flooding his heart, swaying his very soul. There was a voice in the glimmering hall, but not her voice. Nor was it her form that hurried down the steps. It was only the infinitely fortunate maidservant whose progress to the letter-box he watched with a sickening disappointment. There went one who every day could see Lily. Every morning she was privileged to wake her from her rose-fired sleep. Every night she could gossip with her outside the magical door of her room. Lily must sometimes descend into the kitchen, and there they must talk. And yet the idiotic creature was staring curiously at some unutterably dull policeman, and wasting moments she did not appreciate. Then a leaping thought came to Michael, that if she wasted enough time Lily might look round the front-door in search of her. But too soon for such an event the maidservant pattered back; the door slammed; and only the window-panes of dull gold brooded immutably. How long before Lily went up to bed? And did she sleep in a room that fronted the road? Michael could bear it no longer and turned away from the exasperation of her withheld presence; and he made up his mind that he must know every detail of her daily life before he again came sighing ineffectively like this in the night-time.

Michael was vexed to find that he could not even conjure Lily to his side in sleep, but that even there he must be surrounded by the tiresome people of ordinary life. However, there was always a delicious moment, just before he lost complete consciousness, when the image of her dissolved and materialized elusively above the nebulous confines of semi-reality; while always at the very instant of awakening he was aware of her moth-winged kisses trembling upon the first liquid flash of daylight.

In the 'quarter' Michael suggested to Alan that he should come back to Richmond with him, and when Alan looked a little astonished at this Monday night proposal, he explained that he had a lot to talk over.

"I nearly came over at nine o'clock last night," Michael announced.

Alan seemed to realize that it must indeed be something of importance and could scarcely wait for the time when they should be fast alone and primed for confidences.

After dinner Michael proposed a walk up Richmond Hill, and without any appearance of strategy managed to persuade Alan to rest awhile on one of the seats along the Terrace. In this late autumnal time there was no view of the Thames gleaming beneath the sorcery of a summer night. There was nothing now but a vast airiness of mist damascening the blades of light with which the street-lamps pierced the darkness.

"Pretty wet," said Alan distastefully patting the seat.

"We needn't stay long, but it's rather ripping, don't you think?" Michael urged. "Alan, do you remember once we sat here on a night before exams at the end of a summer term?"

"Yes, but it was a jolly sight warmer than it is now," said Alan.

"I know. We were in 'whites,'" said Michael pensively. "Alan, I'm in love. I am really. You mustn't laugh. I was a fool over that first girl, but now I am in love. Alan, she's only seventeen, and she has hair the colour of that rather thick honey you get at chemists. Only it isn't thick, but as foamy as a lemon-sponge. And her mouth is truly a bow and her voice is gloriously deep and exciting, and her eyes are the most extraordinary blue—as blue as ink in a bottle when you hold it up to the light—and her chin is in two pieces rather like yours, and her ankles—well—her ankles are absolutely divine. The extraordinary luck is that she loves me, and I want you to meet her. I'm describing her very accurately like this because I don't want you to think I'm raving or quoting poetry. You see, you don't appreciate poetry, or I could describe her much better."

"I do appreciate poetry," protested Alan.

"Oh, I know you like Kipling and Adam Lindsay Gordon, but I mean real poetry. Well, I'm not going to argue about that. But, Alan, you must be sympathetic and believe that I really am in love. She has a sister called Doris. I haven't met her yet, but she's sure to be lovely, and I think you ought to fall in love with her. Now wouldn't that be splendid? Alan, you do believe I'm in love this time?"

Michael paused anxiously.

"I suppose you must be," said Alan slowly.

"And you're glad?" asked Michael a little wistfully.

"What's going to happen?" Alan wondered.

"Well, of course not much can happen just now. Not much can happen while one is still at school," Michael went on. "But don't let's talk about what is going to be. Let's talk about what is now."

Alan looked at him reproachfully.

"You used to enjoy talking about the future."

"Because it used always to be more interesting," Michael explained.

Alan rose from the seat and taking Michael's arm drew him down the hill.

"And will you come and meet her sister?" Michael asked.

"I expect so," said Alan.

"Hurrah!" cried the lover.

"I suppose this means the end of football, the end of cricket, in fact the end of school as far as you're concerned," Alan complained. "I wish you'd waited a little."

"I told you I was years older than you," Michael pointed out, involuntarily making excuses.

"Only because you would encourage yourself to think so. Well, I hope everything will go well. I hope you won't take it into your head to think you've got to marry her immediately, or any rot like that."

"Don't be an ass," said Michael.

"Well, you're such an impulsive devil. By Jove, the fellow that first called you 'Bangs' was a bit of a spotter."

"It was Abercrombie," Michael reminded him.

"I should think that was the only clever thing he ever did in his life," said Alan.

"Why, I thought you considered him no end of a good man."

"He was a good forward and a good deep field," Alan granted. "But that doesn't make him Shakespeare."

Thence onwards war, or rather sport the schoolboys' substitute, ousted love from the conversation, and very soon solo whist with Mr. and Mrs. Merivale disposed of both.

On Tuesday night Michael in a fever of enthusiasm for Wednesday's approach wrote a letter to Stella.

64 CARLINGTON ROAD,
October, 1900.

My dear Stella,

After this you needn't grouse about my letters being dull, and you can consider yourself jolly honoured because I'm writing to tell you that I'm in love. Her name is Lily Haden. Only, of course, please don't go shouting this all over Germany, and don't write a gushing letter to mother, who doesn't know anything about it. I shouldn't tell you if you were in London, and don't write back and tell me that you're in love with some long-haired dancing-master or one-eyed banjo-player, because I know now what love is, and it's nothing like what you think it is.

Lily is fair—not just fair like a doll, but frightfully *fair. In fact, her hair is like bubbling champagne, I met her in Kensington Gardens. It was truly romantic, not a silly, giggling, gone-on-a-girl sort of meeting. I hope you're getting on with your music. I shall introduce Lily to you just before your first concert, and then if you can't play, well, you never will. You might write me a letter and say what you think of my news. Not a gushing letter, of course, but as sensible as you can make it.*

Your loving brother,
Michael.

Michael had meant to say much more to Stella, but ink and paper seemed to violate the secluded airs in which Lily had her being. However, Stella would understand by his writing at all that he was in deadly earnest, and she was unearthly enough to supply what was missing from his account.

Meanwhile to-morrow was Wednesday, the mate of Saturday and certainly of all the days in the week his second favourite. Monday, of course, was vile. Tuesday was colourless. Thursday was nearly as bad as Monday. Friday was irksome and only a little less insipid than Tuesday. Sunday had many disadvantages. Saturday was without doubt the best day, and Wednesday was next best, for though it was not a half-holiday, as long ago it had been at Randell House, still it had never quite lost its suggestion of holiday. Wednesday—the very word said slowly had a rich individuality. Wednesday—how promptly it sprang to the lips for any occasion of festivity that did not require full-blown reckless Saturday. Monday was dull red. Tuesday was cream-coloured. Thursday was dingy purple. Friday was a harsh scarlet, but Wednesday was vivid apple-green, or was it a clear cool blue? One or the other.

So, tantalizing himself by not allowing a single thought of Lily while he was undressing, Michael achieved bed very easily. Here all trivialities were dismissed, and like one who falls asleep when a star is shining through his window-pane Michael fell asleep, with Lily radiant above the horizon.

It was rather a disappointing Wednesday, for Lily said she could not stay out more than a minute, since her mother was indoors and would wonder what she was doing. However on Saturday she would see Michael again, and announce to her mother that she was going to see him, so that on Sunday Michael could be invited to tea.

"And then if mother likes you, why, you can often come in," Lily pointed out. "That is, if you want to."

"Saturday," sighed Michael.

"Well, don't spoil the few minutes we've got by being miserable."

"But I can't kiss you."

"Think how much nicer it will be when we can kiss," said Lily philosophically.

"I don't believe you care a damn whether we kiss or not," said Michael.

"Don't I?" murmured Lily, quickly touching his hand and as quickly withdrawing it to the prison of the muff.

"Ah, do you, Lily?" Michael throbbed out.

"Of course. Now I must go. Good-bye. Don't forget Saturday in the Gardens, where we met last time. Good-bye, good-bye, good-bye!" She was running from him backwards, forbidding with a wave his sudden step towards her. "No, if you dare to move, I shan't meet you on Saturday. Be good, be good."

By her corner she paused, stood on tiptoe for one provocative instant, blew a kiss, laughed her elfin laugh and vanished more swift than any Ariel.

"Damn!" cried Michael sorely, and forthwith set out to walk round West Kensington at five miles an hour, until his chagrin, his disappointment and his heartsick emptiness were conquered, or at any rate sufficiently humbled to make him secure against unmanly tears.

When Saturday finally did arrive, Michael did not sit reading Verlaine, but wandered from tree-trunk to tree-trunk like Orlando in despair. Then Lily came at last sedately, and brought the good news that to-morrow Michael should come to tea at her house.

"But where does your mother think we met?" he asked in perplexity.

"Oh, I told her it was in Kensington Gardens," said Lily carelessly.

"But doesn't she think I must be an awful bounder?"

"Why, you silly, I told her you were at St. James' School."

"But I never told you I was at school," exclaimed Michael, somewhat aghast.

"I know you didn't, and you never told me that you weren't eighteen yet."

"I am in a month or two," said Michael. "But, good Lord, who have you been talking to?"

"Ah, that's the greatest secret in the world," laughed Lily.

"Oh, no, do tell me."

"Well, I know a boy called Drake who knows you."

"That beast!" cried Michael.

"I think he's quite a nice boy. He lives next door to us and——"

Michael kicked angrily the dead leaves lying about his feet, and almost choked with astonished fury.

"Why, my dear girl, he's absolutely barred. He's as unpopular as anybody I know. I hope you won't discuss me with that hulking brute. What the deuce right has he got to tell you anything about me?"

"Because I asked him, and you needn't look so enraged, because if you want to know why you're coming to tea, it's because I asked Arthur——"

"Who's Arthur?" growled Michael.

"Arthur Drake."

"Go on," said Michael icily.

"I shan't go on, if you look like that."

"I can't help how I look. I don't carry a glass round with me," said Michael. "So I suppose this worm Drake had the cheek to tell your mother I was all right. Drake! Wait till I see the brute on Monday morning."

"Well, if you take my advice," said Lily, "you'll be nice to him, because he's supposed to have introduced us."

"What lies! What lies!" Michael stamped.

"You told me a lie about your age," Lily retorted. "And I've told mother a lie on your account, so you needn't be so particular. And if you think you're going to make me cry, you're not."

She sat down on a seat and looked out at the bare woodland with sullen eyes.

"Has Drake ever dared to make love to you?" demanded Michael.

"That's my business," said Lily. "You've no right to ask me questions like that."

Michael looked at her so adorable even now, and suddenly throwing his dignity to the dead leaves, he sat close beside her caressingly.

"Darling Lily," he whispered, "it was my fault. I lied first. I don't care how much you talked about me. I don't care about anything but you. I'll even say Drake is a decent chap—though he really isn't even moderately decent. Lily, we had such a rotten Wednesday, and to-day ought to be perfect. Will you forgive me? Will you?"

And the quarrel was over.

"But you don't care anything about Drake?" Michael asked, when half an hour had dreamed itself away.

"Of course not," she reassured him. "Arthur likes Doris better than me."

"But he mustn't like Doris," said Michael eagerly. "At least she mustn't like him. Because I've got a friend—at least three million times as decent as Drake—who wants to be in love with Doris, or rather he will want to be when he sees her."

"Why, you haven't seen Doris yourself yet," laughed Lily.

"Oh, of course my plan may all come to nothing," Michael admitted. "But look here, I vote we don't bother about anybody else in the world but ourselves for the rest of the afternoon."

Nor did they.

"Shall I wear a top-hat to-morrow?" Michael asked even in the very poignancy of farewell. "I mean—will your mother prefer it?"

"Oh, no, the people who come to tea with us on Sunday are mostly artists and actors," decided Lily judicially.

"Do lots of people come then?" asked Michael, quickly jealous.

"A good many."

"I might as well have fallen in love with one of the Royal Family," sighed Michael in despair.

"What do you mean?"

"Well, I never can see you alone," he declared.

"Why, we've had the whole of this afternoon," she told him.

"Do you call sitting in the middle of Kensington Gardens being alone? Why, it was crammed with people," he ejaculated in disgust.

"I must go, I must go, I must go," Lily whispered and almost seemed to be preening her wings in the lamplight before she flew away.

"I say, what number is Drake's house?" Michael asked, with a consummate affectation of casual enquiry.

She told him laughingly, and in a most malicious hurry would not even linger a moment to ask him why he wanted to know. Coldly and deliberately Michael after dinner rang the bell of Drake's house.

"Is—er—Master Arthur at home?" he asked the maid.

"Master Arthur," she cried. "Someone to see you."

"Hullo, Bangs," shouted Drake, emerging effusively from a doorway.

"Oh, hullo," said Michael loftily. "I thought I'd call to see if you felt like coming out."

"Right-o," said Drake. "Wait half a tick while I tell my mater. Come in, and meet my people."

"Oh, no," said Michael. "I'm beastly untidy."

He would condescend to Drake for the sake of his love, but he did not think that love demanded the sacrifice of condescending to a possibly more expansive acquaintance with Drake's family.

"So you've met the fair Lily," Drake said, as they strolled along. "Pretty smart, what, my boy?"

"I'm going to tea with them to-morrow," Michael informed him.

"Mrs. Haden's a bit thick," said Drake confidentially. "And Doris is of a very coming-on disposition."

Michael thought of Alan and sighed; then he thought of himself listening to this and he was humiliated.

"But Lily is a bit stand-offish," said Drake. "Of course I never could stand very fair girls, myself. I say, talking of girls, there's a girl in Sherringham Road, well—she's an actress's French maid, as a matter of fact, but, my gad, if you like cayenne, you ought to come along with me, and I'll introduce you. She'll be alone now. Are you on?"

"Oh, thanks very much," said Michael. "But I must get back. Good-night, Drake."

"Well, you're a nice chap to ask a fellow to come out. Come on, don't be an ass. Her name's Marie."

"I don't care if her name's Marie or Mabel or what it is," Michael declared in exasperation. "I'm sorry. I've got to go home. Thanks for coming out."

He turned abruptly and walked off, leaving Drake to apostrophize his eccentricity and seek consolation with Marie.

On Sunday afternoon Michael, torn between a desire to arrive before the crowd of artists and actors who thronged the house and an unwillingness to obtrude upon the Sabbath lethargy of half-past three o'clock, set out with beating heart to invade Lily's home. Love made him reckless and luck rewarded him, for when he enquired for Mrs. Haden the maid told him that only Miss Lily was in.

"Who shall I say?" she asked.

"Mr. Fane."

"Step this way, please. Miss Lily's down in the morning-room."

And this so brief and so bald a colloquy danced in letters of fire across the darkling descent of the enclosed stairs down to the ground-floor.

"Someone to see you, Miss Lily."

Not Iris could have delivered a richer message.

Deep in a wicker chair by a dull red fire sat Lily with open book upon her delicate dress of lavender. The door closed; the daylight of the grey October afternoon seemed already to have fled this room. Dusky in a corner stood a great dolls' house, somewhat sad like a real house that has been left long untenanted.

"Well, now we're alone enough," murmured Lily.

He knelt beside her chair and let his head fall upon her silken shoulder.

"I'm glad you're in your own room," Michael sighed in answer.

Outside, a muffin-man went ringing through the sombre Sabbath chill; and sometimes, disturbing the monotonous railings above the area, absurd legs were seen hurrying to their social tasks. No other sign was given of a life that went on unaware of these two on whom time showered twenty golden minutes.

"Mother and Doris will be back at four," Lily said. "Is my face flushed?"

Fresh carnations would have seemed faded near her, when she looked at Michael for an answer.

"Only very slightly," he reassured her.

"Come up to the drawing-room," she commanded.

"Can I look at your dolls' house?" Michael asked.

"That old thing," said Lily scornfully.

Reverently he pulled aside the front of the battered dwelling-place, and saw the minute furniture higgledy-piggledy.

"I wonder if anyone has ever thought of burning an old dolls' house," said Michael thoughtfully. "It would be rather a rag. I've got an old toy fire-engine somewhere at home."

"You baby," said Lily.

"Well, it depresses me to see that dolls' house all disused and upside down and no good any more. My kiddy sister gave hers to a hospital. What a pity I never thought of burning that," sighed Michael regretfully. "I say, some time we must explore this room. It reminds me of all sorts of things."

"What sort of things?" asked Lily indifferently.

"Oh, being a kid."

"Well, I don't want to be reminded of that," said Lily. "I wish I was older than I am."

"Oh, so do I," said Michael. "I don't want to be a kid again."

Upstairs in the drawing-room it was still fairly light, but the backs of the grey houses opposite and the groups of ghostly trees that filmed the leaden air seemed to call for curtains to be drawn across the contemplation of their melancholy. Yet before they sat down by the crackling fire, Michael and Lily stood with their cheeks against the cold window-panes in a luxury of bodeful silence.

"No, you're not to sit so close now," Lily ordained, when by a joint impulse they turned to inhabit the room in which they had been standing. Michael saw a large photograph album and seized it.

"No, you're not to look in that," Lily cried.

"Why not?" he asked, holding it high above his head.

"Because I don't want you to," said Lily. "Put it down."

"I want to see if there are any photographs of you when you were a kid."

"Well, I don't want you to see them," Lily persisted.

In the middle of a struggle for possession of the album, Mrs. Haden and Doris came in, and Michael felt rather foolish.

"What a dreadfully noisy girl you are, Lily," said Mrs. Haden. "And is this your friend Mr. Fane? How d'ye do?"

"I'm afraid it was my fault," said Michael. "I was trying to bag the photograph album."

"Oh, Lily hates anyone to see that picture of her," Doris interposed. "She's so conceited, and just because——"

"Shut up, you beast," cried Lily.

"Her legs——"

"Doris!" interposed Mrs. Haden. "You must remember you're grown up now."

"Mother, can't I burn the photograph?" said Lily.

"No, she's not to, mother," Doris interrupted. "She's not to, is she? You jealous thing. You'd love to burn it because it's good of me."

"Well, really," said Mrs. Haden, "what Mr. Fane can be thinking of you two girls, I shouldn't like to guess."

The quarrel over the album died down as easily as it had begun, and the entrance of the tea adjusted the conversation to a less excited plane.

Mrs. Haden was a woman whom Michael could not help liking for her open breezy manner and a certain large-handed toleration which suited her loud deep voice. But he was inclined to deprecate her obviously dyed hair and the plentifulness of pink powder; nor could he at first detect in her any likeness to Lily who, though Mrs. Haden persistently reproached her as a noisy girl, stood for Michael as the slim embodiment of a subtle and easy tranquillity. Gradually, however, during the afternoon he perceived slight resemblances between the mother and daughter that showed them vaguely alike, as much alike at any rate as an elk and a roedeer.

Doris Haden was much less fair than Lily, though she could only have been called dark in comparison with her sister. She had a high complexion, wide almond-shaped eyes of a very mutable hazel, and a ripe, sanguine mouth. She was dressed in a coat and skirt of crushed-strawberry frieze, whose cool folds seemed to enhance her slightly exotic air. Michael could not help doubting whether she and Alan were perfectly suited to one another. He could not imagine that she would not care for him, but he wondered about Alan's feelings; and Drake's overnight description stuck unpleasantly in his mind with a sensation of disloyalty to Lily whose sister after all Doris was.

They were not left very long without visitors, for one by one young men came in with a self-possession and an assumption of familiarity that Michael resented very much, and all the more deeply because he felt himself at a disadvantage. He wondered if Lily were despising him, and wished that she would not catch hold of these detestable young men by the lapels of their coats, or submit to their throaty persiflage. Once when the most absolutely self-possessed of all, a tall thin creature with black fuzzy hair and stilted joints, pulled Lily on to his knee to talk to him, Michael nearly dived through the window in a fury of resentment.

All these young men seemed to him to revel in their bad taste, and their conversation, half-theatrical, half-artistic, was of a character that he could not enter into. Mrs. Haden's loud laugh rang out over the clatter of tea-cups; Doris walked about the room smoking a cigarette and humming songs; Lily moved from group to group with a nonchalance that seriously perturbed Michael, who retired more and more deeply behind a spreading palm in the darkest corner of the room. Yet he could not tear himself away from the fascination of watching Lily's grace; he could not surrender her to these marionettes of vulgar fashion; he could not go coldly out into the Sabbath night without the consolation of first hustling these intruders before him.

The afternoon drew on to real dusk; the gas was lighted; songs were sung and music was played. All these young men seemed accomplished performers of insignificant arts. Mrs. Haden recited, and in this drawing-room her heightened air and accentuated voice made Michael blush. Doris went upstairs for a moment and presently came down in a Spanish dancing-dress, in which she swayed about and rattled castanets and banged a tambourine, while the young men sat round and applauded through the smoke of their cigarettes. These cigarettes began to affect Michael's nerves. Wherever he looked he could see their flattened corpses occupying nooks. They were in the flower-pots; they littered the grate; they were strewn on brass ash-trays; and even here and there on uninflammable and level spots they stood up like little rakish mummies slowly and acridly cremating themselves. Michael wondered uneasily what Lily was going to do to entertain these voracious listeners. He hoped she would not debase her beauty by dancing on the hearthrug like her sister. In the end, Lily was persuaded to sing, and her voice very low and sweet singing some bygone coon song, was tremendously applauded.

Supper-time drew on, and at last the parlour-maid came in and enquired with a martyred air how many she should lay for.

"You must all stay to supper," cried Mrs. Haden in deafening hospitality. "Everybody. Mr. Fane, you'll stay, won't you?"

"Oh, thanks very much," said Michael shyly, and wished that these confounded young men would not all look at him as if they had perceived him suddenly for the first time. Everybody seemed as a matter of course to help to get supper ready, and Michael found himself being bumped about and handed plates and knives and glasses and salad-bowls. Even at supper he found himself as far as it was possible to be from Lily, and he thought that never in his life had food tasted so absolutely of nothing. But the evening came to an end, and Michael was consoled for his purgatory by Mrs. Haden's invitation to call whenever he liked. In the hall too Lily came out to see him off, and he besought her anxiously to assure him truthfully that to all these young men she was indifferent.

"Of course, I don't care for any of them. Why, you silly, they all think I'm still a little girl."

Then since a friendly draught had closed the drawing-room door, she kissed him; and he forgot all that had happened before, and sailed home on thoughts that carried him high above the iron-bound sadness of the Sunday night.

Some time early in the week came a letter from Stella in answer to his, and when Michael read it he wished that Stella would come home, since only she seemed to appreciate what love meant. Yet Stella was even younger than Lily.

STUTTGART,
Sunday.

Darling Michael,

I'm writing a sonata about Lily. It's not very good unfortunately, so you'll never be able to hear it. But after all, as you don't understand music, perhaps I will let you hear it. I wish you had told me more about Lily. I think she's lucky. You must be simply a perfect person to be in love with. Most boys are so silly. That's why only men of at least thirty attract me. But of course if I could find someone younger who would be content to love me and not mind whether I loved him, I should prefer that. You say I don't know what love is. How silly you are, Michael. Now isn't it thrilling to take Lily's hand? I do know what love is. But don't look shocked, because if you can still look shocked, you don't know what love is. Don't forget I'm seventeen next month, and don't forget I'm a girl as well as Lily. Lily is a good name for her, if she is very fair. I expect she really has cendré hair. I hope she's rather tall and delicate-looking. I hope she's a violin sort of girl, or like those notes half-way up the treble. It must have been perfect when you met her. I can just imagine you, especially if you like October as much as I do. Did the leaves come falling down all round you, when you kissed her? Oh, Michael, it must have been enchanting. I want to come back soon, soon, soon, and see this Lily of yours. Will she like me? Is she fond of music?

I must have my first concert next summer. Mother must not put me off. Why doesn't she let me come home now? There's some reason for it, I believe. Thank goodness, you'll have left school soon. You must be sick of it, especially since you've fallen in love.

I think of you meeting Lily when I play Schumann, and when I play Chopin I think of you walking about underneath her window, and when I play Beethoven I think of you kissing her.

Darling Michael, I love you more than ever. Be interested in me still, because I'm not interested in anybody but you, except, of course, myself and my music.

Oh, do bring Lily to my first concert, and I'll see you two alone of all the people in the Hall and play you so close together that you'll nearly faint. Now you think I'm gushing, I suppose, so I'll shut up.

With a most tremendous amount of love,

Your delightful sister,
Stella.

"I wonder if she ought to write like that," said Michael to himself. "Oh, well, I don't see why she shouldn't."

Certainly as one grew older a sister became a most valuable property.

Chapter XVIII: *Eighteen Years Old*

TO Michael it seemed almost incredible that school should be able to continue as the great background against which his love stood out like a delicate scene carved by the artist's caprice in an obscure corner of a strenuous and heroic decoration. Michael was hardly less conscious of school on Lily's account, and in class he dreamed neither more nor less than formerly; but his dreams partook more of ecstasy than those nebulous pictures inspired by the ambitions and ideals and books of youth's progress. Nevertheless in the most ultimate refinement of meditation school weighed down his spirit. It is true that games had finally departed from the realm of his consideration, but equally with games much extravagance of intellect and many morbid pleasures had gone out of cultivation. Balancing loss with gain, he found himself at the close of his last autumn term with a surer foothold on the rock-hewn foundations of truth.

Michael called truth whatever of emotion or action or reaction or reason or contemplation survived the destruction he was dealing out to the litter of idols that were beginning to encumber his passage, many of which he thought he had already destroyed when he had merely covered them with a new coat of gilt. During this period he began to enjoy Wordsworth, to whom he came by way of Matthew Arnold, like a wayfarer who crosses green fields and finds that mountains are faint upon the horizon. A successful lover, as he called himself, he began to despise anything in his reading of poetry that could not measure its power with the great commonplaces of human thought.

The Christmas holidays came as a relief from the burden of spending so much of his time in an atmosphere from which he was sure he had drained the last draught of health-giving breath. Michael no longer regarded, save in a contemptuous aside, the microcosm of school; the pleasures of seniority had staled; the whole business was now a tedious sort of mental quarantine. If he had not had Lily to occupy his leisure, he would have expired of restless inanition; and he wondered that the world went on allowing youth's load of education to be

125

encumbered by a dead-weight of superfluous information. Alan, for instance, had managed to obtain a scholarship some time in late December, and would henceforth devote himself to meditating on cricket for one term and playing it hard for another term. It would be nine months before he went to Oxford, and for nine months he would live in a state of mental catalepsy fed despairingly by the masters of the Upper Sixth with the few poor last facts they could scrape together from their own time-impoverished store. Michael, in view of Alan's necessity for gaining this scholarship, had never tried to lure him towards Doris and a share in his own fortune. But he resolved that during the following term he would do his best to galvanize Alan out of the catalepsy that he woefully foresaw was imminent.

Meanwhile the Christmas holidays were here, and Michael on their first night vowed all their leisure to Lily.

There was time now for expeditions farther afield than Kensington Gardens, which in winter seemed to have lost some of their pastoral air. The naked trees no longer veiled the houses, and the city with its dingy railings and dingy people and mud-splashed omnibuses was always an intrusion. Moreover, fellow-Jacobeans used to haunt their privacy; and often when it was foggy in London, out in the country there was winter sunlight.

These were days whose clarity and silence seemed to call for love's fearless analysis, and under a sky of turquoise so faintly blue that scarcely even at the zenith could it survive the silver dazzle of the low January sun, Michael and Lily would swing from Barnet into Finchley with Michael talking all the way.

"Why do you love me?" he would flash.

"Because I do."

"Oh, can't you think of any better reason than that?"

"Because—because—oh, Michael, I don't want to think of reasons," Lily would declare.

"You *are* determined to marry me?" Michael would flash again.

"Yes, some day."

"You don't think you'll fall in love with anybody else?"

"I don't suppose so."

"Only suppose?" Michael would echo on a fierce pause.

"Well, no, I won't."

"You promise?"

"Yes, yes, I promise," Lily would pout.

Then the rhythm of their walk would be renewed, and arm-in-arm they would travel on, until the next foolish perplexity demanded solution. Twilight would often find them still on the road, and when some lofty avenue engulphed their path, the uneasy warmth of the overarching trees would draw them very close, while hushed endearments took them slowly into lampshine.

When the dripping January rains came down, Michael spent many afternoons in the morning-room of Lily's house. Here, subject only to Doris's exaggerated hesitation to enter, Michael would build up for himself and Lily the indissoluble ties of a childhood that, though actually it was spent in ignorance of each other's existence, possessed many links of sentimental communion.

For instance, on the wall hung Cherry Ripe—the same girl in white frock and pink sash who nearly fourteen years ago had conjured for Michael the first hazy intimations of romance. Here she hung, staring down at them as demurely if not quite so sheerly beautiful as of old. Lily observed that the picture was not unlike Doris at the same age, and Michael felt at once that such a resemblance gave it a permanent value. Certainly his etchings of Montmartre and views of the Sussex Downs would never be hallowed by the associations that made sacred this oleograph of a Christmas Annual.

There were the picture-books of Randolph Caldecott tattered identically with his own, and Michael pointed out to Lily that often they must have sat by the fire reading the same verse at the same moment. Was not this thought almost as fine as the actual knowledge of each other's daily life would have been? There were other books whose pages, scrawled and dog-eared, were softened by innumerable porings to the texture of Japanese fairy-books. In a condition practically indistinguishable all of these could be found both in Carlington Road and Trelawny Road.

There were the mutilated games that commemorated Christmas after Christmas of the past. Here was the pack of Happy Families with Mrs. Chip now a widow, Mr. Block the Barber a widower, and the two young Grits grotesque orphans of the grocery. There were Ludo and Lotto and Tiddledy-Winks whose counters, though terribly depleted, were still eloquent with the undetermined squabbles and favourite colours of childhood.

Michael was glad that Lily should spring like a lovely ghost from the dust of familiar and forgotten relics. It had been romantic to snatch her on a dying cadence of Verlaine out of the opalescent vistas of October trees; but his perdurable love for her rested on these immemorial affections whose history they shared.

Lily herself was not so sensitive to this aroma of the past as Michael. She was indeed apt to consider his enthusiasm a little foolish, and would wonder why he dragged from the depths of untidy cupboards so much rubbish that only owed its preservation to the general carelessness of the household. Lily cared very little either for the past or the future, and though she was inclined to envy Doris her dancing-lessons and likelihood of appearing some time next year on the stage, she did not seem really to desire any activity of career for herself. This was a relief to Michael, who frankly feared what the stage might wreak upon their love.

"But I wish you'd read a little more," he protested. "You like such rotten books."

"I feel lazy when I'm not with you," she explained. "And, anyway, I hate reading."

"Do you think of me all the time I'm away from you?" Michael asked.

Lily told him she thought of nothing else, and his pride in her admission led him to excuse her laziness, and even made him encourage it. There was, however, about the atmosphere of Lily's home a laxity which would have overcome more forcible exhortations than Michael's.

He was too much in love with Lily's kisses to do more than vaguely criticize her surroundings. He did not like Mrs. Haden's pink powder, but nevertheless the pink powder made him less sensitive than he might have been to Mrs. Haden's opinion of his daily visits and his long unchaperoned expeditions with Lily. The general laxity tended to obscure his own outlook, and he had no desire to state even to himself his intentions. He felt himself tremendously old when he thought of kisses, but when he tried to visualize Lily and himself even four years hence, he felt hopelessly young. Mrs. Haden evidently regarded him as a boy, and since that fact seemed to relieve her of the slightest anxiety, Michael had no desire to impress upon her his precocity. The only bann that Mrs. Haden laid on his intercourse with Lily was her refusal to allow him to take her out alone at night, but she had no objection to him escorting Doris and Lily together to the theatre; nor did she oppose Michael's plan to celebrate the last night of the holidays by inviting Alan to make a quartette for the Drury Lane pantomime. Alan had only just come back from skating in Switzerland with his father, and he could not refuse to join Michael's party, although he said he was "off girls" at the moment.

"You always are," Michael protested.

"And I'm not going to fall in love, even to please you," Alan added.

"All right," Michael protested. "Just because you've been freezing yourself to death all the holidays, you needn't come back and throw cold water over me."

They all dined with Mrs. Haden, and Michael could not help laughing to see how seriously and how shyly Alan took the harum-scarum feast at which, between every course, one of the girls would rush upstairs to fetch down a fan or a handkerchief or a ribbon.

"I think your friend is charming," said Mrs. Haden loudly, when she and Michael were alone for a minute in the final confusion of not being late. Michael wondered why something in her tone made him resent this compliment. But there was no opportunity to puzzle over his momentary distaste, because it was time to start for the occupation of the box which Mrs. Haden had been given by one of her friends.

"I vote we drive home in two hansoms," suggested Michael as they stood in the vestibule when the pantomime was over.

Alan looked at him quickly and made a grimace. But Michael was determined to enjoy Lily's company during a long uninterrupted drive, and at the same time to give Alan the opportunity of finding out whether he could possibly attach himself to Doris.

Michael's own drive enthralled him. The hot theatre and the glittering performance had made Lily exquisitely tired and languorous, and Michael thought she had never surrendered herself so breathlessly before, that never before had her flowerlike kisses been so intangible and her eyes so drowsily passionate. Lulled by the regularity of the motion, Lily lay along his bended arm as if asleep, and, as he held her, Michael's sense of responsibility became more and more dreamily indistinct. The sensuousness of her abandonment drugged all but the sweet present and the poignant ecstasy of possession.

"I adore you," he whispered. "Lily, are you asleep? Lily! Lily, you are asleep, asleep in my arms, you lovely girl. Can you hear me talking to you?"

She stirred in his embrace like a ruffling bird; she sighed and threw a fevered hand upon his shoulder.

"Michael, why do you make me love you so?" she murmured, and fell again into her warm trance.

"Are you speaking to me from dreams?" he whispered. "Lily, you almost frighten me. I don't think I knew I loved you so much. The whole world seems to be galloping past. Wake up, wake up. We're nearly home."

She stretched herself in a rebellious shudder against consciousness and looked at Michael wide-eyed.

"I thought you were going to faint or something," he said.

Hardly another word they spoke, but sat upright staring before them at the oncoming lamp-posts. Soon Trelawny Road was reached, and in that last good night was a sense of nearness that never before had Michael imagined.

By her house they waited for a minute in the empty street, silent, hand-in-hand, until the other cab swung round the corner. Alan and Michael watched the two girls disappear through the flickering doorway, and then they strolled back towards Carlington Road, where Alan was spending the night.

"Well?" asked Michael. "What do you think of Lily?"

"I think she's very pretty."

"And Doris?"

"I didn't care very much for her really," said Alan apologetically, "She's pretty, not so pretty as Lily, of course; but, I say, Michael, I suppose you'll be offended, but I'd better ask right out ... who are they?"

"The Hadens?"

"Yes. I thought Mrs. Haden rather awful. What's Mr. Haden? or isn't there a Mr. Haden?"

"I believe he's in Burmah," said Michael.

"Burmah?"

"Why shouldn't he be?"

"No reason at all," Alan admitted, "but ... well ... I thought there was something funny about that family."

"You think everything's funny that's just a little bit different from the deadly average," said Michael. "What exactly was funny, may I ask?"

"I don't think Mrs. Haden is a lady, for one thing," Alan blurted out.

"I do," said Michael shortly, "And, anyway, if she weren't, I don't see that that makes any difference to me and Lily."

"But what are you going to do?" Alan asked. "Do you think you're going to marry her?"

"Some day. Life isn't a cricket-match, you know," said Michael sententiously. "You can't set your field just as you would like to have it at the moment."

127

"You know best what's good for you," Alan sighed.

"Yes ... I think I do. I think it's better to live than to stagnate as you're doing."

"What does your mother say?" Alan asked.

"I haven't told her anything about Lily."

"No, because you're not in earnest. And if you're in earnest, Lily isn't."

"What the devil do you know about her?" Michael angrily demanded.

"I know enough to see you're both behaving like a couple of reckless kids," Alan retorted.

"Damn you!" cried Michael in exasperation. "I wish to god you wouldn't try to interfere with what doesn't after all concern you very much."

"You insisted on introducing me," Alan pointed out.

"Because I thought it would be a rag if we were both in love with sisters. But you're turning into a machine. Since you've swotted up into the Upper Sixth, you've turned into a very good imitation of the prigs you associate with. Everybody isn't like you. Some people develop.... I could have been just like you if I had cared to be. I could have been Captain of the School and Scholar of Balliol with my nose ground down to εἰ and ἐάν, hammering out tenth-rate Latin lyrics and reading Theocritus with the amusing parts left out. But what's the good of arguing with you? You're perfectly content and you think you can be as priggish as you like, as long as you conceal it by making fifty runs in the Dulford match. I suppose you consider my behaviour unwholesome at eighteen. Well, I dare say it is by your standards. But are your standards worth anything? I doubt it. I think they're fine up to a point. I'm perfectly willing to admit that we behaved like a pair of little blighters with those girls at Eastbourne. But this is something altogether different."

"We shall see," said Alan simply. "I'm not going to quarrel with you. So shut up."

Michael walked along in silence, angry with himself for having caused this ill-feeling by his obstinacy in making an unsuitable introduction, and angry with Alan because he would accentuate by his attitude the mistake.

By the steps of his house Michael stopped and looked at Alan severely.

"This is the last time I shall attempt to cure you," he announced.

"All right," said Alan with perfect equanimity. "You can do anything you like but quarrel. You needn't talk to me or look at me or think about me until you want to. I shall feel a bit bored, of course, but, oh, my dear old chap, do get over this love-sickness soon."

"This isn't like that silly affair at Bournemouth last Easter," Michael challenged.

"I know that, my dear chap. I wish it was."

With the subject of love finally sealed between him and Alan, Michael receded farther and farther from the world of school. He condescended indeed to occupy a distinguished position by the hot-water pipes of the entrance-hall, where his aloofness and ability to judge men and gods made him a popular, if slightly incomprehensible, figure. Towards all the masters he emanated a compassion which he really felt very deeply. Those whom he liked he conversed with as equals; those whom he disliked he talked to as inferiors. But he pitied both sections. In class he was polite, but somewhat remote, though he missed very few opportunities of implicitly deriding the Liberal views of Mr. Kirkham. The whole school with its ant-like energy, whose ultimate object and obvious result were alike inscrutable to Michael, just idly amused him, and he reserved for Lily all his zest in life.

The Lent term passed away with parsimonious February sunlight, with March lying grey upon the houses until it proclaimed itself suddenly in a booming London gale. The Easter holidays arrived, and Mrs. Fane determined to go to Germany and see Stella. Would Michael come? Michael pleaded many disturbed plans of cricket-practice; of Matriculation at St. Mary's College, Oxford; of working for the English Literature Prize; of anything indeed but his desire to see with Lily April break to May. In the end he had his own way, and Mrs. Fane went to the continent without his escort.

Lily was never eager for the discussions and the contingencies and the doubts of love; in all their walks it had been Michael who flashed the questions, she who let slip her answers. The strange fatigue of spring made much less difference to her than to him, and however insistent he was for her kisses, she never denied him. Michael tried to feel that the acquiescence of the hard, the reasonable, the intellectual side of him to April's passionate indulgence merely showed that he was more surely and more sanely growing deeper in love with Lily every day. Sometimes he had slight tremors of malaise, a sensation of weakening fibres, and dim stirrings of responsibility; but too strong for them was his heart's-ease, too precious was Lily's rose-bloomed grace of submission. The more sharply imminent her form became upon his thought, the more surely deathless did he suppose his love. Michael's mind was always framing moments in eternity, and of all these moments the sight of her lying upon the vivid grass, the slim, the pastoral, the fair immortal girl stood unparagoned by any. There was no landscape that Lily did not make more inevitably composed. There was no place of which she did not become tutelary, whether she lay among the primroses that starred the steep brown banks of woodland or whether she fronted the great sunshine of the open country; but most of all when she sat in cowslips, looking over arched knees at the wind.

Michael fell into the way of talking to her as if he were playing upon Dorian pipes the tale of his love:

"I must buy you a ring, Lily. What ring shall I buy for you? Rings are all so dull. Perhaps your hands would look wrong with a ring, unless I could find a star-sapphire set in silver. I thought you were lovely in autumn, but I think you are more lovely in spring. How the days are going by; it will soon be May. Lily, if you had the choice of everything in the world, what would you choose?"

"I would choose to do nothing."

"If you had the choice of all the people in the world, would you choose me?"

"Yes. Of course."

"Lily, you make me curiously lazy. I want never again to do anything but sit in the sun with you. Why can't we stay like this for ever?"

"I shouldn't mind."

"I wish that you could be turned into a primrose, and that I could be turned into a hazel-bush looking down at you for ever. Or I wish you could be a cowslip and I could be a plume of grass. Lily, why is it that the longer I know you, the less you say?"

"You talk enough for both," said Lily.

"I talk less to you than to anyone. I really only want to look at you, you lovely thing."

But the Easter holidays were almost over, and Michael had to go to Oxford for his Matriculation. On their last long day together, Lily and he went to Hampton Court and dreamed the sad time away. When twilight was falling Michael said he had a sovereign to spend on whatever they liked best to do. Why should they not have dinner on a balcony over the river, and after dinner drive all the way home in a hansom cab?

So they sat grandly on the chilly balcony and had dinner, until Lily in her thin frock was cold.

"But never mind," said Michael. "I'll hold you close to me all the way to London."

They found their driver and told him where to go. The man was very much pleased to think he had a fare all the way to London, and asked Michael if he wanted to drive fast.

"No, rather slow, if anything," said Michael.

The fragrant miles went slowly past, and all the way they drove between the white orchards, and all the way like a spray of bloom Lily was his. Past the orchards they went, past the twinkling roadside houses, past the gates where the shadows of lovers fell across the road, past the breaking limes and lilac, past the tulips stiff and dark in the moonlight, through the high narrow street of Brentford, past Kew Bridge and the slow trams with their dim people nodding, through Chiswick and into Hammersmith where a piano-organ was playing and the golden streets were noisy. It was Doris who opened the door.

"Eleven o'clock," she said. "Mother's rather angry."

"You'd better not come in," said Lily to Michael. "She'll be all right again by next week, when you come back."

"Oh, no, I'll come in," he insisted. "I'd rather explain why we're so late."

"It's no use arguing with mother when she's unreasonable," said Lily. "I shall go up to bed; I don't want to have a row."

"That's right," Doris sneered. "Always take the shortest and easiest way. You are a coward."

"Oh, shut up," said Lily, and without another word went upstairs.

"You've spoilt her," said Doris. "Well, are you going to see mother? She isn't in a very pleasant mood, I warn you."

"She's never been angry before," said Michael hopelessly.

"Well, she has really," Doris explained. "Only she's vented it on me."

"I say, I'm awfully sorry. I had no idea—" Michael began.

"Oh, don't apologize," said Doris. "I'm used to it. Thank god, I'm going on the stage next year; and then Lily and mother will be able to squabble to their heart's content."

Mrs. Haden was sitting in what was called The Cosy Corner; and she treated Michael's entrance with exaggerated politeness.

"Won't you sit down? It's rather late, but do sit down."

All the time she was speaking the plate-rack above The Cosy Corner was catching the back of her hair, and Michael wondered how long it would be before she noticed this.

"Really, I think it's very wrong of you to bring my daughter home at this hour," Mrs. Haden clattered. "I'm sure nobody likes young people to enjoy themselves more than I do. But eleven o'clock! Where is Lily now?"

"Gone to bed," said Doris, who seized the opportunity to depart also.

"I'm awfully sorry, Mrs. Haden," said Michael awkwardly "But as it was my last night, I suggested driving back from Hampton Court. It was all my fault; I do hope you won't be angry with Lily."

"But I am angry with Lily," said Mrs. Haden. "Very angry. She's old enough to know better, and you're old enough to know better. How will people think I'm bringing up my daughters, if they return at midnight with young men in hansoms? I never heard of such a thing. You're presuming on your age. You've no business to compromise a girl like this."

"Compromise?" stammered Michael.

"None of the young people but you has ever ventured to behave like this," Mrs. Haden went on with sharply metallic voice. "Not one of them. And, goodness knows, every Sunday the house is full of them."

"But they don't come to see Lily," Michael pointed out. "They come to see you."

"Are you trying to be rude to me?" Mrs. Haden asked.

"No, no," Michael assured her. "And, honestly, Mrs. Haden, I didn't think you minded me taking Lily out."

"But what's going to happen?" Mrs. Haden demanded.

"Well—I—I suppose I want to marry Lily."

Michael wondered if this statement sounded as absurd to Mrs. Haden as it sounded to himself.

"What nonsense!" she snapped. "What utter nonsense! A schoolboy talking such nonsense. Marriage indeed! You know as well as I do that you've never thought about such a step."

"But I have," said Michael. "Very often, as it happens."

"Then you mustn't go out with Lily again. Why, it's worse than I thought. I'm horrified."

"Do you mean I'm never to come here again?" Michael asked in despair.

"Come occasionally," said Mrs. Haden. "But only occasionally."

"All right. Thanks," said Michael, feeling stunned by this unexpected rebuke. "Good night, Mrs. Haden."

In the hall he found Doris.

"Well?" she asked.

"Your mother says I'm only to come occasionally."

"Oh, that won't last," said Doris encouragingly.

"Yes, but I'm not sure that she isn't right," said Michael. "Oh, Doris, damn. I wish I couldn't always see other people's point of view."

"Mother often has fits of violent morality," said Doris. "And then we always catch it. But really they don't last."

"Doris, you don't understand. It isn't your mother's disapproval I'm worrying over. It's myself. Lily might have waited to say good-night," Michael murmured miserably.

But straight upon his complaint he saw Lily leaning over from the landing above and blowing kisses, and he felt more calm.

"Don't worry too much about Lily," whispered Doris, as she held the door open for him.

"Why?"

"I shouldn't, that's all," she said enigmatically, and closed the door very gently.

At the time Michael was not conscious of any deep impression made by the visit to Oxford for his Matriculation; he was too much worried by the puzzle of his future conduct with regard to Lily. He felt dull in the rooms where he spent two nights alone; he felt shy among the forty or fifty boys from other public-schools; he was glad to go back to London. Vaguely the tall grey tower remained in his mind, and vaguely the cool Gothic seemed to offer a shelter from the problems of behaviour, but that was all.

When he returned, the torment of Lily's desired presence became more acute. His mother wrote to say that she would not be back for three days, and the only consolation was the hint that most probably Stella would come back with her.

Meanwhile this was Saturday, and school did not begin until Tuesday. Time after time Michael set out towards Trelawny Road; time after time he checked himself and fought his way home again. Mrs. Haden had been right; he had behaved badly. Lily was too young to bear the burden of their passionate love. And was she happy without him? Was she sighing for him? Or would she forget him and resume an existence undisturbed by him? But the thought of wasted time, of her hours again unoccupied, of her footsteps walking to places ignorant of him was intolerable.

Sunday came round, and Michael thought that he would fling himself into the stream of callers; but the idea of doing so became humiliating, and instead he circled drearily round the neighbouring roads, circled in wide curves, and sometimes even swooped into the forbidden diameter of Trelawny Road. But always before he could bring himself to pass her very door, he would turn back into his circle and the melancholy Sabbath sunlight of May.

Twilight no more entranced him, and the lovers leaning over to one another languorously in their endearments, moving with intertwined arms and measured steps between the wine-dark houses, annoyed him with their fatuous complacency and their bland eyes. He wanted her, his slim and silent Lily, who blossomed in the night-time like a flower. Her wrists were cool as porcelain and the contact of her form swaying to his progress was light as silk. Everyone else had their contentment, and he must endure wretchedly without the visible expression of his beauty. It was not yet too late to see her; and Michael circled nearer to Trelawny Road. This time he came to Lily's house; he paused within sound of laughter upon the easeful step; and then again he turned away and walked furiously on through the empty Sabbath streets.

In his room, when it was now too late to think of calling, Michael laughed at himself for being so sensitive to Mrs. Haden's reproaches. He told himself that all she said was due to the irritation of the moment, that to-morrow he must go again as if nothing had happened, that people had no right to interfere between lovers. But then, in all its florid bulk, St. James' School rose up, and Michael admitted to himself that to the world he was merely a foolish schoolboy. He, the dauntless lover, must be chained to a desk for five hours every day. A boy and girl affair! Michael ground his teeth with exasperation. He must simply prove by renouncing for a term his part in Lily's life that he was a schoolboy by an accident of time. A man is as old as he feels! He would see Lily once more, and tell her that for the sake of their ultimate happiness, he would give her up for the term of his bondage. Other great and romantic lovers had done the same; they may not have gone to school, but they had accepted menial tasks for the sake of their love.

Yet in the very middle of the night when the thickest darkness seemed to stifle self-deception, Michael knew that he had bowed to authority so easily because his conscience had already told him what Mrs. Haden so crudely hinted. When he was independent of school it would be different. Michael made up his mind that the utmost magnanimity would be possible, if he could see Lily once to tell her of his resolution. But on the next day Lily was out, and Mrs. Haden talked to him instead.

"I've forbidden Lily to go out with you alone," she said. "And I would prefer that you only came here when I am in the house."

"I was going to suggest that I shouldn't come at all until July—until after I had left school, in fact," answered Michael.

"Perhaps that would be best. Then you and Lily will be more sensible."

"Good-bye," said Michael hurriedly, for he felt that he must get out of this stifling room, away from this overwhelming woman with her loud voice and dyed hair and worldly-wise morality. Then he had a sudden conception of himself as part of a scene, perceiving himself in the rôle of the banished lover nobly renouncing all. "I won't write to her. I won't make any attempt to see her," he offered.

"You'll understand," said Mrs. Haden, "that I'm afraid of—that I think," she corrected, "it is quite likely that Lily is just as bad for you as you are for Lily. But of course the real reason I feel I ought to interfere is on account of what people say. If Mr. Haden were not in Burmah ... it would be different."

Michael pitied himself profoundly for the rest of that day; but after a long luxury of noble grief the image of Lily came to agitate and disconcert his acquiescence, and the insurgent fevers of love goaded his solitude.

Mrs. Fane and Stella returned during the first week of school. The great Steinway Grand that came laboriously in through the unsashed window of the third story gave Michael, as it lay like a boulder over Carlington Road, a wonderful sense of Stella's establishment at home. Stella's music-room was next to his bedroom, and when in her nightgown she came to practise in the six o'clock sunshine Michael thought her music seemed the very voice of day. So joyously did the rills and ripples and fountains of her harmony rouse him from sleep that he refrained from criticizing her apparel, and sat contented in the sunlight to listen.

Suddenly Stella wheeled round and said:

"Do tell me about Lily."

"Well, there's been rather a row," Michael began. "You see, I took her to Hampton Court and we drove...." Michael stopped, and for the first time he obtained a cold clear view of his behaviour, when he found he was hesitating to tell Stella lest he might set her a bad example.

"Go on," she urged. "Don't stop."

"Well, we were rather late. But of course it was the first time, and I hope you won't think you can drive back at eleven o'clock with somebody because I did once—only once."

"Why, was there any harm in it?" asked Stella quickly, and, as if to allay Michael's fear by so direct a question, one hand went trilling in scale towards the airy unrealities of the treble.

"No, of course there was no harm in it," said Michael.

"Then why shouldn't I drive back at eleven o'clock if I wanted to?" asked Stella, striking elfin discords as she spoke.

"It's a question of what people think," said Michael, falling back upon Mrs. Haden's line of defence.

"Bother people!" cried Stella, and immediately she put them in their place somewhere very far down in the bass.

"Well, anyway," said Michael, "I understood what Mrs. Haden meant, and I've agreed not to see Lily until after I leave school."

"And then?"

"Well, then I shall see her," said Michael.

"And drive back at eleven o'clock in hansoms?"

"Not unless I can be engaged," Michael surrendered to convention.

"And don't you mind?"

"Of course I mind," he confessed gloomily.

"Why did you agree, then?" Stella asked.

"I had to think about Lily, just as I should have to think about you," he challenged.

"Darling Michael, I love you dreadfully, but I really should not pay the least little tiny bit of attention to you—or anybody else, if that's any consolation," she added. "As it happens, I've never yet met anybody with whom I'd care to drive about in a hansom at eleven o'clock, but if I did, three o'clock in the morning would be the same as three o'clock in the afternoon."

"Stella, you ought not to talk like that," Michael said earnestly. "You don't realize what people would suppose. And really I don't think you ought to practise in your nightgown."

"Oh, Michael, if I practised in my chemise, I shouldn't expect you to mind."

"Stella! Really, you know!"

"Listen," she said, swinging away from him back to the keyboard. "This is the Lily Sonata."

Michael listened, and as he listened he could not help owning to himself that in her white nightgown, straight-backed against the shimmering ebony instrument, little indeed would matter very much among those dancing black and white notes.

"Or in nothing at all," said Stella, stopping suddenly.

Then she ran across to Michael and, after kissing him on the top of his head, waltzed very slowly out of the room.

But not even Stella could for long take away from Michael the torment of Lily's withheld presence. As a month went by, the image of her gained in elusive beauty, and the desire to see became a madness. He tried to evade his promise by haunting the places she would be likely to frequent, but he never saw her. He wondered if she could be in London, and he nearly wrote to ask. There was no consolation to be gained from books; there was no sentiment to be culled from the spots they had known together. He wanted herself, her fragility, her swooning kisses, herself, herself. She was the consummation of idyllic life, the life he longed for, the passionate life of beauty expressed in her. Stella had her music; Alan had his cricket; Mrs. Ross had her son; and he must have Lily. How damnable were these silver nights of June, how their fragrance musk-like even here in London fretted him with the imagination of wasted beauty. These summer nights demanded love; they enraged him with their uselessness.

"Isn't Chopin wonderful?" cried Stella. "Just when the window-boxes are dripping and the earth's warm and damp and the air is all turning into velvet."

"Oh, very wonderful," said Michael bitterly.

And he would go out on the dreaming balcony and, looking down on the motionless lamps, he would hear the murmur and rustle of people. But he was starving amid this rich plenitude of colour and scent; he was idle upon these maddening, these music-haunted, these royal nights that mocked his surrender.

And in the silent heart of the night when the sheets were fibrous and the mattress was jagged, when the pillow seared him and his eyes were like sand, what resolutions he made to carry her away from Kensington; but in the morning how coldly impossible it was to do so at eighteen.

One afternoon coming out of school, Michael met Drake.

131

"Hullo!" said Drake. "How's the fair Lily? I haven't seen you around lately."

"Haven't you?" said Michael. "No, I haven't been round so much lately."

He spoke as if he had suddenly noticed he had forgotten something.

"I asked her about you—over the garden-wall; so don't get jealous," Drake said with his look of wise rakishness. "And she didn't seem particularly keen on helping out the conversation. So I supposed you'd had a quarrel. Funny girl, Lily," Drake went on. "I suppose she's all right when you know her. Why don't you come in to my place?"

"Thanks," said Michael.

He felt that fate had given him this opportunity. He had not sought it. He might be able to speak to Lily, and if he could, he would ask her to meet him, and promises could go to the devil. He determined that no more of summer's treasure should be wasted.

He had a thrill in Drake's dull drawing-room from the sense of nearness to Lily, and from the looking-glass room it was back to back with the more vital drawing-room next door.

Michael could hardly bear to look out of the window into the oblong gardens; two months away from Lily made almost unendurable the thought that in one tremulous instant he might be imparadised in the vision of her reality.

"Hullo! She's there," said Drake from the window. "With another chap."

Michael with thudding heart and flaming cheeks stood close to Drake.

"Naughty girl!" said Drake. "She's flirting."

"I don't think she was," said Michael, but, even as he spoke, the knowledge that she was tore him to pieces.

Chapter XIX: *Parents*

THE brazen sun lighted savagely the barren streets, as Michael left Trelawny Road behind him. His hopeless footsteps rasped upon the pavement. His humiliation was complete. Not even was his personality strong enough to retain the love of a girl for six weeks. Yet he experienced a morbid sympathy with Lily, so unutterably beneath the rest of mankind was he already inclined to estimate himself. Stella opened wide her grey eyes when she greeted his pale disheartened return.

"Feeling ill?" she asked.

"I'm feeling a worthless brute," said Michael, plunging into a dejected acquiescence in the worst that could be said about him.

"Tell me," whispered Stella. "Ah, do."

"I've found out that Lily is quite ready to flirt with anybody. With anybody!"

"What a beastly girl!" Stella flamed.

"Well, you can't expect her to remain true to a creature like me," said Michael, declaring his self-abasement.

"A creature like you?" cried Stella. "Why, Michael, how can you be so absurd? If you speak of yourself like that, I shall begin to think you *are* 'a creature' as you call yourself. Ah, no, but you're not, Michael. It's this Lily who is the creature. Oh, don't I know her, the insipid puss! A silly little doll that lets everybody pull her about. I hate weak girls. How I despise them!"

"But you despise boys, Stella," Michael reminded her. "And this chap she was flirting with was much older than me. Perhaps Lily is like you, and prefers older men."

Michael had no heart left even to maintain his stand against Stella's alarming opinions and prejudices so frankly expressed.

"Like me," Stella cried, stamping her foot. "Like me! How dare you compare her with me? I'm not a doll. Do you think anyone has ever dared to kiss me?"

"I'm sorry," said Michael. "But you talk so very daringly that I shouldn't be surprized by anything you told me. At the same time I can't help sympathizing with Lily. It must have been dull to be in love with a schoolboy—an awkward lout of eighteen."

"Michael! I will not hear you speak of yourself like that. I'm ashamed of you. How can you be so weak? Be proud. Oh, Michael, do be proud—it's the only thing on earth worth being."

Stella stood dominant before him. Her grey eyes flashed; her proud, upcurving mouth was slightly curled: her chin was like the chin of a marble goddess, and yet with that brown hair lapping her wide shoulders, with those long legs, lean-flanked and supple, she was more like some heroic boy.

"Yes, you can be proud enough," said Michael. "But you've got something to be proud of. What have I got?"

"You've got me," said Stella fiercely.

"Why, yes, I suppose I have," Michael softly agreed. "Let's talk about your first appearance."

"I was talking about it to mother when a man called Prescott came."

"Prescott?" said Michael. "I seem to have heard mother speak about him. I wonder when it was. A long time ago, though."

"Well, whoever he was," said Stella, "he brought mother bad news."

"How do you know?"

"Have you ever seen mother cry?"

"Yes, once," said Michael. "It was when I was talking through my hat about the war."

"I've never seen her cry," said Stella pensively. "Until to-day."

Michael forgot about his own distress in the thought of his mother, and he sat hushed all through the evening, while Stella played in the darkness. Mrs. Fane went up to her own room immediately she came in that night, and the next morning, which was Saturday, Michael listlessly took the paper out to read in the garden, while he waited for Stella to dress herself so that they could go out together and avoid the house over which seemed to impend calamity.

Opening the paper, Michael saw an obituary notice of the Earl of Saxby. He scanned the news, only half absorbing it:

"In another column will be found the details—enteric—adds another famous name to the lamentable toll of this war—the late nobleman did not go into society much of late years—formerly Captain in the Welsh Guards—born 1860—married Lady Emmeline MacDonald, daughter of the Earl of Skye, K.T.—raised corps of Mounted Infantry (Saxby's Horse)—great traveller—unfortunately no heir to the title which becomes extinct."

Michael guessed the cause of his mother's unhappiness of yesterday. He went upstairs and told Stella.

"I suppose mother was in love with him," she said.

"I suppose she was," Michael agreed. "I wish I hadn't refused to say good-bye to him. It seems rather horrible now."

Mrs. Fane had left word that she would not be home until after dinner, and Michael and Stella sat apprehensive and silent in the drawing-room. Sometimes they would toss backwards and forwards to each other reassuring words, while outside the livid evening of ochreous oppressive clouds and ashen pavements slowly dislustred into a night swollen with undelivered rain and baffled thunders.

About nine o'clock Mrs. Fane came home. She stood for a moment in the doorway of the room, palely regarding her children. She seemed undecided about something, but after a long pause she sat down between them and began to speak:

"Something has happened, dear children, that I think you ought to know about before you grow any older."

Mrs. Fane paused again and stared before her, seeming to be reaching out for strength to continue. Michael and Stella sat breathless as the air of the night. Mrs. Fane's white kid gloves fell to the floor softly like the petals of a blown rose, and as if she missed their companionship in the stress of explication, she went on more rapidly.

"Lord Saxby has died in the Transvaal of enteric fever, and I think you both ought to know that Lord Saxby was your father."

When his mother said this, the blood rushed to Michael's face and then immediately receded, so that his eyelids as they closed over his eyes to shield them from the room's suddenly intense light glowed greenly; and when he looked again anywhere save directly at his mother, his heart seemed to have been crushed between ice. The room itself went swinging up in loops out of reach of his intelligence, that vainly strove to bring it back to familiar conditions. The nightmare passed: the drawing-room regained its shape and orderly tranquillity: the story went on.

"I have often wished to tell you, Michael, in particular," said his mother, looking at him with great grey eyes whose lustrous intensity cooled his first pained sensation of shamefulness, "Years ago, when you were the dearest little boy, and when I was young and rather lonely sometimes, I longed to tell you. But it would not have been fair to weigh you down with knowledge that you certainly could not have grasped then. I thought it was kinder to escape from your questions, even when you said that your father looked like a prince."

"Did I?" Michael asked, and he fell to wondering why he had spoken and why his voice sounded so exactly the same as usual.

"You see ... of course ... I was never married to your father. You must not blame him, because he wanted to marry me always, but Lady Saxby wouldn't divorce him. I dare say she had a right to nurse her injury. She is still alive. She lives in an old Scottish castle. Your father gave up nearly all his time to me. That was why you were both alone so much. You must forgive me for that, if you can. But I knew, as time went on that we should never be married, and.... Your father only saw you once, dearest Stella, when you were very tiny. You remember, Michael, when you saw him. He loved you so much, for of course, except in name, you were his heir. He wanted to have you to live with him. He loved you."

"I suppose that's why I liked him so tremendously," said Michael.

"Did you, dearest boy?" said Mrs. Fane, and the tears were in her grey eyes. "Ah, how dear it is of you to say that."

"Mother, I can't tell you how sorry I am I never went to say good-bye. I shall never forgive myself," said Michael. "I shall never forgive myself."

"But you must. It was my fault," said his mother. "I dare say I asked you tactlessly. I was so much upset at the time that I only thought about myself."

"Why did he go?" asked Stella suddenly.

"Well, that was my fault. I was always so dreadfully worried over the way in which I had spoilt his life that when he thought he ought to go and fight for his country, I could not bear to dissuade him. You see, having no heir, he was always fretting and fretting about the extinction of his family, and he had a fancy that the last of his name should do something for his country. He had given up his country for me, and I knew that if he went to the war he would feel that he had paid the debt. I never minded so much that we weren't married, but I always minded the feeling that I had robbed him by my love. He was such a very dear fellow. He was always so good and patient, when I begged him not to see you both. That was his greatest sorrow. But it wouldn't have been fair to you, dear children. You must not blame me for that. I knew it was better that you should be brought up in ignorance. It was, wasn't it?" she asked wistfully.

"Better," Michael murmured.

"Better," Stella echoed.

Mrs. Fane stood up, and Michael beheld her tall, tragical form with a reverence he had never felt for anything.

"Children, you must forgive me," she said.

And then simply, with repose and exquisite fitness she left Michael and Stella to themselves. By the door Stella overtook her.

"Mother darling," she cried. "You know we adore you. You do, don't you?"

Mrs. Fane smiled, and Michael thought he would cherish that smile to the end of his life.

"Well?" said Michael, when Stella and he were sitting alone again.

"Of course I've known for years it was something like this," said Stella.

133

"I can't think why I never guessed. I ought to have guessed easily," Michael said. "But somehow one never thinks of anything like this in connection with one's own mother."

"Or sister," murmured Stella, looking up at a spot on the ceiling.

"I wish I could kick myself for not having said good-bye to him," Michael declared. "That comes of talking too much. I talked much too much then. Talking destroys action. What a beast I was. Lily and I look rather small now, don't we?" he went on. "When you think of the amount that mother must have suffered all these years, it just makes Lily and me look like illustrations in a book. It's a curious thing that this business about mother and ... Lord Saxby ought, I suppose, to make me feel more of a worm than ever, but it doesn't. Ever since the first shock, I've been feeling prouder and prouder. I can't make it out."

Then suddenly Michael flushed.

"I say, I wonder how many of our friends have known all the time? Mrs. Carthew and Mrs. Ross both know. I feel sure by what they've said. And yet I wonder if Mrs. Ross does know. She's so strict in her notions that ... I wonder ... and yet I suppose she isn't so strict as I thought she was. Perhaps I was wrong."

"What are you talking about?" Stella asked.

"Oh, something that happened at Cobble Place. It's not important enough to tell you."

"What I'm wondering," said Stella, "is what mother was like when she was my age. She didn't say anything about her family. But I suppose we can ask her some time. I'm really rather glad I'm not 'Lady Stella Fane.' It would be ridiculous for a great pianist to be 'Lady Something.'"

"You wouldn't have been Lady Stella Fane," Michael contradicted. "You would have been Lady Stella Cunningham. Cunningham was the family name. I remember reading about it all when I was interested in Legitimists."

"What are they?" Stella asked. "The opposite of illegitimate?"

Michael explained the difference, and he was glad that the word 'illegitimate' should first occur like this. The pain of its utterance seemed mitigated somehow by the explanation.

"It's an extraordinary thing," Michael began, "but, do you know, Stella, that all the agony of seeing Lily flirting seems to have died away, and I feel a sort of contempt ... for myself, I mean. Flirting sounds such a loathsome word after what we've just listened to. Alan was right, I believe. I shall have to tell Alan about all this. I wonder if it will make any difference to him. But of course it won't. Nothing makes any difference to Alan."

"It's about time I met him," said Stella.

"Why, haven't you?" Michael exclaimed. "Nor you have. Great Scott! I've been so desperately miserable over Lily that I've never asked Alan here once. Oh, I will, though."

"I say, oughtn't we to go up to mother?" said Stella.

"Would she like us to?" Michael wondered.

"Oh, yes, I'm sure she would."

"But I can't express what I feel," Michael complained. "And it will be absurd to go and stand in front of her like two dummies."

"I'll say something," Stella promised; and, "Mother," she said, "come and hear me play to you."

The music-room, with its spare and austere decoration, seemed to Michael a fit place for the quiet contemplation of the tale of love he had lately heard.

Whatever of false shame, of self-consciousness, of shock remained was driven away by Stella's triumphant music. It was as if he were sitting beneath a mountain waterfall that, graceful and unsubstantial as wind-blown tresses, was yet most incomparably strong, and wrought an ice-cold, a stern purification.

Then Stella played with healing gentleness, and Michael in the darkness kissed his mother and stole away to bed, not to dream of Lily that night, not to toss enfevered, but quietly to lie awake, devising how to show his mother that he loved her as much now as he had loved her in the dim sunlight of most early childhood.

About ten days later Mrs. Fane came to Michael and Stella with a letter.

"I want to read you something," she said. "Your father's last letter has come."

"*We are in Pretoria now, and I think the war will soon be over. But of course there's a lot to be done yet. I'm feeling seedy to-night, and I'm rather sighing for England. I wonder if I'm going to be ill. I have a presentiment that things are going wrong with me—at least not wrong, because in a way I would be glad. No, I wouldn't, that reads as if I were afraid to keep going.*

"*I keep thinking of Michael and Stella. Michael must be told soon. He must forgive me for leaving him no name. I keep thinking of those Siamese stamps he asked for when I last saw him. I wish I'd seen him again before I went. But I dare say you were right. He would have guessed who I was, and he might have gone away resentful.*"

Michael looked at his mother, and thanked her implicitly for excusing him. He was glad that his father had not known he had declined to see him.

"*I don't worry so much over Stella. If she really has the stuff in her to make the name you think she will, she does not need any name but her own. But it maddens me to think that Michael is cut out of everything. I can scarcely bear to realize that I am the last. I'm glad he's going to Oxford, and I'm very glad that he chose St. Mary's. I was only up at Christ Church a year, and St. Mary's was a much smaller college in those days. Now of course it's absolutely one of the best. Whatever Michael wants to do he will be able to do, thank God. I don't expect, from what you tell me of him, he'll choose the Service. However, he'll do what he likes. When I come back, I must see him and I shall be able to explain what will perhaps strike him at first as the injustice of his position. I dare say he'll think less hardly of me when I've told him all the circumstances. Poor old chap! I feel that I've been selfish, and yet....*"

134

"I wonder if I'm going to be ill. I feel rotten. But don't worry. Only, if by any chance I can't write again, will you give my love to the children, and say I hope they'll not hate the thought of me? That piano was the best Prescott could get. I hope Stella is pleased with it."

"Thanks awfully for reading us that," said Michael.

Chapter XX: *Music*

MRS. FANE, having momentarily lifted the veil that all these years had hidden her personality from Michael and Stella, dropped it very swiftly again. Only the greatest emotion could have given her the courage to make that avowal of her life. During the days that elapsed between the revelation and the reading of Lord Saxby's last letter, she had lived very much apart from her children, so that the spectacle of her solitary grief had been deeply impressed upon their sensibility.

Michael was reminded by her attitude of those long vigils formerly sustained by ladies of noble birth before they departed into a convent to pray, eternally remote from the world. He himself became endowed with a strange courage by the contemplation of his mother's tragical immobility. He found in her the expression of those most voiceless ideals of austere conduct that until this vision of resignation had always seemed doomed to sink broken-winged to earth. The thought of Lily in this mood became an intrusion, and he told himself that, even if it were possible to seek the sweet unrest of her presence, beneath the sombre spell of this more classic sorrow he would have shunned that lovely and romantic girl. Michael's own realization of the circumstances of his birth occupied a very small part of his thoughts. His mind was fixed upon the aspect of his mother mute and heavy-lidded from the remembrance of that soldier dead in Africa. Michael felt no outrage of fate in these events. He was glad that death should have brought to his father the contentment of his country's honour, that in the grace of reconciliation he should be healed of his thwarted life. Nor could Michael resent that news of death which could ennoble his mother with this placidity of comprehension, this staid and haughty mien of sorrow. And he was grateful, too, that death should upon his own brow dry the fever dew of passion.

But when she had read that last letter, Mrs. Fane strangely resumed her ordinary self. She was always so finely invested with dignity, so exquisitely sheathed, in her repose, Michael scarcely realized that now, after she had read the letter, the vision of her grief was once more veiled against him by that faintly discouraging, tenderly deliberate withdrawal of her personality, and that she was still as seclusive as when from his childhood she had concealed the sight of her love, living in her own rose-misted and impenetrable privacy.

It was Stella who by a sudden request first roused Michael to the realization that his mother was herself again.

"Mother," she said, "what about my first concert? The season is getting late."

"Dearest Stella," Mrs. Fane replied, "I think you can scarcely make your appearance so soon after your father's death."

"But, mother, I'm sure he wouldn't have minded. And after all very few people would know," Stella persisted.

"But I should prefer that you waited for a while," said Mrs. Fane, gently reproachful. "You forget that we are in mourning."

For Michael somehow the conventional expression seemed to disturb the divinity of his mother's carven woe. The world suddenly intervened.

"Well, I don't think I ought to wait for ever," said Stella.

"Darling child, I wonder why you should think it necessary to exaggerate so foolishly," said Mrs. Fane.

"But I'm so longing to begin," Stella went on.

"I don't know that anybody has ever suggested you shouldn't begin," Mrs. Fane observed. "But there is a difference between your recklessness and my more carefully considered plans."

"Mother, will you agree to a definite date?" Stella demanded.

"By all means, dear child, if you will try to be a little less boisterous and impetuous. For one thing, I never knew you were ready to begin at once like this."

"Oh, mother, after all these years and years of practising!" Stella protested.

"But are you ready?" Mrs. Fane enquired in soft surprise. "Really ready? Then why not this autumn? Why not October?"

"Before I go up to Oxford," said Michael quickly.

Stella was immediately and vividly alert with plans for her concert.

"I don't think any of the smaller halls. Couldn't I appear first at one of the big orchestral concerts at King's Hall? I would like to play a Concerto ... Chopin, I think, and nothing else. Then later on I could have a concert all to myself, and play Schumann, and perhaps some Brahms."

So in the end it was settled after numberless interviews, letters, fixtures, cancellations, and all the fuming impediments of art's first presentation at the court of the world.

The affairs and arrangements connected with Stella's career seemed to Michael the proper distraction for his mother and sister during his last two or three weeks of school, before they could leave London. Mrs. Fane had suggested they should go to Switzerland in August, staying at Lucerne, so that Stella would not be hindered in her steady practice.

Michael's last week at school was a curiously unreal experience. As fast as he marshalled the correct sentiments with which to approach the last hours of a routine that had continued for ten years, so fast did they break up in futile disorder. He had really passed beyond the domain of school some time ago when he was always with Lily. It was impossible after that gradual secession, all the more final because it had been so gradual, to gather together now a crowd of associations for the sole purpose of effecting a violent and summary wrench. Indeed, the one action that gave him the expected pang of sentiment was when he went to surrender across the counter of the book-room the key of his locker. The number was seventy-five. In very early days Michael had been proud of possessing, through a happy accident, a locker on the ground-floor very close to the entrance-hall. His junior contemporaries were usually banished to remote corridors in the six-hundreds, waiting eagerly to inherit from departed seniors the more convenient lockers downstairs. But Michael from the day he first heard by the cast of the Laocoön the shuffle of quick feet along the corridor had owned the most convenient locker in all the school. At the last moment Michael thought he would forfeit the half-crown long ago deposited and keep the key, but in the end he, with the rest of his departing contemporaries, callously accepted the more useful half-crown.

School broke up in a sudden heartless confusion, and Michael for the last time stood gossiping outside the school-doors at five o'clock. For a minute he felt an absurd desire to pick up a stone and fling it through the window of the nearest class-room, not from any spirit of indignation, but merely to assure himself of a physical freedom that he had not yet realized.

"Where are you going for the holidays, Bangs?" someone asked.

"Switzerland."

"Hope you'll have a good time. See you next—oh, by Jove, I shan't though. Good-bye, hope you'll have good luck."

"Thanks," said Michael, and he had a fleeting view of himself relegated to the past, one of that scattered host—

Thick as autumnal leaves that strew the brooks

In Vallombrosa—

Old Jacobeans, ghostly, innumerable, whose desks like tombstones would bear for a little while the perishable ink of their own idle epitaphs.

Lucerne was airless; the avenue of pollarded limes sheltered a depressed bulk of dusty tourists; the atmosphere was impregnated with bourgeois exclamations; the very surface of the lake was swarming with humanity, noisy with the click of rowlocks, and with the gutturals that seemed to praise fitly such a theatrical setting.

Mrs. Fane wondered why they had come to Switzerland, but still she asked Michael and Stella whether they would like to venture higher. Michael, perceiving the hordes of Teutonic nomads who were sweeping up into the heart of the mountains, thought that Switzerland in August would be impossible whatever lonely height they gained. They moved to Geneva, whose silverpointed beauty for a while deceived them, but soon both he and Stella became restless and irritable.

"Switzerland is like sitting in a train and travelling through glorious country," said Michael. "It's all right for a journey, but it becomes frightfully tiring. And, mother, I do hate the sensation that all these people round are feeling compelled to enjoy themselves. It's like a hearty choral service."

"It's like an oratorio," said Stella. "I can't play a note here. The very existence of these mobs is deafening."

"Well, I don't mind where we go," said Mrs. Fane. "I'm not enjoying these peculiar tourists myself. Shall we go to the Italian lakes? I used to like them very much. I've spent many happy days there."

"I'd rather go to France," said Michael. "Only don't let's go far. Let's go to Lyons and find out some small place in the country. I was talking to a decent chap—not a tourist—who said there were delightful little red-roofed towns in the Lyonnais."

So they left Switzerland and went to Lyons where, sitting under the shade of trees by the tumbling blue Rhône, they settled with a polite agent to take a small house near Châtillon.

Hither a piano followed them, and here for seven weeks they lived, each one lost in sun-dyed dreams.

"I knew we should like this," Michael said to Stella, as they leaned against tubs of rosy oleanders on a lizard-streaked wall, and watched some great white oxen go smoothly by. "I like this heart of France better than Brittany or Normandy. But I hope mother won't be bored here."

"There are plenty of books," said Stella. "And anyway she wants to lie back and think, and it's impossible to think except in the sun."

The oxen were still in sight along the road that wound upwards to where Châtillon clustered red upon its rounded hill.

"It doesn't look like a real town," said Michael. "It's really not different from the red sunbaked earth all about here. I feel it would be almost a pity ever to walk up that road and find it is a town. I vote we never go quite close, but just sit here and watch it changing colour all through the day. I never want to move out of this garden."

"I can't walk about much," said Stella. "Because I simply must practise and practise and practise and practise."

They always woke up early in the morning, and Michael used to watch Châtillon purple-bloomed with the shadow of the fled night, then hazy crimson for a few minutes until the sun came high enough to give it back the rich burnt reds of the day. All through the morning Michael used to sit among the peach trees of the garden, while Stella played. All through the morning he used to read novel after novel of ephemeral fame that here on the undisturbed shelves had acquired a certain permanence. In the afternoon Stella and he used to wander through the vineyards down to a shallow brown stream bordered by poplars and acacias, or in sun-steeped oak woods idly chase the long lizards splendid with their black and yellow lozenges and shimmering green mail.

Once in a village at harvest-time, when the market-place was a fathom deep in golden corn, they helped in the threshing, and once when the grain had been stored, they danced here with joyful country-folk under the moon.

During tea-time they would sit with their mother beneath an almond tree, while beyond in sunlit air vibrant with the glad cicadas butterflies wantoned with the oleanders, or upon the wall preened their slow fans. Later, they would pace a walk bordered by tawny tea-roses, and out of the globed melons they would scent the garnered warmth of the day floating forth to mingle with the sweet breath of eve. Now was the hour to climb the small hill behind the peach trees. Here across the mighty valley of the Saône they could see a hundred miles away the Alps riding across the horizon, light as clouds. And on the other side over their own little house lay Châtillon cherry-bright in the sunset, then damson-dark for a while, until it turned to a velvet gloom pricked with points of gold and slashed with orange stains.

Michael and Stella always went to bed when the landscape had faded out. But often Michael would sit for a long time and pore upon the rustling, the dark, the moth-haunted night; or if the moon were up he would in fancies swim out upon her buoyant watery sheen.

Sometimes, as he sat among the peach trees, a thought of Lily would come to him; and he would imagine her form swinging round the corner. The leaves and sunlight, while he dreamed of her, dappled the unread pages of his book. He would picture himself with Lily on these sunny uplands of the Lyonnais, and gradually she lost her urban actuality; gradually the disillusionment of her behaviour was forgotten. With the obliteration of Lily's failure the anguish for her bodily form faded out, and Michael began to mould her to an incorporeal idea of first love. In this clear air she stood before him recreated, as if the purifying sun, which was burning him to the likeness of the earth around, had been able at the same time to burn that idea of young love to a slim Etruscan shape which could thrill him for ever with its beauty, but nevermore fret him with the urgency of desire. He was glad he had not spoken to her again after that garden interlude; and though his heart would have leapt to see her motionable and swaying to his glances as she came delicately towards him through the peach trees, Michael felt that somehow he would not kiss her, but that he would rather lead her gravely to the hill-top and set her near him to stay for ever still, for ever young, for ever fair.

So all through that summer the sun burned Michael, while day by day the white unhurried oxen moved, slow as clouds, up the hill towards the town. But Michael never followed their shambling steps, and therefore he never destroyed his dream of Châtillon.

As the time drew nearer and nearer for Stella's concert, she practised more incessantly. Nor would she walk now with Michael through the vineyards down to the shallow poplar-shadowed stream. Michael was seized with a reverence for her tireless concentration, and he never tried to make her break this rule of work, but would always wander away by himself.

One day, when he was lying on a parched upland ridge, Michael had a vision of Alan in green England. Suddenly he realized that in a few weeks they would be setting out together for Oxford. The dazzling azure sky of France lightened to the blown softness of an English April. Cloistral he saw Oxford, and by the base of St. Mary's Tower the people, small as emmets, hurrying. The roofs and spires were wet with rain, and bells were ringing. He saw the faces of all those who from various schools would encounter with him the greyness and the grace of Oxford, and among them was Alan.

How familiar Oxford seemed after all!

The principal fact that struck Michael about Stella in these days of practising for her concert was her capacity for renouncing all extravagance of speech and her steady withdrawal from everything that did not bear directly on her work. She no longer talked of her brilliance; she no longer tried to astonish Michael with predications of genius; she became curiously and impressively diligent, and, without conveying an idea of easy self-confidence, she managed to make Michael feel perfectly sure of her success.

During the latter half of September Michael went to stay with Alan at Richmond, partly because with the nearness of Stella's appearance he began to feel nervous, and partly because he found speculation about Oxford in Alan's company a very diverting pursuit. From Richmond he went up at the end of the month in order to pass Responsions without difficulty. On the sixth of October was the concert at King's Hall.

Michael had spent a good deal of time in sending letters to all the friends he could think of, inviting their attendance on this occasion of importance. He even wrote to Wilmot and many of the people he had met at Edwardes Square. Everyone must help in Stella's triumph.

At the beginning of October Mrs. Ross arrived at the Merivales' house, and for the first time since their conversation in the orchard she and Michael met. He was shy at first, but Mrs. Ross was so plainly anxious to show that she regarded him as affectionately as ever that Michael found himself able to resume his intimacy at once. However, since Stella was always uppermost in his thoughts, he did not test Mrs. Ross with any more surprising admissions.

On the night before the concert Mr. and Mrs. Merivale, Mrs. Ross, Alan and Michael sat in the drawing-room, talking over the concert from every point of view.

"Of course she'll be a success," said Mr. Merivale, and managed to implicate himself as usual in a network of bad puns that demanded the heartiest reprobation from his listeners.

"Dear little girl," said Mrs. Merivale placidly. "How nice it is to see children doing things."

"Of course she'll be a success," Alan vowed. "You've only got to look at her to see that. By gad, what an off-drive she would have had, if she'd only been a boy."

Michael looked at Alan quickly. This was the first time he had ever heard him praise a girl of his own accord. He made up his mind to ask Stella when her concert was over how Alan had impressed her.

"Dear Michael," said Mrs. Ross earnestly, "you must not worry about Stella. Don't you remember how years ago I said she would be a great pianist? And you were so amusing about it, because you would insist that you didn't like her playing."

"Nor I did," said Michael in laughing defence of himself at eight years old. "I used to think it was the most melancholy noise on earth. Sometimes I think so now, when Stella wraps herself up in endless scales. By Jove," he suddenly exclaimed, "what's the time?"

"Half-past eight nearly. Why?" Alan asked.

"I forgot to write and tell Viner to come. It's not very late. I think I'll go over to Notting Hill now, and ask him. I haven't been to see him much lately, and he was always awfully decent to me."

Mr. Viner was reading in his smoke-hung room.

"Hullo," he said. "You've not been near me for almost a year."

"I know," said Michael apologetically. "I feel rather a brute. Some time I'll tell you why."

Then suddenly Michael wondered if the priest knew about Lord Saxby, and he felt shy of him. He felt that he could not talk intimately to him until he had told him about the circumstances of his birth.

"Is that what's been keeping you away?" asked the priest. "Because, let me tell you, I've known all about you for some years. And look here, Michael, don't get into your head that you've got to make this sort of announcement every time you form a new friendship."

"Oh, that wasn't the reason I kept away," said Michael. "But I don't want to talk about myself. I want to talk about my sister. She's going to play at the King's Hall concert to-morrow night. You will come, won't you?"

"Of course I will," said the priest.

"Thanks, and—er—if you could think about her when you're saying Mass to-morrow morning, why, I'd rather like to serve you, if I may. I must tear back now," Michael added. "Good night."

"Good night," said the priest, and as Michael turned in the doorway his smile was like a benediction.

Very early on the next morning through the curdled October mists Michael went over to Notting Hill again. The Mission Church stood obscurely amid a press of mean houses, and as Michael hurried along the fetid narrow thoroughfare, the bell for Mass was clanging among the fog and smoke. Here and there women were belabouring their doorsteps with mangy mats or leaning with grimed elbows on their sills in depressed anticipation of a day's drudgery. From bed-ridden rooms came the sound of children wailing and fighting over breakfast. Lean cats nosed in the garbage strewn along the gutters.

The Mission Church smelt strongly of soap and stale incense, and in the frore atmosphere the coloured pictures on the walls looked more than usually crude and violent. It was the Octave of St. Michael and All Angels, and the white chrysanthemums on the altar were beginning to turn brown. There was not a large congregation—two sisters of mercy, three or four pious and dowdy maiden ladies, and the sacristan. It was more than two years since Michael had served at Mass, and he was glad and grateful to find that every small ceremony still seemed sincere and fit and inevitable. There was an exquisite morning stillness in this small tawdry church, and Michael thought how strange it was that in this festering corner of the city it was possible to create so profound a sense of mystery. Whatever emotion he gained of peace and reconciliation and brooding holiness he vowed to Stella and to her fame and to her joy.

After Mass Michael went back to breakfast with Mr. Viner, and as they sat talking about Oxford, Michael thought how various Oxford was compared with school, how many different kinds of people would be appropriate to their surroundings, and he began with some of the ardour that he had given hitherto to envy of life to covet all varieties of intellectual experience. What a wonderfully suggestive word was University, and how exciting it was to see Viner tabulating introductions for his benefit.

Michael sat by himself at the concert. During the afternoon he had talked to Stella for a few minutes, but she had seemed more than ever immeasurably remote from conversation, and Michael had contented himself with offering stock phrases of encouragement and exhortation. He went early to King's Hall and sat high up in the topmost corner looking down on the orchestra. Gradually through the bluish mist the indefinite audience thickened, and their accumulated voices echoed less and less. The members of the orchestra had not yet entered, but their music-stands stood about with a ridiculous likeness to human beings. In the middle was Stella's piano black and lifeless, a little ominous in its naked and insistent and faintly shining ebon solemnity. One of the orchestra threaded his way through the chairs to where the drums stood in a bizarre group. From time to time this lonely human figure struck his instruments to test their pitch, and the low boom sounded hollowly above the murmurous audience.

A general accession of light took place, and now suddenly the empty platform was filled with nonchalant men who gossiped while they made discordant sounds upon their instruments. The conductor came in and bowed. The audience clapped. There was a momentary hush, followed by a sharp rat-tat of the baton, and the Third Leonora Overture began.

To Michael the music was a blur. It was soundless beside his own beating heart, his heart that thudded on and on, on and on, while the faces of the audience receded farther and farther through the increasing haze. The Overture was finished. From the hall that every moment seemed to grow darker came a sound of ghostly applause. Michael looked at his programme in a fever. What was this unpronounceable German composition, this Tonic Poem that must be played before Stella's turn would arrive? It seemed to go on for ever in a most barbaric and amorphous din; with corybantic crashings, with brazen fanfares and stinging cymbals it flung itself against the audience, while the woodwind howled and the violins were harsh as cats. Michael brooded unreceptive; he had a sense of monstrous loneliness; he could think of nothing. The noise overpowered his beating heart, and he began to count absurdly, while he bit his nails or shivered in alternations of fire and snow. Then his programme fluttered down on to the head of a bald violoncellist, and the ensuing shock of self-consciousness, that was mingled with a violent desire to laugh very loudly, restored him to his normal calm. The Tonic Poem shrieked and tore itself to death. The world became very quiet.

There was a gradual flap of rising applause, and it was Stella who, tall and white, was being handed across the platform. It was Stella who was sitting white and rigid at the black piano that suddenly seemed to have shrunk into a puny insignificance. It was Stella whose fingers were causing those rills of melody to flow. She paused, while the orchestra took up their part, and then again the rills began to flow, gently, fiercely, madly, sadly, wildly. Now she seemed to contend against the mighty odds of innumerable rival instruments; now her own frail instrument seemed to flag; now she was gaining strength; her cool clear harmonies were subduing this welter of violins, this tempest of horns and clarionets, this menace of bass-viols and drums. The audience was extinguished like a candle. The orchestra seemed inspired by the angry forces of Nature herself. The bows of the violins whitened and flickered like willows in a storm, and yet amid this almost intolerable movement Stella sat still as a figure of eternal stone. A faint smile curved more sharply her lips; the black bows in her hair trembled against her white dress; her wonderful hands went galloping away to right and left of her straight back. Plangent as music itself, serene as sculpture, with smiling lips magically crimson, adorably human, she finished her first concerto. And while she bowed to the audience and to the orchestra and the great shaggy conductor, Michael saw ridiculous teardrops bedewing his sleeve, not because he had been moved by the music, but because he was unable to shake by the hand every single person in King's Hall who was now applauding his sister.

It was not until Beethoven's somber knock at the opening of the Fifth Symphony that Michael began to dream upon the deeps of great music, that his thoughts liberated from anxiety went straying into time. Stella, when for a little while he had reveled in her success, was forgotten, and the people in this hall, listening, listening, began to move him with their unimaginable variety. Near him were lovers who in this symphony were fast imparadised; their hands were interlaced; visibly they swayed nearer to each other on the waves of melody. Old men were near him, solitary old men listening, listening ... old men who at the summons of these ringing notes were traversing their past that otherwise might have stayed forever unvoyageable.

Michael sometimes craved for Lily's company, wished that he could clasp her to him and swoon away upon these blinding chords. But she was banished from this world of music, she who had betrayed the beauty of love. There was something more noble in this music than the memory of a slim and lovely girl and of her flower-soft kisses. The world itself surely seemed to travel the faster for this urgent symphony. Michael was spinning face to face with the spinning stars.

And then some thread of simple melody would bring him back to the green world and the little memories of his boyhood. Now more than ever did it seem worth while to live on earth. He recognized, as if suddenly he had come down from incredible heights, familiar faces in the audience. He saw his mother with Mrs. Ross beside her, two figures that amid all this intoxication of speeding life must forever mourn. Now while the flood of music was sounding in his ears, he wished that he could fly down through this dim hall, and tell them, as they sat there in black with memories beside them, how well he loved them, how much he honoured them, how eagerly he demanded from them pride in himself.

After the first emotions of the mighty music had worn themselves out, Michael's imagination began to wander rapidly. At one point the bassoons became very active, and he was somehow reminded of Mr. Neech. He was puzzled for awhile to account for this association of an old form-master with the noise of bassoons. '*For he heard the loud bassoon.*' Out of the past came the vision of old Neech wagging the tail of his gown as he strode backward and forwards over the floor of the Shell class-room. '*The Wedding-Guest here beat his breast, For he heard the loud bassoon.*' Out of the past came the shrill sound of boys ruining The Ancient Mariner, and Michael heard again the outraged apostrophes of Mr. Neech. He began to create from his fancy of Mr. Neech a grotesque symbol of public-school education. Certainly he was the only master who had taught him anything. Yet he had probably tried less earnestly to teach than any other masters. Why did this image of Mr. Neech materialize whenever his thoughts went back to school? Years had passed since he had enjoyed the Shell. He had never talked intimately to Neech; indeed, he had scarcely held any communication with him since he left his form. The influence of Neech must have depended on a personality that demanded from his pupils a stoic bearing, a sense of humour, a capacity for inquisitiveness, an idea of continuity. He could not remember that any of these qualities had been appreciated by himself until he had entered the Shell. Michael regretted very deeply that on the day before he left school he had not thanked Neech for his existence. How nebulous already most of his other masters seemed. Only Neech stood out clear-cut as the intagliation of a sardonyx.

Meditation upon Neech took Michael off to Thackeray. He had been reading Pendennis lately, and the book had given him much the same sensation of finality as his old form-master, and as Michael thought of Thackeray, he began to speculate upon the difference between Michael Fane and the fourteenth Earl of Saxby. Yet he was rather glad that after all he was not the fourteenth Earl of Saxby. It would be interesting to see how his theories of good-breeding were carried out by himself as a nobody with old blood in his veins. He would like to test the common talk that rank was an accident, that old families, old faiths, old education, old customs, old manners, old thoughts, old books were all so much moonshine. Michael wondered whether it were so; whether indeed all men if born with equal chances would not display equal qualities. He did not believe it: he hated the doctrine. Yet people in all their variety called to him still, and as he surveyed the audience he was aware from time to time of a great longing to involve himself in the web of humanity. He was glad that he had not removed himself from the world like Chator. Chator! He must go down to Clere and see how Chator was getting on as a monk. He had not even thought of Chator for a year. But after all Oxford had a monastic intention, and Michael believed that from Oxford he would gain as much austerity of attitude as Chator would acquire from the rule of St. Benedict. And when he left Oxford, he would explore humanity. He would travel through the world and through the underworld and apply always his standard of ... of what? What was his standard? A classic permanence, a classic simplicity and inevitableness?

The symphony stopped. He must hurry out and congratulate Stella. What a possession she was; what an excitement her career would be. How he would love to control her extravagance, and even as he controlled it, how he would admire it. And his mother had talked of taking a house in Chelsea. What various interests were springing into existence. He must not forget to ask Alan what train he was going by to Oxford. They must arrive together. He had not yet bought his china. His china! His pictures! His books! His rooms in college! Life was really astonishing.

The concert was over, and as Michael came swirling down the stairs on the flood of people going home, he had a strange sensation of life beginning all over again.

THE END OF THE
FIRST VOLUME

Volume II

CHAPTER I

THE FIRST DAY

Michael felt glad to think he would start the adventure of Oxford from Paddington. The simplicity of that railway station might faintly mitigate alarms which no amount of previous deliberation could entirely disperse. He remembered how once he had lightly seen off a Cambridge friend from Liverpool Street and, looking back at the suburban tumult of the Great Eastern Railway, he was grateful for the simplicity of Paddington.

Michael had been careful that all his heavy luggage should be sent in advance; and he had shown himself gravely exacting toward Alan in this matter of luggage, writing several times to remind him of his promise not to appear on the platform with more than a portmanteau of moderate size and a normal kit-bag. Michael hoped this precaution would prevent at any rate the porters from commenting upon the freshness of him and his friend.

"Oxford train?" inquired a porter, as the hansom pulled up. Michael nodded, and made up his mind to show his esteem when he tipped this promethean.

"Third class?" the porter went on. Michael mentally doubled the tip, for he had neglected to assure himself beforehand about the etiquette of class, and nothing could have suited so well his self-consciousness as this information casually yielded.

"Let me see, you didn't have any golf-clubs, did you, sir?" asked the porter.

Michael shook his head regretfully, for as he looked hurriedly up and down the platform in search of Alan, he perceived golf-clubs everywhere, and when at last he saw him, actually even he had a golf-bag slung over his shoulder.

"I never knew you played golf," said Michael indignantly.

"I don't. These are the governor's. He's given up playing," Alan explained.

"Are you going to play?" Michael pursued. He was feeling rather envious of the appearance of these veteran implements.

"I may have a shot," Alan admitted.

"You might have told me you were going to bring them," Michael grumbled.

"My dear old ass, I never knew I was, until the governor wanged them into my lap just as I was starting."

Michael turned aside and bought a number of papers, far too many for the short journey. Indeed, all the way they lay on the rack unregarded, while the train crossed and recrossed the silver Thames. At first he was often conscious of the other undergraduates in the compartment, who seemed to be eying him with a puzzled contempt; but very soon, when he perceived that this manner of looking at one's neighbor was general, he became reconciled to the attitude and ascribed it to a habit of mind rather than to the expression of any individual distaste. Then suddenly, as Michael was gazing out of the window, the pearly sky broke into spires and pinnacles and domes and towers. He caught his breath for one bewitched moment, before he busied himself with the luggage on the rack.

On the platform Michael and Alan decided to part company, as neither of them felt sure enough whether St. Mary's or Christ Church were nearer to the station to risk a joint hansom.

"Shall I come and see you this afternoon?" Michael rashly offered.

"Oh, rather," Alan agreed, and they turned away from one another to secure their cabs.

All the time that Michael was driving to St. Mary's, he was regretting he had not urged Alan to visit him first. A growing sensation of shy dread was making him vow that once safe in his own rooms at St. Mary's nothing should drag him forth again that day. What on earth would he say when he arrived at the college? Would he have to announce himself? How would he find his rooms? On these points he had pestered several Old Jacobeans now at Oxford, but none of them could remember the precise ceremonies of arrival. Michael leaned back in the hansom and cursed their inefficient memories.

Then the cab pulled up by the St. Mary's lodge, and events proceeded with unexpected rapidity. A cheerful man with red hair and a round face welcomed his luggage. The cabman was paid the double of his correct fare, and to Michael's relief drove off instantly. From a sort of glass case that filled half the interior of the lodge somebody very much like a family butler inquired richly who Michael was.

"Mr. C. M. S. Fane?" rolled out the unctuous man.

Michael nodded.

"Is there another Fane?" he asked curiously.

"No, sir," said the head porter, and the negative came out with the sound of a drawn cork. "No, sir, but I wished to hessateen if I had your initials down correct in my list. Mr. C. M. S. Fane," he went on, looking at a piece of paper. "St. Cuthbert's. Four. Two pair right. Your servant is Porcher. Your luggage has arrived, and perhaps you'll settle with me presently. Henry will show you to your rooms. Henry! St. Cuthbert's. Four. Two pair right."

The red-headed under-porter picked up Michael's bag, and Michael was preparing to follow him at once, when the unctuous man held up a warning hand. Then he turned to look into a large square pigeon-hole labeled Porcher.

"These letters are for you, sir," he explained pompously. Michael took them, and in a dream followed Henry under a great gothic gateway, and along a gravel path. In a doorway numbered IV, Henry stopped and shouted "Porcher!" From an echoing vault came a cry in answer, and the scout appeared.

"One of your gentlemen arrived," said Henry. "Mr. Fane." Then he touched his cap and retired.

"Any more luggage in the lodge, sir?" Porcher asked.

"Not much," said Michael apologetically.

"There's a nice lot of stuff in your rooms," Porcher informed him. "Come in yesterday morning, it did."

They were mounting the stone stairway, and on each of the floors Michael was made mechanically aware by a printed notice above a water-tap that no slops must be emptied there. This prohibition stuck in his mind somehow as the first ascetic demand of the university.

"These are your rooms, sir, and when you want me, you'll shout, of course. I'm just unpacking Mr. Lonsdale's wine."

Michael was conscious of pale October sunlight upon the heaped-up packing-cases; he was conscious of the unnatural brilliancy of the fire in the sunlight; he was conscious that life at Oxford was conducted with much finer amenities than life at school. Simultaneously he was aware of a loneliness; yet as he once more turned to survey his room, it was a fleeting loneliness which quickly perished in the satisfaction of a privacy that hitherto he had never possessed. He turned into the bedroom, and looked out across the quad, across the rectangle of vivid green grass, across the Warden's garden with its faint gaiety of autumnal flowers and tufted gray walls, and beyond to where the elms of the deer-park were massed against the thin sky and the deer moved in leisurely files about the spare sunlight.

It did not take Michael long to arrange his clothes; and then the problem of undoing the packing-cases presented itself. A hammer would be necessary, and a chisel. He must shout for Porcher. Shouting in the tremulous peace of this October morning would inevitably attract more attention to himself than would be pleasant, and he postponed the summons in favor of an examination of his letters. One after another he opened them, and every one was the advertisement of a tailor or hairdresser or tobacconist. The tailors were the most insistent; they even went so far as to announce that representatives would call upon him at his pleasure. Michael made up his mind to order his cap and gown after lunch. Lunch! How should he obtain lunch? Where should he obtain lunch? When should he obtain lunch? Obviously there must be some precise manner of obtaining lunch, some ritual consecrated by generations of St. Mary's men. The loneliness came back triumphant, and plunged him dejectedly down into a surprisingly deep wicker-chair. The fire crackled in the silence, and the problem of lunch remained insoluble. The need for Porcher's advice became more desperate. Other freshmen before him must have depended upon their scout's experience. He began to practice calling Porcher in accents so low that they acquired a tender and reproachful significance. Michael braced himself for the performance after these choked and muffled rehearsals, and went boldly out on to the stone landing. An almost entranced silence held the staircase, a silence that he could not bring himself to violate. On the door of the rooms opposite he read his neighbor's name—*Mackintosh*. He wished he knew whether Mackintosh were a freshman. It would be delightful to make him share the responsibility of summoning Porcher from his task of arranging Lonsdale's wine. And who was Lonsdale? *No slops must be emptied here! Mackintosh! Fane!* Here were three announcements hinting at humanity in a desolation of stillness. Michael reading his own name gathered confidence and a volume of breath, leaned over the stone parapet of the landing and, losing all his courage in a sigh, decided to walk downstairs and take his chance of meeting Porcher on the way.

On the floor beneath Michael read *Bannerman* over the left-hand door and *Templeton-Collins* over the right-hand door. While he was pondering the personality and status of Templeton-Collins, presumably the gentleman himself appeared, stared at Michael very deliberately, came forward and, leaning over the parapet, yelled in a voice that combined rage, protest, disappointment and appeal with the maximum of sound: "Porcher!" After which, Templeton-Collins again stared very deliberately at Michael and retired into his room, while Michael hurried down to intercept the scout, hoping his dismay at Templeton-Collins' impatience would not be too great to allow him to pay a moment's attention to himself.

However, on the ground floor the silence was still unbroken, and hopelessly Michael read over the right-hand door *Amherst*, over the left-hand door *Lonsdale*. What critical moment had arrived in the unpacking of Lonsdale's wine to make the scout so heedless of Templeton-Collins' call? Again it resounded from above, and Michael looking up involuntarily, caught the downward glance of Templeton-Collins himself.

"I say, is Porcher down there?" the latter asked fretfully.

"I think he's unpacking Lonsdale's wine."

"Who's Lonsdale?" demanded Templeton-Collins. "You might sing out and tell him I want him."

With this request Templeton-Collins vanished, leaving Michael in a quandary. There was only one hope of relieving the intolerable situation, he thought, which was to shout "Porcher" from where he was standing. This he did at the very moment the scout emerged from Lonsdale's rooms.

"Coming, sir," said Porcher in an aggrieved voice.

"I think Mr. Templeton-Collins is calling you," Michael explained, rather lamely he felt, since it must have been obvious to the scout that Michael himself had been calling him.

"And I say," he added hurriedly, "you might bring me up a hammer or something to open my boxes, when you've done."

Leaving Porcher to appease the outraged Templeton-Collins, Michael retreated to the security of his own rooms, where in a few minutes the scout appeared to raise the question of lunch.

"Will you take commons, sir?"

Michael looked perplexed.

"Commons is bread and cheese. Most of my gentlemen takes commons. If you want anything extra, you go to the kitchen and write your name down for what you want."

This sounded too difficult, and Michael gratefully chose commons.

"Ale, sir?"

Michael nodded. If the scout had suggested champagne, he would have assented immediately.

Porcher set to work and undid the cases; he also explained where the china was kept and the wood and the coal. He expounded the theory of roll-calls and chapels, and was indeed so generous with information on every point of college existence that Michael would have been glad to retain his services for the afternoon.

"And the other men on this staircase?" Michael asked, "are any of them freshers?"

"Mr. Mackintosh, Mr. Amherst, and the Honorable Lonsdale is all freshmen. Mr. Templeton-Collins and Mr. Bannerman is second year. Mr. Templeton-Collins had the rooms on the ground floor last term. Very noisy gentleman. Very fond of practicing with a coach-horn. And he don't improve," said Porcher meditatively.

"Do you mean on the coach-horn?" Michael asked.

"Don't improve in the way of noise. Noise seems to regular delight him. He'd shout the head off of a deaf man. Did you bring any wine, sir?"

Michael shook his head.

"Mr. Lonsdale brought too much. Too much. It's easier to order it as you want it from the Junior Common Room. Anything else, sir?"

Michael tried to think of something to detain for a while the voluble service of Porcher, but as he seemed anxious to be gone, he confessed there was nothing.

Left alone again, Michael began to unpack his pictures. Somehow those black and red scenes of Montmartre and the landscapes of the Sussex downs with a slight atmosphere of Japan seemed to him unsatisfactory in this new room, and he hung them forthwith in his bedroom. For his sitting-room he resolved to buy certain pictures that for a long time he had coveted—Mona Lisa and Primavera and Rembrandt's Knight in Armor and Montegna's St. George. Those other relics of faded and jejune aspirations would label him too definitely. People would see them hanging on his walls and consider him a decadent. Michael did not wish to be labeled in his first term. Oxford promised too much of intellectual romance and adventure for him to set out upon his Odyssey with the stepping-stones of dead tastes hung round his neck. Oxford should be approached with a stainless curiosity. Already he felt that she would only yield her secret in return for absolute surrender. This the grave city demanded.

After his pictures Michael unpacked his books. The deep shelves set in the wall beside the fireplace looked alluring in their emptiness, but when he had set out in line all the books he possessed, they seemed a scanty and undistinguished crowd. The pirated American edition of Swinburne alone carried itself with an air: the Shelley and the Keats were really editions better suited to the glass and gloom of a seaside lodging: the school-books looked like trippers usurping the gothic grandeur of these shelves. Moreover, the space was eked out with tattered paper editions that with too much room at their disposal collapsed with an appearance of ill-favored intoxication. Michael examined his possessions in critical discontent. They seemed to symbolize the unpleasant crudity of youth. In the familiar surroundings of childhood they had seemed on the contrary to testify to his maturity. Now at Oxford he felt most abominably young again, yet he was able to console himself with the thought that youth would be no handicap among his peers. He took down the scenes of Montmartre even from the walls of his bedroom and pushed them ignominiously out of sight under the bed.

Michael abandoned the contemplation of his possessions, and looked out of his sitting-room window at the High. There was something salutary in the jangle of the trams, in the vision of ordinary people moving unconsciously about the academic magnificence of Oxford. An undergraduate with gown wrapped carelessly round his neck flashed past on a bicycle, and Michael was discouraged by the sense of his diabolic ease. The luxury of his own rooms, the conviction of his new independence, the excitement of an undiscovered life all departed from him, and he was left with nothing but a loneliness more bitter even than when at Randell House he had first encountered school.

Porcher came in presently with lunch, and the commons of bread and cheese with the ale foaming in a silver tankard added the final touch to Michael's depression. He thought that nothing in the world, could express the spirit of loneliness so perfectly as a sparse lunch laid for one on a large table. He wandered away from its melancholy invitation into the bedroom and looked sadly down into the quad. In every doorway stood knots of senior men talking: continually came new arrivals to hail familiarly their friends after the vacation: scouts hurried to and fro with trays of food: from window to window gossip, greetings, appointments were merrily shouted. Michael watched this scene of intimate movement played against the background of elms and gray walls. The golden fume of the October weather transcended somehow all impermanence, and he felt with a sudden springing of imagination that so had this scene been played before, that so forever would it be played for generations to come. Yet for him as yet outside the picture remained, fortunately less eternal, that solitary lunch. He ate it hurriedly and as soon as he had finished set out to find Alan at Christ Church.

Freedom came back with the elation of walking up the High; and in the Christ Church lodge Michael was able to ask without a blush for Alan's rooms. The great space of Tom quad by absorbing his self-consciousness allowed him to feel himself an unit of the small and decorative population that enhanced the architecture there. The scattered, groups of friends whose voices became part of the very air itself like the wings of the pigeons and the perpetual tapping of footsteps, the two dons treading in slow confabulation that wide flagged terrace, even himself were here forever. Michael captured again in that moment the crystallized vision of Oxford which had first been vouchsafed to him long ago by that old print of St. Mary's tower. He turned reluctantly away from Tom quad, and going on to seek Alan in Meadows, by mistake found himself in Peckwater. A tall fair undergraduate was standing alone in the center of the quad, cracking a whip. Suddenly Michael realized that his father had been at Christ Church; and this tall fair whip-cracker served for him as the symbol of his father. He must have often stood here so, cracking a whip; and Michael never came into Peckwater without recreating him so occupied on a fine autumn afternoon, whip in hand, very tall and very fair in the glinting sunlight.

143

Dreams faded out, when Michael ran up the staircase to Alan's rooms; but he was full-charged again with all that suppressed intellectual excitement which he had counted upon finding in Oxford, but which he had failed to find until the wide tranquillity of Tom quad had given him, as it were, the benediction of the University.

"Hullo, Alan!" he cried. "How are you getting on? I say, why do they stick 'Mr.' in front of your name over the door? At St. Mary's we drop the 'Mr.' or any other sort of title. Aren't you unpacked *yet?* You are a slacker. Look here, I want you to come out with me at once. I've got to get some more picture-wire and a gown and a picture of Mona Lisa."

"Mona how much?" said Alan.

"La Gioconda, you ass."

"Sorry, my mistake," said Alan.

"And I saw some rattling book-shops as I came up the High," Michael went on. "What did you have for lunch? I had bread and cheese—commons we call it at St. Mary's. I say, I think I'm glad I don't have to wear a scholar's gown."

"I'm an exhibitioner," said Alan.

"Well, it's the same thing. I like a commoner's gown best. Where did you get that tea-caddy? I don't believe I've got one. Pretty good view from your window. Mine looks out on the High."

"Look here," asked Alan very solemnly, "where shall I hang this picture my mater gave me?"

He displayed in a green frame The Soul's Awakening.

"Do you like it?" Michael asked gloomily.

"I prefer these grouse by Thorburn that the governor gave me, but I like them both in a way," Alan admitted.

"I don't think it much matters where you hang it," Michael said. Then, thinking Alan looked rather hurt, he added hastily: "You see it's such a very square room that practically it might go anywhere."

"Will you have a meringue?" Alan asked, proffering a crowded plate.

"A meringue?" Michael repeated.

"We're rather famous for our meringues here," said Alan gravely. "We make them in the kitchen. I ordered a double lot in case you came in."

"You seem to have found out a good deal about Christ Church already," Michael observed.

"The House," Alan corrected. "We call it—in fact everybody calls it the House."

Michael was inclined to resent this arrogation by a college not his own of a distinct and slightly affected piece of nomenclature, and he wished he possessed enough knowledge of his own peculiar college customs to counter Alan's display.

"Well, hurry up and come out of the House," he urged. "You can't stay here unpacking all the afternoon."

"Why do you want to start buying things straight away?" Alan argued.

"Because I know what I want," Michael insisted.

"Since when?" Alan demanded. "I'm not going to buy anything for a bit."

"Come on, come on," Michael urged. He was in a hurry to enjoy the luxury of traversing the quads of Christ Church in company, of strolling down the High in company, of looking into shop windows in company, of finally defeating that first dismal loneliness with Alan and his company.

It certainly proved to be a lavish afternoon. Michael bought three straight-grained pipes so substantially silvered that they made his own old pipes take on an attenuated vulgarity. He bought an obese tobacco jar blazoned with the arms of his college and, similarly blazoned, a protuberant utensil for matches. He bought numerous ounces of those prodigally displayed mixtures of tobacco, every one of which was vouched for by the vendor as in its own way the perfect blend. He bought his cap and his gown and was measured by the tailor for a coat of Harris tweed such as everybody seemed to wear. He found the very autotype of Mona Lisa he coveted, and farther he was persuaded by the picture-dealer to buy for two guineas a signed proof of a small copperplate engraving of the Primavera. This expenditure frightened him from buying any more pictures that afternoon and seemed a violent and sudden extravagance. However, he paid a visit to the Bank where, after signing his name several times, he was presented with a check book. In order to be perfectly sure he knew how to draw a check, he wrote one then and there, and the five sovereigns the clerk shoveled out as irreverently as if they were chocolate creams, made him feel that his new check-book was the purse of Fortunatus.

Michael quickly recovered from the slight feeling of guilt that the purchase of the Botticelli print had laid upon his conscience, and in order to assert his independence in the face of Alan's continuous dissuasion, he bought a hookah, a miniature five-barred gate for a pipe-rack, a mother-of-pearl cigarette-holder which he dropped on the pavement outside the shop and broke in pieces, and finally seven ties of knitted silk.

By this time Michael and Alan had reached the Oriental Café in Cornmarket Street; and since it was now five o'clock and neither of them felt inclined to accept the responsibility of inviting the other back to tea, they went into the café and ate a quantity of hot buttered toast and parti-colored cakes. The only thing that marred their enjoyment and faintly disturbed their equanimity was the entrance of three exquisitely untidy undergraduates who stood for a moment in the doorway and surveyed first the crowded café in general, and then more particularly Michael and Alan with an expression of outraged contempt. After a prolonged stare one of them exclaimed in throaty scorn:

"Oh, god, the place is chock full of damned freshers!"

Whereupon he and his companions strode out again.

Michael and Alan looked at each other abashed. The flavor had departed from the tea: the brilliant hues of the cakes had paled: the waitress seemed to have become suddenly critical and haughty. Michael and Alan paid their bill and went out.

"Are you coming back to my rooms?" Michael asked. Yet secretly he half hoped that Alan would refuse. Dusk was falling, and he was anxious to be alone while the twilight wound itself about this gray city.

Alan said he wanted to finish unpacking, and Michael left him quickly, promising to meet him again to-morrow.

Michael did not wander far in that dusk of fading spires and towers, for a bookshop glowing like a jewel in the gloom of an ancient street lured him within. It was empty save for the owner, a low-voiced man with a thin pointed beard who as he stood there among his books seemed to Michael strangely in tune with his romantic surroundings, as much in tune as some old painting by Vandyck would have seemed leaning against the shelves of books.

A little wearily, almost cynically, Mr. Lampard bade Michael good evening.

"May I look round?" Michael asked.

The bookseller nodded.

"Just come up?" he inquired.

"To-day," Michael confessed.

"And what sort of books are you interested in?"

"All books," said Michael.

"This set of Pater for instance," the bookseller suggested, handing Michael a volume bound in thick sea-green cloth and richly stamped with a golden monogram. "Nine volumes. Seven pounds ten, or six pounds fifteen cash." This information he added in a note of disdainful tolerance.

Michael shook his head and looked amused by the offer.

"Of course, nobody really cares for books nowadays," Mr. Lampard went on. "In the early 'nineties it was different. Then everybody cared for books."

Michael resented this slur upon the generation to which he belonged.

"Seven pounds ten," he repeated doubtfully. How well those solid sea-green volumes would become the stately bookshelves of his room.

"What college?" asked Mr. Lampard. "St. Mary's? Ah, there used to be some great buyers there. Let me see, Lord William Vaughan, the Marquis of Montgomery's son, was at St. Mary's, and Mr. Richard Meysey. I published his first volume of poems—of course, you've read his books. He was at St. Mary's. Then there was Mr. Chalfont and Mr. Weymouth. You've heard of The Patchbox? I still have some copies of the first number, but they're getting very scarce. All St. Mary's men and all great book buyers. But Oxford has changed in the last few years. I really don't know why I go on selling books, or rather why I go on not selling them."

Mr. Lampard laughed and twisted his beard with fingers that were very thin and white. Outside in the darkness a footfall echoed along some entry. The sound gave to Michael a sense of communion with the past, and the ghosts of bygone loiterers were at his elbow.

"Perhaps after all I will take the Pater," he said. "Only I may not be able to pay you this term."

The bookseller smiled.

"I don't think I shall worry you. Do you know this set—Boccaccio, Rabelais, Straparola, Masuccio, etc. Eleven guineas bound in watered silk. They'll always keep their price, and of course all the photogravures are included."

"All right. You might send them too."

Michael could not resist the swish of the watered silk as Volume One of the Decameron was put back into its vacancy. And as he hurried down to College the thought that he had spent nineteen pounds one shilling scarcely weighed against the imagination of lamplight making luminous those silken backs of faded blue and green and red and gold, against those silk markers and the consciousness that now at last he was a buyer of books, a buyer whose spirit would haunt that bookshop. He had certainly never regretted the seventeen-and-sixpence he had spent on the pirated works of Swinburne, and then he was a wretched schoolboy balanced on the top of a ladder covetous of unattainable splendors, a pitiable cipher in the accounts of Elson's bookshop. At Lampard's he was already a personality.

All that so far happened to Michael not merely in one day at Oxford, but really during his whole life was for its embarrassment nothing in comparison with the first dinner in hall. As he walked through the Cloisters and heard all about him the burble of jolly and familiar conversation, he shuddered to think what in a minute he must face. The list of freshmen, pinned up on the board in the Lodge, was a discouraging document to those isolated members of public schools other, than Eton, Winchester, Harrow or Charterhouse. These four seemed to have produced all but six or seven of the freshmen. Eton alone was responsible for half the list. What chance, thought Michael, could he stand against such an impenetrable phalanx of conversation as was bound to ensue from such a preponderance? However, he was by now at the top of the steps that led up to hall, and a mild old butler was asking his name.

"You'll be at the second freshmen's table. On the right, sir. Mr. Wedderburn is at the head of your table, sir."

Michael was glad to find his table at the near end of hall, and hurriedly taking his seat, almost dived into the soup that was quickly placed before him. He did not venture to open a conversation with either of his neighbors, but stared instead at the freshman occupying the armchair at the head of the table, greatly impressed by his judicial gravity of demeanor, his neat bulk and the profundity of his voice.

"How do you become head of a table?" Michael's left-hand neighbor suddenly asked.

Michael said he really did not know.

"Because what I'm wondering," the left-hand neighbor continued, "is why they've made that ass Wedderburn head of our table."

"Why, is he an ass?" Michael inquired.

"Frightful ass," continued the left-hand neighbor, whom Michael perceived to be a small round-faced youth, very fair and very pink. "Perfectly harmless, of course. Are you an Harrovian?"

Michael shook his head.

"I thought you were a cousin of my mother," said the left-hand neighbor.

Michael looked astonished.

"His name's Mackintosh. What's your name?"

Michael told him.

"My name's Lonsdale. I think we're on the same staircase—so's Mackintosh. It's a pity he's an Harrovian, but I promised my mother I'd look him up."

Then, after surveying the table, Lonsdale went on in a confidential undertone:

"I don't mind telling you that the Etonians up here are a pretty poor lot. There are two chaps from my house who are not so bad—in fact rather good eggs—but the rest! Well, look at that ass Wedderburn. He's typical."

"I think he looks rather a good sort," said Michael.

"My dear chap, he was absolutely barred. M' tutor used to like him, but really—well—I don't mind telling you, he's really an æsthete."

With this shocked condemnation, Lonsdale turned to his other neighbor and said in his jerky and somewhat mincing voice that was perfectly audible to Michael:

"I say, Tommy, this man on my right isn't half bad. I don't know where he comes from, His name's Fane."

"He's from St. James'."

"Where on earth's that?"

"London."

"Why, I thought it was a kind of charity school," said Lonsdale. Then he turned to Michael again:

"I say, are you really from St. James'?"

Michael replied coldly that he was.

"I say, come and have coffee with me after hall. One or two O. E.'s are coming in, but you won't mind?"

"Why, do you want to find out something about St. James'?" demanded Michael, frowning.

"Oh, I say, don't be ratty. It's that ass Tommy. He always talks at the top of his voice."

Lonsdale, as he spoke, looked so charmingly apologetic and displayed such accomplished sang-froid that Michael forgave him immediately and promised to come to coffee.

"Good egg!" Lonsdale exclaimed with the satisfaction of having smoothed over an awkward place. "I say," he offered, "if you'd like to meet Wedderburn, I'll ask him, too. He seems to have improved since he's been up at the Varsity. Don't you think that fat man Wedderburn has improved, Tommy?"

Tommy nodded.

"One day's done him no end of good."

"I say," Lonsdale offered, "you haven't met Fane. Mr. Fane—Mr. Grainger. I was just saying to Fane that the Etonians are a rotten lot this term."

"One or two are all right," Grainger admitted with evident reluctance.

"Well, perhaps two," Lonsdale agreed. "This dinner isn't bad, what?"

By this time the conversation at the table had become more general, and Michael gradually realized that some of the alarm he had felt himself had certainly been felt by his companions. Now at any rate there was a perceptible relaxation of tension. Still the conversation was only general in so much as that whenever anybody spoke, the rest of the table listened. The moment the flow of his information dried up, somebody else began pumping forth instruction. These slightly nervous little lectures were delivered without any claim to authority and they came up prefaced by the third person of legendary narrative.

"They say we shall all have to interview the Warden to-morrow."

"They say on Sunday afternoon the Wagger makes the same speech to the freshers that he's made for twenty years."

"They say we ought to go head of the river this year."

"They say the freshers are expected to make a bonner on Sunday night."

"They say any one can have commons of bread and cheese by sending out word to the buttery. It's really included in the two-and-fourpence for dinner."

"They say they charge a penny for the napkin every night."

So the information proceeded, and Michael had just thought to himself that going up to Oxford was very much like going to school again, when from the second-year tables crashed the sound of a concerted sneeze. The dons from high table looked coldly down the hall, expressing a vague, but seemingly impotent disapproval, for immediately afterward that sternutation shook the air a second time.

Michael thought the difference between school and Oxford might be greater than he had supposed.

The slowest eater at the second freshmen's table had nervously left half his savory; Wedderburn without apparent embarrassment had received the Sub-Warden's permission to rise from dinner; Lonsdale hurriedly marshaled as many of his acquaintances as he could, and in a large and noisy group they swarmed through the moonlight toward his rooms.

Michael was interested by Lonsdale's sitting-room, for he divined at once that it was typical, just a transplanted Eton study with the addition of smoking paraphernalia. The overmantel was plumed with small photographs of pleasant young creatures in the gay nautical costumes of the Fourth of June and festooned hats of Alexandra or Monarch, of the same pleasant young creatures at an earlier and chubbier age, of the same pleasant young creatures with penciled mustaches and the white waistcoat of Pop. In addition to their individual commemorations the pleasant young creatures would appear again in house groups, in winning house elevens, and most exquisitely of all in Eton Society. Michael always admired the photographs of Pop, for they seemed to him to epitomize all the traditions of all the public-schools of England, to epitomize them moreover with something of that immortality of captured action expressed by great Athenian sculpture. In comparison with Pop the Harrow Philathletic Society was a barbarous group, with all the self-consciousness of a deliberate archaism. Besides the personal photographs in Lonsdale's room there were studies of grouse by Thorburn; and Michael, remembering Alan's grouse, felt in accord with Lonsdale and with all that Lonsdale stood for. Knowing Alan, he felt that he knew Lonsdale, and at once he became more at ease with all his contemporaries in Lonsdale's room. Michael looked at the colored prints of Cecil Aldin's pictures and made up his mind he would buy a set for Alan: also possibly he would buy for Alan the Sir Galahad of Watts which was rather better than The Soul's Awakening.

After Lonsdale's pictures Michael surveyed Lonsdale's books, the brilliantly red volumes of Jorrocks, the two or three odd volumes of the Badminton library, and the school books tattered and ink-splashed. More interesting than such a library were the glossy new briars, the virgin meerschaum, the patent smoking-tables and another table evidently designed to make drinking easy, but by reason of the complexity of its machinery actually more likely to discourage one forever from refreshment. The rest of the space, apart from the furniture bequeathed by the noisy Templeton-Collins when he moved to larger rooms above, was crowded with the freshmen whom after hall Lonsdale had so hastily gathered together unassorted.

"I ordered coffee for sixteen," announced the host. "I thought it would be quicker than making it in a new machine that my sister gave me. It just makes enough for three, and the only time I tried, it took about an hour to do that ... who'll drink port?"

Michael thought the scout's prophecies about the superfluity of Lonsdale's wine were rather premature, for it seemed that everybody intended to drink port.

"I believe this is supposed to be rather good port," said Lonsdale.

"It is jolly good," several connoisseurs echoed.

"I don't know much about it myself. But my governor's supposed to be rather a judge. He said 'this is wasted on you and your friends, but I haven't got any bad wine to give you.'"

Here everybody held up their glasses against the light, took another sip and murmured their approval.

"Do you think this is a good wine, Fane?" demanded Lonsdale, thereby drawing so much attention to Michael that he blushed to nearly as deep a color as the port itself.

"I like it very much," Michael said.

"Do you like it, Wedderburn?" asked Lonsdale, turning to the freshman who had sat in the armchair at the head of the second table.

"Damned good wine," pronounced Wedderburn in a voice so rich with appreciation and so deep with judgment that he immediately established a reputation for worldly knowledge, and from having been slightly derided at Eton for his artistic ambitions was ever afterward respected and consulted. Michael envied his air of authority, but trembled for Wedderburn's position when he heard him reproach Lonsdale for his lack of any good pictures.

"You might stick up one that can be looked at for more than two seconds," Wedderburn said severely.

"What sort of picture?" asked Lonsdale.

"Primavera, for instance," Wedderburn suggested, and Michael's heart beat in sympathy.

"Never heard of the horse," Lonsdale answered. "Who owned her?"

"My god," Wedderburn rumbled, "I'll take you to buy one to-morrow, Lonny. You deserve it after that."

"Right-O!" Lonsdale cheerfully agreed. "Only I don't want my room to look like the Academy, you know."

Wedderburn shook his head in benevolent contempt, and the conversation was deflected from Lonsdale's artistic education by a long-legged Wykehamist with crisp chestnut hair and a thin florid face of dimpling smiles.

"Has anybody been into Venner's yet?" he asked.

"I have," proclaimed a dumpy Etonian whose down-curving nose hung over a perpetually open mouth. "Marjoribanks took me in just before hall. But he advised me not to go in by myself yet awhile."

"The second-year men don't like it," agreed the long-legged Wykehamist with a wise air. "They say one can begin to go in occasionally in one's third term."

"What is Venner's?" Michael asked.

"Don't you know?" sniffed the dumpy Etonian who had already managed to proclaim his friendship with Marjoribanks, the President of the Junior Common Room, and therefore presumably had the right to open his mouth a little wider than usual at Michael.

"I'm not quite sure myself," said Lonsdale quickly. "I vote that Cuffe explains."

"I'm not going to explain," Cuffe protested, and for some minutes his mouth was tightly closed.

"Isn't it just a sort of special part of the J. C. R.?" suggested the smiling Wykehamist, who seemed to wish to make it pleasant for everybody, so long as he himself would not have to admit ignorance. "Old Venables himself is a ripper. They say he's been steward of the J. C. R. for fifty years."

"Thirty-two years," corrected Wedderburn in his voice of most reverberant certitude. "Venner's is practically a club. You aren't elected, but somehow you know just when you can go in without being stared at. There's nothing in Oxford like that little office of Venner's. It's practically made St. Mary's what it is."

All the freshmen, sipping their port and lolling back in their new gowns, looked very reverent and very conscious of the honor and glory of St. Mary's which they themselves hoped soon to affirm more publicly than they could at present. Upon their meditations sounded very loud the blast of a coach-horn from above.

147

"That's Templeton-Collins," said Michael.

"Who's he?" several demanded.

"He's the man who used to live in these rooms last year," said Lonsdale lightly, as if that were the most satisfactory description for these freshmen, as indeed for all its youthful heartlessness it was.

"Let's all yell and tell him to shut up that infernal row," suggested Wedderburn sternly. Already from sitting in an armchair at the head of a table of freshmen he was acquiring an austere seniority of his own.

"To a second-year blood?" whispered somebody in dread surprise.

"Why not take away the coach-horn?" Lonsdale added.

However, this the freshmen were not prepared to do, although with unanimity they invited Templeton-Collins to refrain from blowing it.

"Keep quiet, little boys," shouted Templeton-Collins down the stairs.

The sixteen freshmen retreated well pleased with their audacity, and the long-legged Wykehamist proclaimed delightedly that this was going to be a hot year. "I vote we have a bonner."

"Will you light it, Sinclair?" asked another Wykehamist in a cynical drawl.

"Why not?" Sinclair retorted.

"Oh, I don't know. But you always used to be better at theory than practice."

"How these Wykehamists love one another," laughed an Etonian.

This implied criticism welded the four Winchester men present in defiance of all England, and Michael was impressed by their haughty and bigoted confidence.

"Sunday night is the proper time for a bonner," said Wedderburn. "After the first 'after.'"

"'After'?" queried another.

"Oh, don't you know? Haven't you heard?" several well-informed freshmen began, but Wedderburn with his accustomed gravity assumed the burden of instruction, and the others gave way.

"Every Sunday after hall," he explained, "people go up to the J. C. R. and take wine and dessert. Healths are drunk, and of course the second-year men try to make the freshers blind. Then everybody goes round to one of the large rooms in Cloisters for the 'after Common Room.' People sing and do various parlor tricks. The President of the J. C. R. gives the first 'after' of the term. The others are usually given by three or four men together. Whisky and cigars and lemon-squash. They usually last till nearly twelve. Great sport. They're much better than private wines, better for everybody. That's why we have them on Sunday night," he concluded rather vaguely.

The unwieldy bulk of sixteen freshmen was beginning to break up into bridge fours. Friendships were already in visible elaboration. The first evening had wonderfully brought them together. Something deeper than the superficial amity of chance juxtaposition at the same table was now begetting tentative confidences that would ultimately ripen to intimacies. Etonians were discovering that all Harrovians were not the dark-blue bedecked ruffians of Lords nor the aggressive boors of Etonian tradition. Harrovians were beginning to suspect that some Etonians might exist less flaccid, less deliberately lackadaisical, less odiously serene than the majority of those they had so far only encountered in summer holidays. Carthusians found that athletic prowess was going to count pleasantly in their favor. Even the Wykehamists extended a cordiality that was not positively chilling, and though they never lost an opportunity to criticize implicitly all other schools, and though their manners were so perfect that they abashed all but the more debonair Etonians, still it was evident they were sincerely trying to acknowledge a little merit, a little good-fellowship among these strange new contemporaries, however exuberantly uneducated they might appear to Wykeham's adamantine mold.

Michael did not thrust himself upon any of these miniature societies in the making, because the rather conscious efforts of diverse groups to put themselves into accord with one another made him shy and restless. Nobody yet among these freshmen seemed able to take his neighbor for granted, and Michael fancied that himself as the product of a day-school appeared to these cloistered catechumens as surprising and disconcerting and vaguely improper as a ballet-girl or a French count. At the same time he sympathized with their bewilderment and gave them credit for their attempt not to let him think he confused their social outlook. But the obviously sustained attempt depressed him with a sense of fatigue. After all, his trousers were turned up at the bottom and the last button of his waistcoat was undone. Failure to comply with the Draconic code of dress could not be attributed to him, as mercilessly it had served to banish into despised darkness a few scholars whose trousers frayed themselves upon their insteps and whose waistcoats were ignobly buttoned to the very end.

"An Old Giggleswickian," commented some one in reference to one of these disgraced scholars, with such fanatic modishness that Michael was surprised to see he wore the crude tie of the Old Carthusians; such inexorable scorn consorted better with the rich sobriety of the Old Wykehamist colors.

"Why, were you at school with him?" asked Michael quickly.

"Me? At Giggleswick?" stammered the Carthusian.

"Why not?" said Michael. "You seem to know all about him."

"Isn't your name Fane?" demanded the Carthusian abruptly, and when Michael nodded, he said he remembered him at his private school.

"That'll help me along a bit, I expect," Michael prophesied.

"We were in the same form at Randell's. My name's Avery."

"I remember you," said Michael coldly. And he thought to himself how little Avery's once stinging wit seemed to matter now. Really he thought Avery was almost attractive with his fresh complexion and deep blue eyes and girlish sensitive mouth, and when he rose to go out of Lonsdale's room, he was not sorry that Avery rose too and walked out with him into the quad.

"I say," Avery began impulsively. "Did I make an ass of myself just now? I mean, do you think people were sick with me?"

"What for?"

"I mean did I sound snobbish?" Avery pursued.

"Not more than anybody else," Michael assured him, and as he watched Avery's expression of petulant self-reproach he wondered how it was possible that once it mattered whether Avery knew he had a governess and wore combinations instead of pants and vest.

"I say, aren't you rather keen on pictures? I heard you talking to Wedderburn. Do come up to my room some time. I'm in Cloisters. Are you going out? You'll have to buck up. It's after nine."

They had reached the lodge, and Michael, nodding good-night, was ushered out by the porter. As he reached the corner of Longwall, Tom boomed his final warning, and over the last echoing reverberation sounded here and there the lisp of footsteps in the moonlight.

Michael wandered on in meditation. From lighted windows in the High came a noise of laughter and voices that seemed to make more grave and more perdurable the spires and towers of Oxford, deepening somehow the solemnity of the black entries and the empty silver spaces before them. Michael pondered the freshmen's chatter and apprehended dimly how this magical sublunary city would convert all that effusion of naïve intolerance to her own renown. He stood still for a moment rapt in an ecstasy of submission to this austere beneficence of stone that sheltered even him, the worshiper of one day, with the power of an immortal pride. He wandered on and on through the liquid moonshine, gratefully conscious of his shadow that showed him in his cap and gown not so conspicuous an intruder as he had seemed to himself that morning.

So for an hour he wandered in a tranced revelry of aspirations, until at last breathlessly he turned into the tall glooms of New College Street and Queen's Lane, where as he walked he touched the cold stones, forgetting the world.

In the High he saw his own college washed with silver, and the tower tremulous in the moonlight, fine-spun and frail as a lily.

It was pleasant to nod to one or two people standing in the lodge. It was pleasant to turn confidently under the gateway of St. Cuthbert's quad. It was pleasant to be greeted by his own name at the entrance of his staircase. It was the greatest contentment he had ever known to see the glowing of his fire, and slowly to untie under the red-shaded light the fat parcels of his newly-bought books.

Outside in the High a tram rumbled slowly past. The clock struck ten from St. Mary's tower. The wicker chair creaked comfortably. The watered silk of the rich bindings swished luxuriously. This was how Boccaccio should be read. Michael's mind was filled with the imagination of that gay company, secluded from the fever, telling their gay stories in the sunlight of their garden. This was how Rabelais should be read: the very pages seemed to glitter like wine.

Midnight chimed from St. Mary's tower. One by one the new books went gloriously to their gothic shelves. The red lamp was extinguished. Michael's bedroom was scented with the breath of the October night. It was too cold to read more than a few sentences of Pater about some splendid bygone Florentine. Out snapped the electric light: the room was full of moonshine, so full that the water in the bath tub was gleaming.

CHAPTER II

THE FIRST WEEK

The first two or three days were busy with interviews, initiations, addresses, and all the academic panoply which Oxford brings into action against her neophytes.

First of all, the Senior Tutor, Mr. Ardle, had to be visited. He was a deaf and hostile little man whose side-whiskers and twitching eyelid and manner of exaggerated respect toward undergraduates combined to give the impression that he regarded them as objectionable discords in an otherwise justly modulated existence.

Michael in his turn went up the stairs to Mr. Ardle's room, knocked at the door and passed in at the don's bidding to where he sat sighing amid heaps of papers and statistical sheets. The glacial air of the room was somehow increased by the photographs of Swiss mountains that crowded the walls.

"Mr.?" queried the Senior Tutor. "Oh, yes, Mr. Fane. St. James'. Your tutor will be the Dean—please sit down—the Dean, Mr. Ambrose. What school are you proposing to read?"

"History, I imagine," said Michael. "History!" he repeated, as Mr. Ardle blinked at him.

"Yes," said the Senior Tutor in accents of patient boredom. "But we have to consider the immediate future. I suggest Honor Moderations and Literæ Humaniores."

"I explained to you that I wanted to read History," said Michael, echoing himself involuntarily the don's tone of patient boredom.

"I have you down as coming from St. James'," snapped the Senior Tutor. "A school reputed to send out good classical scholars, I believe."

"I'm not a scholar," Michael interrupted. "And I don't intend to take Honor Mods."

"That will be for the college to decide."

"Supposing the college decided I was to read Chinese?" Michael inquired.

"There is no need for impertinence. Well, well, for the present I have put you down for the lectures on Pass Moderations. You will attend my lectures on Cicero, Mr. Churton on the Apologia, Mr. Carder on Logic, and Mr. Vereker for Latin Prose. The weekly essay set by the Warden for freshmen you will read to your tutor Mr. Ambrose."

Then he went on to give instructions about chapels and roll-calls and dining in hall and the various regulations of the college, while the Swiss mountains stared bleakly down at the chilly interview.

"Now you'd better go and see Mr. Ambrose," said the Senior Tutor, and Michael left him. On the staircase he passed Lonsdale going up.

"What's he like?" asked Lonsdale.

"Pretty dull," said Michael.

"Does he keep you long?"

Michael shook his head.

"Good work," said Lonsdale cheerfully. "Because I've just bought a dog." And he whistled his way upstairs.

Michael wondered what the purchase of a dog had got to do with the Senior Tutor, but relinquished the problem on perceiving Mr. Ambrose's name on the floor below.

The Dean's room was very much like the Senior Tutor's, and the interview, save that it was made slightly more tolerable by the help of a cigarette, was of much the same chilliness owing to Michael's reiterated refusal to read Honor Moderations.

"I expected a little keenness," said Mr. Ambrose.

"I shall be keen enough when I've finished with Pass Mods," said Michael. "Though what good it will be for me to read the Pro Milone and the Apology all over again, when I read them at fifteen, I don't know."

"Then take Honor Moderations?" the Dean advised.

"I've given up classics," Michael argued, and as the cigarette was beginning to burn his fingers and the problem of disposing of it in the Dean's room seemed insoluble, he hurried out.

Lonsdale was whistling his way downstairs from his interview with Mr. Ardle.

"Hallo, Fane, what did he say to you?"

"I think all these dons are very much like schoolmasters," growled Michael resentfully.

"They can't help it," said Lonsdale. "I asked old Ardle if I could keep a dog in college, and he turned as blue as an owl. Any one would think I'd asked him if I could breed crocodiles."

In addition to these personal interviews the freshmen had certain communal experiences to undergo. Among these was their formal reception into the University, when they trooped after the Senior Tutor through gothic mazes and in some beautiful and remote room received from the Vice-Chancellor a bound volume of Statuta et Decreta Universitatis. This book they carried back with them to college, where in many rooms it shared with Ruff's Guide and Soapy Sponge's Sporting Tour an intellectual oligarchy. Saturday morning was spent in meeting the Warden at the Warden's Lodgings, where they shook hands with him in nervous quartets. Michael when he discussed this experience with his fellows fancied that the Warden's butler had left a deeper impression than the Warden himself. On Sunday afternoon, however, when they gathered in the hall to hear the annual address of welcome and exhortation, the great moon-faced Warden shone undimmed.

"You have come to Oxford," he concluded, "some of you to hunt foxes, some of you to wear very large and very unusual overcoats, some of you to row for your college and a few of you to work. But all of you have come to Oxford to remain English gentlemen. In after life when you are ambassadors and proconsuls and members of Parliament you will never remember this little address which I have the honor now of delivering to you. That will not matter, so long as you always remember that you are St. Mary's men and the heirs of an honorable and ancient foundation."

The great moon-faced Warden beamed at them for one moment, and after thanking them for their polite attention floated out of the hall. The pictures of cardinals and princes and poets in their high golden frames seemed in the dusk faintly to nod approval. The bell was ringing for evening chapel, and the freshmen went murmurously along the cloisters to take their places, feeling rather proud that the famous quire was their quire and looking with inquisitive condescension at the visitors who sat out of sight of those candle-starred singers.

In hall that night the chief topic of conversation was the etiquette and ritual of the first J. C. R. wine.

Michael to his chagrin found himself seated next to Mackintosh, for Mackintosh, cousin though he was of the sparkish Lonsdale, was a gloomy fellow scornful of the general merriment. As somebody had quickly said, sharpening his young wit, he was more of a wet-blanket than a Mackintosh.

"I suppose you're coming to the J. C. R.?" Michael asked.

"Why should I? Why should I waste my time trying to keep sober for the amusement of all these fools?"

"I expect it will be rather a rag," said Michael hopefully, but he found it tantalizing to hear farther down the table snatches of conversation that heard more completely would have enlightened him on several points he had not yet mastered in the ceremony of wine in the J. C. R. However, it was useless to speculate on such subjects in the company of the lugubrious Mackintosh. So they talked instead of Sandow exercises and mountain-climbing in Cumberland, neither of which topics interested Michael very greatly.

Hall was rowdy that evening, and the dons looked petulantly down from high table, annoyed to think that their distinguished visitors of Sunday evening should see so many pieces of bread flung by the second-year men. The moon-faced Warden was deflected from his intellectual revolutions round a Swedish man of science, and sent the butler down to whisper a remonstrance to the head of one of the second-year tables. But no sooner had the butler again taken his place behind the Warden's chair than a number of third-year men whose table had been littered by the ammunition of their juniors retaliated without apparent loss of dignity, and presently both years combined to bombard under the Scholars. Meanwhile the freshmen applauded with laughter, and thought their seniors were wonderful exemplars for the future.

After hall everybody went crowding up the narrow stairs to the J. C. R., and now most emphatically the J. C. R. presented a cheerful sight, with the red-shaded lamps casting such a glow that the decanters of wine stationed before the President's place looked like a treasure of rubies. The two long tables were set at right angles to one another, and the President sat near their apex. All along their shining length at regular intervals stood great dishes of grapes richly bloomed, of apples and walnuts and salted almonds and deviled biscuits. The freshmen by instinct rushed to sit altogether at the end of the table more remote from the door. As Michael looked at his contemporaries, he perceived that of the forty odd freshmen scarcely five-and-twenty had come to this, the first J. C. R. Vaguely he realized that already two sets were manifest in the college, and he felt depressed by the dullness of those who had not come and some satisfaction with himself for coming.

The freshmen stared with awe at Marjoribanks, the President of the J. C. R., and told one another with reverence that the two men on either side of him were those famous rowing blues from New College, Permain and Strutt; while some of them who had known these heroes at school sat anxiously unaware of their presence and spoke of them familiarly as Jack Permain and Bingey. There were several other cynosures from New College and University near the President's chair, a vivid bunch of Leander ties. There were also one or two old St. Mary's men who had descended to haunt for a swift week-end the place of their renown, and these were pointed out by knowing freshmen as unconcernedly as possible.

One by one the President released the decanters, and round and round they came. Sometimes they would be held up by an interesting conversation; and when the sherry and the port and the burgundy were all standing idle, a shout of "pass along the wine" would go up, after which for a time the decanters would swing vigorously from hand to hand. Then suddenly Marjoribanks was seen to be bowing to Permain, and Permain was bowing solemnly back to his host. This was a plain token to everybody that the moment for drinking healths had arrived. A great babel of shouted names broke out at the end of the Common Room remote from the freshmen, so tremendous a din that the freshmen felt the drinking of their own healths at their end would pass unnoticed. So they drank to one another, bowing gravely after the manner of their seniors.

Michael had determined to take nothing but burgundy, and when he had exchanged sentiments with the most of his year, he congratulated himself upon the comparative steadiness of his head. Already in the case of one or two reckless mixers he noticed a difficulty in deciding how many times it was necessary to clip a cigar, an inclination to strike the wrong end of a match and a confusion between right and left when the decanters in their circulation paused before them.

After the first tumult of good wishes had died down, Marjoribanks lifted his glass, looked along to where the freshmen were sitting and shouted "Cuffe!" Cuffe hastily lifted his glass and answering "Marjorie!" drained his salute of acknowledgment. Then he sat back in his chair with an expression, Michael thought, very like that of an actress who has been handed a bouquet by the conductor. But Cuffe was not to be the only recipient of honor, for immediately afterward Marjoribanks sang out "Lonsdale!" Lonsdale was at the moment trying to explain to Tommy Grainger some trick with the skin of a banana which ought to have been an orange and a wooden match which ought to have been a wax vesta. Michael, who was sitting next to him, prodded anxiously his ribs.

"What's the matter?" demanded Lonsdale indignantly. "Can't you see I'm doing a trick?"

"Marjoribanks is drinking your health," whispered Michael in an agony that Lonsdale would be passed over.

"Hurrah!" shouted Lonsdale, rising to his feet and scandalizing his fellows by his intoxicated audacity. "Where is the old ripper!" Then "Mark over!" he shouted and collapsed into Tommy Grainger's lap. Everybody laughed, and everybody, even the cynosures from New College and University, began to drink Lonsdale's health without heel-taps.

"No heelers, young Lonsdale," they called mirthfully.

Lonsdale pulled himself together, stood up, and, balancing himself with one hand on Michael's shoulder, replied:

"No heelers, you devils? No legs, you mean!" Then he collapsed again.

Soon all the freshmen found that their healths were now being drunk, all the freshmen, that is, from Eton or Winchester or Harrow. Michael and one or two others without old schoolfellows among the seniors remained more sober. But then suddenly a gravely indolent man with a quizzical face, who the day before in the lodge had had occasion to ask Michael some trifling piece of information, cried "Fane!" raising his glass. Michael blushed, blessed his unknown acquaintance inwardly and drank what was possibly the sincerest sentiment of the evening. Other senior men hearing his name, followed suit, even the great Marjoribanks himself; and soon Michael was very nearly as full as Lonsdale. An immense elation caressed his soul, a boundless sense of communal life, a conception of sublime freedom that seemed to be illimitable forever. The wine was over. Down the narrow stone stairs everybody poured. At the foot on the right was a little office—the office of Venables, the steward of the J. C. R., the eleusinian and impenetrable sanctum of seniority called Venner's. Wine-chartered though they were, the freshmen did not venture even to peep round the corner of the door, but hurried out into the cloisters, where they walked arm-in-arm shouting.

Michael could have fancied himself at a gathering of mediæval witches. The moon temporarily clouded over by the autumnal fog made the corbels and gargoyles and sculptured figures above the cloisters take on a grotesque vivacity, as the vapors curled around them. The wine humming in his head: the echoing shouts of his companions: the decorative effect of the gowns: the chiming high above of the bells in the tower: all combined to create for Michael a nightmare of exultation. He was aware of a tremendous zest in doing nothing, and there flowed over him a consciousness that this existence of shout and dance along these cloisters was really existence lived in a perpetual expression of the finest energy. The world seemed to be going round so much faster than usual that in order to keep up with this new pace, it was necessary for the individual like himself to walk faster, to talk faster, to think faster, and finally to raise to incoherent speed every coherent faculty. Another curious effect of the wine, for after all Michael admitted to himself that his mental exhilaration must be due to burgundy, was the way in which he found himself at every moment walking beside a different person. He would scarcely have finished an excited acceptance of Wedderburn's offer to go to-morrow and look at some Dürer woodcuts, when he would suddenly find himself discussing sympathetically with Lonsdale the iniquity of the dons in refusing to let him keep his new dog in one of the scouts' pigeon-holes in the lodge.

"After all," Lonsdale pointed out earnestly, "they're never really full, and the dog isn't large—of course I don't expect to keep him in a pigeon-hole when he's full grown, but he's a puppy."

"It's absurd," Michael agreed.

"That's the word I've been looking for," Lonsdale exclaimed. "What was it again? Absurd! You see what I say is, when one scout's box is full, move the poor little beast into another. It isn't likely they'd all be full at the same time. What was that word you found just now? Absurd! That's it. It is absurd. It's absurd!"

"And anyway," Michael pointed out, "if they were all full they could chain him to the leg of the porter's desk."

151

"Of course they could. I say, Fane, you're a damned good sort," said Lonsdale. "I wish you'd come and have lunch with me to-morrow. I don't think I've asked very many chaps: I want to show you that dog. He's in a stable off Holywell at present. Beastly shame! I'm not complaining, of course, but what I want to ask our dons is how would they like to be bought by me and shut up in Holywell?"

And just when Michael had a very good answer ready, he found himself arm-in-arm with Wedderburn again, who was saying in his gravest voice that over a genuine woodcut by Dürer it was well worth taking trouble. But before Michael could disengage Wedderburn's Dürer from Lonsdale's dog, he found himself running very fast beside Tommy Grainger who was shouting:

"Five's late again! Six, you're bucketing! Bow, you're late! Two, *will* you get your belly down!"

Then Grainger stopped suddenly and asked Michael in a very solemn tone whether he knew what was the matter with the crew. Michael shook his head and watched the others steer their devious course toward him and Grainger.

"They're too drunk to row," said Grainger.

"Much too drunk," Michael agreed.

When he had pondered for a moment or two his last remark, he discovered it was extraordinarily funny. So he was seized with a paroxysm of laughter, and the more he laughed, the more he wanted to laugh. When somebody asked him what he was laughing at, he replied it was because he had left the electric light burning in his room. Several people seemed to think this just as funny as Michael thought it, and they joined him in his mirth, laughing unquenchably until Wedderburn observed severely in his deepest voice:

"Buck up, you're all drunk, and they're coming out of Venner's."

Then like some patient profound countryman he shepherded them all up to the large room on a corner staircase of Cloisters, where the "after" was going to be held. The freshmen squeezed themselves together in a corner and were immensely entertained by the various performers, applauding with equal rapture a light comedian from Pembroke, a tenor from Corpus, a comic singer from Oriel and a mimic from professional London. They drank lemon squashes to steady themselves: they joined in choruses: they cheered and smoked cigars and grew more and more conscious as the evening progressed that they belonged to a great college called St. Mary's. Their enthusiasm reached its zenith, when the captain of the Varsity Eleven (a St. Mary's man even as they were St. Mary's men) sang the St. Mary's song in a voice whose gentleness of utterance and sighing modesty in no way abashed the noisy appreciation of the audience. It was a wonderful song, all about the triumphs of the college on river and cricket-field, in the Schools, in Parliament and indeed everywhere else. It had a fine rollicking chorus which was repeated twice after each verse. And as there were about seventeen verses, by the time the song was half over the freshmen had learned the words and were able to sing the final chorus with a vigor which positively detonated against the windows and contrasted divertingly with the almost inaudible soloist.

Last of all came Auld Lang Syne, when everybody stood up on chairs and joined hands, seniors, second-year men and freshmen. Auld Lang Syne ended with perhaps the noisiest moment of all because although Lonsdale had taken several lemon squashes to steady himself, he had not taken enough to keep his balance through the ultimate energetic repetition, when he collapsed headlong into a tray of syphons and glasses, dragging with him two other freshmen. But nobody seemed to have hurt himself, and downstairs they all rushed, shouting and hulloaing, into the cool moonlight.

The guests from New College and University and the "out-of-college" men hurried home, for it was close upon midnight. In the lodge the freshmen foregathered for a few minutes with the second-year men, and as they talked they knew that the moment was come when they must proclaim themselves free from the restrictions of school, and by the kindling of a bonfire prove that they were now truly grown up. Bundles of faggots were seized from the scouts' holes: in the angle of St. Cuthbert's quad where the complexion of the gravel was tanned by the numberless bonfires of past generations the pile of wood grew taller and taller: two or three douches of paraffin made the mass readily inflammable: a match was set, and with a roar the bonfire began. From their windows second-year men, their faces lighted by the ascending blaze, looked down with pleasant patronage upon the traditional pastime of their juniors. The freshmen danced gleefully round the pyre of their boyhood, feeding it with faggots and sometimes daringly and ostentatiously with chairs: the heat became intense: the smoke surged upward, obscuring the bland aspectful moon. Slowly upon the group of law-breakers fell a silence, as they stood bewitched by the beauty of their own handiwork. The riotous preparations and annunciatory yells had died away to an intimate murmur of conversation. From the lodge came Shadbolt the unctuous head-porter to survey for a moment this mighty bonfire: conscious of their undergraduate dignity the freshmen chaffed him, until he retired with muttered protests to summon the Dean.

"What will the Dean do?" asked one or two less audacious ones as they faded into various doorways, ready to obliterate their presence as soon as authority should arrive upon the scene.

"What does the Dean matter?" cried others, flinging more faggots on to the fire until it crackled and spat and bellowed more fiercely than ever, lighting up with its wavy radiance the great elms beyond the Warden's garden and the Palladian fragment of New quad whence the dons like Georgian squires pondered their prosperity.

Presently against the silvery space framed by the gateway of St. Cuthbert's tower appeared the silhouette of the Dean, lank and tall with college cap tip-tilted down on to his nose and round his neck a gown wrapped like a shawl. Nearer he came, and involuntarily the freshmen so lately schoolboys took on in their attitude a certain anxiety. Somehow the group round the bonfire had become much smaller. Somehow more windows looking upon the quad were populated with flickering watchful faces.

"Great Scott! What can Ambrose do?" demanded Lonsdale despairingly, but when at last the Dean reached the zone of the fire, there only remained about eight freshmen to ascertain his views and test his power. The Dean stood for a minute or two, silently warming his hands. In a ring the presumed leaders eyed him, talking to each other the while with slightly exaggerated carelessness.

"Well, Mr. Fane?" asked the Dean.

"Well, sir," Michael replied.

"Damned good," whispered Lonsdale ecstatically in Michael's ear. "You couldn't have said anything better. That's damned good."

Michael under the enthusiastic congratulations of Lonsdale began to feel he had indeed said something very good, but he hoped he would soon have an opportunity to say something even better.

"Enjoying yourself, Mr. Lonsdale?" inquired the Dean.

"Yes, sir. Are you?" answered Lonsdale.

"Splendid," murmured Michael.

A silence followed this exchange of courtesies. The bonfire was beginning to die down, but nobody ventured under the Dean's eye to put on more faggots. Under-porters were seen drawing near with pails of water, and though a cushion aimed from a window upset one pail, very soon the bonfire was a miserable mess of smoking ashes and the moon resumed her glory. From an upper window some second-year men chanted in a ridiculous monotone:

"The Dean—he was the Dean—he was the Dean—he was the Dean! The Dean—he was the Dean he was—the Dean he was—the Dean!!"

Mr. Ambrose did not bother to look up in the direction of the glee, but took another glance at Michael, Lonsdale, Grainger and the other stalwarts. Then he turned away.

"Good night," Lonsdale called after the retreating figure of the tall hunched don, and not being successful in luring him back, he poured his scorn upon the defaulters safe in their rooms above.

"You are a lot of rotters. Come down and make another."

But the freshmen were not yet sufficiently hardy to do this. One by one they melted away, and Lonsdale marked his contempt for their pusillanimity by throwing two syphons and his gown into the Warden's garden. After which he invited Michael and his fellow die-hards to drink a glass of port in his rooms. Here for an hour they sat, discussing their contemporaries.

In the morning Shadbolt was asked if anybody had been hauled for last night's bonner.

"Mr. Fane, Mr. Grainger and the Honorable Lonsdale," he informed the inquirer. Together those three interviewed the Dean.

"Two guineas each," he announced after a brief homily on the foolishness and inconvenience of keeping everybody up on the first Sunday of term. "And if you feel aggrieved, you can get up a subscription among your co-lunatics to defray your expenses."

Michael, Grainger and Lonsdale sighed very movingly, and tried to look like martyrs, but they greatly enjoyed telling what had happened to the other freshmen and several second-year men. It was told, too, in a manner of elaborate nonchalance with many vows to do the same to-morrow.

CHAPTER III

THE FIRST TERM

His first term at Oxford was for Michael less obviously a period of discovery than from his pre-figurative dreams he had expected. He had certainly pictured himself in the midst of a society more intellectually varied than that in which he found himself; and all that first term became in retrospect merely a barren noisy time from which somehow after numberless tentative adjustments and developments emerged a clear view of his own relation to the college, and more particularly to his own "year." These trials of personality were conducted with all the help that sensitiveness could render him. But this sensitiveness when it had registered finely and accurately a few hazardous impressions was often sharp as a nettle in its action, so sharp indeed sometimes that he felt inclined to withdraw from social encounters into a solitude of books. Probably Michael would have become a recluse, if he had not decided on the impulse of the moment to put down his name for Rugby football. He was fairly successful in the first match, and afterward Carben, the secretary of the college club, invited him to tea. This insignificant courtesy gave Michael a considerable amount of pleasure, inasmuch as it was the first occasion on which he had been invited to his rooms by a second-year man. With Carben he found about half a dozen other seniors and a couple of freshmen whom he did not remember to have noticed before; and the warm room, whose murmurous tinkle was suddenly hushed as he entered, affected him with a glowing hospitality.

Michael had found it so immediately easy to talk that when Carben made a general observation on the row of Sunday night's celebration, Michael proclaimed enthusiastically the excellence of the bonfire.

"Were you in that gang?" Carben asked in a tone of contemptuous surprise.

"I was fined," Michael announced, trying to quench the note of exultation in deference to the hostility he instinctively felt he was creating.

"I say," Carben sneered, "so at last one of the 'bloods' is going to condescend to play Rugger. Jonah," he called to the captain of the Fifteen who was lolling in muscular grandeur at the other end of the room, "we've got a college blood playing three-quarter for us."

"Good work," said Jones, with a toast-encumbered laugh. "Where is he?"

Carben pointed to Michael who blushed rather angrily.

"No end of a blood," Carben went on. "Lights bonfires and gets fined all in his first week."

The two freshmen sniggered, and Michael made up his mind to consult Lonsdale about their doom. He was pensively damned if these two asses should laugh at him. There had already been talk of ragging one or two freshmen whose raw and mediocre bearing had offended the modish perceptions of the majority. When the proscription was on foot, Michael promised his injured pride that he would denounce them with their red wrists and their smug insignificance.

"You were at St. James', weren't you?" asked Jones. "Did you know Mansfield?"

"I didn't know him—exactly," said Michael, "but—in fact—we thought him rather a tick."

"Thanks very much and all that," said Jones. "He was a friend of mine, but don't apologize."

There was a general laugh at Michael's expense from which Carben's guffaw survived. "Jonah was never one for moving in the best society," he said with an implication in his tone that the best society was something positively contemptible.

Michael retired from the conversation and sat silent, counting with cold dislike the constellated pimples on Carben's face. Meanwhile the others exercised their scornful wit upon the "bloods" of the college.

"Did you hear about Fitzroy and Gingold?" Carben indignantly demanded. "Gingold was tubbing yesterday and Fitzroy was coaching. 'Can't you keep your fat little paunch down? I don't want to look at it,' said Fitzroy. That's pretty thick from a second-year man to a third-year man in front of a lot of freshers. Gingold's going to jack rowing, and he's quite right."

"Quite right," a chorus echoed.

Michael remembered Fitzroy very blithely intoxicated at the J. C. R.; he remembered, too, that Fitzroy had drunk his health. This explosion of wrath at the insult offered to Gingold's dignity irritated Michael. He felt sure that Gingold had a fat little paunch and that he thoroughly deserved to be told to keep it out of sight. Gingold was probably as offensive as Jones and Carben.

"These rowing bloods think they've bought the college," somebody was wisely propounding.

"We ought to go head of the river this year, oughtn't we?" Michael inquired with as much innocence as he could muster to veil the armed rebuke.

"Well, I think it would be a d'd good thing, if we dropped six places," Carben affirmed.

How many pimples there were, thought Michael, looking at the secretary, and he felt he must make some excuse to escape from this room whose atmosphere of envy and whose castrated damns were shrouding Oxford with a dismal genteelness.

"Oh, by the way, before you go," said Carben, "you'd better let me put your name down for the Ugger."

"The what?" Michael asked, with a faint insolence.

"The Union."

Michael, occupied with the problem of adjustment, had no intention of committing himself so early to the Union and certainly not under the sponsorship of Carben.

"I don't think I'll join this term."

He ran down the stairs from Carben's rooms and stood for a moment apprehensively upon the lawn. Then sublime in the dusk he saw St. Mary's tower and, refreshed by that image of an aspiration, he shook off the memory of Carben's tea-party as if he had alighted from a crowded Sunday train and plunged immediately into deep country.

In hall that night Lonsdale asked Michael what he had been doing, and was greatly amused by his information, so much amused that he called along the table to Grainger:

"I say, Tommy, do you know we've got a Rugger rough with us?"

Several people murmured in surprise.

"I say, have you really been playing Rugger?"

"Well, great Scott!" exclaimed Michael, "there's nothing very odd in that."

"But the Rugger roughs are all very bad men," Lonsdale protested.

"Some are," Michael admitted. "Still, it's a better game than Socker."

"But everybody at St. Mary's plays Socker," Lonsdale went on.

Michael felt for a while enraged against the pettiness of outlook that even the admired Lonsdale displayed. How ridiculous it was to despise Rugby football because the college was so largely composed of Etonians and Harrovians and Wykehamists and Carthusians. It was like schoolboys. And Michael abruptly realized that all of them sitting at this freshmen's table were really schoolboys. It was natural after all that with the patriotism of youth they should disdain games foreign to their traditions. This, however, was no reason for allowing Rugby to be snuffed out ignominiously.

"Anyway I shall go on playing Rugger," Michael asserted.

"Shall I have a shot?" suggested Lonsdale.

"It's a most devilish good game," Michael earnestly avowed.

"Tommy," Lonsdale shouted, "I'm going to be a Rugger rough myself."

"I shall sconce you, young Lonsdale, if you make such a row," said Wedderburn severely.

"My god, Wedders, you are a prize ass," chuckled the offender.

Wedderburn whispered to the scout near him.

"Have you sconced me?" Lonsdale demanded.

The head of the table nodded.

Lonsdale was put to much trouble and expense to avenge his half-crown. Finally with great care he took down all the pictures in Wedderburn's room and hung in their places gaudy texts. Also for the plaster Venus of Milo he caused to be made a miniature chest-protector. It was all very foolish, but it afforded exquisite entertainment to Lonsdale and his auxiliaries, especially when in the lodge they beheld Wedderburn's return from a dinner out of college, and when presently they visited him in his room to enjoy his displeasure.

Michael's consciousness of the sharp division in the college between two broad sections prevented him from retiring into seclusion. He continued to play Rugby football almost entirely in order to hear with a delighted irony the comments of the "bad men" on the "bloods." Yet many of these "bad men" he rather liked, and he would often defend them to his critical young contemporaries, although on the "bad men" of his own year he was as hard as the rest of the social leaders. He was content in this first term to follow loyally, with other heedless ones, the trend of the moment. He made few attempts to enlarge the field of his outlook by cultivating acquaintanceship outside his own college. Even Alan he seldom visited, since in these early days of Oxford it seemed to him essential to move cautiously and always under the protection of numbers. These freshmen in their first term found a curious satisfaction in numbers. When they lunched together, they lunched in eights and twelves; when they dined out of college, as they sometimes did, at the Clarendon or the Mitre or the Queen's, they gathered in the lodge almost in the dimensions of a school-treat.

"Why do we always go about in such quantity?" Michael once asked Wedderburn.

"What else can we do?" answered Wedderburn. "We must subject each other to—I mean—we haven't got any clubs yet. We're bound to stick together."

"Well, I'm getting rather fed up with it," said Michael. "I feel more like a tourist than a Varsity man. Every day we lunch and dine and take coffee and tea in great masses of people. I'm bored to tears by half the men I go about with, and I'm sure they're bored to tears with me. We don't talk about anything but each other's schools and whether A is a better chap than B, or whether C is a gentleman and if it's true that D isn't really. I bought for my own pleasure some rather decent books; and every other evening about twelve people come and read them over each other's shoulders, while I spend my whole time blowing cigarette ash off the pictures. And when they've all read the story of the nightingale in the Decameron, they sit up till one o'clock discussing who of our year is most likely to be elected president of the J. C. R. four years from now."

But for all Michael's grumbling through that first term he was beginning to perceive the blurred outlines of an intimate society at Oxford which in the years to come he would remember. There was Wedderburn himself whose square-headed solidity of demeanor and episcopal voice masked a butterfly of a temperament that flitted from flower to flower of artistic experiment or danced attendance upon freshmen, the honey of whose future fame he seemed always able to probe.

"I wonder if you really are the old snob you try to make yourself," said Michael. "And yet I don't think it is snobbishness. I believe it's a form of collecting. It's a throw back to primitive life in a private school. One day in your fourth year you'll give a dinner party for about twelve bloods and I shall come too and remind you just when and how and where you picked them all up before their value was perfectly obvious. Partly of course it's due to being at Eton where you had nothing to do but observe social distinction in the making and talk about Burne-Jones to your tutor."

"My dear fellow," said Wedderburn deeply, "I have these people up to my rooms because I like them."

"But it is convenient always to like the right people," Michael argued. "There are lots of others just as pleasant whom you don't like. For instance, Avery——"

"Avery!" Wedderburn snorted.

"He's not likely ever to be captain of the 'Varsity Eleven," said Michael. "But he's amusing, and he can talk about books."

"Patronizing ass," Wedderburn growled.

"That's exactly what he isn't," Michael contradicted.

"Damnable poseur," Wedderburn rumbled.

"Oh, well, so are you," said Michael.

He thought how willfully Wedderburn would persist in misjudging Avery. Yet himself had spent most delightful hours with him. To be sure, his sensitiveness made him sharp-tongued, and he dressed rather too well. But all the Carthusians at St. Mary's dressed rather too well and carried about with them the atmosphere of a week-end in a sporting country-house owned by very rich people. This burbling prosperity would gradually trickle away, Michael thought, and he began to follow the course of Avery four years hence directed by Oxford to—to what? To some distinguished goal of art, but whether as writer or painter or sculptor he did not know, Avery was so very versatile. Michael mentally put him on one side to decorate a conspicuous portion of the ideal edifice he dreamed of creating from his Oxford society. There was Lonsdale. Lonsdale really possessed the serene perfection of a great work of art. Michael thought to himself that almost he could bear to attend for ever Ardle's dusty lectures on Cicero in order that for ever he might hear Lonsdale admit with earnest politeness that he had not found time to glance at the text the day before, that he was indeed sorry to cause Mr. Ardle such a mortification, but that unfortunately he had left his Plato in a sadler's shop, where he had found it necessary to complain of a saddle newly made for him.

"But I am lecturing on Cicero, Mr. Lonsdale. The Pro Milone was not delivered by Plato, Mr. Lonsdale."

"What's he talking about?" Lonsdale whispered to Michael.

"Nor was it delivered by Mr. Fane," added the Senior Tutor dryly.

Lonsdale looked at first very much alarmed by this suggestion, then seeing by the lecturer's face that something was still wrong, he assumed a puzzled expression, and finally in an attempt to relieve the situation he laughed very heartily and said:

"Oh, well, after all, it's very much the same." Then, as everybody else laughed very loudly, Lonsdale sat down and leaned back, pulling up his trousers in gentle self-congratulation.

"Rum old buffer," he whispered presently to Michael. "His eye gets very glassy when he looks at me. Do you think I ought to ask him to lunch?"

Michael thought that Avery, Wedderburn and Lonsdale might be considered to form the nucleus of the intimate ideal society which his imagination was leading him on to shape. And if that trio seemed not completely to represent the forty freshmen of St. Mary's, there might be added to the list certain others for qualities of athletic renown that combined with charm of personality gave them the right to be set up in Michael's collection as types. There was Grainger, last year's Captain of the Boats at Eton, who would certainly row for the 'Varsity in the spring. Michael liked to sit in his rooms and watch his sprawling bulk and listen for an hour at a time to his naïve theories of life. Grainger seemed to shed rays of positive goodness, and Michael found that he exercised over this splendid piece of youth a fascination which to himself was surprising.

"Great Scott, you are an odd chap," Grainger once ejaculated.

"Why?"

"Why, you're a clever devil, aren't you, and you don't seem to do anything. Have I talked a lot of rot?"

"A good deal," Michael admitted. "At least, it would be rot if I talked it, but it would be ridiculous if you talked in any other way."

"You *are* a curious chap. I can't make you out."

"Why should you?" asked Michael. "You were never sent into this world to puzzle out things. You were sent here to sprawl across it just as you're sprawling across that sofa. When you go down, you'll go into the Egyptian Civil Service and you'll sprawl across the Sahara in exactly the same way. I rather wish I were like you. It must be quite comfortable to sit down heavily and unconcernedly on a lot of people. I can't imagine a more delightful mattress; only I should feel them wriggling under me."

"I suppose you're a Radical. They say you are," Grainger lazily announced through puffed-out fumes of tobacco.

"I suppose I might be," said Michael, "if I wanted to proclaim myself anything at all, but I'd much rather watch you sprawling effectively and proclaiming yourself a supporter of Conservatism. I've really very little inclination to criticize people like you. It's only in books I think you're a little boring."

Term wore on, and a pleasurable anticipation was lent to the coming vacation by a letter which Michael received from his mother.

CARLINGTON ROAD,
November 20th.

Dearest Michael,

I'm so glad you're still enjoying Oxford. I quite agree with you it would be better for me to wait a little while before I visit you, though I expect I should behave myself perfectly well. You'll be glad to hear that I've got rid of this tiresome house. I've sold it to a retired Colonel— such an objectionable old man, and I'm really so pleased he's bought it. It has been a most worrying autumn because the people next door were continually complaining of Stella's piano, and really Carlington Road has become impossible. Such an air of living next door, and whenever I look out of the window the maid is shaking a mat and looking up to see if I'm interested. We must try to settle on a new house when you're back in town. We'll stay in a hotel for a while. Stella has had to take a studio, which I do not approve of her doing, and I cannot bear to see the piano going continually in and out of the house. There are so many things I want to talk to you about—money, and whether you would like to go to Paris during the holidays. I daresay we could find a house at some other time.

Your loving
Mother.

From Stella about the same time, Michael also received a letter.

My dear old Michael,

I seem to have made really a personal success at my concert, and I've taken a studio here because the man next door—a most frightful bounder—said the noise I made went through and through his wife. As she's nearly as big round as the world, I wasn't flattered. Mother is getting very fussy, and all sorts of strange women come to the house and talk about some society for dealing with Life with a capital letter. I think we're going to be rather well off, and Mother wants to live in a house she's seen in Park Street, but I want to take a house in Cheyne Walk. I hope you like Cheyne Walk, because this house has got a splendid studio in the garden and I thought with some mauve brocades it would look perfectly lovely. There's a very good paneled room that you could have, and of course the studio would be half yours. I am working at a Franck concerto. I'm being painted by rather a nice youth, at least he would be nice, if he weren't so much like a corpse. I suppose you'll condescend to ask me down to Oxford next term.

Yours ever,
Stella.

P.S.—I've come to the conclusion that mere brilliancy of execution isn't enough. Academic perfection is all very well, but I don't think I shall appear in public again until I've lived a little. I really think life is rather exciting—unless it's spelt with a capital letter.

Michael was glad that there seemed a prospect of employing his vacation in abolishing the thin red house in Carlington Road. He felt he would have found it queerly shriveled after the spaciousness of Oxford. He was sufficiently far along in his first term to be able to feel the privilege of possessing the High, and he could think of no other word to describe the sensation of walking down that street in company with Lonsdale and Grainger and others of his friends.

Term drew to a close, and Michael determined to mark the occasion by giving a dinner in which he thought he would try the effect of his friends all together. Hitherto the celebrations of the freshmen had been casual entertainments arranged haphazard out of the idle chattering groups in the lodge. This dinner was to be carefully thought out and balanced to the extreme of nice adjustment. This terminal dinner might, Michael thought, almost become with him a regular function, so that people would learn to speak with interest and respect of Fane's terminal dinners. In a way, it would be tantamount to forming a club, a club strictly subjective, indeed so personal in character as really to preclude the employment of the sociable world. At any rate, putting aside all dreams of the future, Michael made up his mind to try the effect of the first. It should be held in the Mitre, he decided, since that would give the company an opportunity of sailing homeward arm-in-arm along the whole length of the High. The guests should be Avery, Lonsdale, Wedderburn, Grainger, and Alan. Yet when Michael came to think about it, six all told seemed a beggarly number for his first terminal dinner. Already Michael began to think of his dinner as an established ceremony of undergraduate society. He would like to choose a number that should never vary every term. He knew that the guests would change, that the place of its celebration would alter, but he felt that some permanency must be kept, and Michael fixed upon eleven as the number, ten guests and himself. For this first dinner five more must be invited, and Michael without much further consideration selected five freshmen whose athletic prowess and social amiableness drew them into prominence. But when he had given all the invitations Michael was a little depressed by the conventional appearance of his list. With the exception of Alan as a friend from another college, and Avery, his list was exactly the same as any that might have been drawn up by Grainger. As Michael pondered it, he scented an effluence of correctness that overpowered his individuality. However, when he sat at the head of the table in the private room at the Mitre, and surveyed round the table his terminal dinner party, he was after all glad that on this occasion he had deferred to the prejudices of what in a severe moment of self-examination he characterized as "snobbishness." In this room at the Mitre with its faded red paper and pictures of rod and gun and steeplechase, with its two waiters whiskered and in their garrulous subservience eloquent of Thackerayan scenes, with its stuffed ptarmigan and snipe and glass-enshrined giant perch, Michael felt that a more eclectic society would have been out of place.

Only Avery's loose-fronted shirt marred the rigid convention of the group.

"*Who's* that man wearing a pie-frill?" whispered Alan sternly from Michael's right.

Michael looked up at him with an expression of amused apprehension.

"Avery allows himself a little license," said Michael. "But, Alan, he's really all right. He always wears his trousers turned up, and if you saw him on Sunday you'd think he was perfectly dressed. All Old Carthusians are."

But Alan still looked disapprovingly at Avery, until Lonsdale, who had met Alan several times at the House, began to talk of friends they had in common.

Michael was not altogether pleased with himself. He wished he had put Avery on his left instead of Wedderburn. He disliked owning to himself that he had put Avery at the other end of the table to avoid the responsibility of listening to the loudly voiced opinions which he felt grated upon the others. He looked anxiously along toward Avery, who waved a cheery hand. Michael perceived with pleasure and faint relief that he seemed to be amusing his neighbor, a Wykehamist called Castleton.

Michael was glad of this, for Castleton in some respects was the strongest influence in Michael's year, and his friendship would be good for Avery. Wedderburn had implied to Michael that he considered Castleton rather over-rated, but there was a superficial similarity between the two in the sort of influence they both possessed, and jealousy, if jealousy could lurk in the deep-toned and immaculate Wedderburn, might be responsible for that opinion. Michael sometimes wondered what made Castleton so redoubtable, since he was no more apparently than an athlete of ordinary ability, but Wykehamist opinion in the college was emphatic in proclaiming his solid merit, and as he seemed utterly unaware of possessing any quality at all, and as he seemed to add to every room in which he sat a serenity and security, he became each day more and more a personality impossible to neglect.

Opposite to Avery was Cuffe, and as Michael looked at Cuffe he was more than ever displeased with himself. The invitation to Cuffe was a detestable tribute to public opinion. Cuffe was a prominent freshman, and Michael had asked him for no other reason than because Cuffe would certainly have been asked to any other so representative a gathering of St. Mary's freshmen as this one might be considered. But a representative gathering of this kind was not exactly what Michael had intended to achieve with his terminal dinner. He looked at Cuffe with distaste. Then, too, in the middle of the table were Cranborne, Sterne, and Sinclair, not one of whom was there from Michael's desire to have him, but from some ridiculous tradition of his suitableness. However, it was useless to resent their presence now and, as the champagne went round, gradually Michael forgot his predilections and was content to see his first terminal dinner a success of wine and good-fellowship.

Soon Lonsdale was on his feet making a speech, and Michael sat back and smiled benignly on the company he had collected, while Lonsdale discussed their individual excellencies.

"First of all," said Lonsdale, "I want to propose the health of our distinguished friend, Mr. Merivale of Christ Church. For he's a jolly good fellow and all that. My friend Mr. Wedderburn's a jolly good fellow, too, and my friend Mr. Sterne on my center is a jolly good fellow and a jolly good bowler and so say all of us. As for my friend Tommy Grainger—whom I will not call Mister, having known him since we were boys together—I will here say that I confidently anticipate he will get his blue next term and show the Tabs that he's a jolly good fellow. I will not mention the rest of us by name—all jolly good fellows—except our host. He's given us a good dinner and good wine and good company, which nobody can deny. So here's his health."

Then, in a phantasmagoria in which brilliant liqueurs and a meandering procession of linked arms and the bells of Oxford and a wet night were all indistinguishably confused in one strong impression, Michael passed through his first terminal dinner.

CHAPTER IV

CHEYNE WALK

The Christmas vacation was spent in searching London for a new house. Mrs. Fane, when Carlington Road was with a sigh of relief at last abandoned, would obviously have preferred to go abroad at once and postpone the consideration of a future residence; but Michael with Stella's support prevailed upon her to take more seriously the problem of their new home.

Ultimately they fixed upon Chelsea, indeed upon that very house Stella had chosen for its large studio separated by the length of a queer little walled garden from the rest of the house. Certainly 173 Cheyne Walk was better than 64 Carlington Road, thought Michael as, leaning back against the parapet of the Embankment, he surveyed the mellow exterior in the unreal sunlight of the January noon. Empty as it was, it diffused an atmosphere of beauty and comfort, of ripe dignity and peaceful solidity. The bow windows with their half-opaque glass seemed to repulse the noise and movement of the world from the tranquil interior they so sleekly guarded. The front door with its shimmering indigo surface and fanlight and dolphin-headed knocker and on either side of the steps the flambeaux-stands of wrought iron, the three-plaster medallions and the five tall windows of the first story all gave him much contemplative pleasure. He and his mother and Stella had in three weeks visited every feasible quarter of London and as Michael thought of Hampstead's leaf-haunted by-streets, of the still squares of Kensington, even of Camden Hill's sky-crowned freedom, he was sure he regretted none of them in the presence of this sedate house looking over the sun-flamed river and the crenated line of the long Battersea shore.

Michael was waiting for Mrs. Fane, who as usual was late. Mr. Prescott was to be there to give his approval and advice, and Michael was anxious to meet this man who had evidently been a very intimate friend of his father. He saw Prescott in his mind as he had seen him years ago, an intruder upon the time-shrouded woes of childhood, and as he was trying to reconstruct the image of a florid jovial man, whose only definite impression had been made by the gold piece he had pressed into Michael's palm, a hansom pulled up at the house and someone, fair and angular with a military awkwardness, alighting from it, knocked at the door. Michael crossed the road quickly and asked if he were Mr. Prescott. Himself explained who he was and, opening the front door, led the way into the empty house. He was conscious, as he showed room after room to Prescott, that the visitor was somehow occupied less with the observation of the house than with a desire to achieve in regard to Michael himself a tentative advance toward intimacy. The January sun that sloped thin golden ladders across the echoing spaces of the bare rooms expressed for Michael something of the sensation which Prescott's attitude conveyed to him, the sensation of a benign and delicate warmth that could most easily melt away, stretching out toward certain unused depths of his heart.

"I suppose you knew my father very well," said Michael at last, blushing as he spoke at the uninspired obviousness of the remark.

"About as well as anybody," said Prescott nervously. "Like to talk to you about him some time. Better come to dinner. Live in Albany. Have a soldier-servant and all that, you know. Must talk sometimes. Important you should know just how your affairs stand. Suppose I'm almost what you might call your guardian. Of course your mother's a dear woman. Known her for years. Always splendid to me. But she mustn't get too charitable."

"Do you mean to people's failings?" Michael asked.

Michael did not ask this so much because he believed that was what Prescott really meant as because he wished to encourage him to speak out clearly at once so that, when later they met again, the hard shyness of preliminary encounters would have been softened. Moreover, this empty house glinting with golden motes seemed to encourage a frankness and directness of intercourse that made absurd these roundabout postponements of actual problems.

"Charitable to societies," Prescott explained. "I don't want her to think she's got to endow half a dozen committees with money and occupation."

"Stella's a little worried about mother's charities," Michael admitted.

"Awful good sort, Stella," Prescott jerked out. "Frightens me devilishly. Never could stand very clever people. Oh, I like them very much, but I always feel like a piece of furniture they want to move out of their way. Used to be in the Welsh Guards with your father," he added vaguely.

"Did you know my father when he first met my mother?" Michael asked directly, and by his directness tripped up Prescott into a headlong account.

"Oh, yes, rather. I sent in my papers when he did. Chartered a yacht and sailed all over the Mediterranean. Good gracious, twenty years ago! How old we're all getting. Poor old Saxby was always anxious that no kind of"—Prescott gibbed at the word for a moment or two— "no kind of slur should be attached.... I mean, for instance, Mrs. Fane might have had to meet the sort of women, you know, well, what I mean is ... there was nothing of the sort. Saxby was a Puritan, and yet he was always a rattling good sort. Only of course your mother was always cut off from women's society. Couldn't be helped, but I don't want her now to overdo it. Glad she's taken this house, though. What are you going to be?"

Michael was saved from any declaration of his intentions by a ring at the front door, which shrilled like an alarm through the empty house. Soon all embarrassments were lost in his mother's graceful and elusive presence that seemed to furnish every room in turn with rich associations of leisure and tranquillity, and with its fine assurance to muffle all the echoes and the emptiness. Stella, who had arrived with Mrs. Fane, was rushing from window to window, trying patterns of chintz and damask and Roman satin; and all her notions of decoration that she flung up like released birds seemed to flutter for a while in a confusion of winged argument between her and Michael, while Mr. Prescott listened with an expression on his wrinkling forehead of admiring perplexity. But every idea would quickly be gathered in by Mrs. Fane, and when she had smoothed its ruffled doubts and fears, it would fly with greater certainty, until room by room and window by window and corner by corner the house was beautifully and sedately and appropriately arranged.

"I give full marks to Prescott," said Stella later in the afternoon to Michael. "He's like a nice horse."

"I think we ought to have had green curtains in the spare room," said Michael.

"Why?" demanded Stella.

And when Michael tried to discover a reason, it was difficult to find one.

"Well, why not?" he at last very lamely replied.

There followed upon that curiously staccato conversation between Michael and Prescott in the empty house a crowded time of furnishing, while Mrs. Fane with Michael and Stella stayed at the Sloane Street Hotel, chosen by them as a convenient center from which to direct the multitudinous activities set up by the adventure of moving. Michael, however, after the first thrills of selection had died down, must be thinking about going up again and be content to look forward on the strength of Stella's energetic promises to coming down for the Easter vacation and entering 173 Cheyne Walk as his home.

Michael excused himself to himself for not having visited any old friends during this vacation by the business of house-hunting. Alan had been away in Switzerland with his father, but Michael felt rather guilty because he had never been near his old school nor even walked over to Notting Hill to give Viner an account of his first term. It seemed to him more important that he had corresponded with Lonsdale and Wedderburn and Avery than that he should have sought out old friends. All that Christmas vacation he was acutely conscious of the flowing past of old associations and of a sense of transition into a new life that though as yet barren of experience contained the promise of larger and worthier experiences than it now seemed possible to him could have happened in Carlington Road.

On the night before he went up Michael dined with Prescott at his rooms in the Albany. He enjoyed the evening very much. He enjoyed the darkness of the room whose life seemed to radiate from the gleaming table in its center. He enjoyed the ghostly motions of the soldier-servant and the half-obscured vision of stern old prints on the walls of the great square room, and he enjoyed the intense silence that brooded outside the heavily curtained windows. Here in the Albany Michael was immeasurably aware of the life of London that was surging such a little distance away; but in this modish cloister he felt that the life he was aware of could never be dated, as if indeed were he to emerge into Piccadilly and behold suddenly crinolines or even powdered wigs they would not greatly surprise him. The Albany seemed to have wrung the spirit from the noisy years that swept on their course outside, to have snatched from each its heart and in the museum of this decorous glass arcade to have preserved it immortally, exhibiting the frozen palpitations to a sensitive observer.

"You're not talking much," said Prescott.

"I was thinking of old plays," said Michael.

Really he was thinking of one old play to which his mother had been called away by Prescott on a jolly evening forgotten, whose value to himself had been calculated at half-a-sovereign pressed into his hand. Michael wished that the play could be going to be acted to-night and that for half-a-sovereign he could restore to his mother that jolly evening and that old play and his father. It seemed to him incommunicably sad, so heavily did the Albany with its dead joys rest upon his imagination, that people could not like years be frozen into a perpetual present.

"Don't often go to the theater nowadays," said Prescott. "When Saxby was alive"—Michael fancied that "alive" was substituted for something that might have hurt his feelings—"we used to go a lot, but it's dull going alone."

"Must you go alone?" asked Michael.

"Oh, no, of course I needn't. But I seem to be feeling oldish. Oldish," repeated the host.

Michael felt the usurpation of his own youth, but he could not resist asking whether Prescott thought he was at all like his father, however sharply this might accentuate the usurpation.

"Oh, yes, I think you are very like," said Prescott. "Good Lord, what a pity, what a pity! Saxby was always a great stickler for law and order, you know. He hated anything that seemed irregular or interfered with things. He hated Radicals, for instance, and motor cars. He had much more brain than many people thought, but of course," Prescott hurriedly added, as if he wished to banish the slightest hint of professional equipment, "of course he always preferred to be perfectly ordinary."

"I like to be ordinary," Michael said; "but I'm not."

"Never knew anybody at your age who was. I remember I tried to write some poetry about a man who got killed saving a child from being run over by a train," said Prescott in a tone of wise reminiscence. "You know, I think you're a very lucky chap," he added. "Here you are all provided for. In your first term at Oxford. No responsibilities except the ordinary responsibilities of an ordinary gentleman. Got a charming sister. Why, you might do anything."

"What, for example?" queried Michael.

"Oh, I don't know. There's the Diplomatic Service. But don't be in a hurry. Wait a bit. Have a good time. Your allowance is to be four hundred a year at St. Mary's. And when you're twenty-one you come into roughly seven hundred a year of your own, and ultimately you'll have at least two thousand a year. But don't be a young ass. You've been brought up quietly. You haven't *got* to cut a dash. Don't get in a mess with women, and, if you do, come and tell me before you try to get out of it."

"I don't care much about women," said Michael. "They're disappointing."

"What, already?" exclaimed Prescott, putting up his eyeglass.

Michael murmured a dark assent. The glass of champagne that owing to the attention of the soldier-servant was always brimming, the dark discreet room, and the Albany's atmosphere of passion squeezed into the mold of contemporary decorum or bound up to stand in a row of Thackeray's books, all combined to affect Michael with the idea that his life had been lived. He felt himself to belong to the period of his host, and as the rubied table glowed upon his vision more intensely, he beheld the old impressionable Michael, the nervous, the self-conscious, the sensitive slim ghost of himself receding out of sight into the gloom. Left behind was the new Michael going up to the Varsity to-morrow morning for his second term, going up with the assurance of finding delightful friends who would confirm his distaste for the circumscribed past. Only a recurrent apprehension that under the table he seemed called upon to manage a number of extra legs, or perhaps it was only a slight uncertainty as to which leg was crossed over the other at the moment, made him wonder very gently whether after all some of this easy remoteness were not due to the champagne. The figure of his host was receding farther and farther every moment, and his conversation reached Michael across a shimmering inestimable space of light, while finally he was aware of his own voice talking very rapidly and with a half-defiant independence of precisely what he wished to say. The evening swam past comfortably, and gradually from the fumes of the cigar smoke the figure of Prescott leaning back in his shadowy armchair took on once again a definite corporeal existence. A clock on the mantelpiece chimed the twelve strokes of midnight in a sort of silvery apology for obtruding the hour. Michael came back into himself with a start of confusion.

"I say, I must go."

Prescott and he walked along the arcade toward Albany Courtyard.

"I say," said Michael, with his foot on the step of the hansom, "I think I must have talked an awful lot of rot to-night."

"No, no, no, my dear boy; I've been very much interested," insisted Prescott.

And all the jingling way home Michael tried to rescue from the labyrinth of his memory some definite conversational thread that would lead him to discover what he could have said that might conceivably have mildly entertained his host.

"Nothing," he finally decided.

Next morning Michael met Alan at Paddington, and they went up to Oxford with all the rich confidence of a term's maturity. Even in the drizzle of a late January afternoon the city assumed in place of her eternal and waylaying beauty a familiarity that for Michael made her henceforth more beautiful.

After hall Avery came up to Michael's room, and while the rain dripped endlessly outside, they talked lazily of life with a more clearly assured intimacy than either of them could have contemplated the term before.

159

Michael spoke of the new house, of his sister Stella, of his dinner with Prescott at the Albany, almost indeed of the circumstances of his birth, so easy did it seem to talk to Avery deep in the deep chair before the blazing fire. He stopped short, however, at his account of the dinner.

"You know, I think I should like to turn ultimately into a Prescott," he affirmed. "I think I should be happy living in rooms at the Albany without ever having done a very great deal. I should like to feel I was perfectly in keeping with my rooms and my friends and my servant."

"But you wouldn't be," Avery objected, "if you thought about it."

"No, but I shouldn't think about it," Michael pointed out. "I should have steeled myself all my life not to think about it, and when your eldest son comes to see me, Maurice, and drinks a little too much champagne and talks as fast as his father used to talk, I shall know just exactly how to make him feel that after all he isn't quite the silly ass he will be inclined to think himself about the middle of his third cigar."

Michael sank farther back into the haze of his pipe and, contemplating dreamily the Mona Lisa, made up his mind that she would not become his outlook thirty years hence. Some stern old admiral with his hand on the terrestrial globe and a naval engagement in the background would better suit his mantelpiece.

"I wonder what I shall be like at fifty," he sighed.

"It depends what you do in between nineteen and fifty," said Avery. "You can't possibly settle down at the Albany as soon as you leave the Varsity. You'll have to do something."

"What, for example?" Michael asked.

"Oh, write perhaps."

"Write!" Michael scoffed. "Why, when I can read all these"—he pointed to his bookshelves—"and all the dozens and dozens more I intend to buy, what a fool I should be to waste my time in writing."

"Well, I intend to write," said Avery. "In fact, I don't mind telling you I intend to start a paper as soon as I can."

Michael laughed.

"And you'll contribute," Avery went on eagerly.

"How much?"

"I'm talking about articles. I shall call my paper—well, I haven't thought about the title—but I shall get a good one. It won't be like the papers of the nineties. It will be more serious. It will deal with art, of course, and literature, and politics, but it won't be decadent. It will try to reflect contemporary undergraduate thought. I think it might be called The Oxford Looking-Glass."

"Yes, I expect it will be a looking-glass production," said Michael. "I should call it The World Turned Upside Down."

"I'm perfectly serious about this paper," said Avery reproachfully.

"And I'm taking you very seriously," said Michael. "That's why I won't write a line. Are you going to have illustrations?"

"We might have one drawing. I'm not quite sure how much it costs to reproduce a drawing. But it would be fun to publish some rather advanced stuff."

"Well, as long as you don't publish drawings that look as if the compositor had suddenly got angry with the page and thrown asterisks at it, and as long as——"

"Oh, shut up," interrupted the dreaming editor, "and don't fall into that tiresome undergraduate cynicism. It's so young."

"But I am young," Michael pointed out with careful gravity. "So are you. And, Maurice, really you know for me my own ambitions are best. I've got a great sense of responsibility, and if I were to start going through life trying to do things, I should worry myself all the time. The only chance for me is to find a sort of negative attitude to life like Prescott. You'll do lots of things. I think you're capable of them. But I'd rather watch. At least in my present mood I would. I'd give anything to feel I was a leader of men or whatever it is you are. But I'm not. I've got a sister whom you ought to meet. She's got all the positive energy in our family. I can't explain, Maurice, just exactly what I'm feeling about existence at this moment, unless I tell you more about myself than I possibly can—anyway yet a while. I don't want to do any harm, and I don't think I could ever feel I was in a position to do any good. Look here, don't let's talk any more. I meant to dream myself into an attitude to-night, and you've made me talk like an earnest young convert."

"I think I'll go round and consult Wedderburn about this paper," said Avery excitedly.

"He thinks you're patronizing," Michael warned him.

Avery pulled up, suddenly hurt:

"Does he? I wonder why."

"But he won't, if you ask his advice about reproducing advanced drawings."

"Doesn't he like me?" persisted Avery. "I'd better not go round to his rooms."

"Don't be foolish, Maurice. Your sensitiveness is really all spoiled vanity."

When Avery had hesitatingly embarked upon his expedition to Wedderburn, Michael thought rather regretfully of his presence and wished he had been more sympathetic in his reception of the great scheme. Yet perhaps that was the best way to have begun his own scheme for not being disturbed by life. Michael thought how easily he might have had to reproach himself over Lily Haden. He had escaped once. There should be no more active exposure to frets and fevers. Looking back on his life, Michael came to the conclusion that henceforth books should give him his adventures. Actually he almost made up his mind to retire even from the observation of reality, so much had he felt, all this Christmas vacation, the dominance of Stella and so deeply had he been impressed by Prescott's attitude of inscrutable commentary.

Michael was greatly amused when two or three evenings later he strolled round to Wedderburn's rooms to find him and Maurice Avery sitting in contemplation of about twenty specimen covers of The Oxford Looking-Glass that were pinned against the wall on a piece of old

160

lemon-colored silk. He was greatly amused to find that the reconciling touch of the Muses had united Avery and Wedderburn in a firm friendship—so much amused indeed that he allowed himself to be nominated to serve on the obstetrical committee that was to effect the birth of this undergraduate bantling.

"Though what exactly you want me to do," protested Michael, "I don't quite know."

"We want money, anyway," Avery frankly admitted. "Oh, and by the way, Michael, I've asked Goldney, the Treasurer of the O.U.D.S. to put you up."

"What on earth for?" gasped Michael.

"Oh, they'll want supers. They're doing The Merchant of Venice. Great sport. Wedders is going to join. I want him to play the Prince of Morocco."

"But are you running the Ouds as well as The Oxford Looking-Glass?" Michael inquired gently.

In the end, however, he was persuaded by Avery to become a member, and not only to join himself but to persuade other St. Mary's freshmen, including Lonsdale, to join. The preliminary readings and the rehearsals certainly passed away the Lent term very well, for though Michael was not cast for a speaking part, he had the satisfaction of seeing Wedderburn and Avery play respectively the Princes of Morocco and Arragon, and of helping Lonsdale to entertain the professional actresses who came up from London to take part in the production.

"I think I ought to have played Lorenzo," said Lonsdale seriously to Michael, just before the first night. "I think Miss Delacourt would have preferred to play Jessica to my Lorenzo. As it is I'm only a gondolier, an attendant, and a soldier."

Michael was quite relieved when this final lament burst forth. It seemed to set Lonsdale once more securely in the ranks of the amateurs. There had been a dangerous fluency of professional terminology in "my Lorenzo."

"I'm only a gondolier, an attendant, and a mute judge," Michael observed.

"And I don't think that ass from Oriel knows how to play Lorenzo," Lonsdale went on. "He doesn't appreciate acting with Miss Delacourt. I wonder if my governor would be very sick if I chucked the Foreign Office and went on the stage. Do you think I could act, if I had a chance? I'm perfectly sure I could act with Miss Delacourt. Don't forget you're lunching with me to-morrow. I don't mind telling you she threw over a lunch with that ass from Oriel who's playing Lorenzo. I never heard such an idiotic voice in my life."

Such conversations coupled with requests from Wedderburn and Maurice Avery to hear them their two long speeches seemed to Michael to occupy all his leisure that term. At the same time he enjoyed the rehearsals in the lecture rooms at Christ Church, and he enjoyed escaping sometimes to Alan's rooms and ultimately persuading Alan to become a gondolier, an attendant and a soldier. Moreover, he met various men from other colleges, and he began to realize faintly thereby the individuality of each college, but most of all perhaps the individuality of his own college, as when Lonsdale came up to him one day with an expression of alarm to say that he had been invited to lunch by the man who played Launcelot Gobbo.

"Well, what of it?" said Michael. "He probably wants to borrow your dog."

"He says he's at Lincoln," Lonsdale stammered.

"So he is."

"Well, I don't know where Lincoln is. Have you got a map or something of Oxford?"

The performance of The Merchant of Venice took place and was a great success. The annual supper of the club took place, when various old members of theatrical appearance came down and made speeches and told long stories about their triumphs in earlier days. Next morning the auxiliary ladies returned to London, and in the afternoon the disconsolate actors went down to the barges and encouraged their various Toggers to victory.

Lonsdale forgot all about Miss Delacourt when he saw Tommy Grainger almost swinging the St. Mary's boat into the apprehensive stern of the only boat which stood between them and the headship, and that evening his only lament was that the enemy had on this occasion escaped. The Merchant of Venice with its tights and tinsel and ruffs faded out in that Lenten week of drizzling rain, when every afternoon Michael and Lonsdale and many others ran wildly along the drenched towing-path beside their Togger. And when in the end St. Mary's failed to catch the boat in front, Michael and Lonsdale and many others felt each in his own way that after all it had been greatly worth while to try.

Michael came down for the Easter vacation with the pleasant excitement of seeing 173 Cheyne Walk furnished and habitable. In deference to his mother's particular wish he had not invited anybody to stay with him, but he regretted he had not been more insistent when he saw each room in turn nearly twice as delightful as he had pictured it.

There was his mother's own sitting-room whose rose du Barri cushions and curtains conformed exactly to his own preconceptions, and there was Stella's bedroom very white and severe, and his own bedroom pleasantly mediæval, and the dining-room very cool and green, and the drawing-room with wallpaper of brilliant Chinese birds and in a brass cage a blue and crimson macaw blinking at the somber Thames. Finally there was the studio to which he was eagerly escorted by Stella.

"I haven't done anything but just have it whitewashed," she said. "I wanted you to choose the scheme, as I'm going to make all the noise."

The windy March sunlight seemed to fill the great room when Michael and his sister entered it.

"But it's absolutely empty," he exclaimed, and indeed there was nothing in all that space except Stella's piano, looking now almost as small and graceful as in Carlington Road it had seemed ponderous.

"You shall decorate the room," she said. "What will you choose?"

Michael visualized rapidly for a moment, first a baronial hall with gothic chairs and skins and wrought-iron everywhere, with tapestries and blazonries and heavy gold embroideries. Then he thought of crude and amazing contrasts of barbarous reds and vivid greens and purples, with Persian rugs and a smell of joss-sticks and long low divans. Yet, even as Michael's fancy decked itself with kaleidoscopic intentions, his mind swiftly returned to the keyboard's alternations of white and black, so that in a moment exotic splendors were merged in esoteric significance.

"I don't think we want anything," he finally proclaimed. "Just two or three tall chairs and a mask of somebody—Beethoven perhaps—and black silk curtains. You see the piano wouldn't go with elaborate decorations."

So every opportunity of prodigal display was neglected, and the studio remained empty. To Michael, all that windy Eastertide, it was an infallible thrill to leave behind him the sedate Georgian house and, crossing the little walled rectangle of pallid grass, to pause and listen to the muffled sound of Stella's notes. Never had any entrance seemed to him so perfect a revelation of joy within as now when he was able to fling wide open the door of the studio and feel, while the power and glory of the sonata assailed him, that this great white room was larger even than the earth itself. Sitting upon a high-backed chair, Michael would watch the white walls melting like clouds in the sun, would see their surface turn to liquid light, and fancy in these clear melodies of Stella that he and she and the piano and the high-backed chair were in this room not more trammeled than by space itself. Alan sometimes came shyly to listen, and while Stella played and played, Michael would wonder if ever these two would make for him the union that already he was aware of coveting. Alan was rosy with the joy of life on the slopes of the world, and Stella must surely have always someone fresh and clean and straight like Alan to marvel at her.

"By Jove, she must have frightfully strong wrists and fingers," said Alan.

Just so, thought Michael, might a shepherd marvel at a lark's powerful wings.

April went her course that year with less of sweet uncertainty than usual, and Michael walked very often along the Embankment dreaming in the sunshine as day by day, almost hour by hour, the trees were greening. Chelsea appealed to his sense of past greatness. It pleased him to feel that Carlyle and Rossetti might have walked as he was walking now during some dead April of time. Moreover, such heroes were not too far away. Their landscape was conceivable. People who had known them well were still alive. Swinburne and Meredith, too, had walked here, and themselves were still alive. In Carlington Road there had been none of this communion with the past. Nobody outside the contemporary residents could ever have walked along its moderately cheerful uniformity.

Michael, as he pondered the satisfaction which had come from the change of residence, began to feel a sentimental curiosity about Carlington Road and its surrounding streets. It was not yet a year since he had existed there familiarly, almost indigenously; but the combination of Oxford and Cheyne Walk made him feel a lifetime had passed since he had been so willingly transplanted. One morning late in April and just before he was going up for the summer term, he determined to pay a visit to the scenes of his childhood. It was an experience more depressing than he had imagined it would be. He was shocked by the sensation of constraint and of slightly contemptible limitation that was imposed upon his fancy by the pilgrimage. He thought to himself, as he wandered between the rows of thin red houses, that after the freedom of the river Carlington Road was purely intolerable. It did not possess the narrowness that lent a mysterious intimacy. The two rows of houses did not lean over and meet one another as houses lean over, almost seeming to gossip with one another, in ancient towns. They gave rather the impression of two mutually unattractive entities propelled into contiguity by the inexorable economy of the life around. The two rows came together solely for the purpose of crowding together a number of insignificant little families whose almost humiliating submission to the tyranny of city life was expressed pathetically by the humble flaunting of their window-boxes and in their front gardens symbolically by the dingy parterres of London Pride. Michael wondered whether a spirit haunting the earth feels in the perception of its former territory so much shame as he felt now in approaching 64 Carlington Road. When he reached the house itself, he was able to expel his sentiment for the past by the trivial fact that the curtains of the new owner had dispossessed the house of its personality. Only above the door, the number in all its squat assurance was able to convince him that this was indeed the house where he had wrestled so long and so hardly with the problems of childhood. There, too, was the plane-tree that, once an object of reproach, now certainly gave some distinction to the threshold of this house when every area down the road owned a lime-tree identical in age and growth.

Yet with all his distaste for 64 Carlington Road Michael could scarcely check the impulse he had to mount the steps and, knocking at the door, inform whomsoever should open it that he had once lived in this very house. He passed on, however, remembering at every corner of every new street some bygone unimportant event which had once occupied his whole horizon. Involuntarily he walked on and on in a confusion of recollections, until he came to the corner of the road where Lily Haden lived.

It was with a start of self-rebuke that he confessed to himself that here was the ultimate object of his revisitation. He had scarcely thought of Lily since the betrayal of his illusions on that brazen July day when last he had seen her in the garden behind her house. If he had thought of her at all, she had passed through his mind like the memory, or less even than the definite memory, like the consciousness that never is absent of beautiful days spent splendidly in the past. Sometimes during long railway journeys Michael had played with himself the game of vowing to remember an exact moment, some field or effect of clouds which the train was rapidly passing. Yet though he knew that he had done this a hundred times, it was always as impossible to conjure again the vision he had vowed to remember as it had been impossible ever to remember the exact moment of falling asleep.

After all, however, Lily could not have taken her place with these moments so impossible to recapture, or he would not have come to himself with so acute a consciousness of her former actuality here at the corner of Trelawney Road. It was almost as uncanny as the poem of Ulalume, and Michael found himself murmuring, "Of my most immemorial year," half expectant of Lily's slim form swaying toward him, half blushful already in breathless anticipation of the meeting.

Down the road a door opened. Michael's heart jumped annoyingly out of control. It was indeed her door, and whoever was coming out hesitated in the hall. Michael went forward impulsively, but the door slammed, and a man with a pencil behind his ear ran hurriedly down the steps. Michael saw that the windows of the house were covered with the names of house-agents, that several "to let" boards leaned confidentially over the railings to accost passers-by. Michael caught up the man, who was whistling off in the opposite direction, and asked him if he knew where Mrs. Haden had gone.

"I wish I did," said the man, sucking his teeth importantly. "No, sir, I'm afraid I don't. Nor anybody else."

"You mean they went away in a hurry," said Michael shamefaced.

"Yes, sir."

162

"And left no address?"

"Left nothing but a heap of tradesmen's bills in the hall."

Michael turned aside, sorry for the ignominious end of the Hadens, but glad somehow that the momentary temptation to renew his friendship with the family, perhaps even his love for Lily, was so irremediably defeated.

In the sunset that night, as he and Stella sat in the drawing-room staring over the incarnadined river, Michael told his sister of his discovery.

"I'm glad you're not going to start that business again," she said. "And, Michael, do try not to fall in love for a bit, because I shall soon have such a terrible heap of difficulties that you must solve for me disinterestedly and without prejudice."

"What sort of difficulties?" Michael demanded, with eyes fixed upon her cheeks warm with the evening light.

"Oh, I don't know," she half whispered. "But let's go away together in the summer and not even take a piano."

CHAPTER V

YOUTH'S DOMINATION

On May Morning, when the choir boys of St. Mary's hymned the rising sun, Michael was able for the first time to behold the visible expression of his own mental image of Oxford's completeness, to pierce in one dazzling moment of realization the cloudy and elusive concepts which had restlessly gathered and resolved themselves in beautiful obscurity about his mind. He was granted on that occasion to hold the city, as it were, imprisoned in a crystal globe, and by the intensity of his evocation to recognize perfectly that uncapturable quintessence of human desire and human vision so supremely displayed through the merely outward glory of its repository.

All night Michael and a large party of freshmen, now scarcely to be called freshmen so much did they feel they possessed of the right to live, had sustained themselves with dressed crab and sleepy bridge-fours. During the gray hour of hinted dawn they wandered round the college, rousing from sleep such lazy contemporaries as had vowed that not all the joys and triumph of May Morning on the tower should make them keep awake, during the vigil. Even so with what it contained of ability to vex other people that last hour hung a little heavily upon the enthusiasts. Slowly, however, the sky lightened: slowly the cold hues and blushes of the sun's youth, that stood as symbol for so much here in St. Mary's, made of the east one great shell of lucent color. The gray stones of the college lost the mysterious outlines of dawn and sharpened slowly to a rose-warmed vitality. The choir boys gathered like twittering birds at the base of the tower: energetic visitors came half shyly through the portal that was to give such a sense of time's rejuvenation as never before had they deemed possible: dons came hurrying like great black birds in the gathering light: and at last the tired revelers, Michael and Wedderburn, Maurice Avery and Lonsdale and Grainger and Cuffe and Castleton and a score besides equipped in cap and gown went scrambling and laughing up the winding stairs to the top.

For Michael the moment of waiting for the first shaft of the sun was scarcely to be endured: the vision of the city below was almost too poignant during the hush of expectancy that preceded the declaration of worship. Then flashed a silver beam in the east: the massed choir boys with one accord opened their mouths and sang just exactly, Michael said to himself, like the morning stars. The rising sun sent ray upon ray lancing over the roofs of the outspread city until with all its spires and towers, with all its domes and houses and still, unpopulous streets it sparkled like the sea. The hymn was sung: the choir boys twittered again like sparrows, and, bowing their greetings to one another, the dons cawed gravely like rooks. The bells incredibly loud here on the tower's top crashed out so ardently that every stone seemed to nod in time as the tower trembled and swayed backward and forward while the sun mounted into the day.

Michael leaned over the parapet and saw the little people busy as emmets at the base of the tower on whose summit he had the right to stand. Intoxicated with repressed adoration, the undergraduates sent hurtling outward into the air their caps, and down below the boys of the town scrambled and fought for these trophies of May Morning.

Michael through all the length of that May day dreamed himself into the heart of England. He had refused Maurice's invitation to a somewhat mannered breakfast-party at Sandford Lasher, though when he saw the almost defiantly jolly party ride off on bicycles from the lodge, he was inclined to regret his refusal. He wished he had persuaded Alan, now sleeping in the stillness of the House unmoved by May Morning celebrations, to rise early and come with him on some daylong jaunt far afield. It was a little dull to sit down to breakfast in the college shorn of revelers, and for another two hours unlikely to show any sign of life on the part of those who had declined for sleep the excitement of eating dressed crab and playing bridge through the vigil. After breakfast it would still be only about seven o'clock with a hot-eyed languor to anticipate during the rest of the morning. Michael almost decided to go to bed. He turned disconsolately out of the lodge and walked round Cloisters, out through one of the dark entries on to the lawns of New Quad gold-washed in the morning stillness. It seemed incredible that no sign should remain here of that festal life which had so lately thronged the scene. Michael went up to the J.C.R. and ate a much larger breakfast than usual, after which, feeling refreshed, he extracted his bicycle from the shed and at the bidding of a momentary impulse rode out of Oxford toward Lechlade.

It had been an early spring that year, and the country was far more typical than usual of old May Morning. Michael nowadays disliked the sensation of riding a bicycle, and though gradually the double irritation of no sleep and a long ride unaccompanied wore off, he was glad to see Lechlade spire and most glad of all to find himself deep in the grass by the edge of the river. Lying on his back and staring up at the slow clouds, he was glad he had refused to attend Maurice's mannered breakfast. Soon he fell asleep, and when he woke the morning had gone and it was time for lunch. Michael felt magnificently at ease with the country after his rest, and when he had eaten at the inn, he went back to the river's bank and slept away two hours more. Then for a while in the afternoon, so richly endowed with warmth and shadows that it seemed to have stolen a summer disguise, he walked about level water-meadows very lush and vivid, painted with gay and simple flowers and holding in their green embroidered lap all England. Riding back to Oxford, Michael thought he would have tea at an inn that stood beside a dreaming ferry. He was not sure of the inn's name, and deliberately he did not ask what sweet confluence of streams here happened, whether it were Windrush or Evenlode or some other nameless tributary that was flowing into the ancestral Thames.

163

Michael thought he would like to stay on to dinner and ride back to Oxford by moonlight. So with dusk falling he sat in the inn garden that was faintly melodious with the plash of the river and perfumed with white stocks. A distant clock chimed the hour, and Michael, turning for one moment to salute the sunset, went into the somber inn parlor.

At the table another undergraduate was sitting, and Michael hoped a conversation might ensue since he was attracted to this solitary inmate. His companion, however, scarcely looked up as he took his seat, but continued to stare very hard at a small piece of writing-paper on the table before him. He scarcely seemed to notice what was put on the table by the serving-maid, and he ate absently with his eyes still fixed upon his paper. Michael wondered if he were trying to solve a cipher and regretted his preoccupation, since the longer he spent in his silent company the more keenly he felt the attraction of this strange youth with the tumbled hair and drooping lids and delicately carved countenance. At last he put away the pencil he had been chewing instead of his food, and slipped the paper into the pocket of his waistcoat. Then with an expression of curiosity so intense as to pucker up his pale forehead into numberless wrinkles the pensive undergraduate examined the food on the plate before him.

"I think it's rather cold by now," said Michael, unable to keep silence any longer in the presence of this interesting stranger.

"I was trying to alter the last line of a sonnet. If I knew you better, I'd read you the six alternative versions. But if I read them to you now, you'd think I was an affected ass," he drawled.

Michael protested he would like to hear them very much.

"They're all equally bad," the poet proclaimed gloomily. "What made you come to this inn? I didn't know that anybody else except me had ever been here. You're at the Varsity, I suppose?"

Michael with a nod announced his college.

"I'm at Balliol. At Balliol you find the youngest dons and the oldest undergraduates in Oxford."

"I think just the reverse is true of St. Mary's," Michael suggested.

"Well, certainly the youngest thing I ever met is a St. Mary's man. I refer to the ebullient Avery whom I expect you know."

"Oh, rather. In fact, he's rather a friend of mine. He's keen on starting a paper just at present."

"I know. I know," said the poet. "He's asked me to be one of the forty-nine sub-editors. Are you another?"

"I was invited to be," Michael admitted. "But instead I'm going to subscribe some of the capital required. My name's Fane."

"Mine's Hazlewood. It's rather jolly to meet a person in this inn. Usually I only meet fishermen more flagrantly mendacious than anywhere else. But they've got bored with me because I always unhesitatingly go two pounds better than the biggest juggler of avoirdupois present. Have you ever thought of the romance in Troy measure? I can imagine Paris weighing the charms of Helen—no—on second thoughts I'm being forced. Don't encourage me to talk for effect. How did you come to this inn?"

"I don't know," said Michael, wrestling as he spoke with the largest roast chicken he had ever seen. "I think I missed a turning. I've been at Lechlade all day."

"We may as well ride back together," Hazlewood proposed.

After dinner they talked and smoked for a while in the inn parlor, and then with half-a-moon high in the heavens they scudded back to Oxford. Hazlewood invited Michael to come up to his rooms for a drink.

"Do you know many Balliol people?" he asked.

Michael named a few acquaintances who had been the fruit of his acting in The Merchant of Venice.

"I daresay some of that push will be in my rooms. Other people use my rooms almost more than I do myself. I think they have a vague idea they're keeping a chapel, or else it's a relief from the unparagoned brutality of the college architecture."

Hazlewood was right in his surmise, for when he and Michael reached his rooms, they seemed full of men. It was impossible to say at once how many were present because the only light was given by two gigantic wax candles that stood on either side of the fireplace in massive candlesticks of wrought iron.

"Mr. Fane of St. Mary's," said Hazlewood casually, and Michael was dimly aware of multitudinous nods of greeting and an unanimous murmur of expostulation with Hazlewood for his lateness.

"I suppose you know that this is a meeting of the Chandos, Guy?" the chorus sighed, in a climax of exasperated patience.

"Forgot all about it," said Hazlewood. "But I suppose I can bring a visitor."

Michael made a move to depart, feeling embarrassed by the implied criticism of the expostulation.

"Sit down," said Hazlewood peremptorily. "If I can't bring a visitor I resign from the Society, and the five hundred and fiftieth meeting will have to be held somewhere else. I call upon Lord Comeragh to read us his carefully prepared paper on The Catapult in Mediæval Warfare."

"Don't be an affected ass, Guy," said Comeragh. "You know you yourself are reading a paper on The Sonnet."

"Rise from the noble lord," said Hazlewood. "The first I've had in a day's fishing. I say, Fane, don't listen to this rot."

The company settled back in anticipation of the paper, while the host and reader searched desperately in the dim light for his manuscript.

Michael found the evening a delightful end to his day. He was sufficiently tired by his nocturnal vigil to be able to accept the experience without any prickings of self-consciousness and doubt as to whether this Balliol club resented his intrusion. Hazlewood's room was the most personal that so far he had seen in Oxford. It shadowed forth for Michael possibilities that in the sporting atmosphere of St. Mary's he had begun to forget. He would not have liked Tommy Grainger or Lonsdale to have rooms like this one of Hazlewood's, nor would he have exchanged the society of Grainger and Lonsdale for any other society in Oxford; but he was glad to think that Hazlewood and his rooms existed. He lay back in a deep armchair watching the candlelight flicker over the tapestries, and the shadows of the listeners in giant size upon their martial and courtly populations. He heard in half-a-dream the level voice of Hazlewood enunciating his theories in graceful singing sentences, and the occasional fizz of a replenished glass. The tobacco smoke grew thicker and thicker, curling in spirals about the emaciated loveliness of an ivory saint. The paper was over: and before the discussion was started somebody rose and drew back the dull green curtains sown with golden fleur-de-lys. Moonbeams came slanting in and with them the freshness of the May night: more richly blue gathered the tobacco smoke: more magical became the room, and more perfectly the decorative expression of all Oxford stood for. One by one the members of the Chandos Society rose up to comment on the paper, mocking and earnest, affected and sincere, always clever, sometimes humorous, sometimes truly wise with an apologetic wisdom that was the more delightful.

Michael came to the conclusion that he liked Balliol, that most unjustly had he heard its atmosphere stigmatized as priggish. He made up his mind to examine more closely at leisure this atmosphere, so that from it he might extract the quintessential spirit. Walking with Hazlewood to the lodge, he asked him if the men he had met in his room would stand as representatives of the college.

"Yes, I should think so," said Hazlewood. "Why, are you making exhaustive researches into the social aspects of Oxford life? It takes an American to do that really well, you know."

"But what is the essential Balliol?" Michael demanded.

"Who could say so easily? Perhaps it's the same sort of spirit, slightly filtered down through modern conditions, as you found in Elizabethan England."

Michael asked for a little more elaboration.

"Well, take a man connected with the legislative class, directly by birth and indirectly by opportunities, give him at least enough taste not to be ashamed of poetry, give him also enough energy not to be ashamed of football or cricket, and add a profound satisfaction with Oxford in general and Balliol in particular, and there you are."

"Will that description serve for yourself?" Michael asked.

"For me? Oh, great scott, no! I'm utterly deficient in proconsular ambitions."

They had reached the lodge by now, and Michael left his new friend after promising very soon to come to lunch and pursue further his acquaintance with Balliol.

When Michael got back to college, Avery was hard at work with Wedderburn drawing up the preliminary circular of The Oxford Looking-Glass. Both the promoters insisted that Michael should listen to their announcement before he told them anything about himself or his day.

"The Oxford Looking-Glass" Avery began, *"is intended to reflect contemporary undergraduate thought."*

"I prefer 'will reflect,'" Wedderburn interrupted, in bass accents of positive opinion.

"I don't think it very much matters," said Michael, "as long as you don't think that 'contemporary undergraduate thought' is too pretentious. The question is whether you can see a ghost in a mirror, for a spectral appearance is just about as near as undergraduate thought ever reaches toward reality."

Neither Avery nor Wedderburn condescended to reply to his criticism, and the chief promoter went on:

"Some of the subjects which The Oxford Looking-Glass will reflect will be Literature, Politics, Painting, Music, and the Drama."

"I think that's a rotten sentence," Michael interrupted.

"Well, of course, it will be polished," Avery irritably explained. "What Wedders and I have been trying to do all the evening is to say as simply and directly as possible what we are aiming at."

"Ah!" Michael agreed, smiling. "Now I'm beginning to understand."

"It may be assumed," Avery went on, *"that the opinion of those who are 'knocking at the door'* (in inverted commas)——"

"I shouldn't think anybody would ever open to people standing outside a door in inverted commas," Michael observed.

"Look here, Michael," Avery and Wedderburn protested simultaneously, "will you shut up, or you won't be allowed to contribute."

"Haven't you ever heard of the younger generation knocking at the door in Ibsen?" fretfully demanded Maurice. *"That the opinion of those who are knocking at the door,"* he continued defiantly, *"is not unworthy of an audience."*

"But if they're knocking at a door," Michael objected, "they can't be reflected in a mirror; unless it's a glass door, and if it's a glass door, they oughtn't to be knocking on it very hard. And if they don't knock hard, there isn't much point——"

"The Editor in chief," pursued Maurice, undaunted by Michael's attempt to reduce to absurdity the claims of The Oxford Looking-Glass, *"will be M. Avery (St. Mary's), with whom will be associated C. St. C. Wedderburn (St. Mary's), C. M. S. Fane (St. Mary's), V. L. A. Townsend (B.N.C.).* I haven't asked him yet, as a matter of fact, but he's sure to join because he's very keen on Ibsen. *W. Mowbray (Univ.).* Bill Mowbray's very bucked at the scheme. He's just resigned from the Russell and joined the Canning. They say at the Union that a lot of the principal speakers are going to follow Chamberlain's lead for Protection. *N. R. Stewart (Trinity).* Nigel Stewart is most tremendously keen, and rather a good man to have, as he's had two poems taken by The Saturday Review already. *G. Hazlewood (Balliol)*——"

"That's the man I've come to talk about," said Michael. "I met him to-day."

Avery asked if Michael liked old Guy and was obviously pleased to hear he had been considered interesting. "For in his own way," said Avery solemnly, "he's about the most brilliant man in the Varsity. I'd sooner have him under me than all the rest put together, except of course you and Wedders," he added quickly. "I'm going to take this prospectus round to show him to-morrow. He may have some suggestions to make."

Michael joined with the Editor in supposing that Hazlewood might have a large number of suggestions. "And he's got a sense of humor," he added consolingly.

For a week or two Michael found himself deeply involved in the preliminaries of The Oxford Looking-Glass, and the necessary discussions gave many pleasant excuses for dinner parties at the O.U.D.S. or the Grid to which Townsend and Stewart (both second-year men) belonged. Vernon Townsend wished to make The Oxford Looking-Glass the organ of advanced drama; but Avery, though he was willing for Townsend to be as advanced as he chose within the limits of the space allotted to his progressive pen, was unwilling to surrender the whole of the magazine to drama, especially since under the expanding ambitions of editorship he had come to the conclusion he was a critic himself, and so was the more firmly disinclined to let slip the trenchant opportunity of pulverizing the four or five musical comedies that would pass through the Oxford theater every term. However, Townsend's demand for the drama and nothing but the drama was mitigated by his determination as a Liberal that The Oxford Looking-Glass should not be made the mouthpiece of the New Toryism represented by Mowbray; and Maurice was able to recover the control of the dramatic criticism by representing to Townsend the necessity for such unflinching exposition of Free Trade and Palmerston Club principles as would balance Mowbray's torrential leadership of the Tory Democrats. "So called," Townsend bitterly observed, "because as he supposed they were neither Tories nor Democrats."

Mowbray at the end of his second year was certainly one of the personalities of undergraduate Oxford. For a year and a term he had astonished the Russell Club by the vigor of his Radicalism; and then just when they began to talk of electing him President and were looking forward to this Presidency of the Russell as an omen of his future Presidency of the Union itself, he resigned from the Russell, and figuratively marched across the road to the Canning, taking with him half a dozen earnest young converts and galvanizing with new hopes and new ambitions the Oxford Tories now wilting under the strain of the Boer war. Mowbray managed to impart to any enterprise the air of a conspiracy, and Michael never saw him arrive at a meeting of The Oxford Looking-Glass without feeling they should all assume cloaks and masks and mutter with heads close together. Mowbray did indeed exist in an atmosphere of cabals, and his consent to sit upon the committee of The Oxford Looking-Glass was only a small item in his plot to overthrow Young Liberalism in Oxford. His rooms at University were always thronged with satellites, who at a word from him changed to meteors and whizzed about Oxford feverishly to outshine the equally portentous but less dazzling exhalations of Liberal opinion.

Stewart of Trinity represented an undergraduate type that perhaps had endured and would endure longer than any of the others. He would have been most in his element if he had come up in the early nineties, but yet with all his intellectual survivals he did not seem an anachronism. Perhaps it was as well that he had not come up in the nineties, since much of his obvious and youthful charm might have been buried beneath absurdities which in those reckless decadent days were carried sometimes to moral extremes that destroyed a little of the absurdity. As it was, Stewart was perhaps the most beloved member of Trinity, whether he were feeding Rugger blues on plovers' eggs or keeping an early chapel with the expression of an earthbound seraph or playing tennis in the Varsity doubles or whether, surrounded by Baudelaire and Rollinat and Rops and Huysmans, he were composing an ode to Satan, with two candles burning before his shrine of King Charles the Martyr and a ramshorn of snuff and glasses of mead waiting for casual callers.

With Townsend, Mowbray, and Stewart, thought Michael, added to Wedderburn's Pre-Raphaelitism and staid Victorian romance, to Hazlewood's genuine inspiration, and with Maurice Avery to whip the result into a soufflée of exquisite superficiality, it certainly seemed as if The Oxford Looking-Glass might run for at least a year. But what exactly was himself doing on the committee? He could contribute, outside money, nothing of force to help in driving the new magazine along to success. Still, somehow he had allowed his name to appear in the preliminary circular, and next October when the first number was published somehow he would share however indirectly in the credit or reproach accruing. Meanwhile, there were the mere externals of this first summer term to be enjoyed, this summer term whose beginning he had hailed from St. Mary's tower, this dream of youth's domination set against the gray background of time's endurance that was itself spun of the fabric of dreams.

Divinity and Pass Moderations would occur some time at the term's end, inexplicable as such a dreary interruption seemed in these gliding river-days which only rain had power for a brief noontide or evening to destroy. Yet, as an admission that time flies, the candidates for Pass Mods and Divvers attended a few sun-drowsed lectures and never omitted to lay most tenderly underneath the cushions of punt or canoe the text-books of their impertinent examinations. Seldom, however, did Cicero or the logical Jevons emerge in that pool muffled from sight by trellised boughs of white and crimson hawthorn. Seldom did Socrates have better than a most listless audience or St. Paul the most inaccurate geographers, when on the upper river the punt was held against the bank by paddles fast in the mud; for there, as one lay at ease, the world became a world of tall-growing grasses, and the noise of life no more than the monotony of a river's lapping, or along the level water meadows a faint sibilance of wind. This was the season when supper was eaten by figures in silhouette against the sunset, figures that afterward drifted slowly down to college under the tree-entangled stars and flitting assiduous bats, with no sound all the way but the rustle of a bird's wing in the bushes and the fizz of a lighted match dropped idly over the side of the canoe. This was the season when for a long while people sat talking at open windows, and from the Warden's garden came sweetly up the scent of May flowers.

Sometimes Michael went to the Parks to watch Alan play in one or two of the early trial matches, and sometimes they sat in the window of Alan's room looking out into Christ Church meadows. Nothing that was important was ever spoken during these dreaming nights, and if Michael tried to bring the conversation round to Stella, Alan would always talk of leg-drives and the problems that perpetually presented themselves to cover-point. Yet the evenings were always to Michael in retrospect valuable, betokening a period of perfect happiness from the lighting of the first pipe to the eating of the last meringue.

Eights Week drew near, and Michael decided after much deliberation that he would not ask either his mother or Stella to take part in the festival. One of his reasons, only very grudgingly admitted, for not inviting Stella was his fear lest Alan might be put into the shade by certain more brilliant friends whom he would feel bound to introduce to her. Having made up his own mind that Alan represented the perfection of normal youth, he was unwilling to admit dangerous competitors. Besides, though by now he had managed to rid himself of most of his self-consciousness, he was not sure he felt equal to charging the battery of eyes that mounted guard in the lodge. The almost savage criticism of friends and relatives indulged in by the freshmen's table was more than he could equably contemplate for his own mother and sister.

So Eights Week arrived with Michael unencumbered and delightfully free to stand in the lodge and watch the embarrassed youth, usually so debonair and self-possessed, herding a long trail of gay sisters and cousins toward his room where even now waited the inevitable salmon mayonnaise. Lonsdale in a moment of filial enthusiasm had invited his father and mother and only sister to come up, and afterward had spent two days of lavish regret for the rashness of the undertaking.

166

"After all, they can only spend the day," he sighed hopefully to Michael, "You'll come and help me through lunch, won't you, and we'll rush them off by the first train possible after the first division is rowed. I was an ass to ask them. You won't mind being bored a bit by my governor? I believe he's considered quite a clever man."

Michael, remembering that Lord Cleveden had been a distinguished diplomatist, was prepared to accept his son's estimate.

"They're arriving devilish early," said Lonsdale, coming up to Michael's room with an anxious face on the night before.

Ever since his fatal display of affection, he had taken to posting, as it were, bulletins of the sad event on Michael's door.

"Would you be frightfully bored if I asked you to come down to the station and meet them? It will be impossible for me to talk to the three of them at once. I think you'd better talk about wine to the governor. It'll buck him rather to think his port has been appreciated. Tell him how screwed we made the bobby that night when we were climbing in late from that binge on the Cher, and let down glass after glass of the governor's port from Tommy's rooms in Parsons' Quad."

Michael promised to do his best to entertain the father, and without fail to support the son at the ceremony of meeting his people next morning.

"I say, you've come frightfully early," Lonsdale exclaimed, as Lord and Lady Cleveden with his sister Sylvia alighted from the train.

"Well, we can walk round my old college," suggested Lord Cleveden cheerfully. "I scarcely ever have an opportunity to get up to Oxford nowadays."

"I say, I'm awfully sorry to let you in for this," Lonsdale whispered to Michael. "Don't encourage the governor to do too much buzzing around at the House. Tell him the mayonnaise is getting cold or something."

Soon they arrived at Christ Church, and Michael rather enjoyed walking round with Lord Cleveden and listening to his stately anecdotes of bygone adventure in these majestic quadrangles.

"I wonder if Lord Saxby was up in your time?" asked Michael as they stood in Peckwater.

"Yes, knew him well. In fact, he was a connection of mine. Poor chap, he died in South Africa. Where did you meet him? He never went about much."

"Oh, I met him with a chap called Prescott," said Michael hurriedly.

"Dick Prescott? Good gracious!" Lord Cleveden exclaimed, "I haven't seen him for years. What an extraordinary mess poor Saxby made of his life, to be sure."

"Did he?" asked Michael, well aware of the question's folly, but incapable of not asking it.

"Terrible! Terrible! But it was never a public scandal."

"Oh," gulped Michael humbly, wishful he had never asked Lord Cleveden about his father.

"I can't remember whether my old rooms were on that staircase or this one. Saxby's I think were on this, but mine surely were on that one. Let's go up and ask the present owner to let us look in," Lord Cleveden proposed, peering the while in amiable doubt at the two staircases.

"Oh, no, I say, father, really, no, no," protested his son. "No, no; he may have people with him. Really."

"Ah, to be sure," Lord Cleveden agreed. "What a pity!"

"And I think we ought to buzz round St. Mary's before lunch," Lonsdale announced.

"Do they make meringues here nowadays?" inquired Lord Cleveden meditatively.

"No, no," Lonsdale assured him. "They've given up since the famous cook died. Look here, we absolutely must buzz round St. Mary's. And our crème caramel is a much showier sweet than anything they've got at the House."

The tour of St. Mary's was conducted with almost incredible rapidity, because Lonsdale knew so little about his own college that he omitted everything except the J.C.R., the hall, the chapel, the buttery and the kitchen.

"Why didn't you ask Duncan Mackintosh to lunch, Arthur dear?" Lady Cleveden inquired.

"My dear mother," said Arthur, "he's quite impossible."

"But Sir Hugh Mackintosh is such a charming man," said Lady Cleveden, "and always asks us to stay with him when we're in Scotland."

"Yes, but we never are," Lonsdale pointed out. "And I'm sorry to hurt your feelings, mother, about a relation of yours, but Mackintosh is really absolutely impossible. He's the very worst type of Harrovian."

Michael felt bound to support his friend by pointing out that Mackintosh was so eccentric as to dislike entertainment of any kind, and urged a theory that even if he had been asked, he would certainly have declined rather offensively.

"He's not a very bonhomous lad," said Lonsdale, and with that sentence banished Mackintosh for ever from human society.

After lunch the host supposed in a whisper to Michael that they ought to take his people out in a punt. Michael nodded agreement, and weighed down by cushions the party walked through the college to where the pleasure craft of St. Mary's bobbed at their moorings.

Lonsdale on the river possessed essentially the grand manner, and his sister who had been ready to laugh at him gently was awed into respectful admiration. Even Lord Cleveden seemed inclined to excuse himself, if ever in one of the comprehensive and majestic indications of his opinion he disturbed however slightly the equilibrium of the punt. Lonsdale stood up in the stern and handled the ungainly pole with the air of a Surbiton expert. His tendency toward an early rotundity was no longer noticeable. His pink and cheerful face assumed a grave superciliousness of expression that struck with apologetic dismay the navigators who impeded his progress. Round his waist the rich hues of the Eton Ramblers glowed superbly.

"Thank you, sir. Do you mind letting me through, sir? Some of these toshers ought not to be trusted with a punt of their own." This comment was for Michael and uttered in a voice of most laryngeal scorn so audible that the party of New College men involved reddened with dull fury. "Try and get along, please, sir. You're holding up the whole river, sir. I say, Michael, this is an absolute novices' competition."

After an hour of this slow progress Lonsdale decided they must go back to college for tea, an operation which required every resource of sangfroid to execute successfully. When he had landed his father and mother and sister, he announced that they must all be quick over tea and then buzz off at once to see the first division row.

"I think we shall go head to-night," Lonsdale predicted very confidentially. "I told Tommy Grainger he rowed like a caterpillar yesterday."

But after all it was not to be the joyful privilege of Lonsdale's people to see St. Mary's bump New College in front of their own barge, and afterward to behold the victorious boat row past in triumph with the westering sun making glow more richly scarlet the cox's blazer and shine more strangely beautiful the three white lilies in his buttonhole.

"Now you've just got time to catch your train," said Lonsdale, when the sound of the last pistol-shots and plaudits had died away. And "Phew!" he sighed, as he and Michael walked slowly down the station-hall, "how frightfully tiring one's people are when imported in bulk!"

Eights Week came to an end with the scarlet and lilies still second; and without the heartening effect of a bump-supper the candidates for Pass Mods applied themselves violently to the matter in hand. At the end of the examination, which was characterized by Lonsdale as one of the most low-down exhibitions of in-fighting he had ever witnessed, the candidates had still a week of idleness to recover from the dastardly blows they had received below their intellectual belts.

It was the time of the midsummer moon; and the freshmen in this the last week of their state celebrated the beauty of the season with a good deal of midsummer madness. Bonfires were lit for the slightest justification, and rowdy suppers were eaten in college after they had stayed on the river until midnight, rowdy suppers that demanded a great expense of energy before going to bed, in order perhaps to stave off indigestion.

On one of these merry nights toward one o'clock somebody suggested that the hour was a suitable one for the ragging of a certain Smithers who had made himself obnoxious to the modish majority not from any overt act of contumely, but for his general bearing and plebeian origin. This derided Smithers lived on the ground floor of the Palladian fragment known as New Quad. The back of New Quad looked out on the deer-park, and it was unanimously resolved to invade his rooms from the window, so that surprise and alarm would strike at the heart of Smithers.

Half a dozen freshmen—Avery, Lonsdale, Grainger, Cuffe, Sinclair, and Michael—all rendered insensitive to the emotions of other people by the amount of champagne they had drunk, set out to harry Smithers. Michael alone possibly had a personal slight to repay, since Smithers had been one of the freshmen who had sniggered at his momentary mortification in the rooms of Carben, the Rugby secretary, during his first week. The others were more vaguely injured by Smithers' hitherto undisturbed existence. Avery disliked his face: Lonsdale took exception to his accent: Grainger wanted to see what he looked like: Cuffe was determined to be offensive to somebody: and Sinclair was anxious to follow the fashion.

Not even the magic of the moonlit park deterred these social avengers from their vendetta. They moved silently indeed over the filmy grass and paused to hearken when in the distance the deer stampeded in alarm before their progress, but the fixed idea of Smithers' reformation kept them to their project, and perhaps only Michael felt a slight sense of guilt in profaning this fairy calm with what he admitted to himself might very easily be regarded as a piece of stupid cruelty. Outside Smithers' open window they all stopped; then after hoisting the first man onto the dewy sill, one by one they climbed noiselessly into the sitting-room of the offensive Smithers. Somebody turned on the electric light, and they all stood half-abashed, surveying one another in the crude glare that in contrast with the velvet depths and silver shadows of the woodland they had traversed seemed to illuminate for one moment an unworthy impulse in every heart.

The invaders looked round in surprise at the photographs of what were evidently Smithers' people, photographs like the groups in the parlors of country inns or the tender decorations of a housemaid's mantelpiece.

"I say, look at that fringe," gurgled Avery, and forthwith he and Lonsdale collapsed on the sofa in a paroxysm of strangled mirth.

Michael, as he gradually took in the features of Smithers' room, began to feel very much ashamed of himself. He recognized the poverty that stood in the background of this splendid "college career" of Percy or Clarence or whatever other name of feudal magnificence had been awarded to counterbalance "Smithers." No doubt the champagne in gradual reaction was over-charging him with sentiment, but observing in turn each tribute from home that adorned with a pathetic utility this bleak room dedicated for generations to poor scholars, Michael felt very much inclined to detach himself from the personal ragging of Smithers and go to bed. What seemed to him in this changed mood so particularly sad was that on the evidence of his books Smithers was not sustained by the ascetic glories of learning for the sake of learning. He was evidently no classical scholar with a future of such dignity as would compensate for the scraping and paring of the past. To judge by his books, he was at St. Mary's to ward off the criticism of outraged Radicals by competing on behalf of the college and the university in scientific knowledge with newer foundations like Manchester or Birmingham. Smithers was merely an advertisement of Oxford's democratic philanthropy, and would only gain from his university a rather inferior training in chemistry at a considerably greater personal cost but with nothing else that Oxford could and did give so prodigally to others more fortunately born.

At this point in Michael's meditations Smithers woke up, and from the bedroom came a demand in startled cockney to know who was there. The reformers were just thinking about their reply, when Smithers, in a long nightgown and heavy-eyed with sleep, appeared in the doorway between his two rooms.

"Well, I'm jiggered!" he gasped. "What are you fellers doing in my sitting-room?"

It happened that Cuffe at this moment chose to take down from the wall what was probably an enlarged portrait of Smithers' mother in order to examine it more closely. The son, supposing he meant to play some trick with it, sprang across the room, snatched it from Cuffe's grasp, and shouting an objurgation of his native Hackney or Bermondsey, fled through the open window into the deer-park.

Cuffe's expression of dismay was so absurd that everybody laughed very heartily; and the outburst of laughter turned away their thoughts from damaging Smithers' humble property and even from annoying any more Smithers himself with proposals for his reformation.

"I say, we can't let that poor devil run about all night in the park with that picture," said Grainger. "Let's catch him and explain we got into his rooms by mistake."

"I hope he won't throw himself into the river or anything," murmured Sinclair anxious not to be involved in any affair that might spoil his reputation for enjoying every rag without the least reproach ever lighting upon him personally.

"I say, for goodness' sake, let's catch him," begged Michael, who had visions of being sent to explain to a weeping mother in a mean street that her son had died in defending her enlargement.

Out into the moon-washed park the pursuers tumbled, and through its verdurous deeps of giant elms they hurried in search of the outlaw.

"It's like a scene in The Merry Wives of Windsor," Michael said to Avery, and as he spoke he caught a glimpse of the white-robed Smithers, running like a young druid across a glade where the moonlight was undimmed by boughs.

He called to Smithers to go back to his rooms, but whether he went at once or huddled in some hollow tree half the night Michael never knew, for by this time the unwonted stampeding of the deer and the sound of voices in the Fellows' sacred pleasure-ground had roused the Dean, who supported by the nocturnal force of the college servants was advancing against the six disturbers of the summer night. The next hour was an entrancing time of hot pursuit and swift evasion, of crackling dead branches and sudden falls in lush grass, of stealthy procedure round tree-trunks, and finally of scaling a high wall, dropping heavily down into the rose-beds of the Warden's garden and by one supreme effort of endurance going to ground in St. Cuthbert's quad.

"By Jove, that was a topping rag," puffed Lonsdale, as he filled six glasses with welcome drink. "I think old Shadbolt recognized me. He said: 'It's no use you putting your coat over your 'ead, sir, because I knows you by your gait.'"

"I wonder what happened to Smithers," said Michael.

"Damned good thing if he fell into the Cher," Avery asserted. "I don't know why on earth they want to have a bounder like that at St. Mary's."

"A bounder like what?" asked Castleton, who had sloped into the room during Avery's expression of opinion.

Castleton was greeted with much fervor, and a disjointed account of the evening's rag was provided for his entertainment.

"But why don't you let that poor devil alone?" demanded the listener.

At this time of night nobody was able to adduce any very conclusive reason against letting Smithers alone, although Maurice Avery insisted that men like him were very bad for the college.

Dawn was breaking when Michael strolled round Cloisters with Castleton, determined to probe through the medium of Castleton's common sense and Wykehamist notions the ethical and æsthetic rights of people like Smithers to obtain the education Oxford was held to bestow impartially.

"After all, Oxford wasn't founded to provide an expensive three years of idleness for the purpose of giving a social cachet to people like Cuffe," Castleton pointed out.

"No, no," Michael agreed, "but no institution has ever yet remained true to the principles of its founder. The Franciscans, for instance, or Christianity itself. The point surely is not whether it has evolved into something inherently worthless, but whether, however much it may have departed from original intentions, it still serves a useful purpose in the scheme of social order."

"Oh, I'm not grumbling at what Oxford is," Castleton went on. "I simply suggest that the Smitherses have the right, being in a small minority, to demand courtesy from the majority, and, after all, Oxford is serving no purpose at all, if she cannot foster good manners in people who are supposed to be born with a natural tendency toward good manners. I should be the first to regret an Oxford with the Smitherses in the majority, but I think that those Smitherses who have fought their way in with considerable difficulty should not go down with the sense of hatred which that poor solitary creature must surely feel against all of us."

Michael asked Castleton if he had ever talked to him.

"No, I'm afraid I haven't. I'm afraid I'm too lazy to do much more than deplore theoretically these outbursts of rowdy superiority. Now, as I'm beginning to talk almost as priggishly as a new sub-editor of The Spectator might talk, to bed."

The birds were singing, as Michael walked back from escorting Castleton to his rooms. St. Mary's tower against the sky opening like a flower seemed to express for him a sudden aspiration of all life toward immortal beauty. In this delicate hour of daybreak all social distinctions, all prejudices and vulgarities became the base and clogging memories of the night before. He felt a sudden guilt in beholding this tranquil college under this tranquil dawn. It seemed, spread out for his solitary vision, too incommunicable a delight. And suddenly it struck him that perhaps Smithers might be standing outside the gate of this dream city, that he, too, might wish to salute the sunrise. He blushed with shame at the thought that he had been of those who rushed to drive him away from his contemplation.

Straightway when Michael reached his own door, he sat down and wrote to invite Smithers to his third terminal dinner, never pausing to reflect that so overwhelming an hospitality after such discourtesy might embarrass Smithers more than ever. Yet, after he had worried himself with this reflection when the invitation had been accepted, he fancied that Smithers sitting on his right hand next to Guy Hazlewood more charming than Michael had ever known him, seemed to enjoy the experience, and triumphantly he told himself that contrary to the doctrine of cynics quixotry was a very effective device.

CHAPTER VI

GRAY AND BLUE

When Michael, equipped with the prospect of reading at least fifty historical works in preparation for the more serious scholastic enterprise of his second year, came down for the Long Vacation, he found that somehow his mother had changed. In old days she had never lost for an instant that air of romantic mystery with which Michael as a very little boy for his own satisfaction had endowed her, and with which, as he grew older, he fancied she armed herself against the world of ordinary life. Now after a month or two of Chelsea's easy stability Mrs. Fane had put behind her the least hint of the unusual and seemed exceptionally well suited by her surroundings. Michael at first thought that perhaps in Carlington Road, to which she always came from the great world, however much apart from the great world her existence had been when she was in it, his mother had only evoked a thought of romance because the average inhabitant was lower down the ladder of the more subtly differentiated social grades than herself, and that now in Cheyne Walk against an appropriate background her personality was less conspicuous. Yet when he had been at home for a week or two he realized that indeed his mother had changed profoundly.

Michael put together the few bits of outside opinion he could muster and concluded that an almost lifelong withdrawal from the society of other women had now been replaced by an exaggerated pleasure in their company. What puzzled him most was how to account for the speed with which she had gathered round her so many acquaintances. It was almost as if his father in addition to bequeathing her money enough to be independent of the world had bequeathed also enough women friends to make her forget that she had ever stood in any other relation to society.

"Where does mother get hold of all these women?" Michael asked Stella irritably, when he had been trapped into a rustling drawing-room for the whole of a hot summer afternoon.

"Oh, they're all interested in something or other," Stella explained. "And mother's interested in them. I expect, you know, she had rather a rotten time really when she was traveling round."

"But she used always to be so vague and amusing," said Michael, "and now she's as fussy and practical as a vicar's wife."

"I think I know why that is," Stella theorized meditatively. "I think if I ever gave up everything for one man I should get to rely on him so utterly that when he wasn't with me any sort of contact with other people would make me vague."

"Yes, but then she would be more vague than ever now," Michael argued.

"No; the reaction against dependence on one person would be bound to make her change tremendously, if, as I think, a good deal of the vagueness came after she ran away with father."

Michael looked rather offended by Stella's blunt reference.

"I rather wish you wouldn't talk quite so easily about all of that," he said. "I think the best thing for you to do is to forget it."

"Like mother, in fact," Stella pointed out. "Do you know, Michael, I believe by this time she is entirely oblivious of the fact that in her past there has been anything which was not perfectly ordinary, almost dull. Really by the way she worries me about the simplest little things, you'd think—however, as I know you have rather a dread of perfect frankness in your only sister, I'll shut up and say no more."

"What things?" asked Michael sharply. Stella's theories about the freedom of the artist had already worried him a good deal, and though he had laughed them aside as the extravagant affectations of a gifted child, now that, however grudgingly he must admit the fact, she was really grown up, it would never do for her without a protest from him to turn theories into practice.

"Oh, Michael!" Stella laughed reprovingly. "Don't put on that professorial or priestly air or whatever you call it, because if you ever want confidences from me you'll have just to be humbly sympathetic."

Michael sternly demanded if she had been keeping up her music, which made Stella dance about the studio in tempestuous mirth.

"I don't see anything to giggle at in such a question," Michael grumbled, and simultaneously reproached himself for a method of obloquy so cheap. "Anyway, you never talk about your music now, and whatever you may say, you don't practice as much as you used. Why?"

For answer Stella sat down at the piano, and played over and over again the latest popular song until Michael walked out of the studio in a rage.

A few days later at breakfast he broached the subject of going away into the country.

"My dear boy, I'm much too busy with the Bazaar," said Mrs. Fane.

Michael sighed.

"I don't think I can possibly get away until August, and then I've half promised to go to Dinard with Mrs. Carruthers. She has just taken up Mental Science—so interesting and quite different from Christian Science."

"I hate these mock-turtle religions," said Michael savagely.

Mrs. Fane replied that Michael must learn a little toleration in very much the same tone as she might have suggested a little Italian.

"But why don't you and Stella go away somewhere together? Stella has been quite long enough in London for the present."

"I've got to practice hard for my next concert," said Stella, looking coldly at her brother. "You and Michael are so funny, mother. You grumble at me when I don't practice all day, and yet when it's really necessary for me to work, you always suggest going away."

"I never suggested your coming away," Michael contradicted. "As a matter of fact, I've been asked to join a reading-party in Cornwall, and I think I'll go."

The reading-party in question consisted besides Michael of Maurice Avery, Guy Hazlewood, Castleton, and Stewart. Bill Mowbray also joined them for the first two days, but after receiving four wires in reference to the political candidature of a friend in the north of England, he decided that his presence was necessary to the triumph of Tory Democracy and left abruptly in the middle of the night with a request to forward his luggage when it arrived. When it did arrive, the reading-party sent it to await at Univ Mowbray's arrival in October, arguing that such an arrangement would save Bill and his friends much money, as he would indubitably spend during the rest of the vacation not more than forty-eight hours on the same spot.

The reading-party had rooms in a large farmhouse near the Lizard; and they spent a very delightful month bathing, golfing, cliff-climbing, cream-eating, fishing, sailing, and talking. Avery and Stewart also did a certain amount of work on the first number of The Oxford Looking-Glass, work which Hazlewood amused himself by pulling to pieces.

"I'm doing an article for the O.L.G. on Cornwall," Avery announced one evening.

"What, a sort of potted guide?" Hazlewood asked.

Maurice made haste to repudiate the suggestion.

"No, no; it's an article on the uncanny place influence of Cornwall."

"I think half of that uncanniness is due to the odd names hereabouts," Castleton observed. "The sign-posts are like incantations."

"Much more than that," Avery earnestly assured him. "It really affects me profoundly sometimes."

Hazlewood laughed.

"Oh, Maurice, not profoundly. You'll never be affected profoundly by anything," he prophesied.

Maurice clicked his thumbs impatiently.

"You always know all about everybody and me in particular, Guy, but though, as you're aware, I'm a profound materialist——"

"Maurice is plumbing the lead to-night," Hazlewood interrupted, with a laugh. "He'll soon transcend all human thought."

"Here in Cornwall," Maurice pursued, undaunted, "I really am affected sometimes with a sort of horror of the unknown. You'll all rag me, and you can, but though I've enjoyed myself frightfully, I don't think I shall ever come to Cornwall again."

With this announcement he puffed defiance from his pipe.

"Shut up, Maurice!" Hazlewood chaffed. "You've been reading Cornish novelists—the sort of people who write about over-emotionalized young men and women acting to the moon in hut-circles or dancing with their own melodramatic Psyches on the top of a cromlech."

"Do you believe in presentiments, Guy?" Michael broke in suddenly.

"Of course I do," said Hazlewood. "And I'd believe in the inherent weirdness of Cornwall, if people in books didn't always go there to solve their problems and if Maurice weren't always so facile with the right emotion at the right moment."

"I've got a presentiment to-night," said Michael, and not wishing to say more just then, though he had been compelled against his will to admit as much, he left the rest of the party, and went up to his room.

Outside the tamarisks lisped at intervals in a faint wind that rose in small puffs and died away in long sighs. Was it a presentiment he felt, or was it merely thunder in the air?

Next morning came a telegram from Stella in Paris:

join me here rather quickly.

Michael left Cornwall that afternoon, and all the length of the harassing journey to London he thought of his friends bathing all day and talking half through the intimate night, until gradually, as the train grew hotter, they stood out in his memory like cool people eternally splashed by grateful fountains. Yet at the back of all his regrets for Cornwall, Michael was thinking of Stella and wondering whether the telegram was merely due to her impetuous way or whether indeed she wanted him more than rather quickly.

It was dark when he reached London, and in the close August night the street-lamps seemed to have lost all their sparkle, seemed to glow luridly like the sinister lamps of a dream.

"I'm really awfully worried," he said aloud to himself, as through the stale city air the hansom jogged heavily along from Paddington to Charing Cross.

Michael arrived at Paris in the pale burning blue of an August morning, and arriving as he did in company with numerous cockney holiday-makers, something of the spirit of Paris was absent. The city did not express herself immediately as Paris unmistakable, but more impersonally as the great railway-station of Europe, a center of convenience rather than the pulsing heart of pleasure. However, as soon as Michael had taken his seat in the bony fiacre and had ricocheted from corner to corner of half a dozen streets, Paris was herself again, with her green jalousies and gilded letterings, her prodigality of almost unvarying feminine types, those who so neatly and so gayly hurried along the pavements and those who in soiled dressing-jackets hung listlessly from upper windows.

Stella's address was near the Quai d'Orsay; and when Michael arrived he found she was living in rooms over a bookseller's shop with a view of the Seine and beyond of multitudinous roofs that in the foreground glistened to the sun like a pattern of enamel, until with distance they gradually lost all definition and became scarcely more than a woven damascene upon the irresolute horizon of city and sky.

Michael never surrendered to disillusion the first impression of his entrance that August morning. In one moment of that large untidy room looking over the city that most consciously of all cities has taken account of artists he seemed to capture the symbol of the artist's justification. Stella's chestnut hair streamed down her straight back like a warm drift of autumn leaves. She had not finished dressing yet, and the bareness of her arms seemed appropriate to that Hungarian dance she played. All the room was permeated with the smell of paint, and before an easel stood a girl in long unsmocked gown of green linen. This girl Michael had never seen, but he realized her personality as somehow inseparably associated with that hot-blooded Bacchante on whose dewy crimson mouth at the moment her brush rested. Geranium flowers, pierced by the slanting rays of the sun, stood on the window-sill of an inner room whose door was open. Stella did not stop to finish the dance she was playing, but jumped up to greet Michael, and in the fugitive silence that followed his introduction to her friend Clarissa Vine, he heard the murmur of ordinary life without which drowned by the lightest laugh nevertheless persisted unobtrusive and imperturbable.

Yet, for all Michael's relief at finding Stella at least superficially all right, he could not help disapproving a little of that swift change of plan which, without a word of warning to himself before the arrival of the telegram in Cornwall, had brought her from London to Paris. Nor could he repress a slight feeling of hostility toward Miss Clarissa Vine whose exuberant air did not consort well with his idea of a friend for Stella. He was certainly glad, whether he were needed or not, that he had come rather quickly. Clarie was going to paint all that morning, and Michael, who was restless after his journey, persuaded Stella to abandon music for that day and through the dancing streets of Paris come walking.

The brother and sister went silently for a while along the river's bank.

171

"Well," said Michael at last, "why did you wire for me?"

"I wanted you."

Stella spoke so simply and so naturally that he was inclined to ask no more questions and to accept the situation as one created merely by Stella's impetuousness. But he could not resist a little pressure, and begged to know whether there were no other reason for wanting him but a fancy for his company.

Stella agreed there might be, and then suddenly she plunged into her reasons. First, she took Michael back to last autumn and a postscript she had written to a letter.

"Do you remember how I said that academic perfection was not enough for an artist, that there was also life to be lived?"

Michael said he remembered the letter very well indeed, and asked just how she proposed to put her theory to the test.

"I told you that a youth was painting me."

"But you also said he looked like a corpse," Michael quickly interjected. "You surely haven't fallen in love with somebody who looks like a corpse?"

"I'm not in love with his outside, but I am fascinated by his inside," Stella admitted.

Michael looked darkly for a moment, overshadowed by the thought of the fellow's presumption.

"I never yet met a painter who had very much inside," he commented.

"But then, my dearest Michael, I suppose you'll confess that your acquaintanceship with the arts as practiced not talked about is rather small."

Michael looked round him and eyed all Paris with comprehensive hostility.

"And I suppose this chap is in Paris now," he said. "Well, I can't do anything. I suppose for a long time now you've been making a fool of yourself over him. What have you fetched me to Paris for?"

He felt resentful to think that his hope of Stella and Alan falling in love with one another was to be broken up by this upstart painter whom he had never seen.

"I've certainly not been making a fool of myself," Stella flamed. "But I thought I would rather you were close at hand."

"And who's this Clarissa Vine?" Michael indignantly demanded.

"She's the girl I traveled with to Paris."

"But I never heard of her before. All this comes of your taking that studio before we moved to Cheyne Walk."

By the token that Stella did not contradict him, Michael knew that all this had indeed come from that studio, and to show his disapproval of the studio, he began to rail at Clarissa.

"I can't bear that overblown type of girl. I suppose every night she'll sit and talk hot air till three o'clock in the morning. I shall go mad," Michael exclaimed, aghast at the prospective futility of the immediate future.

Stella insisted that Clarissa was a good sort, that she had had an unhappy love-affair, that she thought nothing of men but only of her art, that she made one want to work and was therefore a valuable companion, and, finally, to appease if possible Michael's mistrust of Clarie by advertising her last advantage, Stella said that she could not stand George Ayliffe.

Michael announced that, as Miss Vine had scarcely condescended to address a single word to him in the quarter of an hour he was waiting for Stella to dress, it was impossible for him to say whether he could stand her or not, but that he was still inclined to think she was thoroughly objectionable.

"Well, to-night at our party, you shall sit next to her," Stella promised.

"Party?" interrogated Michael, in dismay.

"We're having a party in our rooms to-night."

"And this fellow Ayliffe is coming, I suppose?"

She nodded.

"And I shall have to meet him?"

She nodded again very cheerfully.

They went back to fetch Clarie out to lunch, but rather decently, Michael was bound to admit, she made some excuse for not coming, so that he and Stella were able to spend the afternoon together. It was a jolly afternoon, for though Stella had closed her lips tightly to any more confidences, she and Michael enjoyed themselves wandering in a light-hearted dream, grasping continually at those airy bubbles of vitality that floated upward sparkling from the debonair streets.

The party at the girls' rooms that evening seemed to Michael, almost more than he cared to admit to the side of him conscious of being Stella's brother, a recreation of ideal Bohemia. He knew the influence of the rich August moon was responsible for most of the enchantment and that the same people encountered earlier in the day in the full glare of the sunlight would have seemed to him too keenly aware of the effect at which they were aiming. But to resist their appeal, coming as they did from the heart of Paris to this long riverside room with its lamps and shadows, was impossible. Each couple that entered seemed to relinquish slowly on the threshold a mysterious intimacy which set Michael's heart beating in the imagination of what altitudes it might not have reached along the path of romantic passions. Every young woman or young man who entered solitary and paused in the doorway, blinking in search of familiar faces, moved him with the respect owed by lay worldlings to great artists. Masterpieces brooded over the apartment, and Michael tolerated in his present mood of unqualified admiration personalities so pretentious, so vain, so egotistical, as would in his ordinary temper have plunged him into speechless gloom.

Oxford after this assembly of frank opinions and incarnate enthusiasms seemed a colorless shelter for unfledged reactionaries, a nursery of callow men in the street. Through the open windows the ponderous and wise moon commented upon the scintillations of the outspread city whose life reached this room in sound as emotionally melodious, as romantically real as the sea-sound conjured by a shell. Here were gathered people who worked always in that circumfluent inspiration, that murmur of liberty, that whisper of humanity. What could Oxford give but the bells of out-worn beliefs, and the patter of aimless footsteps? How right Stella had been to say that academic perfection was vain without the breath of life. How right she was to find in George Ayliffe someone whose artistic sympathy would urge her on to achievements impossible to attain under Alan's admiration for mere fingers and wrists.

Michael watched this favorite of his sister all through the evening. He tried to think that Ayliffe's cigarette-stained fingers were not so very unpleasant, that Ayliffe's cadaverous exterior was just a noble melancholy, that Ayliffe's high pointed head did not betray an almost insufferable self-esteem, and, what was the hardest task of all, he tried to persuade himself that Ayliffe's last portrait of Stella had not transformed his splendidly unconcerned sister into a self-conscious degenerate.

"How do you like George's picture of Stella?"

The direct inquiry close to his ear startled Michael. He had been leaning back in his chair, listening vaguely to the hum of the guests' conversation and getting from it nothing more definite than a sense of the extraordinary ease of social intercourse under these conditions. Looking round, he saw that Clarissa Vine had come to sit next to him and he felt half nervous of this concentrated gaze that so evidently betokened a determination to probe life and art and incidentally himself to the very roots.

"I think it's a little thin, don't you?" said Clarie.

Michael hated to have his opinion of a painting invited, and he resented the painter's jargon that always seemed to apply equally to the subject and the medium. It was impossible to tell from Miss Vine's question whether she referred to Stella's figure or to Ayliffe's expenditure upon paint.

"I don't think it's very like Stella," Michael replied, and consoled himself for the absence of subtlety or cleverness in such an answer by the fact that at least it was a direct statement of what he thought.

"I know what you mean," said Clarissa, nodding seriously.

Michael hoped that, she did. He could not conceive an affirmation of personal opinion delivered more plainly.

"You mean he's missed the other Stella," said Clarissa.

Michael bowed remotely. He told himself that contradiction or even qualified agreement would be too dangerous a proceeding with a person of Clarissa's unhumorous earnestness.

"I said so when I first saw it," cried Clarissa triumphantly. "I said, 'my god, George, you've only given us half of her!'"

Michael took a furtive glance at the portrait to see whether his initial impression of a full-length study had been correct, and, finding that it was, concluded Clarissa referred to some metaphysical conception of her own.

From the amplification of this he edged away by drawing attention to the splendor of the moon.

"I know what you mean," said Clarissa. "But I like sunshine effects best."

"I wasn't really thinking about painting at that moment," Michael observed, without remembering that all his mind was supposed to be occupied with it.

"You know you're very paintable," Clarissa went on. "I suppose you've sat to heaps of people. All the same, I wish you'd let me paint you. I should like to bring out an aspect I daresay lots of people have never noticed."

Michael was not proof against this attack, and, despising the while his weak vanity, asked Clarissa what was the aspect.

"You're very passionate, aren't you?" she said, shaking Michael's temperament in the thermometer of her thought.

"No; rather the reverse," said Michael, as he irritably visualized himself in a tiger-skin careering across one of Clarissa's florid canvases.

"All the same, I wish you would sit for me," persisted Clarissa.

Michael made up his mind he must speak seriously to Stella about this friend of hers. It was really very unfair to involve him in this way with a provocative young paintress who, however clever she might be, was most obviously unsympathetic to him. What a pity Maurice Avery was not here! He would so enjoy skating on the thin ice of her thought. Yet ice was scarcely an appropriate metaphor to use in connection with her. There should be some parallel with strawberries to illustrate his notion of Clarissa, who was after all with her precious aspirations and constructive fingers a creature of the sun. Yet it was strange and rather depressing to think that English girls could never get any nearer to the Mænad than the evocation of the image of a farouche dairymaid.

All the time that Michael had been postulating these conclusions to himself, he had been mechanically shaking his head to Clarissa's request. "What can you be thinking about?" she asked, and at the moment mere inquisitiveness unbalanced the solemnity of her search for truth. Stella had gone to the piano, and someone with clumsy hair was testing the pitch of his violin. So Michael assumed the portentous reverence of a listening amateur and tried to suggest by his attitude that he was beyond the range of Clarissa's conversation. He did not know who had made the duet that was being played, nor did he greatly care, since, aside from his own participation in what it gave of unified emotion to the room, on its melodies he, as it were, voyaged from heart to heart of everyone present. There had been several moments during his talk with Clarissa when he had feared to see vanish that aureole with which he had encircled this gathering, that halo woven by the mist of his imagination and illuminated by the essential joy of the company. But now, when all were fused by the power of the music in a brilliance that actually pierced his apprehension with the sense of its positive being, Michael's aureole gleamed with the same comparative reality. Traveling from heart to heart, he drew from each the deepdown sweetness which justified all that was extravagant in demeanor and dress, all that was flaunting in voice and gesture, all that was weak in achievement and ambition. Even Clarissa's prematurity seemed transferred from the cause to the effect of her art, so that here and there some strain of music was strong enough to sustain her personality up to the very point of abandon at which her pictures aimed. As for George Ayliffe, Michael watching him was bound to acknowledge that, seen thus in repose with all the wandering weaknesses of his countenance temporarily held in check by the music, Stella's affection for him was just intelligible. He might be said to possess now at least some of the graceful melancholy of a pierrot, and suddenly Michael divined that Ayliffe was much more in love with Stella than she was or ever could be in love with him. He

173

realized that Ayliffe, with fixed eyes sitting back and absorbing her music, was aware of the hopelessness of his desire, aware it must be for ever impossible for Stella to love him, as impossible as it was for him to paint a great portrait of her. Michael was sorry for Ayliffe because he knew that those anxious and hungry eyes of his were losing her continually even now in complexities that could never by him be unraveled, in depths that could never be plumbed.

More suggestive, however, than the individual listeners were the players themselves, so essentially typical were they of their respective instruments; and they were even something more than typical, for they did ultimately resemble them. The violinist must himself have answered in these harmonious wails to the lightest question addressed to him. His whole figure had surely that very look of obstinate surprise which belongs to a violin. The bones in that lean body of his might have been of catgut, so much did he play with his whole frame, so little observably with his hands merely. As for Stella, apart from the simplicity of her coloring, it was less easy to find physically a resemblance to the piano, and yet how well her personality consorted with one. Were she ignorant of the instrument, it would still be possible to compare her to a piano with her character so self-contained and cool and ordered that yet, played upon by people or circumstances, could reveal with such decorous poignancy the emotion beneath, emotion, however, that was always kept under control, as in a piano the pressure or release of a pedal can swell or quell the most expressive chord.

There was something consolatory to Michael in the way Stella's piano part corrected the extreme yearning of the violin. On ascending notes of the most plangent desire the souls of the listeners were drawn far beyond the capacity of their own artistic revelation. It became almost tragical to watch their undisciplined soaring regardless of the height from which they must so swiftly fall. Yet when the violin had thoughtlessly lured them to such a zenith that had the music stopped altogether on that pole a reaction into disappointed sobs might not have been surprising, Stella with her piano brought them back to the normal course of their hopes, seemed to bear tenderly each thwarted spirit down to earth and to set it back in the lamps and shadows of this long riverside room, while with the wistfulness of that cool accompaniment she mitigated all the harshness of disillusion. Michael looked sharply across at Ayliffe during this rescue and wondered how often by Stella herself had he been just as gently treated.

The duet came to an end, and was followed by absurd games and absurdly inadequate refreshments, until almost all together the guests departed. From the street below fainter and fainter sounded their murmurous talk, until it died away, swallowed up in the nightly whisper of the city.

Ayliffe stayed behind for a time, but he could not survive Michael's too polite "Mr. Ayliffe," although he did not perhaps realize all the deadliness of this undergraduate insult. Clarissa went off to bed after expressing once more her wish that Michael would sit for her.

"Oh, what for? Of course he will, Clarie," cried Stella.

"Of course I won't," said Michael, ruffling.

"What do you want him to sit for?" Stella persisted, paying not the least regard to Michael's objection.

"Oh, something ascetic," said Clarie, staring earnestly into space as if the pictorial idea was being dangled from the ceiling.

"Just now it was to be something passionate," Michael pointed out scornfully. He suspected Clarissa's courage in the presence of Stella's disdainful frankness.

"Ah, perhaps it will be both!" Clarie promised, and "Good night, most darling Stella," she murmured intensely. Then with one backward look of reproach for Michael she walked with rather self-conscious sinuousness out of the room and up to bed.

"My hat, Stella, where did you pick up that girl? She's like a performing leopard!" Michael burst out. "She's utterly stupid and utterly second-rate and she closes her eyes for effect and breathes into your face and doesn't wear stays."

"I get something out of all these queer people," Stella explained.

"New-art flower-vases, I should think," scoffed Michael. "Why on earth you wanted to fetch me from Cornwall to look after you in this crowd of idiots I can't imagine. I may not be a great pianist in the making, and I'm jolly glad I'm not, if it's to make one depend on the flattery of these fools."

"You know perfectly well that most of the evening you enjoyed yourself very much. And you oughtn't to be horrid about my friends. I think they're all so dreadfully touching."

"Yes, and touched," Michael grumbled. "You're simply playing at being in Bohemia. You'd be the first to laugh at me, if I dressed up Alan and Maurice Avery and half a dozen of my friends in velvet jackets and walked about Paris with them, smelling of onions."

"My dear Michael," Stella argued, "do get out of your head the notion that I dressed these people up. I found them like that. They're not imported dolls."

"Well, you're not bound to know them. I tell you they all hang on to you because you have money. That compensates for any jealousy they might feel because you are better at your business than any of them are at theirs."

"Rot!" Stella ejaculated.

However, the argument that might have gone on endlessly was quenched suddenly by the vision of the night seen by Stella and Michael simultaneously. They hung over the sill entranced, and Michael was so closely held by the sorcery of the still air that he was ready to surrender instantly his provocative standpoint of intolerance. The contest between prejudice and sentiment was unequal in such conditions. No one could fail to forgive the most outrageous pretender on such a night; no one could wish for Stella better associates than the moonstruck company which had entered so intangibly, had existed in reality for a while so blatantly, but was now again dissolved into elusive specters of a legendary paradise.

"I suppose what's really been the matter with me all the evening," confessed Michael, on the verge of going to bed, "is that I've felt out of it all, not so much out of sympathy with them as acutely aware that for them I simply didn't exist. That's rather galling. Now at Oxford, supposing your friend Ayliffe were suddenly shot down among a lot of men in my year, he would be out of sympathy with us, and we should be out of sympathy with him, even up to the point of debagging him, but we should all be uncomfortably aware of his existence. Seriously, Stella, why did you send for me? Not surely just to show me off to these unappreciative enthusiasts?"

"Perhaps I wanted a standard measure," Stella whispered, with a gesture of disarming confidingness. "Something heavy and reliable."

"My dear girl, I'm much too much of a weathercock, or if you insist on me being heavy, let's say a pendulum. And there's nothing quite so confoundedly unreliable as either. Enough of gas. Good night."

There followed a jolly time in Paris, but for Michael it would have been a jollier time if he could have let himself go with half the ridiculous pleasure he had derived from lighting bonfires in St. Cuthbert's quad or erecting a cocoanut shy in the Warden's garden. He was constantly aware of a loss of dignity which worried him considerably and for which he took himself to task very sternly. Finally he attributed it to one of two reasons, either that he felt a sense of constraint in Stella's presence on her account, or that his continued holding back was due to his difficulty in feeling any justification for extravagant behavior, when he had not the slightest intention of presenting the world with the usufruct of his emotions in terms of letters or color or sound.

"I really think I'm rather jealous of all these people," he told Stella. "They always seem to be able to go on being excited, and everything that happens to them they seem able to turn to account. Now, I can do nothing with my experience. I seize it, I enjoy it for a very short time. I begin to observe it with a warm interest, then to criticize, then to be bored by it, and finally I forget it altogether and remain just as I was before it occurred except that I never can seize the same sort of experience again. Perhaps it's being with you. Perhaps you absorb all the vitality."

Stella looked depressed by this suggestion.

"Let's go away and leave all these people," she proposed. "Let's go to Compiègne together, and we'll see if you're depressed by me then. But if you are, oh, Michael, I shan't know what to do! Only you won't be, if we're in Compiègne. It was such a success last time. In a way, you know, we really met each other there for the first time."

It was a relief to say farewell to Clarissa and her determination to produce moderately good pictures, to Ayliffe and his morbid hopes, to all that motley crowd, so pathetic and yet so completely self-satisfied. It was pleasant to arrive in Compiègne and find that Madame Regnier's house had not changed in three years, that the three old widows had not suffered from time's now slow and kindly progress, that M. Regnier still ate his food with the same noisy recklessness, that the front garden blazed with just the same vermilion of the geranium flowers.

For a week they spent industrious days of music and reading, and long mellow afternoons of provincial drowsiness that culminated in the simple pleasures of cassis and billiards at night. Michael wrote a sheaf of long letters to all his friends, among others to Lonsdale, who on hearing that he was at Compiègne wrote immediately to Prince Raoul de Castéra-Verduzan, an Eton contemporary, and asked him to call upon Michael. The young prince arrived one morning in a 70 h.p. car and by his visit made M. Regnier the proudest bourgeois in France. Prince Raoul, who was dressed, so Stella said, as brightly as it was possible even for a prince to dress nowadays, insisted that Michael and his sister must become temporary members of the Société du Sport de Compiègne. This proposal at first they were inclined to refuse, but M. Regnier and Madame Regnier and the three old widows were all so highly elated at the prospect of knowing anybody belonging to this club, and were so obviously cast down when their guests seemed to hesitate, that Michael and Stella, more to please the Pension Regnier than themselves, accepted Prince Raoul's offer.

It was amusing, too, this so excessively aristocratic club where every afternoon Princesses and Duchesses and the wives of Greek financiers sat at tea or watched the tennis and polo of their husbands and brothers and sons. Stella and Michael played sets of tennis with Castéra-Verduzan and the vicomte de Miramont, luxurious sets in which there were always four little boys to pick up the balls and at least three dozen balls to be picked up. Stella was a great success as a tennis-player, and their sponsor introduced the brother and sister to all the languidly beautiful women sitting at tea, and also to the over-tailored sportsmen who were cultivating a supposedly Britannic seriousness of attitude toward their games. Soon Michael and Stella found themselves going out to dinner and playing bridge and listening to much admiration of England in a Franco-cockney accent that was the result of a foreign language mostly acquired from grooms. With all its veneer of English freedom, it was still a very ceremonious society, and though money had tempered the rigidity of its forms and opinions, there was always visible in the background of the noisiest party Black Papalism, a dominant Army and the hope of the Orleanist succession. Verduzan also took them for long drives in the forest, and altogether time went by very gayly and very swiftly, until Stella woke up to the fact that her piano had been silent for nearly a fortnight. Verduzan was waiting with his impatient car in the prim road outside the Pension Regnier when she made this discovery, and he looked very much mortified when she told him that to-day she really ought to practice.

"But you must come because I have to go away to-morrow," he declared.

"Ah, but I've been making such wonderful resolutions ever since the sun rose," Stella said, shaking her head. "I must work, mustn't I, Michael?"

"Oh, rot, she must come for this last time, mustn't she, Fane?"

Michael thought that once more might not spoil her execution irreparably.

"Hurrah, you can't get out of it, Miss Fane!"

The car's horn tooted in grotesque exultation. Stella put on her dust-cloak of silver-gray, and in a few minutes they were racing through the forest so fast that the trees on either side winked in a continuous blur or where the forest was thinner seemed like knitting-needles to gather up folds of landscape.

After they had traversed all the wider roads at this speed, somewhere in the very heart of the forest Raoul turned sharply off along a wagoner's track over whose green ruts the car jolted abominably, but just when it would have been impossible to go on, he stopped and they all got out.

"You don't know why I've brought you here," he laughed.

Michael and Stella looked their perplexity to the great delight of the young man. "Wait a minute and you'll see," he chuckled. He was leading the way along a narrow grass-grown lane whose hedges on either side were gleaming with big blackberries.

"We shall soon be right out of the world," said Stella. "Won't that worry you, Monsieur?"

"Well, yes, it would for a very long time," replied the Prince, in a tone of such wistfulness as for the moment made him seem middle-aged. "But, look," he cried, and triumphant youth returned to him once more.

The lane had ended in a forest clearing whose vivid turf was looped with a chain of small ponds blue as steel. On the farther side stood a cottage with diamonded lattices and a gabled roof and a garden full of deep crimson phlox glowing against a background of gnarled and somber hawthorns. Cottage and clearing were set in a sweeping amphitheater of beechwoods.

"It reminds me of Gawaine and the Green Knight," said Michael.

"I'll take you inside," Raoul offered.

They walked across the small common silently, so deeply did they feel they were trespassing on some enchantment. From the cottage chimney curled a film of smoke that gave a voiceless voice to the silence, and when as they paused in the lych-gate, Castéra-Verduzan clanged the bell, it seemed indeed the summons to waken from a spell sleepers long ago bewitched.

"Surely nobody is going to answer that bell," said Stella.

"Why, yes, of course, Ursule will open it. Ursule! Ursule!" he cried. "C'est moi, Monsieur Raoul."

The cottage door opened and, evidently much delighted, Ursule came stumping down the path. She was an old woman whose rosy face was pectinated with fine wrinkles as delicate as the pluming of a moth's wing, while everything about her dress gave the same impression of extreme fineness, though the stuff was only a black bombazine and the tippet round her shoulders was of coarse lace. When she and Raoul had talked together in rapidest French, Ursule like an old queen waved them graciously within.

They sat in the white parlor on tall chairs of black oak among the sounds of ticking clocks and distant bees and a smell of sweet herbs and dryness.

"And there's a piano!" cried Stella, running to it. She played the Cat's Fugue of Domenico Scarlatti.

"You could practice on that piano?" Raoul anxiously inquired. "It belonged to my sister who often came here. More than any of us do. She's married now."

The sadness in Raoul's voice had made Michael suppose he was going to say his sister was dead.

"Then this divine place belongs to you?" Stella asked.

"To my sister and me. Ursule was once my nurse. Would you be my guests here, although I shall be away? For as long as you like. Ursule will look after you. Do say 'yes.'"

"Why, what else could we say?" Michael and Stella demanded simultaneously.

It was a disappointment to the Regniers when Michael and Stella came back to announce their retreat into the fast woodland, but perhaps M. Regnier found compensation in going down to his favorite café that afternoon and speaking of his guests, Monsieur and Mademoiselle Fêne, now staying with M. le prince de Castéra-Verduzan at his hunting-lodge in the forest.

Later that afternoon with their luggage and music Raoul brought Michael and Stella back to the cottage in his car, after which he said good-bye. Ursule was happy to have somebody to look after, and the cottage that had seemed so very small against the high beeches of the steep country behind was much larger when it was explored. It stretched out a rectangular wing of cool and shadowed rooms toward the forest. In this portion Ursule lived, and there was the pantry, and the kitchen embossed with copper pans, and the still-room which had garnered each flowery year in its course. Coterminous with Ursule's wing was a flagged court where a stone well-head stained with gray and orange lichen mirrored a circumscribed world. Beyond into an ancient orchard whose last red apples ripened under the first outstretched boughs of the forest tossed an acre of garden with runner-beans still in bloom.

In the part of the cottage where Stella and Michael lived, besides the white parlor with the piano, there was the hall with a great hooded fireplace and long polished dining-table lined and botched by the homely meals of numberless dead banqueters; and at either end of the cottage there were two small bedrooms with frequent changing patterns in dimity and chintz, with many tinted china ornaments and holy pictures that all combined to present the likeness of two glass cases enshrining an immoderately gay confusion of flowers and fruit and birds.

Here in these ultimate September days of summer's reluctant farewell life had all the rich placidity of an apricot upon a sun-steeped wall. Michael, while Stella practiced really hard, read Gregorovius' History of the Papacy; and when she stopped suddenly he would wake half-startled from the bloody horrors of the tenth century narrated laboriously with such cold pedantry, and hear above the first elusive silence swallows gathering on the green common, robins in their autumnal song, and down a corridor the footfalls and tinkling keys of Ursule.

It was natural that such surroundings should beget many intimate conversations between Michael and Stella, and if anything were wanting to give them a sense of perfect ease the thought that here at Compiègne three years ago they had realized one another for the first time always smoothed away the trace of shyness.

"Whether I had come out to Paris or not," asked Michael earnestly, "there never would have been anything approaching a love-affair between you and that fellow Ayliffe?" He had to recur to this uneasy theme.

"There might have been, Michael. I think that people who like me grow to rely tremendously on themselves require rather potty little people to play about with. It's the same sort of pleasure one gets from eating cheap sweets between meals. With somebody like George, one feels no need to bother to sustain one's personality at highest pitch. George used to be grateful for so little. He really wasn't bad."

"But didn't you feel it was undignified to let him even think you might fall in love with him? I don't want to be too objectionably fraternal, but if Ayliffe was as cheap as you admit, you ran the risk of cheapening yourself."

"Only to other people," Stella argued, "not to myself. My dear Michael, you've no idea what a relief it is sometimes to play on the piano a composition that is really easy—ridiculously, fatuously easy."

"But you wouldn't choose that piece for public performance," Michael pointed out. He was beginning to feel the grave necessity of checking Stella's extravagance.

"Surely the public you saw gathered round me in Paris wasn't very important?" She laughed in almost contemptuous remembrance.

"Then why did you wire for me if the whole affair was so trivial as you make out now?"

"I wanted a corrective," Stella explained.

"But how am I a corrective outside the fact that I'm your brother? And, you know, I don't believe you would consider that relationship had much to do with my importance one way or the other."

"In fact," said Stella, laughing, "what you're really trying to do is to work the conversation round to yourself. One reason why you're a corrective to George is that you're a gentleman."

"There you are!" cried Michael excitedly, and as if with that word she had released a spring that was holding back all the pent-up conclusions of some time past, he launched forth upon the display of his latest excavation of life. "We all half apologize for using the word 'gentleman,' but we can't get on without it. People say it means nothing nowadays. Although if it ever meant anything, it should mean more nowadays than it did in the past, since every generation should add something to its value. I haven't been able to talk this out before, because you're the only person who knows what I was born and at the same time is able to understand that for me to think about my circumstances rather a lot doesn't imply any very morbid self-consciousness. *You're* all right. You have this astonishing gift which would have guaranteed you self-expression whatever you had been born. When one sees an artist up to your level, one doesn't give a damn for his ancestors or his family or his personal features apart from the security of the art's consummation. Perhaps I have a vague inclination toward art myself, but inclinations are no good without something to lean up against at the end. These people who came to your party that night in Paris are in a way much happier, or rather much more secure than me. However far they incline without support, they're most of them inclining away from a top-heavy suburban life. So if they become failures, they'll always have the consolation of knowing they had either got to incline outward or be suffocated."

Michael stopped for a while and stared out through the cottage lattices at the stretch of common, at the steel-blue chain of ponds and the narrow portal that led to this secluded forest-world, and away down the lane to where on either side of the spraying brambles a plantation of delicate birch-trees was tinted with the diaphanous brown and gold and pale fawn of their last attiring.

"If I could only find in life itself," said Michael, sighing, "a path leading to something like this cottage."

"But, meanwhile, go on," Stella urged. "Do go on with your self-revelation. It's so fascinating to me. It's like a chord that never resolves itself, or a melody flitting in and out of a symphony."

"Something rather pathetic in fact," Michael suggested.

"Oh, no, much too elusive and independent to be pathetic," she assured him.

"My difficulty is that by natural inheritance I'm the possessor of so much I can never make use of," Michael began again. "I'm not merely discontented from a sense of envy. That trivial sort of envy doesn't enter my head. Indeed, I don't think I'm ever discontented or even resentful for one moment, but if I *were* the head of a great family I should have my duties set out in a long line before me, and all my theories of what a gentleman owes to the state would be weighted down with importance, or at any rate with potential significance, whereas now——" he shrugged his shoulders.

"I don't see much difference really," Stella said. "You're not prevented from being a gentleman and proving it on a smaller scale perhaps."

"Yes, yes," Michael plunged on excitedly. "But crowds of people are doing that, and every day more and more loudly the opinion goes up that these gentlemen are accidental ornaments, rather useless, rather irritating ornaments of contemporary society. Every day brings another sneer at public schools and universities. Every new writer who commands any attention drags out the old idol of the Noble Savage and invites us to worship him. Only now the Noble Savage has been put into corduroy trousers. My theory is that a gentleman leavens the great popular mass of humanity, and however superficially useless he may seem, his existence is a pledge of the immanence of the idea. Popular education has fired thousands to prove themselves not gentlemen in the present meaning of the term, but something much finer than any gentleman we know anything about. And they are *not*, they simply and solidly are *not*. The first instinct of the gentleman is respect for the past with all it connotes of art and religion and thought. The first instinct of the educated unfit is to hate and destroy the past. Now I maintain that the average gentleman, whatever situation he is called upon to face, will deal with it more effectively than these noble savages who have been armed with weapons they don't know how to use and are therefore so much the more dangerous, since every weapon to the primitive mind is a weapon of offense. Had I been Lord Saxby instead of Michael Fane, I could have proved my theory on the grand scale, and obviously the grand scale even for a gentleman is the only scale that is any good nowadays."

"I wonder if you could," murmured Stella. "Anyway, I don't see why you shouldn't ultimately attain to the grand scale, if you begin with the small scale."

"But the small scale means just a passive existence that hurts nobody and fades out of memory at the moment of death," Michael grumbled.

"Well, if your theory of necessary ornaments is valid," Stella pointed out, "you'll find your niche."

"I shall be a sort of Prescott. That's the most I can hope for," Michael gloomily announced. "Yet after all that's pretty good."

Stella looked at him in surprise, and said that though she had known Michael liked Prescott, she had no idea he had created such an atmosphere of admiration. She was eager to find out what Michael most esteemed in him, and she plied him indeed with so many questions that he finally asked her if she did not approve of Prescott.

"Of course I approve of him. No one could accept a refusal so wonderfully without being approved. But naturally I wanted to find out your opinion of him. What could be more interesting to a girl than to know the judgment of others on a person she might have married?"

Michael gazed at her in astonishment and demanded her reason for keeping such an extraordinary event so secret.

"Because I didn't want to introduce an atmosphere of curiosity into your relationship with him. You know, Michael, that if I had told you, you would always have been examining him when you thought he wasn't looking. And of course I never told mother, who would have examined him through her lorgnettes whether he were looking or not."

It seemed strange to Michael, as he and Stella sat here with the woodland enclosing them, that she could so fearlessly accept or refuse what life offered. And yet he supposed the ability to do so made of her the artist she was. Thinking of her that night, as he sat up reading in the clock-charmed room where lately she had played him through the dawn of the English Constitution, he told himself that even this cottage which so essentially became them both, was the result of Stella's appeal to Raoul de Castéra-Verduzan, an appeal in which his own personality had scarcely entered. Castéra-Verduzan! Prescott! Ayliffe! What folly it had been for him to make his own plans for her and Alan. Yet it had seemed so obvious and so easy that these two should fall in love with each other. Michael wondered whether he were specially privileged in being able to see through to a sister's heart, whether other brothers went blindly on without an inkling that their sisters were loved. It was astonishing to think that the grave Prescott had stepped so far and so rashly from his polite seclusion as to accept the risk of ridicule for proposing to a girl whose mother's love for a friend of his own he had spent his life in guarding. Michael put out the lamp and, lighting a candle, went along the corridor to bed. From the far end he heard Stella's voice calling to him and turned back to ask her what she wanted. She was sitting up in bed very wide-eyed, and, in that dainty room of diminutive buds and nosegays all winking in the soft candlelight, she seemed with her brown hair tied up with a scarlet bow someone disproportionately large and wild, yet someone whom for all her largeness and wildness it would still be a joy devotedly to cherish and protect.

"Michael, I've been thinking about what you said," she began, "and you mustn't get cranky. I wish you wouldn't bother so much about what you're going to be. It will end in your simply being unhappy."

"I don't really bother a great deal," Michael assured her. "But I do feel a sort of responsibility for being a nobody, so very definitely a nobody."

"The people who ought to have felt that responsibility were mother and father," said Stella.

"Yes, logically," Michael agreed. "But I think father did feel the responsibility rather heavily, and it's a sort of loyalty I have for him which makes me so determined to justify myself."

That night the equinoctial gales began. Stella and Michael had only two or three walks more down the wide glades where the fallen leaves trundled and swirled, and then it would be time to leave this forest house. Raoul did not manage to come back to Compiègne in time to say good-bye, and so at the moment of departure they took leave of old Ursule and the cottage very sadly, for it seemed, so desolate and gusty was the October morning, that never again would they possess for their own that magical corner of the world.

The equinoctial gales died away in a flood of rain, and the fine weather came back. London welcomed their return with a gracious calm. The Thames was a sheet of trembling silver, and the distant roofs and spires and trees of the Surrey shore no more than breath upon a glass. In this luminous and immaterial city the house in Cheyne Walk stood out with the pleasant aspect of its demure reality, and Mrs. Fane like one of those clouded rose pastels on the walls of her room was to both of them after their absence from London herself for a while as they had known her in childhood.

"Dear children, how charming to see you looking so well. I'm not quite sure I like that very Scotch-looking skirt, darling Stella. I'm so glad you've enjoyed yourselves together. Is it a heather mixture? And I was in France, too. But the trains are so oddly inconvenient. Mrs. Carruthers' most interesting! I wish, darling Stella, you would take up Mental Science. Ah, but I forgot, you have your practicing."

It was time to go up to Oxford after the few days that Stella and Michael spent in making arrangements for a series of Brahms recitals in one of the smaller concert halls. Alan met Michael on the platform at Paddington. This custom they had loyally kept up each term, although otherwise their paths seemed to be diverging.

"Good vac?" Michael asked.

"Oh, rather! I've been working at rather a tricky slow leg-break. Fifty-five wickets for 8.4 during the vac. Not bad for a dry summer. I was playing for the Tics most of the time. What did you do?"

Michael during the journey up talked mostly about Stella.

CHAPTER VII

VENNER'S

The most of Michael's friends had availed themselves of the right of seniority to move into more dignified rooms for their second year. These "extensions of premises," as Castleton called them, reached the limit of expansion in the case of Lonsdale who, after a year's residence in two small ground-floor rooms of St. Cuthbert's populous quad, had acquired the largest suite of three in Cloisters. Exalted by palatial ambitions, he spent the first week of term in buttonholing people in the lodge, so that after whatever irrelevant piece of chatter he had seized upon as excuse he might wind up the conversation by observing nonchalantly:

"Oh, I say, have you chaps toddled round to my new rooms yet? Rather decent. I'm quite keen on them. I've got a dining-room now. Devilish convenient. Thought of asking old Wedders to lay in a stock of pictures. It would buck him up rather."

"But why do you want these barracks?" Michael asked.

"Oh, binges," said Lonsdale. "We ought to be able to run some pretty useful binges here. Besides, I'm thinking of learning the bagpipes."

Wedderburn had moved into the Tudor richness of the large gateway room in St. Cuthbert's tower. Avery had succeeded the canorous Templeton-Collins on Michael's staircase, and had brought back with him from Flanders an alleged Rubens to which the rest of the furniture and the honest opinions of his friends were ruthlessly sacrificed. Michael alone had preferred to remain in the rooms originally awarded to him. He had a sentimental objection to denying them the full period of their participation in his own advance along the lines he had marked out for himself. As he entered them now to resume the tenure interrupted by the Long Vacation he compared their present state with the negative effect they had produced a year ago. Being anxious to arrange some decorative purchases he had made in France, Michael had ordered commons for himself alone. How intimate and personal that sparse lunch laid for one on a large table now seemed! How trimly crowded was now that inset bookcase and what imprisoned hours it could release to serve his pleasure! There was not now indeed a single book that did not recall the charmed idleness of the afternoon it commemorated. Nor was there one volume that could not conjure for him at midnight with enchantments eagerly expected all the day long.

It was a varied library this that in three terms he had managed to gather together. When he began, ornate sets like great gaudy heralds had proclaimed those later arrivals which were after all so much the more worshipful. The editions of luxury had been succeeded by the miscellanies of mere information, works that fired the loiterer to acquire them for the sake of the knowledge of human by-ways they generally so jejunely proffered. And yet perhaps it was less for their material contents that they were purchased than for the fact that in some dead publishing season more extravagant buyers had spent four or five times as much to partake of their accumulated facts and fortuitous illustrations. With Michael the passion for remainders was short-lived, and he soon pushed them ignobly out of the way for the sake of those stately rarities that combined a decorous exterior with the finest flavor of words and a permanent value that was yet subject to mercantile elation and depression.

If among these ambassadors of learning and literature was to be distinguished any predominant tone, perhaps the kindliest favor had been extended toward the more unfamiliar and fantastic quartos of the seventeenth century, those speculative compendiums of lore that though enriched by the classic Renaissance were nevertheless more truly the eclectic consummation of the Middle Ages. The base of their thought may have been unsubstantial, a mirage of philosophy, offering but a Neo-Platonic or Gnostic kaleidoscope through which to survey the universe; but so rich were their tinctures and apparels, so diverse was the pattern of their ceremonious commentary, and so sonorous was their euphony that Michael made of their reading a sanctuary where every night for a while he dreamed upon their cadences resounding through a world of polychromatic images and recondite jewels, of spiritual maladies and minatory comets, of potions for revenge and love, of talismans, to fortune, touchstones of treasure and eternal life, and strange influential herbs. Mere words came to possess Michael so perilously that under the spell of these Jacobeans he grew half contemptuous of thought less prodigally ornate. The vital ideas of the present danced by in thin-winged progress unperceived, or rather perceived as bloodless and irresolute ephemerides. When people reproached him for his willful prejudice, he pointed out how easy it would always be to overtake the ideas of the present and how much waste of intellectual breath would be avoided by letting his three or four Oxford years account for the most immediately evanescent. Oxford seemed to him to provide an opportunity, and more than an opportunity—an inexpugnable command to wave with most reluctant hands farewell to the backward of time, around whose brink rose up more truthful dreams than those that floated indeterminate, beckoning through the mist across the wan mountains of the future.

On the walls Michael's pictures had been collected to achieve through another medium the effect of his books. Mona Lisa was there not for her lips or eyes, but rather for that labyrinth of rocks and streams behind; and since pictures seldom could be found to provide what he sought in a picture, there were very few of them in his sitting-room. One hour of the Anatomy of Melancholy or of Urn Burial could always transform the pattern of the terra-cotta wall paper to some diagrammatic significance. Apart from the accumulation of books and pictures, he had changed the room scarcely at all. Curtains and covers, chairs and tables, all preserved the character of the room itself as something that existed outside the idiosyncrasies of the transient inhabitants who read and laughed and ate and talked for so comparatively fleeting a space of time between its four walls. With all that he had imposed of what in the opinion of his contemporaries were eccentricities of adornment, the rooms remained, as he would observe to any critic, essentially the same as his own. Instead of college groups which marked merely by the height of the individual's waistcoat-opening the almost intolerable fugacity of their record, there were Leonardo and Blake and Frederick Walker to preserve the illusion of permanence, or at least of continuity. Instead of the bleached and desiccated ribs of momentarily current magazines cast away in sepulchral indignity, there were a hundred quartos whose calf bindings had the durableness and sober depth of walnut furniture, furniture, moreover, that was still in use.

Yet it was in Venner's office where Michael found the perfect fruit of time's infinitely fastidious preservation, the survival not so much of the fittest as of the most expressive. Here, indeed, whatever in his own rooms might affect him with the imagination of the eternal present of finite conceptions, was the embodiment of the possible truth of those moments in which at intervals he had apprehended, whether through situations or persons or places, the assurance of immortality. Great pictures, great music and most of all great literature would always remain as the most obvious pledge of man's spiritual potentiality, but these subtler intimations of momentary vision had such power to impress themselves that Michael could believe in the child Blake when he spoke of seeing God's forehead pressed against the window panes, could believe that the soul liberated from the prison of the flesh had struggled in the very instant of her recapture to state the ineffable. To him Blake seemed the only poet who had in all his work disdained to attempt the recreation of anything but these moments of positive faith. Every other writer seemed clogged by human conceptions of grandeur. Most people, seeking the imaginative reward of their sensibility, would obtain the finest thrill that Oxford could offer from the sudden sight of St. Mary's tower against a green April afterglow, or of the moon-parched High Street in frost. Michael, however, found in Venner's office, just as he had found in that old print of St. Mary's tower rather than in the tower itself, the innermost shrine of Oxford, the profoundest revelation of the shining truth round which the mysterious material of Oxford had grown through the Middle Ages.

Michael with others of his year had during the summer term ventured several times into Venner's, but the entrance of even a comparatively obscure senior had always driven them out. They had not yet enjoyed the atmosphere of security without which a club unlike an orchard never tastes sweet. Now, with the presence of a new year's freshmen and with the lordship of the college in their own hands, since to the out-of-college men age with merciless finger seemed already to be beckoning, Michael and his contemporaries in their pride of prime marched into Venner's after hall and drank their coffee.

Venner's office was one of the small ground-floor rooms in Cloisters, but it had long ago been converted to the present use. An inner storeroom, to which Venner always retired to make a cup of squash or to open a bottle of whisky, had once been the bedroom. The office itself was not luxuriously furnished, and the accommodation was small. A window-seat with a view of the college kitchens, a square table, and a couple of Windsor chairs were considered enough for the men who frequented Venner's every night after hall, and who on Sunday nights after wine in J.C.R. clustered there like a swarm of bees. Venner's own high chair stood far back in the corner behind his high sloping desk on which, always spread open, lay the great ledger of J.C.R. accounts. On the shelves above were the account books of bygone years in which were indelibly recorded the extravagances of more than thirty years of St. Mary's men. Over the fireplace was a gilt mirror of Victorian design stuck round with the fixture cards of the university and the college, with notices of grinds and musical clubs and debating societies; in fact, with all the printed petty news of Oxford. A few photographs of winning crews, a book-case with stores of college stationery, a Chippendale sideboard with a glass case of priced cigars on top, and an interesting drawerful of Venner's relics above the varnished wainscot completed the furniture. The wall-paper was of that indefinite brownish yellow which one finds in the rooms of old-fashioned solicitors, and of that curious oily texture which seems to produce an impression of great age and at the same time of perfect modernity.

Yet the office itself, haunted though it was by the accumulated personalities of every generation at St. Mary's, would scarcely have possessed the magical effect of fusion which it did possess, had not all these personalities endured in a perpetual present through the conservative force of Venner himself. John Venables had been Steward of the Junior Common Room for thirty-three years, but he seemed to all these young men that came within the fragrancy of his charm to be as much an intrinsic part of the college as the tower itself. The moon-faced Warden, the dry-voiced dons, the deer park, the elms, the ancient doors and traceries, the lawns and narrow entries, the groinings and the lattices, were all subordinate in the estimation of the undergraduates to Venner. He knew the inner history of every rag; he realized why each man was popular or unpopular or merely ignored; he was a treasure-house of wise counsel and kindly advice; he held the keys of every heart. He was an old man with florid, clean-shaven face, a pair of benignant eyes intensely blue, a rounded nose, a gentle voice and most inimitable laugh. Something there was in him of the old family butler, a little more of the yeoman-farmer, a trace of the head game-keeper, a suspicion of the trainer of horses, but all these elements were blended to produce the effect of someone wise and saintly and simple who could trouble himself to heal the lightest wounds and could rouse with a look or a gesture undying affection.

With such a tutelary spirit, it was not surprising the freedom of Venner's should have been esteemed a privilege that could only be conferred by the user's consciousness of his own right. There was no formal election to Venner's: there simply happened a moment when the St. Mary's man entered unembarrassed that mellow office and basked in that sunny effluence. In this ripe old room, generous and dry as sherry wine, how pleasant it was to sit and listen to Venner's ripe old stories: how amazingly important seemed the trivial gossip of the college in this historic atmosphere: how much time was apparently wasted here between eight and ten at night, and what a thrill it always was to come into college about half-past nine of a murky evening and stroll round Cloisters to see if there was anybody in Venner's. It could after all scarcely be accounted a waste of time to sit and slowly mature in Venner's, and sometimes about half-past nine the old man would be alone, the fire would be dying down and during the half-hour that remained of his duty, it would be possible to peel a large apple very slowly and extract from him more of the essence of social history than could be gained from a term's reading of great historians even with all the extra lucidity imparted by a course of Mr. So-and-So's lectures.

Michael found that Venner summed up clearly for him all his own tentative essays to grasp the meaning of life. He perceived in him the finest reaction to the prejudice and nobility, the efficiency and folly of aristocratic thought. He found in him the ideal realization of his own most cherished opinions. England, and all that was most inexplicable in the spirit of England, was expressed by Venner. He was a landscape, a piece of architecture, a simple poem of England. One of Venner's applauded tricks was to attach a piece of string to the tongs for a listener to hold to his ears, while Venner struck the tongs with the poker and evoked the sound of St. Mary's chimes. But the poker and tongs were unnecessary, for in Venner's own voice was the sound of all the bells in England. Communion with this gracious, this tranquil, this mellow presence affected Michael with a sense of the calm certainty of his own life. It lulled all the discontent and all the unrest. It indicated for the remainder of his Oxford time a path which, if it did not lead to any outburst of existence, was at least a straight path, green bordered and gay with birdsong, with here and there a sight of ancient towers and faiths, and here and there an arbor in which he and his friends could sit and talk of their hopes.

"Venner," said Lonsdale one evening, "do you remember the Bishop of Cirencester when he was up? Stebbing his name was. My mother roped him in for a teetotal riot she was inciting this vac."

"Oh, yes, I think he was rather a wild fellow," Venner began, full of reminiscence. "But we'll look him up."

Down came some account-book of the later seventies, and all the festive evenings of the Bishop, spent in the period when undergraduates were photographed with mutton-chop whiskers and bowler hats, lay revealed for the criticism of his irreverent successors.

"There you are," chuckled Venner triumphantly. "What did I say? One dozen champagne. Three bottles of brandy. All drunk in one night, for there's another half dozen put down for the next day. Ah, but the men are much quieter nowadays. Not nearly so much drinking done in college as there used to be. Oh, I remember the Bishop—Stebbing he was then. He put a cod-fish in the Dean's bed. Oh, there was a dreadful row about it! The old Warden kicked up such a fuss."

And, as easily as one Arabian night glides into another, Venner glided from anecdote to anecdote of episcopal youth.

"I thought the old boy liked the governor's port," laughed Lonsdale. "'What a pity everybody can't drink in moderation,' said Gaiters. Next time he cocks his wicked old eye at me, I shall ask him about that cod-fish."

"What's this they tell me about your bringing out a magazine?" Venner inquired, turning to Maurice Avery.

"Out next week, Venner," Maurice announced importantly.

"Why, whatever do you find to write about?" asked Venner. "But I suppose it's amusing. I've often been asked to write my own life. What an idea! As if I had any time. I'm glad enough to go to bed when I get home, though I always smoke a pipe first. We had two men here once who brought out a paper. Chalfont and Weymouth. I used to have some copies of it somewhere. They put in a lot of skits of the college dons. The Warden was quite annoyed. 'Most scurrilous, Venables,' he said to me, I remember. 'Most scurrilous.'" Venner chuckled at the remembrance of the Warden's indignation.

"This is going to be a very serious affair, Venner," explained somebody. "It's going to put the world quite straight again."

"Ho-ho, I suppose you're one of these Radicals," said Venner to the editor. "Dear me, how anyone can be a Radical I can't understand. I've always been a Conservative. We had a Socialist come up here to lecture once in a man's rooms—a great Radical this man was—Sir Hugh Gaston—a baronet—there's a funny thing, fancy a Radical baronet. Well, the men got to hear of this Socialist coming up and what do you think they did?" Venner chuckled in anticipatory relish. "Why, they cropped his hair down to nothing. Sir Hugh Gaston was quite upset about it, and when he made a fuss, they cut his hair too, though it was quite short already. There was a terrible rowdy set up then. The men are very much quieter nowadays."

The door opened as Venables finished his story, and Smithers came in to order rather nervously a tin of biscuits. The familiar frequenters of Venner's eyed in cold silence his entrance, his blushful wait and his hurried exit.

"That's a scholar called Smithers," Venner explained. "He's a very quiet man. I don't suppose any of you know him even by sight."

"We ragged him last term," said Michael, smiling at his friends.

"He's a bounder," declared Avery obstinately.

"He hasn't much money," said Venner. "But he's a very nice fellow. You oughtn't to rag him. He's very harmless. Never speaks to anybody. He'll get a first, I expect, but there, you don't think anything of that, I know. But the dons do. The Warden often has him to dinner. I shouldn't rag him any more. He's a very sensitive fellow. His father's a carpenter. What a wonderful thing he should have a son come up to St. Mary's."

The rebuke was so gently administered that only the momentary silence betrayed its efficacy.

One day Michael brought Alan to be introduced to Venables, and it was a pleasure to see how immediately the old man appreciated Alan.

"Why ever didn't you come to St. Mary's?" asked Venner. "Just the place for you. Don't you find Christ Church a bit large? But they've got some very good land. I've often done a bit of shooting over the Christ Church farms. The Bursar knows me well. 'Pleased to see you, Mr. Venables, and I hope you'll have good sport.' That's what he said to me last time I saw him. Oh, he's a very nice man! Do they still make meringues at your place? I don't suppose you ever heard the story of the St. Mary's men who broke into Christ Church. It caused quite a stir at the time. Well, some of our men were very tipsy one night at the Bullingdon wine, and one of them left his handkerchief in the rooms of a Christ Church man, and what do you think they did? Why, when they got back to college, this man said he wasn't going to bed without his handkerchief. Did you ever hear of such a thing? So they all climbed out of St. Mary's at about two in the morning and actually climbed into Christ Church. At least they thought it was Christ Church, but it was really Pembroke. Do you know Pembroke? I don't suppose you've even been there. Our men always cheer Pembroke in the Eights—Pemmy, as they call it—because their barge is next to us. But fancy breaking in there at night to look for a handkerchief. They woke up every man in the college, and there was a regular set-to in the quad, and the night porter at Pembroke got a most terrible black eye. The President of the J.C.R. had to send an apology, and it was all put right, but this man who lost his handkerchief, Wilberforce his name was, became a regular nuisance, because for ever afterward, whenever he got drunk, he used to go looking for this old handkerchief. There you see, that's what comes of going to the Bullingdon wine. Are you a member of the Bullingdon?"

"He's a cricketer, Venner," Michael explained.

"So was this fellow Wilberforce who lost his handkerchief, and what do you think? One day when we were playing Winchester—you're not a Wykehamist, are you?—he came out to bat so drunk that the first ball he hit, he went and ran after it himself. It caused quite a scandal. But you don't look one of that sort. Will you have a squash and a biscuit? The men like these biscuits very much. There's been quite a run on them."

Michael was anxious to know how deep an impression Venner had made on Alan.

"You've got nobody like him at the House?" he asked.

Alan was bound to admit there was indeed nobody.

"He's an extraordinary chap," said Michael. "He's always different, and yet he's always absolutely the same. For me he represents Oxford. When one's in his company, one feels one's with him for ever, and yet one knows that people who have gone down can feel just the same, and that people who haven't yet come up will feel just the same. You know, I do really think that what it sets out to do St. Mary's does better than any other college. And the reason of that is Venner's. It's the only successful democracy in the world."

"I shouldn't have called it a democracy," said Alan. "Everybody doesn't go there."

"But everybody can go there. It depends entirely on themselves."

"What about that fellow Smithers you were talking about?" Alan asked. "He seems barred."

"But he won't be," Michael urged hopefully.

"He'd be happier at the House all the same," Alan said. "He'd find his own set there."

"But so he can at St. Mary's."

"Then it isn't a democracy," Alan stoutly maintained.

"I say, Alan," exclaimed Michael, in surprise. "You're getting quite a logician."

"Well, you always persist in treating me like an idiot," said Alan. "But I *am* reading Honor Mods. It's a swat, but I've got to get some sort of a class."

"You'll probably get a first," said Michael.

Yet how curious it was to think of Alan, whom he still regarded as chiefly a good-looking and capable athlete, taking a first class in a school he himself had indolently passed over. Of course he would never take a first. He was too much occupied with the perfection of new leg-breaks. And what would he do after his degree, his third in greats? A third was the utmost Michael mentally allowed him in the Final Schools.

"I suppose you'll ultimately try for the Indian Civil?" Michael asked. "Do you remember when we used to lie awake talking in bed at Carlington Road? It was always going to be me who did everything intellectual; you were always the sportsman."

"I am still. Michael, I think I've got a chance of my blue this year. If I can keep that leg-break," he added fervidly. "There's no slow right-hander of much class in the Varsity. I worked like a navvy at that leg-break last vac."

"I thought you were grinding for Mods," Michael reminded him, with a smile.

"I worked like a navvy at Mods," said Alan.

"You'll be a proconsul, I really believe." Michael looked admiringly at his friend. "And do you know, Alan, in appearance you're turning into a regular viking."

"I meant to have my hair cut yesterday," said Alan, in grave and reflective self-reproof.

"It's not your hair," cried Michael. "It's your whole personality. I never appreciated you until this moment."

"I think you talk more rot nowadays than you used to talk even," said Alan. "So long, I must go back and work."

The tall figure with the dull gold hair curling out from the green cap of Harris tweed faded away in the November fog that was traveling in swift and smoky undulations through the Oxford streets. What a strangely attractive walk Alan had always had, and now it had gained something of determination, whether from leg-breaks or logic Michael did not know. But the result was a truer grace in the poise of his neck; a longer and more supple swing from his tapering flanks.

Michael went on up the High and stood for a moment, watching the confusion caused by the fog at Carfax, listening to the fretful tinkles of the numerous bicycles and the jangling of the trams and the shouts of the paper-boys. Then he walked down Cornmarket Street past the shops splashing through the humid coils of vapor their lights upon the townspeople, loiterers and purchasers who thronged the pavements. Undergraduates strolled along, linked arm in arm and perpetually staring. How faithfully each group resembled its forerunners and successors. All had the same fresh complexions, the same ample green coats of Harris tweed, the same gray flannel trousers. Only in the casual acknowledgments of his greeting when he recognized acquaintances was there the least variation, since some would nod or toss their heads, others would shudder with their chins, and a few would raise their arms in a fanlike gesture of social benediction. Michael turned round into the Broad where the fog made mysterious even the tea-tray gothic of Balliol, and Trinity with its municipal ampelopsis. A spectral cabman saluted him interrogatively from the murk. A fox-terrier went yapping down the street at the heels of a don's wife hurrying back to Banbury Road. A belated paper-boy yelled, "Varsity and Blackheath Result," hastening toward a more profitable traffic. The fog grew denser every minute, and Michael turned round into Turl Street past many-windowed Exeter and the monastic silence of Lincoln. There was time to turn aside and visit Lampard's bookshop. There was time to buy that Glossary of Ducange which he must have, and perhaps that red and golden Dictionary of Welby Pugin which he ought to have, and ultimately, as it turned out, there was time to buy half a dozen more great volumes whose connection with mediæval history was not too remote to give an excuse to Michael, if excuse were needed, for their purchase. Seven o'clock chimed suddenly, and Michael hurried to college, snatched a black coat and a gown out of Venner's and just avoided the sconce for being more than a quarter of an hour late for hall.

Michael was glad he had not missed hall that night. In Lampard's alluring case of treasures he had been tempted to linger on until too late, and then to take with him two or three new books and in their entertainment to eat a solitary and meditative dinner at Buol's. But it would have been a pity to have missed hall when the electric light failed abruptly and when everybody had just helped themselves to baked potatoes. It would have been sad not to have seen the Scholars' table so splendidly wrecked or heard the volleys of laughter resounding through the darkness.

"By gad," said Lonsdale, when the light was restored and the second year leaned over their table in triumphant exhaustion. "Did you see that bad man Carben combing the potatoes out of his hair with a fork? I say, Porcher," he said to his old scout who was waiting at the table, "do bring us some baked potatoes."

"Isn't there none left?" inquired Porcher. "Mr. Lonsdale, sir, you'd better keep a bit quiet. The Sub-Warden's looking very savage—very savage indeed."

At this moment Maurice Avery came hurrying in to dinner.

"Oh, sconce him!" shouted everybody. "It's nearly five-and-twenty past."

"Couldn't help it," said Maurice very importantly. "Just been seeing the first number of the O.L.G. through the press."

"By gad," said Lonsdale. "It's a way we have in the Buffs and the Forty Two'th. Look here, have we all got to buy this rotten paper of yours? What's it going to cost?"

"A shilling," said Maurice modestly.

"A bob!" cried Lonsdale. "But, my dear old ink-slinger, I can buy the five-o'clock Star for a half-penny."

Maurice had to put up with a good deal of chaff from everybody that night.

"Let's have the program," Sinclair suggested.

The editor was so much elated at the prospect of to-morrow's great event that he rashly produced from his pocket the contents bill, which Lonsdale seized and immediately began to read out:

"THE OXFORD LOOKING-GLASS.

No. I.

"*Some Reflections. By Maurice Avery.*

"What are you reflecting on, Mossy?"

"Oh, politics," said Maurice lightly, "and other things."

"My god, he'll be Prime Minister next week," said Cuffe.

"*Socrates at Balliol. By Guy Hazlewood.*

"And just about where he ought to have been," commented Lonsdale. "Oh, listen to this! Whoo-oop!

"*The Failure of the Modern Illustrator.*

"But wait a minute, who do you think it's by? C. St. C. Wedderburn! Jolly old Wedders! The Failure of the Modern Illustrator. Wedders! My god, I shall cat with laughing. Wedders! A bee-luddy author."

"Sconce Mr. Lonsdale, please," said Wedderburn, turning gravely to the recorder by his chair.

182

"What, half a crown for not really saying bloody?" Lonsdale protested.

That night after hall there was much to tell Venner of the successful bombardment with potatoes, and there was some chaff for Avery and Wedderburn in regard to their forthcoming magazine. Parties of out-of-college men came in after their dinner, and at half-past eight o'clock the little office was fuller than usual, with the college gossip being carried on in a helter-skelter of unceasing babble. Just when Fitzroy the Varsity bow was enunciating the glories of Wet Bobbery and the comparative obscurities of Dry Bobbery and just when all the Dry Bobs present were bowling the contrary arguments at him from every corner at once, the door opened and a freshman, as fair and floridly handsome as a young Bacchus, walked with curious tiptoe steps into the very heart of the assembly.

Fitzroy stopped short in his discourse and thrummed impatiently with clenched fists upon his inflated chest, as gorillas do. The rest of the company eyed the entrance of the newcomer in puzzled, faintly hostile silence.

"Oh, Venner," said the intruder, in loftiest self-confidence and unabashed clarity of accent. "I haven't had those cigars yet."

He hadn't had his cigars yet! Confound his impudence, and what right had he to buy cigars, and what infernal assurance had led him to suppose he might stroll into Venner's in the third raw week of his uncuffed fresherdom? Who was he? What was he? Unvoiced, these questions quivered in the wrathful silence.

"The boy was told to take them up, sir," said Venner. Something in Venner's manner toward this newcomer indicated to the familiars that he might have deprecated this deliberate entrance armored in self-satisfaction. Something there was in Venner's assumption of impersonal civility which told the familiars that Venner himself recognized and sympathized with their as yet unspoken horror of tradition's breach.

"I rather want them to-night," said the newcomer, and then he surveyed slowly his seniors and even nodded to one or two of them whom presumably he had known at school. "So if the boy hasn't taken them up," he continued, "you might send up another box. Thanks very much."

He seemed to debate for a moment with himself whether he should stay, but finally decided to go. As he reached the door, he said that, by Jove, his cigarette had gone out, and "You've got a light," he added to Lonsdale, who was standing nearest to him. "Thanks very much." The door of Venner's slammed behind his imperturbableness, and a sigh of pent-up stupefaction was let loose.

"Who's your young friend, Lonny?" cried one.

"He thought Lonny was the Common Room boy," cried another.

"Venner, give the cigars to Mr. Lonsdale to take up," shouted a third.

"He's very daring for a freshman," said Venner. "Very daring. I thought he was a fourth year Scholar whom I'd never seen, when he first came in the other day. Most of the freshmen are very timid at first. They think the senior men don't like their coming in too soon. And perhaps it's better for them to order what they want when I'm by myself. I can talk to them more easily that way. With all the men wanting their coffee and whiskies, I really can't attend to orders so well just after hall."

"Who is he, Venner?" demanded half a dozen indignant voices.

"Mr. Appleby. The Honorable George Appleby. But you ought to know him. He's an Etonian."

Several Etonians admitted they knew him, and the Wykehamists present seized the occasion to point out the impossibility of such manners belonging to any other school.

"He's a friend of yours, then?" said Venner to Lonsdale.

"Good lord, no, Venner!" declared Lonsdale.

"He seemed on very familiar terms with you," Venner chuckled wickedly.

Lonsdale thought very hard for two long exasperated moments and then announced with conviction that Appleby must be ragged, severely ragged this very night.

"Now don't go making a great noise," Venner advised. "The dons don't like it, and the Dean won't be in a very good temper after that potato-throwing in hall."

"He must be ragged, Venner," persisted Lonsdale inexorably. "There need be no noise, but I'm hanged if I'm going to have my cigarette taken out of my hand and used by a damned fresher. Who's coming with me to rag this man Appleby?"

The third-year men seemed to think the correction beneath their dignity, and the duty devolved naturally upon the second-year men.

"I can't come," said Avery. "The O.L.G.'s coming out to-morrow."

"Look here, Mossy, if you say another word about your rotten paper, I won't buy a copy," Lonsdale vowed.

Michael offered to go with Lonsdale and at any rate assist as a spectator. He was anxious to compare the behavior of Smithers with the behavior of Appleby in like circumstances. Grainger offered to come if Lonny would promise to fight sixteen rounds without gloves, and in the end he, with Lonsdale, Michael, Cuffe, Sinclair, and three or four others, marched up to Appleby's rooms.

Lonsdale knocked upon the door, and as he opened it assumed what he probably supposed to be an expression of ferocity, though he was told afterward he had merely looked rather more funny than usual.

"Oh, hullo, Lonsdale," said Appleby, as the party entered. "Come in and have a smoke. How's your governor?"

Lonsdale seemed to choke for breath a moment, and then sat down in a chair so deep that for the person once plunged into its recesses an offensive movement must have been extremely difficult.

"Come in, you chaps," Appleby pursued in hospitable serenity. "I don't know any of your names, but take pews, take pews. Venner hasn't sent up the cigars I ordered."

"We know," interrupted Lonsdale severely.

"But I've some pretty decent weeds here," continued Appleby, without a tremor of embarrassment. "Who's for whisky?"

"Look here, young Apple-pip, or whatever your name is, what you've got to understand is that...."

Appleby again interrupted Lonsdale.

"Can we make up a bridge four? Or are you chaps not keen on cards?"

"What you require, young Appleby," began Lonsdale.

"You've got it right this time," said Appleby encouragingly.

"What you require is to have your room bally well turned upside down."

"Oh, really?" said Appleby, with a suave assumption of interest.

"Yes," answered Lonsdale gloomily, and somehow the little affirmative that was meant to convey so much of fearful intent was so palpably unimpressive that Lonsdale turned to his companions and appealed for their more eloquent support.

"Tell him he mustn't come into Venner's and put on all that side. It's not done. He's a fresher," gasped Lonsdale, obviously helpless in that absorbing chair.

"All right," agreed Appleby cheerfully. "I'll send the order up to you next time."

Immediately afterward, though exactly how it happened Lonsdale could never probably explain, he found himself drinking Appleby's whisky and smoking one of Appleby's cigars. This seemed to kindle the spark of his resentment to flame, and he sprang up.

"We ought to debag him!" he cried.

Appleby was thereupon debagged; but as he made no resistance to the divestiture and as he continued to walk about trouserless and dispense hospitality without any apparent loss of dignity, the debagging had to be written down a failure. Finally he folded up his trousers and put on a dressing-gown of purple velvet, and when they left him, he was watching them descend his staircase and actually was calling after them to remind Venner about the cigars, if the office were still open.

"Hopeless," sighed Lonsdale. "The man's a hopeless ass."

"I think he had the laugh, though," said Michael.

CHAPTER VIII

THE OXFORD LOOKING-GLASS

Roll-calls were not kept at St. Mary's with that scrupulousness of outward exterior which, in conjunction with early rising, such a discipline may have been designed primarily to secure. On the morning after the attempted adjustment of Appleby's behavior, a raw and vaporous November morning, Michael at one minute to eight o'clock ran collarless, unbrushed, unshaven, toward the steps leading up to hall at whose head stood the Dean beside the clerkly recorder of these sorry matutinal appearances. Michael waited long enough to see his name fairly entered in the book, yawned resentfully at the Dean, and started back on the taciturn journey that must culminate in the completion of his toilet. Crossing the gravel space between Cloisters and Cuther's worldly quad, he met Maurice Avery dressed finally for the day at one minute past eight o'clock. Such a phenomenon provoked him into speech.

"What on earth.... Are you going to London?" he gasped.

"Rather not. I'm going out to buy a copy of the O.L.G."

Michael shook his head, sighed compassionately, and passed on. Twenty minutes later in Common Room he was contemplating distastefully the kedgeree which with a more hopeful appetite he had ordered on the evening before, when Maurice planked down beside his place the first number of The Oxford Looking-Glass.

"There's a misprint on page thirty-seven, line six. It ought to be 'yet' not 'but.' Otherwise I think it's a success. Do you mind reading my slashing attack on the policy of the Oxford theater? Or perhaps you'd better begin at the beginning and go right through the whole paper and give me your absolutely frank opinion of it as a whole. Just tell me candidly if you think my Reflections are too individual. I want the effect to be more——"

"Maurice," Michael interrupted, "do you like kedgeree?"

"Yes, very much," Maurice answered absently. Then he plunged on again. "Also don't forget to tell me if you think that Guy's skit is too clever. And if you find any misprints I haven't noticed, mark them down. We can't alter them now, of course, but I'll speak to the compositor myself. You like the color? I wonder whether it wouldn't have been better to have had dark blue after all. Still——"

"Well, if you like kedgeree," Michael interrupted again, "do you like it as much in the morning as you thought you were going to like it the night before?"

"Oh, how the dickens do I know?" exclaimed Maurice fretfully.

"Well, will you just eat my breakfast and let me know if you think I ought to have ordered eggs and bacon last night?"

"Aren't you keen on the success of this paper?" Maurice demanded.

"I'll tell you later on," Michael offered. "We'll lunch together quietly in my rooms, and the little mulled claret we shall drink to keep out this filthy fog will also enormously conduce to the amiableness of my judgment."

"And you won't come out with me and Nigel Stewart to watch people buying copies on their way to leckers?" Maurice suggested in a tone of disappointment. Lonsdale arrived for breakfast at this moment, just in time to prevent Michael's heart from being softened. The newcomer was at once invited to remove the editor.

"Have you bought your copy of the O.L.G. yet, Lonny?" Maurice demanded, unabashed.

"Look here, Moss Avery," said Lonsdale seriously, "if you promise to spend the bob you screw out of me on buying yourself some soothing syrup, I'll ..."

But the editor rejected the frivolous attentions of his audience, and left the J.C.R. Michael, not thinking it very prudent to remind Lonsdale of last night's encounter with Appleby, examined the copy of The Oxford Looking-Glass that lay beside his plate.

It was a curious compound of priggishness and brilliance and perspicacity and wit, this olive-green bantling so meticulously hatched, and as Michael turned the pages and roved idly here and there among the articles that by persevering exhortation had been driven into the fold by the editor, he was bound to admit the verisimilitude of the image of Oxford presented. Maurice might certainly be congratulated on the variety of the opinions set on record, but whether he or that Academic Muse whose biographies and sculptured portraits nowhere exist should be praised for the impression of corporate unanimity that without question was ultimately conveyed to the reader, Michael was not sure. It was a promising fancy, this of the Academic Muse; and Michael played with the idea of elaborating his conception in an article for this very Looking-Glass which she invisibly supported. The Oxford Looking-Glass might serve her like the ægis of Pallas Athene, an ægis that would freeze to academic stone the self-confident chimeras of the twentieth century. Michael began to feel that his classical analogies were enmeshing the original idea, involving it already in complexities too manifold for him to unravel. His ideas always fled like waking dreams at the touch of synthesis. Perhaps Pallas Athene was herself the Academic Muse. Well enough might the owl and the olive serve as symbols of Oxford. The owl could stand for all the grotesque pedantry, all the dismal hootings of age, all the slow deliberate sweep of the don's mind, the seclusions, the blinkings in the daylight and the unerring destruction of intellectual vermin; while the olive would speak of age and the grace and grayness of age, of age each year made young again by its harvest of youth, of sobriety sun-kindled to a radiancy of silver joy, of wisdom, peace, and shelter, and Attic glories.

Michael became so nearly stifled by the net of his fancies that he almost rose from the table then and there, ambitious to take pen in hand and test the power of its sharpness to cut him free. He clearly saw the gray-eyed goddess as the personification of the spirit of the university: but suddenly all the impulse faded out in self-depreciation. Guy Hazlewood would solve the problem with his pranked-out allusiveness, would trace more featly the attributes of the Academic Muse and establish more convincingly her descent from Apollo or her identity with Athene. At least, however, he could offer the idea and if Guy made anything of it, the second number of The Oxford Looking-Glass would hold more of Michael Fane than the ten pounds he had laid on the table of its exchequer. Inspired by the zest of his own fancy, he read on deliberately.

Some Reflections. By Maurice Avery.

The editor had really succeeded in reflecting accurately the passing glance of Oxford, although perhaps the tortuous gilt of the frame with which he had tried to impart style to his mirror was more personal to Maurice Avery than general to the university. Moreover, his glass would certainly never have stood a steady and protracted gaze. Still with all their faults these paragraphic reflections did show forth admirably the wit and unmatured cynicism of the various Junior Common Rooms, did signally flash with all the illusion of an important message, did suggest a potentiality for durable criticism.

Socrates at Balliol. By Guy Hazlewood.

There was enough of Guy in his article to endear it to Michael, and there was so much of Oxford in Guy that whatever he wrote spontaneously would always enrich the magazine with that adventurous gaiety and childlike intolerance of Athene's favorites.

The Failure of the Modern Illustrator.
By C. St. C. Wedderburn.

Here was Wedders writing with more distinction than Michael would have expected, but not with all the sartorial distinction of his attire.

"Let us turn now to the illustrators of the sixties and seventies, and we shall see...." Wedderburn in the plural scarcely managed to convey himself into print. The neat bulk began to sprawl: the solidity became pompous: the profundity of his spoken voice was lacking to sustain so much sententiousness.

Quo Vadis? By Nigel Stewart.

Nigel's plea for the inspiration of modernity to make more vital the decorative Anglicanism whose cause he had pledged his youth to advance, was with all its predetermined logic and emphasis of rhetorical expression an appealing document. Michael did not think it would greatly serve the purpose for which it had been written, but its presence in The Oxford Looking-Glass was a guarantee that the youngest magazine was not going to ignore the force that perhaps more than any other had endowed Oxford with something that Cambridge for all her poets lacked. Michael himself had since he came up let the practice of religion slide, but his first fervors had not burned themselves out so utterly as to make him despise the warmth they once had kindled. His inclination in any argument was always toward the Catholic point of view, and though he himself allowed to himself the license of agnostic speech and agnostic thought, he was always a little impatient of a skeptical non-age and very contemptuous indeed of an unbelief which had never been tried by the fire of faith. He did not think Stewart's challenge with its plaintive under-current of well-bred pessimism would be effective save for the personality of the writer, who revealed his formal grace notwithstanding the trumpeting of his young epigrams and the tassels of his too conspicuous style. With all the irritation of its verbal cleverness, he rejoiced to read *Quo Vadis?* and he felt in reading it that Oxford would still have silver plate to melt for a lost cause.

Under the stimulus of Nigel Stewart's article, Michael managed to finish his breakfast with an appetite. As he rose to leave the Common Room, Lonsdale emerged from the zareba of illustrated papers with which he had fortified his place at table.

"Have you been reading that thing of Mossy's?" he asked incredulously.

Michael nodded.

"Isn't it most awful rot?"

"Some of it," Michael assured him.

"I suppose it would be only sporting to buy a copy," sighed Lonsdale. "I suppose I ought to buzz round and buck the college up into supporting it. By Jove, I'll write and tell the governor to buy a copy. I want him to raise my allowance this year, and he'll think I'm beginning to take an interest in what he calls 'affairs.'"

Michael turned into Venner's before going back to his own rooms.

"Hullo, is that the paper?" asked Venner. "Dear me, this looks very learned. You should tell him to put some more about sport into it— our fellows are all so dreadfully wild about sport. They'd be sure to buy it then. Going to work this morning? That's right. I'm always advising the men to work in the morning. But bless you, they don't pay any attention to me. They only laugh and say, 'what's old Venner know about it?'"

Michael, sitting snugly in the morning quiet of his room, leaned over to poke the fire into a blaze, eyed with satisfaction November's sodden mists against his window, and settled himself back in the deep chair to The Oxford Looking-Glass.

Oxford Liberalism. By Vernon Townsend.
A Restatement of Tory Ideals. By William Mowbray.

These two articles Michael decided to take on trust. From their perusal he would only work himself up into a condition of irritated neutrality. Indeed, he felt inclined to take all the rest of the magazine on trust. The tranquillity of his own room was too seductive. Dreaming became a duty here. It was so delightful to count from where he sat the books on the shelves and to arrive each time at a different estimate of their number. It was so restful to stare up at Mona Lisa and traverse without fatigue that labyrinth of rocks and streams. His desk not yet deranged by work or correspondence possessed a monumental stability of neatness that was most soothing to contemplate. It had the restfulness of a well-composed landscape where every contour took the eye easily onward and where every tree grew just where it was needed for a moment's halt. The olive-green magazine dropped unregarded onto the floor, and there was no other book within reach. The dancing fire danced on. Far away sounded the cries of daily life. The chimes in St. Mary's tower struck without proclaiming any suggestion of time. How long these roll-call mornings were and how rapidly dream on dream piled its drowsy outline. Was there not somewhere at the other end of Oxford a lecture at eleven o'clock? This raw morning was not suitable for lectures out of college. Was not Maurice coming to lunch? How deliciously far off was the time for ordering lunch. He really must get out of the habit of sitting in this deep wicker-chair, until evening licensed such repose.

Some people had foolishly attended a ten-o'clock lecture at St. John's. What a ludicrous idea! They had ridden miserably through the cold on their bicycles and with numb fingers were now trying to record scraps of generalization in a notebook that would inevitably be lost long before the Schools. At the same time it was rather lazy to lie back like this so early in the morning. Why was it so difficult to abandon the Sirenian creakings of this chair? He wanted another match for his second pipe, but even the need for that was not violent enough to break the luxurious catalepsy of his present condition.

Then suddenly Maurice Avery and Nigel Stewart burst into the room, and Michael by a supreme effort plunged upward onto his legs to receive them.

"My hat, what a frowst!" exclaimed Maurice, rushing to the window and letting in the mist and the noise of the High.

"We're very hearty this morning," murmured Stewart. "I heard Mass at Barney's for the success of the O.L.G."

"Nigel and I have walked down the High, rounded the Corn, and back along the Broad and the Turl," announced Maurice. "And how many copies do you think we saw bought by people we didn't know?"

"None," guessed Michael maliciously.

"Don't be an ass. Fifteen. Well, I've calculated that at least four times as many were being sold, while we were making our round. That's sixty, and it's not half-past ten yet. We ought to do another three hundred easily before lunch. In fact, roughly I calculate we shall do five hundred and twenty before to-night. Not bad. After two thousand we shall be making money."

"Maurice bought twenty-two copies himself," said Stewart, laughing, and lest he should seem to be laughing at Maurice thrust an affectionate arm through his to reassure him.

"Well, I wanted to encourage the boys who were selling them," Maurice explained.

"They'll probably emigrate with the money they've made out of you," predicted Michael. "And what on earth are you going to do with twenty-two copies? I find this one copy of mine extraordinarily in the way."

"Oh, I shall send them to well-known literary people in town. In fact, I'm going to write round and get the best-known old Oxford men to give us contributions from time to time, without payment, of course. I expect they'll be rather pleased at being asked."

"Don't you think it may turn their heads?" Michael anxiously suggested. "It would be dreadful to read of the sudden death of Quiller-Couch from apoplectic pride or to hear that Hilaire Belloc or Max Beerbohm had burst with exultation in his bath."

"It's a pity you can't be funny in print," said Maurice severely. "You'd really be some use on the paper then."

"But what we've really come round to say," interposed Stewart, "is that there's an O.L.G. dinner to-night at the Grid; and then afterward we're all going across to my digs opposite."

"And what about lunch with me?"

Both Maurice and Nigel excused themselves. Maurice intended to spend all day at the Union. Nigel had booked himself to play fug-socker with three hearty Trindogs of Trinity.

"But when did you join the Union?" Michael asked the editor.

"I thought it was policy," he explained. "After all, though we laugh at it here, most of the Varsity does belong. Besides, Townsend and Bill Mowbray were both keen. You see they think the O.L.G. is going to have an influence in Varsity politics. And, after all, I am editor."

"You certainly are," Michael agreed. "Nothing quite so editorial was ever conceived by the overwrought brain of a disappointed female contributor."

Michael always enjoyed dining at the Grid. Of all the Oxford clubs it seemed to him to display the most completely normal undergraduate existence. Vincent's, notwithstanding its acknowledged chieftaincy, depended ultimately too much on a mechanically apostolic succession. It was an institution to be admired without affection. It had every justification for calling itself The Club without any qualifying prefix, but it produced a type too highly specialized, and was too definitely Dark Blue and Leander Pink. In a way, too, it belonged as much to Cambridge, and although violently patriotic had merged its individuality in brawn. By its substitution of co-option for election, its Olympic might was now scarcely much more than the self-deification of Roman Emperors. Vincent's was the last stronghold of muscular supremacy. Yet it was dreadfully improbable, as Michael admitted to himself, that he would have declined the offer of membership.

The O.U.D.S. was at the opposite pole from Vincent's, and if it did not offend by its reactionary encouragement of a supreme but discredited spirit, it offended even more by fostering a premature worldliness. For an Oxford club to take in The Stage and The Era was merely an exotic heresy. On the walls of its very ugly room the pictures of actors that in Garrick Street would have possessed a romantic dignity produced an effect of strain, a proclamation of mounte-bank-worship that differed only in degree from the photographs of actresses on the mantelpiece of a second-rate room in a second-rate college. The frequenters of the O.U.D.S. were always very definitely Oxford undergraduates, but they lacked the serenity of Oxford, and seemed already to have planted a foot in London. The big modern room over the big cheap shop was a restless place, and its pretentiousness and modernity were tinged with Thespianism. Scarcely ever did the Academic Muse enter the O.U.D.S., Michael thought. She must greatly dislike Thespianism with all that it connoted of mildewed statuary in an English garden. Yet it would be possible to transmute the O.U.D.S., he dreamed. It had the advantage of a limited membership. It might easily become a grove where Apollo and Athene could converse without quarreling. Therefore, he could continue to frequent its halls.

The Bullingdon was always delightful; the gray bowlers and the white trousers striped with vivid blue displayed its members, in their costume, at least, as unchanging types, but the archaism made it a club too conservative to register much more than an effect of peculiarity. The Bullingdon had too much money, and not enough unhampered humanity to achieve the universal. The Union, on the other hand, was too indiscriminate. Personality was here submerged in organization. Manchester or Birmingham could have produced a result very similar.

The Grid, perhaps for the very fact that it was primarily a dining-club, was the abode of discreet good-fellowship. Its membership was very strictly limited, and might seem to have been confined to the seven or eight colleges that considered themselves the best colleges, but any man who deserved to be a member could in the end be sure of his election. The atmosphere was neither political nor sporting nor literary, nor financial, but it was very peculiarly and very intimately the elusive atmosphere of Oxford herself. The old rooms looking out on the converging High had recently been redecorated in a very crude shade of blue. Members were grumbling at the taste of the executive, but Michael thought the unabashed ugliness was in keeping with its character. It was as if unwillingly the club released its hold upon the externals of Victorianism. Such premises could afford to be anachronistic, since the frequenters were always so finely sensitive to fashion's lightest breath. Eccentricity was not tolerated at the Grid except in the case of the half-dozen chartered personalities who were necessary to set off the correctness of the majority. The elective committee probably never made a mistake, and when somebody like Nigel Stewart was admitted, it was scrupulously ascertained beforehand that his presence would evoke affectionate amusement rather than the chill surprise with which the Grid would have greeted the entrance of someone who, however superior to the dead level of undergraduate life, lacked yet the indefinable justification for his humors.

Michael on the evening of the Looking-Glass dinner went up the narrow stairs of the club in an aroma of pleasant anticipation, which was not even momentarily dispersed by the sudden occurrence of the fact that he had forgotten to take his name off hall, and must therefore pay two shillings and fourpence to the college for a dinner he would not eat. In the Strangers' Room were waiting the typical guests of the typical members. Here and there nods were exchanged, but the general atmosphere was one of serious expectancy. In the distance the rattle of crockery told of dinners already in progress. Vernon Townsend came in soon after Michael, and as Townsend was a member, Michael lost that trifling malaise of waiting in a club's guest-room which the undergraduate might conceal more admirably than any other class of man, but nevertheless felt acutely.

"Not here yet, I suppose," said Townsend.

It was unnecessary to mention a name. Nigel Stewart's habits were proverbial.

"Read my article?" asked Townsend.

"Splendid," Michael murmured.

"It's going to get me the Librarianship of the Union," Townsend earnestly assured Michael.

Michael was about to congratulate the sanguine author without disclosing his ignorance of the article's inside, when Bill Mowbray rushed breathlessly into the room. Everybody observed his dramatic entrance, whereupon he turned round and rushed out again, pausing only for one moment to exclaim in the doorway:

"Good god, that fool will never remember!"

"See that?" asked Townsend darkly, as the Tory Democrat vanished.

Michael admitted that he undoubtedly had.

"Bill Mowbray has become a poseur," Townsend declared. "Or else he knows his ridiculous article on Toryism was too badly stashed by mine," he added.

"We shan't see him again to-night," Michael prophesied.

Townsend shrugged his shoulders.

"We shall, if he can make another effective entrance," he said a little bitterly.

Maurice Avery and Wedderburn arrived together. The combination of having just been elected to the Grid and the birth of the new paper had given Maurice such an effervescence of good spirits as even he seldom boasted. Wedderburn in contrast seemed graver, supplying in company with Maurice a solidity to the pair of them that was undeniably beneficial to their joint impression. They were followed almost immediately by Guy Hazlewood, who with his long legs came sloping in as self-possessed as he always was. Perhaps his left eyelid drooped a little lower than it was accustomed, and perhaps the sidelong smile that gave him a superficial resemblance to Michael was drawn down to a sharper point of mockery, but whatever stored-up flashes of mood and fancy Guy had to deliver, he always drawled them out in the same half-tired voice emphasized by the same careless indolence of gesture. And so this evening he was the same Guy

Hazlewood, sure of being with his clear-cut pallor and effortless distinction of bearing, the personality that everyone would first observe in whatever company he found himself.

"Nigel not here, of course," he drawled. "Let's have a sweep on what he's been doing. Five bob all round. I say he's just discovered Milton to be a great poet and is now, reading Lycidas to a spellbound group of the very heartiest Trindogs in Trinity."

"I think he saw The Perfect Flapper," said Maurice "and has been trying ever since to find out whether she were a don's daughter or a theatrical bird of passage."

"I think he's forgotten all about it," pronounced Wedderburn very deeply indeed.

"I hope he saw that ass Bill Mowbray tearing off in the opposite direction and went to fetch him back," said Townsend.

"I think he's saying Vespers for the week before last," Michael proposed as his solution.

Stewart himself came in at that moment, and in answer to an united demand to know the reason of his lateness embraced in that gentle and confiding air of his all the company, included them all as it were in an intimate aside, and with the voice and demeanor of a strayed archangel explained that the fearful velocity of a pill was responsible for his unpunctuality.

"But you're quite all right now, Nigel?" inquired Guy. "You could almost send a testimonial?"

"Oh, rather," murmured Nigel, with tender assurance lighting up his great, innocent eyes. "I expect, you know, dinner's ready." Then he plunged his arm through Guy's, and led the way toward the private dining-room he had actually not forgotten to command.

Dinner, owing to Avery's determined steering of the conversation, was eaten to the accompaniment of undiluted shop. Never for a moment was any topic allowed to oust The Oxford Looking-Glass from discussion. Even Guy was powerless against the editor intoxicated by ambition's fulfillment. Maurice sat in triumphant headship with only Mowbray's vacant place to qualify very slightly the completeness of his satisfaction. He hoped they all liked his scheme of inviting well-known, even celebrated, old Oxford men to contribute from time to time. He flattered himself they would esteem the honor vouchsafed to them. He disclaimed the wish to monopolize the paper's criticism and nobly invited Townsend to put in their places a series of contemporary dramatists. He congratulated Guy upon his satiric article and assured him of his great gifts. He reproached Michael for having written nothing, and vowed that many of the books for which he had already sent a printed demand to their publishers must in the December issue be reviewed by Michael. He arranged with Nigel Stewart and Wedderburn at least a dozen prospective campaigns to harry advertisers into unwilling publicity.

At nine-o'clock, the staff of The Oxford Looking-Glass, reflecting now a very roseate world, marched across the High to wind up the evening in Stewart's digs. On the threshold the host paused in sudden dismay.

"Good lord, I quite forgot. There's a meeting of the De Rebus Ecclesiasticis in my digs to-night. They'll all be there; what shall I do?"

"You can't possibly go," declared everybody.

"Mrs. Arbour," Nigel called out, hurriedly dipping into the landlady's quarters. "Mrs. Arbour."

Mrs. Arbour assured him comfortably of her existence as she emerged to confer with him in the passage.

"There may be one or two men waiting in my rooms. Will you put out syphons and whisky and explain that I shan't be coming."

"Any reason to give, sir?" asked Mrs. Arbour.

The recalcitrant shook his seraphic head.

"No, sir," said Mrs. Arbour cheerfully, "quite so. Just say you're not coming? Yes, sir. Oh, they'll make themselves at home without you, I'll be bound. It's not likely to be a very noisy party, is it, sir?"

"Oh, no. It's the De Rebus Ecclesiasticis, Mrs. Arbour."

"I see, sir. Foreigners. I'll look after them."

Nigel having disposed of the pious debaters, joined his friends again, and it was decided to adjourn to Guy's digs in Holywell. Arm in arm the six journalists marched down the misted High. Arm in arm they turned into Catherine Street, and arm in arm they walked into the Proctor outside the Ratcliffe Camera. To him they admitted their membership of the university. To him they proffered very politely their names and the names of their colleges, and with the same politeness agreed to visit him next morning. The Proctor raised his cap and with his escort faded into the fog. Arm in arm the six journalists continued their progress into Holywell. Guy had digs in an old house whose gabled front leaned outward, whose oriel windows were supported by oaken beams worm-eaten and grotesquely carved. Within, a wide balustraded staircase went billowing upward unevenly. Guy's room that he shared with two intellectual athletes from his own college was very large. It was paneled all round up to the ceiling, and it contained at least a dozen very comfortable armchairs. He had imposed upon his partners his own tastes and with that privilege had cut off electric light and gas, so that lit only by two Pompeian lamps, the room was very shadowy when they all came in.

"Comeragh and Anstruther are working downstairs, I expect," Guy explained, as one by one, while his guests waited in the dim light, he made a great illumination with wax candles. Then he poked up the fire and set glasses ready for anyone's need. Great armchairs were pulled round in a semicircle: pipes were lit: the stillness and mystery of the Oxford night crept along the ancient street, a stillness which at regular intervals was broken by multitudinous chimes, or faintly now and then by passing footfalls. Unexcited by argument the talk rippled in murmurous contentment.

Michael was in no mood himself for talking, and he sat back listening now and then, but mostly dreaming. He thought of the conversation in that long riverside room in Paris with its extravagance and pretentiousness. Here in this time-haunted Holywell Street was neither. To be sure, Christianity and the soul's immortality and the future of England and contemporary art were running the gauntlet of youth's examination, but the Academic Muse had shown the company her ægis, had turned everything to unpassionate stone, and softened all presumption with her guarded glances. It was extraordinary how under her guidance every subject was stripped of obtrusive reality, how even women, discussed never so grossly, remained untarnished; since they ceased to be real women, but mere abstractions wanton or chaste in accordance with the demands of wit. The ribaldry was Aristophanic or Rabelaisian with as little power to offend, so much was it consecrated and refined by immemorial usages. Michael wished that all the world could be touched by the magical freedom and equally magical restraint of the Academic Muse, and as he sat here in this ancient room, hoped almost violently that never again would he be compelled to smirch the present clarity and steadiness of his vision.

CHAPTER IX

THE LESSON OF SPAIN

Perhaps Michael enjoyed more than anything else during his accumulation of books the collection of as many various editions of Don Quixote as possible. He had brought up from London the fat volume illustrated by Doré over which he had fallen asleep long ago and of which owing to Nurse's disapproval he had in consequence been deprived. Half the pages still showed where they had been bent under the weight of his small body: this honorable scar and the familiar musty smell and the book's unquestionable if slightly vulgar dignity prevented Michael from banishing it from the shelf that now held so many better editions. However much the zest in Doré's illustrations had died away in the flavor of Skelton's English, Michael could not abandon the big volume with what it held of childhood's first intellectual adventure. The shelf of Don Quixotes became in all his room one of the most cherished objects of contemplation. There was something in the "Q" and the "X" repeated on the back of volume after volume that positively gave Michael an impression in literal design of the Knight's fantastic personality. The very soul of Spain seemed to be symbolized by those sere quartos of the seventeenth century, nor was it imperceptible even in Smollett's cockney rendering bound in marbled boards. Staring at the row of Don Quixotes on a dull December afternoon, Michael felt overwhelmingly a desire to go to Spain himself, to drink at the source of Cervantes' mighty stream of imagination which with every year's new reading seemed to him to hold more and more certainly all that was most vital to life's appreciation. He no longer failed to see the humor of Don Quixote, but even now tears came more easily than laughter, and he regretted as poignantly as the Knight himself those times of chivalry which with all the extravagance of their decay were yet in essence superior to the mode that ousted them into ignominy. Something akin to Don Quixote's impulsive dismay Michael experienced in his own view of the twentieth century. He felt he needed a constructive ideal of conduct to sustain him through the long pilgrimage that must ensue after these hushed Oxford dreams.

Term was nearly over. Michael had heard from Stella that she was going to spend two or three months in Germany. Her Brahms recitals, she wrote, had not been so successful as she ought to have made them. In London she was wasting time. Mother was continually wanting her to come to the theater. It seemed almost as if mother were trying to throw her in the way of marrying Prescott. He had certainly been very good, but she must retreat into Germany, and there again work hard. Would not Michael come too? Why was he so absurdly prejudiced against Germany? It was the only country in which to spend Christmas.

The more Stella praised Germany, the more Michael felt the need of going to a country as utterly different from it as possible. He did not want to spend the vacation in London. He did not want his mother to talk vaguely to him of the advantage for Stella in marrying Prescott. The idea was preposterous. He would be angry with his mother, and he would blurt out to Prescott his dislike of such a notion. He would thereby wound a man whom he admired and display himself in the light of the objectionably fraternal youth. In the dreary and wet murk of December the sun-dried volumes of Cervantes spoke to him of Spain.

Maurice Avery came up to his room, fatigued with fame and disappointed that Castleton with whom he had arranged to go to Rome had felt at the last moment he must take his mother to Bath. To him Michael proposed Spain.

"But why not Rome?" Maurice argued. "As I originally settled."

"Not with me," Michael pointed out. "I don't want to go to Rome now. I always feel luxuriously that there will occur the moment in my life when I shall say, 'I am ready to go to Rome. I must go to Rome.' It's a fancy of mine and nothing will induce me to spoil it by going to Rome at the wrong moment."

Maurice grumbled at him, told him he was affected, unreasonable, and even hinted Michael ought to come to Rome simply for the fact that he himself had been balked of his intention by the absurdly filial Castleton.

"I do think mothers ought not to interfere," Maurice protested. "My mother never interferes. Even my sisters are allowed to have their own way. Why can't Mrs. Castleton go to Bath by herself? I'm sure Castleton overdoes this 'duty' pose. And now you won't come to Rome. Well, will you come to Florence?"

"Yes, and be worried by you to move on to Rome the very minute we arrive there," said Michael. "No, thanks. If you don't want to come to Spain, I'll try to get someone else. Anyway, I don't mind going by myself."

"But what shall we do in Spain?" asked Maurice fretfully.

Michael began to laugh.

"We can dance the fandango," he pointed out. "Or if the fandango is too hard, there always remains the bolero."

"If we went to Rome," Maurice was persisting, but Michael cut him short.

"It's absolutely useless, Mossy. I am not going to Rome."

"Then I suppose I shall have to go to Spain," said Maurice, in a much injured tone.

So in the end it was settled chiefly, Michael always maintained, because Maurice found out it was advisable to travel with a passport. As not by the greatest exaggeration of insecurity could a passport be deemed necessary for Rome, Maurice decided it was an overrated city and became at once fervidly Spanish, even to the extent of saying "gracias" whenever the cruet was passed to him in hall. Wedderburn at the last moment thought he would like to join the expedition: so Maurice with the passport in his breast pocket preferred to call it.

There were two or three days of packing in London, while Maurice stayed at 173 Cheyne Walk and was a great success with Mrs. Fane. The Rugby match against Cambridge was visited in a steady downpour. Wedderburn fetched his luggage, and the last dinner was eaten together at Cheyne Walk. Mrs. Fane was tenderly, if rather vaguely, solicitous for their safety.

"Dearest Michael," she said, "do be careful not to be gored by a bull. I've never been to Spain. One seems to know nothing about it. Mr. Avery, do have some more turkey. I hope you don't dreadfully dislike garlic. Such a pungent vegetable. Michael darling, why are you laughing? Isn't it a vegetable? Mr. Wedderburn, do have some more turkey. A friend of mine, Mrs. Carruthers, who is a great believer in Mental Science ... Michael always laughs at me when I try to explain.... Hark, there is the cab, really. I hope it won't be raining in Spain. 'Rain, rain, go to Spain.' So ominous, isn't it? Good-bye, dearest boy, and write to me at Mrs. Carruthers, High Towers, Godalming."

"I say, I know Mrs. Carruthers. She lives near us," Maurice exclaimed.

"Come on," his friends insisted. "You haven't time now to explain the complications of Surrey society."

"I'm so glad," said Mrs. Fane. "Because you'll be able to see that Michael remembers the address."

"I never forget addresses, mother," protested Michael.

"No, I know. I always think everyone is like me. Merry Christmas, and do send a post card to Stella. She was so hurt you wouldn't go to Germany."

In the drench and soak of December weather they drove off in the four-wheeler. On such a night it seemed more than ever romantic to be setting out to Spain, and all the way to Victoria Maurice tried to decide by the occasional gleam of a blurred lamp-light how many pesetas one received for an English sovereign.

The crossing to Dieppe was rough, but all memories of the discomfort were wiped out when next day they saw the Sud Express looking very long and swift and torpedo-like between the high platforms of that white drawing-room, the Gare d'Orleans. Down they went all day through France with rain speckling the windows of their compartment, past the naked poplar trees and rolling fallows until dusk fell sadly on the flooded agriculture. Dawn broke as they were leaving behind them the illimitable Landes. Westward the Atlantic clouds swept in from the Bay of Biscay, parting momentarily to reveal rifts of milky turquoise sky. Wider and wider grew the rifts, and when the train passed close to the green cliffs of St. Jean de Luz, the air was soft and fragrant: the sea was blue. At Irun they were in Spain, and Michael, as he walked up and down the platform waiting for déjeuner, watched, with a thrill of conviction that this was indeed a frontier, the red and blue toy soldiers and the black and green toy soldiers dotted about the toy landscape.

Maurice was rather annoyed that nobody demanded their passports and that every official should seem so much more anxious to examine their railway tickets, but when they reached Madrid and found that no bull-fights would be held before the spring, he began to mutter of Rome and was inclined to obliterate the Spaniards from the category of civilization, so earnestly had he applied himself by the jiggling light of the train to the mastery of all the grades from matador to banderillo.

In Seville, however, Maurice admitted he could not imagine a city more perfectly adapted to express all that he desired from life. Seville with her guitars and lemon-trees, her castanets and oranges and fans, her fountains and carnations and flashing Andalusians, was for him the city to which one day he would return and dream. Here one day he could come when seriously he began to write or paint or take up whatever destiny in art was in store for him. Here he would forget whatever blow life might hold in the future. He would send everybody he knew to Seville, notwithstanding Michael's objection that such generosity would recoil upon himself in his desire to possess somewhere on earth the opportunity of oblivion. Maurice and Wedderburn both bought Spanish cloaks and hats and went with easels to sit beside the Guadalquiver that sun-stained to the hue of its tawny banks was so contemptuous of their gentlemanly water-colors, as contemptuous as those cigarette-girls that came chattering from the tobacco-factory every noon. Michael preferred to wander over the roofs of the cathedral, until drowsed by the scent of warm stone he would sit for an hour merely conscious that the city lay below and that the sky was blue above.

After Seville they traveled to Granada, to Cadiz and Cordova and other famous cities; and in the train they went slowly through La Mancha where any windmill might indeed be mistaken for Pentapolin of the Naked Arm, and where at the stations the water-carriers even in January cried "agua, agua," so that already the railway-carriages seemed parched by the fierce summer sun. They traveled to Salamanca and Toledo, and last of all they went to Burgos where Maurice and Wedderburn strove in vain to draw corner after corner of the cathedral, in the dust and shadows of whose more remote chantries Michael heard many Masses. A realization of the power of faith was stirred in him by these Masses that every day of every year were said without the recognition of humanity. These mumblings of ancient priests, these sanctus-bells that rattled like shaken ribs, these interminable and ceremonious shufflings were the outward expression of the force that sustained this fabric of Burgos and had raised in Seville a cathedral that seemed to crush like a stupendous monster the houses scattered about in its path, insignificant as a heap of white shells. Half of these old priests, thought Michael, were probably puppets who did not understand even their own cracked Latinity, yet their ministrations were almost frightening in their efficacy: they were indeed the very stones of Burgos made vocal.

Listening to these Masses, Michael began to regret he had allowed all his interest in religion to peter out in the irritation of compulsory chapel-keeping at Oxford. Here in Burgos, he felt less the elevating power of faith than the unrelenting and disdainful inevitableness of its endurance. At Bournemouth, when he experienced the first thrill of conversion, he had been exultingly aware of a personal friendliness between himself and God. Here in Burgos he was absorbed into the divine purpose neither against his will nor his desire, since he was positively aware of the impotency of his individuality to determine anything in the presence of omnipotence. He told himself this sense of inclusion was a sign of the outpouring once more of the grace of God, but he wished with a half whimsical amusement that the sensation were rather less like that of being contemptuously swept by a broom into the main dust-heap. Yet as on the last morning of his stay in Burgos Michael came away from Mass, he came away curiously fortified by his observation of the moldy confessionals worn down by the knees of so many penitents. That much power of impression at least had the individual on this cathedral.

When Michael lay awake in the train going northward he remembered very vividly the sense of subordination which in retrospect suddenly seemed to him to reveal the essential majesty of Spain. The train stopped at some French station. Their carriage was already full enough, but a bilious and fussy Frenchman insisted there was still room, and on top of him broke in a loud-voiced and assertive Englishman with a meek wife. It was intolerable. Michael, Wedderburn, and Maurice displayed their most polite obstructiveness, but in the end each of them found himself upright, stiff-backed and exasperated. Michael thought regretfully of Spain, and remembered those peasants who shared their crusts, those peasants with rank skins of wine and flopping turkeys, those peasants who wrought so inimitably their cigarettes and would sit on the floor of the carriage rather than disarrange the comfort of the three English travelers. Michael went off into an uneasy sleep trying to arrange synthetically his deductions, trying to put Don Quixote and Burgos Cathedral and the grace of God

190

and subordination and feudalism and himself into a working theory of life. And just when the theory really seemed to be shaping itself, he was awakened by the Englishman prodding his wife.

"What is it, dear?" she murmured.

"Did you pack those collars that were in the other chest of drawers?"

"I think so, dear."

"I wish you'd know something for a change," the husband grumbled.

The Frenchman ground his teeth in swollen sleep, exhaling himself upon the stale air of the compartment. Maurice was turning over the pages of a comic paper. Wedderburn snored. It was difficult to achieve subordination of one's personality in the presence of other personalities so insistently irritating.

Stella had not come back from Germany when Michael reached home, which was a disappointment as he had looked forward to planning with her a journey back to Spain as soon as possible. His mother during this vacation had lapsed from Mental Science into an association to prevent premature burial.

"My dearest boy, you have no idea of the numbers of people buried alive every year," she said. "I have been talking to Dick Prescott about it. I cannot understand his indifference. I intend to devote all my time to it. We are going to organize a large bazaar next season. Banging their foreheads against the coffins! It's dreadful to think of. Do be careful, Michael. I have written a long letter to Stella explaining all the precautions she ought to take. Who knows what may happen in Germany? Such an impulsive nation. At least the Kaiser is. Don't laugh, my dear boy, it's so much more serious than you think. Would you like to come with me to Mrs. Carruthers' and hear some of the statistics? Gruesome, but most instructive. At three o'clock. You needn't wait for tea, if you're busy. The lecturer is an Eurasian. Where *is* Eurasia, by the by?"

Michael kissed his mother with affectionate amusement.

"Will you wear the mantilla I brought you from Spain? Look, it's as light as burnt tissue paper."

"Dearest Michael," she murmured reproachfully, "you ought not to laugh about sacred subjects.... I don't really see why we shouldn't have a car. We must have a consultation with Dick Prescott."

After dinner that night Michael wrapped up some stained and faded vestments he had brought for Viner and went off to see him at Netting Hill. He told himself guiltily in the hansom that it was more than a year since he had been to see old Viner, but the priest was so heartily glad to welcome him and accepted so enthusiastically his propitiatory gifts, that he felt as much at ease as ever in the smoke-hung room.

"Well, how's Oxford? I was coming up last term, but I couldn't get away. Have you been to see Sandifer yet? Or Pallant at Cowley, or Canon Harrowell?"

Michael said he had not yet taken advantage of Viner's letters of introduction to these dignitaries. He had indeed heard Pallant preach at the church of the Cowley Fathers, but he had thought him too much inclined to sacrifice on the altar of empirical science.

"I hate compromise," said Michael.

"I don't think Pallant compromises, but I think he does get hold of men by offering them Catholic doctrine in terms of the present."

Michael shrugged his shoulders.

"This visit to Spain seems to have made you very bigoted," Viner observed, smiling.

"I haven't made up my mind one way or the other about Christianity," Michael said. "But when I do I won't try to include everybody, to say to every talkative young Pragmatist with Schiller's last book in his pocket, 'come inside, you're really one of us.' I shan't invite every callow biologist to hear Mass just because a Cowley Dad sees nothing in the last article on spontaneous generation that need dismay the faithful. I'm getting rather fed up with toleration, really; the only people with any fanaticism now are the rationalists. It's quite exhilarating sometimes to see the fire of disbelief glowing in the eyes of a passionate agnostic."

"Our Lord Himself was very tolerant," said Viner.

"Yes, tolerant to the weaknesses of the flesh, tolerant to the woman taken in adultery, tolerant to the people without wine at Cana, but he hadn't much use for people who didn't believe just as He believed."

"Isn't it rather risky to slam the door in the face of the modern man?"

"But, Mr. Viner," Michael protested, "you can't betray the myriads of the past because the individual of to-day finds his faith too weak to sustain him in their company, because the modern man wants to reëdit spiritual truths just as he has been able to reëdit a few physical facts that apparently stand the test of practical experiment. While men have been rolling along intoxicated by the theory of physical evolution, they may have retrograded spiritually."

"Of course, of course," the priest agreed. "By the way, your faith seems to be resisting the batterings of external progress very stoutly. I'm glad, old chap."

"I'm not sure that I have much faith, but I certainly haven't given up hope," Michael said gravely. "I think, you know, that hope, which is after all a theological virtue, has never had justice at the hands of the theologians. Oh, lord, I wish earnest young believers weren't so smug and timid. Or else I wish that I didn't feel the necessity of coordinating my opinions and accepting Christianity as laid down by the Church. I should love to be a sort of Swedenborgian with all sorts of fanciful private beliefs. But I want to force everything within the convention. I hate Free Thought, Free Love, and Free Verse, and yet I hate almost equally the stuffy people who have never contemplated the possibility of their merit. Do you ever read a paper called The Spectator? Now I believe in what The Spectator stands for, and I admire its creed enormously, but the expression of its opinions makes me spue. If only earnest young believers wouldn't treat Almighty God with the same sort of proprietary air that schoolgirls use toward a favorite mistress."

"Michael, Michael!" cried Viner, "where are you taking me with your coördinating impulses and your Spectators and your earnest young believers? What undergraduate paradox are you trying to wield against me? Remember, I've been down nearly twenty years. I can no longer turn mental somersaults. I thought you implied *you* were a believer."

"Oh, no, I'm watching and hoping. And just now I'm afraid the anchor is dragging. Hope does have an anchor, doesn't she? I'm not asking, you know, for the miracle of a direct revelation from God. The psychologists have made miracles of that sort hardly worth while. But I'm hoping with all my might to see bit by bit everything fall away except faith. Perhaps when I behold God in one of his really cynical moods ... I'm groping in the dark after a hazy idea of subordination. That's something, you know. But I haven't found my own place in the scheme."

"You see you're very modern, after all," said Viner, "with your coördinations and subordinations."

"But I don't want to assert myself," Michael explained. "I want to surrender myself, and I'm not going to surrender anything until I am sure by faith that I'm not merely surrendering the wastage of myself."

Michael left Viner with a sense of the pathetic sameness of the mission-priest's existence. He had known so well before he went that, because it was Monday, he would find him sitting in that armchair, smoking that pipe, reading that novel. Every other evening he would be either attending to parochial clubs in rooms of wood and corrugated iron, or his own room would be infested with boys who from year to year, from month to month, never changed in general character, but always gave the same impression of shrill cockney, of boisterous familiarity, of self-satisfied election. To-morrow morning he would say Mass to the same sparse congregation of sacristan and sisters-of-mercy and devout old maids. The same red-wristed server would stump about his liturgical business in Viner's wake, and the same coffee pot put in the same place on the same table by the same landlady would await his return. There was a dreariness about the ministrations of this Notting Hill Mission which had been absent from the atmosphere of Burgos Cathedral. No doubt superficially even at Burgos there was a sameness, but it was a glorious sameness, a sameness that approximated to eternity. Long ago had the priests learned subordination. They had been absorbed into the omnipotence of the church against which the gates of hell could not prevail. Viner remained, however much as he might have surrendered of himself to his mission work, essentially an isolated, a pathetic individual.

As usual, Michael met Alan at Paddington, and he was concerned to see that Alan looked rather pale and worried.

"What problems have you been solving this vac?" Michael asked.

"Oh, I've been swatting like a pig for Mods," said Alan hopelessly. "You are a lucky lazy devil."

Even during the short journey to Oxford Alan furtively fingered his text-books, while he talked to Michael about a depressing January in London.

"Never mind. Perhaps you'll get your Blue next term," said Michael. "And if you aren't determined to play cricket all the Long, we'll go away and have a really sporting vac somewhere."

"If I'm plowed," said Alan gloomily, "I've settled to become a chartered accountant."

Michael enjoyed his second Lent term. With an easy conscience he relegated Rugby football into the limbo of the past. He decided such violent exercise was no longer necessary, and he was getting to know so many people at other colleges that the cultivation of new personalities occupied all his leisure. After Maurice and Wedderburn came back from Spain, they devoted much of their time to painting, and The Oxford Looking-Glass became a very expensive business on account of the reproduction of their drawings. Moreover, the circulation decreased in ratio with the increase of these drawings, and the five promoters who did not wish to practice art in the pages of their magazine convoked several meetings of protest. Finally Maurice was allowed to remain editor only on condition that he abstained from publishing any more drawings.

Nigel Stewart's meeting of the De Rebus Ecclesiasticis together with the visit to Spain induced Michael to turn his attention to that side of undergraduate life interested in religion. He went to see Canon Harrowell, and even accepted from him an invitation to a breakfast at which he met about half a dozen Klebe men who talked about bishops. Afterward Canon Harrowell seemed anxious to have a quiet talk with him in the library, but Michael made an excuse, not feeling inclined for self-revelation so quickly on top of six Klebe men and the eggs and bacon. He went to see Father Pallant at Cowley, but Father Pallant appeared so disappointed that he had brought him no scientific problems to reconcile with Catholic dogma, and was moreover so contemptuous of Dom Cuthbert Manners, O.S.B. and Clere Abbey that Michael never went to see him again. He preferred old Sandifer, who with all the worldly benefits of good wine, good food, and pleasant company, offered in addition his own courtly Caroline presence that added to wit and learning and trenchant theology made Michael regret he had not called upon him sooner.

Nigel Stewart took Michael to a meeting of De Rebus Ecclesiasticis, at which he met not only the six Keble men who had talked about bishops at Canon Harrowell's breakfast, but about twenty more members of the same college, all equally fervid and in his opinion equally objectionable. Michael also went with Nigel Stewart to Mass at St. Barnabas', where he saw the same Keble men all singing conspicuously and all conveying the impression that every Sunday they occupied the same place. By the end of the term Michael's aroused interest in religion at Oxford died out. He disliked the sensation of belonging to a particular school of thought within a university. The ecclesiastical people were like the ampelopsis at Trinity: they were highly colored, but so inappropriate to Oxford, that they seemed almost vulgar. It was ridiculous they should have to worship in Oxford at a very ugly modern church in the middle of very ugly modern slums, as ridiculous as it was to call in the aid of American creepers to cover up the sins of modern architects.

Yet Michael was at a loss to explain to himself why the ecclesiastical people were so obviously out of place in Oxford. After all, they were the heirs of a force which had persisted there for many years almost in its present aspect: they were the heirs after a fashion of the force that kept the Royal Standard flying against the Parliament. But they had not inherited the spirit of mediæval Oxford. They were too self-conscious, too congregational. As individuals, perhaps they were in tone with Oxford, but, eating bacon and eggs and talking about bishops, they belonged evidently to Keble, and Michael could not help feeling that Keble like Mansfield and Ruskin Hall was in Oxford, but not in the least of Oxford. The spirit of mediæval Oxford was more typically preserved in the ordinary life of the ordinary graduate; and yet it was a mistake to think of the spirit of Oxford at any date. That spirit was dateless and indefinable, and each new manifestation which

Michael was inclined to seize upon, even a manifestation so satisfying as Venner's, became with the very moment that he was aware of it as impossible to determine as a dream which leaves nothing behind but the almost violent knowledge that it was and exasperatingly still is.

The revived interest lasted a very short time in its communal aspect, and Michael retreated into his mediæval history, still solicitous of Catholicism in so far as to support the papacy against the Empire in the balance of his judgment, but no longer mingling with the Anglican adherents of the theory, nor even indeed committing himself openly to Christianity as a general creed. Indeed, his whole attitude to religion was the result of a reactionary bias rather than of any impulse toward constructive progression. He would have liked to urge himself forward confidently to proclaim his belief in Christianity, but he could acquire nothing more positive than a gentle skepticism of the value of every other form of thought, a gentleness that only became scornfully intolerant when provoked by ignorance or pretentious statement.

Meanwhile, The Oxford Looking-Glass, though inclining officially to neither political party, was reflecting a widespread interest in social reform. Michael woke up to this phenomenon as he read through the sixth number on a withering March day toward the end of term. Knowing Maurice to be a chameleon who unconsciously acquired the hue of his surroundings, Michael was sure that The Oxford Looking-Glass by this earnest tone indicated the probable tendency of undergraduate energy in the hear future. Yet himself, as he surveyed his acquaintances, could not perceive in their attitude any hint of change. In St. Mary's the debating clubs were still debating the existence of ghosts: the essay clubs were still listening to papers that took them along the by-ways of archæology or sport. Throughout the university the old habit of mind persisted apparently. The New College manner that London journalists miscalled the Oxford manner still prevailed in the discussion of intellectual subjects. In Balliol when any remark trembled on the edge of a generalization, somebody in a corner would protest, "Oh, shut up, fish-face!" and the conversation at once veered sharply back to golf or scandal, while the intellectual kitten who had been playing with his mental tail would be suddenly conscious of himself or his dignity and sit still. In Exeter the members of the Literary Society were still called the Bloody Lits. Nothing anywhere seemed as yet to hint that the traditional flippancy of Oxford which was merely an extension of the public-school spirit was in danger of dying out. Oxford was still the apotheosis of the amateur. It was still surprising when the Head of a House or a don or an undergraduate achieved anything in a manner that did not savor of happy chance. It was still natural to regard Cambridge as a provincial university, and to take pleasure in shocking the earnest young Cambridge man with the metropolitan humors and airy self-assurance of Oxford.

Yet The Oxford Looking-Glass reflected another spirit which Michael could not account for and the presence of which he vaguely resented.

"The O.L.G. is getting very priggish and serious and rather dull," he complained to Maurice.

"Not half so dull as it would be if I depended entirely on casual contributions," replied the editor. "I don't seem to get anything but earnestness."

"Oxford is becoming the home of living causes," sighed Michael. "That's a depressing thought. Do you really think these Rhodes Scholars from America and Australia and Germany are going to affect us?"

"I don't know," Maurice said. "But everybody seems keen to speculate on the result."

"Why don't you take up a strong line of patronage? Why don't you threaten these pug-nosed invaders with the thunders of the past?" Michael demanded fiercely.

"Would it be popular?" asked Maurice. "Personally of course I don't care one way or the other, but I don't want to let the O.L.G. in for a lot of criticism."

"You really ought to be a wonderful editor," said Michael. "You're so essentially the servant of the public."

"Well, with all your grumbles,", said Maurice, "ours is the only serious paper that has had any sort of a run of late years."

"But it lacks individuality," Michael complained. "It's so damned inclusive. It's like The Daily Telegraph. It's voluminous and undistinguished. It shows the same tepid cordiality toward everything, from a man who's going to be hanged for murder to a new record at cricket. Why can't you infect it with some of the deplorable but rather delightfully juvenile indiscretion of The Daily Mail?"

"The Daily Mail," Maurice scoffed. "That rag!"

"A man once said to me," Michael meditatively continued, "that whenever he saw a man in an empty railway compartment reading The Daily Telegraph, he always avoided it. You see, he knew that man. He knew how terrible it would be to listen to him when he had finished his Telegraph. I feel rather like that about the O.L.G. But after all," he added cheerfully, "nobody does read the O.L.G. The circulation depends on the pledges of their pen sent round to their friends and relations by the casual contributors. And nobody ever meets a casual contributor. Is it true, by the way, that the fossilized remains of one were found in-that great terra incognita—Queen's College?"

But Maurice had left him, and Michael strolled down to the lodge to see if there were any letters. Shadbolt handed him an invitation to dinner from the Warden. As he opened it, Lonsdale came up with a torn replica of his own.

"I say, Michael, this is a rum sort of binge for the Wagger to give. I spotted all the notes laid out in a row by old Pumpkin-head's butler. You. Me. Tommy Grainger. Fitzroy. That ass Appleby. That worm Carben. And Smithers. There may have been some others too. I hope I don't get planted next the Pumpkinette."

"Miss Wagger may not be there," said Michael hopefully. "But if she is, you're bound to be next her."

"I say, Shadbolt," Lonsdale demanded, "is this going to be a big squash at the Wagger's?"

"The Warden has given me no instruction, sir, about carriages. And so I think we may take it for granted as it will be mostly confined to members of the college, sir. His servant tells me as the Dean is going and the Senior Tutor."

"And there won't be any does?"

"Any what, sir?"

"Any ladies?"

"I expect as Miss Crackanthorpe will be present. She very rarely absconds from such proceedings," said Shadbolt, drawing every word with the sound of popping corks from the depths of his pompousness.

Michael and Lonsdale found out that to the list of guests they had established must be added the names of Maurice, Wedderburn and two freshmen who were already favorably reported through the college as good sportsmen.

Two evenings later, at seven o'clock, Michael, Maurice, Lonsdale, Wedderburn, and Grainger, bowed and starched, stood in Venner's, drinking peach bitters sharpened by the addition of gin.

"The men have gone in to hall," said Venner. "You ought to start round to the Warden's lodgings at ten past seven. Now don't be late. I expect you'll have a capital dinner."

"Champagne, Venner?" asked Lonsdale.

"Oh, bound to be! Bound to be," said Venner. "The Warden knows how to give a dinner. There's no doubt of that."

"Caviare, Venner?" asked Maurice.

"I wouldn't say for certain. But if you get an opportunity to drink any of that old hock, be sure you don't forget. It's a lovely wine. I wish we had a few dozen in the J.C.R. Now don't go and get tipsy like some of our fellows did once at a dinner given by the Warden."

"Did they, Venner?" asked everybody, greatly interested.

"It was just after the Transvaal war broke out. Only three or four years ago. There was a man called Castleton, a cousin of our Castleton, but a very different sort of man, such a rowdy fellow. He came out from the Warden's most dreadfully tipsy, and the men were taking him back to his rooms, when he saw little Barnaby, a Science don, going across New quad. He broke away from his friends and shouted out, 'there's a blasted Boer,' and before they could stop him, he'd knocked poor little Barnaby, a most nervous fellow, down in the wet grass and nearly throttled him. It was hushed up, but Castleton was never asked again you may be sure, and then soon after he volunteered for the front and died of enteric. So you see what comes of getting tipsy. Now you'd better start."

Arm in arm the five of them strolled through Cloisters until they came to the gothic door of the Warden's Lodgings. Up the Warden's majestic staircase they followed the butler into the Warden's gothic drawing-room where they shook hands with the great moon-faced Warden himself, and with Miss Crackanthorpe, who was very much like her brother, and nearly as round on a much smaller scale. They nodded to the Dean, mentally calculating how many roll-calls they were behind, for the Dean notwithstanding the geniality of his greeting had one gray eye that seemed unable to forget it belonged to the Dean. They nodded to Mr. Ardle, the Senior Tutor, who blinked and sniffed and bowed nervously in response. Fitzroy beamed at them: Smithers doubtfully eyed them. The two freshmen reputed to be good sportsmen smiled grateful acknowledgments of their condescension. Appleby waved his hand in a gesture of such bland welcome that Lonsdale seemed to gibber with suppressed mortification and rage.

"Will you lay five to one in bobs that I don't sit next the Pumpkinette?" whispered Lonsdale to Michael, as they went downstairs to dinner.

"Not a halfpenny," laughed Michael. "You will. And I shall get Ardle."

Upon the sage-green walls of the dining-room hung the portraits of three dead Wardens, and though the usual effect of family pictures was to make the living appear insignificant beside them, Michael felt that Pumpkin-head even in the presence of his three ferocious and learned forerunners had nothing to fear for his own preëminence. Modern life found in him a figure carved out of the persistent attributes of his office, and therefore already a symbol of the universal before his personality had been hallowed by death or had expressed itself in its ultimate form under the maturing touch of art and time. This quality in the host diffused itself through the room in such a way that the whole dinner party gained from it a dignity and a stability which made more than usually absurd the superficial actions of eating and drinking, and the general murmur of infinitely fugacious talk.

Michael taking his first glance round the table after the preliminary shynesses of settling down, was as much thrilled by his consciousness of the eternal reality of this dinner party as he would have been if by a magical transference he could have suddenly found himself pursuing some grave task in the picture of a Dutch master. He had been to many dinners in Oxford of which commemorative photographs had been made by flashlight, and afterward when he saw the print he could scarcely believe in his own reality, still less in that of the dinner, so ludicrously invented seemed every group. He wished now that a painter would set himself the problem of preserving by his art some of these transitory entertainments. He began to imagine himself with the commission to set on record the present occasion. He wished for the power to paint those deeper shadows in which the Warden's great round face inclined slowly now toward Fitzroy with his fair complexion and military rigor of bearing, now toward Wedderburn whose evening dress acquired from the dignity of its owner the richness of black velvet. More directly in the light of the first lamp sat Maurice and Appleby opposite to one another, both imparting to the assemblage a charming worldliness, Maurice by his loose-fronted shirt, Appleby by the self-esteem of his restless blue eyes. The two freshmen on either side of the Dean wonderfully contrasted with his gauntness, and even more did the withered Ardle, who looked like a specimen of humanity dried as plants are dried between heavy books, contrast with the sprawling bulk of Grainger. On the other side, Michael watched with amusement Miss Crackanthorpe with shining apple-face bobbing nervously between Smithers pale and solid and domed like a great cheese, and Lonsdale cool and pink as an ice. In the background from the shadows at either end of the room the sage-green walls materialized in the lamplight: the three dead Wardens stared down at the table: and every fifteen minutes bells chimed in St. Mary's tower.

"And how is The Oxford Looking-Glass progressing, Avery?" inquired the Warden, shining full upon the editor in a steady gaze. "No doubt it takes up a great deal of your valuable time?"

The Dean winked his gray decanal eye at the champagne: the Senior Tutor coughed remotely like a grasshopper: Lonsdale prodded Michael with his elbow and murmured that "the Wagger had laid Mossy a stymie."

Maurice admitted the responsibility of the paper for occupying a considerable amount of his *leisure*, but consoled himself for this by the fact that certainly, The Oxford Looking-Glass was progressing very well indeed.

"We don't altogether know what attitude to take up over the Rhodes Bequest," said Maurice. Then boldly he demanded from the Warden what would be the effect of these imposed scholars from America and Australia and Africa.

"The speculation is not without interest," declared the Warden. "What does Fitzroy think?"

Fitzroy threw back his shoulders as if he were going to abuse the Togger and said he thought the athletic qualifications were a mistake. "After all, sir, we don't want the Tabs—I mean to say we don't want to beat Cambridge with the help of a lot of foreigners."

"Foreigners, Fitzroy? Come, come, we can scarcely stigmatize Canadians as foreigners. What would become of the Imperial Idea?"

"I think the Imperial Idea will take a lot of living up to," said Wedderburn, "when we come face to face with its practical expression. Personally I loathe Colonials except at the Earl's Court Exhibition."

"Ah, Wedderburn," said the Warden, "you are luckily young enough to be able to be particular. I with increasing age begin to suffer from that terrible disease of age—toleration."

"But the Warden is not so very old," whispered Miss Crackanthorpe to Lonsdale and Michael.

"Oh, rather not," Lonsdale murmured encouragingly.

"I think they'll wake up Oxford," announced Smithers; then, as everyone turned to hear what more he would say, Smithers seemed inclined to melt into silence, but with a sudden jerk of defiance, he hardened himself and became volubly opinionative.

"There's no doubt," he continued, "that these fellows will make the average undergrad look round him a bit." As Smithers curtailed undergraduate to the convention of a lady-novelist, a shudder ran round the dinner party. Almost the butler instead of putting ice into the champagne might have slipped it down the backs of the guests.

"In fact, what ho, she bumps," whispered Lonsdale. "Likewise pip-ip, and tootle-oo."

"Anyway, he won't be able to ignore them," said Smithers.

"We hope not, indeed," the Warden gravely wished. "What does Lonsdale think? Lord Cleveden wrote to me to say how deeply interested he was by the whole scheme—a most appreciative letter, and your father has had a great experience of colonial conditions."

"Has he?" said Lonsdale. "Oh, yes, I see what you mean. You mean when he was Governor. Oh, rather. But I never knew him in those days." Then under his breath he muttered to Michael: "Dive in, dive in, you rotter, I'm getting out of my depth."

"I think Oxford will change the Rhodes Scholars much more profoundly than the Rhodes Scholars will change Oxford," said Michael. "At least they will if Oxford hasn't lost anything lately. Sometimes I'm worried by that, and then I'm not, for I do really feel that they must be changed. Civilization must have some power, or we should all revert."

"And are we to regard these finished oversea products as barbarians?" asked the Warden.

"Oh, yes," said Michael earnestly. "Just as much barbarians as any freshmen."

Everybody looked at the two freshmen on either side of the Dean and laughed, while they laughed too and tried to appear pleasantly flattered by the epithet.

"And what will Oxford give them?" asked the Dean dryly. He spoke with that contempt of generalizations of which all dons made a habit.

"Oh, I don't know," said Michael. "But vaguely I would say that Oxford would cure them of being surprised by themselves or of showing surprise at anybody else. Marcus Aurelius said what I'm trying to say much better than I ever can. Also they will gain a sense of humor, or rather they will ripen whatever sense they already possess. And they'll have a sense of continuity, too, and perhaps—but of course this will depend very much on their dons—perhaps they'll take as much interest in the world as in Australia."

"Why will that depend on their dons?" challenged Mr. Ambrose.

"Oh, well, you know," explained Michael apologetically, "dons very often haven't much capacity for inquisitiveness. They get frightened very easily, don't they?"

"Very true, very true," said the Warden. "But, my dear Fane, your optimism and your pessimism are both quixotic, immensely quixotic."

Later on in the quad when the undergraduate members of the dinner party discussed the evening, Maurice rallied Michael on his conversation.

"If you can talk your theories, why can't you write them?" he complained.

"Because they'd be almost indecently diaphanous," said Michael.

"Good old Fane!" said Grainger. "But, I say, you are an extraordinary chap, you know."

"He did it for me," said Lonsdale. "Pumpkin-head would have burst, if I'd let out I didn't know what part of the jolly old world my governor used to run."

CHAPTER X

STELLA IN OXFORD

Alan, when he met Michael at Paddington, was a great deal more cheerful than when they had gone up together for the previous term. He had managed to achieve a second class in Moderations, and he had now in view a term of cricket whose energy might fortunately be crowned with a blue. Far enough away now seemed Greats and not very alarming Plato and Aristotle at these first tentative encounters.

Michael dined with Alan at Christ Church after the Seniors' match, in which his host had secured in the second innings four wickets at a reasonable price. Alan casually nodded to one or two fellow hosts at the guest table, but did not offer to introduce Michael. All down the hall, men were coming in to dinner and going out of dinner as unconcernedly as if it had been the dining-saloon of a large hotel.

"Who is that man just sitting down?" Michael would ask.

"I don't know," Alan would reply, and in his tone would somehow rest the implication that Michael should know better than to expect him to be aware of each individual in this very much subdivided college.

"Did you hear the hockey push broke the windows of the socker push in Peck?" asked one of the Christ Church hosts.

"No, really?" answered Alan indifferently.

After hall as they walked back to Meadows', Michael tried to point out to him that the St. Mary's method of dining in hall was superior to that of the House.

"The dinner itself is better," Alan admitted. "But I hate your system of all getting up from table at the same time. It's like school."

"But if a guest comes to St. Mary's he sits at his host's regular table. He's introduced to everybody. Why, Alan, I believe if you'd had another guest to-night, you wouldn't even have introduced me to him. He and I would have had to drink coffee in your rooms like a couple of dummies."

"Rot!" said Alan. "And whom could you have wanted to meet this evening? All the men at the guests' table were absolute ticks."

"I've never met a House man who didn't think every other House man impossible outside the four people in his own set," retorted Michael. "And yet, I suppose, you'll say it's the best college?"

"Of course," Alan agreed.

Up in his rooms they pondered the long May day's reluctant death, while the coffee-machine bubbled and fizzed and The Soul's Awakening faintly kindled by the twilight was appropriately sentimental.

"Will you have a meringue?" Alan asked. "I expect there's one in the cupboard."

"I'm sure there is," said Michael. "It's very unlikely that there is a single cupboard in the House without a meringue. But no, thanks, all the same."

They forsook the window-seat and pulled wicker-chairs very near to the tobacco-jar squatting upon the floor between them: they lit their pipes and sipped their coffee. For Alan the glories of the day floated before him in the smoke.

"It's a pity," he said, "Sterne missed that catch in the slips. Though of course I wasn't bowling for the slips. Five for forty-eight would have looked pretty well. Still four for forty-eight isn't so bad in an innings of 287. The point is whether they can afford to give a place to another bowler who's no earthly use as a bat. It seems a bit of a tail. I went in eighth wicket both innings. Two—first knock. Blob—second. Still four for forty-eight was certainly the best. I ought to play in the first trial match." So Alan voiced his hopes.

"Of course you will," said Michael. "And at Lord's. I think I shall ask my mother and sister up for Eights," he added.

Alan looked rather disconcerted.

"What's the matter?" Michael asked. "You won't have to worry about them. I'll explain you're busy with cricket. Stella inquired after you in a letter this week."

During the Easter vacation Alan had stayed once or twice in Cheyne Walk, and Stella who had come back from an arduous time with music and musical people in Germany had seemed to take a slightly sharper interest in his existence.

"Give her my—er—love, when you write," said Alan very nonchalantly. "And I don't think I'd say anything about those four wickets for forty-eight. I don't fancy she's very keen on cricket. It might bore her."

No more was said about Stella that evening, and nothing indeed was said about anything except the seven or eight men competing for the three vacancies in the Varsity eleven. At about a quarter to ten Alan announced as usual that "those men will be coming down soon for cocoa."

"Alan, who are these mysterious creatures that come down for cocoa at ten?" asked Michael. "And why am I never allowed to meet them?"

"They'd bore you rather," said Alan. "They're people who live on this staircase. I don't see them any other time."

Michael thought Alan would be embarrassed if he insisted on staying, so to his friend's evident relief he got up to go.

"You House men are like a lot of old bachelors with your fads and regularities," he grumbled.

"Stay, if you like," said Alan, not very heartily. "But I warn you they're all awfully dull, and I've made a rule to go to bed at half-past ten this term."

"So long," said Michael hurriedly, and vanished.

A few days later Michael had an answer from his mother to his invitation for Eights Week:

173 CHEYNE WALK,
S.W.
May 5.

My dearest Michael,

I wish you'd asked me sooner. Now I have made arrangements to help at the Italian Peasant Jewelry Stall in this big bazaar at Westminster Hall for the Society for the Improvement of the Condition of Agricultural Laborers all over the world. I think you'd be interested. It's all about handicrafts. Weren't you reading a book by William Morris the other day? His name is mentioned a great deal always. I've been meeting so many interesting people. If Stella comes, why not ask Mrs. Ross to chaperone her? Such a capital idea. And do be nice about poor Dick Prescott. Stella is so young and impulsive. I wish she could understand how much much happier she would be married to a nice man, even though he may be a little older than herself. This tearing all over Europe cannot be good for her. And now she talks of going to Vienna and studying under somebody with a perfectly impossible name beginning with L. Not only that, but she also talks of unlearning all she has learned and beginning all over again. This is most absurd, and I've tried to explain to her. She should have thought of this man beginning with L before. At her age to start scales and exercises again does seem ridiculous. I really dread Stella's coming of age. Who knows what she may not take it into her head to do? I can't think where she gets this curious vein of eccentricity. I'll write to Mrs. Ross if you like. Stella, of course, says she can go to Oxford by herself, but that I will not hear of, and I beg you not to encourage the idea, if she suggests it to you.

Your loving
Mother.

Michael thought Mrs. Ross would solve the difficulty, and he was glad rather to relieve himself of the responsibility of his mother at Oxford. He would have had to be so steadily informative, and she would never have listened to a word. Stella's view of the visit came soon after her mother's.

173 CHEYNE WALK,
S.W.
May 8.

Dear M.,

What's all this about Mrs. Ross chaperoning me at Oxford? Is it necessary? At a shot I said to mother, "No, quite unnecessary." But of course, if I should disgrace you by coming alone, I won't. Isn't Mrs. Ross a little on the heavy side? I mean, wouldn't she rather object to me smoking cigars?

"Great scott!" interjaculated Michael.

I'm going to Vienna soon to begin music all over again, so be very charming to your only sister,
Stella.

P.S.—Do crush mother over Prescott.

Michael agreed with his mother in thinking a chaperone was absolutely necessary for Stella's visit to Oxford, and since the threat of cigars he cordially approved of the suggestion that Mrs. Ross should come. Moreover, he felt his former governess would approve of his own attitude toward Oxford, and he rather looked forward to demonstrating it to her. In the full-blooded asceticism of Oxford Michael censured his own behavior when he was seventeen and looked back with some dismay on the view of himself at that time as it appeared to him now. He was as much shocked by that period now as at school in his fifteenth year he had been shocked by the memory of the two horrid little girls at Eastbourne. Altogether this invitation seemed an admirable occasion to open the door once again to Mrs. Ross and to let her personality enter his mind as the sane adjudicator of whatever problems should soon present themselves. It would be jolly for Alan, too, if his aunt came up and saw him playing for the Varsity in whatever cricket match was provided to relieve the tedium of too much rowing.

So finally, after one or two more protests from Stella, it was arranged that she should come up for Eights Week under the guardianship of Mrs. Ross.

Michael took care some time beforehand to incorporate a body of assistant entertainers. Lonsdale in consideration of Michael having helped him with his people for one day last year was engaged for the whole visit. Maurice was made to vow attendance for at least every other occasion. Wedderburn volunteered his services. Guy Hazlewood, who was threatened with Schools, was let off with a lunch. Nigel Stewart spoke mysteriously of a girl whose advent he expected on which account he could not pledge himself too straightly. Rooms were taken in the High. Trains were looked out. On Saturday morning Lonsdale and Michael went down to the station to meet Mrs. Ross and Stella.

"I think it was a very bad move bringing me," said Lonsdale, as they waited on the platform. "Your sister will probably think me an awful ass, and ..."

But the train interrupted Lonsdale's self-depreciation, and he sustained himself well through the crisis of the introductions. Michael thought Mrs. Ross had never so well been suited by her background as now when tall and straight and in close-fitting gray dress she stood in the Oxford sunlight. Stella, too, in that flowered muslin relieved Michael instantly of the faint anxiety he had conceived lest she might appear in a Munich garb unbecoming to a reserved landscape. It was a very peculiarly feminine dress, but somehow she had never looked more like a boy, and her gray eyes, as for one moment she let them rest wide open on the city's towers and spires, were more than usually gray and pellucid.

"I say, I ordered a car to meet us," said Lonsdale. "I thought we should buzz along quicker."

"What you really thought," said Michael, "was that you would have to drive my sister in a hansom."

"Oh, no, I say, really," protested Lonsdale.

"I'm much more frightened of you than you could ever be of me," Stella declared.

"Oh no, I say, really, are you? But I'm an awful ass, Miss Fane," said Lonsdale encouragingly. "Hallo, here's the jolly old car."

As they drove past the castle, Lonsdale informed Stella it was the county gaol, and when they reached the gaol he told her it was probably Worcester College, or more familiarly Wuggins.

"You'll only have to tell her that All Souls is the County Asylum and that Queens is a marmalade factory, and she'll have a pretty good notion of the main points of interest in the neighborhood," said Michael.

"He always rags me," explained Lonsdale, smiling confidentially round at the visitors. "I say, isn't Alan Merivale your nephew?" he asked Mrs. Ross. "He's playing for the Varsity against Surrey. Sent down some very hot stuff yesterday. We ought to buzz round to the Parks after lunch and watch the game for a bit."

Wedderburn, who had been superintending the preparations for lunch, met them in the lodge with a profound welcome, having managed to put at least twenty years on to his age. Lunch had been laid in Lonsdale's rooms, since he was one of the few men in college who possessed a dining-room in addition to a sitting-room. Yet, notwithstanding that Michael had invited the guests and that they were lunching in Lonsdale's rooms, to Wedderburn by all was the leadership immediately accorded.

197

The changeless lunch of Eights Week with its salmon mayonnaise and cold chicken and glimpses through the windows of pink and blue dresses going to and fro across the green quadrangles, with its laughter and talk and speculations upon the weather, with its overheated scout and scent of lilac and hawthorn, went its course: as fugitive a piece of mirthfulness as the dance of the mayflies over the Cher.

After lunch they walked to the Parks to watch Alan playing for the Varsity. Wedderburn, who with people to entertain feared nothing and nobody, actually went coolly into the pavilion and fetched out Alan who was already in pads, waiting to go in. Michael watched very carefully Alan's meeting with Stella, watched Alan's face fall when he saw her beside Maurice and marked how nervously he fidgeted with his gloves. There was a broken click from the field of play. It was time for Alan to go in. Michael wished very earnestly he could score a brilliant century so that Stella hearing the applause could realize how much there was in him to admire. Yet ruefully he admitted to himself the improbability of Stella realizing anything at all about the importance of cricket. However, he had scarcely done with his wishing, when he saw Alan coming gloomily back from the wicket, clean bowled by the very first ball he had received.

"Of course, you know, he isn't played for his batting," he hastened to explain to Stella.

She, however, was too deeply engaged in discussing Vienna with Maurice to pay much attention, even when Alan sat down despondently beside them, unbuckling his pads. It was just as Michael had feared, fond though he was of Maurice.

The last Varsity player was soon out, and Wedderburn proposed an early tea in his rooms to be followed by the river. Turning into Holywell, they met Guy Hazlewood, who said without waiting to be introduced to Mrs. Ross and Stella:

"My dear people, I fall upon your necks. Suggest something for me to do that for one day and one night will let me entirely forget Schools. We can't bear our digs any longer."

"Why don't you give a party there on Monday night," suggested Wedderburn deeply.

"Let me introduce you to Mrs'sss ... my sissss ... Mr. H'wood," mumbled Michael in explanation of Wedderburn's proposal.

"What a charming idea," drawled Guy. "But isn't it rather a shame to ask Miss Fane to play? Anyway, I daren't."

"Oh, no," said Stella. "I should rather like to play in Oxford."

So after a kaleidoscope of racing and a Sunday picnic on the upper river, when everybody ate as chickens drink with a pensive upward glance at the trend of the clouds, occurred Guy Hazlewood's party in Holywell, which might more truly have been called Wedderburn's party, since he at once assumed all responsibility for it.

The digs were much more crowded than anybody had expected, chiefly on account of the Balliol men invited.

"Half Basutoland seems to be here," Lonsdale whispered to Michael.

"Well, with Hazlewood, Comeragh and Anstruther, all sons of Belial, what else can you expect?" replied Michael.

Stella had seemed likely at first to give the favor of her attention more to Hazlewood than to anybody else, but Maurice was in a dauntless mood and, with Guy handicapped by having to pretend to assent to Wedderburn's suggestions for entertainment, he managed at last to monopolize Stella almost entirely. Alan had declined the invitation with the excuse of wanting a steady hand and eye for to-morrow. But Michael fancied there was another reason.

Stella played three times and was much applauded.

"Very sporting effort, by Jove," said Lonsdale, and this was probably the motive of most of the commendation, though there was a group of really musical people in the darkest corner who emerged between each occasion and condoled with Michael on having to hear his sister play in such inadequate surroundings.

Michael himself was less moved by Stella's playing than he had ever been. Nor was this coldness due to any anxiety for her success. He was sure enough of that in this uncritical audience.

"Do you think Stella plays as well as she did?" he asked Mrs. Ross.

"Perhaps this evening she may be a little excited," Mrs. Ross suggested.

"Perhaps," said Michael doubtfully. "But what I mean is that, if she isn't going to advance quite definitely, there really isn't any longer an excuse for her to arrogate to herself a special code of behavior."

"Stella says a great deal more than she does," Mrs. Ross reassured him. "You'd be surprised, as indeed I was surprised, to find how simple and childlike she really is. I think an audience is never good for her."

"But, after all, her life is going to be one audience after another in quick succession," Michael pointed out.

"Gradually an audience will cease to rouse her into any violence of thought or accentuation of superficial action—oh, Michael," Mrs. Ross exclaimed, breaking off, "what dreadfully long words you're tempting me to use, and why do you make me talk about Stella? I'd really rather talk about you."

"Stella is becoming a problem to me," said Michael.

"And you yourself are no longer a problem to yourself?" Mrs. Ross inquired.

"Not in the sense I was, when we last talked together."

Michael was a little embarrassed by recalling that conversation. It seemed to link him too closely for his pleasure to the behavior which had led up to it, to be a part of himself at the time, farouche and uncontrolled.

"And all worries have passed away?" persisted Mrs. Ross.

"Yes, yes," said Michael quickly. "For one thing," he added as if he thought he had been too abrupt, "I'm too comfortably off to worry much about anything. Boredom is the only problem I shall ever have to face. Seriously though, Mrs. Ross, I really am rather shocked when I think of myself as sixteen and seventeen." Michael was building brick by brick a bridge for Mrs. Ross to step over the chasm of three years. "I seem to see myself," he persevered, "with very untidy hair, with very loose joints, doing and saying and thinking the most impossible things. I blush now at the memory of myself, just as I should blush now with Oxford snobbishness to introduce a younger brother like myself then, say to the second-year table in hall." Michael paused for a moment, half hoping Mrs. Ross would assure him he had caricatured his former self, but as she said nothing, he continued: "When I came up to Oxford I found that the natural preparation for Oxford was not a day-school like St. James', but a boarding-school. Therefore I had to acquire in a term what most of my contemporaries had been given several years to acquire. I remember quite distinctly my father saying to my mother, 'By gad, Valérie, he ought to go to Eton, you know,' and my mother disagreeing, 'No, no, I'm sure you were right when you said St. James'.' That's so like mother. She probably had never thought the matter out at all. She was probably perfectly vague about the difference between St. James' and Eton, but because it had been arranged so, she disliked the idea of any alteration. I'm telling you all this because, you know, you provided as it were the public-school influence for my early childhood. After you I ought to have passed on to a private school entirely different from Randell House, and then to Eton or Winchester. I'm perfectly sure I could have avoided everything that happened when I was sixteen or seventeen, if I'd not been at a London day-school."

"But is it altogether fair to ascribe everything to your school?" asked Mrs. Ross. "Alan for instance came very successfully, as far as normality is concerned, through St. James'."

"Yes, but Alan has the natural goodness of the average young Englishman. Possibly he benefited by St. James'. Possibly at Eton, and with a prospect of money, he would have narrowed down into a mere athlete, into one of the rather objectionable bigots of the public-school theory. Now I was never perfectly normal. I might even have been called morbid and unhealthy. I should have been, if I hadn't always possessed a sort of curious lonely humor which was about twice as severe as the conscience of tradition. At the same time, I had nothing to justify my abnormality. No astounding gift of genius, I mean."

"But, Michael," interrupted Mrs. Ross, "I don't fancy the greatest geniuses in the world ever justified themselves at sixteen or seventeen."

"No, but they must have been upheld by the inner consciousness of greatness. You get that tremendously through all the despondencies of Keats' letters for instance. I have never had that. Stella absorbed all the creative and interpretative force that was going. I never have and never shall get beyond sympathy, and even the value that gives my criticism is to a certain extent destroyed by the fact that the moment I try to express myself more permanently than by mouth, I am done."

"But still, I don't see why a day-school should have militated against the development of that sympathetic and critical faculty."

"It did in this way," said Michael. "It gave me too much with which to sympathize before I could attune my sympathy to criticism. In fact I was unbalanced. Eton would have adjusted this balance. I'm sure of that, because since I've been at Oxford I find my powers of criticism so very much saner, so very much more easily economized. I mean to say, there's no wastage in futile emotions. Of course, it's partly due to being older."

"Really, Michael," Mrs. Ross protested, "if you talk like this I shall begin to regret your earlier extravagance. This dried-up self-confidence seems to me not quite normal either."

"Ah, that's only because I'm criticizing my earlier self. I really am now in a delightful state of cool judgment. Once I used to want passionately to be like everybody else. I thought that was the goal of social happiness. Then I wanted to be violently and conspicuously different from everybody else. Now I seem to be getting near the right mean between the two extremes. I'm enjoying Oxford enormously. I can't tell you how happy I am here, how many people I like. And I appreciate it so much the more because to a certain extent at first it was a struggle to find that wide normal road on which I'm strolling along now. I'm so positive that the best of Oxford is the best of England, and that the best of England is the best of humanity that I long to apply to the world the same standards we tacitly respect—we undergraduates. I believe every problem of life can be solved by the transcendency of the spirit which has transcended us up here. You remember I used to say you were like Pallas Athene? Well, just those qualities in you which made me think of that resemblance I find in Oxford. Don't ask me to say what they are, because I couldn't explain."

"I think you have a great capacity for idealization," said Mrs. Ross gravely. "I wonder how you are going to express it practically. I wonder what profession you'll choose."

"I don't suppose I shall choose a profession at all," said Michael. "There's no financial reason—at any rate—why I should."

"Well, you won't have to decide against a profession just yet," said Mrs. Ross. "And now tell me, just to gratify my curiosity, why you think Stella's playing has deteriorated—if you really think it has."

"Oh, I didn't say it had," Michael contradicted in some dismay. "I merely said that to-night it did not seem up to her level. Perhaps she was anxious. Perhaps she felt among all these undergraduates, as I felt in my first week. Perhaps she's thinking what schoolboys they all are, and how infinitely youthful they appear beside those wild and worldly-wise Bohemians to whose company she has been accustomed for so long. I long to tell her that these undergraduates are really so much wiser, even if literature means Mr. Soapy Sponge's Sporting Tour, and art The Soul's Awakening, and religion putting on a bowler to go and have a hot breakfast at the O.U.D.S. after chapel, and politics the fag-ends of paternal or rather ancestral opinion, and life a hot bath and changing after a fox-hunt or a grouse-drive."

Farther conversation was stopped by Wedderburn driving everybody down to supper with pastoral exhortations in his deepest bass. Michael, after his talk with Mrs. Ross, was relieved to find himself next to Lonsdale and sheltered by a quivering rampart of jellies from more exacting company.

"These Basutos aren't so bad when you talk to them," said Lonsdale. "Comeragh was at m'tutor's. I wonder if he still collects bugs. I rather like that man Hazlewood. I thought him a bit sidy at first, but he's rather keen on fishing. I don't think much of the girl that Trinity man—what's his name—Stewart has roped in. She looks like something left over from a needlework stall. I say, your sister jolly well knows how to punch a piano. Topping, what? Mossy's been very much on the spot to-night. He and Wedders are behaving like a couple of theatrical managers. Why didn't Alan Merivale turn up? I was talking to some of the cricket push at the Club, and it doesn't look a hundred quid to a tanner on his Blue. Bad luck. He's a very good egg."

Michael listened vaguely to Lonsdale's babble. He was watching the passage of the cigars and cigarettes down the table. Thank heaven, Stella had let the cigars go by.

The party of 196 Holywell broke up. Outside in the shadowy street of gables they stood laughing and talking for a moment. Guy Hazlewood, Comeragh and Anstruther looked down from the windows at their parting guests.

"It's been awfully ripping," these murmured to their hosts. The hosts beamed down.

"We've been awfully bucked up by everything. Special vote of thanks to Miss Fane."

"You ought all to get Firsts now," said Wedderburn.

Then he and Lonsdale and Michael and Maurice set off with Stella and Mrs. Ross to the High Street rooms. In different directions the rest of the party vanished on echoing footsteps into the moon-bright spaces, into the dark and narrow entries. Voices faint and silvery rippled along the spell-bound airs of the May night. The echoing footsteps died out to whispers. There was a whizzing of innumerable clocks, and midnight began to clang.

"We must hurry," said the escort, and they ran off down the High toward St. Mary's, reaching the lodge on the final stroke.

"Shall I come up to your rooms for a bit?" Maurice suggested to Michael.

"I'm rather tired," objected Michael, who divined that Maurice was going to talk at great length about Stella.

He was too jealous of Alan's absence that evening to want to hear Maurice's facile enthusiasm.

CHAPTER XI

SYMPATHY

Mrs. Ross and Stella left Oxford two days after the party, and Michael was really glad to be relieved of the dread that Stella in order to assert her independence of personality would try to smash the glass of fashion and dint the mold of form. Really he thought the two occasions during her visit on which he liked her best and admired her most were when she was standing on the station platform. Here she was expressed by that city of spires confusing with added beauty that clear sky of Summer. Here, too, her personality seemed to add an appropriate foreground to the scene, to promise the interpretation that her music would give, a promise, however, that Michael felt she had somehow belied.

Alan dropped out of the Varsity Eleven the following week, and he was in a very gloomy mood when Michael paid him a visit of condolence.

"These hard wickets have finished me off," he sighed. "I shall take up golf, I think."

The bag of clubs he had brought up on his first day was lying covered with gray fluff under the bed.

"Oh, no, don't play golf," protested Michael, "you've got two more years to get your Blue and all your life to play golf, which is a rotten game and has ruined Varsity cricket."

"But one can be alone at golf," said Alan.

"Alone?" repeated Michael. "Why on earth should you want to play an outdoor game alone?"

"Because I get depressed sometimes," Alan explained. "What good am I?"

Michael began to laugh.

"It's nothing to laugh at," said Alan sadly. "I've been thinking of my future. I shall never have enough money to marry. I shall never get my Blue. I shall get a fourth in Greats. Perhaps I shan't even get into the Egyptian Civil Service. I expect I shall end as a bank clerk. Playing cricket for a suburban club on Saturday afternoons. That's all I see before me. When is Stella going to Vienna?"

"I don't know that she is going," said Michael. "She always talks a great deal about things which don't always come off."

"I was rather surprised she seemed to like that man Avery so much," Alan said. "But I suppose he pretended to know an awful lot about music. I don't think I care for him."

"Some people don't," Michael admitted. "I think women always like him, though."

"Yes, I should think they did," Alan agreed bitterly. "Sorry I'm so depressing. Have a meringue or something."

"Alan, why, are you in love with Stella?" Michael challenged.

"What made you think I was?" countered Alan, looking alarmed.

"It's pretty obvious," Michael said. "And curiously enough I can quite understand it. Generally, of course, a brother finds it difficult to understand what other people can see in his sister, but I'm never surprised when they fall in love with Stella."

"A good many have?" asked Alan, and his blue eyes were sharpened by a pain deeper than that of seeing a catch in the slips missed off his bowling.

Michael nodded.

"Oh, I've realized for a long time how utterly hopeless it was for me," Alan sighed. "I'm evidently going to be a failure."

"Would you care for some advice?" inquired Michael very tentatively.

"What sort of advice?" Alan asked.

Michael took this for assent, and plunged in.

"Let her alone," he adjured his friend. "Let her absolutely alone. She's very young, you know, and you're not very old. Let her alone for at least a year. I suggest two years. Don't see much of her, and don't let her think you care. That would interest her for a week, and really, Alan, it's not good for Stella to think that everybody falls in love with her. I don't mind about Maurice. It would do him good to be turned down."

"Would he be?" demanded Alan gloomily.

"Of course, of course ... it seems funny to be talking to you about love ... you used to be so very scornful about it.... I expect you know you'll fall in love pretty deeply now.... Alan, I'm frightfully keen you should marry Stella. But let her alone. Don't let her interfere with your cricket. Don't take up golf on account of her."

Michael was so much in earnest with his exhortation to Alan that he picked up a meringue and was involved in the difficulties of eating it before he was aware he was doing so. Alan began to laugh, and the heavy airs of disappointment and hopelessness were lightened.

"It's funny," said Michael, "that I should have an opportunity now of talking to you about love and cricket."

"Funny?" Alan repeated.

"Don't you remember three years ago on the river one night how I wished you would fall in love, and you said something about it being bad for cricket?"

"I believe I do remember vaguely," said Alan.

Michael saw that after the explanation of his depression he wanted to let the subject drop, and since that was the very advice he had conferred upon Alan, he felt it would be unfair to tempt him to elaborate this depression merely to gratify his own pleasure in the retrospect of emotion. So Stella was not discussed again for a long while, and as she did after all go to Vienna to study a new technique, the abstention was not difficult. Michael was glad, since he had foreseen the possibility of a complication raveled by Maurice. Her departure straightened this out, for Maurice was not inclined to gather strength from absence. Other problems more delicate of adjustment even than Stella began to arise, problems connected with the social aspects of next term.

Alan would still be in college. Scholars at Christ Church were allowed sometimes to spend even the whole of their four years in college. Michael tried in vain to persuade him to ask leave to go into digs. Alan offered his fourth year to companionship with Michael, but nothing would induce him to emerge from college sooner. And why did Michael so particularly want him? There were surely men in his own college with whom he was intimate enough to share digs. Michael admitted there were many, but he did not tell Alan that the real reason he had been so anxious for his partnership was to have an excuse to escape from an arrangement made lightly enough with Maurice Avery in his first or second term that in their third year they should dig together. Maurice had supposed the other day that the arrangement stood, and Michael, not wishing to hurt his feelings, had supposed so too. A few days later Maurice had come along with news of rooms in Longwall. Should he engage them? Michael said he hated Longwall as a prospective dwelling-place, and Maurice had immediately deferred to his prejudice.

It was getting unpleasantly near a final arrangement, for the indefatigable Maurice would produce address after address, until Michael seemed bound ultimately to accept. Lonsdale and Grainger had invited him to dig with them at 202 High. Michael suggested Maurice as well, but they shook their heads. Wedderburn was already partially sharing, that is to say, though he had his own sitting-room he was in the same house and would no doubt join in the meals. Maurice was not to be thought of. Maurice was a very good fellow but—Maurice was—but—and Michael in asking Lonsdale and Grainger why they declined his company, asked himself at the same time what were his own objections to digging with Maurice. He tried to state them in as kindly a spirit as he could, and for a while he told himself he wished to be in digs with people who represented the broad stream of normal undergraduate life; he accused himself in fact of snobbishness, and justified the snobbishness by applying it to undergraduate Oxford as a persistent attribute. As time went by, however, and Maurice produced rooms on rooms for Michael's choice, he began almost to dislike him, to resent the assumption of a desire to dig with him. Where was Maurice's sensitiveness that it could not react to his unexpressed hatred of the idea of living with him? Soon it would come to the point of declaring outright that he did not want to dig with him. Such an announcement would really hurt his feelings, and Michael did not want to do that. As soon as Maurice had receded into the background of casual encountership, he would take pleasure in his company again. Meanwhile, however, it really seemed as if Maurice were losing all his superficial attractiveness. Michael wondered why he had never before noticed how infallibly he ran after each new and petty phase of art, how vain he was too, and how untidy. It was intolerable to think of spending a year's close association with all those paint-boxes and all that modeling wax and all those undestroyed proof-sheets of The Oxford Looking-Glass. Finally, he had never noticed before how many cigarettes Maurice smoked and with what skill he concealed in every sort of receptacle the stained and twisted stumps that were left over. That habit would be disastrous to their friendship, and Michael knew that each fresh cigarette lighted by him would consume a trace more of the friendship, until at last he would come to the state of observing him with a cold and mute resentment. He was in this attitude of mind toward his prospective companion, when Maurice came to see him. He seemed nervous, lighting and concealing even more cigarettes than usual.

"About digs in Longwall," he began.

"I won't live in Longwall," affirmed Michael.

"Do you think you could find anybody else?"

"Why, have you got hold of some digs for three?" asked Michael hopefully. This would be a partial solution of the difficulty, as long as the third person was a tolerably good egg.

Maurice seemed embarrassed.

"No; well, as a matter of fact, Castleton rather wants to dig with me. The New College man he was going to live with is going down, and he had fixed up some rather jolly digs in Longwall. He offered me a share, but of course I said I was digging with you, and there's no room for a third."

"I can go in with Tommy Grainger and Lonny," said Michael quickly.

Maurice looked much relieved.

"As long as you don't feel I've treated you badly," he began.

"That's all right," said Michael, resenting for the moment Maurice's obvious idea that he was losing something by the defection. But as soon as he could think of Maurice unlinked to himself for a year, his fondness for him began to return and his habit of perpetually smoking cigarettes was less irritating. He accepted Maurice's invitation to stay at Godalming in July with an inward amusement roused by the penitence which had prompted it.

Stella's unexpectedly prompt departure to Vienna had left Michael free to make a good many visits during the Long Vacation. He enjoyed least the visit to High Towers, because he found it hard not to be a little contemptuous of the adulation poured out upon Maurice by his father and mother and sisters. Mr. Avery was a stockbroker with a passion for keeping as young as his son. Mrs. Avery was a woman who, when her son and her husband were not with her, spoiled the dogs, and sometimes even her daughters. She was just as willing to spoil Michael, especially when his politeness led him into listening in shady corners of the tennis-lawn to Mrs. Avery's adorations of Maurice. He found Godalming oppressive with the smart suburbanity of Surrey. He disliked the facility of life there, the facile thought, the facile comfort, the facile conversation. Everything went along with a smoothness that suited the civilized landscape, the conventional picturesqueness and the tar-smeared roads. After a week Michael was summoned away by a telegram. Without a ruse, he would never have escaped from this world of light-green Lovat tweeds, of fashionable rusticity and carefully pressed trousers.

"Dear Mrs. Avery," he wrote, preening himself upon the recuperative solitude of empty Cheyne Walk whence his mother had just departed to France. "I enjoyed my visit so much, and so much wish I had not been called away on tiresome business. I hope the garden-party at the Nevilles was a great success, and that the High Towers croquet pair distinguished themselves. Please remember me to Mr. Avery."

"Thank Heaven that's done!" he sighed, and lazily turned the pages of Bradshaw to discover how to reach Wedderburn in the depths of South Wales.

The vacation went by very quickly with quiet intervals in London between his visits, of which he enjoyed most the fortnight at Cressingham Hall—a great Palladian house in the heart of the broad Midlands. It was mid-August with neither shooting nor golf to disturb the pastoral calm. Lonsdale was trying under Lord Cleveden's remonstrances to obtain a grasp of rural administration. So he and his sister Sylvia with Michael drove every day in a high dogcart to various outlying farms of the estate. Lonsdale managed to make himself very popular, and after all as he confided to Michael that was the main thing.

"And how's his lordship, sir?" the tenant would inquire.

"Oh, very fit," Lonsdale would reply. "I say, Mr. Hoggins, have you got any of that home-brewed beer on draught? My friend Mr. Fane has heard a good deal about it."

In a cool farm-parlor Lonsdale and Michael would toast the health of agriculture and drink damnation to all Radicals, while outside in the sun were Sylvia with Mrs. Hoggins, looking at the housewife's raspberries and gooseberries.

"I envy your life," said Michael.

"A bit on the slow side, don't you think?"

"Plenty of time for thinking."

"Ah," said Lonsdale. "But then I've got no brains. I really haven't, you know. The poor old governor's quite worried about it."

However, when after dinner Lord Cleveden bade his son and his guest draw up their chairs and when, as he ceremoniously circulated the port, he delivered majestic reminiscences of bygone celebrities and notorieties, Michael scarcely thought that anything would ever worry him very much, not even a dearth of partridges, still less a dearth of brains in his only son.

"Dear Lady Cleveden," he wrote, when once again he sat in the empty house in Cheyne Walk. "London is quite impossible after Cressingham."

And so it was with the listless August people drooping on the Embankment, the oily river and a lack-luster moon.

Michael was surprised at such a season to get a telegram from Prescott, inviting him to dine at the Albany. His host was jaded by the hot London weather, and the soldier-servant waited upon him with more solicitude than usual. Prescott and Michael talked of the commonplace for some time, or rather Michael talked away rather anxiously while Prescott lent him a grave attention. At last Michael's conversation exhausted itself, and for a few minutes there was silence, while Prescott betrayed his nervousness by fidgeting with the ash on his cigar. At last he burnt himself and throwing away the cigar leaped forthwith into the tide of emotion that was deepening rapidly around his solitary figure.

"Daresay your mother told you I wanted to marry Stella. Daresay Stella told you. Of course, I realize it's quite absurd. Said so at once, and of course it's all over now. Phew! it's fearfully hot to-night. Always feel curiously stranded in London in August, but I suppose that's the same with most people."

Michael had an impulse to ask Prescott to come away with him, but the moment for doing so vanished in the shyness it begot, and a moment later the impulse seemed awkwardly officious. Yet by Prescott's confidence Michael felt himself committed to a participation in his existence that called for some response. But he could not with any sincerity express a regret for Stella's point of view.

"Mother was very anxious she should accept you," said Michael, and immediately he had a vision of Prescott like the puppet of an eighteenth-century novelist kneeling to receive Stella's stilted declaration of her refusal.

"Your mother was most extraordinarily gracious and sympathetic. But of course I'm a man of fifty. I suppose you thought the idea very ridiculous."

"I don't think Stella is old enough to marry," said Michael.

"But don't you think it's better for girls to marry when they're young?" asked Prescott, and as he leaned forward, Michael saw his eyes were very bright and his actions feverish. "I've noticed that tendencies recur in families. Time after time. I don't like this Viennese business, yet if Stella had married me I shouldn't have interfered with her," he added, with a wistfulness that was out of keeping with his severely conventional appearance. "Still, I should have always been in the background."

"Yes, I expect that was what she felt," said Michael.

He did not mean to be brutal, but he saw at once how deeply he had wounded Prescott, and suddenly in a panic of inability to listen any longer, he rose and said he must go.

As he was driving to Waterloo Station on the following afternoon to go down to Basingstead, he saw vaguely on the posters of the starved August journals "Suicide of a Man About Town." At Cobble Place newspapers were read as an afterthought, and it was not until late on the day after that above a short paragraph the headline "Tragedy in the Albany" led him on to learn that actually Prescott was the man about town who had killed himself.

Michael's first emotion was a feeling of self-interest in being linked so closely with an event deemed sufficiently important to occupy the posters of an evening paper. For the moment the fact that he had dined with Prescott a few hours beforehand seemed a very remarkable coincidence. It was only after he had had to return to London and attend the inquest, to listen to the coroner's summing up of the evidence of depression and the perspiring jury's delivery of their verdict of temporary insanity he began to realize that in the crisis of a man's life his own words or behavior might easily have altered the result. He was driving to Waterloo Station again in order to take up the thread of his broken visit. On the posters of the starved August journals he read now with a sharp interest "Cat Saves Household in Whitechapel Fire." This cat stood for him as the symbol of imaginative action. He bought the evening papers at Waterloo, and during the journey down to Hampshire read about this cat who had saved a family from an inquest's futile epitaph, and who even if unsuccessful would have been awarded the commendatory platitudes of the coroner.

Michael had not said by what train he would arrive, and so after the journey he was able to walk to Basingstead through lanes freshening for evening. By this time the irony of the cat's fortuitous interference was blunted, and Michael was able to see himself in clearer relation to the fact of Prescott's death. He was no longer occupied by the strange sensation of being implicated in one of the sufficiently conspicuous daily deaths exalted by the press to the height of a tragedy. Yet for once the press had not been so exaggerative. Prescott's life was surely a tragedy, and his death was only not a tragedy because it had violated all the canons of good form and had falsified the stoicism of nearly fifty years. Yet why should not the stoic ideal be applied to such a death? It was an insult to such perfect manners to suppose that a hopeless love for a girl had led him to take his life. Surely it would be kinder to ascribe it to the accumulative boredom of August in London, or possibly to a sudden realization of vulgarity creeping up to the very portals of the Albany.

Michael was rather anxious to believe in this theory, because he was beginning to reproach himself more seriously than when the cat had first obtruded a sardonic commentary on his own behavior in having given away to the panic of wishing to listen no longer to the dead man's confidences. With all his personal regrets it was disconcerting to think of a man whose attitude to life had seemed so correct making this hurried exit, an exit too that left his reputation a prey to the public, so that his whole existence could be soiled after death by the inquisitive grubbing of a coroner. Prescott had always seemed secure from an humiliation like this. The mezzotints of stern old admirals, the soldier-servant, the fashionable cloister in which he lived, the profound consciousness he always betrayed of the importance of restraint whether in morals or cravats had seemed to combine in unrelaxing guardianship of his good form. The harder Michael thought about the business, the more incredible it appeared. Himself in an earlier mood of self-distrust had accepted Prescott as an example to whose almost contemptuous attitude of withdrawal he might ultimately aspire. He had often reproached himself for outlived divergencies of thought and action, and with the example of Prescott he had hammered into himself the possibility of eternal freedom from their recurrence. And now he must admit that mere austerity unless supported by a spiritual encouragement to endure was liable at any moment to break up pitiably into suicide. The word itself began to strike him with all the force of its squalid associations. The fresh dust of the Hampshire lanes became a gray miasma. Loneliness looped itself slowly round his progress so that he hurried on with backward glances. The hazel-hedges were somber and monotonous and defiled here and there by the rejected rags of a tramp. The names of familiar villages upon the signposts lost their intimations of sane humanity, and turned to horrible abstractions of the dead life of the misshapen boot or empty matchbox at their foot. The comfortable assurance of a prosperous and unvexed country rolling away to right and left forsook him, and only the pallid road writhed along through the twilight. "My nerves are in a rotten state," he told himself, and he was very glad to see Basingstead Manor twinkling in the night below, while himself was still walking shadowless in a sickly dusk.

In the drawing-room of Cobble Place all was calm, as indeed, Michael thought, why on earth should it not be? Mrs. Carthew's serene old age drove out the last memory of the coroner's court, and here was Mrs. Ross coming out of a circle of lamplight to greet him, and here in Cobble Place was her small son sleeping.

"You look tired and pale, Michael," said Mrs. Ross. "Why didn't you wire which train you were coming by? I would have met you with the chaise."

"Poor fellow, of course he's tired!" said Mrs. Carthew. "A most disturbing experience. Come along. Dinner will do him good."

The notion of suicide began to grow more remote from reality in this room, which had always been to Michael soft and fragrant like a great rose in whose heart, for very despair of being able ever to express in words the perfection of it, one swoons to be buried. The evening went the calm course of countless evenings at Cobble Place. Michael played at backgammon with Mrs. Carthew: Joan Carthew worked at the accounts of a parochial charity: May Carthew knitted: Mrs. Ross, reading in the lamplight, met from time to time Michael's glances with a concern that never displayed itself beyond the pitch of an unexacting sympathy. He was glad, as the others rustled to greet the ten strokes of the clock, to hear Mrs. Ross say she would stay up for a while and keep him company.

"Unless you want to work?" she added.

Michael shook his head.

When the others had gone to bed, he turned to her:

"Do you know, Mrs. Ross, I believe I could have prevented Prescott's death. He began to talk about Stella, and I felt embarrassed and came away."

"Oh, my dear Michael, I think you're probably accusing yourself most unfairly. How could you have supposed the terrible sequel to your dinner?"

"That's just it. I believe I did know."

"You thought he was going to kill himself?"

"No, I didn't think anything so definite as that, but I had an intuition to ask him to come away with me, and I was afraid he'd think it rather cheek and, oh, Mrs. Ross, what on earth good am I? I believe I've got the gift of understanding people, and yet I'm afraid to use it. Shall I ever learn?"

Michael looked at Mrs. Ross in despair. He was exasperated by his own futility. He went on to rail at himself.

"The only gift I have got! And then my detestable self-consciousness wrecks the first decent chance I've had to turn it to account."

They talked for some time. At first Mrs. Ross consoled him, insisting that imagination affected by what had happened later was playing him false. Then she seemed to be trying to state an opinion which she found it difficult to state. She spoke to Michael of qualities which in the future with one quality added would show his way in the world clear and straight before him. He was puzzled to guess at what career she was hinting.

"My dear Michael, I would not tell you for anything," she affirmed.

"Why not?"

"Why not? Why, because with all the ingenuous proclamations of your willingness to do anything that you're positive you can do better than anything else, I'm quite, quite sure you're still the rather perverse Michael of old, and as I sit here talking to you I remember the time when I told you as a little boy that you would have been a Roundhead in the time of the Great Rebellion. How angry you were with me! So what I think you're going to do—I almost said when you're grown up—but I mean when you leave Oxford, I shall have to tell you after you have made up your own mind. I shall have to give myself merely the pleasure of saying, 'I knew it.'"

"I suppose really I know what you think I shall do," said Michael slowly. "But you're wrong—at least, I think you're wrong. I lack the mainspring of the parson's life. Talk to me about Kenneth instead of myself. How's he getting on?"

"Oh, he's splendid at five years old, but I want to give him something more than I ever managed to give you."

"Naturally," said Michael, smiling. "He's your son."

"Michael, would you be surprised if I told you that I thought of...." Mrs. Ross broke off abruptly. "No, I won't tell you yet."

"You're full of unrevealed mysteries," said Michael.

"Yes, it's bedtime for me. Good night."

Two mornings later Michael had a letter from his mother in London. He wondered why he should be vaguely surprised by her hurried return. Surely Prescott's death could not have been a reason to bring her home.

173 CHEYNE WALK,
S.W.

My dearest Michael,

I'm so dreadfully upset about poor Dick Prescott. I have so few old friends, so very few, that I can't afford to lose him. His devotion to your father was perfectly wonderful. He gave up everything to us. He remained in society just enough to be of use to your father, but he was nearly always with us. I think he was fond of me, but he worshiped him. Perhaps I was wrong in trying to encourage the idea of marrying Stella. But I console myself by saying that that had nothing to do with this idea of his to take his own life. You see, when your father died, he found himself alone. I've been so selfishly interested in reëntering life. He had no wish to do so. Michael, I can't write anything more about it. Perhaps, dearest boy, you wouldn't mind giving up some of your time with the Carthews, and will come back earlier to be with me in London for a little time.

Your loving
Mother.

P.S.—I hope the funeral was properly done.

Michael realized with a start the loneliness of his mother, and in his mood of self-reproachfulness attacked himself for having neglected her ever since the interests of Oxford had arisen to occupy his own life so satisfyingly. He told Mrs. Ross of the letter, and she agreed with him in thinking he ought to go back to London at once. Michael had only time for a very short talk with old Mrs. Carthew before the chaise would arrive.

"There has been a fate upon this visit," said the old lady. "And I'm sorry for it. I'd promised myself a great many talks with you. Besides, you'll miss Alan now, and he'll disappointed, and as for Nancy, she'll be miserable."

"But I must go," Michael said.

"Of course you must go," said Mrs. Carthew, thumping with her stick on the gravel path. "You must always think first of your mother."

"You told me that before on this very path a long time ago," said Michael thoughtfully. "I didn't understand so well why at the time. Now, of course," he added shyly, "I understand everything. I used to wonder what the mystery could be. I used to imagine all sorts of the most extraordinary things. Prisons and lunatic asylums among others."

Mrs. Carthew chuckled to herself.

"It's surprising you didn't imagine a great deal more than you did. How's Oxford?"

"Ripping," said Michael. "And so was your advice about Oxford. I've never forgotten. It was absolutely right."

"I always am absolutely right," said Mrs. Carthew.

The wheels of the chaise were audible; and Michael must go at once.

"If I'm alive in two years, when you go down," said Mrs. Carthew, "I'd like to give you some advice about the world. I'm even more infallible about the world. Although I married a sailor, I'm a practical and worldly old woman."

Michael said good-bye to all the family standing by the gate of Cobble Place, to Mrs. Ross with the young Kenneth now in knickerbockers by her side and soon, thought Michael, a subject fit for speculation; to delightful May and Joan; to the smiling Carthew cook; all waving to him in the sunlight with the trim cotoneaster behind them.

It gave Michael a consciousness of a new and most affectionate intimacy to find his mother alone in the house in Cheyne Walk. It was scarcely yet September, and the desolation of London all around seemed the more sharply to intagliate upon his senses the fineness of his mother's figure set in the frame of that sedate house. They had tea together in her own room, and it struck him with a sudden surprise to see her once again in black. The room with its rose du Barri and clouded pastels sustained her beauty and to her somber attire lent a deeper poignancy; or perhaps it was something apart from the influence of the room, this so incontestable pathos, and was rather the effect of the imprisonment of her elusiveness by a chain whose power Michael had not suspected. Always, for nearly as many years as he could remember, when he had kissed her she had seemed to evade the statement of any positive and ordinary affection. Her personality had fluttered for a moment to his embrace and fled more than swiftly. In one moment as Michael kissed her now, the years were swept away, and he was sitting up for an extra half hour at the seaside, while she with her face flushed by another August sunset was leaning over him. The river became the sea, and the noise of the people on the Embankment were the people walking on the promenade below. In one moment as Michael kissed her now, her embrace gave to him what it had not given during all the years between—a consciousness that he depended upon her life.

"Dearest boy," she murmured, "how good of you to come back so quickly from the Carthews!"

"But I would much rather be with you," said Michael.

Indeed, as he sat beside her holding her hand, he wondered to himself how he had been able to afford to miss so many opportunities of sitting like this, and immediately afterward wondered at himself for being able to sit like this without any secret dread that he was making himself absurd by too much demonstrativeness. After all, it was very easy to show emotion even to one's mother without being ridiculous.

"Poor Dicky Prescott," she said, and tears quickly blurred her great gray eyes and hung quivering on the shadowy lashes beneath. Michael held her hand closer when he saw she was beginning to cry. He felt no awe of her grief, as he had when she told him of his father's death. This simpler sorrow brought her so much nearer to him. She was speaking of Prescott's death as she might have spoken of the loss of a cherished possession, a dog perhaps or some familiar piece of jewelry.

"I shall never get used to not having him to advise me. Besides, he was the only person to whom I could talk about Charles—about your father. Dicky was so bound up with all my life. So long as he was alive, I had some of the past with me."

Michael nodded with comprehending gravity of assent.

"Darling boy, I don't mean that you and darling Stella are not of course much more deeply precious to me. You are. But I can't help thinking of that poor dear man, and the way he and Charles used to walk up and down the quarter-deck, and I remember once Charles lent him a stud. It's the silly little sentimental memories like that which are so terribly upsetting when they're suddenly taken away."

Now she broke down altogether, and Michael with his arms about her, held her while she wept.

"Dearest mother, when you cry I seem to hold you very safely," he whispered. "I don't feel you'll ever again be able to escape."

She had ceased from her sobbing with a sudden shiver and catch of the breath and looked at him with frightened eyes.

"Michael, he once said that to me ... before you were born. Before ... on a hillside it was ... how terribly well I remember."

Michael did not want her to speak of his father. He felt too helpless in the presence of that memory. The death of Prescott was another matter, a trivial and pathetic thing. Quickly he brought his mother back to that, until she was tired with the flowing of many tears.

Michael spent the rest of the Long Vacation with his mother in London, and gradually he made himself a companion to her. They went to theaters together, because it gave her a sentimental pleasure to think how much poor Dicky Prescott would have enjoyed this piece once upon a time. Between them was the unspoken thought of how much somebody else would have enjoyed this piece also. Michael teased his mother lightly about her bazaars, until she told him he was turning into a second Prescott himself. He discussed seriously the problem of Stella, but he did not say a word of his hope that she would fall in love with Alan. Alan, however, who was already back in town, came to spend week-ends that were very much like the week-ends spent at Carlington Road in the past. Mrs. Fane enjoyed dining with her son and his friend. She asked the same sort of delightfully foolish questions about Oxford that she used to ask about school. In October Mrs. Carruthers arrived back in town, and by this time Mrs. Fane was ready to begin again to flit from charity to charity, and from fad to fad. Yet, however much she seemed to become again her old elusive, exquisite self, Michael never again let her escape entirely from the intimacy which had been created by the sentimental shock of Prescott's death, and he went up for his third year at Oxford with a feeling that somehow during this vacation he had grown more sure of himself and to his mother more precious.

"What have you done this vac?" they asked him in Venner's on the night of reunion.

"Nothing very much," he said, and to himself he thought less than usual in fact, and yet really in one way such a very great deal.

CHAPTER XII

2O2 HIGH

The large room at 202 High Street which Michael shared with Grainger and Lonsdale was perhaps in the annals of university lodgings the most famous. According to tradition, the house was originally part of the palace of a cardinal. Whether it had been the habitation of ecclesiastical greatness or not, it had certainly harbored grandeur of some kind; to this testified the two fireplaces surmounted by coats-of-arms in carved oak that enhanced this five-windowed room with a dignity which no other undergraduate lodging could claim. The house at this period was kept by a retired college cook, who produced for dinner parties wonderful old silver which all his tenants believed to have been stolen from the kitchen of his college. The large room of 202 High gave the house its character, but there were many other rooms besides. Wedderburn, for instance had on the third story a sitting-room whose white paneling and Georgian grace had been occupied by generations of the transitory exquisites of art and fashion. Downstairs in the aqueous twilight created by a back garden was the dining-room which the four of them possessed in common. As for the other lodgers, none were St. Mary's men, and their existence was only alluded to by Michael and his friends when the ex-cook charged them for these strangers' entertainments.

Michael was the first to arrive at Two Hundred and Two, and he immediately set to work to arrange in the way that pleased him best the decorative and personal adjuncts contributed by Grainger, Lonsdale, and himself. For his own library he found a fine set of cupboards which he completely filled. The books of Grainger and Lonsdale he banished to the dining-room, where their scant numbers competed for space on the shelves with jars of marmalade, egg-cups, and toast-racks. The inconvenience of the confusion was helpfully obviated first by the fact that their collection, or rather their accumulation, was nearly throughout in duplicate owing to the similar literary tastes and intellectual travaux forcés of Grainger and Lonsdale, and secondly by the fact that for a year to neither taste nor intellect was there frequent resort. With their pictures Michael found the same difficulty of duplication, but as there were two fireplaces he took an ingenious delight in supporting each fireplace with similar pictures, so that Thorburn's grouse, Cecil Aldin's brilliant billiard-rooms, Sir Galahad and Eton Society were to be found at either end. Elsewhere on the spacious walls he hung his own Blakes and Frederick Walkers, and the engraving of the morning stars singing together he feathered with the photographic souvenirs of Lonsdale's fagdom. As for the pictures that belonged to the ex-cook, mostly very large photogravures of Marcus Stone such as one sees in the corridors of theaters, these he took upstairs and with them covered Wedderburn's white-paneled walls after he had removed the carefully hung Dürers to the bathroom. This transference wasted a good deal of time, but gave him enough amusement when Wedderburn arrived to justify the operation. The pictures all disposed, he called for a carpenter to hang Grainger's triumphal oars and Lonsdale's hunting trophies of masks, pads and brushes, and surveyed with considerable satisfaction the accumulative effect of the great room now characterized by their joint possessions. Michael was admiring his work when Lonsdale arrived and greeted him boisterously.

"Hullo! I say, are we all straight? How topping! But wait a bit. I've got something that's going to put the jolly old lid on this jolly old room. What's the name of the joker who keeps these digs? Macpherson?"

He shouted from the landing to the ex-cook.

"I say, send up the packing-case that's waiting for me downstairs."

Michael inquired what was inside.

"Wait a bit, my son," said the beaming owner. "I've got something in there that's going to make old Wedders absolutely green. I've thought this out. I told my governor I was going into digs with some of the æsthetic push and didn't want to be cut out, so he's lent me this."

"What on earth is it?" Michael asked on a note of ambiguous welcome.

The packing-case shaped like a coffin had been set down on the floor by the ex-cook and his slave. Lonsdale was wrenching off the top.

"I had a choice between a mummy and a what d'ye call it, and I chose the what d'ye call it," said Lonsdale.

He had torn the last piece of the cover away, and lying in straw was revealed the complete armor of a Samurai.

"Rum-looking beggar. Worth twenty of those rotten statues of Wedderburn's. It was a present to the governor from somebody in the East, but as I promised not to go to dances in it, he lent it to me. Rather sporting of him, what? Where shall we put him?"

"I vote we hide it till this evening," suggested Michael, "and then put it in Wedder's bed. He'll think he's in the wrong room."

"Ripping!" cried Lonsdale. "In pyjamas, what?"

That Japanese warrior never occupied the æsthetic niche that Lord Cleveden from his son's proposal may have thought he would occupy. Otherwise he played an important part in the life of Two Hundred and Two. Never did any visitor come to stay for the week-end, but Sammy, as he was soon called, was set to warm his bed. To Lonsdale, returning home mildly drunk from Trinity Clareter or Phoenix Wine, he was always ready to serve as a courteous listener of his rambling account of an evening's adventures. He was borrowed by other digs to annoy the landladies: he went for drives in motor cars to puzzle country inns. Lonsdale tried to make him into a college mascot, and he drove in state to the St. Mary's grind on the box seat of the coach. He was put down on the pavement outside the lodge with a plate for pennies and a label "Blind" round his neck. But Sammy's end was a sad one. He had been sent to call on the Warden, and was last seen leaning in a despondent attitude against the Warden's gothic door. Whether the butler broke him up when Sammy fell forward onto his toes, or whether he was imprisoned eternally in a coal cellar, no one knew. Lord Cleveden was informed he had been stolen.

If Michael had tried hard to find two people in whose company it would be more difficult to work than with any other pair in the university, he could scarcely have chosen better than Lonsdale and Grainger. Neither of them was reading an Honor School, and the groups called H2 or C3 or X26, that with each term's climax they were compelled to pass in order to acquire the degree of bachelor of arts, produced about a week before their ordeal a state of irritable industry, but otherwise were unheeded. Michael was not sorry to let his own reading beyond the irreducible minimum slide during this gay third year. He promised himself a fourth year, when he would withdraw from this side of Oxford life and in some cloistered digs work really hard. Meanwhile, he enjoyed 202 High as the quintessence of youth's amenity.

Some of the most enduring impressions of Oxford were made now, though they were not perhaps impressions that marked any development in himself by intellectual achievements or spiritual crises. In fact, at the time the impressions seemed fleeting enough; and it was only when the third year was over, when Two Hundred and Two was dismantled of every vestige of this transient occupation that Michael in summoning these impressions from the past recaptured, often from merely pictorial recollections, as much of Oxford as was necessary to tell him how much Oxford had meant.

There were misty twilights in November when Lonsdale came back spattered with mud after a day with the Bicester or the V.W.H. At such an hour Michael, who had probably been sitting alone by the roaring fire, was always ready to fling away his book, and, while Lonsdale grunted and labored to pull off his riding-boots to hear the tale of a great run across a great piece of country.

There was the autumn afternoon when Grainger stroked St. Mary's to victory in the Coxwainless Fours. Another oar was hung in Two Hundred and Two, and a bonfire was made in Cuther's quad to celebrate the occasion. Afterward Grainger himself triumphantly drunk between Michael and Lonsdale was slowly persuaded along the High and put to bed, while Wedderburn prescribed in his deepest voice a dozen remedies.

There were jovial dinner parties when rowing men from Univ and New College sat gigantically round the table and ate gigantically and laughed gigantically, and were taken upstairs to Wedderburn's dim-lit room to admire his statues of Apollo, his old embroideries and his Dürer woodcuts. These giants in their baggy blanket trousers, their brass-buttoned coats and Leander ties nearly as pink as their own faces, made Wedderburn's white Apollos look almost mincing and the embroideries rather insipid. There were other dinner parties even more jovial when the Palace of Delights, otherwise 202 High, entertained the Hotel de Luxe, otherwise 230 High, the abode of Cuffe, Sterns, and Sinclair, or the Chamber of Horrors, otherwise 61 Longwall, where Maurice and Castleton lived. After dinner the guests and the hosts would march arm in arm down to college and be just in time to make a tremendous noise in Venner's, after which they would visit some of the second-year men, and with bridge to wind up the evening would march arm in arm up the High and home again.

In the Lent term there were windy afternoons with the St. Mary's beagles, when after a long run Lonsdale and Michael would lose the college drag and hire a dogcart in which they would come spanking back to Oxford with the March gale dying in their wake and the dusk gathering fast. In the same term there was a hockey cup-match, when St. Mary's was drawn to play an unfamiliar college on the enemy's ground. 202 High wondered how on earth such an out-of-the-way ground could possibly be reached, and the end of it was that a coach was ordered in which a dozen people drove the mile or so to the field of play, with Lonsdale blowing the horn all the way down High Street and Cornmarket Street and the Woodstock Road.

Michael during the year at Two Hundred and Two scarcely saw anybody who was not in the heart of the main athletic vortex of the university. In one way, his third year was a retrogression, for he was nearer to the life of his first year than to his second. The Oxford Looking-Glass had created for him a society representing various interests. This was now broken up, partly by the death of the paper, partly by the more highly intensified existence of the founders. Maurice certainly remained the same and was already talking of starting another paper. But Wedderburn was beginning to think of a degree and was looking forward to entering his father's office and becoming in another year a prosperous partner in a prosperous firm. Guy Hazlewood had gone down and was away in Macedonia, trying to fulfill a Balliol precept to mix yourself up in the affairs of other nations or your own as much as possible. Townsend and Mowbray thought now of nothing but of being elected President of the Union, and as Michael was not a member and hated politics he scarcely saw them. Nigel Stewart had gone to Ely Theological College. The Oxford Looking-Glass was shattered into many pieces. Alan, however, Michael saw more often than last year, because Alan was very popular at Two Hundred and Two.

Michael more and more began to assume the opinions and the attitude of his companions. He began more and more rigidly to apply their somewhat naïve standards in his judgment of the world. He was as intolerant and contemptuous as his friends of any breach of what he almost stated to himself as the public-school tradition. Oxford was divided into Bad Men and Good Eggs. The Bad Men went up to London and womanized—some even of the worst womanized in Oxford: they dressed in a style that either by its dowdiness or its smartness stamped them: they wore college colors round their straw hats and for their ties: they were quiet, surreptitious, diligent, or blatantly rowdy in small sections, and at least half the colleges in the Varsity contained nothing but Bad Men. The Good Eggs went up to London and got drunk; and if they womanized no one must know anything about it. Drink was the only vice that should be enjoyed communely; in fact, if it were enjoyed secretly, it transformed the victim into the very worst of Bad Men. The Good Eggs never made a mistake in dress: they only wore old school colors or Varsity club colors: they were bonhomous, hearty, careless, and rowdy in large groups. Only the men from about eight colleges were presumed to be Good Eggs: the rest of the Varsity had to demonstrate its goodness.

Michael sometimes had misgivings about this narrowly selected paucity of Good Eggs. He never doubted that those chosen were deservedly chosen, but he did sometimes speculate whether in the masses of the Bad Men there might not be a few Good Eggs unrecognized as Eggs, unhonored for their Goodness. Yet whenever he made an excursion into the midst of the Bad Men, he was always bound to admit the refreshment of his very firm prejudice in favor of the Good Eggs. What was so astonishing about Good Eggery was the members' obvious equipment for citizenship of the world as opposed to the provincialism of Bad Mannery. Unquestionably it was possible to meet the most intelligent, the most widely read Bad Men; but intellect and culture were swamped by their barbarous self-proclamation. They suffered from an even bitterer snobbishness than the Good Eggs. In the latter case, the snobbishness was largely an inherited pride: with the Bad Men it was obviously an acquired vanity. Where, however, Michael found himself at odds with Good Eggery was in the admission to titular respect of the Christ Church blood. This growing toleration was being conspicuously exemplified in the attitude of St. Mary's, that most securely woven and most intimate nest of Good Eggery.

When Michael had first come up there had been an inclination at his college to regard with as much contemptuous indifference an election to the Bullingdon as an election to the Union. It was tacitly understood at St. Mary's that nothing was necessary to enhance the glory of being a St. Mary's man. Gradually, however, the preponderance of Etonian influence outweighed the conventional self-sufficiency of the Wykehamists, and several men in Michael's year joined the Bullingdon, one of the earliest of these destroyers of tradition being Lonsdale. The result of this action was very definitely a disproportion in the individual expenditure of members of the college. St. Mary's had always been a college for relatively rich men, but in accordance with the spirit of the college to form itself into an aristocratic republic, it had for long been considered bad form to spend more than was enough to sustain each member of this republic on an equality with his fellows.

Now Lonsdale was so obviously a Good Egg that it did not matter when he played with equal zest roulette and polo or hunted three times a week or wore clothes of the last extreme of fashion. But Michael and Grainger were not sure they cared very much for all of Lonsdale's friends from the House. Certainly they were Etonians and members of the Bullingdon, but so many of their names were curiously familiar from the hoardings of advertisements that neither Michael nor Grainger could altogether believe in their assumption of the privilege of exclusion on the ground of inherited names.

"I think these Bullingdon bloods are rather rotters," protested Michael, after an irritating evening of vacuous wealth.

"I *must* ask them in sometimes," apologized Lonsdale.

"Why?" rumbled Wedderburn, and on his note of interrogation the Bullingdon bloods were impaled to swing unannaled.

207

"I don't think all this sort of thing is very good for the college," debated Grainger. "It's all very well for you, Lonny, but some of the second-year men behave rather stupidly. Personally I hate roulette at St. Mary's. As for some of the would-be fresher bloods, they're like a lot of damned cavalry subalterns."

"You can't expect the college to be handed over entirely to the rowing push," said Lonsdale.

"That's better than turning Venner's into Tattersall's," said Wedderburn.

The effect of enlarging the inclusiveness of Good Eggery was certainly to breed a suspicion that it was largely a matter of externals; and therefore among the St. Mary's men who disliked the application of money as a social standard an inclination grew up to suppose that Good Eggery might be enlarged on the other side. The feeling of the college, that elusive and indefinable aroma of opinion, declared itself unmistakably in this direction, and many Bad Men became Good Eggs.

"We're all growing older," said Michael to Wedderburn in explanation of the subtle change manifesting itself. "And I suppose a little wiser. Castleton will be elected President of the J.C.R. at the end of this year. Not Tommy Grainger, although he'll be President of the O.U.B.C., not Sterne, although he'll be in the Varsity Eleven. Castleton will be elected because he never has believed and he never will believe in mere externals."

Nevertheless for all of his third year, with whatever fleeting doubts he had about the progress of St. Mary's along the lines laid down by the Good Eggery of earlier generations, Michael remained a very devoted adherent of the principle. He was able to perceive something more than mere externals in the Best Eggery. This was not merely created by money or correct habiliment or athletic virtuosity. This existed inherently in a large number of contemporary undergraduates. Through this they achieved the right to call themselves the Best. It was less an assertion of snobbishness than of faith. Good Eggery had really become a religion. It was not inconsistent with Christianity: indeed, it probably derived itself from Christianity through many mailclad and muscular intercedents. Yet it shrank from anything definitely spiritual as it would have shrunk from the Salvation Army. Men who intended to be parsons were of course exceptions, but parsons were regarded as a facet of the existing social order rather than as trustees for the heirs of universal truth. Social service was encouraged by fashion, so long as it meant no more than the supporting of the College Mission in the slums of Bristol by occasional week-ends. Members of the college would play billiards in the club for dockhands under or over seventeen, would subscribe a guinea a year, and as a great concession would attend the annual report in the J.C.R. There must, however, be no more extravagance in religion and social service than there should be in dress. The priestly caste of Good Eggery was represented not by the parsons, but by the schoolmasters and certain dons. The schoolmasters were the most powerful, and tried to sustain the legend common to all priestly castes that they themselves made the religion rather than that they were mere servants of an idea. Mature Good Eggs affected to laugh at the schoolmasters whose leading-strings they had severed, but an instinctive fear endured, so that in time to come Good Egglets would be handed over for the craft to mold as they had molded their fathers. It could scarcely be denied that schoolmasters like priests were disinclined to face facts: it was indubitable that they lived an essentially artificial life: it was certain that they fostered a clod-headed bigotry, that they were tempted to regard themselves as philanthropists, that they feared dreadfully the intrusion of secular influence. It could scarcely be denied that the Schoolmasterdom of England was a priestcraft as powerful and arrogant as any which had ever been. But they were gentlemen, that is to say they shaved oftener than Neapolitan priests; they took a cold bath in the morning, which probably Calvin's ministers never did; they were far more politely restrained than the Bacchantes and not less chaste than the Vestal Virgins. These clean and honest, if generally rather stupid gentlemen, were the wielders of that afflatus, the public-school spirit, and so far as Michael could see at present, Good Eggs were more safe morally with that inspiration than they might have been with any other. And if a touch of mysticism were needed, it might be supplied by Freemasonry at the Apollo Lodge; while the Boy Scouts were beginning to show how admirably this public-school spirit could blow through the most unpromising material of the middle classes.

Michael so much enjoyed the consciousness of merit which is the supreme inducement offered by all successful religions, and more than any by Good Eggery, that he made up his mind quite finally that Good Eggery would carry him through his existence, however much it were complicated by the problem of Bad Mannery. During that year at Two Hundred and Two he grew more and more deeply convinced that to challenge any moral postulate of Good Eggery was merely contumacious self-esteem. One of the great principles of Good Eggery was that the Good Egg must only esteem himself as a valuable unit in Good Eggery. His self-esteem was entitled to rise in proportion with the distance he could run or kick or throw or hit.

Analyzed sharply, Michael admitted that Good Eggery rested on very frail foundations, and it was really surprising with what enthusiasm it managed to sustain the Good Eggs themselves, so that apparently without either spiritual exaltation or despair, without disinterested politics or patriotism, without any deep humanity even, the Good Eggs were still so very obviously good. Certainly the suicide of Prescott made Michael wonder how much that rather ignominious surrender by such a Good Egg might have been avoided with something profounder than Good Eggery at the back of life's experience. But suicide was an accident, Michael decided, and could not be used in the arguments against the fundamental soundness of Good Eggery as the finest social nourishment in these days of a bourgeoning century.

Meanwhile, at St. Mary's the Good Eggs flourished, and time went by with unexampled swiftness. In the last days of the Lent term, after St. Mary's had been defeated by Christ Church in the final of the Association Cup, Michael, Grainger and Lonsdale determined to drown woe by a triple Twenty-firster. Every contemporary Good Egg in St. Mary's and several from other colleges were invited. Forty Good Eggs, groomed and polished and starched, sat down at the Clarendon to celebrate this triple majority. Upon that banquet age did not lay one hesitant touch. The attainment of discretion was celebrated in what might almost have been hailed as a debauch of youthfulness. Forty Good Eggs drank forty-eight bottles of Perrier Jouet '93. They drank indeed the last four dozen gages of that superb summer stored in the J.C.R., the last four dozen lachrymatories of the 1893 sun, nor could it be said that vintage of Champagne had funeral games unworthy of its foam and fire. Forty Good Eggs went swinging out of the Clarendon about half-past nine o'clock, making almost more noise than even the Corn had ever heard. Forty Good Eggs went swinging along toward Carfax, swinging and singing, temporarily deified by the last four dozen of Perrier Jouet '93. Riotous feats were performed all down the High. Two trams were unhorsed. Hansoms were raced. Bells were rung. Forty Good Eggs, gloriously, ravishingly drunk, surged into the lodge. There was just time to see old Venner. In the quiet office was pandemonium. Good Eggs were dancing hornpipes; Good Eggs were steadying themselves with cognac; Good Eggs were gently herded out of the little office as ten o'clock chimed. "Bonner! Bonner!" the forty Good Eggs shouted, and off they went not to St. Cuthbert's, but actually to the great lawn in front of New Quad. Third-year men when they did come into college roaring drunk took no half-measures of celebration. Excited freshmen and second-year men came swarming out of Cloisters, out of Parsons' Quad, out of Cuther's to support these wild seniors. What a bonfire it was! Thirty-one chairs, three tables, two doors, twelve lavatory seats, every bundle of faggots in college and George Appleby's bed. Somebody had brought Roman candles. O exquisite blue and emerald stars! Somebody else had brought Chinese crackers as big as red chimneys. O sublime din! Lonsdale was on the roof of Cloisters trying to kill a gargoyle with hurtling syphons. Michael was tossing up all by himself to decide whether he should tell the Senior Tutor or the Warden what he really thought of him. A fat welterweight, a straggler from New College, had been shorn of his coat-tails, and was plunging about like an overgrown Eton boy. With crimson faces and ruffled hair and scorched shirt-fronts the guests of the Twenty-firster acclaimed to-night as the finest tribute ever paid to years of discretion.

Next morning the three hosts paid ten guineas each to the Dean.

"I thought you people were supposed to have come of age," he said sardonically.

So incomparably slight was the hang-over from Perrier Jouet '93 that Grainger, Lonsdale, and Michael smiled very cheerfully, produced their check books, and would, if Mr. Ambrose had not been so discouraging, have been really chatty.

After Collections of Lent term, that opportunity accepted by the college authorities to be offensive in bulk, Michael felt his historical studies were scarcely betraying such an impulse toward research as might have been expected of him at this stage. Mr. Harbottle, the History tutor, an abrupt and pleasant man with the appearance of a cat and the manners of a dog, yapped vituperations from where he sat with all the other dons in judgment along the High Table in Hall.

The Warden turned on his orbit and shone full-faced upon Michael.

"A little more work, Mr. Fane, will encourage us all. Your Collection papers have evidently planted a doubt in Mr. Harbottle's mind."

"He never does a stroke of honest work, Warden," yapped the History tutor. "If he stays up ten years he'll never get a Fourth."

"In spite of Mr. Harbottle's discouraging prophecy, we must continue to hope, Mr. Fane, that you will obtain at least a Second next term."

"Next term!" Michael gasped. "But I was expecting to take Schools next year."

"I'm afraid," said the Warden, "that according to Mr. Ambrose the fabric of the college will scarcely survive another year of your residence. I believe I echo your views, Mr. Ambrose?"

The Dean blinked his gray eye and finally said that possibly Mr. Fane would change next term, adding that a more immediately serious matter was a deficit of no less than seven chapels. Michael pointed out that he designed in his fourth year to go as it were into industrious solitude far away from St. Mary's.

"Are you suggesting Iffley?" inquired the Warden.

"Oh, no, not so far as that; but right away," said Michael. "Somewhere near Keble. Miles away."

"But we have to consider next term," the Warden urged. "Next term, I take it, you will still be occupied with the fashionable distractions of High Street?"

"I'll make an offer," barked Mr. Harbottle. "If he likes to do another Collection paper at the beginning of next term, and does it satisfactorily, I will withdraw my opposition, and as far as I'm concerned he can take his Schools next year."

"What luck?" asked everybody in the lodge when Michael had emerged from the ordeal.

"I had rather a hot time," said Michael. "Still Harbottle behaved like a gentleman on the whole."

Maurice arrived in the lodge soon after Michael, and conveyed the impression that he had left the tutorial forces of the college reeling under the effect of his witty cannonade. Then Michael went off to interview the Dean in order to adjust the difficulty which had been created by the arrears of his early rising. With much generosity he admitted the whole seven abstentions, and was willing not merely to stay up a week to correct the deficit, but suggested that he should spend all the Easter vacation working in Oxford.

So it fell out that Michael managed to secure his fourth year, and in the tranquillity of that Easter vacation it seemed to him that he began to love Oxford for the first time with a truly intense passion and that a little learning was the least tribute he could offer in esteem. It was strange how suddenly history became charged with magic. Perhaps the Academic Muse sometimes offered this inspiration, if one spent hours alone with her. Michael was sad when the summer term arrived in its course. So many Good Eggs would be going down for ever after this term, and upon Two Hundred and Two High brooded the shadow of dissolution. Alan again hovered on the edge of the Varsity Eleven, but a freshman who bowled rather better the same sort of ball came up, and it seemed improbable he would get his Blue. However, the disappointment was evidently not so hard for Alan to bear nowadays. He was indeed becoming gravely interested in philosophy, and Michael was forced to admit that he seemed to be acquiring most unexpectedly a real intellectual grasp of life. So much the better for their companionship next year in those rooms in St. Giles' which Michael had already chosen.

The summer term was going by fast. It was becoming an experience almost too fugitive to be borne, this last summer term at Two Hundred and Two. Michael, Grainger, and Lonsdale had scarcely known how to endure some offensive second-year men from Oriel being shown their room for next year. They resented the thought of these Oriel men leaning out of the window and throwing cushions at their friends and turning to the left to keep a chapel at Oriel, instead of scudding down to St. Mary's on the right. Wedderburn was always the one who voiced sentimentally the unexpressed regrets of the other three. He it was who spoke of the grime and labor of the paternal office, of Life with a capital letter as large as any lady novelist's, and of how one would remember these evenings and the leaning-out over a cushioned window-sill and the poring upon this majestic street.

"We don't realize our good luck until it's too late really," said Wedderburn seriously. "We've wasted our time, and now we've got to go."

"Well, dash it all, Wedders," said Lonsdale, "don't talk as if we were going to bolt for a train before hall. We aren't going down for three weeks yet, and jolly old Michael and jolly old Tommy aren't going down for another year."

"Lucky devils!" sighed Wedderburn. "By gad, if I only had my time at the Varsity all over again."

But just when Wedderburn had by his solemnity almost managed really to impress the company with a sense of fleeting time, and when even upon Lonsdale was descending the melancholy of the deep-dyed afternoon, across the road they could see sauntering three men whom they all knew well.

"Tally-ho-ho-ho-whooop!" shouted Lonsdale.

The three men saluted thus came upstairs to the big room of Two Hundred and Two, and a bout of amiable ragging and rotting passed away the hour before dinner and restored to the big room itself the wonted air of imperishable good-fellowship.

"Lucky you lads turned up," said Lonsdale. "Old Wedders has been moping in his window-seat like a half-plucked pigeon. We're dining in hall to-night, are you?"

The newcomers were dining in hall, and so in a wide line of brilliant ties and ribbons the seven of them strolled down to college.

There were very few people in hall that night, and Venner's was pleasantly empty. Venner himself was full of anecdotes, and as they sat on the table in the middle of the room, drinking their coffee, it seemed impossible enough to imagine that they would not be forever here drinking their coffee on a fine June evening.

"Going down soon, Venner," said Wedderburn, who was determined to make somebody sad.

"What a pity you're not taking a fourth year!" said Venner. "You ought to have read an Honor School. I always advise the men to read for honors. The dons like it, you know."

"Got to go and earn my living, Venner," said Wedderburn.

"That's right," said Venner cheerfully. "Then you'll be married all the sooner, or perhaps you're not a marrying man."

"Haven't found the right girl yet, Venner," said Wedderburn.

"Oh, there's plenty of time," chuckled Venner. "You don't want to be thinking about girls up here. Some of our men go getting engaged before they've gone down, and it always messes them up in the Schools."

Maurice Avery came in while Venner was speaking. He seemed restless and worried, and as Venner went on his restlessness increased.

"But very few of our men have got into trouble here with girls. We had one man once who married a widow. He was dreadfully chaffed about it, and couldn't stand it any longer. The men never let him alone."

"Married a widow, while he was still up?" people asked incredulously.

"Why, yes," said Venner. "And actually brought her down for Eights and introduced her to the Warden on the barge. She was a most severe-looking woman, and old enough to be his mother. There was some trouble once at 202 High—that's where you are, isn't it?" He turned to Lonsdale. "But there won't be any more trouble because Macpherson vowed he wouldn't have a servant-girl in the house again."

"I suppose that's why we have that perspiring boy," grumbled Wedderburn. "But what happened, Venner?"

"Well, the usual thing, of course. There were five of our men living there that year, and she picked out the quietest one of the lot and said it was him. He had to pay fifty pounds, and when he'd paid it all, the other four came up to him one by one and offered to pay half."

Everybody laughed, and Maurice suddenly announced that he was in a devil of a fix with a girl.

"A girl at a village near here," he explained. "There's no question of her having a baby or anything like that, you know; but her brother followed me home one night, and yesterday her father turned up. I got Castleton to talk to him. But it was damned awkward. He and old Castleton were arguing like hell in our digs."

Maurice stopped and, lighting a cigarette, looked round him as if expectant of the laughter which had hailed Venner's story. Nobody seemed to have any comment to make, and Michael felt himself blushing violently for his friend.

"Bit chilly in here to-night, Venner," said Lonsdale.

"You are a confounded lot of prigs!" said Maurice angrily, and he walked out of Venner's just as Castleton came in.

"My dear old Frank Castleton," said Lonsdale immediately, "I love you very much and I think your hair is beautifully brushed, but you really must talk to our Mr. Avery very, very seriously. He mustn't be allowed to make such a bee-luddy fool of himself by talking like a third-rate actor."

"What do you mean?" asked Castleton gruffly.

Lonsdale explained what Maurice had done, and Castleton looked surprised, but he would not take part in the condemnation.

"You're all friends of his in here," he pointed out. "He probably thought it was a funny story." There was just so much emphasis on the pronoun as made the critics realize that Castleton himself was really more annoyed than he had superficially appeared.

An awkwardness had arisen through the inculpation of Maurice, and everybody found they had work to do that evening. Quickly Venner's was emptied.

Michael, turning out of Cloisters to stroll for a while on the lawns of New Quad before he gave himself to the generalizations of whatever historian he had chosen to beguile this summer night, came up to Maurice leaning over the parapet by the Cher.

"Hullo, are you going to condescend to speak to me after the brick I dropped in Venner's?" asked Maurice bitterly.

"I wish you wouldn't be so theatrically sarcastic," complained Michael, who was half-unconsciously pursuing the simile which lately Lonsdale had found for Maurice's behavior.

"Well, why on earth," Maurice broke out, "it should be funny when Venner tells a story about some old St. Mary's man and yet be"—he paused, evidently too vain, thought Michael a little cruelly, to stigmatize himself—"and yet be considered contrary to what is *done* when I tell a story about myself, I don't quite know, I must admit."

"It was the introduction of the personal element which made everybody feel uncomfortable," said Michael. "Venner's tale had acquired the impersonality of a legend."

"Oh, god, Michael, you do talk rot sometimes!" said Maurice fretfully. "It's nothing on earth but offensive and very youthful priggishness."

"I wonder if I sounded like you," said Michael, "when I talked rather like you at about seventeen."

Maurice spluttered with rage at this, and Michael saw it would be useless to remonstrate with him reasonably. He blamed himself for being so intolerant and for not having with kindlier tact tried to point out why he had made a mistake; and yet with all his self-reproach he could not rid himself of what was something very near to active dislike of Maurice at that moment.

But Maurice went on, unperceiving.

"I hate this silly pretense up here—and particularly at St. Mary's—that nobody ever looks at a woman. It's nothing but infernal hypocrisy. Upon my soul, I'm glad I'm going down this term. I really couldn't have stood another year, playing with the fringe of existence. It seems to me, Michael, if you're sincere in this attitude of yours, you'll have a very dismal waking up from your dream. As for all the others, I don't count them. I'm sick of this schoolboy cant. Castleton's worth everybody else in this college put together. He was wonderful with that hulking fellow who came banging at the door of our digs. I wonder what you'd have done, if you'd been digging with me."

"Probably just what Castleton did," said Michael coldly. "You evidently weren't at home. Now I must go and work. So long."

He left Maurice abruptly, angry with him, angry with himself. What could have induced Maurice to make such a fool of himself in Venner's? Why hadn't he been able to perceive the difference of his confession from Venner's legendary narration which, unfettered by the reality of present emotions, had been taken under the protection of the comic spirit? The scene in retrospect appeared improbable, just as improbable in one way, just as shockingly improbable as the arrival of an angry rustic father at some Varsity digs in Longwall. And why had he made the recollection worse for himself by letting Maurice enlarge upon his indignation? It had been bad enough before, but that petulant outbreak had turned an accidental vulgarity into vulgarity itself most cruelly vocal. Back in Two Hundred and Two, Michael heard the comments upon Maurice, and as Grainger and Lonsdale delivered their judgment, he felt they had all this time tolerated the offender merely for a certain capacity he possessed for entertainment. They spoke of him now, as one might speak of a disgraced servant.

"Oh, let Maurice drop," said Michael wearily. "It was one of those miserable aberrations from tact which can happen to anybody. I've done the same sort of thing myself. It's an involuntary spasm of bad-manners, like sneezing over a crowded railway-carriage."

"Well, I suppose one must make allowances," said Grainger. "These artistic devils are always liable to breaks."

"That's right," said Michael. "Hoist the Union Jack. It's an extraordinary thing, the calm way in which an Englishman is always ready to make art responsible for everything."

Next day Maurice overtook Michael on the way to a lecture.

"I say," he began impetuously, "I made an awful fool of myself yesterday evening. What shall I do?"

"Nothing," said Michael.

"I was really horribly worried, you know, and I think I rather jumped at the opportunity to get the beastly business off my chest, as a sort of joke."

"Come and dine at the Palace of Delights this evening," Michael invited. "And tell Frank Castleton to come."

"We can't afford to be critical during the last fortnight of jolly old Two Hundred and Two," said Michael to Lonsdale and Grainger, when they received rather gloomily at first the news of the invitation.

Maurice in the course of the evening managed to reinstate himself. He so very divertingly drew old Wedders on the subject of going down.

The last week of the summer term arrived, and really it was very depressing that so many Good Eggs were irrevocably going to be lost to the St. Mary's J.C.R.

"I think my terminal dinner this term will have to be the same as my first one," said Michael. "Only twice as large."

So they all came, Cuffe and Sterne and Sinclair and a dozen more. And just because so many of the guests were going down, not a word was said about it. The old amiable ragging and rotting went on as if the college jokes of to-night would serve for another lustrum yet, as if Two Hundred and Two would merely be empty of these familiar faces for the short space of a vacation. Not a pipe was gone from its rack; not a picture was as yet deposed; not a hint was given of change, either by the material objects of the big room or by the merry and intimate community that now thronged it. Then the college tenor was called upon for a song, and perhaps without any intention of melancholy he sang O Moon of My Delight. Scarcely was it possible even for these Good Eggs, so rigidly conscious of each other's rigidity, not to think sentimentally for a moment how well the turning down of that empty glass applied to them. The new mood that descended upon the company expressed itself in reminiscence; and then, as if the sadness must for decency's sake be driven out, the college jester was called upon for the comic song whose hebdomadal recurrence through nine terms had always provoked the same delirious encore. Everything was going on as usual, and at a few minutes to midnight Auld Lang Syne ought not to have been difficult. It had been sung nearly as often as the comic song, but it was shouted more fervently somehow, less in tune somehow, and the silence at its close was very acute. Twelve o'clock was sounding; the guests went hurrying out; and, leaning from the windows of Two Hundred and Two, Grainger, Lonsdale, Wedderburn, and Michael heard their footsteps clattering down the High.

"I suppose we'd better begin sorting out our things to-morrow," said Michael.

CHAPTER XIII

PLASHERS MEAD

Stella came back from Vienna for a month in the summer. Indeed she was already arrived, when Michael reached Cheyne Walk. He was rather anxious to insist directly to her that her disinclination to marry Prescott had nothing to do with his death. Michael did not feel it would be good for Stella at nineteen to believe to that extent in her power. One or two of her letters had betrayed an amount of self-interest that Michael considered unhealthy. With this idea in view, he was surprised when she made no allusion to the subject, and resented a little that he must be the one to lead up to it.

"Oh, don't let's talk of what happened nearly a year ago," protested Stella.

"You were very much excited by it at the time," Michael pointed out.

"Ah, but lots of things have happened since then."

"What sort of things?"

He disapproved of the suggestion that the suicide of a lifelong friend was a drop in the ocean of incident that swayed round Stella.

"Oh, loves and deaths and jealousies and ambitions," said she lightly. "Things do happen in Vienna. It's much more eventful than Paris. I don't know what made me come back to London. I'm missing so much fun."

This implication that he and his mother were dull company for her was really rather irritating.

"You'd better go and look up some of your Bohemian friends," he advised severely. "They're probably all hanging about Chelsea still. It's not likely that any of them is farther on with his art than he was two years ago. Who was that bounder you were so fond of, and that girl who painted? Clarissa Vine, wasn't she called? What about her?"

"Poor old George," said Stella. "I really must try and get hold of him. I haven't seen Clarie for some time. She made a fool of herself over some man."

The result of Michael's sarcastic challenge was actually a tea-party in the big studio at 173 Cheyne Walk, which Stella herself described as being like turning out a lumber-room of untidy emotions.

"They're as queer as old-fashioned clothes," she said. "But rather touching, don't you think, Michael? Though after all," she added pensively, "I haven't gone marching at a very great pace along that triumphant career of mine. I don't know that I've much reason to laugh at them. Really in one way poor Clarie is in a better position than me. At least she can afford to keep the man she's living with. As for George Ayliffe, since he gave up trying to paint the girls he was in love with, he has become 'one of our most promising realists.'"

"He looks it," said Michael sourly.

What had happened to Stella during this last year? She had lost nearly all her old air of detachment. Formerly a radiance of gloriously unpassionate energy had shielded her from any close contact with the vulgar or hectic or merely ordinary life round her. Michael had doubted once or twice the wisdom of smoking cigars and had feared that artistic license of speech and action might be carried too far, but, looking back on his earlier opinion of Stella, he realized he had only been doubtful on his own account. He had never really thought she ran the least danger of doing anything more serious in its consequence than would have been enough to involve him or his mother in a brief embarrassment. Now, though he was at a loss to explain how he was aware of the change, she had become vulnerable. With this new aspect of her suddenly presented, he began to watch Stella with a trace of anxiety. He was worried that she seemed so restless, so steadily bored in London. He mistrusted the brightening of her eyes, when she spoke of soon going back to Vienna. Then came a week when Stella was much occupied with speculations about the Austrian post, and another week when she was perturbed by what she seemed anxious to suppose its vagaries. A hint from Michael that there was something more attractive in Vienna than a new technique of the piano made her very angry; and since she had always taken him into her confidence before, he tried to persuade himself that his suspicion was absurd and to feel tremendously at ease when Stella packed up in a hurry and went back with scarcely two days' warning of her departure to Vienna.

It was a sign of the new intimacy of relation between himself and his mother that Michael was able to approach naturally the subject of Stella's inquietude.

"My dear boy, I'm just as much worried as you are," Mrs. Fane assured him. "I suppose I ought to have been much more unpleasant than I can ever bear to make myself. No doubt I ought to have forbidden her quite definitely to go back—or perhaps I should have insisted on going back with her. Though I don't know what I would have done in Vienna. They make pastry there, don't they? I daresay there are very good tea-shops."

"I think it would have been better," said Michael firmly. Mrs. Fane turned to him with a shrug of helplessness.

"My dear boy, you know how very unpleasant Stella can be when she is crossed. Really very unpleasant indeed. Girls are so much more difficult to manage than boys. And they begin by being so easy. But after eighteen every month brings a new problem. Their clothes, you know. And of course their behavior."

"It's quite obvious what's the matter," said Michael. "Funny thing. I've never concerned myself very much with Stella's love-affairs before, but this time she seemed less capable of looking after herself."

"Would you like to go out to Vienna?" she suggested.

"Oh, no, really, I must go away and work. Besides I shouldn't do any good. Nor would you," Michael added abruptly.

"I wish Dick Prescott were alive," his mother sighed. "Really, you know, Michael, I was shocked at Stella's callousness over that business."

"Well, my dear mother, be fair. It wasn't anything to do with Stella, and she has no conventional affections. That's one comfort—you do know where you are with her. Now, let's leave Stella alone and talk about your plans. You're sure you don't mind my burying myself in the country? I must work. I'm going down into Oxfordshire with Guy Hazlewood."

Michael had met Guy the other evening in the lobby of a theater. He had come back from Macedonia with the intention of settling somewhere in the country. He was going to devote himself to poetry, although he exacted Michael's pledge not to say a word of this plan for fear that people would accuse him of an affected withdrawal. He was sensitive to the strenuous creed of his old college, to that atmosphere of faint contempt which surrounded a man who was not on the way toward administering mankind or acres. He had not yet chosen his retreat. That would be revealed in a flash, if his prayer were to be granted. Meanwhile why should not Michael accompany him to some Cotswold village? They would ride out from Oxford on bicycles and when they had found the ideal inn, they would stay there through August and September, prospecting the country round. Michael was flattered by Guy's desire for his companionship. Of all the men he had known, he used to admire Guy the most. Two months with him would be a pleasure he would not care to forego, and it was easy enough to convince himself that he would be powerless to influence Stella in any direction and that anyway, whether he could or could not, it would be more serviceable for her character to win or lose her own battles.

Michael and Guy left Oxford in the mellow time of an afternoon in earliest August and rode lazily along the Cheltenham road. At nightfall, just as the stripling moon sank behind a spinney of firs that crowned the farthest visible dip of that rolling way ahead across the wold, they turned down into Wychford. The wide street of the town sloped very rapidly to a valley of intertwining streams whence the air met them still warm with the stored heat of the day, yet humid and languorous after the dry upland. On either side, as they dipped luxuriously down with their brakes gently whirring, mostly they were aware of many white hollyhocks against the gray houses that were already bloomed with dusk and often tremulous with the voyaging shadows of candle-light. At the Stag Inn they found a great vaulted parlor, a delicate roast of lamb, a salad very fragrant with mint and thyme, cream and gooseberries and ale.

"This is particularly good ale," said Guy.

"Wonderful ale," Michael echoed.

Once again they filled their pewter mugs.

"It seems to me exceptionally rich and tawny," said Guy.

"And it has a very individual tang," said Michael. "Another quart, I think, don't you?"

"Two, almost," Guy suggested, and Michael agreed at once.

"I vote we stay here," said Guy.

"I'll wire them to send along my books to-morrow," decided Michael.

After supper they went on down the street and came to the low parapet of a bridge in one of whose triangular bays they stood, leaning over to count in the stream below the blurred and jigging stars. Behind them in the darkness was the melodious roar of falling water, and close at hand the dusty smell of ivy. Farther exploration might have broken the spell of mystery; so in silence they pored upon the gloom, until the rhythmic calm and contemplation were destroyed by a belated wagon passing over the bridge behind them. They went back to the Stag and that night in four-posters slept soundly.

Next morning Michael and Guy went after breakfast to visit the bridge on which they had stood in the starlight. It managed curiously to sustain the romantic associations with which they had endowed it on the night before. A mighty sycamore, whose roots in their contest with the floods had long grappled in desperate convolutions with the shelving bank of the stream below, overshadowed the farther end: here also at right angles was a line of gabled cottages crumbling into ruin and much overgrown with creepers. They may have been old almshouses, but there was no sign of habitation, and they seemed abandoned to chattering sparrows whose draggled nests were everywhere visible in the ivy. Beyond on the other side of the bridge the stream gurgled toward a sluice that was now silent; and beyond this, gray buildings deep embowered in elms and sycamores surrounded what was evidently a mill pool. They walked on to where the bridge became a road that in contrast with the massed trees all round them shone dazzlingly in the sunshine. A high gray wall bounded the easterly side; on the west the road was bordered by a low quickset hedge that allowed a view of a wide valley through which the river, having gathered once more its vagrant streams and brooks, flowed in prodigal curves of silver as far as the eye could follow. The hills that rose to right and left of the valley in bald curves were at this season colorless beside the vivider green of the water-meadows at their base, which was generally indeterminate on account of plantations whence at long intervals the smoke of hidden mills and cottages ascended. When the road had traversed the width of the valley, it trifurcated. One branch followed westward the gentle undulations of the valley; a second ran straight up the hill, disappearing over a stark sky-line almost marine in its hint of space beyond. The main branch climbed the hill diagonally to the right and conveyed a sense of adventure with a milestone which said fifty miles to an undecipherable town.

Michael and Guy took this widest road for a while, but they soon paused by a gate to look back at Wychford. The sun shone high, and the beams slanting transversely through the smoke of the chimneys in tier upon tier gave the clustered gray roofs a superficial translucence like that of an uncut gem. The little town built against the hill nowhere straggled, and in its fortified economy and simplicity of line it might have been cut on wood by a mediæval engraver. Higher up along the hill's ridge went rocketing east and west the windswept highway from Oxford over the wold to Gloucestershire. They traced its course by the telegraph-poles whose inclinations had so long been governed by the wind that the mechanic trunks were as much a natural feature of the landscape as the trees, themselves not much less lean and sparse. It was a view of such extension that roads more remote were faint scars on the hills, and the streams of the valley narrowed ultimately to thin blades of steel. The traffic of generations might be thought to have converged upon this town, so much did it produce the effect of waiting upon that hillside, so little sense did it have of seeming to obtrude its presence upon the surroundings.

Gradually the glances of Guy and Michael came back from the fading horizons of this wide country to concentrate first upon the town and then upon the spire that with glittering weather-vane rose lightly as smoke from the gray fabric of its church, until finally they must have rested simultaneously upon a long low house washed by one stream and by another imprisoned within a small green island.

"It's to let," said Michael.

"I know," said Guy.

The unspoken thought that went sailing off upon the painted board was only expressed by the eagerness with which they stared at the proffered house.

"I might be able to take it," said Guy at last.

Michael looked at him in admiration. Such a project conceived in his company did very definitely mark an altogether new stage and, as it seemed to him, a somewhat advanced stage in his relationship with the world.

They discovered the entrance immediately behind the almshouses in the smell of whose ivy they had lingered on the bridge last night. They passed through a wooden gateway in a high gray wall and, walking down a stained gravel path between a number of gnarled fruit

213

trees trimmed as espaliers to conform with an antique mode of insuring fertility, they came at last round an overgrown corner close against the house. Seen from the hillside, it had quickly refined itself to be for them at least the intention of that great view, of that wide country of etched-in detail. The just background had been given, the only background that would have enabled them to esteem all that was offered here in this form of stone well-ordered, gray, indigenous, the sober crown of the valley.

Guy from the moment he saw it had determined to take this house: his inquiries about the rent and the drains, his discussion of the terms of the agreement, of the dampness within, of the size of the garden were the merest conventions of the house-hunter, empty questions whose answers really had very slight bearing on the matter in hand. Here he said to Michael he would retire: here he would live and write poetry: here life would be escorted to the tread of great verse: here an eremite of art he would show forth the austerity of his vocation.

Meanwhile, Michael's books arrived, and at Guy's exhortation he worked in the orchard of Plashers Mead—so the small property of some twenty acres was called. Guy was busy all day with decorators and carpenters and masons. The old landlord had immediately surrendered his house to so enterprising a tenant; an agreement for three years had been signed; and Guy was going to make all ready in summer that this very autumn with what furniture he had he might inhabit his own house set among these singing streams.

Michael found it a little hard to pay the keenest attention to Anson's or to Dicey's entertainment of his curiosity about the Constitution, too much did the idea of Guy's emancipation alluringly rustle as it were in the tree-tops, too much did the thought of Guy's unvexed life draw Michael away from his books. And even if he could blot out Guy's prospect, it was impossible not to follow in fancy the goldfinches to their thistle-fields remote and sunny, the goldfinches with their flighted song.

Summer passed, and Michael did not find that the amount of information he had absorbed quite outweighed a powerful impression, that was shaping in his mind, of having wasted a good deal of time in staring at trees and the funnels of light between them, in listening to the wind and the stream, to the reapers and the progress of time.

One evening in mid-September he and Guy went after supper to see how some newly painted room looked by candlelight. They sat on a couple of borrowed windsor chairs in the whitewashed room that Guy had chosen for his own. Two candles stuck on the mantelpiece burned with motionless spearheads of gold, and showed to their great satisfaction that by candlelight as well as by day the green shelves freshly painted were exactly the green they had expected. When they blew out the candles, they realized, such a plenitude of silver light was left behind, that the full moon of harvest was shining straight in through the easterly bow window which overhung the stream.

"By gad, what a glorious night!" sighed Guy, staring out at the orchard. "We'll take a walk, shall we?"

They went through the orchard where the pears and pippins were lustered by the sheen and glister of the moon. They walked on over grass that sobbed in the dewfall beneath their footsteps. They faded from the world into a web of mist when trees rose suddenly like giants before them and in the depths of whose white glooms on either side they could hear the ceaseless munching of bullocks at nocturnal pasturage. Then in a moment they had left the mist behind them and stood in the heart of the valley, watching for a while the willows jet black against the moon, and the gleaming water at their base.

"I wish you were going to be up next term," said Michael. "I really can hardly bear to think of you here. You are a lucky devil."

"Why don't you come and join me?" Guy suggested,

"I wish I could. Perhaps I will after next year. And yet what should I do? I've dreamed enough. I must decide what I'm going to *try* to do, at any rate. You see, I'm not a poet. Guy, you ought to start a sort of lay monastery—a house for people to retreat into for the purpose of meditation upon their careers."

"As a matter of fact, it would be a jolly good thing if some people did do that."

"I don't know," said Michael. "I should get caught in the web of the meditation. I should hear the world as just now we heard those bullocks. Guy, Wychford is a place of dreams. You'll find that. You'll live on and on at Plashers Mead until everything about you turns into the sort of radiant unreality we've seen to-night."

The church-clock with raucous whizz and clangor sounded ten strokes.

"And time," Michael went on, "will come to mean no more than a brief disturbance of sound. Really I'm under the enchantment already. I'm beginning to wonder if life really does hold a single problem that could not be dissolved at once by this powerful moonshine."

Next day Michael said he must go back to London to-morrow since he feared that if he dallied he would never go back. Guy could not dissuade him from his resolve.

"I don't want to spoil my picture of you in this valley," Michael explained. "You know, I feel inclined to put Plashers Mead into the farthest recesses of my heart, so that whatever happens when I go down next year, it will be so securely hidden that I shall have the mere thought of it for a refuge."

"And more than the thought of it, you silly ass," Guy drawled.

They drove together to the railway station five miles away. In the sleepy September heat the slow train puffed in. Hot people with bunches of dahlias were bobbing to one another in nearly all the compartments. Michael sighed.

"Don't go," said Guy. "It's much too hot."

Michael shook his head.

"I must."

Just then a porter came up to tell Guy there were three packing-cases awaiting his disposal in the luggage-office.

"Some of my books," he shouted, as the train was puffing out. Michael watched from the window Guy and the porter, the only figures among the wine-dark dahlias of the platform.

"What fun unpacking them," he thought, and leaned back regretfully to survey the placid country gliding past.

Yet even after that secluded and sublunary town where Guy in retrospect seemed to be moving as remotely as a knight in an old tale, London, or rather the London which shows itself in the neighborhood of great railway termini, impressed Michael with nearly as sharp a romantic strangeness, so dreadfully immemorial appeared the pale children, leaning over scabrous walls to salute the passing train. Always, as one entered London, one beheld these children haunting the backs of houses whose frontal existence as a mapped-out street was scarcely credible. To Michael they were goblins that lived only in this gulley of fetid sunlight through which the trains endlessly clanged. Riding through London in a hansom a few minutes later, the people of the city became unreal to him, and only those goblin-children remained in his mind as the natural inhabitants. He drove on through the quiet streets and emerged in that space of celestial silver which was called Chelsea; but the savage roar of the train, as it had swept through those gibbering legions of children, was still in Michael's ears when the hansom pulled up before the sedate house in Cheyne Walk.

The parlormaid showed no surprise at his unexpected arrival, and informed him casually with no more indication of human interest than would have been given by a clock striking its mechanical message of time that Miss Stella was in the studio. That he should have been unaware of his sister's arrival seemed suddenly to Michael a too intimate revelation of his personality to the parlormaid, and he actually found himself taking the trouble to deceive this machine by an affectation of prior knowledge. He was indeed caught up and imprisoned by the coils of infinitely small complications that are created by the social stirrings of city life. The pale children seen from the train sank below the level of ordinary existence, no longer conspicuous in his memory, no longer even faintly disturbing. As for Plashers Mead and the webs of the moon, they were become the adventure of a pleasant dream. He was in fact back in town.

Michael went quickly to the studio and found Stella not playing as he hoped, but sitting listless. Then he realized how much at the very moment the parlormaid told him of Stella's return he had feared such a return was the prelude to disaster. Almost he had it on his lips to ask abruptly what was the matter. It cost him an effort to greet her with just that amount of fraternal cordiality which would not dishonor by its demonstrativeness this studio of theirs. He was so unreasonably glad to see her back from Vienna that a gesture of weakness on her side would have made him kiss her.

"Hullo, I didn't expect to see you," was, however, all he said.

"Nor did I you," was what she answered.

Presently she began to give him an elaborate account of the journey from Austria, and Michael knew that exactly in proportion to its true insignificance was the care she bestowed upon its dreariness and dust.

Michael began to wish it were not exactly a quarter-of-an-hour before lunch. Such a period was too essentially consecrated to orderly ideas and London smoothness for it to admit the intrusion of anything more disturbing than the sound of a gong. What could have brought Stella back from Vienna?

"Did you come this morning?" he asked.

"Oh, no. Last night. Why?" she demanded. "Do I look as crumpled as all that?"

For Stella to imply so directly that something had happened which she had expected to change materially even her outward appearance was perhaps a sign he would soon be granted her confidence. He rather wished she would be quick with it. If he were left too long to form his own explanations, he would be handicapped at the crucial moment. Useless indeed he were imagining all this, he thought in supplement, as the lunch-gong restored by its clamor the atmosphere of measured life where nothing really happens.

After lunch Stella went up to her room: the effect of the journey, she turned round to say, still called for sleep. Michael did not see her again before dinner. She came down then, looking very much older than he had ever seen her, whether because she was dressed in oyster-gray satin or was in fact much older, Michael did not know. She grumbled at him for not putting on a dinner jacket.

"Don't look so horrified at the notion," she cried petulantly. "Can't you realize that after a year with long-haired students I want a change?"

After dinner Michael asked her to come and play in the studio.

"Play?" she echoed. "I'm never going to play again."

"What perfect rot you are talking," said Michael, in a damnatory generalization which was intended to cover not merely all she had been saying, but even all she had been doing almost since she first announced her intention of going to Vienna.

Stella burst into tears.

"Come on, let's go to the studio," said Michael. He felt that Stella's tears were inappropriate to the dining-room. Indeed, only the fact that she was wearing this evening frock of oyster-gray satin, and was therefore not altogether the invulnerable and familiar and slightly boyish Stella imprinted on his mind, prevented him from being shocked to the point of complete emotional incapacity. It seemed less of an outrage to fondle however clumsily this forlorn creature in gray satin, even though he did find himself automatically and grotesquely saying to himself "Enter Tilburina stark mad in white satin and the Confidante stark mad in white muslin."

"Come along, come along," he begged her. "You must come to the studio."

Michael went on presenting the studio with such earnestness that he himself began to endow it with a positively curative influence; but when at last Stella had reached the studio, not even caring apparently whether on the way the parlormaid saw her tears, and when she had plunged disconsolately down upon the divan, still weeping, Michael looked round at their haven with resentment. After all, it was merely an ungainly bleak whitewashed room, and Stella was crying more bitterly than before.

"Look here, I say, why don't you tell me what you're crying about? You can't go on crying forever, you know," Michael pointed out. "And when you've stopped crying, you'll feel such an ass if you haven't explained what it was all about."

"I couldn't possibly tell anybody," said Stella, looking very fierce. Then suddenly she got up, and so surprising had been her breakdown that Michael scarcely stopped to think that her attitude was rather unusually dramatic.

"But I'm damned if I *will* give up playing," she proclaimed; and, sitting down at the piano, forthwith she began to play into oblivion her weakness.

It was a very exciting piece she played, and Michael longed to ask her what it was called, but he was afraid to provoke in her any renewal of self-consciousness; so he enjoyed the fiery composition and Stella's calm with only a faint regret that he would never know its name and would never be able to ask her to play it again. When she had finished, she swung round on the stool and asked him what had happened to Lily Haden.

"I don't know—really—they've left Trelawny Road," he said, feeling vaguely an unfair flank attack was being delivered.

"And you never think of her, I suppose?" demanded Stella.

"Well, no, I don't very much."

"Yet I can remember," said Stella, "when you were absolutely miserable because she had been flirting with somebody else."

"Yes, I was very miserable," Michael admitted. "And you were rather contemptuous about it, I remember. You told me I ought to be more proud."

"And don't you realize," Stella said, "that just because I did remember what I told you, I made my effort and began to play the piano again?"

Michael waited. He supposed that she would now take him into her confidence, but she swung round to the keyboard, and when she had finished playing she had become herself again, detached and cool and masterful. It was incredible that the wet ball of a handkerchief half hidden by a cushion could be her handkerchief.

Michael made up his mind that Stella's unhappiness was due to a love-affair which had been wrecked either by circumstance or temperament, and he tried to persuade himself of his indignation against the unknown man. He was sensible of a desire to punch the fellow's head. With the easy exaggerations of the night-time he could picture himself fighting duels with punctilious Austrian noblemen. He went so far as mentally to indite a letter to Alan and Lonsdale requesting their secondary assistance. Then the memory of Lily began to dance before him. He forgot about Stella in speculations about Lily. Time had softened the trivial and shallow infidelity of which she had been guilty. Time with night for ally gave her slim form an ethereal charm. He had been reading this week of the great imaginative loves of the Middle Ages, and of that supple and golden-haired girl he began to weave an abstraction of passion like the Princess of Trebizond. He slept upon the evocation of her beauty just as he was setting forth upon a delicate and intangible pursuit. Next morning Michael suggested to Stella they should revisit Carlington Road.

"My god, to think we once lived here!" exclaimed Stella, as they stood outside Number 64. "To me it seems absolutely impossible, but then of course I was much more away from it than you ever were."

Stella was so ferocious in her mockery of their childish haunts and habitations that Michael began to perceive her old serene contempt was become tinged with bitterness. This morning she was too straightly in possession of herself. It was illogical after last night.

"Well, thank heaven, everything does change," she murmured. "And that ugly things become even more ugly."

"Only for a time," objected Michael. "In twenty years if we visit Carlington Road we shall think how innocent and intimate and pretty it all is."

"I wasn't thinking so much of Carlington Road," said Stella. "I was really thinking of people."

"Even they become beautiful again after a time," argued Michael.

"It would take a very long time for some," said Stella coldly.

Michael had rather dreaded his mother's return, with Stella in this mood, and he was pleased when he found that his fears had been unjustifiable. Stella in fact was very gentle with her mother, as if she and not herself had suffered lately.

"I'm so glad you're back, darling Stella, and so delighted to think you aren't going to Petersburg to-morrow, because the man at Vienna whose name begins with that extraordinary letter...."

"Oh, mother," Stella laughed, "the letter was quite ordinary. It was only L."

"But the name was dreadful, dear child. It always reminded one of furs. A most oppressive name. So that really you'll be in London all this winter?"

"Yes, only I shan't play much," said Stella.

"Mrs. Carruthers is so anxious to meet you properly," Mrs. Fane said. "And Mabel Carruthers is really very nice. Poor girl! I wish you could be friends with her. She's interested in nothing her mother does."

Michael was really amazed when Stella, without a shrug, without even a wink at him, promised simply to let Mrs. Carruthers "meet her properly," and actually betrayed as much interest in Mabel Carruthers as to inquire how old she was.

Maurice arrived at Cheyne Walk, just before Michael went up for term, to say he had taken a most wonderful studio in Grosvenor Road. He was anxious that Michael should bring his sister to see it, but Stella would not go.

"Thanks very much, my dear," she said to him, "but I've seen too much of the real thing. I'm in no mood just now for a sentimental imitation."

"I think you ought to come," said Michael. "It would be fun to see Maurice living in Grosvenor Road with all the Muses. Castleton will have such a time tidying up after them when he joins him next year."

But Stella would not go.

CHAPTER XIV

99 ST. GILES

It was strange to come up to Oxford and to find so many of the chief figures in the college vanished. For a week Michael felt that in a way he had no business still to be there, so unfamiliar was the college itself inhabited by none of his contemporaries save a few Scholars. Very soon, however, the intimacy of the rooms in St. Giles which he shared with Alan cured all regrets, and with a thrill he realized that this last year was going to be of all the years at Oxford the best, indeed perhaps of all the years of his life the best.

College itself gave Michael a sharper sense of its entity than he had ever gathered before. He was still sufficiently a part of it not to feel the implicit criticism of his presence that in a year or two, revisiting Oxford, he would feel; and he was also far enough away from the daily round to perceive and admire the yearly replenishment which preserved its vigor notwithstanding the superficially irreparable losses of each year. There were moments when he regretted 202 High with what now seemed its amazingly irresponsible existence, but 202 High had never given him quite the same zest in returning to it as now 99 St. Giles could give. Nothing had ever quite equaled those damp November dusks, when after a long walk through silent country Michael and Alan came back to the din of Carfax and splashed their way along the crowded and greasy Cornmarket toward St. Giles, those damp November dusks when they would find the tea-things glimmering in the firelight. Buttered toast was eaten; tea was drunk; the second-best pipe of the day was smoked to idle cracklings of The Oxford Review and The Star; a stout landlady cleared away, and during the temporary disturbance Michael pulled back the blinds and watched the darkness and fog slowly blotting out St. John's and the alley of elm-trees opposite, and giving to the Martyrs' Memorial and even to Balliol a gothic and significant mystery. The room was quiet again; the lamps and the fire glowed; Michael and Alan, settled in deep chairs, read their History and Philosophy; outside in the November night footsteps went by; carts and wagons occasionally rattled; bells chimed; outside in the November murk present life was manifesting its continuity; here within, the battles and the glories, the thoughts, the theories and the speculations of the past for Michael and Alan moved across printed pages under the rich lamplight.

Dinner dissolved the concentrated spell of two hours. But dinner at 99 St. Giles was very delightful in the sea-green dining-room whose decorations had survived the departing tenant who created them. Michael and Alan did not talk much; indeed, such conversation as took place during the meal came from the landlady. She possessed so deft a capacity for making apparently the most barren observations flower and fruit with intricate narrations, that merely an inquiry as to the merit of the lemon-sole would serve to link the occasion with an intimate revelation of her domestic past.

After dinner Michael and Alan read on toward eleven o'clock, at which hour Alan usually went to bed. It was after his departure that in a way Michael enjoyed the night most. The mediæval chronicles were put back on their shelf; Stubbs or Lingard, Froude, Freeman, Guizot, Lavisse or Gregorovius were put back; round the warm and silent room Michael wandered uncertain for a while; and at the end of five minutes down came Don Quixote or Adlington's Apuleius, or Florio's Montaigne, or Lucian's True History. The fire crumbled away to ashes and powder; the fog stole into the room; outside was now nothing but the chimes at their measured intervals, nothing but the noise of them to say a city was there; at that hour Oxford was truly austere, something more indeed than austere, for it was neither in time nor in space, but the abstraction of a city. Only when the lamps began to reek did Michael go up to bed by candlelight. In his vaporous room, through whose open window the sound of two o'clock striking came very coldly, he could scarcely fancy himself in the present. The effort of intense reading, whether of bygone institutions or of past adventure, had left him in the condition of physical freedom that saints achieve by prayer. He was aware of nothing but a desire to stay forever like this, half feverish with the triumph of tremendous concentration, to undress in this stinging acerbity of night air, and to lie wakeful for a long time in this world of dreaming spires.

99 St. Giles exercised just that industrious charm which Michael had anticipated from the situation. The old house overlooked such a wide thoroughfare that the view, while it afforded the repose of movement, scarcely ever aroused a petty inquisitiveness into the actions of the passers-by. The traffic of the thoroughfare like the ships of the sea went by merely apprehended, but not observed. The big bay-window hung over the street like the stern-cabin of a frigate, and as Michael sat there he had the impression of being cut off from communication, the sense of perpetually leaving life astern. The door of 99 St. Giles did not open directly on the street, but was reached by a tortuous passage that ran the whole depth of the house. This entrance helped very much the illusion of separation from the ebb and flow of ordinary existence, and was so suggestive of a refuge that involuntarily Michael always hurried through it that the sooner he might set his foot on the steep and twisted staircase inside the house. There was always an excitement in reaching this staircase again, an impulse to run swiftly up, as if this return to the sitting-room was veritably an escape from the world. Here the books sprawled everywhere. At 202 High they had filled the cupboards in orderly fashion. Here they overflowed in dusty cataracts, and tottered upward in crazy escalades and tremulous piles. All the shelves were gorged with books. Moreover, Michael every afternoon bought more books. The landlady held up her hands in dismay as, crunching up the paper in which they had been wrapped, he considered in perplexity their accommodation. More space was necessary, and the sea-green dining-room was awarded shelves. Here every morning after breakfast came the exiles, the dull and the disappointing books which had been banished from the sitting-room. Foot by foot the sea-green walls disappeared behind these shelves. In Lampard's bookshop Michael was certainly a personality. Lampard himself even came to tea, and sat nodding his approbation.

As for Alan, he used to stay unmoved by the invading volumes. He had stipulated at the beginning that one small bookcase should be reserved for him. Here Plato and Aristotle, Herodotus and Thucydides always had room to breathe, without ever being called upon to endure the contamination of worm-eaten bibliophily.

"Where the deuce has my Stubbs got to?" Michael would grumble, delving into the musty cascade of old plays and chap books which had temporarily obliterated the current literature of the week's work.

Alan would very serenely take down Plato from his own trim and unimpeded shelves, and his brow would already be knitted with the effort of fixing half-a-dozen abstractions before Michael had decided after a long excavation that Stubbs had somehow vanished in the by-ways of curious reading.

Yet notwithstanding the amount of time occupied by arranging and buying and finding books, Michael did manage to absorb a good deal of history, even of that history whose human nature has to be sought arduously in charters, exchequer-rolls and acts of parliament. Schools were drawing near; the dates of Kings and Emperors and Popes in their succession adorned the walls of his bedroom, so that even while he was cleaning his teeth one fact could be acquired.

Only on Sunday evenings did Michael allow himself really to reënter the life of St. Mary's. These Sunday evenings had all the excitement of a long-interrupted reunion. To be sure, Venner's was thronged with people who seemed to be taking life much too lightly; but Tommy Grainger was there, still engaged with a pass-group. People spoke hopefully of going head this year. Surely with Tommy and three other Blues in the boat, St. Mary's must go head. The conversation was so familiar that it was almost a shock to find so many of the faces altered. But Cuffe was still there with his mouth perpetually open just as wide as ever. Sterne was still there and likely, so one heard, to make no end of runs next summer. George Appleby was very much in evidence since Lonsdale's departure. George Appleby was certainly there, and Michael rather liked him and accepted an invitation to lunch. In hall the second-year men were not quite as rowdy as they used to be, and when they were rowdy, somehow to Michael and the rest of the fourth year they seemed to lack the imagination of themselves when they—but after all the only true judges of that were the Princes and Cardinals and Poets staring down from their high golden frames. The dons, too, at High Table might know, for there they sat, immemorial as ever.

Wine in Common Room was just the same, and it really was very jolly to be sitting between Castleton—that very popular President of J.C.R.—and Tommy Grainger. There certainly was a great and grave satisfaction in leading off with a more ceremonious health drinking than had ever been achieved in the three years past. Michael found it amusing to catch the name of some freshman and, shouting abruptly a salute, to behold him wriggle and blush and drink his answer and wonder who on earth was hailing *him*. Michael often asked himself if it really were possible he could appear to that merry rout at the other end of J.C.R. in truly heroic mold. He supposed, with a smile at himself for so gross a fraud, that he really did for them pass mortal stature and that already he had a bunch of legends dangling from his halo. Down in Venner's after wine, Michael fancied the shouts of the freshmen wandering round Cloisters were more raucous than once they had seemed. Sometimes really they were almost irritating, but the After was capital, although the new comic song of the new college jester lacked perhaps a little the perfect lilt of "Father says we're going to beat them." Yet, after all, the Boer war had been over three years now: no doubt "Father says we're going to beat them" would have sounded a little stale. Last term, however, at Two Hundred and Two it had rung as fresh as ever. But the singer was gone now. It was meet his song should perish with his withdrawal from the Oxford scene. Still the After was quite good sport, and Michael was glad to think he and Grainger and Sterne were giving the last After but one of this term. He bicycled back to the digs with his head full of chatter, of clinking glasses and catchy tunes. Nevertheless, all consciousness of the evening's merriment faded out, as he hurried up the crooked staircase to the sitting-room where Alan, upright at the table amid Thucydidean commentaries, was reading under the lamp's immotionable rays, his hair glinting with what was now rare gold.

During this autumn term neither Michael nor Alan spoke of Stella except as an essentially third person. She was in London, devoting so much of herself so charmingly to her mother that Mrs. Fane nearly abandoned every other interest in her favor. There were five Schumann recitals, of which press notices were sent to 99 St. Giles. Michael as he read them handed them on to Alan.

"Jolly good," said he, in a tone of such conventional praise that Michael really began to wonder whether he had after all changed his mind instead of merely concealing his intention. However, since conversation between these two had been stripped to the bare bones of intercourse, Michael could not bring himself to violate this habit of reserve for the sake of a curiosity the gratification of which in true friendship should never be demanded, nor even accepted with deeper attention than the trivial news of the day casually offered. Nor would Michael have felt it loyal to Alan to try from Stella to extract a point of view regarding him. Anyway, he reassured himself, nothing could be done at present.

Toward the end of term Mrs. Ross wrote a letter to Michael whose news was sufficiently unexpected to rouse the two of them to a conversation of greater length than any they had had since term began.

COBBLE PLACE,
November 30.

My dear Michael,

You will be surprised to hear that I have become a Catholic, or I suppose I should say to you, if you still adhere to your theories, a Roman Catholic. My reasons for this step, apart of course from the true reason—the grace of God—were, I think, connected a good deal with my boy. When your friend Mr. Prescott killed himself, I felt very much the real emptiness of such a life that on the surface was so admirable, in some ways so enviable. I am dreadfully anxious that Kenneth—he is Kenneth Michael now—I hope you won't be vexed I should have wished him to have Michael also—well, as I was saying—that Kenneth should grow up with all the help that the experience of the past can give him. It has become increasingly a matter of astonishment to me how so many English boys manage to muddle through the crises of their boyhood without the Sacraments. I'm afraid you'll be reading this letter in rather a critical spirit, and perhaps resenting my implication that you, for instance, have come through so many crises without the Sacraments. But I'm not yet a good enough theologian to argue with you about the claims of your Church. Latterly I've felt positively alarmed by the prospect of grappling with Kenneth's future. I have seen you struggle through, and I know I can say win a glorious victory over one side of yourself. But I have seen other things happen, even from where I live my secluded life. If my husband had not been killed I might not perhaps have felt this dread on Kenneth's account. But I like to think that God in giving me that great sorrow has shown His purpose by offering me this new and unimagined peace and security and assurance. I need scarcely say I have had a rather worrying time lately. It is strange how when love and faith are the springs of action one must listen with greater patience than one could listen for any lesser motive to the opinions of other people.

Joan and Mary whom I've always thought of as just wrapped up in the good works of their dear good selves, really rose in their wrath and scorched me with the fieriest opposition. I could not have believed they had in them to say as much in all their lives as they said to me when I announced my intention. Nor had I any idea they knew so many English clergymen. I believe that to gratify them I have interviewed half the Anglican ministry. Even a Bishop was invoked to demonstrate my apostasy. Nancy, too, wrote furious letters. She was not outraged so much theologically, but her sense of social fitness was shattered.

My darling old mother was the only person who took my resolve calmly. "As long as you don't try to convert me," she said, "and don't leave incense burning about the house, well—you're old enough to know your own mind." She was so amusing while Joan and Mary were marshaling arguments against me. She used to sit playing "Miss Milligan" with a cynical smile, and said, when it was all over and in spite of everyone I had been received, that she had really enjoyed Patience for the first time, as Joan and Mary were too busy to prevent her from cheating.

How are you and dear old Alan getting on? Of course you can read him this letter. I've not written to him because I fancy he won't be very much interested. Forgive me that I did not take you into my confidence beforehand, but I feared a controversy with a real historian about the continuity of the Anglican church.

My love to you both at Oxford.

Your affectionate
Maud Ross.

"Great scott!" Michael exclaimed, as he finished the letter. "Alan! could you ever in your wildest dreams have imagined that Mrs. Ross, the most inveterate Whig and Roundhead and Orange bigot, at least whenever she used to argue with me, would have gone over?"

"What do you mean?" Alan asked, sinking slowly to earth from his Platonic *ονρανος*. "Gone over where?"

"To Rome—become a Roman Catholic."

"Who?" gasped Alan, staggered now more than Michael. "Mrs. Ross—Aunt Maud?"

"It's the most extraordinary thing I ever heard," said Michael. "She—and Kenneth," he added rather maliciously, seeing that Alan's Britannic prejudice was violently aroused. "I'll read you her letter."

Plato was shut up for the evening before Michael was halfway through, and almost before the last sentence had been read, Alan's wrath exploded.

"It's all very fine for her to laugh like that at Joan and Mary and Nancy," he said, coloring hotly. "But they were absolutely right, and Mrs. Ross—I mean Aunt Maud——"

"I was afraid you were going to disown the relationship," Michael laughed.

"Aunt Maud is absolutely wrong. Why, my uncle would have been furious. Even if *she* became a Catholic she had no business to take Kenneth with her. The more I think of it—you know, it really is a bit thick."

"Why do you object?" Michael asked curiously. "I never knew you thought about religion at all, except so far as occasionally to escort your mother politely to Matins, and that was after all to oblige her more than God. Besides, you're reading Greats, and I always thought that the Greats people in their fourth year abstained from anything like a definite opinion for fear of losing their First."

"I may not have a definite opinion about Christianity," said Alan. "But Catholicism is ridiculous, anyway—it doesn't suit English people."

"There you're treading on the heels of the School of Modern History which you affect to despise. You really don't know, if I may say so, what could or could not suit the English people unless you know what has or has not suited them."

"Why don't you become a Catholic yourself," challenged Alan, "if you're so keen on them?"

"For a logician," said Michael, "your conclusion is bad, being entirely unrelated to any of our premises. Secondly, were I inclined to label myself as anything, I should be disposed to label myself as a Catholic already."

"Oh, I know that affectation!" scoffed Alan.

"Well, the net result of our commentary is that you, like everybody else, object to Mrs. Ross changing her opinions, because you don't like it. Her position is negligible, the springs of action being religious. Now if my mother went over to Rome I should be rather bucked on her account."

"My dear chap, if you don't mind my saying so," suggested Alan as apologetically as his outraged conventionality would allow, "your mother has always been rather given to—er—all sorts of new cults, and it wouldn't be so—er—noticeable in her case. But supposing Stella——"

Michael looked at him sharply.

"Supposing Stella did?" he asked.

"Oh, of course she's artistic and she's traveled and—oh, well, I don't know—Stella's different."

At any rate, thought Michael, he was still in love with Stella. She was evidently beyond criticism.

"You needn't worry," said Michael. "I don't think she ever will."

"You didn't think Aunt Maud ever would," Alan pointed out.

"And, great scott, it's still absolutely incredible," Michael murmured.

Although in the face of Alan's prejudice Michael had felt very strongly that Mrs. Ross had done well by her change of communion, or rather by her submission to a communion, for he never could remember her as perfervid in favor of any before, at the same time to himself he rather regretted the step, since it destroyed for him that idea he had kept of her as one who stood gravely holding the balance. He dreaded a little the effect upon her of a sudden plunge into Catholicism, just as he had felt uneasy when eight or nine years ago Alan had first propounded the theory of his uncle being in love with her. Michael remembered how the suggestion had faintly shocked his conception of Miss Carthew. It was a little disconcerting to have to justify herself to Nancy, or indeed to anyone. It seemed to weaken her status. Moreover, his own deep-implanted notion of "going over to Rome" as the act of a weakling and a weather-cock was hard to allay. His own gray image of Pallas Athene seemed now to be decked with meretricious roses. He was curious to know what his mother would think about the news. Mrs. Fane received it as calmly as if he had told her Mrs. Ross had taken up palmistry; to her Catholicism was only one of the numberless fads that made life amusing. As for Stella, she did not comment on the news at all. She was too much occupied with the diversions of the autumn season. Yet Stella was careful to impress on Michael that her new mode of life had not been dictated by any experience in Vienna.

"Don't think I'm drowning care," she wrote. "I made a damned fool of myself and luckily you're almost the only person who knows anything about it. I've wiped it out as completely as a composition I've learned and played and done with. Really I find this pottering life that mother and I lead very good for my music. I'm managing to store up a reserve of feeling. The Schumann recitals were in some ways my best efforts so far. Just now I'm absolutely mad about dancing and fencing; and as mother's life is entirely devoted to the theory of physical culture at this exact moment, we're both happy."

Michael told Alan what Stella said about dancing and fencing, and he was therefore not surprised when Alan informed him, with the air of one who really has discovered something truly worth while, that there was a Sword club at Oxford.

219

"Hadn't you better join as well next term?" he suggested. "Rather good ecker, I fancy."

"Much better than golf," said Michael.

"Oh, rather," Alan agreed, in lofty innocence of any hidden allusion to his resolve of last summer.

For the Christmas vacation Michael went to Scotland, partly because he wanted to brace himself sharply for the last two terms of his Oxford time, but more because he had the luxurious fancy to stay in some town very remote from Oxford, there meditating on her spires like gray and graceful shapes of mist made perdurable forever. Hitherto Oxford had called him back, as to a refuge most severe, from places whose warmth or sensuousness or gaiety was making her cold beauty the more desirable. Now Michael wished to come back for so nearly his ultimate visit as to a tender city of melting outlines. Therefore to fulfill this vision of return he refused Guy Hazlewood's invitation to Plashers Mead. It seemed to him that no city nearer than Aberdeen would give him the joy of charging southward in the train, back to the moist heart of England and that wan aggregation of immaterial domes and spires.

Aberdeen was spare and harsh enough even for Michael's mood, and there for nearly five weeks of northeasterly weather he worked at political economy. It was a very profitable vacation; and that superb and frozen city of granite indifferent to the howling North sent him back more ready to combat the perilous dreams which like the swathes of mist destroying with their transmutations the visible fabric of Oxford menaced his action.

Certainly it needed the physical bracing of his sojourn at Aberdeen to keep Michael from dreaming away utterly his last Lent term. February was that year a month of rains from silver skies, of rains that made Oxford melodious with their perpetual trickling. They were rains that lured him forth to dabble in their gentle fountains, to listen at the window of Ninety-nine to their rippling monody, and at night to lie awake infatuated.

Still, even with all the gutterspouts in Oxford jugging like nightingales and with temptation from every book of poetry to abandon history, Michael worked fairly steadily, and when the end of term surprised him in the middle of his industry, he looked back with astonishment at the amount of apposite reading accomplished in what seemed, now so cruelly swift were the hours, a mere week of rain.

He obtained leave to stay up during the Easter vacation, and time might have seemed to stand still, but that Spring on these rathe mornings of wind and scudded blue sky was forward with her traceries, bringing with every morning green Summer visibly nearer. The urgency of departure less than the need for redoubled diligence in acquiring knowledge obsessed Michael all this April. Sitting in the bay-window at Ninety-nine on these luminous eves of Spring, he vexed himself with the thought of disturbing so soon his books, of violating with change the peaceful confusion achieved in two terms. The fancy haunted him that for the length of the Long Vacation 99 St. Giles would drowse under the landlady's nick-nacks brought out to replace his withdrawn treasures; that nothing would keep immortal the memory of him and Alan save their photographs in frames of almost royal ostentation. Vaguely through his mind ran the notion of becoming a don, that forever he might stay here in Oxford, a contemplative intellectual cut-off from the great world. For a week the notion ripened swiftly, and Michael worked very hard in his determination to proceed from a First to the competition for a Fellowship. The notion ripened too swiftly, however, and fell with a plump, fit for nothing, when he suddenly realized he would have to stay on in Oxford alone, since of all his friends he could see not one who would be likely in the academic cloister to accompany his meditations. With a gesture of weary contempt Michael flung Stubbs into the corner, and resolved that, come what might in the History Schools, for what remained of his time at Oxford he would enjoy the proffered anodyne.

After he had disowned his work, he took to wandering rather aimlessly about the streets; but their aspect, still unfrequented as yet by the familiar figures of term-time, made him feel sad. Guy Hazlewood was summoned by telegram from where at Plashers Mead he was presumed to have found abiding peace. He came bicycling in from the Witney road at noon of a blue April day so richly canopied with rolling clouds that the unmatured season took on some of June's ampler dignity. After lunch they walked to Witham Woods, and Guy tried to persuade Michael to come to Wychford when the summer term was over. He was full of the plan for founding that lay monastery, that cloister for artists who wished between Oxford and the world a space unstressed by anything save ordered meditation. Michael was captured anew by the idea he had first propounded, and they talked gayly of its advantages, foreseeing, if the right people could be induced to come, a period of intense stimulation against a background of serenity. Then Guy began to talk of how day by day he was subduing words to rhyme and meter.

"And you, what would you do?" he asked.

At once Michael realized the futility of their scheme for him.

"I should only dream away another year," he said rather sadly, "and so if you don't mind, old chap, I think I won't join you."

"Rot!" Guy drawled. "I've got it all clear now in my mind. Up at seven. At breakfast we should take it in turns to read aloud great poetry. From eight to ten retire to our cells, and work at a set piece—a sonnet or six lines of prose. Ten to eleven a discussion on what we'd done. Eleven to one work at our own stuff. One o'clock lunch with some reading aloud. All the afternoon to do what we like. Dinner at seven with more reading aloud, and in the evening reading to ourselves. Not a word to be spoken after nine o'clock, and bed at eleven. After tea twice a week we might have academic discussions."

"It sounds perfect," said Michael, "if you're already equipped with the desire to be an artist, and what is more important if deep down in yourself you're convinced you have the least justification for ambition. But, Guy, what a curious chap you are. You seem to have grown so much younger since you went down."

Guy laughed on a note of exultation that sounded strange indeed in one whom when still at Balliol Michael had esteemed as perhaps the most perfect contemporary example of the undergraduate tired by the consciousness of his own impeccable attitude. Guy had always possessed so conspicuously that Balliol affectation of despising accentuations of seriousness, of humor, of intention, of friendship, of everything indeed except parlor rowdiness with cushions and sofas, that Michael was almost shocked to hear the elaborately wearied Guy declare boisterously:

"My dear chap, that is the great secret. The moment you go down, you do grow younger."

220

He must be in love, thought Michael suddenly; and, so remote was love seeming to him just now, he blushed in the implication by his inner self of having penetrated uninvited the secret of a friend.

Guy talked all tea-time of the project, and when they had eaten enough bread and honey, they set out for Oxford by way of Godstow. The generous sun was blanched by watery clouds. A shrewd wind had risen while they sat in the inn, and the primroses looked very wan in the shriveled twilight. Michael had Guy's company for a week of long walks and snug evenings, but the real intimacy which he had expected would be consummated by this visit never effected itself somehow. Guy was more remote in his mood of communal ambitions than he was at Oxford, living his life of whimsical detachment. After he went back to Plashers Mead, Michael only missed the sound of his voice, and was not conscious of that more violent wrench when the intercourse of silence is broken.

It happened that year St. Mark's Eve fell upon a Sunday, and Michael, having been reading the poems of Keats nearly all the afternoon, was struck by the coincidence. Oxford on such an occasion was able to provide exactly the same sensation for him as Winchester had given to the poet. Michael sat in his window-seat looking out over the broad thoroughfare of St. Giles, listening to the patter and lisp of Sabbath footfalls, to the burden of the bells; and as he sat there with the city receding in the wake of his window, he was aware more poignantly than ever of how actually in a few weeks it would recede. The bells and the footsteps were quiet for a while: the sun had gone: it was the vesper stillness of evening prayer: slowly the printed page before him faded from recognition. Already the farther corners of the room were black, revealing from time to time, as a tongue of flame leaped up in the grate, the golden blazonries of the books on the walls. It was everywhere dark when the people came out of church, and the footsteps were again audible. Michael envied Keats the power which he had known to preserve forever that St. Mark's Eve of eighty years ago in Winchester. It was exasperating that now already the footfalls were dying away, that already their sensation was evanescent, that he could not with the wand of poetry forbid time to disturb this quintessential hour of Oxford. Art alone could bewitch the present in the fashion of that enchantress in the old fairy tale who sent long ago a court to sleep.

What was the use of reading history unless the alchemy of literature had transcended the facts by the immortal presentation of them? These charters and acts of parliament, these exchequer-rolls and raked-up records meant nothing. Ivanhoe held more of the Middle Ages than all of Maitland's fitting and fussing, than all of Stubbs' ponderous conclusions. The truth of Ivanhoe, the truth of the Ingoldsby Legends, the truth of Christabel was indeed revealed to the human soul through the power of art to unlock for one convincing moment truth with the same directness of divine exposition as faith itself.

Now here was Oxford opening suddenly to him her heart, and he was incapable of preserving the vision. The truth would state itself to him, and as he tried to restate it, lo, it was gone. Perhaps these moments that seemed to demand expression were indeed mystical assurances of human immortality. Perhaps they were not revealed for explanation. After all, when Keats had wrought forever in a beautiful statement the fact of a Sabbath eve, the reader could not restate why he had wrought it forever. Art could do no more than preserve the sense of the fact: it could not resolve it in such a way that life would cease to be the baffling attempt it was on the individual's part to restate to himself his personal dreams.

Oh, this clutching at the soul by truth, how damnably instantaneous it was, how for one moment it could provoke the illusion of victory over all the muddled facts of existence: how a moment after it could leave the tantalized soul with a despairing sense of having missed by the breadth of a hair the entry into knowledge. By the way, was there not some well-reasoned psychological explanation of this physical condition?

The sensation of St. Mark's Eve was already fled. Michael forsook the chilling window-seat and went with lighted candle to search for the psychological volume which contained a really rational explanation of what he had been trying to apprehend. He fumbled among his books for a while, but he could not find the one he wanted. Then, going to pull down the blinds, he was aware of Oxford beyond the lamplit thoroughfare, with all her spires and domes invisible in the darkness, the immutable city that neither mist nor modern architects could destroy, the immortal academy whose spirit would surely outdare the menace of these reforming Huns armed with Royal Commissions, and wither the cowardly betrayers of her civilization who, even now before the barbarian was at her gates, were cringing to him with offers to sell the half of her heritage of learning. Michael, aware of Oxford all about him in the darkness, wished he could be a member of Convocation and make a flaming speech in defense of compulsory Greek. That happened to be the proposed surrender to modern conditions which at the moment was agitating his conservative passion.

"Thank heaven I live when I do," he said to himself. "If it were 2000 A.D., how much more miserable I should be."

He went down to dinner and, propping The Anatomy of Melancholy against the cruet, deplored the twentieth century, but found the chicken rather particularly good.

CHAPTER XV

THE LAST TERM

Michael meant to attend the celebration of May Morning on St. Mary's tower, but when the moment came it was so difficult to get out of bed that he was not seen in the sun's eye. This lapse of enthusiasm saddened him rather. It seemed to conjure a little cruelly the vision of speeding youth.

The last summer-term was a period of tension. Michael found that notwithstanding his vow of idleness the sight of the diligence of the other men in view of Schools impelled him also to labor feverishly. He was angry with himself for his weakness, and indeed tried once or twice to join on the river the careless parties of juniors, but it was no good. The insistent Schools forbade all pleasure, and these leafy days were spent hour after hour of them at his table. Eights Week came round, and though the college went head of the river, for Michael the achievement was merely a stroke of irony. For three years he and his friends, most of whom were now fled, had waited for this moment, had counted upon this bump-supper, had planned a hundred diversions for this happy date. Michael now must attend without the majority of them, and he went in rather a critical frame of mind, for though to be sure Tommy Grainger was drunk in honor of his glorious captaincy, it was not the bump-supper of his dreams. Victory had come too late.

Tired of the howling and the horse-play, tired of the fretful fireworks, he turned into Venner's just before ten o'clock.

"Why aren't you with your friends, making a noise?" asked Venner.

"Ought to go home and work," Michael explained.

"But surely you can take one night off. You used always to be well to the fore on these occasions."

"Don't feel like it, Venner."

"You mustn't work too hard, you know," said the old man, blinking kindly at him.

"Oh, it's not work, Venner. It's age."

"Why, what a thing to say. Hark! They're having a rare time to-night. I don't expect the dons'll say much. They expect a bit of noise after a bump-supper. Why ever don't you go out and do your share?"

Venner was ready to go home, and Michael leaving the little office in his company paused irresolutely in Cloisters for a moment. It was no good. He could not bring himself to be flung into that vortex of ululation. He turned away from its direction and walked with Venner to the lodge.

"Don't forget to mark me down as out of college, Shadbolt," he warned the porter. "I don't want to be hauled to-morrow morning for damage done in my absence."

The porter held up his hand in unctuous deprecation.

"There is no fear of my making a mistake, Mr. Fane. I was observing your egress, sir," he said pompously, "and had it registered in my book before you spoke."

Shadbolt unlocked the door for Michael and Venner to pass out into the High. Michael walked with Venner as far as St. Mary's bridge, and when the old man had said good night and departed on his way home, he stood for a while watching the tower in the May moonlight. He could hear the shouts of those doing honor to the prowess of the Eight. From time to time the sky was stained with blue and green and red from the Roman candles. To himself standing here now he seemed as remote from it all as the townsfolk loitering on the bridge in the balmy night air to listen to the fun. Already, thought Michael, he was one of the people, small as emmets, swarming at the base of this slim and lovely tower. He regretted sharply now that he had not once more, even from distant St. Giles, roused himself to salute from the throbbing summit May Morning. It was melancholy to stand here within the rumor of the communal joy, but outside its participation; and presently he started to walk quickly back to his digs, telling himself with dreadful warning as he went that before Schools now remained scarcely more than a week.

Alan was in a condition of much greater anxiety even than Michael. Michael had nothing much beyond a moral pact with the college authorities to make him covet a good class: to Alan it was more important, especially as he had given up the Sudan and was intending to try for the Home Civil Service.

"However, I've given up thinking of a First, and if I can squeeze a Second, I shall be jolly grateful," he told Michael.

The day of Schools arrived. The Chief Examiner had caused word to be sent round that he would insist on the rigor of the law about black clothes. So that year many people went back to the earlier mode of the university examination and appeared in evening-dress. The first four days went by with their monotony of scratching pens, their perspiring and bedraggled women-candidates, their tedious energy and denial of tobacco. Alan grew gloomier and gloomier. He scarcely thought he had even escaped being plowed outright. For the fourth night preparatory to the two papers on his Special Subject, Michael ordered iced asparagus and quails in aspic, a bottle of champagne and two quarts of cold black coffee. He sat up all night, and went down tight-eyed and pale-faced to the final encounter. In the afternoon he emerged, thanked heaven it was all over, and, instead of celebrating his release as he had intended with wine and song, slept in an armchair through the benign June evening. Alan, who had gone to bed at his usual hour the night before, spent his time reading the credentials of various careers offered to enterprising young men by the Colonies. The day after, however, nothing seemed to matter except that the purgatorial business was done forever, and that Oxford offered nearly a fortnight of impregnable idleness.

This fortnight, when she was so prodigal with her beauty and when her graciousness was a rich balm to the ordeal she had lately exacted, was not so poignant as Michael had expected. Indeed, it was scarcely poignant at all so far as human farewells went, though there was about it such an underlying sadness as deepens the mellow peace of a fine autumn day.

It seemed to Michael that in after years he would always think of Oxford dowered so with Summer, and brooding among her trees. Matthew Arnold had said she did not need June for beauty's heightening. That was true. Her beauty was not heightened now, but it was displayed with all the grave consciousness of an unassertive renown. Michael dreaded more the loss of this infoliated calm than of any of the people who were enjoying its amenity. There were indeed groups upon the lawns that next year would not form themselves, that forever indeed would be irremediably dispersed; but the thought of himself and other members scattered did not move him with as much regret as the knowledge that next year himself would have lost the assurance that he was an organic part of this tutelary landscape. The society of his contemporaries was already broken up: the end of the third year had effected that. This farewell to Oxford herself was harder, and Michael wished that from the very first moment of his arrival he had concentrated upon the object of a Fellowship. Such a life would have suited him well. He would not have withered like so many dons: he would each year have renewed his youth in the stream of freshmen. He would have been sympathetic, receptive, and worldly enough not to be despised by each generation in its course. Now, since he had not aimed at such a career, he must go. The weather opulently fine mocked his exit.

Michael and Alan had decided to stay up for Commemoration. Stella and Mrs. Fane had been invited: Lonsdale and Wedderburn were coming up: Maurice was bringing his mother and sisters. For a brief carnival they would all be reunited, and rooms would be echoing to the voices of their rightful owners. Yet after all it would be but a pretense of reviving their merry society. It was not a genuine reunion this, that was requiring women to justify it. Oxford, as Michael esteemed her, was already out of his reach. She would be symbolized in the future by these rooms at 99 St. Giles, and Michael made up his mind that no intrusion of women should spoil for him their monastic associations. He would stay here until the last day, and for Commemoration he would try to borrow his old rooms in college, thus fading from this wide thoroughfare without a formal leave-taking. He would drop astern from the bay-window whence for a time he had watched the wrack and spume of the world drifting toward the horizon in its wake. Himself would recede so with the world, and without him the bay-window would hold a tranquil course, unrocked by the loss or gain of him or the transient voyagers of each new generation. Very few eves and sunsets were still his to enjoy from this window-seat. Already the books were being stacked in preparation for their removal to the studio at 173 Cheyne Walk. Dusty and derelict belongings of him and Alan were already strewn about the landings outside their bedrooms. Even the golf-bag of Alan's first term, woolly now with the accumulated mildew of neglect, had been dragged from its obscurity. Perhaps it would be impossible to drop astern as imperceptibly as he would have liked. Too many reminders of departure littered the rooms with their foreboding of finality.

"I'm shore I for one am quite sorry you're going," said the landlady. "I never wish to have a nicer norer quieter pair of gentlemen. It's to be hoped, I'm shore, that next term's comings-ins from St. John's will be half as nice. Yerse, I shall be very pleased to have these coverlets—I suppose you would call them coverlets—and you're leaving the shelves in the dining-room? Yerse, I'm shore they'll be as handy as anything for the cruets and what not. And so you're going to have a dinner here to eleven gentlemen—oh, eleven in all, yerse, I see."

It was going to be rather difficult, Michael thought, to find exactly the ten people he wished to invite to this last terminal dinner. Alan, Grainger, and Castleton, of course. Bill Mowbray and Vernon Townsend. And Smithers. Certainly, he would ask Smithers. And why not George Appleby, who was Librarian of the Union this term, and no longer conceivable as that lackadaisical red rag which had fluttered Lonsdale to fury? What about the Dean? And if the Dean, why not Harbottle, his History tutor? And for the tenth place? It was really impossible to choose from the dozen or so acquaintances who had an equal claim upon it. He would leave the tenth place vacant, and just to amuse his own fancy he would fill it with the ghost of himself in the December of his first term.

Michael, when he saw his guests gathered in the sea-green dining-room of 99 St. Giles, knew that this last terminal dinner was an anachronism. After all, the prime and bloom of these eclectic entertainments had been in the two previous years. This was not the intimate and unusual society he had designed to gather round him as representative of his four years at the Varsity. This was merely representative of the tragical incompleteness of Oxford. It was certainly a very urbane evening, but it was somehow not particularly distinctive of Oxford, still less of Michael's existence there. Perhaps it had been a mistake to invite the two dons. Perhaps everyone was tired under the strain of Schools. Michael was glad when the guests went and he sat alone in the window-seat with Alan.

"To-morrow, my mother and Stella are coming up," he reminded Alan. "It's rather curious my mother shouldn't have been up all the time, until I'm really down."

"Is that man Avery coming up?" Alan asked.

Michael nodded.

"I suppose your people see a good deal of him now he's in town," said Alan, trying to look indifferent to the answer.

"Less than before he went," said Michael. "Stella's rather off studios and the Vie de Bohême."

"Oh, he has a studio?"

"Didn't you know?"

"I don't take very much interest in his movements," Alan loftily explained.

They smoked on for a while without speaking.

"I must go to bed," announced Alan at last.

"Not yet, not yet," Michael urged him. "I don't think you've quite realized that this is our last night in Ninety-nine."

"I've settled to stay on here during Commem Week," said Alan. "Your people are staying at the Randolph?"

Michael nodded, wondering to himself if it were possible that Alan could really have been so far-sighted as to stay on in St. Giles for the sake of having the most obvious right to escort his mother and Stella home. "But why aren't you going into college?" he asked.

"Oh, I thought it would be rather a fag moving in for so short a time. Besides, it's been rather ripping in these digs."

Michael looked at him gratefully. He had himself feared to voice his appreciation of this last year with Alan: he was feeling sentimental enough to dread on Alan's side a grudging assent to his enthusiasm.

"Yes, it has been awfully ripping," he agreed.

"I should like to have had another year," sighed Alan. "I think I was just beginning to get a dim sort of a notion of philosophy. I wonder how much of it is really applicable?"

"To what? To God?" asked Michael.

"No, the world—the world we live in."

"I don't fancy, you know," said Michael, "that the intellectual part of Oxford is directly applicable to the world at all. What I mean to say is, that I think it can only be applied to the world through our behavior."

"Well, of course," said Alan, "that's a truism."

Michael was rather disconcerted. The thought in his mind had seemed more worthy of expression.

"But the point is," Alan went on, "whether our philosophic education, our mental training has any effect on our behavior. It seems to me that Oxford is just as typically Oxford whatever a man reads."

"That wasn't the case at school," said Michael. "I'm positive for instance the Modern side was definitely inferior to the Classical side—in manners and everything else. And though at Oxford other circumstances interfere to make the contrast less violent, it doesn't seem to me one gains the quintessence of the university unless one reads Greats. Even History only supplies that in the case of men exceptionally sensitive to the spirit of place. I mean to say sensitive in such a way that Oxford, quite apart from dons and undergraduates, can herself educate. I'm tremendously anxious now that Oxford should become more democratic, but I'm equally anxious that, in proportion as she offers more willingly the shelter of her learning to the people, the learning she bestows shall be more than ever rigidly unpractical, as they say."

"So you really think philosophy is directly applicable?" said Alan.

"How Socratic you are," Michael laughed. "Perhaps the Rhodes Scholars will answer your question. I remember reading somewhere lately that it was confidently anticipated the advent of the Rhodes Scholars would transform a provincial university into an imperial one. That may have been written by a Cambridge man bitterly aware of his own provincial university. Yet a moment's reflection should have taught him that provincialism in academic matters is possibly an advantage. Florence and Athens were provincial. Rome and London and Oxford are metropolitan—much more dangerously exposed to the metropolitan snares of superficiality and of submerged personality with the corollary of vulgar display. Neither Rome nor London nor Oxford has produced her own poets. They have always been sung by the envious but happy provincials. Rome and London would have treated Shelley just as Oxford did. Cambridge would have disapproved of him, but a bourgeois dread of interference would have let him alone. As for an imperial university, the idea is ghastly. I figure something like the Imperial Institute filled with Colonials eating pemmican. The Eucalyptic Vision, it might be called."

"And you'd make a distinction between imperial and metropolitan?" Alan asked.

"Good gracious, yes. Wouldn't you distinguish between New York and London? Imperialism is the worst qualities of the provinces gathered up and exhibited to the world in the worst way. A metropolis takes provincialism and skims the cream. It is a disintegrating, but for itself a civilizing, force. A metropolis doesn't encourage creative art by metropolitans. It ought to be engaged all the time in trying to make the provincials appreciate what they themselves are doing."

"I think you're probably talking a good deal of rot," said Alan severely. "And we seem to have gone a long way from my question."

"About the application of philosophy?"

Alan nodded.

"Dear man, as were I a Cantabrian provincial, I should say. Dear man! Doesn't it make you shiver? It's like the 'Pleased to meet you,' of Americans and Tootingians. It's so terribly and intrusively personal. So informative and unrestrained, so gushing and——"

"I wish you'd answer my question," Alan grumbled, "and call me what you like without talking about it."

"Now I've forgotten my answer," said Michael. "And it was a wonderful answer. Oh, I remember now. Of course, your philosophy is applicable to the world. You coming from a metropolitan university will try to infect the world with your syllogisms. You will meet Cambridge men much better educated than yourself, but all of them incompetent to appreciate their own education. You will gently banter them, trying to allay their provincial suspicion of your easy manner. You will——"

"*You* will simply not be serious," said Alan. "And so I shall go to bed."

"My dear chap, I'm only talking like this because if I were serious, I couldn't bear to think that to-night is almost the end of our fourth year. It is, in fact, the end of 99 St. Giles."

"Well, it isn't as if we were never going to see each other again," said Alan awkwardly.

"But it is," said Michael. "Don't you realize, even with all your researches into philosophy, that after to-night we shall only see each other in dreams? After to-night we shall never again have identical interests and obligations."

"Well, anyway, I'm going to bed," said Alan, and with a good-night very typical in its curtness of many earlier ones uttered in similar accents, he went upstairs.

Michael, when he found himself alone, thought it wiser to follow him. It was melancholy to watch the moon above the empty thoroughfare, and to hear the bells echoing through the spaces of the city.

CHAPTER XVI

THE LAST WEEK

Michael's old rooms in college were lent to him for three or four days as he had hoped they would be. The present occupant, a freshman, was not staying up for Commemoration, and though next term he would move into larger rooms for his second year, his effects had not yet been transferred. Michael found it interesting to deduce from the evidence of his books and pictures the character of the owner with whom he had merely a nodding acquaintance. On the whole, he seemed to be a dull young man. The photographs of his relatives were dull: his books were dull and unkempt: his pictures were dull, narrative rather than decorative. Probably there was nothing in the room that was strictly individual, nothing that he had acquired to satisfy his own taste. Every picture had probably been brought to Oxford because its absence would not be noticed in whatever spare bedroom it had previously been hung. Every book seemed either a survival of school or the inexpensive pastime of a railway journey. The very clock on the mantelpiece, which was still drearily ticking, looked like the first prize of a consolation race, rather than the gratification of a personal choice. Michael reproached the young man for being able to spend three terms a year without an attempt to garnish decently the gothic bookshelves, without an effort to leave upon this temporary abode the impression of his lodging. He almost endowed the room itself with a capacity for criticism, feeling it must deplore three terms of such undistinguished company. Yet, after all, he had left nothing to tell of his sojourn here. Although he and the dull young freshman had both used this creaking wicker-chair, for their successors neither of them could preserve the indication of their precedence. One relic of his own occupation, however, he did find in the fragments of envelopes which he had stuck to the door on innumerable occasions to announce the time of his return. These bits of paper that straggled in a kite's tail over the oak door had evidently resisted all attempts to scrub them off. There were usually a few on every door in college, but no one had ever so extensively advertised his movements as Michael, and to see these obstinate bits of tabs gave him a real pleasure, as if they assured him of his former existence here. Each one had marked an ubiquitous hour that was recorded more indelibly than many other occasions of higher importance.

There was not, however, much time for sentimentalizing over the past, as somewhere before one o'clock his mother and Stella would arrive, and they must be met. Alan came with him to the railway station, and it was delightful to see Wedderburn with them, and in another part of the train Maurice with his mother and sisters. They must all have lunch at the Randolph, said Wedderburn immediately. Mrs. Fane was surprised to find the Randolph such a large hotel, and told Michael that if she had known it were possible to be at all comfortable in Oxford, she would have come up to see him long before. In the middle of lunch Lonsdale appeared, having according to his own account traced Michael's movements with tremendous determination. He was introduced to Mrs. Fane, who evidently took a fancy to him. She was looking, Michael thought, most absurdly young as Lonsdale rattled away to her, himself quite unchanged by a year at Scoone's and a recent failure to enter the Foreign Office.

"I say, this is awfully sporting of you, Mrs. Fane. You know, one feels fearfully out of it, coming up like this. Terribly old, and all that. I've been mugging away for the Diplomatic and I've just made an awful ass of myself. So I thought I wouldn't ask my governor to come up. He's choking himself to pieces over my career at present, but I've had an awfully decent offer from a man I know who runs a motor business, and I don't think I've got the ambassadorial manner, do you? I think I shall be much better at selling cars, don't you? I say, which balls are you going to? Because I must buzz round and see about tickets."

Lonsdale's last question seemed to demand an answer, and Mrs. Fane looked at Michael rather anxiously.

"Michael, what balls are we going to?" she inquired.

"Trinity, the House, and the Apollo," he told her.

"What house is that? and I don't think I ever heard of Apollo College. It sounds very attractive. Have I said something foolish?" Mrs. Fane looked round her, for everyone was laughing.

"The House is Christ Church, mother," said Michael, and then swiftly he remembered his father might have made that name familiar to her. If he had, she gave no sign; and Michael blushing fiercely, went on quickly to explain that the Apollo was the name of the Masonic Lodge of the university. Stella and Mrs. Fane rested that afternoon, and Michael with Wedderburn, Lonsdale, and several other contemporaries spent a jolly time in St. Mary's, walking round and reviving the memories of former rags. Alan had suggested that, as he would be near the Randolph, he might as well call in and escort Mrs. Fane and Stella down to tea in Michael's rooms. Mrs. Avery with Blanche and Eileen Avery had also been invited, and there was very little space left for teacups. Wedderburn, however, assisted by Porcher on whom alone of these familiar people time had not laid a visible finger, managed to make everybody think they had enjoyed their tea. Afterward there was a general move to the river for a short time, but as Lonsdale said, it must be for a very short time in order that everyone might be in good form for the Trinity ball. Mrs. Fane thought she would like to stay with Michael and talk to him for a while. It was strange to see her sitting here in his old room, and to be in a way more sharply aware of her than he had ever been, as he watched her fanning herself and looking round at the furniture, while the echoes of laughter and talk died away down the stone staircase without.

"Dear Michael," she said. "I wish I'd seen this room when you lived in it properly."

He laughed.

"When I lived in it properly," he answered, "I should have been made so shy by your visit that I think you'd have hated me and the room."

"You must have been so domestic," said his mother. "Such a curious thing has happened."

"Apropos of what?" asked Michael, smiling.

"You know Dick Prescott left Stella all his money, well——"

"But, mother, I didn't know anything about it."

"It was rather vague. He left it first to some old lady whom he intended to live four or five years, but she died this week, and so Stella inherits it at once. About two thousand a year. It's all in land, and will have to be managed. Huntingdonshire, or some country nobody believes in. It's all very difficult. She must marry at once."

"But, mother, why because she is to be better off and own land in Huntingdonshire, is she to marry at once?" asked Michael.

"To avoid fortune-hunters, odd foreign counts, and people."

"But she's not twenty-one yet," he objected.

"My dearest boy, I know, I know. That's why she must marry. Don't you see, when she's of age, she'll be able to marry whom she likes, and you know how headstrong Stella is."

"Mother," said Michael suddenly, "supposing she married Alan?"

"Delightful boy," she commented.

"You mean he's too young?"

"For the present, yes."

"But you wouldn't try to stop an engagement, would you?" he asked very earnestly.

"My dearest Michael, if two young people I were fond of fell in love, I should be the last person to try to interfere," Mrs. Fane promised.

"Well, don't say anything to Alan about Stella having more money. I think he might be sensitive about it."

"Darling Stella!" she sighed. "So intoxicated with poverty—the notion of it, I mean."

"Mother," said Michael suddenly and nervously, "you know, don't you, that the day after to-morrow is the House ball—the Christ Church ball?"

"Where your father was?" she said gently, pondering the past.

He nodded.

"I'll show you his old rooms," Michael promised.

"Darling boy," she murmured, putting out her hand. He held it very tightly for a moment.

Next day after the Trinity ball Alan, who was very cheerful, told Michael he thought it would be good sport to invite everybody to tea at 99 St. Giles.

"Oh, I particularly didn't want that to happen," said Michael, taken aback.

Alan was puzzled to know his reason.

"You'll probably think me absurd," said Michael. "But I rather wanted to keep Ninety-nine for a place that I could remember as more than all others the very heart of Oxford, the most intimate expression of all I have cared for up here."

"Well, so you can, still," said Alan severely. "My asking a few people there to tea won't stop you."

"All the same, I wish you wouldn't," Michael persisted. "I moved into college for Commem just to avoid taking anybody to St. Giles."

"Not even Stella?" demanded Alan.

Michael shook his head.

"Well, of course, if you don't want me to, I won't," said Alan grudgingly. "But I think you're rather ridiculous."

"I am, I know," Michael agreed. "But thanks for honoring me. Do you think Stella has altered much since she was in Vienna, and during this year in town?"

"Not a bit," Alan declared enthusiastically. "And yet in one way she has," he corrected himself. "She seems less out of one's reach."

"Or else you know better how to stretch," Michael laughed.

"Oh, I wasn't thinking of her attitude to me," said Alan a little stiffly.

"Most generalizations come down to a particular fact," Michael answered. But he would not tease Alan too much because he really wished him to have confidence.

After the Trinity ball it seemed to Michael now not very rash to sound Stella about her point of view with regard to Alan. For this purpose he invited her to come in a canoe with him on the Cher. Yet when together they were gliding down the green tunnels of the stream, when all the warmth of June was at their service, when neither question nor answer could have cast on either more than a momentary shadow, Michael could not bring himself to approach the subject even indirectly. They discussed lazily the success of the Trinity ball, without reference to the fact that Stella had danced three-quarters of her program with Alan. She did not even bother to say he was a good dancer, so much was the convention of indifference demanded by the brother and sister in their progress along this fronded stream.

That night in the Town Hall Michael did not dance a great deal himself at the Masonic ball. He sat with Lonsdale in the gallery, and together they much diverted themselves with the costumes of the Freemasons. It was really ridiculous to see Wedderburn in a red cloak and inconvenient sword dancing the Templars quadrille.

"I think the English are curious people," said Michael. "How absurd that all these undergraduates should belong to an Apollo Lodge and wear these aprons and dress up like this! Look at Wedders!"

"Enter Second Ruffian, what?" Lonsdale chuckled.

"I suppose it does take the place of religion," Michael ejaculated, in a tone of bewilderment. "Can you see my sister and Alan Merivale anywhere?" he added casually.

"When's that coming off?" asked Lonsdale. He had taken to an eyeglass since he had been in London, and the enhanced eye glittered very wisely at Michael.

"You think?"

"What? Rather! My dear old bird, I'll lay a hundred to thirty. Look at them now."

"They're only dancing," said Michael.

"But what dancing! Beautiful action. I never saw a pair go down so sweetly to the gate. By the way, what are you going to do now you're down?"

Michael shrugged his shoulders.

"I suppose you wouldn't like to come into the motor business?"

"No, thanks very much," said Michael.

"Well, you must do something, you know," said Lonsdale, letting fall his eyeglass in disapproval. "You'll find that out in town."

Michael was engaged for the next dance to one of Maurice's sisters. Amid the whirl of frocks, as he swung round this pretty and insipid creature in pink crêpe-de-chine, he was dreadfully aware that neither his nor her conversation mattered at all, and that valuable time was being robbed from him to the strains of the Choristers waltz. Really he would have preferred to leave Oxford in a manner more solemn than this, not tangled up with frills and misses and obvious music. Looking down at Blanche Avery, he almost hated her. And to-morrow there would be another ball. He must dance with her again, with her and with her sister and with a dozen more dolls like her.

Next morning, or rather next noon, for it was noon before people woke after these balls that were not over until four o'clock, Michael looked out of his bedroom window with a sudden dismay at the great elms of the deer park, deep-bosomed, verdurous, entranced beneath the June sky.

"This is the last whole day," he said, "the last day when I shall have a night at the end of it; and it's going to be absolutely wasted at a picnic with all these women."

Michael scarcely knew how to tolerate that picnic, and wondered resentfully why everybody else seemed to enjoy it so much.

"Delicious life," said his mother, as he punted her away from the tinkling crowd on the bank. "I'm not surprised you like Oxford, dear Michael."

"I like it—I liked it, I mean, very much more when it was altogether different from this sort of thing. The great point of Oxford—in fact, the whole point of Oxford—is that there are no girls."

"How charmingly savage you are, dear boy," said his mother. "And how absurd to pretend you don't care for girls."

"But I don't," he asserted. "In Oxford I actually dislike them very much. They're out of place except in Banbury Road. Dons should never have been allowed to marry. Really, mother, women in Oxford are wrong."

"Of course, I can't argue with you. But there seem to me to be a great many of them."

"Great scott, you don't think it's like this in term-time, do you?"

"Isn't it?" said Mrs. Fane, apparently very much surprised. "I thought undergraduates were so famously susceptible. I'm sure they are, too."

"Do you mean to say you really thought this Commem herd was always roaming about Oxford?"

"Michael, your Oxford expressions are utterly unintelligible to me."

"Don't you realize you are up here for Commem—for Commemoration?" he asked.

"How wonderful!" she said. "Don't tell me any more. It's so romantic, to be told one is 'up' for something."

Michael began to laugh, and the irritation of seeing the peaceful banks of the upper river dappled with feminine forms, so that everywhere the cattle had moved away to browse in the remote corners of the meadows, vanished.

The ball at Christ Church seemed likely to be the most successful and to be the one that would remain longest in the memories of those who had taken part in this Commemoration. Nowhere could an arbiter of pleasure have found so perfect a site for his most elaborate entertainment. There was something very strangely romantic in this gay assembly dancing in the great hall of the House, so that along the cloisters sounded the unfamiliar noise of fiddles; but what gave principally the quality of romance and strangeness was that beyond the music, beyond the fantastically brilliant hall, stretched all around the dark quadrangles deserted now save where about their glooms dresses indeterminate as moths were here and there visible. The decrescent moon would scarcely survive the dawn, and meanwhile there would be darkness everywhere away from the golden heart of the dance in that great hall spinning with light and motion.

Alan was evidently pleased that he was being able to show Stella his own college. He wore about him an air of confidence that Michael did not remember to have seen so plainly marked before. He and Stella were dancing together all the time here at Christ Church, and Michael felt he, too, must dance vigorously, so that he should not find himself overlooking them. He was shy somehow of overlooking them, and when Blanche Avery and Eileen Avery and half a dozen more cousins and sisters of friends had been led back to their chaperones, Michael went over to his mother and invited her to walk with him in the quadrangles of Christ Church. She knew why he wanted her to walk with him, and as she took his arm gently, she pressed it to her side. He thought again how ridiculously young she seemed and how the lightness of her touch was no less than that of the ethereal Eileen or the filmy Blanche. He wished he had asked her to dance with him, but yet on second thoughts was glad he had not, since to walk with her thus along these dark cloisters, down which traveled fainter and fainter the fiddles of the Eton Boating Song, was even better than dancing. Soon they were in Peckwater, standing silent on the gravel, almost overweighted by that heavy Georgian quadrangle.

"He lived either on that staircase or that one," said Michael. "But all the staircases and all the rooms in Peck are just the same, and all the men who have lived in them for the past fifty years are just the same. The House is a wonderful place, and the type it displays best changes less easily than any other."

"I didn't know him when he lived here," she murmured.

With her hand still resting lightly upon his sleeve, Michael felt the palpitation of long-stored-up memories and emotions. As she stood here pensive in the darkness, the years were rolling back.

"I expect if he were alive," she went on softly, "he would wonder how time could have gone by so quickly since he was here. People always do, don't they, when they revisit places they've known in younger days? When he was here, I must have been about fifteen. Funny, severe, narrow-minded old father!"

Michael waited rather anxiously. She had never yet spoken of her life before she met his father, and he had never brought himself to ask her.

"Funny old man! He was at Cambridge—Trinity College, I think it was called."

Then she was silent for a while, and Michael knew that she was linking her father and his father in past events; but still she did not voice her thoughts, and whatever joys or miseries of that bygone time were being recalled were still wrapped up in her reserve: nor did Michael feel justified in trying to persuade her to unloose them, even here in this majestic enclosure that would have engulfed them all as soon as they were free.

"You're not cold?" he tenderly demanded.

Surely upon his arm she had shivered.

"No, but I think we'll go back to the ballroom," she sighed.

Michael felt awed when their feet grated again in movement over the gravel. Behind them in the quadrangle there were ghosts, and the noise of walking here seemed sacrilegious upon this moonless and heavy summer night. Presently, however, two couples came laughing into the lamplight at the corner. The sense of decorous creeds outraged by his mother's behavior of long ago vanished in the relief that present youth gave with its laughing company and fashionable frocks. Beside such heedlessness it were vain to conjure too remorsefully the past. After all, Peckwater was a place in which young men should crack whips and shout to one another across window-boxes; here there should be no tombs. Michael and his mother went on their way to the hall, and soon the music of the waltzing filled magically the lamplit entries of the great college, luring them to come back with light hearts, so importunate was the gaiety.

Michael rather reproached himself afterward for not trying to take advantage of his mother's inclination to yield him a more extensive confidence. He was sure Stella would not have allowed the opportunity to slip by so in a craven embarrassment; or was it rather a fine sensitiveness, an imaginative desire to let the whole of that history lie buried in whatever poor shroud romance could lend it? As he was thinking of Stella, herself came toward him over the shining floor of the ballroom emptied for the interval between two dances. How delicately flushed she was and how her gray eyes were lustered with joy of the evening, or perhaps with fortunate tidings. Michael was struck by the direct way in which she was coming toward him without bothering through self-consciousness to seem to find him unexpectedly.

"Come for a walk with me in the moonlight," she said, taking his arm.

"There's no moon yet, but I'll take you for a walk."

The clock was striking two, as they reached Tom quad, and the decrescent moon to contradict him was already above the roofs. They strolled over to the fountain and stood there captured by loveliness, silent themselves and listening to the talk and laughter of shimmering figures that reached them subdued and intermittent from the flagged terraces in the distance.

"I suppose," said Stella suddenly, "you're very fond of Alan?"

"Rather, of course I am."

"So am I."

Then she blushed, and her cheeks were very crimson in the moonlight. Michael had never seen her blush like this, had never been aware before of her maidenhood that now flooded his consciousness like a bouquet of roses. Hitherto she had always been for Michael a figure untouched by human weakness. Even when last summer he had seen her break down disconsolate, he had been less shocked by her grief than by its incongruity in her. This blush gave to him his only sister as a woman.

"The trouble with Alan is that he thinks he can't marry me because I have money, whereas he will be dependent on what he earns. That's rubbish, isn't it?"

"Of course," he agreed warmly. "I'll tell him so, if you like."

"I don't think he'd pay much attention," she said. "But you know, poor old Prescott left me a lot of land."

Michael nodded.

"Well, it's got to be managed, hasn't it?"

"Of course," said Michael. "You'll want a land agent."

"Why not Alan?" she asked. "I don't want to marry somebody in the Home Civil Service. I want him to be with me all day. Wouldn't you?"

"You've not told mother?" Michael suggested cautiously.

"Not yet. I shall be twenty-one almost at once, you know."

"What's that got to do with it?"

He was determined that in Stella's behavior there should be no reflection, however pale, of what long ago had come into the life of an undergraduate going down from Christ Church. He wished for Stella and Alan to have all the benisons of the world. "You've no right to assume that mother will object," he told her.

But Stella did not begin to speak, as she was used, of her determination to have her own way in spite of everybody. She was a softer Stella to-night; and that alone showed to Michael how right he had been to wish with all his heart that she would fall in love with Alan.

"There he is!" she cried, clapping her hands.

Michael looked up, and saw him coming across the great moonlit space, tall and fair and flushed as he should be coming like this to claim Stella. Michael punched Alan to express his pleasure, and then he quickly left them standing by the fountain close together.

CHAPTER XVII

THE LAST DAY

At sunrise when the stones of Oxford were the color of lavender, a photograph was taken of those who had been dancing at the Christ Church ball; after which, their gaiety recorded, the revelers went home. Michael was relieved when Alan offered to drive his mother and Stella back to the Randolph. He was not wishing for company that morning, but rather to walk slowly down to college alone. He waited, therefore, to see the dancers disappear group by group round various corners, until the High was desolate and he was the only human figure under this virginal sky. In his bedroom clear and still and sweet with morning light he did not want to go to bed. The birds fluttering on the lawns, the sun sparkling with undeterrent rays of gold not yet high and fierce, and all the buildings of the college dreaming upon the bosom of this temperate morn made him too vigilant for beauty. It would be wrong to sleep away this Oxford morning. With deliberate enjoyment he changed from ruffled evening dress into flannels.

In the sitting-room Michael looked idly through the books, and glanced with dissatisfaction at the desquamating backs of the magazines. There was nothing here fit to occupy his attention at such a peerless hour. Yet he still lingered by the books. Habit was strong enough to make him feel it necessary at least to pretend to read during the hours before breakfast. Finally in desperation he pulled out one of the magazines, and as he did so a small volume bound in paper fell onto the floor. It was Manon Lescaut, and Michael was pleased that the opportunity was given to him of reading a book he had for a long time meant to read. Moreover, if it were disappointing, this edition was so small that it would fit easily into his pocket and be no bother to carry. He wondered rather how Manon Lescaut had come into this bookshelf, and he opened it at an aquatint of ladies deject and lightly clothed—*c'est une douzaine de filles de joie*, said the inscription beneath. Here, Michael feared, was the explanation of how the Abbé Prévost found himself squeezed away between Pearson's and The Strand. Here at last was evidence in these rooms of a personal choice. Here spoke, if somewhat ignobly, the character of the purchaser. Michael slipped the small volume into his pocket and went out.

The great lawns in front of New Quad stretched for his solitary pleasure in the golden emptiness of morn. At such an hour it were vain to repine; so supreme was beauty like this that Michael's own departure from Oxford appeared to him as unimportant as the fall of a petal unshaken by any breath of summer wind. With the air brimming to his draught and with early bees restless along the herbaceous border by the stream's parapet, Michael began to read Manon Lescaut. He would finish this small volume before breakfast, unless the fumes of the sun should drug him out of all power to award the Abbé his fast attention. The great artist was stronger than the weather, and Michael read on while the sun climbed the sky, while the noises of a new day began, while the footsteps of hurrying scouts went to and fro.

It was half-past eight when he finished that tale of love. For a few moments he sat dazed, visualizing that dreadful waste near New Orleans where in the sand it was so easy for the star-crossed Chevalier to bury the idol of his heart.

Porcher was surprised to find Michael up and wide awake.

"You oughtn't to have gone and tired yourself like that, sir," he said reproachfully.

Michael rather resented putting back the little book among those magazines. He felt it would be almost justifiable to deprive the owner of what he so evidently did not esteem, and he wondered if, when he had cut the pages with his prurient paper-knife the purchaser had wished at the end of this most austere tale that he had not spent his money so barrenly. *C'est une douzaine de filles de joie.* It was a bitter commentary on human nature, that a mere aquatint of these poor naked creatures jolting to exile in their tumbril should extort half a crown from an English undergraduate to probe their history.

"Dirty-minded little beast," said Michael, as he confiscated the edition of Manon Lescaut, placing it in his suitcase. Then he went out into St. Mary's Walks, and at the end of the longest vista sat down on a garden-bench beside the Cherwell. Before him stretched the verdurous way down which he had come; beyond, taking shape among the elms, was the college; to right and left were vivid meadows where the cattle were scarcely moving, so lush was the pasturage here; and at his side ran the slow, the serpentine, the tree-green tranquil Cher.

As he sat here among the bowers of St. Mary's, the story he had just read came back to him with a double poignancy. He scarcely thought that any tale of love could purify so sharply every emotion but that of pity too profound for words. He wondered if his father had loved with such a devotion of self-destruction as had inspired des Grieux. It was strange himself should have been so greatly moved by a story of love at the moment when he was making ready to enter the world. He had not thought of love during all the time he had been up at Oxford. Now he went back in memory to the days when Lily had the power to shake his soul, even as the soul of des Grieux had been shaken in that inn-yard of Amiens, when coming by the coach from Arras he first beheld Manon. How trivial had been Lily's infidelity compared with Manon's: how shallow had been his own devotion beside the Chevalier's. But the love of des Grieux for Manon was beyond the love of ordinary youth. The Abbé by his art had transmuted a wild infatuation, a foolish passion for a wanton into something above even the chivalry of the noblest lover of the Middle Ages. It was beyond all tears, this tale; and the dry grief it now exacted gave to Michael in some inexplicable way a knowledge of life more truly than any book since Don Quixote. It was an academic tale, too: it was told within the narrowest confines of the most rigid form. There was not in this narrative one illegitimate device to excite an easy compassion in the reader: it was literature of a quality marmoreal, and it moved as only stone can move. The death of Manon in the wilderness haunted him even as he sat here: almost he too could have prostrated himself in humiliation before this tragedy.

"There is no story like it," said Michael to the sleek river. *N'exigez point de moi que je vous décrive mes sentiments, ni que je vous rapporte mes dernières expressions.* And it was bought by an undergraduate for half a crown because he wanted to stare like the peasant-folk. *C'est une douzaine de filles de joie.* How really promising that illustration must have looked: how the coin must have itched in his pocket: how carefully he must have weighed the slimness of the book against his modesty: how easy it had been to conceal behind those magazines.

But he could not sit here any longer reconstructing the shamefaced curiosity of a dull young freshman, nor even, with so much to arrange this last morning, could he continue to brood upon the woes of the Chevalier des Grieux and Manon Lescaut. It was time to go and rouse Lonsdale. Lonsdale had slept long enough in those ground-floor rooms of his where on the first day of the first term the inextricable Porcher had arranged his wine. It did not take long to drag Lonsdale out of bed.

"You slack devil, I've not been to bed at all," said Michael.

"More silly ass you," Lonsdale yawned. "Now don't annoy me while I'm dressing with your impressions of the sunrise." Michael watched him eat his breakfast, while he slowly and with the troublesome aid of his eyeglass managed to focus once again the world.

"I was going to tell you something deuced interesting about myself when you buzzed off this morning. You've heard of Queenie Molyneux—well, Queenie ..."

"Wait a bit," Michael interrupted. "I haven't heard of Queenie Molyneux."

"Why, she's in the Pink Quartette."

Michael still looked blank, and Lonsdale adjusting his eyeglass looked at him in amazement.

"The Pink Quartette in My Mistake."

"Oh, that rotten musical comedy," said Michael. "I haven't seen it."

Lonsdale shook his head in despair, and the monocle tinkled down upon his plate. When he had wiped it clean of marmalade, he asked Michael in a compassionate voice if he *never* went to the theater, and with a sigh returned to the subject of Queenie.

"It's the most extraordinary piece of luck. A girl that everyone in town has been running after falls in love with me. Now the question is, what ought I to do? I can't afford to keep her, and I'm not cad enough to let somebody else keep her, and use the third latchkey. My dear old chap, I don't mind telling you I'm in the deuce of a fix."

"Are you very much in love with her?" Michael asked.

"Of course I am. You don't get Queenies chucked at your head like turnips. Of course I'm frightfully keen."

"Why don't you marry her?" Michael asked.

"What? Marry her? You don't seem to understand who I'm talking about. Queenie Molyneux! She's in the Pink Quartette in My Mistake."

"Well?"

"Well, I can't marry a chorus-girl."

"Other people have," said Michael.

"Well, yes, but—er—you know, Queenie has rather a reputation. I shouldn't be the first."

"The problem's too hard for me," said Michael.

In his heart he would have liked to push Manon Lescaut into Lonsdale's hands and bid him read that for counsel. But he could not help laughing to himself at the notion of Lonsdale wrestling with the moral of Manon Lescaut, and if the impulse had ever reached his full consciousness, it died on the instant.

"Of course, if this motor-car business is any good," Lonsdale was saying, "I might be able in a year or two to compete with elderly financiers. But my advice to you ..."

"You asked for my advice," said Michael, with a smile.

"I know I did. I know I did. But as you haven't ever been to see My Mistake—the most absolutely successful musical comedy for years— why, my dear fellow, I've been thirty-eight times!... and my advice to you is 'avoid actresses.' Oh, yes, I know it's difficult, I know, I know."

Lonsdale shook his head so often that the monocle fell on the floor, and his wisdom was speechless until he could find it again.

Michael left him soon afterward, feeling rather sadly that the horizon before him was clouding over with feminine forms. Alan would soon be engaged to his sister. It was delightful, of course, but in one way it already placed a barrier between their perfect intercourse. Maurice would obviously soon be thinking of nothing but women. Already even up at Oxford a great deal of his attention had been turned in that direction: and now Lonsdale had Queenie. This swift severance from youth by all his friends, this preoccupation with womanhood was likely to be depressing, thought Michael, unless himself also fell in love. That was very improbable, however. Love filled him with fear. The Abbé Prévost that morning had expressed for him in art the quintessence of what he knew with sharp prevision love for him would mean. He felt a dread of leaving Oxford that quite overshadowed his regret. Here was shelter—why had he not shaped his career to stay forever in this cold peace? And, after all, why should he not? He was independent. Why should he enter the world and call down upon himself such troubles and torments as had vexed his youth in London? From the standpoint of moral experience he had a right to stay here: and yet it would be desolate to stay here without a vital reason, merely to grow old on the fringe of the university. Could he have been a Fellow, it would have been different: but to vegetate, to dream, to linger without any power of art to put into form even what he had experienced already, that would inevitably breed a pernicious melancholy. On the other hand, he might go to Plashers Mead. He might almost make trial of art. Guy would inspire him, Guy living his secluded existence with books above a stream. Whatever occurred to him in the way of personal failure, he could on his side encourage Guy. His opinion might be valuable, for although he seemed to have no passion to create, he was sure his judgment was good. How Guy would appreciate Manon; and perhaps like so many classics he had taken it as read, nor knew yet what depths of pity, what profundities of beauty awaited his essay.

Michael made up his mind that instead of going to London this afternoon he would ride over to Wychford and either stay with Guy or in any case announce his speedy return to stay with him for at least the rest of the summer. Alan would escort his mother and Stella home. It would be easier for Alan that way. His mother would be so charming to him, and everything would soon be arranged. With this plan to unfold, Michael hurried across to Ninety-nine. Alan was already up. Everything was packed. Michael realized he could already regard the digs without a pang for the imminence of final departure. Perhaps the Abbé Prévost had deprived him of the capacity for a merely sentimental emotion, at any rate for the present.

Alan looked rather doubtful over Michael's proposal.

"I hate telling things in the train," he objected.

"You haven't got to tell anything in the train," Michael contradicted. "My mother is sure to invite you to dinner to-night, and you can tell her at home. It's much better for me to be out of it. I shall be back in a few days to pack up various things I shall want for Plashers Mead."

"It's a most extraordinary thing," said Alan slowly, "that the moment you think there's a chance of my marrying your sister, you drop me like a hot brick."

Michael touched his shoulder affectionately.

"I'm more pleased about you and her than about anything that has ever happened," he said earnestly. "Now are you content?"

"Of course, I oughtn't to have spoken to her," said Alan. "I really don't know, looking back at last night, how on earth I had the cheek. I expect I said a lot of rot. I ought certainly to have waited until I was in the Home Civil."

"You must chuck that idea," said Michael. "Stella would loathe the Civil Service."

"I can't marry ..." Alan began.

"You've got to manage her affairs. She has a temperament. She also has land." Then Michael explained about Prescott, and so eloquent was he upon the need for Stella's happiness that Alan began to give way.

"I always thought I should be too proud to live on a woman," he said.

"Don't make me bring forward all my arguments over again," Michael begged. "I'm already feeling very fagged. You'll have all your work cut out. To manage Stella herself, let alone her piano and let alone her land, is worth a very handsome salary. But that's nothing to do with it. You're in love with each other. Are you going to be selfish enough to satisfy your own silly pride at the expense of her happiness? I could say lots more. I could sing your praises as ..."

"Thanks very much. You needn't bother," interrupted Alan gruffly.

"Well, will you not be an ass?"

"I'll try."

"Otherwise I shall tell you what a perfect person you are."

"Get out," said Alan, flinging a cushion.

Michael left him and went down to the Randolph. He found Stella already dressed and waiting impatiently in the lobby for his arrival. His mother was not yet down.

"It's all right," he began, "I've destroyed the last vestige of Alan's masculine vanity. Mother will be all right—if," said Michael severely, pausing to relish the flavor of what might be the last occasion on which he would administer with authority a brotherly admonition. "*If* you don't put on a lot of side and talk about being twenty-one in a couple of months. Do you understand?"

Stella for answer flung her arms round his neck, and Michael grew purple under the conspicuous affront she had put upon his dignity.

"You absurd piece of pomposity," she said. "I really adore you."

"For God's sake don't talk in that exaggerated way," Michael muttered. "I hope you aren't going to make a public ass of Alan like that. He'd be rather sick."

"If you say another word," Stella threatened, "I'll clap my hands and go dancing all round this hotel."

At lunch Michael explained that he was not coming to town for a day or two, and his mother accepted his announcement with her usual gracious calm. Just before they were getting ready to enter their cab to go to the station, Michael took her aside.

"Mother, you'll be very sympathetic, won't you?" Then he whispered to her, fondling her arm. "They really are so much in love, but Alan will never be able to explain how much, and I swear to you he and Stella were made for each other."

"But they don't want to be married at once?" asked Mrs. Fane, in some alarm.

"Oh, not to-morrow," Michael admitted. "But don't ask them to have a year's engagement. Will you promise me?"

"Why don't you come back to-night and talk to me about it?" she asked.

"Because they'll be so delightful talking to you without me. I should spoil it. And don't forget—Alan is a *slow* bowler, but he gets wickets."

Michael watched with a smile his mother waving to him from the cab while still she was vaguely trying to resolve the parting metaphor he had flung at her. As soon as the cab had turned the corner, he called for his bicycle and rode off to Wychford.

He went slowly with many roadside halts, nor was there the gentlest rise up which he did not walk. It was after five o'clock when he dipped from the rolling highway down into Wychford. There were pink roses everywhere on the gray houses. As he went through the gate of Plashers Mead, he hugged himself with the thought of Guy's pleasure at seeing him so unexpectedly on this burnished afternoon of midsummer. The leaves of the old espalier rustled crisply: they were green and glossy, and the apples, still scarcely larger than nuts, promised in the autumn when he and Guy would be together here a ruddy harvest. The house was unresponsive when he knocked at the door. He waited for a minute or two, and then he went into the stone-paved hall and up the steep stairs to the long corridor, at whose far end the framed view of the open doorway into Guy's green room glowed as vividly as if it gave upon a high-walled sunlit garden. The room itself was empty. There were only the books and a lingering smell of tobacco smoke, and through the bay-window the burble of the stream swiftly flowing. Michael looked out over the orchard and away to the far-flung horizon of the wold beyond.

Here assuredly, he told himself, was the perfect refuge. Here in this hollow waterway was peace. From here sometimes in the morning he and Guy would ride into Oxford, whence at twilight they would steal forth again and, dipping down from the bleak road, find Plashers Mead set safe in a land that was tributary only to the moon. Guy's diamond pencil, with which he was wont upon the window to inscribe mottoes, lay on the sill. Michael picked it up and scratched upon the glass: *The fresh green lap of fair King Richard's land*, setting the date below.

Then suddenly coming down past the house with the stream he saw in a canoe Guy with a girl. The canoe swept past the window and was lost round the bend, hidden immediately by reeds and overarching willows. Yet Michael had time to see the girl, to see her cheeks of frailest rose, to know she was a fairy's child and that Guy was deep in love. Although the fleet vision thrilled him with a romantic beauty, Michael was disheartened. Even here at Plashers Mead, where he had counted upon finding a cloister, the disintegration of life's progress had begun. It would be absurd for him to intrude now upon Guy. He would scarcely be welcomed now in this June weather. After all, he must go to London; so he left behind him the long gray house and walked up the slanting hill that led to the nearest railway station. By the gate where he and Guy had first seen Plashers Mead, he paused to throw one regret back into that hollow waterway, one regret for the long gray house on its green island circled by singing streams.

There were two hours to wait at the station before the train would arrive. He would be in London about half-past nine. Discovering a meadow pied with daisies, Michael slept in the sun.

When he woke, the grass was smelling fresh in the shadows, and the sun was westering. He went across to the station and, during the ten minutes left before his train came in, walked up and down the platform in the spangled airs of evening, past the tea-roses planted there, slim tawny buds and ivory cups dabbled with creamy flushes.

It was dark when Michael reached Paddington, and he felt depressed, wishing he had come back with the others. No doubt they would all be at the theater. Or should he drive home and perhaps find them there?

"Know anything about this golf-bag, Bill?" one porter was shouting to another.

Michael went over to look at the label in case it might be Alan's bag. But it was an abandoned golf-bag belonging to no one: there were no initials even painted on the canvas. This forsaken golf-bag doubled Michael's depression, and though he had always praised Paddington as the best of railway stations, he thought to-night it was the gloomiest in London. Then he remembered in a listless way that he had forgotten to inquire about his suit case, which had been sent after him from Oxford to Shipcott, the station for Wychford. It must be lying there now with Manon Lescaut inside. He made arrangements to recapture it, which consummated his depression. Then he called a hansom and drove to Cheyne Walk. They had all gone to the Opera, the parlormaid told him. Michael could not bear to stay at home to-night alone: so, getting back into the hansom, he told the man to drive to the Oxford Music-hall. It would be grimly amusing to see on the programs there the theatrical view of St. Mary's tower.

THE END OF THE FIRST BOOK

BOOK TWO
ROMANTIC EDUCATION

Sancta ad vos anima atque istius inscia culpae

descendam, magnorum haud umquam indignus
avorum.

VIRGIL.

For Fancy cannot live on real food:

In youth she will despise familiar joy

To dwell in mournful shades, as they grow
real,

Then buildeth she of joy her fair ideal.

ROBERT BRIDGES.

CHAPTER I

OSTIA DITIS

When Michael reached the Oxford Music-hall he wondered why he had overspurred his fatigue to such a point. There was no possibility of pleasure here, and he would have done better to stay at home and cure with sleep what was after all a natural depression. It had been foolish to expect a sedative from contact with this unquiet assemblage. In the mass they had nothing but a mechanical existence, subject as they were to the brightness or dimness of the electrolier that regulated their attention. Michael did not bother to buy a program. From every podgy hand he could see dangling the lithograph of St. Mary's tower with its glazed moonlight; and he was not sufficiently aware of the glib atom who bounced about the golden dazzle of the stage to trouble about his name. He mingled with the slow pace of the men and women on the promenade. They were going backward and forward like flies, meeting for a moment in a quick buzz of colloquy and continuing after a momentary pause their impersonal and recurrent progress. Michael was absorbed in this ceaseless ebb and flow of motion where the sidelong glances of the women, as they brushed his elbow in the passing crowd, gave him no conviction of an individual gaze. Once or twice he diverted his steps from the stream and tried to watch in a half-hearted way the performance; but as he leaned over the plush-covered barrier a woman would sidle up to him, and he would move away in angry embarrassment from the questioning eyes under the big plumed hat. The noise of popping corks and the chink of glasses, the whirr of the ventilating fans, the stentorophonic orchestra, the red-faced raucous atom on the stage combined to irritate him beyond further endurance; and he had just resolved to walk seven times up and down the promenade before he went home, when somebody cried in heartiest greeting over his shoulder, "Hullo, Bangs!"

Michael turned and saw Drake, and so miserable had been the effect of the music-hall that he welcomed him almost effusively, although he had not seen him during four years and would probably like him rather less now than he had liked him at school.

"*My* lord! fancy seeing you again!" Drake effused.

Michael found himself shaken warmly by the hand in support of the enthusiastic recognition. After the less accentuated cordiality of Oxford manners, it was strange to be standing like this with clasped hands in the middle of this undulatory crowd.

"I *say*, Bangs, old man, we must have a drink on this."

Drake led the way to the bar and called authoritatively for two whiskies and a split Polly.

"Quite a little-bit-of-fluffy-all-right," he whispered to Michael, seeming to calculate with geometrical eyes the arcs and semicircles of the barmaid's form. She with her nose in the air poured out the liquid, and Michael wondered how any of it went into the glass. As a matter of fact, most of it splashed onto the bar, whence Drake presently took his change all bedewed with alcohol, and, lifting his glass, wished Michael a jolly good chin-chin.

"'D luck," Michael muttered in response.

"*My* lord!" Drake began again. "Fancy meeting you of all people. And not a bit different. I said to myself: 'I'm jiggered if that isn't old Bangs,' and—well, *my* lord! but I was surprised. Do you often come out on the randan?"

"Not very often," Michael admitted. "I just happened to be alone to-night."

"Good for you, old sport. What have you been doing since you left school?"

"I'm just down from Oxford," Michael informed him.

"Pretty good spree up there, eh?"

"Oh, yes, rather," said Michael.

"Well, I had the chance to go," said Drake. "But it wasn't good enough. It's against you in the City, you know. Waste of time really, except of course for a parson or a schoolmaster."

"Yes, I expect it would have been rather a waste of time for you," Michael agreed.

"Oh, rotten! So you moved from—where was it?—Carlington Road?"

"Yes, we moved to Cheyne Walk."

"Let's see. That's in Hampstead, isn't it?"

"Well, it's rather nearer the river," suggested Michael. "Are you still in Trelawny Road?"

"Yes, still in the same old hovel. My hat! Talking of Trelawny Road, it *is* a small world. Who do you think I saw last week?"

"Not Lily Haden?" Michael asked, in spite of a wish not to rise so quickly to Drake's hook.

232

"You're right. I saw the fair Lily. But where do you think I saw her? Bangs, old boy, I tell you I'm not a fellow who's easily surprised. But this knocked me. Of course, you'll understand the Hadens flitted from Trelawny Road soon after you stopped calling. So who knows what's happened since? I give you three guesses where I saw her."

"I hate riddles," said Michael fretfully.

"At the Orient," said Drake solemnly. "The Orient Promenade. You could have knocked me down with a feather."

Michael stared at Drake, scarcely realizing the full implication of what he just announced. Then suddenly he grasped the horrible fact that revealed to him here in a music-hall carried a double force. His one instinct for the moment was to prevent Drake from knowing into what depths his news had plunged him.

"Has she changed?" asked Michael, and could have kicked himself for the question.

"Well, of course there was a good deal of powder," said Drake. "I'm not easily shocked, but this gave me a turn. She was with a man, but even if she hadn't been, I doubt if I'd have had the nerve to talk to her. I wouldn't have known what to say. But, of course, you know, her mother was a bit rapid. That's where it is. Have another drink. You're looking quite upset."

Michael shook his head. He must go home.

"Aren't you coming down West a bit?" asked Drake, in disappointment. "The night's still young."

But Michael was not to be persuaded.

"Well, don't let's lose sight of each other now we've met. What's your club? I've just joined the Primrose myself. Not a bad little place. You get a rare good one-and-sixpenny lunch. You ought to join. Or perhaps you're already suited?"

"I belong to the Bath," said Michael.

"Oh, of course, if you're suited, that's all right. But any time you want to join the Primrose just let me know and I'll put you up. The sub isn't really very much. Guinea a year."

Michael thanked him and escaped as quickly as he could. Outside even in Oxford Street the air was full of summer, and the cool people sauntering under the sapphirine sky were as welcome to his vision as if he had waked from a fever. His head was throbbing with the heat of the music-hall, and the freshness of night-air was delicious. He called a hansom and told the driver to go to Blackfriars Bridge, and from there slowly along the Embankment to Cheyne Walk. For a time he leaned back in the cab, thinking of nothing, barely conscious of golden thoroughfares, of figures in silhouette against the glitter, and of the London roar rising and falling. Presently in the quiet of the shadowy cross-streets he began to appreciate what seemed the terrible importance to himself of Drake's news.

"It concerns me," he began to reiterate aloud. "It concerns me—me—me. It's useless to think that it doesn't. It concerns me."

Then a more ghastly suggestion whispered itself. How should he ever know that he was not primarily responsible? The idea came over him with sickening intensity; and upright now he saw in the cracked mirrors of the cab a face blanched, a forehead clammy with sweat, and over his shoulder like a goblin the wraith of Lily. It was horrible to see so distorted that beautiful memory which time had etherealized out of a reality, until of her being nothing had endured but a tenuous image of earliest love. Now under the shock of her degradation he must be dragged back by this goblin to face his responsibility. He must behold again close at hand her shallow infidelity. He must assure himself of her worthlessness, hammer into his brain that from the beginning she had merely trifled with him. This must be established for the sake of his conscience. Where the devil was this driver going?

"I told you down the Embankment," Michael shouted through the trap.

"I can't go down the Embankment before I gets there, can I, sir?" the cabman asked reproachfully.

Michael closed the trap. He was abashed when he perceived they were still only in Fleet Street. Why had he gone to The Oxford to-night? Why had he spoken to Drake? Why had he not stayed at Wychford? Why had he not returned to London with the others? Such regrets were valueless. It was foredoomed that Lily should come into his life again. Yet there was no reason why she should. There was no reason at all. Men could hardly be held responsible for the fall of women, unless themselves had upon their souls the guilt of betrayal or desertion. It was ridiculous to argue that he must bother because at eighteen he had loved her, because at eighteen he had thought she was worthy of being loved. No doubt the Orient Promenade was the sequel of kissing objectionable actors in the back gardens of West Kensington. Yet the Orient Promenade? That was a damnable place. The Orient Promenade? He remembered her kisses. Sitting in this cab, he was kissing her now. She had ridden for hours deep in his arms. Not Oxford could cure this relapse into the past. Every spire and every tower had crashed to ruins around his staid conceptions, so that they too presently fell away. Four years of plastic calm were unfashioned, and she was again beside him. Every passing lamp lit up her face, her smoldering eyes, her lips, her hair. The goblin took her place, the goblin with sidelong glances, tasting of scent, powdered, pranked, soulless, lost. What was she doing at this moment? What invitation glittered in her look? Michael nearly told the driver to turn his horse. He must reach the Orient before the show was done. He must remonstrate with her, urge her to go home, help her with money, plead with her, drag her by force away from that procession. But the hansom kept on its way. All down the Embankment, all along Grosvenor Road the onrushing street-lamps flung their balls of light with monotonous jugglery into the cab. To-night, anyhow, it was too late to find her. He would sleep on whatever resolve he took, and in the morning perhaps the problem would present itself in less difficult array.

Michael reached home before the others had come back from the Opera, and suddenly he knew how tired he was. To-day had been the longest day he could ever remember. Quickly he made up his mind to go to bed so that he would not be drawn into the discussion of the delightful engagement of Stella and Alan. He felt he could hardly face the irony of their happiness when he thought of Lily. For a while he sat at the window, staring at the water and bathing his fatigue in the balm of the generous night. Even here in London peace was possible, here where the reflected lamps in golden pagodas sprawled across the width of the river and where the glutted tide lapped and sucked the piers of the bridge, nuzzled the shelving strand and swirled in sleepy greed around the patient barges at their moorings. A momentary breeze frilled the surface of the stream, blurring the golden pagodas of light so that they jigged and glittered until the motion died away. Eastward in the sky over London hung a tawny stain that blotted out the stars.

233

From his window Michael grew more and more conscious of the city stirring in a malaise of inarticulate life beneath that sinister stain. He was aware of the stealthy soul of London transcending the false vision of peace before his eyes. There came creeping over him the dreadful knowledge that Lily was at this moment living beneath that London sky, imprisoned, fettered, crushed beneath that grim suffusion, that fulvid vile suffusion of the nocturnal sky. He began to spur his memory for every beautiful record of her that was stamped upon it. She was walking toward him in Kensington Gardens: not a contour of her delicate progress had been blunted by the rasp of time. Five years ago he had been the first to speak: now, must it be she who sometimes spoke first? Seventeen she had told him had been her age, and they had kissed in the dark midway between two lamps. No doubt she had been kissed before. In that household of Trelawny Road anything else was inconceivable. The gray streets of West Kensington in terrace upon terrace stretched before him, and now as he recalled their barren stones it seemed to him there was not one corner round which he might not expect to meet her face to face. "*Michael, why do you make me love you so?*" That was her voice. It was she who had asked him that question. Never before this moment had he realized the import of her demand. Now, when it was years too late to remedy, it came out of the past like an accusation. He had answered it then with closer kisses. He had released her then like a ruffled bird, secure that to-morrow and to-morrow and to-morrow she would nestle to his arms for cherishing. And now if he thought more of her life beneath that lurid stain he would go mad; if he conjured to himself the vision of her now—had not Drake said she was powdered and painted? To this had she come. And she was here in London. Last week she had been seen. It was no nightmare. It was real, horrible and real. He must go out again at once and find her. He must not sit dreaming here, staring at the silly Thames, the smooth and imperturbable Thames. He must plunge into that phantasmagoric city; he must fly from haunt to haunt; he must drag the depths of every small hell; he must find her to-night.

Michael rose, but on the instant of his decision his mother and Stella drove up. Alan was no longer with them. He must have gone home to Richmond. How normal sounded their voices from the pavement below. Perhaps he would after all go down and greet them. They might wonder otherwise if something had happened. Looking at himself as he passed the mirror on his way down, he saw that he really was haggard. If he pleaded a headache, his countenance would bear him out. In the end he shouted to them over the balusters, and both of them wanted to come up with remedies. He would not let them. The last thing his mood desired was the tending of cool hands.

"I'm only fagged out," he told them. "I want a night's sleep."

Yet he knew how hard it would be to fall asleep. His brain was on fire. Morning, the liquid morning of London summer, was unimaginable. He shut the door of his room and flung himself down upon the bed. Contact with the cool linen released the pent-up tears, and the fire within burnt less fiercely as he cried. His surrender to self-pity must have lasted half an hour. The pillow-case was drenched. His body felt battered. He seemed to have recovered from a great illness. The quiet of the room surprised him, as he looked round in a daze at the familiar objects. The cataclysm of emotion so violently expressed had left him with a sense that the force of his grief must have shaken the room as it had shaken him. But everything was quiet; everything was the same. Now that he had wept away that rending sense of powerlessness to aid her, he could examine the future more calmly. Already the numbness was going, and the need for action was beginning to make itself felt. Yet still all his impulses were in confusion. He could not attain to any clear view of his attitude.

He was not in love with her now. He was neither covetous of her kisses nor in any way of her bodily presence. To his imagination at present she appeared like one who has died. It seemed to him that he desired to bring back a corpse, that over a lifeless form he wished to lament the loss of beauty, of passion and of youth. But immediately afterward, so constant was the impression of her as he had last known her, so utterly incapable was Drake's account to change his outward picture of her, he could not conceive the moral disintegration wrought by her shame. It seemed to him that could he be driving with her in a hansom to-night, she would lie still and fluttered in his arms, the Lily of five years ago whom now to cherish were an adorable duty.

Therefore, he was in love with her. Otherwise to every prostitute in London he must be feeling the same tenderness. Yet they were of no account. Were they of no account? *C'est une douzaine de filles de joie.* When he read Manon this morning—how strange! this morning he had been reading Manon at Oxford—he was moved with pity for all poor light women. And Lily was one of them. They did not banish them to New Orleans nowadays, but she was not less an outcast. It was not because he was still in love with her that he wished to find her. It was because he had known her in the old days. He bore upon his own soul the damning weight that in the past she had said, "*Michael, why do you make me love you so?*" If there was guilt, he shared the guilt. If there was shame, he was shameful. Others after him had sinned against her casually, counting their behavior no more than a speck of dust in the garbage of human emotion with which she was already smirched. He may not have seduced her, but he had sinned against her, because while loving her he had let her soul elude him. He had made her love him. He had trifled with her sensuousness, and to say that he was too young for blame was cowardly. It was that very youth which was the sin, because under society's laws, whatever fine figure his love might seem to him to have cut, he should have known that it was a profitless love for a girl. He shared in the guilt. He partook of the shame. That was incontrovertible.

Suddenly a new aspect of the situation was painfully visible. Had not his own mother been sinned against by his father? That seemed equally incontrovertible. Prescott had known it in his heart. Prescott had said to him in the Albany on the night he killed himself that he wanted to marry Stella in order to be given the right to protect her. Prescott must always have deplored the position in which his friend's mistress had been placed. That was a hard word to use for one's mother. It seemed to hiss with scorn. No doubt his father would have married her, if Lady Saxby had divorced him. No doubt that was the salve with which he had soothed his conscience. Something was miserably wrong with our rigid divorce law, he may have said. He must have cursed it innumerable times in order to console his conscience, just as himself at eighteen had cursed youth when he could not marry Lily. His mother had been sinned against. Nothing could really alter that. It was useless to say that the sinner had in the circumstances behaved very well, that so far as he was able he had treated her honorably. But nothing could excuse his father's initial weakness. The devotion of a lifetime could not wash out his deliberate sin against—and who was she? Who was his mother? Valérie ... and her father was at Trinity, Cambridge ... a clergyman ... a gentleman. And his father had taken her away, had exposed her to the calumny of the world. He had afterward behaved chivalrously at any rate by the standards of romance. But by what small margin had his own mother escaped the doom of Lily? All his conceptions of order and safety and custom tottered and reeled at such a thought. Surely such a realization doubled his obligation to atone by rescuing Lily, out of very thankfulness to God that his own mother had escaped the evil which had come to her. How wretchedly puny now seemed all his own repinings. All he had gained for his own character had been a vague dissatisfaction that he could not succeed to the earldom in order to prove the sanctity of good breeding. There had been no gratitude; there had been nothing but a hurt conceit. The horror of Drake's news would at least cure him forever of that pettiness. Already he felt the strength that comes from the sight of a task that must be conquered. He had been moved that morning by the tale of Manon Lescaut. This tale of Lily was in comparison with that as an earthquake to the tunneling of a mole beneath a croquet-lawn. And now must he regard his father's memory with condemnation? Must he hate him? He must hate him, indeed, unless by his own behavior he could feel he had accepted in substitution the burden of his father's responsibility. And he had admired him so much dying out there in Africa for his country. He had resented his death for the sake of thousands more unworthy living comfortably at home.

"All my standards are falling to pieces," thought Michael. "Heroes and heroines are all turning into cardboard. If I don't make some effort to be true to conviction, I shall turn to cardboard with the rest."

He began to pace the room in a tumult of intentions, vows and resolutions. Somehow before he slept he must shape his course. Four years had dreamed themselves away at Oxford. Unless all that education was as immaterial as the fogs of the Isis, it must provide him now with an indication of his duty. He had believed in Oxford, believed in her infallibility and glory, he had worshiped all she stood for. He had surrendered himself to her to make of him a gentleman, and unless these four years had been a delusion, his education must bear fruit now.

Michael made up his mind suddenly, and as it seemed to him at the moment in possession of perfect calm and clarity of judgment, that he would marry Lily. He had accepted marriage as a law of his society. Well, then that law should be kept. He would test every article of the creed of an English gentleman. He would try in the fire of his purpose honor, pride, courtesy, and humility. All these must come to his aid, if he were going to marry a whore. Let him stab himself with the word. Let him not blind himself with euphemisms. His friends would have no euphemisms for Lily. How Lonsdale had laughed at the idea of marrying Queenie Molyneux, and she might have been called an actress. How everybody would despise his folly. There would not be one friend who would understand. Least of all would his mother understand. It was a hard thing to do; and yet it would be comparatively easy, if he could be granted the grace of faith to sustain him. Principles were rather barren things to support the soul in a fight with convention. Principles of honor when so very personal were apt to crumple in the blast of society's principles all fiercely kindled against him. Just now he had thought of the thankfulness he owed to God. Was it more than a figure of speech, an exaggerative personification under great emotion of what most people would call chance? At any rate, here was God in a cynical mood, and the divine justice of this retributive situation seemed to hint at something beyond mere luck. And if principles were strong enough to sustain him to the onset, faith might fire him to the coronation of his self-effacement. He made up his mind clearly and calmly to marry Lily, and then he quickly fell into sleep, where as if to hearten him he saw her slim and lovely, herself again, treading for his dreams the ways of night like a gazelle.

Next morning when Michael woke, his resolve purified by sleep of feverish and hysterical promptings was fresh upon his pillow. In the fatigue and strain of the preceding night the adventure had caught a hectic glow of exaltation. Now, with the sparrows twittering and the milkman clanking and yodeling down Cheyne Walk and the young air puffing the curtains, his course acquired a simplicity in this lucid hour of deliberation, which made the future normal and even obvious. There was a great relief in this fresh following breeze after the becalmed inaction of Oxford: it seemed an augury of life's importance that so immediately on top of the Oxford dream he should find such a complete dispersion of mist and so urgent a fairway before him. The task of finding Lily might easily occupy him for some time, for a life like hers would be made up of mutable appearances and sudden strange eclipses. It might well be a year before she was seen again on the Orient Promenade. Yet it was just as likely that he would find her at once. For a moment he caught his breath in thinking of the sudden plunge which that meeting would involve. He thought of all the arguments and all the dismay that the revelation of his purpose would set in motion. However, the marriage had to be. He had threshed it all out last night. But he might reasonably hope for a brief delay. Such a hope was no disloyalty to his determination.

Stella was already at breakfast when he came downstairs. Michael raised his eyebrows in demand for news of her and Alan.

"Mother was the sweetest thing imaginable," she said. "And so we're engaged. I wanted to come and talk to you last night, but I thought you would rather be left alone."

"I'm glad you're happy," he said gravely. "And I'm glad you're safe."

Stella looked at him in surprise.

"I've never been anything but safe," she assured him.

"Haven't you?" he asked, looking at her and reproving himself for the thought that this gray-eyed sister of his could ever have exposed herself to the least likelihood of falling into Lily's case. Yet there had been times when he had felt alarmed for her security and happiness. There had been that fellow Ayliffe, and more serious still there had been that unknown influence in Vienna. Invulnerable she might seem now in this cool dining-room on a summer morning, but there had been times when he had doubted.

"What are you looking at?" she asked, flaunting her imperious boyishness in his solemn countenance.

"You. Thinking you ought to be damned grateful."

"What for?"

"Everything."

"You included, I suppose," she laughed.

Still it had been rather absurd, Michael thought, as he tapped his egg, to suppose there was anything in Stella's temperament which could ever link her to Lily. Should he announce his quest for her approbation and sympathy? It was difficult somehow to begin. Already a subtle change had taken place in their relation to each other since she was engaged to Alan. Of course, his reserve was ridiculous, but he could not bring himself to break through now. Besides, in any case it were better to wait until he had found Lily again. It would all sound very pretentiously noble in anticipation, and though she would have every right to laugh, he did not want her to laugh. When he stood on the brink of marriage, they would none of them be able to laugh. There was a grim satisfaction in that.

"When does mother suggest you should be married?" he asked.

"We more or less settled November. Alan has given up the Civil Service. That's my first piece of self-assertion. He's coming for me this morning, and we're going to lunch at Richmond."

"You've never met Mr. and Mrs. Merivale?"

Stella shook her head.

"Old Merivale's a ripping old boy. Always making bad puns. And Mrs. Merivale's a dear."

"They must both be perfect to have been the father and mother of Alan," said Stella.

"I shouldn't get too excited over him," Michael advised. "Or over yourself, either. You might give me the credit of knowing all about it long before either of you."

"Darling Michael," she cried, bounding at him like a puppy.

"When you've done making an ass of yourself you might chuck me a roll."

Alan arrived soon after breakfast, and he and Michael had a few minutes together, while Stella was getting ready to go out.

"Were your people pleased?" Michael asked.

"Oh, of course. Naturally the mater was a little nervous. She thought I seemed young. Talked a good deal about being a little boy only yesterday and that sort of rot."

"And your governor?"

"He supposed I was determined to steal her," said Alan, with a whimsical look of apology for the pun. "And having worked that off he spent the rest of the evening relishing his own joke."

Stella came down ready to start for Richmond. Both she and Alan were in white, and Michael said they looked like a couple of cricketers. But he envied them as he waved them farewell from the front door through which the warm day was deliciously invading the house. Their happiness sparkled on the air as visibly almost as the sunshine winking on the river. Those Richmond days belonged imperishably to him and Alan, yet for Alan this Saturday would triumph over all the others before. Michael turned back into the house rather sadly. The radiance of the morning had been dislustered by their departure, and Michael against his will had to be aware of the sense of exclusion which lovers leave in their wake. He waited indoors until his mother came down. She was solicitous for the headache of last night, and while he was with her he was not troubled by regrets for the break-up of established intercourse. He asked himself whether he should take her into his confidence by announcing the tale of Lily. Yet he did not wish to give her an impression of being more straightly bound to follow his quest than by the broadest rules of conduct. He felt it would be easier to explain when the marriage had taken place. How lucky for him that he was not financially dependent! That he was not, however, laid upon him the greater obligation. He could find, even if he wished one, no excuse for unfulfillment.

Michael and his mother talked for a time of the engagement. She was still somewhat doubtful of Alan's youth, when called upon to adapt itself to Stella's temperament.

"I think you're wrong there," said Michael. "Alan is rather a rigid person in fundamentals, you know, and his youth will give just that flexibility which Stella would demand. In another five years he would have been ensconced behind an Englishman's strong but most unmanageable barrier of prejudice. I noticed so much his attitude toward Mrs. Ross when she was received into the Roman Church. I asked him what he would say if Stella went over. He maintained that she was different. I think that's a sign he'll be ready to apply imagination to her behavior."

"Yes, but I hope he won't think that whatever she does is right," Mrs. Fane objected.

"Oh, no," laughed Michael. "Imagination will always be rather an effort for Alan. Mother, would you be worried if I told you I wanted to go away for a while—I mean to say, go away and perhaps more or less not be heard of for a while?"

"Abroad?" she asked.

"Not necessarily abroad. I'm not going to involve myself in a dangerous undertaking; but I'm just sufficiently tired of my very comfortable existence to wish to make an experiment. I may be away quite a short time, but I might want to be away a few months. Will you promise me not to worry yourself over my movements? Some of the success of this undertaking will probably depend on a certain amount of freedom. You can understand, can't you, that the claims of home, however delightful, might in certain circumstances be a problem?"

"I suppose you're taking steps to prepare my mind for something very extremely unpleasant," she said.

"Let's ascribe it all to my incurably romantic temperament," Michael suggested.

"And I'm not to worry?"

"No, please don't."

"But when are you going away?"

"I'm not really going away at all," Michael explained. "But if I didn't come back to dinner one night or even the next night, would you be content to know quite positively that I hadn't been run over?"

"You're evidently going to be thoroughly eccentric. But I suppose," she added wistfully, "that after your deserted childhood I can hardly expect you to be anything else. Yet it seems so comfortable here." She was looking round at the chairs.

"I'm not proposing to go to the North Pole, you know," Michael said, "but I don't want to obey dinner-gongs."

"Very noisy and abrupt," she agreed.

Soon they were discussing all kinds of substitutions.

"Mother, what an extraordinary lot you know about noise," Michael exclaimed.

"Dearest boy, I'm on the committee of a society for the abatement of London street noises."

"So deeply occupied with reform," he said, patting her hand.

"One must do something," she smiled.

"I know," he asserted. "And therefore you'll let me ride this new hobby-horse I'm trying without thinking it bucks. Will you?"

"You know perfectly well that you will anyhow," said Mrs. Fane, shaking her head.

Michael felt justified in letting the conversation end at this admission. Maurice Avery had invited him to come round to the studio in order to assist at Castleton's induction, and Michael walked along the Embankment to 422 Grosvenor Road.

The large attic which ran all the width of the Georgian house was in a state of utter confusion, in the midst of which Castleton was hard at work hammering, while Maurice climbed over chairs in eager advice, and at the Bechstein Grand a tall dark young man was playing melodies from Tchaikovsky's symphonies.

"Just trying to make this place a bit comfortable," said Castleton. "Do you know Cunningham?" He indicated the player, and Michael bowed.

"Making it comfortable," Michael repeated. "My first impression was just the reverse. I suppose it's no good asking you people to give me lunch?"

"Rather, of course," Maurice declared. "Castleton, it's your turn to buy lunch."

"One extraordinary thing, Michael," said Castleton, "is the way in which Maurice can always produce a mathematical reason for my doing something. You'd think he kept a ledger of all our tasks."

"We can send old Mother Wadman if you're tired," Maurice offered. Castleton, however, seemed to think he wanted some fresh air; so he and Cunningham went out to buy things to eat.

"I was fairly settled before old Castleton turned up," Maurice explained, "but we shall be three times as comfortable when he's finished. He's putting up divans."

Maurice indicated with a gesture the raw material on which Castleton was at work. They were standing by the window which looked out over multitudinous roofs.

"What a great rolling sense of human life they do give," said Michael. "A sea really with telegraph poles and wires for masts and rigging, and all that washing like flotillas of small boats. And there's the lighthouse," he pointed to the campanile of Westminster Chapel.

"The sun sets just behind your lighthouse, which is a very bad simile for anything so obscurantist as the Roman Church," said Maurice. "We're having such wonderful green dusks now. This is really a room made for a secret love-affair, you know. Such nights. Such sunny summer days. What is it Browning says? Something about sparrows on a housetop lonely. We two were sparrows. You know the poem I mean. Well, no doubt soon I shall meet the girl who's meant to share this with me. Then I really think I could work."

Michael nodded absently. He was wondering if an attic like this were not the solution of what might happen to him and Lily when they were married. Whatever bitterness London had given her would surely be driven out by life in a room like this with a view like this. They would be suspended celestially above all that was worst in London, and yet they would be most essentially and intimately part of it. The windows of the city would come twinkling into life as incomprehensibly as the stars. Whatever bitterness she had guarded would vanish, because to see her in a room like this would be to love her. How well he understood Maurice's desire for a secret love-affair here. Nobody wanted a girl to perfect Plashers Mead. Even Guy's fairy child at Plashers Mead had seemed an intrusion; but here, to protect one's loneliness against the overpowering contemplation of the life around, love was a necessity. And perhaps Maurice would begin to justify the ambition his friends had for his career. It might be so. Perhaps himself might find an inspiration in an attic high up over roofs. It might be. It might be so.

"What are you thinking about?" Maurice asked.

"I was thinking you were probably right," said Michael.

Maurice looked pleasantly surprised. He was rather accustomed to be snubbed when he told Michael of his desire for feminine companionship.

"I don't want to get married, you know," he hastily added.

"That would depend," said Michael. "If one married what is called an impossible person and lived up here, it ought to be romantic enough to make marriage rather more exciting than any silvery invitation to St. Thomas' Church at half-past two."

"But why are you so keen about marriage?" Maurice demanded.

"Well, it has certain advantages," Michael pointed out.

"Not among the sparrows," said Maurice.

"Most of all among the sparrows," Michael contradicted. He was becoming absorbed by his notion of Lily in such surroundings. It seemed to remove the last doubt he had of the wisdom or necessity of the step he proposed to take. They would be able to reënter the world after a long retirement. For her it should be a convalescence, and for him the opportunity which Oxford denied to test academic values on the touchstone of human emotions. It was obvious that his education lacked something, though his academic education was finished. He supposed he had apprehended dimly the risk of this incompletion in Paris during that first Long Vacation. It was curious how already the quest of Lily had assumed less the attributes of a rescue than of a personal desire for the happiness of her company. No doubt he must be ready for a shock of disillusion when they did meet, but for the moment Drake's account of her on the Orient Promenade lost all significance of evil. The news had merely fired him with the impulse to find her again.

"It is really extraordinarily romantic up here," Maurice exclaimed, bursting in upon his reverie.

"Yes, I suppose that's the reason," Michael admitted.

"The reason of what?" Maurice asked.

"Of what I was thinking," Michael said.

Maurice waited for him to explain further, but Michael was silent; and almost immediately Castleton came back with provision for lunch.

Soon after they had eaten Michael said he would leave them to their hammering. Then he went back to Cheyne Walk and, finding the house still and empty in the sunlight, he packed a kit-bag, called a hansom-cab, and told the driver to go to the Seven Sisters Road.

CHAPTER II

NEPTUNE CRESCENT

The existence of the Seven Sisters Road had probably not occurred to Michael since in the hazel-coppices of Clere Abbey he had first made of it at Brother Aloysius' behest the archetype of Avernus, and yet his choice of it now for entrance to the underworld was swift as instinct. The quest of Lily was already beginning to assume the character of a deliberate withdrawal from the world in which he familiarly moved. With the instant of his resolve all that in childhood and in youth he had apprehended of the dim territory, which in London sometimes lay no farther away than the other side of the road, demanded the trial of his experience.

That he had never yet been to the Seven Sisters Road gave it a mystery; that it was not very far from Kentish Town gave it a gruesomeness, for ever since Mrs. Pearcey's blood-soaked perambulator Kentish Town had held for him a macaber significance: of the hellish portals mystery and gruesomeness were essential attributes. The drive was for a long time tediously pleasant in the June sunshine; but when the cab had crossed the junction of the Euston Road with the Tottenham Court Road, unknown London with all its sly and labyrinthine romance lured his fancy onward. Maple's and Shoolbred's, those outposts of shopping civilization, were left behind, and the Hampstead Road with a hint of roguery began. He was not sure what exactly made the Hampstead Road so disquieting. It was probably a mere trick of contrast between present squalor and the greenery of its end. The road itself was merely grim, but it had a nightmare capacity for suggesting that deviation by a foot from the thoroughfare itself would lead to obscure calamities. Those bright yellow omnibuses in which he had never traveled, how he remembered them from the days of Jack the Ripper, and the horror of them skirting the Strand by Trafalgar Square on winter dusks after the pantomime. Even now their painted destinations affected him with a dismay that real people could be familiar with this sinister route.

Here was the Britannia, a terminus which had stuck in his mind for years as situate in some gray limbo of farthest London. Here it was, a tawdry and not very large public-house exactly like a hundred others. Now the cab was bearing round to the right, and presently upon an iron railway bridge Michael read in giant letters the direction Kentish Town behind a huge leprous hand pointing to the left. The hansom clattered through the murk beneath, past the dim people huddled upon the pavement, past a wheel-barrow and the obscene skeletons and outlines of humanity chalked upon the arches of sweating brick. Here then was Kentish Town. It lay to the left of this bridge that was the color of stale blood. Michael told the driver to stop for one moment, and he leaned forward over the apron of the cab to survey the cross-street of swarming feculent humanity that was presumably the entering highway. A train roared over the bridge; a piano organ gargled its tune; a wagon-load of iron girders drew near in a clanging tintamar of slow progress. Michael's brief pause was enough to make such an impression of pandemoniac din as almost to drive out his original conception of Kentish Town as a menacing and gruesome suburb. But just as the cab reached the beginning of the Camden Road, he caught sight of a slop-shop where old clothes smothered the entrance with their mucid heaps and, just beyond, of three houses from whose surface the stucco was peeling in great scabs and the damp was oozing in livid arabesques and scrawls of verdigris. This group restored to Kentish Town a putative disquiet, and the impression of mere dirt and noise and exhalations of fried fish were merged in the more definite character allotted by his prefiguration.

The Camden Road was, in contrast with what had gone before, a wide and easy thoroughfare which let in the blue summer sky; and it was not for some minutes that Michael began to notice what a queerness came from the terraces that branched off on either side. The suggestion these terraces could weave extended itself to the detached houses of the main road. In the gaps between them long parallelograms of gardens could be seen joining others even longer that led up to the backs of another road behind. Sometimes it seemed that fifty gardens at once were visible, circumscribed secretive pleasure-grounds in the amount of life they could conceal, the life that could prosper and decay beneath their arbors merely for that conspiracy of gloating windows. It was impossible not to speculate upon the quality of existence in these precise enclosures; and to this the chapels of obscure sects that the cab occasionally passed afforded an indication. To these arid little tabernacles the population stole out on Sunday mornings. There would be something devilish about these reunions. Upon these pinchbeck creeds their souls must surely starve, must slowly shrink to desiccated imps. Anything more spiritually malevolent than those announcements chalked upon the black notice-board of the advent of the hebdomadal messiah, the peregrine cleric, the sacred migrant was impossible to imagine. With what apostolic cleverness would he impose himself upon these people, and how after the gravid midday meal of the Sabbath he would sit in those green arbors like a horrible Chinese fum. The cabman broke in upon Michael's fantastic depression by calling down through the trap that they were arrived at the Nag's Head and what part of Seven Sisters Road did he want.

Michael was disappointed by the Seven Sisters Road. It seemed to be merely the garish mart of a moderately poor suburban population. There was here nothing to support the diabolic legend with which under the suggestion of Brother Aloysius he had endowed it. Certainly of all the streets he had passed this afternoon there had been none less inferential of romance than this long shopping street.

"What number do you want, sir?" the driver repeated.

"Well, really I want rooms," Michael explained. "Only this seems a bit noisy."

"Yes, it is a bit boisterous," the cabman agreed.

Michael told him to drive back along the Camden Road; but when he began to examine the Camden Road as a prospective place of residence, it became suddenly very dull and respectable. The locked-up chapels and the quiet houses declined from ominousness into respectability, and he wondered how he had managed only a quarter of an hour ago to speculate upon the inner life they adumbrated. Nothing could be less surreptitious than those chatting nursemaids, and actually in one of the parallelograms of garden a child was throwing a scarlet ball high into the air. The cab was already nearing the iron railway bridge of Kentish Town, and Michael had certainly no wish to lodge in a noisy slum.

"Try turning off to the left," he called to the driver through the roof.

The maneuver seemed likely to be successful, for they entered almost immediately a district of Victorian terraces, where the name of each street was cut in stone upon the first house; and so fine and well-proportioned was each superscription that the houses' declension from gentility was the more evident and melancholy.

Michael was at last attracted to a crescent of villas terminating an unfrequented gray street and, for the sake of a pathetic privacy, guarded in front by a sickle-shaped inclosure of grimy Portugal laurels. Neptune Crescent, partly on account of its name and partly on account of the peculiar vitreous tint which the stone had acquired with age, carried a marine suggestion. The date *1805* in spidery numerals and the iron verandas, which even on this June day were a mockery, helped the illusion that here was a forgotten by-way in an old sea-port. A card advertising Apartments stood in the window of Number Fourteen. Michael signaled the driver to stop: then he alighted and rang the bell. The Crescent was strangely silent. Very far away he could hear the whistle of a train. Close at hand there was nothing but the jingle of the horse's harness and the rusty mewing of a yellow cat which was wheedling its lean body in and out of the railings of the falciform garden.

Soon the landlady opened the door and stood inquisitively in the narrow passage. She was a woman of probably about thirty-five with stubby fingers; her skin was rather moist, but she had a good-natured expression, and perhaps when the curl-papers were taken out from her colorless hair, and when lace frills and common finery should soften her turgid outlines she would be handsome in a labored sort of way. The discussion with Mrs. Murdoch about her vacant rooms did not take long. Michael had made up his mind to any horrors of dirt and discomfort, and he was really pleasantly surprised by their appearance. As for Mrs. Murdoch, she was evidently too much interested to know what had brought Michael to her house to make any difficulties in the way of his accommodation.

"Will you want dinner to-night?" she asked doubtfully.

"No, but I'd like some tea now, if you can manage it; and I suppose you can let me have a latchkey?"

"I've got the kettle on the boil at this moment. I was going out myself for the evening. Meeting my husband at the Horseshoe. There's only one other lodger—Miss Carlyle. And she's in the profession."

As Mrs. Murdoch made this announcement, she looked up at the fly-frecked ceiling, and Michael thought how extraordinarily light and meaningless her eyes were and how curiously dim and heavy this small sitting-room was against the brilliancy of the external summer.

"Well, then, tea when I can get it," said Mrs. Murdoch cheerfully. "And the double-u is just next your bedroom on the top floor. That's all, I think."

She left him with a backward smile over her shoulder, as if she were loath to relinquish the study of this unusual visitor to Neptune Crescent.

Michael when he was alone examined the chairs that were standing about the room as stiff as grenadiers in their red rep. He stripped them of their antimacassars and pulled the one that looked least uncomfortable close to the window. Outside, the yellow cat was still mewing; but the cab was gone and down the gray street that led to Neptune Crescent here and there sad-gaited wayfarers were visible. Two or three sparrows were cheeping in a battered laburnum, and all along the horizon the blue sky descending to the smoke of London had lost its color and had been turned to the similitude of tarnished metal. A luxurious mournfulness was in the view, and he leaned out over the sill scenting the reasty London air.

It was with a sudden shock of conviction that Michael realized he was in Neptune Crescent, Camden Town, and that yesterday he had actually been in Oxford. And why was he here? The impulse which had brought him must have lain deeper in the recesses of his character than those quixotic resolutions roused by Drake's legend of Lily. He would not otherwise have determined at once upon so complete a demigration. He would have waited to test the truth of Drake's story. His first emotional despair had vanished with almost unaccountable ease. Certainly he wanted to be independent of the criticism of his friends until he had proved his purpose unwavering, and he might ascribe this withdrawal to a desire for a secluded and unflinching contemplation of a life that from Cheyne Walk he could never focus. But ultimately he must acknowledge that his sojourn here, following as it did straight upon his entrance into the underworld through the disappointing portals of the Seven Sisters Road, was due to that ancient lure of the shades. This experience was foredoomed from very infancy. It was designated in childish dreams to this day indelible. He could not remember any period in his life when the speculum of hidden thought had not reflected for his fear that shadow of evil which could overcast the manifestations of most ordinary existence. Those days of London fog when he had sat desolately in the pinched red house in Carlington Road; those days when on his lonely walks he had passed askance by Padua Terrace; the shouting of murders by newspaper-boys on drizzled December nights; all those dreadful intimations in childhood had procured his present idea of London. With the indestructible truth of earliest impressions they still persisted behind the outward presentation of a normal and comfortable procedure in the midst of money, friends, and well-bred conventions. Nor had that speculum been merely the half-savage fancy of childhood, the endowment by the young of material things with immaterial potencies. Phantoms which had slunk by as terrors invisible to the blind eyes of grown-ups had been abominably incarnate for him. Brother Aloysius had been something more than a mere personification, and that life which the ex-monk had indicated as scarcely even below the surface, so easy was it to enter, had he not entered it that one night very easily?

Destiny, thought Michael, had stood with pointed finger beside the phantoms and the realities of the underworld. There for him lay very easily discernible the true corollary to the four years of Oxford. They had been years of rest and refreshment, years of armament with wise and academic and well-observed theories of behavior that would defeat the victory of evil. It was very satisfactory to discover definitely that he was not a Pragmatist. He had suspected all that crew of philosophers. He would bring back Lily from evil, not from any illusion of evil. He would not allow himself to disparage the problem before him by any speciousness of worldly convenience. It was imperative to meet Lily again as one who moving in the shadows meets another in the nether gloom. They had met first of all as boy and girl, as equals. Now he must not come too obviously from the world she had left behind her. Such an encounter would never give him more than at best a sentimental appeal; at worst it could have the air of a priggish reclamation, and she would forever elude him, she with secret years within her experience. His instinct first to sever himself from his own world must have been infallible, and it was on account of that instinct that now he found himself in Neptune Crescent leaning over the window-sill and scenting the reasty London air.

And how well secluded was this room. If he met Lonsdale or Maurice or Wedderburn, it would be most fantastically amusing to evade them at the evening's end, to retreat from their company into Camden Town; into Neptune Crescent unimaginable to them; into this small room with its red rep chairs and horsehair sofa and blobbed valances and curtains; to this small room where the dark blue wall-paper inclosed him with a matted vegetation and the picture of Belshazzar's Feast glowered above the heavy sideboard; to this small room made rich by the two thorny shells upon the mantelpiece, by the bowl of blond goldfish in ceaseless dim circumnatation, and by those colored pampas plumes and the bulrushes in their conch of nacreous glass.

Mrs. Murdoch came in with tea which he drank while she stood over him admiringly.

"Do you think you'll be staying long?" she inquired.

Michael asked if she wanted the rooms for anyone else.

"No. No. I'm really very glad to let them. You'll find it nice and quiet here. There's only Miss Carlyle, who's in the profession and comes in sometimes a little late. Mr. Murdoch is a chemist. But of course he hasn't got his own shop now."

She paused, and seemed to expect Michael would comment on Mr. Murdoch's loss of independence; so he said, "Of course not," nodding wisely.

"There was a bit of trouble through his being too kind-hearted to a servant-girl," said Mrs. Murdoch, looking quickly at the door and shaking her curl-papers. "Yes. Though I don't know why I'm telling you straight off as you might say. But there, I'm funny sometimes. If I take to anybody, there's nothing I won't do for them. Alf—that *is* my old man—he gets quite aggravated with me over it. So if you happen to get into conversation with him, you'd better not let on you know he used to have a shop of his own."

Michael, wondering how far off were these foreshadowed intimacies with his landlord, promised he would be very discreet, and asked where Mr. Murdoch was working now.

"In a chemist's shop. Just off of the Euston Road. You know," she said, beaming archly. "It's what you might call rather a funny place. Only he gets good money, because the boss knows he can trust him."

Michael nodded his head in solemn comprehension of Mr. Murdoch's reputation, and asked his landlady if she had such a thing as a postcard.

"Well, there. I wonder if I have. If I have, it's in the kitchen dresser, that's a sure thing. Perhaps you'd like to come down and see the kitchen?"

Michael followed her downstairs. There were no basements in Neptune Crescent, and he was glad to think his bedroom was above his sitting-room and on the top floor. It would have been hot just above the kitchen.

"Miss Carlyle has her room here," said Mrs. Murdoch, pointing next door to the kitchen. "Nice and handy for her as she's rather late sometimes. I hate to hear anybody go creaking upstairs, I do. It makes me nervous."

The kitchen was pleasant enough and looked out upon a narrow strip of garden full of coarse plants.

"They'll be very merry and bright, won't they?" said Mrs. Murdoch, smiling encouragement at the greenery. "It's wonderful what you can do nowadays for threepence."

Michael asked what they were.

"Why, sunflowers, of course, only they want another month yet. I have them every year—yes. They're less trouble than rabbits or chickens. Now where did I see that postcard?"

She searched the various utensils, and at last discovered the postcard stuck behind a mutilated clock.

"What *will* they bring out next?" demanded Mrs. Murdoch, surveying it with affectionate approbation. "Pretty, I call it."

A pair of lovers in black plush were sitting enlaced beneath a pink frosted moon.

"Just the thing, if you're writing to your young lady," said Mrs. Murdoch, offering it to Michael.

He accepted it with many expressions of gratitude, but when he was in his own room he laughed very much at the idea of sending it to his mother in Cheyne Walk. However, as he must write and tell her he would not be home for some time, he decided to go out and buy both writing materials and unillustrated postcards. When he came back he found Mrs. Murdoch feathered for the evening's entertainment. She gave him the latchkey, and from his window Michael watched her progress down Neptune Crescent. Just before her lavender dress disappeared behind the Portugal laurels she turned round and waved to him. He wondered what his mother would say if she knew from what curious corner of London the news of his withdrawal would reach her to-night.

The house was very still, and the refulgence of the afternoon light streaming into the small room fused the raw colors to a fiery concordancy. Upon the silence sounded presently a birdlike fidgeting, and Michael going out onto the landing to discover what it was, caught to his surprise the upward glance of a thin little woman in untidy pink.

"Hulloa!" she cried. "I never knew there was anybody in—you did give me a turn. I've only just woke up."

Michael explained the situation, and she seemed relieved.

"I've been asleep all the afternoon," she went on. "But it's only natural in this hot weather to go to sleep in the afternoon if you don't go out for a walk. Why don't you come down and talk to me while I have some tea?"

Michael accepted the invitation with a courtesy which he half suspected this peaked pink little creature considered diverting.

"You'll excuse the general untidiness," she said. "But really in this weather anyone can't bother to put their things away properly."

Michael assented, and looked round at the room. It certainly was untidy. The large bed was ruffled where she had been lying down, and the soiled copy of a novelette gave it a sort of stale slovenry. Over the foot hung an accumulation of pink clothes. On the chairs, too, there were clothes pink and white, and the door bulged with numberless skirts. Miss Carlyle herself wore a pink blouse whose front had escaped the constriction of a belt. Even her face was a flat unshaded pink, and her thin lips would scarcely have showed save that the powder round the edges was slightly caked. Yet there was nothing of pink's freshness and pleasant crudity in the general effect. It was a tired, a frowsy pink like a fondant that has lain a long while in a confectioner's window.

"Take a chair and make yourself at home," she invited him. "What's your name?"

He told her "Fane."

"You silly thing, you don't suppose I'm going to call you Mr. Fane, do you? What's your other name? Michael? That's Irish, isn't it? I used to know a fellow once called Micky Sullivan. I suppose they call you Micky at home."

He was afraid he was invariably known as Michael, and Miss Carlyle sighed at the stiff sort of a name it was.

"Mine's Poppy," she volunteered. "That's much more free and easy. Or I think so," she added rather doubtfully, as Michael did not immediately celebrate its license by throwing pillows at her. "Are you really lodging here?" she went on. "You don't look much like a pro."

Michael said that was so much the better, as he wasn't one.

"I've got you at last," cried Poppy. "You're a shop-walker at Russell's."

He could not help laughing very much at this, and the queer pink room seemed to become more faded at the sound of his merriment. Poppy looked offended by the reception of her guess, and Michael hastened to restore her good temper by asking questions of her.

"You're on the stage, aren't you?"

"I usually get into panto," she admitted.

"Aren't you acting now?"

"Yes, I don't think. You needn't be funny."

"I wasn't trying to be funny."

"You mind your business," she said bitterly. "And I'll look after mine."

"There doesn't seem to be anything very rude in asking if you're acting now," said Michael.

"Oh, shut up! As if you didn't know."

"Know what?" he repeated.

He looked so genuinely puzzled that Poppy seemed to make an effort to overcome her suspicion of his mockery.

"It's five years since I went on the game," she said.

Michael blushed violently, partly on her account, partly for his own stupidity, and explained that Mrs. Murdoch had told him she was in the profession.

"Well, you didn't expect her to say 'my ground-floor front's a gay woman,' did you?"

He agreed that such an abrupt characterization would have surprised him.

"Well, I'm going out to get dinner now," she announced.

"Why don't you dine with me?" Michael suggested.

She looked at him doubtfully.

"Can you afford it?"

"I think I could manage it."

"Because if we *are* in the same house that doesn't say you've got to pay my board, does it?" she demanded proudly.

"Once in a way won't matter," Michael insisted. "And we might go on to a music hall afterward."

"Yes, we might, if I hadn't got to pay the woman who's looking after my kid for some clothes she's made for him," said Poppy. "And sitting with you at the Holborn all night won't do that. No, you can give me dinner and then I'll P.O. I'm not going to put on a frock even for you, because I never get off only when I'm in a coat and skirt."

Michael rose to leave the room while Poppy got ready.

"Go on, sit down. As you're going to take me out to dinner, you can talk to me while I dress as a reward."

In this faded pink room where the sun was by now shining with a splendor that made all the strewn clothes seem even more fusty and overblown, Michael could not have borne to see a live thing take shape as it were from such corruption. He made an excuse therefore of letters to be written and left Poppy to herself, asking to be called when she was ready.

Michael's own room upstairs had a real solidity after the ground-floor front. He wondered if it were possible that Lily was inhabiting at this moment such a room as Poppy's. It could not be. It could not be. And he realized that he had pictured Lily like Manon in the midst of luxury, craving for magnificence and moving disdainfully before gilded mirrors. This Poppy Carlyle of Neptune Crescent belonged to another circle of the underworld. Lily would be tragical, but this little peaked creature downstairs was scarcely even pathetic. Indeed, she was almost grotesque with the coat and skirt that was to insure her getting off. Of course her only chance was to attract a jaded glance by her positive plainness, her schoolma'am air, her decent unobtrusiveness. Yet she was plucky, and she had accepted the responsibility of supporting her child. There was, too, something admirable in the candor with which she had treated him. There was something friendly and birdlike about her, and he thought how when he had been first aware of her movements below he had compared them to a bird's fidgeting. There was something really appealing about the gay woman of the ground-floor front. He laughed at her description; and then he remembered regretfully that he had allowed her to forego what might after all have been for her a pleasant evening because she must pay for some clothes the woman who was looking after her child. He could so easily have offered to give her the money. No matter, he could make amends at once and offer it to her now. It would be doubtless an unusual experience for her to come into contact with someone whose rule of life was not dictated by the brutal self-interest of those with whom her commerce must generally lie. She would serve to bring to the proof his theory that so much of the world's beastliness could be cleansed by having recourse to the natural instincts of decent behavior without any grand effort of reformation. Nevertheless, Michael did feel very philanthropic when he went down to answer Poppy's summons.

241

"I say," he began at once. "It was stupid of me just now not to suggest that I should find the money for your kid's clothes. Look here, we'll go to the Holborn after dinner and——" he paused. He felt a delicacy in inquiring how much exactly she might expect to lose by giving him her company—"and—er—I suppose a couple of pounds would buy something?"

"I say, kiddie, you're a sport," she said. "Only look here, don't go and spend more than what you can afford. It isn't as if we'd met by chance, as you might say."

"Oh no, I can afford two pounds," Michael assured her.

"Where shall we go? I know a nice room which the woman lets me have for four shillings. That's not too much, is it?"

He was touched by her eager consideration for his purse, and he stammered, trying to explain as gently as he could that the two pounds was not offered for hire.

"But, kiddie, I can't bring you back here. Not even if you do lodge here. These aren't gay rooms."

"I don't want to go anywhere with you," said Michael. "The money is a present."

"Oh, is it?" she flamed out. "Then you can keep your dirty money. Thanks, I haven't come down to charity. Not yet. If I'm not good enough for you, you can keep your money. I believe you're nothing more than a dirty ponce. I've gone five years without keeping a fellow yet. And I'm not going to begin now. That's very certain. Are you going out or am I going out? Because I don't want to be seen with you. You and your presents. Gard! I should have to be drunk on claret and lemon before I went home with you."

Michael had nothing to say to her and so he went out, closing the front door quickly upon her rage. His first impression when he gained the fresh air was of a fastidious disgust. Here in the Crescent the orange lucency of the evening shed such a glory that the discoloration of the houses no longer spoke of miserably drawn-out decay, but took on rather the warmth of live rock. The deepening shadows of that passage where the little peaked creature had spat forth her fury made him shudder with the mean and vicious passions they now veiled. Very soon, however, his disgust died away. Looking back at Neptune Crescent, he knew there was not one door in all that semicircle which did not putatively conceal secrets like those of Number Fourteen. Like poisonous toadstools in rankness and gloom, the worst of human nature must flourish here. It was foolish to be disgusted; indeed, already a half-aroused curiosity had taken its place, and Michael regretted that he had not stayed to hear what more she would have said. How far she had been from appreciating the motives that prompted his offer of money. Poppy's injustice began to depress him. He felt, walking southward to Piccadilly, an acute sense of her failure to be grateful from his point of view. It hurt him to find sincerity so lightly regarded. Then he realized that it was her vanity which had been touched. *Hell knows no fury like a woman scorned.* The ability to apply such a famous generalization directly to himself gave Michael a great satisfaction. It was strange to be so familiar with a statement, and then suddenly like this to be staggered by its truth. He experienced a sort of pride in linking himself on to one of the great commonplaces of rhetoric. He need no longer feel misjudged, since Poppy had played a universal part. In revulsion he felt sorry for her. He hated to think how deeply her pride must have been wounded. He could not expect her to esteem the reason which had made him refuse her. She could have little comprehension of fastidiousness and still less could she grasp the existence of an abstract morality that in its practical expression must have seemed to her so insulting. That, however, did not impugn the morality, nor did it invalidate the desire to befriend her. Impulse had not really betrayed him: the mistake had been in his tactlessness, in a lack of worldly knowledge. Moreover, Poppy was only an incident, and until Lily was found he had no business to turn aside. Nevertheless, he had learned something this evening; he had seen proved in action a famous postulate of feminine nature, and the truth struck him with a sharpness that no academic demonstration had ever had the power to effect.

On the whole, Michael was rather pleased with himself as he rode on the front seat of the omnibus down Tottenham Court Road in the cool of the evening.

At the Horseshoe he alighted and went into the saloon bar on the chance of seeing what Mr. Murdoch looked like; but there was no sign of the landlady and her husband. The saloon bar smelt very strongly of spilt stout; and a number of men, who looked like draymen in tailcoats and top-hats, were arguing about money. He was glad to leave the tavern behind; and in a Soho restaurant he ate a tranquil dinner, listening with much amusement to the people round him. He liked to hear each petty host assure his guests that he had brought them to a place of which very few but himself knew. All the diners under the influence of this assurance stared at one another like conspirators.

Just before nine o'clock. Michael reached the Orient Palace of Varieties, and with excitement bubbling up within him, notwithstanding all his efforts to stay unmoved, he joined the throng of the Promenade. He looked about him at first in trepidation. Although all the way from Camden Town he had practiced this meeting with Lily, now at its approach his presence of mind vanished, and he felt that to meet her suddenly without a longer preparation would lead him to make a fool of himself. However, in the first quick glance he could not see anyone who resembled her, and he withdrew to the secluded apex of the curving Promenade whence he could watch most easily the ebb and flow of the crowd. That on the stage a lady of the haute école was with a curious wooden rapidity putting a white horse through a number of tricks did not concern his attention beyond the moment. For him the Promenade was the performance. Certainly at the Orient it was a better staged affair than that weary heterogeneous mob at The Oxford. At the Orient there was an unity of effect, an individuality, and a conscious equipment. At The Oxford the whole business had resembled a suburban parade. Here was a real exposition of vice like the jetty of Alexandria in olden days. Indeed, so cynical was the function of the Orient Promenade that the frankness almost defeated its object, and the frequenters instead of profiting by the facilities for commerce allowed themselves to be drugged into perpetual meditation upon an attractive contingency.

Seen from this secluded corner, the Promenade resembled a well-filled tank in an aquarium. The upholstery of shimmering green plush, the dim foreground, the splash of light from the bar in one corner, the gliding circumambient throng among the pillars and, displayed along the barrier, the bright-hued ladies like sea-anemones—there was nothing that spoiled the comparison. Moreover, the longer Michael looked, the more nearly was the effect achieved. At intervals women whose close-fitting dresses seemed deliberately to imitate scales went by: and generally the people eyed one another with the indifferent frozen eyes of swimming fish. There was indeed something cold-blooded in the very atmosphere, and it was from, this rapacious and vivid shoal of women that he was expecting Lily to materialize. Yet he was better able to imagine her in the luxury of the Orient than sleeping down the sun over a crumpled novelette in such a room as Poppy's in Camden Town.

242

The evening wore itself away, and the motion in that subaqueous air was restful in its continuity. Michael was relieved by the assurance that he had still a little time in which to compose himself to face the shock he knew he must ultimately expect from meeting Lily again. The evening wore itself away. The lady of the haute école was succeeded by a band of Caucasian wrestlers, by a troupe of Bolivian gymnasts, by half a dozen cosmopolitan ebullitions of ingenuity. The ballet went its mechanical course, and as each line of dancers grouped themselves, it was almost possible to hear the click of the kaleidoscope's shifting squares and lozenges. Michael wondered vaguely about the girls in the ballet and whether they were happy. It seemed absurd to think that down there on the stage there were eighty or ninety individuals each with a history, so little more did they seem from here than dolls. And on the Promenade where it was quite certain that every woman had a history to account for her presence there, how utterly living had quenched life. The ballet was over, and he passed out into the streets.

For a fortnight Michael came every evening to the Orient without finding Lily. They were strange evenings, these that were spent in the heart of London without meeting anyone he knew. It was no doubt by the merest chance that none of his friends saw him at the Orient, and yet he began to fancy that actually every evening he did, as it were, by some enchantment fade from the possibility of recognition. He felt as if his friends would not perceive his presence, so much would they in that circumambient throng take on the characteristics of its eternal motion. They too, he felt, irresponsive as fish, would glide backward and forward with the rest. Nor did Michael meet anyone whom he knew at any of the restaurants or cafés to which he went after the theater. By the intensity of his one idea, the discovery of Lily, he cut himself off from all communion with the life of the places he visited. He often thought that perhaps acquaintances saw him there, that perhaps he had seemed deliberately to avoid their greetings and for that reason had never been hailed. Yet he was aware of seeing women whom he had seen the night before, mostly because they bore a superficial likeness to Lily; and sometimes he would be definitely conscious of a dress or a hat, perceiving it in the same place at the same hour, but never meeting the wearer's glance.

He did not make any attempt to be friendly with Poppy after their unpleasant encounter, and he always tried to be sure they would not meet in the hall or outside the front door. That he was successful in avoiding her gave him a still sharper sense of the ease with which it was possible to seclude one's self from the claims of human intercourse. He was happy in his room at Neptune Crescent, gazing out over the sickle-shaped garden of Portugal laurels, listening in a dream to the distant cries of railway traffic and reading the books which every afternoon he brought back from Charing Cross Road, so many books indeed that presently the room in 14 Neptune Crescent came curiously to resemble rooms in remote digs at Oxford, where poor scholars imposed their books on surroundings they could not afford to embellish. Mrs. Murdoch could not make Michael out at all. She used to stand and watch him reading, as if he were performing an intricate surgical operation.

"I never in all my life saw anyone read like you do," she affirmed. "Doesn't it tire your eyes?"

Then she would move a step nearer and spell out the title of the book, looking sideways at it like a fat goose.

"Holy Living and Holy Dying. Ugh! Enough to give you the horrors, isn't it? And only this morning they hung that fellow at Pentonville. This *is* Tuesday, isn't it?"

After three or four days of trying to understand him, Mrs. Murdoch decided that Alf must be called in to solve his peculiarity.

Mr. Alfred Murdoch was younger than Michael had expected. He could scarcely have been more than forty, and Michael had formed a preconception of an elderly chemist reduced by misfortune and misdeeds to the status of one of those individuals who with a discreet manner somewhere between a family doctor and a grocer place themselves at the service of the public in an atmosphere of antiseptics. Mr. Murdoch was not at all like this. He was a squat swarthy man with one very dark eye that stared fixedly regardless of the expression of its fellow. Michael could not make up his mind whether this eye were blind or not. He rather hoped it was, but in any case its fierce blankness was very disconcerting. Conversation between Michael and Mr. Murdoch was not very lively, and Mrs. Murdoch's adjutant inquisitiveness made Michael the more monosyllabic whenever her husband did commit himself to a direct inquiry.

"I looked for you in the Horseshoe the other evening," said Michael finally, at a loss how in any other way to give Mr. Murdoch an impression that he took the faintest interest in his existence.

"In the Horseshoe?" repeated Mr. Murdoch, in surprise. "I never go to the Horseshoe only when a friend asks me in to have one."

Michael saw Mrs. Murdoch frowning at him, and, perceiving that there was a reason why her husband must not suppose she had been to the Horseshoe on the evening of his arrival, he said he had gathered somehow, he did not exactly know where or why or when, that Mr. Murdoch was often to be found in the Horseshoe. He wished this awkward and unpleasant man would leave him and cock his rolling eye anywhere else but in his room.

"Bit of a reader, aren't you?" inquired the chemist.

Michael admitted he read a good deal.

"Ever read Jibbon's Decline and Fall of the Roman Empire?" continued the chemist.

"Some of it."

Mr. Murdoch said in that case it was just as well he hadn't bought some volumes he'd seen on a barrow in the Caledonian Road.

"Four-and-six, with two books out in the middle," he proclaimed.

Michael could merely nod his comment, though he racked his brains to think of some remark that would betray a vestige of cordiality. Mr. Murdoch got up to retire to the kitchen. He evidently did not find his tenant sympathetic. Outside on the landing Michael heard him say to his wife: "Stuck up la-di-da sort of a ——, isn't he?"

Presently the wife came up again.

"How did you like my old man?"

"Oh, very much."

"Did you notice his eye?"

Michael said he had noticed something.

"His brother Fred did that for him."

She spoke proudly, as if Fred's act had been a humane achievement. "When they were boys," she explained. "It gives him a funny look. I remember when I first met him it gave me the creeps, but I don't notice it really now. Would you believe he couldn't see an elephant with it?"

"I wondered if it were blind," said Michael.

"Blind as a leg of mutton," said Mrs. Murdoch, and still there lingered in her accents a trace of pride. Then suddenly her demeanor changed and there crept over her countenance what Michael was bound to believe to be an expression of coyness.

"Don't say anything more to Alf about the Horseshoe. You see, I only gave you the idea I was meeting him, because I didn't really know you very well at the time. Of course really I'd gone to see my sister. No, without a joke, I was spending the evening with a gentleman friend."

Michael looked at her in astonishment.

"My old man wouldn't half knock me about, if he had the least suspicion. But it's someone I knew before I was married, and that makes a difference, doesn't it?"

"Does your husband go out with lady friends he knew before he was married?" Michael asked, and wondered if Mrs. Murdoch would see an implied reproof.

"What?" she shrilled. "I'd like to catch him nosing after another woman. He wouldn't see a hundred elephants before I'd done with him. I'd show him."

"But why should you have freedom and not he?" Michael asked.

"Never mind about him. You let him try. You see what he'd get."

Michael did not think the argument could be carried on very profitably. So he showed signs of wanting to return to his book, and Mrs. Murdoch retired. What extraordinary standards she had, and how bitterly she was prepared to defend a convention, for after all in such a marriage the infidelity of the husband was nothing but a conventional offense: she obviously had no affection for him. The point of view became very topsyturvy in Neptune Crescent, Michael decided.

On the last evening of the fortnight during which he had regularly visited the Orient, Michael went straight back to Camden Town without waiting to scan the cafés and restaurants until half-past twelve as he usually had. This abode in Neptune Crescent was empty, and as always when that was the case the personality of the house was very vivid upon his imagination. As he turned up the gas-jet in the hall, the cramped interior with its fusty smell and its thread-bare staircarpet disappearing into the upper gloom round the corner seemed to be dreadfully closing in upon him. The old house conveyed a sense of having the power to choke out of him every sane and orderly and decent impulse. For a whim of tristfulness, for the luxury of consummating the ineffable depression the house created in him, Michael prepared to glance at every one of the five rooms. The front door armed with the exaggerated defenses of an earlier period in building tempted him to lock and double-lock it, to draw each bolt and to fasten the two clanking chains. He had the fantastic notion to do this so that Mr. and Mrs. Murdoch and Poppy might stay knocking and ringing outside in the summer night, while himself escaped into the sunflowers of the back garden and went climbing over garden wall and garden wall to abandon this curious mixture of salacity and respectableness, of flimsiness and solidity, this quite indefinably raffish and sinister and yet in a way strangely cozy house. He opened gingerly the door of the ground-floor front. He peered cautiously in, lest Poppy should be lying on her bed. The gas-jet was glimmering with a scarcely perceptible pinhead of blue flame, but the light from the passage showed all her clothes still strewn about. From the open door came out the faint perfume of stale scent which mingled with the fusty odor of the passage in a most subtle expression of the house's personality. He closed the door gently. In the silence it seemed almost as if the least percussion would rouse the very clothes from their stupor of disuse. In the kitchen was burning another pinhead of gas, and the light from the passage reaching here very dimly was only just sufficient to give all the utensils a ghostly sheen and to show the mutilated hands at a quarter past five upon the luminous face of the clock. This unreal hour added the last touch to unreality, and when Michael went upstairs and saw the books littering his room, even they were scarcely guarantors of his own actuality. He had a certain queasiness in opening the door of the Murdochs' bedroom, and he was rather glad when he was confronted here by a black void whose secrecy he did not feel tempted to violate. With three or four books under his arm he went upstairs to bed. As he leaned out of the window two cats yawled and fizzed at one another among the laurels, and then scampered away into muteness. From a scintillation of colored lights upon the horizon he could hear the scrannel sounds of the railway come thinly along the night air. Nothing else broke the silence of the nocturnal streets. Michael felt tired, and he was disappointed by his failure to find Lily. Just as he was dozing off, he remembered that his Viva Voce at Oxford was due some time this week. He must go back to Cheyne Walk to-morrow, and on this resolution he fell asleep.

Michael woke up with a start and instantly became aware that the house was full of discordant sounds. For a minute or two he lay motionless trying to connect the noise with the present, trying to separate his faculties from the inspissate air that seemed to be throttling them. He was not yet free from the confusion of sleep, and for a few seconds he could only perceive the sound almost visibly churning the clotted darkness that was stifling him. Gradually the clamor resolved itself into the voices of Mr. Murdoch, Mrs. Murdoch and Poppy at the pitch of excitement. Nothing was intelligible except the oaths that came up in a series of explosions detached from the main din. He got out of bed and lit the gas, saw that it was one o'clock, dressed himself roughly, and opened the door of his room.

"Yes, my lad, you thought you was very clever."

"No, I didn't think I was clever. Now then."

"Yes! You can spend all your money on that muck. The sauce of it. In a hansom!"

Here Poppy's voice came in with a malignant piping sound.

"Muck yourself, you dirty old case-keeper!"

"You call me a case-keeper? What men have I ever let you bring back here?"

Mrs. Murdoch's voice was swollen with wrath.

"You don't know how many men I haven't brought back. So now, you great ugly mare!" Poppy howled.

"The only fellow you've ever brought to my house is that one-eyed —— who calls himself my husband. Mister *Mur*doch! Mis-ter *Murdoch!* And you get out of my house in the streets where you belong. I don't want no two-and-fours in *my* house."

"Hark at her!" Poppy cried, in a horrible screaming laugh. "Why don't you go back on the streets yourself? Why, I can remember you as one of the old fourpenny Hasbeens when I was still dressmaking; a dirty drunken old teat that couldn't have got off with a blind tramp."

Michael punctuated each fresh taunt and accusation with a step forward to interfere; and every time he held himself back, pondering the impossibility of extracting from these charges and countercharges any logical assignment of blame. It made him laugh to think how extraordinarily in the wrong they all three were and at the same time how they were all perfectly convinced they were right. The only factor left out of account was Mrs. Murdoch's own behavior. He wondered rather what effect that gentleman friend would produce on the husband. He decided that he had better go back to bed until the racket subsided. Then, just as he was turning away in the midst of an outpouring of vileness far more foul than anything uttered so far, he heard what sounded like a blow. That of course could not be tolerated, and he descended to intervene.

The passage was the field of battle, and the narrow space seemed to give not only an added virulence to the fight, but also an added grotesquery. When Michael arrived at the head of the staircase, Alf had pinned his wife to the wall and was shouting to Poppy over his shoulder to get back into her own room. Poppy would go halfway, but always a new insult would occur to her, and she would return to fling it at Mrs. Murdoch, stabbing the while into its place again a hatpin which during her retreats she always half withdrew.

As for Mrs. Murdoch, she was by now weeping hysterically and occasionally making sudden forward plunges that collapsed like jelly.

Michael paused at the head of the stairs, wondering what to say. It seemed to him really rather a good thing that Alf was restraining his wife. It would be extremely unpleasant to have to separate the two women if they closed with each other. He had almost decided to retire upstairs again, when Poppy caught sight of him and at once turned her abuse in his direction.

"What's it got to do with you?" she screamed. "What's the good in you standing gaping there? We all know what *you* are. We all know what she's always going up to *your* room for."

Mrs. Murdoch was heaving and puffing and groaning, and while Alf held her, his rolling eye with fierce and meaningless stare nearly made Michael laugh. However, he managed to be serious, and gravely advised Poppy to go to bed.

"Don't you dare try to order me about!" she shrieked. "Keep your poncified ways for that fat old maggot which her husband can't hardly hold, and I don't blame him. She's about as big as a omnibus."

"Oh, you wicked woman," sobbed Mrs. Murdoch. "Oh, you mean, hateful snake-in-the-grass! Oh, you filth!"

"Hold your jaw," commanded Alf. "If you don't want me to punch into you."

"All day she's in his room. Let him stand up and deny it if he can, the dirty tyke. Why don't you punch into *him*, Alf?" Poppy screamed.

Still that wobbling eye, blank and ferocious, was fixed upon vacancy.

"Let *me* look after Mrs. Murdoch I *don't* think!" shouted Poppy. "And be a man, even if you can't keep your old woman out of the lodger's room. —— ——! I wouldn't half slosh his jaw in, if I was a man, the —— ——!"

It was a question for Michael either of laughing outright or of being nauseated at the oaths streaming from that little woman's thin magenta lips. He laughed. Even with her paint, she still looked so respectable. When he began to laugh, he laughed so uncontrollably that he had to hold on to the rail of the balusters until they rattled like ribs.

Michael's laughter stung the group to frenzied action. Mrs. Murdoch spat in her husband's face, whereupon he immediately loosed his grip upon her shoulders. In a moment she and Poppy were clawing each other. Michael, though he was still laughing unquenchably, rushed downstairs to part them. He had an idea that both of the women instantly turned and attacked him. The hat-stand fell over: the scurfy front-door mat slid up and down the oil cloth: there was a reek of stale scent and dust and spirituous breath.

At last Michael managed to secure Poppy's thin twitching arms and to hold her fast, though she was kicking him with sharp-heeled boots and he was weak with inward laughter. Mrs. Murdoch in the lull began fecklessly to gather together the strands of her disordered hair. Alf, who had gone to peep from the window of the ground-floor front in case a policeman's bull's-eye were glancing on Neptune Crescent, reappeared in the doorway.

"What a smell of gas!" he exclaimed nervously.

There was indeed a smell of gas, and Michael remembered that Poppy in her struggle had grasped the bracket. She must have dislocated the lead pipe rather badly, for the light was already dimming and the gas was rushing out fast. The tumultuous scene was allayed. Mr. Murdoch hurried to cut off the main. Poppy retired into her room, slammed and locked the door. Michael went upstairs to bed, and just as darkness descended upon the house he saw his landlady painfully trying to raise the hat-stand, while with the other arm she felt aimlessly for strands of tumbled hair.

Next morning Michael was surprised to see Mrs. Murdoch enter very cheerfully with his tea; her hair that so short a time since had seemed eternally intractable had now shriveled into subjugatory curl-papers: of last night's tear-smudged face remained no memory in this beaming countenance.

"Quite a set-out we had last night, didn't we?" she said expansively. "But that Poppy, really, you know, she is the limit. Driving home with my old man in a hansom cab. There's a nice game to get up to. I was bound to let her have it. I couldn't have held myself in."

"I suppose you'll get rid of her now," said Michael.

"Oh, well, she's not so bad in some ways, and very quiet as a rule. She was a bit canned last night, and I suppose I'd had one or two myself. Oh, well, it wouldn't do, would it, if we never had a little enjoyment in this life?"

She left him wondering how he would ever be able to readjust his standards to the topsyturvy standards of the underworld, the topsyturvy feuds and reconciliations, the hatreds; the loves and jealousies and fears. But to-day he must leave this looking-glass world for a time.

Mrs. Murdoch was very much upset by his departure from Neptune Crescent.

"It seems such a pity," she said. "And just as I was beginning to get used to your ways. Oh, well, we'll meet again some day, I hope, this side of the cemetery."

Michael felt some misgivings about ordering a hansom after last night, but Mrs. Murdoch went cheerfully enough to fetch one. He drove away from Neptune Crescent, waving to her where she stood in the small doorway looking very large under that rusty frail veranda. He also waved rather maliciously to Poppy, as he caught sight of her sharp nose pressed against the panes of the ground-floor front.

CHAPTER III

THE CAFÉ D'ORANGE

Michael came back to Cheyne Walk with a sense of surprise at finding that it still existed; and when he saw the parlormaid he half expected she would display some emotion at his reappearance. After Neptune Crescent, it was almost impossible to imagine a female who was not subject to the violence of her mutable emotions. Yet her private life, the life of the alternate Sunday evening out, might be as passionate and gusty as any scene in Neptune Crescent. He looked at the tortoise-mouthed parlormaid with a new interest, until she became waxily pink under his stare.

"Mrs. Fane is in the drawing-room, sir." It was as if she were rebuking his observation.

His mother rose from her desk when he came to greet her.

"Dearest boy, how delightful to see you again, and so thoughtful of you to send me those postcards."

If she had asked him directly where he had been, he would have told her about Neptune Crescent, and possibly even about Lily. But as she did not, he could reveal nothing of the past fortnight. It would have seemed to him like the boring recitation of a dream, which from other people was a confidence he always resented.

"Stella and Alan are in the studio," she told him.

They chatted for a while of unimportant things, and then Michael said he would go and find them. As he crossed the little quadrangle of pallid grass and heard in the distance the sound of the piano he could not keep back the thought of how utterly Alan's company had replaced his own. Not that he was jealous, not that he was not really delighted; but a period of life was being rounded off. The laws of change were being rather ruthless just now. Both Alan and Stella were so obviously glad to see him that the fleck of bitterness vanished immediately, and he was at their service.

"Where have you been?" Stella demanded. "We go to Richmond. We send frantic wires to you to join us on the river, and when we come back you're gone. Where have you been?"

"I've been away," Michael answered, with a certain amount of embarrassment.

"My dear old Michael, we never supposed you'd been hiding in the cistern-cupboard for a fortnight," said Stella, striking three chords of cheerful contempt.

"I believe he went back to Oxford," suggested Alan.

"I am going up to-morrow," Michael said. "When is your Viva?"

"Next week. Where are you going to stay?"

"In college, if I can get hold of a room."

"Bother Oxford," interrupted Stella. "We want to know where you've been this fortnight."

"You do," Alan corrected.

"I'll tell you both later on," Michael volunteered. "Just at present I suppose you won't grudge me a secret. People who are engaged to be married should show a very special altruism toward people who are not."

"Michael, I will not have you being important and carrying about a secret with you," Stella declared.

"You can manage either me or Alan," Michael offered. "But you simply shall not manage both of us. Personally, I recommend you to break-in Alan."

With evasive banter he succeeded in postponing the revelation of what he was, as Stella said, up to.

"We're going in for Herefords," Alan suddenly announced without consideration for the trend of the talk. "You know. Those white-faced chaps."

Michael looked at him in astonishment.

"I was thinking about this place of Stella's in Huntingdonshire," Alan explained. "We went down to see it last week."

"Oh, Alan, why did you tell him? He doesn't deserve to be told."

"Is it decent?" Michael asked.

"Awfully decent," said Alan. "Rather large, you know."

"In fact, we shall belong to the squirearchy," cried Stella, crashing down upon the piano with the first bars of Chopin's most exciting Polonaise and from the Polonaise going off into an absurd impromptu recitative.

"We shall have a dog-cart—a high and shining dog-cart—and we shall go bowling down the lanes of the county of Hunts—because in books about people who live in the county and of the county and by with or from the county dog-carts invariably bowl—we shall have a herd of Herefordshire bulls and bullocks and bullockesses—and my husband Alan with a straw in his mouth will go every morning with the bailiff to inspect their well-being—— and three days every week from November to March we shall go hunting in Huntingdon—and when we aren't actually hunting in Huntingdon we shall be talking about hunting—and we shall also talk about the Primrose League and the foot-and-mouth disease and the evolutions of the new High Church Vicar—we shall...."

But Michael threw a cushion at her, and the recitative came to an end.

They all three talked for a long while more seriously of plans for life at Hardingham Hall.

"You know dear old Prescott requested me in his will that I would hyphen his name on to mine, whether I were married or single," said Stella. "So we shall be Mr. and Mrs. Prescott-Merivale. Alan has been very good about that, though I think he's got a dim idea it's putting on side. Stella Prescott-Merivale or The Curse of the County! And when I play I'm going to be Madame Merivale. I decline to be done out of the Madame! and everybody will pronounce it Marivahleh and I shall receive the unanimous encomia of the critical press."

"Life will be rather a rag," said Michael, with approbation.

"Of course it's going to be simply wonderful. Can't you see the headlines? From Chopin to Sheep. Madame Merivale, the famous Virtuosa, and her Flock of Barbary Long-tails."

It was all so very remote from Neptune Crescent, Michael thought. They really were going to be so ridiculously happy, these two, in their country life. And now they were talking of finding him a house close to Hardingham Hall. There must be just that small Georgian house, they vowed, where with a large garden of stately walks and a well-proportioned library of books he could stay in contented retreat. They promised him, too, that beyond the tallest cedar on the lawn a gazebo should command the widest, the greenest expanse of England ever beheld.

"It would so add to our reputation in the county of Hunts," said Stella, "if you were near by. We should feel so utterly Augustan. And of course you'd ride a nag. I'm not sure really that you wouldn't have to wear knee-breeches. I declare, Michael, that the very idea makes me feel like Jane Austen, or do I mean Doctor Johnson?"

"I should make up your mind which," Michael advised.

"But you know what I mean," she persisted. "The doctor's wife would come in to tea and tell us that her husband had dug up a mummy or whatever it was the Romans left about. And I should say, 'We must ask my brother about it. My brother, my dear Mrs. Jumble, will be sure to know. My brother knows everything.' And she would agree with a pursed-up mouth. 'Oh, pray do, my dear Mrs. Prescott-Merivale. Everyone says your brother is a great scholar. It's such a pleasure to have him at the Lodge. So very distinguished, is it not?'"

"If you're supposed to be imitating Jane Austen, I may as well tell you at once that it's not a bit like it."

"But I think you ought to come and live near us," Alan solemnly put in.

"Of course, my dear, he's coming," Stella declared.

"Of course I'm not," Michael contradicted. But he was very glad they wanted him; and then he thought with a pang how little they would want him with Lily in that well-proportioned library. How little Lily would enjoy the fat and placid Huntingdon meadows. How little, too, she would care to see the blackbird swagger with twinkling rump by the shrubbery's edge or hear him scatter the leaves in shrill affright. In the quick vision that came to him of a sleek lawn possessed by birds, Michael experienced his first qualm about the wisdom of what he intended to do.

"And how about Michael's wife?" Alan asked.

Michael looked quite startled by a query so coincident with his own.

"Oh, of course we shall find someone quite perfect for him," Stella confidently prophesied.

"No, really," said Michael to hide his embarrassment. "I object. Matchmaking ought not to begin during an engagement."

Stella paid no heed to the protest, and she began to describe a lady-love who should well become the surroundings in which she intended to place him.

"I think rather a Quakerish person, don't you, Alan? Rather neat and tiny with a great sense of humor and...."

"In fact, an admirable sick nurse," Michael interposed, laughing.

Soon he left them in the studio and went for a walk by the side of the river, thinking, as he strolled in the shade of the plane-trees, how naturally Stella would enter the sphere of English country life now that by fortune the opportunity had been given to her of following in the long line of her ancestors. That she would be able to do so seemed to Michael an additional reason why he should consider less the security of his own future, and he was vexed with himself for that fleeting disloyalty to his task.

Michael stayed at 202 High for his Viva. He occupied Wedderburn's old white-paneled room, which he noted with relief was still sacred to the tradition of a carefully chosen decorousness. The Viva was short and irrelevant. He supposed he had obtained a comfortable third, and really it seemed of the utmost unimportance in view of what a gulf now lay between him and Oxford. However, he mustered enough interest to stay in Cheyne Walk until the lists were out, and during those ten days he made no attempt to find Lily.

Alan got a third in Greats and Michael a first in History. Michael's immediate emotion was of gladness that Alan had no reason now to feel the disappointment. Then he began to wonder how on earth he had achieved a first. Many letters of congratulation arrived; and one or two of the St. Mary's dons suggested he should try for a fellowship at All Souls. The idea occupied his fancy a good deal, for it was attractive to have anything so remote come suddenly within the region of feasibleness. He would lose nothing by trying for it, and if he succeeded what a congenial existence offered itself. With private means he would be able to divide his time between Oxford and London. There would really be nothing to mar the perfect amenity of the life that seemed to stretch before him. Since he apparently had some talent (he certainly had not worked hard enough to obtain a first without some talent) he would prosecute the study of history. He would make himself famous in a select sort of way. He would become the authority of a minor tributary to the great stream of research. A set of very scholarly, very thorough works would testify to his reputation. There were plenty of archaic problems still to be solved. He cast a proprietary glance over the centuries, and he had almost decided to devote himself to the service of Otto I and Sylvester II, when in a moment the thought of Lily, sweeping as visibly before his mind as the ghost in an Elizabethan play, made every kind of research into the past seem a waste of resolution. He tore up the congratulatory letters and decided to let the future wait a while. This pursuit of Lily was a mad business, no doubt, but to come to grips with the present called for a certain amount of madness.

Alan remonstrated with him, when he heard that he had no intention of trying for All Souls.

"You are an extraordinary chap. You were always grumbling when you were up that you didn't know what you ought to do, and now when it's perfectly obvious you won't make the slightest attempt to do it."

"Used I to grumble?" asked Michael.

"Well, not exactly grumble. But you were always asking theoretical questions which had no answer," said Alan severely.

"What if I told you I'd found an answer to a great many of them?"

"Ever since I've been engaged to Stella you've found it necessary to be very mysterious. What are you playing at, Michael?"

"It's imaginable, don't you think, that I might be making up my mind to do something which I considered more vital for me than a fellowship at All Souls?"

"But it seems so obvious after your easy first that you should clinch it."

"I tell you it was a fluke."

"My third wasn't a fluke," said Alan. "I worked really hard for it."

"Thirds and firsts are equally unimportant in the long run," Michael argued. "You have already fitted into your place with the most complete exactitude. There's no dimension in your future that can possibly trouble you. Supposing I get this fellowship? It will either be too big for me, in which case I shall have to be perpetually puffing out my frills and furbelows to make a pretense of filling it, or it will be too small, and I shall have to pare down my very soul in order to squeeze into it most uncomfortably."

"You'll never do anything," Alan prophesied. "Because you'll always be doubting."

"I might get rid finally of that sense of insecurity," Michael pointed out. "With all doubts and hesitations I'm perfectly convinced of one great factor in human life—the necessity to follow the impulse which lies deeper than any reason. Reason is the enemy of civilization. Reason carried to the nth power can always with absurd ease be debauched by sentiment, and sentiment is mankind's wretched little lament for disobeying impulse. Women preserve this divinity because they are irrational. The New Woman claims equality with man because she claims to be as reasonable as men. She has fixed on voting for a Member of Parliament as the medium to display her reasonableness. The franchise is to be endowed with a sacramental significance. If the New Women win, they will degrade themselves to the slavery of modern men. But of course they won't win, because God is so delightfully irrational. By the way, it's worth noting that the peculiar vestment with which popular fancy has clothed the New Woman is called rational costume. You often hear of 'rationals' as a synonym for breeches. What was I saying? Oh, yes, about God being irrational. You never know what he'll do next. He is a dreadful problem for rationalists. That's why they have abolished him."

"You're confusing two different kinds of reason," said Alan. "What you call impulse—unless your impulse is mere madness—is what I might call reason."

"In that case I recommend you as a philosopher to set about the reconstruction of your terminology. I'm not a philosopher, and therefore I've given this vague generic name 'impulse' to something which deserves, such a powerful and infallible and overmastering impetus does it give to conduct, a very long name indeed."

"But if you're going through life depending on impulse," Alan objected, "you'll be no better off than a weathercock. You can't discount reason in this way. You must admit that our judgments are modified by experience."

"The chief thing we learn from experience is to place upon it no reliance whatever."

"It's no good arguing with you," Alan said. "Because what you call impulse I call reason, and what you call reason I call imperfect logic."

"Alan, I can't believe you only got a third. For really, you know, your conversation is a model of the philosophic manner. Anyway, I'm not going to try to be a Fellow of All Souls and you are going to be a country squire. Let's hold on to what certainties we can."

Michael would have liked to lead him into a discussion of the problem of evil, so that he might ascertain if Alan had ever felt the intimations of evil which had haunted his own perceptions. However, he thought he had tested to the utmost that third in Greats, and therefore he refrained.

There was a discussion that evening about going away. August was already in sight and arrangements must be made quickly to avoid the burden of it in London. In the end, it was arranged that Mrs. Fane and Stella and Alan should go to Scotland, where Michael promised to join them, if he could get away from London.

"If you can get away!" Stella scoffed. "What rot you do talk."

But Michael was not to be teased out of his determination to stay where he was, and in three or four days he said good-bye to the others northward bound, waving to them from the steps of 173 Cheyne Walk on which already the August sun was casting a heavy heat untempered by the stagnant sheen of the Thames.

That evening Michael went again to the Orient Promenade; but there was no sign of Lily, and it seemed likely that she had gone away from London for a while. After the performance he visited the Café d'Orange in Leicester Square. He had never been there yet, but he had often noticed the riotous exodus at half-past twelve, and he argued from the quality of the frequenters who stood wrangling on the pavement that the Café d'Orange would be a step lower than any of the night-resorts he had so far attended. He scarcely expected to find Lily here. Indeed, he was rather inclined to think that she was someone's mistress and that Drake's view of her at the Orient did not argue necessarily that she had yet sunk to the promiscuous livelihood of the Promenade.

Downstairs at the Café d'Orange was rather more like a corner of hell than Michael had anticipated. The tobacco smoke which could not rise in these subterranean airs hung in a blue murk round the gaudy hats and vile faces, while from the roof the electric lamps shone dazzlingly down and made a patchwork of light and shade and color. In a corner left by the sweep of the stairs a quartet of unkempt musicians in seamy tunics of beer-stained scarlet frogged with debilitated braid were grinding out ragtime. The noisy tune in combination with the talking and laughter, the chink of glasses and the shouted acknowledgments of the waiters made such a din that Michael stood for a moment in confusion, debating the possibility of one more person threading his way through the serried tables to a seat.

There were three arched recesses at the opposite end of the room, and in one of these he thought he could see a table with a vacant place. So paying no heed to the women who hailed him on the way he moved across and sat down. A waiter pounced upon him voraciously for orders, and soon with an unrequited drink he was meditating upon the scene before him in that state of curious tranquillity which was nearly always induced by ceaseless circumfluent clamor. Sitting in this tunnel-shaped alcove, he seemed to be in the box of a theater whence the actions and voices of the contemplated company had the unreality of an operatic finale. After a time the various groups and individuals were separated in his mind, so that in their movements he began to take an easily transferred interest, endowing them with pleasant or unpleasant characteristics in turn. Round him in the alcove there were strange contrasts of behavior. At one table four offensive youths were showing off with exaggerated laughter for the benefit of nobody's attention. Behind them in the crepuscule of two broken lamps a leaden-lidded girl; ivory white and cloying the air with her heavy perfume, was arguing in low passionate tones with a cold-eyed listener who with a straw was tracing niggling hieroglyphics upon a moist surface of cigarette-ash. In the deepest corner a girl with a high complexion and bright eyes was making ardent love to a partially drunk and bearded man, winking the while over her shoulder at whoever would watch her comedy. The other places were filled by impersonal women who sipped from their glasses without relish and stared disdainfully at each other down their powdered noses. At Michael's own table was a blotchy man who alternately sucked his teeth and looked at his watch; and immediately opposite sat a girl with a merry, audacious and somewhat pale face of the Gallic type under a very large and round black hat trimmed with daisies. She was twinkling at Michael, but he would not catch her eye, and he looked steadily over the brim of her hat toward the raffish and rutilant assemblage beyond. Along two sides of the wall were large mirrors painted with flowers and bloated Naiads; here in reflection the throng performed its antics in numberless reduplications. Advertisements of drink decorated the rest of the space on the walls, and at intervals hung notices warning ladies that they must not stay longer than twenty minutes unless accompanied by a gentleman, that they must not move to another table unless accompanied by a gentleman, and with a final stroke of ironic propriety that they must not smoke unless accompanied by a gentleman. The tawdry beer hall with its reek of alcohol and fog of tobacco smoke, with its harborage of all the flotsam of the underworld, must preserve a fiction of polite manners.

Michael was not allowed to maintain his attitude of disinterested commentary, for the girl in the daisied hat presently addressed him, and he did not wish to hurt her feelings by not replying.

"You're very silent, kiddie," she said. "I'll give you a penny for them."

"I really wasn't thinking about anything in particular," said Michael. "Will you have a drink?"

"Don't mind if I do. Alphonse!" she shouted, tugging at the arm of the overloaded waiter who was accomplishing his transit. "Bring me a hot whisky-and-lemon. There's a love."

Alphonse made the slightest sign of having heard the request and passed on. Michael held his breath while the girl was giving her order. He was expecting every moment that the waiter would break over the alcove in a fountain of glass.

"I've taken quite a fancy to whisky-and-lemon hot," she informed Michael. "You know. Anyone does, don't they? Get a sudden fit and keep on keeping on with one drink, I mean. This'll be my sixth to-night. But I'm a long way off being drunk, kiddie. Do you like my new hat? I reckon it'll bring me luck."

"I expect it will," Michael said.

"You are serious, aren't you? When I first saw you I thought you was the spitting image of a fellow I know—Bert Saunders, who writes about the boxing matches for Crime Illustrated. He's more of a bright-eyes than you are, though."

The whisky-and-lemon arrived, and she drank Michael's health.

"Funny-tasting stuff when you come to think of it," she said meditatingly. "What's your name, kiddie?"

He told her.

"Michael," she repeated. "You're a Jew, then?"

He shook his head.

"Well, kid, I suppose you know best, but Michael is a Jewish name, isn't it? Michael? Of course it is. I don't mind Jew fellows myself. One or two of them have been very good to me. My name's Daisy Palmer."

The conversation languished slightly, because Michael since his encounter with Poppy at Neptune Crescent was determined to be very cautious.

"You look rather French," was his most audacious sally toward the personal.

"Funny you should have said that, because my mother was a stewardess on the Calais boat. She was Belgian herself."

Again the conversation dropped.

"I'm waiting for a friend," Daisy volunteered. "She's been having a row with her fellow, and she promised to come on down to the Orange and tell me about it. Dolly Wearne is her name. She ought to have been here by now. What's the time, kid?"

It was after midnight, and Daisy began to look round anxiously.

"I'm rather worried over Doll," she confided to Michael, "because this fellow of hers, Hungarian Dave, is a proper little tyke when he turns nasty. I said to Doll, I said to her, 'Doll, that dirty rotter you're so soft over'll swing for you before he's done. Why don't you leave him,' I said, 'and come and live along with me for a bit?'"

"And what did she say?" Michael asked.

But there was no answer, for Daisy had caught sight of Dolly herself coming down the stairs, and she was now hailing her excitedly.

"Oh, doesn't she look shocking white," exclaimed Daisy. "Doll!" she shouted, waving to her. "Over here, duck."

The four offensive youths near them in the alcove mimicked her in exaggerated falsetto.

"—— to you," she flung scornfully at them over her shoulder. There was a savage directness, a simple coarseness in the phrase that pleased Michael. It seemed to him that nothing except that could ever be said to these young men. Whatever else might be urged against the Café d'Orange, at least one was able to hear there a final verdict on otherwise indescribable humanity.

By this time Dolly Wearne, a rather heavy girl with a long retreating chin and flabby cheeks, had reached her friend's side. She began immediately a voluble tale:

"Oh, Daisy, I put it across him straight. I give you my word, I told him off so as he could hardly look me in the face. 'You call yourself a man,' I said, 'why, you dirty little alien.' That's what I called him. I did straight, 'you dirty little—— '"

"This is my friend," interrupted Daisy, indicating Michael, who bowed. It amused him to see how in the very middle of what was evidently going to be a breathless and desperate story both the girls could remember the convention of their profession.

"Pleased to meet you," said Dolly, offering a black kid-gloved hand with half-a-simper.

"What will you drink?" asked Michael.

"Mine's a brandy and soda, please. 'You dirty little alien,' I said." Dolly was helter-skelter in the track of her tale again.

"Go on, did you? And what did he say?" asked Daisy admiringly.

"He never said nothing, my dear. What could he say?"

"That's right," nodded Daisy wisely.

"'For two years,' I said, 'you've let a girl keep you,' I said, 'and then you can go and give one of my rings to that Florrie. Let me get hold of her,' I said. 'I'll tear her eyes out.' 'No, you won't, now then,' he said. 'Won't I? I will, then,' and with that I just lost control of my feelings, I felt that wild...."

"What did you do, Doll?" asked Daisy, plying her with brandy to soothe the outraged memory.

"What did I do? Why, I spat in his tea and came straight off down to the Orange. 'Yes,' I said, 'you can sit drinking tea while you break my heart.' Don't you ever go and have a fancy boy, Daise. Why, I was a straight girl when I first knew him. Straight—well, anyway not on the game like what I am now." Here Dolly Wearne began to weep with bitter self-compassion. "I've slaved for that fellow, and now he serves me like dirt."

"Go on. Don't cry, duck," Daisy begged. "Come home with me to-night and we can send and fetch your things away to-morrow. I wouldn't cry over him," she said fiercely. "There's no fellow worth crying over. The best of them isn't worth crying over."

The four offensive youths in the alcove began to mock Dolly's tears, and Michael, who was already bitten with some of the primitive pugnacity of the underworld, rose to attack them.

"Sit down," Daisy commanded. "I wouldn't mess my hands, if I was you, with such a pack of filth. Sit down, you stupid boy. You'll get us all into trouble."

Michael managed by a great effort to resume his seat, but for a minute or two he saw the beerhall through a mist of rage.

Gradually Dolly's tears ceased to flow, and after another brandy she became merely more abusive of the faithless Dave. Her cheeks swollen with crying seemed flabbier than ever, and her long retreating chin expressed a lugubrious misanthropy.

"Rotten, I call it, don't you?" said the sympathetic Daisy, appealing to Michael.

He agreed with a profound nod.

"And she's been that good to him. You wouldn't believe."

Michael thought it was rather risky to embark upon an enumeration of Dolly's virtuous acts. He feared another relapse into noisy grief.

At this moment the subject of Daisy's eulogy rose from her seat and stared very dramatically at a corner of the main portion of the beerhall.

"My God!" she said, with ominous calm.

"What is it, duck?" asked Daisy, anxiously peering.

"My God!" Daisy repeated intensely. Then suddenly she poured forth a volley of obloquy, and with an hysterical scream caught up her glass evidently intending to hurl it in the direction of her abuse. Daisy seized one arm: Michael gripped the other, and together they pulled her back into her chair. She was still screaming loudly, and the noise of the beerhall, hitherto scattered and variable in pitch, concentrated in a low murmur of interest. Round about them in the alcove the neighbors began to listen: the girl who had been arguing so passionately with the cold-eyed man stopped and stared; the partially drunk and bearded man collapsed into a glassy indifference, while his charmer no longer winked over her shoulder at the spectators of her wooing; the four offensive youths gaped like landed trout; even the blotchy-faced man ceased to look at his watch and confined himself to sucking steadily his teeth.

It seemed probable, Michael thought, that there was going to be rather a nasty row. Dolly would not listen to persuasion from him or her friend. She was going to attack that Florrie; she was going to mark that Florrie for life with a glass; she was going to let her see if she could come it over Doll Wearne. It would take more than Florrie to do that; yes, more than half-a-dozen Florries, it would.

The manager of the Orange had been warned, and he was already edging his way slowly toward the table. The friends of Florrie were using their best efforts to remove her from the temptation to retaliate. Though she declared loudly that nothing would make her quit the Orange, and certainly that Dolly less than anybody, she did suffer herself to be coaxed away.

Dolly, when she found her rival had retreated, burst into tears again and was immediately surrounded by a crowd of inquisitive sympathizers, which made her utterly hysterical. Michael, without knowing quite how it had happened, found that he was involved in the fortunes and enmities and friendships of a complete society. He found himself explaining to several bystanders the wrong which Dolly had been compelled to endure at the hands of Hungarian Dave. It was extraordinary how suddenly this absurd intrigue of the underworld came to seem tremendously important. He felt that all his sense of proportion was rapidly disappearing. In the middle of an excited justification of Dolly's tears he was aware that he and his surroundings and his attitude were to himself incredible. He was positively in a nightmare, and a prey to the inconsequence of dreams. Or was all his life until this moment a dream, and was this reality? One fact alone presented itself clearly, which was the necessity to see the miserable Dolly safely through the rest of the evening. He felt very reliant upon Daisy, who was behaving with admirable composure, and when he asked her advice about the course of action, he agreed at once with her that Dolly must be persuaded into a cab and be allowed in Daisy's rooms in Guilford Street a freedom of rage and grief that was here, such was the propriety of the Orange, a very imprudent display of emotion.

"She'll be barred from coming down here," said Daisy. "Come on, let's get her home."

"Where's that Florrie?" screamed Dolly.

"She's gone home. So what's the use in your carrying on so mad? The manager's got his eye on us, Doll. Come on, Doll, let's get on home. I tell you the manager's looking at us. You are a silly girl."

"—— the manager," said Dolly obstinately. "Let him look."

"Why don't you come and see if you can find Florrie outside?" Daisy suggested.

Dolly was moved by this proposal, and presently she agreed to vacate the Orange, much to Michael's relief, for he was expecting every moment to see her attack the manager with the match-stand that was fretting her fingers. As it happened, Daisy's well-meant suggestion was very unlucky because Hungarian Dave, the cause of all the bother, was standing on the pavement close to the entrance.

Daisy whispered to Michael to get a cab quickly, because Hungarian Dave was close at hand. He looked at him curiously, this degraded individual in whose domestic affairs he was now so deeply involved. A very objectionable creature he was, too, with his greasy hair and large red mouth. His cap was pulled down over the eyes, and he may have wished not to be seen; but an instinct for his presence made Dolly turn round, and in a moment she was in the thick of the delight of telling him off for the benefit of a crowd increasing with every epithet she flung. It was useless now to attempt to get her away, and Michael and Daisy could only drag her back when she seemed inclined to attack him with finger-nails or hatpin.

"Get a cab," cried Daisy. "Never mind what she says. Get a cab, and we'll put the silly thing into it and drive off. The coppers will be here in a moment."

Michael managed to hail a hansom immediately, but when he turned back to the scene of the pavement the conditions of the dispute were entirely changed. Hungarian Dave, infuriated or frightened, had knocked Dolly down, and she was just staggering to her feet, when a policeman stepped into the circle.

"Come on, move along," he growled.

The bully had merged himself in the ring of onlookers, and Dolly, with a cry of fury, flung herself in his direction.

"Stop that, will you?" the policeman said savagely, seizing her by the arm.

"Go on, it's a dirty shame," cried Daisy. "Why don't you take the fellow as knocked her down?"

Michael by this time had forced his way through the crowd, rage beating upon his brain like a great scarlet hammer.

"You infernal ass," he shouted to the constable. "Haven't you got the sense to see that this woman was attacked first? Where is the blackguard who did it?" he demanded of the stupid, the gross, the vilely curious press of onlookers. No one came forward to support him, and Hungarian Dave had slipped away.

"Move on, will you?" the policeman repeated.

"Damn you," cried Michael. "Will you let go of that woman's arm?"

The constable with a bovine density of purpose proceeded apparently to arrest the wretched Dolly, and Michael maddened by his idiocy felt that the only thing to do was to hit him as hard as he could. This he did. The constable immediately blew his whistle. Other masses of inane bulk loomed up, and Michael was barely able to control himself sufficiently not to resist all the way to Vine Street, as two of them marched him along, and four more followed with Daisy and Dolly. A spumy trail of nocturnal loiterers clung to their wake.

Next morning Michael appeared before the magistrate. He listened to the charge against him and nearly laughed aloud in court, because the whole business so much resembled the trial in Alice in Wonderland. It was not that the magistrate was quite so illogical as the King of Hearts; but he was so obviously biassed in favor of the veracity of a London policeman, that the inconsequence of the nightmare which had begun last night was unalterably preserved. Michael, aware of the circumstances which had led up to what was being made to appear as wantonly riotous behavior in Leicester Square, could not fail to be exasperated by the inability of the magistrate to understand his own straightforward story. He began to sympathize with the lawless population. The law could only seem to them an unintelligent machine for crushing their freedom. If the conduct of this case were a specimen of administration, it was obvious that arrest must be synonymous with condemnation. The magistrate in the first place seemed dreadfully overcome by the sorrow of beholding a young man in Michael's position on the police-court.

"I cannot help wondering when I see a young man who has had every opportunity ..." the magistrate went on in a voice that worked on the stale air of the court like a rusty file.

"I'm not a defaulting bank clerk," Michael interrupted. "Is it impossible for you to understand——"

"Don't speak to me like that. Keep quiet. I've never been spoken to like that in all my experience as a magistrate. Keep quiet."

Michael sighed in compassion for his age and stupidity.

"Are there any previous convictions against Wearne and Palmer?" the magistrate inquired. He was told that the woman Palmer had not hitherto appeared, but that Wearne had been previously fined for disorderly conduct in Shaftesbury Avenue. "Ah!" said the magistrate. "Ah!" he repeated, looking over the rim of his glasses. "And the case against the male defendant? I will take the evidence of Constable C11254."

"Your worship, I was on duty yesterday evening at 12.25 in Leicester Square. Hearing a noise in the direction of the Caffy Dorringe and observing a crowd collect, I moved across the road to disperse it. The defendant Wearne was using obscene language to an unknown man; and wishing to get her to move on I took hold of her arm. The male defendant, also using very obscene language, attempted to rescue her and struck me on the chest. I blew my whistle...."

The ponderous constable with his thick red neck continued a sing-song narrative.

When Michael's turn came to refute some of the evidence against him, he merely shrugged his shoulders.

"It's really useless, you know, for me to say anything. If 'damn you' is obscene, then I was obscene. If a girl is knocked down by a bully and on rising to her feet is instantly arrested by a dunderhead in a blue uniform, and if an onlooker punches this functionary, then I did assault the constable."

"This sort of insolence won't do," said the magistrate trembling with a curious rarefied passion. "I have a very good mind to send you to prison without the option of a fine, but in consideration...."

Somehow or other it was made to appear a piece of extraordinary magnanimity on the part of the magistrate that Michael was only fined three guineas and costs.

"I wish to pay the fines of Miss Palmer and Miss Wearne," he announced.

Later in the morning Michael, with the two girls, emerged into the garish summer day. Not even yet was the illusion of a nightmare dissipated, for as he looked at his two companions, feathered, frilled and bedraggled, who were walking beside him, he could scarcely acknowledge even their probable reality here in the sun.

"I shan't drink hot whisky-and-lemon again in a hurry," vowed Daisy. "I knew it was going to bring me bad luck when I said it tasted so funny."

"But you said your hat was going to be lucky," Michael pointed out.

"Yes, I've been properly sucked in over that," Daisy agreed.

"Nothing ever brings me luck," grumbled Dolly resentfully.

As Michael looked at the long retreating chin and down-drawn mouth he was inclined to agree that nothing could invigorate this fatal mournfulness with the prospect of good fortune.

"I reckon I'll go home and have a good lay down," said Daisy. "Are you going to have dinner with me?" she asked, turning to Dolly.

"Dinner?" echoed Dolly. "Nice time to talk to anyone about their dinner, when they've got the sick like I have! Dinner!"

They had reached Piccadilly Circus by now, and Michael wondered if he might not put them into a cab and send them back to Guilford Street. He found it embarrassing when the people slowly turned away from Swan and Edgar's window to stare instead at him and his companions.

Daisy pressed him to come back with them, but he promised he would call upon her very soon. Then he slipped into her hand the change from the second five-pound note into which the law had broken.

"Is this for us?" she asked.

He nodded.

"You are a sport. Mind you come and see us. Come to tea. Doll's going to live with me a bit now, aren't you, Doll?"

"I suppose so," said Doll.

Michael really admired the hospitality which was willing to shelter this lugubrious girl, and as he contemplated her, looking in the sunlight like a moist handkerchief, he had a fleeting sympathy with Hungarian Dave.

When the girls had driven off, Michael recovered his ordinary appearance by visiting a barber and a hosier. The effect of the shampoo was almost to make him incredulous of the night's event, and he could not help paying a visit to the Café d'Orange, to verify the alcove in which he had sat. The entrance of the beerhall was closed, however, and he stood for a moment like a person who passes a theater which the night before he has seen glittering. As Michael was going out of the bar, he thought he recognized a figure leaning over the counter. Yes, it was certainly Meats. He went up and tapped him on the shoulder, addressing him by name. Meats turned round with a start.

"Don't you remember me?" asked Michael.

"Of course I do," said Meats nervously. "But for the love of Jerusalem drop calling me by that name. Here, let's go outside."

In the street Michael asked him why he had given up being Meats.

"Oh, a bit of trouble, a bit of trouble," said Meats.

"You are a strange chap," said Michael. "When I first met you it was Brother Aloysius. Then it was Meats. Now——"

"Look here," said Meats, "give over, will you? I've told you once. If you call me that again I shall leave you. Barnes is what I am now. Now don't forget."

"Come and have a drink, and tell me what you've been doing in the four years since we met," Michael suggested.

"B-a-r-n-e-s. Have you got it?"

Michael assured him that everything but Barnes as applicable to him had vanished from his mind.

"Come on, then," said Barnes. "We'll go into the Afrique, upstairs."

Michael fancied he had met Barnes this time in a reincarnation that was causing him a good deal of uneasiness. He had lost the knowingness which had belonged to Meats and the sheer lasciviousness which had seemed the predominant quality of Brother Aloysius. Instead, sitting at the round marble table opposite Michael saw an individual who resembled an actor out of work in the lowest grades of his profession. There was the cheesy complexion, and the over-fashioned suit of another season too much worn and faded now to flaunt itself objectionably, but with its dismoded exaggerations still conveying an air of rococo smartness; perhaps, thought Michael, these signs had always been obvious and it had merely been his own youth which had supposed a type to be an exception. Certainly Barnes could not arouse now anything but a compassionate amusement. How this figure with its grotesque indignity as of a puppet temporarily put out of action testified to his own morbid heightening of common things in the past. How incredible it seemed now that this Barnes had once been able to work upon his soul with influential doctrine.

"What have you been doing with yourself?" Michael asked again.

"Oh, hopping and popping about. I've got the rats at present."

"Where are you living?"

Barnes looked at Michael in suspicious astonishment. "What do you want to know for?" he asked.

"Mere inquisitiveness," Michael assured him. "You really needn't treat me like a detective, you know."

"My mistake," said Barnes. "But really, Fane. Let's see, that is your name? Thought it was. I don't often forget a name. No, without swank, Fane, I've been hounded off my legs lately. I'm living in Leppard Street. Pimlico way."

"I'd like to come and see you some time," said Michael.

"Here, straight, what *is* your game?" Barnes could not conceal his suspicion.

"Inquisitiveness," Michael declared again. "Also I rather want a Sancho Panza."

"Oh, of course, any little thing I can do to oblige," said Barnes very sarcastically.

It took Michael a long time to convince him that no plot was looming, but at last he persuaded him to come to 173 Cheyne Walk, and after that he knew that Barnes could not refuse to show him Leppard Street.

CHAPTER IV

LEPPARD STREET

While they were driving to Cheyne Walk, Michael extracted from Barnes an outline of his adventures since last they had met. The present narrative was probably not less cynical than the account of his life related to Michael on various occasions in the past; but perhaps because his imagination had already to some extent been fed by reality, he could no longer be shocked. He received the most sordid avowals calmly, neither blaming Barnes nor indulging himself with mental goose-flesh. Yet amid all the frankness accorded to him he could not find out why Barnes had changed his name. He was curious about this, because he could not conceive any shamelessness too outrageous for Barnes to reveal. It would be interesting to find out what could really make even him pause; no doubt ultimately, with the contrariness of the underworld, it would turn out to be something that Michael himself would consider trivial in comparison with so much of what Barnes had boasted. Anyway, whether he discovered the secret or not, it would certainly be interesting to study Barnes, since in him good and evil might at any moment display themselves as clearly as a hidden substance to a reagent flung into a seething alembic. It might perhaps be assuming too much to say that there was any good in him; and yet Michael was unwilling to suppose that all his conversions were merely the base drugs of a disordered morality. Apart from his philosophic value, Barnes might very actually be of service in the machinery of finding Lily.

At 173 Cheyne Walk Barnes looked about him rather bitterly.

"Easy enough to behave yourself in a house like this," he commented.

Here spoke the child who imagines that grown-up people have no excuse to be anything but very good. There might be something worth pursuing in that thought. A child might consider itself chained more inseverably than one who apparently possesses the perfectiveness of free-will. Had civilization complicated too unreasonably the problem of evil? It was a commonplace to suppose that the sense of moral responsibility increased with the opportunity of development, and yet after all was not the reverse true?

"Why should it be easier to behave here than in Leppard Street?" Michael asked. "I do wish you could understand it's really so much more difficult. I can't distinguish what is wrong from what is right nearly so well as you can."

"Well, in my experience, and my experience has done its bit I can tell you," said Barnes in self-satisfied parenthesis. "In my experience most of the difficulties in this world come from wanting something we haven't got. I don't care what it is—a woman or a drink or a new suit of clothes. Money'll buy any of them. Give me ten pounds a week, and I could be a bloody angel."

"Supposing I offered you half as much for three months," suggested Michael. "Do you think you'd find life any easier while it lasted?"

"Well, don't be silly," said Barnes. "Of course I should. If you'd walked home every night with your eyes on the gutter in case anybody had dropped a threepenny bit, you'd think it was easier. It's not a bit of good your running me down, Fane. If you were me, you'd be just the same. Those monks at the Abbey used to jaw about holy poverty. The man who first said that ought to be walking about hell with donkey's ears on his nob. What's it done for me? I ask you. Why, it's made me so that I'd steal a farthing from one blind man to palm it off as half-a-quid on another."

"Tell me about Leppard Street," said Michael, laughing. "What's it like?"

"Well, you go and punch a few holes in a cheese rind. That's what it looks like. And then go and think yourself a rat who's lost all his teeth, and you've got what it feels like to be living in it."

"Supposing I said I'd like to try?" asked Michael. "What would you think?"

"Think? I shouldn't think two seconds. I should know you were having a game. What good's Leppard Street to you, when you can sit here bouncing up and down all day on cushions?"

"Experience," said Michael.

"Oh, rats! Nothing's experience that you haven't had to do."

"Well, I'll give you five pounds a week," Michael offered, "if you'll keep yourself free to do anything I want you to do. I shouldn't want anything very dreadful, of course," he added.

It was difficult for Michael to persuade Barnes that he was in earnest, so difficult indeed that, even when he produced five sovereigns and offered them directly to him, he had to disclose partially his reason for wishing to go to Leppard Street.

"You see, I want to find a girl," he explained.

"Well, if you go and live in Leppard Street you'll lose the best girl you've got straight off. That's all there is to it."

"You don't understand. This girl I used to know has gone wrong, and I want to find her and marry her."

It seemed to Michael that Barnes' manner changed in some scarcely definable way when he made this announcement. He pocketed the five pounds and invited Michael to come to Leppard Street whenever he liked. He was evidently no longer suspicious of his sincerity, and a perky, an almost cunning cordiality had replaced the disheartened cynicism of his former attitude. It encouraged Michael to see how obviously his resolve had impressed Barnes. He accepted it as an augury of good hap. Involuntarily he waited for his praise; and when Barnes made no allusion to the merit of his action, he ascribed his silence to emotion. This was proving really a most delightful example of the truth of his theory. And it was clever of Barnes—it was more than clever, it was truly imaginative of him—to realize without another question the need to leave for a while Cheyne Walk.

"But is there a vacant room?" Michael asked in sudden dread of disappointment.

"Look here, you'd better see the place before you decide on leaving here," Barnes advised. "It isn't a cross between Buckingham Palace and the Carlton, you know."

"I suppose it's the name that attracts me," said Michael. "It sounds ferocious."

"I don't know about the name, but old Ma Cleghorne who keeps the house is ferocious enough. Never mind." He jingled the five sovereigns.

"I'll go up and pack," said Michael. "By the way, I haven't told you yet that I was run in last night."

"In quod you mean?" asked Barnes. "Whatever for?"

"Drunk and disorderly in Leicester Square."

"These coppers are the limit," said Barnes emphatically. "The absolute limit. Really. They'll pinch the Archbishop of Canterbury for looking into Stagg and Mantle's window before we know where we are."

Michael left Barnes in the drawing-room, and as he turned in the doorway to see if he was at his ease, he thought the visitor and the macaw on its perch were about equally exotic.

They started immediately after lunch and, as always, the drive along the river inspired Michael with a jolly conception of the adventurousness of London. It was impossible to hear the gurgle of the high spring-tide without exulting in the movement of the stream that was washing out with its flood all the listlessness of the hot August afternoon. When Chelsea Bridge was left behind, the mystery of the banks of a great river sweeping through a great city began to be more evident. The whole character of the Embankment changed at every hundred yards. First there was that somber canal which, flowing under the road straight from the Thames, reappeared between a cañon of gloomy houses and vanished again underground not very unlike the Styx. Then came what was apparently a large private house which had been gutted of the tokens of humanity and filled with monstrous wheels and cylinders and pistons, all moving perpetually and slowly with a curious absence of noise. Under Grosvenor Road Bridge they went, the horse clattering forward and a train crashing overhead. Out again from slimy bricks and girders dripping with the excrement of railway-engines, they came into Grosvenor Road. They passed the first habitations of Pimlico, two or three terraces and isolated houses all different in character. There could scarcely be another road in London so varied as this. Maurice had been wise to have his studio in Grosvenor Road. From the Houses of Parliament to Chelsea Bridge was an epitome of London.

The hansom turned to the left up Clapperton Street, a very wide thoroughfare of houses with heavy porticoes, a very wide and very gray street, of a gray that almost achieved the effect of positive color, so insistent was it. Michael remembered that there had been a Clapperton Street murder, and he wondered behind which of those muslin curtains the poison had been mixed. It was a street of quite extraordinarily sinister respectableness. It brooded with a mediocre prosperity, very wide and very gray and very silent. The columns of the porticoes were checked off by the window of the cab with dull regularity, and the noise of the horse's hoofs echoed hollowly down the empty street, to which every evening men with black shiny bags would come hurrying home. It was impossible to imagine a nursemaid lolling over a perambulator in Clapperton Street. It was impossible to imagine that anyone lived here but dried-up little men with greenish-white complexions and hatchet-shaped whiskers and gnawed mustaches, dried-up little men whose wives kept arsenic in small triangular cupboards by the bed.

"I wouldn't mind having lodgings here," said Barnes. He had caught sight of a square of cardboard at the farther end of the street. This was the outpost of an array of apartment cards, for the next street was full of them. The next street was evidently a little nearer to the period of final dilapidation; but Michael fancied that, in comparison with the middle-aged respectableness of Clapperton Street, this older and now very swiftly decaying warren of second-rate apartments was almost attractive. Street followed street, each one, as they drew nearer to Victoria Station, being a little more raffish than its predecessor, each one being a little less able to resist the corrosion of a persistently inquinating migration. Sometimes, and with a sharp effect of contrast, occurred prosperous squares; but even these, with their houses so uniformly tall and ocherous, delivered a presage of irremediable decadency.

Suddenly the long ranks of houses, which were beginning to seem endless, vanished upon the margin of a lake of railway lines. Just before the hansom would have mounted the slope of an arcuated bridge, it swung to the right into Leppard Street, S.W. The beginning of the street ran between two high brown walls crowned with a ruching of broken glass: these guarded on one side the escarp of the railway, on the other a coal yard. At the farther end the street swept round to an exit between two rows of squalid dwellings called Greenarbor Court, an exit, however, that was barred to vehicles by a row of blistered posts. Some fifty yards before this the wall deviated to form a recess in which five very tall houses rose gauntly against the sky from the very edge of the embankment. Standing as they did upon a sort of bluff and flanked on either side by blind walls, these habitations gave an impression of quite exceptional height. This was emphasized by the narrow oblong windows of which there may have been nearly fifty. The houses were built of the same brick as the walls, and they had deepened from yellow to the same fuscous hue. This promontory seemed to serve as an appendix for the draff of the neighborhood's rubbish. The ribs of an umbrella; a child's boot; a broken sieve; rags of faded color, lay here in the gutter undisturbed, the jetsam of a deserted beach.

"Here we are," said Barnes. "Here's Leppard Street that you've been so anxious to see."

"It looks rather exciting," Michael commented.

"Oh, it's the last act of a Drury Lane melodrama I don't think. Exciting?" Barnes repeated. "You know, Fane, there's something wrong with you. If you think this is exciting, you'd go raving mad when I showed you some of the places where I've lived. Well, here we are, anyhow. Number One—the corner house."

They walked up the steps which were gradually scaling in widening ulcers of decay: the handle of the bell-pull hung limply forward like a parched tongue: and the iron railings of a basement strewn with potato parings were flaked with rust, and here and there decapitated.

Barnes opened the door.

"We'll take your bag up to my room first, and then we'll go downstairs and talk to Ma Cleghorne about your room, that is if you don't change your mind when you've seen the inside."

Michael had no time to notice Barnes' room very much. But vaguely he saw a rickety bed with a patchwork counterpane and frowzy recesses masked by cheap cretonnes in a pattern of disemboweled black and crimson fruits. After that glimpse they went down again over the grayish staircarpet that was worn to the very filaments. Barnes shouted to the landlady in the basement.

"She'll have a fit if she hears me calling down to her," he said to Michael. "You see, just lately I've been very anxious to avoid meeting her."

He jingled with satisfaction the sovereigns in his pocket.

They descended into the gloom that smelt of damp cloths and the stale soapiness of a sink. They peeped into the front room, as they went by: here a man in shirt-sleeves was lying under the scattered sheets of a Sunday paper upon a bed that gave an effect of almost oriental luxury, so much was it overloaded with mattresses and coverlets. Indeed; the whole room seemed clogged with woolly stuffs, and the partial twilight of its subterranean position added to the impression of airlessness. It was as if these quilted chairs and heavy hairy curtains had suffocated everything else.

"That's Cleghorne," said Barnes. "I reckon he'd sleep Rip van Winkle barmy."

"What's he do?" whispered Michael, as they turned down the passage.

"He snores for a living, he does," said Barnes.

They entered the kitchen, and through the dim light Michael saw the landlady with her arms plunged into a steaming cauldron. Outside, two trains roared past in contrary directions; the utensils shivered and chinked; the ceiling was obscured by pendulous garments which exhaled a moist odorousness; on the table a chine of bacon striated by the carving-knife was black with heavy-winged flies.

"I've brought a new lodger, Mrs. Cleghorne," said Barnes.

"Have you brought your five weeks' rent owing?" she asked sourly.

He laid two pounds on the table, and Mrs. Cleghorne immediately cheered up, if so positive an expression could be applied to a woman whose angularities seemed to forbid any display of good-will. Michael thought she looked rather like one of the withered nettles that overhung the wall of the sunken yard outside the kitchen window.

"Well, he can have the top-floor back, or he can have the double rooms on the ground floor which of course is unfurnished. Do you want me to come up and show you?"

She inquired grudgingly and rubbed the palm of her hand slowly along her sharp nose as if to express a doubtful willingness.

"Perhaps Mr. Cleghorne ..." Michael began.

"Mis-ter Cleghorne!" she interrupted scornfully, and immediately she began to dry her arms vigorously on a roller-towel which creaked continuously.

"Oh, I don't want to disturb him," said Michael.

"Disturb him!" she sneered. "Why, half Bedlam could drive through his brains in a omnibus before he'd move a little finger to trouble hisself. Yes," she shouted, "Yes!" Her voice mingling with the creak of the roller seemed to be grating the air itself, and with every word it grew more strident. "Why, the blessed house might burn before he'd even put on his boots, let alone go and show anyone upstairs, though his wife can work herself to the bone for him. Disturb him! Good job if anyone could disturb him. If I found a regiment of soldiers in the larder, he'd only grunt. Asthmatic! Yes, some people 'ud be very pleased to be asthmatic, if they could lie snorting on a bed from morning to night."

Mrs. Cleghorne's hands were dry now, and she led the way along the passage upstairs, sniffing as she passed her crapulous husband. She unlocked the door of the ground-floor rooms, and they entered. It was not an inspiring lodging as seen thus in its emptiness, with drifts of fluff along the bare dusty boards. The unblacked grate contained some dried-up bits of orange peel; with the last summons of the late tenant the bellrope had broken, and it now lay invertebrate; by the window, catching a shaft of sunlight, stood a drain pipe painted with a landscape in cobalt-blue and probably once used as an umbrella stand.

"That's all I got for two months' rent," said Mrs. Cleghorne bitterly, surveying it. "And it's just about fit for my old man to go and bury his good-for-nothing lazy head in, and that's all. The bedroom's in here, of course." She opened the folding doors whose blebs of paint had been picked off up to a certain height above the floor, possibly as far as some child had been able to reach.

The bedroom was rather dustier than the sitting-room, and it was much darker owing to a number of ferns which had been glued upon the window-panes. Through this mesh could be seen the nettle-haunted square of back garden; and beyond, over a stucco wall pocked with small pebbles, a column of smoke was belching into the sky from a stationary engine on the invisible lake of railway lines.

255

"Do you want to see the top-floor back?" Mrs. Cleghorne asked.

"Well, if you wouldn't mind." Michael felt bound to apologize to her, whatever was suggested.

She sighed her way upstairs, and at last flung open a door for them to enter the vacant room.

The view from here was certainly more spacious, and a great deal of the permeating depression was lightened by looking out as it were over another city across the railway, a city with streamers of smoke, and even here and there a flag flying. At the same time the room itself was less potentially endurable than the ground-floor; there was no fireplace and the few scraps of furniture were more discouraging than the positive emptiness downstairs. Michael shuddered as he looked at the gimcrack washstand through whose scanty paint the original wood was visible in long fibrous sores. He shuddered, too, at the bedstead with its pleated iron laths furred by dust and rust, and at the red mattress exuding flock like clustered maggots.

"This is furnished, of course," said Mrs. Cleghorne, complacently sucking a tooth. "Well, which will you have?"

"I think perhaps I'll take the ground-floor rooms. I'll have them done up."

"Oh, they're quite clean. The last people was a bit dirty. So I gave them an extra-special clear-out."

"But you wouldn't object to my doing them up?" persisted Michael.

"Oh, no, I shouldn't *object,*" said Mrs. Cleghorne, and in her accent was the suggestion that equally she would not be likely to derive very much pleasure from the fruition of Michael's proposal.

They were going downstairs again now, and Mrs. Cleghorne was evidently beginning to acquire a conviction of her own importance, because somebody had contemplated with a certain amount of interest those two empty rooms on the ground floor; in the gratification of her pride she was endowing them with a value and a character they did not possess.

"I've always said that, properly cared for, those two rooms are worth any other two rooms in the house. And of course that's the reason I'm really compelled to charge a bit more for them. I always say to everyone right out—if you want the two best rooms in the house, why, you must pay according. They're only empty now because I've always been particular about letting them. I won't have anybody, and that's a fact. Mr. Barnes here knows I'm really fond of those rooms."

They had reentered them, and Mrs. Cleghorne stood with arms admiringly akimbo.

"They really are a beautiful lodging," she declared. "When would you want them from?"

"Well, as soon as I can get them done up," said Michael.

"I see. Perhaps you could explain a little more clearly just what you was thinking of doing?"

Michael gave some of his theories of decoration, while Mrs. Cleghorne waited in critical audience; as it were, feeling the pulse of the apartments under the stimulus of Michael's sketch of their potentiality.

"All white?" the landlady echoed pessimistically. "That sounds very gloomy, doesn't it? More like a outhouse or a coal-cellar than a nice couple of rooms."

"Well, they couldn't look rottener than what they do at present," Barnes put in. "So if you take my advice, you'll say 'yes' and be very thankful. They'll look clean, anyway."

The landlady threw back her head and surveyed Barnes like a snake about to strike.

"Rotten?" she sniffed. "I'm sure this gentleman here isn't likely to find a nicer and cheaper pair of rooms or a more convenient and a quieter pair of rooms anywhere in Pimlico. A lot of people is very anxious to be in this neighborhood."

Mrs. Cleghorne was much offended by Barnes' criticism, and there was a long period of dubiety before it was settled that Michael should be accepted as a tenant.

"I've never cared for white," she said, in final protest. "Not since I was married."

Reminded of Mr. Cleghorne's existence in the basement, she hurried forthwith to rout him out. As she disappeared, Michael saw that she was searching in the musty folds of her skirt in order to deposit in her purse the month's rent he had paid in advance.

A couple of weeks passed while the decorators worked hard; and Michael returned from an unwilling visit to Scotland to find them ready for him. He got together a certain amount of furniture, and toward the end of August he moved into Leppard Street.

Barnes on account of the prosperity which had come to him through Michael's money had managed to dress himself in a series of outrageously new and fashionable suits, and on the afternoon of his patron's arrival he strutted about the apartments.

"Very nice," he said. "Very nice, indeed. I reckon old Ma Cleghorne ought to be very pleased with herself. Some of these pictures are a bit too religious for me just at present, but everyone to their own taste, that's what I always say. To their own taste," he repeated. "Otherwise, what's the good in being given an opinion of your own?"

Michael felt it was time to explain to Barnes more particularly his quest of Lily.

"You don't know a girl called Lily Haden?" he asked.

"Lily Haden," said Barnes thoughtfully. "Lily Hopkins. A great fat girl with red...."

"No, no," Michael interrupted. "Lily Haden. Tall. Slim. Very fair hair. Of course she may have another name now."

"That's it, you see," said Barnes wisely.

"Wherever she is, whatever she's doing, I must find her," Michael went on.

"Well, if you go about it in that spirit, you'll soon find her," Barnes prophesied.

Michael looked at him sharply. He thought he noticed in Barnes' manner a suggestion of humoring him. He rather resented the way in which Barnes seemed to encourage him as one might encourage a child.

"You understand I want to marry her?" Michael asked fiercely.

"That's all right, old chap. I'm not trying to stop you, am I?"

"But why are you talking as if I weren't in earnest?" Michael demanded. "When I first told you about it you were evidently very pleased, and now you've got a sneer which frankly I tell you I find extraordinarily objectionable."

Barnes looked much alarmed by Michael's sudden attack, and explained that he meant nothing by his remarks beyond a bit of fun.

"Is it funny to marry somebody?" Michael demanded.

"Sometimes it's very funny to marry a tart," said Barnes.

Michael flushed. This was a directness of speech for which he was not prepared.

"But when I first told you," Michael said, "you seemed very pleased."

"I was very pleased to find I'd evidently struck a nice-mannered lunatic," said Barnes. "You offered me five quid a week, didn't you? Well, you didn't offer me that to give you good advice, now did you?"

Michael tried to conceal the mortification that was being inflicted upon him. He had been very near to making a fool of himself by supposing that his announcement had aroused admiration. Instead of admiring him, Barnes evidently regarded him as an idiot whom it were politic to encourage on account of the money this idiot could provide. It was an humiliating discovery. The chivalry on which he congratulated himself had not touched a single chord in Barnes. Was it likely that in Lily herself he would find someone more responsive to what he still obstinately maintained to himself was really rather a fine impulse? Michael began to feel half sorry for Barnes because he could not appreciate nobility of motive. It began to seem worth while trying to impose upon him the appreciation which he felt he owed. Michael was sorry for his uncultivated ideals, and he took a certain amount of pleasure in the thought of how much Barnes might benefit from a close association with himself. He did not regret the whim which had brought them to Leppard Street. Whatever else might happen, it would always be consoling to think that he would be helping Barnes. In half a dream Michael began to build up the vision of a newer and a finer Barnes, a Barnes with sensitiveness and decent instincts, a Barnes who would forsake very willingly the sordid existence he had hitherto led in order to rise under Michael's guidance and help to a wider and better life. Michael suddenly experienced a sense of affection for Barnes, the affection of the missionary for the prospective convert. He forgave him his cynical acceptance of the five pounds a week, and he made up his mind not to refer to Lily again until Barnes should be able to esteem at its true value the step he proposed to take.

Michael looked round at the new rooms he had succeeded in creating out of the ground floor of 1 Leppard Street. These novel surroundings would surely be strong enough to make the first impression upon Barnes. He could not fail to be influenced by this whiteness and cleanliness, so much more white and clean where everything else was dingy and vile. It was all so spare and simple that it surely must produce an effect. Barnes would see him living every day in perfect contentment with a few books and a few pictures. He must admire those cherry-red curtains and those green shelves. He must respect the cloistral air Michael had managed to import even into this warren of queer inhabitants whom as yet he had scarcely seen. It was romantic to come like this into a small secluded world which did not know him; to bring like this a fresh atmosphere into a melancholy street of human beings who lived perpetually in a social twilight. Michael's missionary affection began to extend beyond Barnes and to embrace all the people in this house. He felt a great fondness for them, a great desire to identify himself with their aspirations, so that they would be glad to think he was living in their midst. He began to feel very poignantly that his own existence hitherto had been disgracefully unprofitable both to himself and everybody else. He was grateful that destiny had brought him here to fulfill what was plainly a purpose. But what did fate intend should be his effect upon these people? To what was he to lead them? Michael had an impulse to kneel down and pray for knowledge. He wished that Barnes were not in this white room. Otherwise he would surely have knelt down, and in the peace of the afternoon sunlight he might have resigned himself to a condition of spirit he had coveted in vain for a very long time.

Just then there was a tap at the door, and a middle-aged man with blinking watery eyes and a green plush smoking-cap peeped round the corner.

"Come in," Michael cheerfully invited him.

The stranger entered in a slipshod hesitant manner. He looked as if all his clothes were on the verge of coming off, so much like a frayed accordion did his trousers rest upon the carpet slippers; so wide a space of shirt was visible between the top of the trousers and the bottom of the waistcoat; so utterly amorphous was his gray alpaca coat.

"What I really came down for was a match," the stranger explained.

Michael offered him a box, and with fumbling hands he stored it away in one of his pockets.

"You don't go in for puzzles, I suppose?" he asked tentatively. "But any time I can help. I'm the Solutionist, you know. Don't let me keep you. Good afternoon, Mr. Barnes. I'm worrying out this week's lot in The Golden Penny very slowly. I've really had a sort of a headache the last few days—a very nasty headache. Do you know anything about cricketers?" he asked, turning to Michael. "Famous cricketers, of course, that is? For instance, I cannot think what this one can be."

He produced after much uncertainty a torn and dirty sheet of some penny weekly.

"I've got all the others," he said to Michael. "But one picture will often stump you like this. No joke intended." He smiled feebly and pointed to a woman holding in one hand the letter S, in the other the letter T.

"What about Hirst?" Michael asked.

"Hirst," repeated the Solutionist. "Her S T. That's it. That's it." In his excitement he began to dribble. "I'm very much obliged to you, sir. Her S. T. Yes, that's it."

He began to shuffle toward the door.

"Anything you want solved at any time," he said to Michael. "I'm only just upstairs, you know, in the room next to Mr. Barnes. I shall be most delighted to solve anything—anything!"

He vanished, and Michael smiled to think how completely some of his problems would puzzle the Solutionist.

"What's his name?" he inquired of Barnes.

"Who? Barmy Sid? Sydney Carvel, as he calls himself. Yet he makes a living at it."

"At what?" Michael asked.

"Solving those puzzles and sending solutions at so much a time. He took fifteen-and-six last week, or so he told me. You can see his advertisement in Reynolds. Barmy Sid I call him. He says he used to be a conjurer and take his ten pounds a week easily. But he looks to me more like one of these here soft fellows who ought to be shut up. You should see his room. All stuck over with bits of paper. Regular dust-hole, that's what it is. Did you hear what he said? Solve anything—anything! He hasn't solved how to earn more than ten bob a week, year in year out. Silly——! That's what he is, barmy."

Michael's hope of entering into a close relation with all the lodgers of 1 Leppard Street was falsified. None of them except Barmy Sid once visited his rooms; nor did he find it at all easy to strike up even a staircase acquaintance. Vaguely he became aware of the various personalities that lurked behind the four stories of long narrow windows. Yet so fleeting was the population that the almost weekly arrivals and departures perpetually disorganized his attempts to observe them as individuals or to theorize upon them in the mass. No doubt Barnes himself would have left by now, had he not been sustained by Michael's subsidy; and it was always a great perplexity to Michael how Mrs. Cleghorne managed to pay the rent, since apparently half the inquilines of a night and even some of the less transient lodgers ultimately escaped owing her money.

It was a silent and a dreary house, and although children would doubtless have been a nuisance, Michael sometimes wished that the landlady's strict regulation no longer to take them in could be relaxed. All the five houses of Leppard Street seemed to be untenanted by children, which certainly added a touch to their decrepitude. In Greenarbor Court close at hand the pavements writhed with children, and occasionally small predatory bands advanced as far as Leppard Street to play in a half-hearted manner with some of the less unpromising rubbish that was moldering there. On the steps of Number Three, two pale little girls in stammel petticoats used to sit for hours over a grocer's shop of grit and waste paper and refined mud. They apparently belonged to the basement of Number Three, for Michael often saw them disappear below at twilight. Michael thought of the children who swarmed above the walls of the embankment before Paddington Station, and he wondered what sort of a desolate appearance these five houses must present for voyagers to and from Victoria. They must surely stand up very forbidding in abandonment to those who were traveling back to their cherished dolls-houses in Dulwich. From his bedroom window he could not actually see the trains, but always he could hear their shrieking and their clangor, and he looked almost with apprehension at St. Ursula in her high serene four-poster reposing tranquilly upon the white wall. Nothing except the trains could vex her sleep; for in this house was a perpetual silence. Even when Mrs. Cleghorne was vociferously arguing with her husband, the noise of her rage down in the basement among the quilts and coverlets never penetrated beyond the door at the head of the inclosing staircase, save in sounds of fury greatly minified. So silent was the house that had it not been for the variety of the smells, Michael might easily have supposed that it really was empty and that life here was indeed an illusion. The smells, however, of onions or hot blankets or machine-oil or tom-cats or dirty bicycles proclaimed emphatically that a community shared these ascending mustard-colored walls, that human beings passed along the stale landings to frowst behind those finger-stained doors of salmon-pink. Sometimes, too, Michael emerging into the passage from his room would hear from dingy altitudes descend the noise of a door hurriedly slammed; and sometimes he would see go down the ulcerous steps in front of the house depressing women in black, or unshaven men with the debtor's wary and furtive eye. The only lodgers who seemed to be permanent were Barnes and Carvel the Solutionist. Barnes on the strength of Michael's allowance used to go up West, as he described it, every night. He used to assure Michael, when toward two o'clock of the next afternoon he extracted himself from bed, that he devoted himself with the greatest pertinacity to obtaining definite news of Lily Haden. The Solutionist occasionally visited Michael with a draggled piece of newspaper, and often he was visible in the garden attending to a couple of Belgian hares who lived in a packing-case marked Fragile among the nettles of the back-yard.

After he had spent a week or so in absorbing the atmosphere of Leppard Street, Michael felt it was time for him to move forth again at any rate into that underworld whose gaiety, however tawdry and feverish, would be welcome after this turbid backwater. There was here the danger of being drugged by the miasma that rose from this unreflecting surface. He felt inclined to renew his acquaintance with Daisy Palmer, and to hear from her the sequel to the affair of Dolly Wearne and Hungarian Dave. He found her card with the Guilford Street address and went over to Bloomsbury, hoping to find her in to tea. The landlady looked surprised when he inquired for Miss Palmer.

"Oh, she's been gone this fortnight," the woman informed him. Michael asked where she was living now.

"I don't know, I'm sure," said the landlady, and as she was already slowly and very unpleasantly closing the door, Michael came away a little disconsolate. These abrupt dematerializations of the underworld were really very difficult to grapple with. It gave him a sense of the futility of his search for Lily (though lately he had prosecuted it somewhat lazily) when girls, who a month ago offered what was presumably a permanent address, could have vanished completely a fortnight later. Perhaps Daisy would be at the Orange. He would take Barnes with him this evening and ask his opinion of her and Dolly and Hungarian Dave.

The beerhall downstairs looked exactly the same as when he had visited it a month ago. Michael could sympathize with the affection such places roused in the hearts of their frequenters. There was a great deal to be said for an institution that could present, day in, day out, a steady aspect to a society whose life was spent in such extremes of elation and despair, of prosperity and wretchedness, and whose actual lodging was liable to be changed at any moment for better or worse.

"Not a bad place, is it?" said Barnes, looking round in critical approval at the prostitutes and bullies hoarded round the tables puddly with the overflow of mineral waters and froth of beer.

"You really like it?" Michael asked.

"Oh, it's cheerful," said Barnes. "And that's something nowadays."

Michael perceived Daisy before they were halfway across the room. He greeted her with particular friendliness as an individual among these hard-eyed constellations.

"Hulloa!" she cried. "Wherever have you been all this time?"

"I called at Guilford Street, but you were gone."

"Oh, yes. I left there. I couldn't stand the woman there any longer. Sit down. Who's your friend?"

Michael brought Barnes into the conversation, and suggested moving into one of the alcoves where it was easier to talk.

"No, come on, sit down here. Fritz won't like it, if we move."

Michael looked round for the protector, and she laughed.

"You silly thing! Fritz is the waiter."

Michael presently grew accustomed to being jogged in the back by everyone who passed, and so powerful was the personality of the Orange that very soon he, like the rest of the crowd, was able to discuss private affairs without paying any heed to the solitary smoking listeners around.

"Where's Dolly?" he asked.

"Oh, I had to get rid of her very sharp," said Daisy. "She served me a very nasty trick after I'd been so good to her. Besides, I've taken up with a fellow. Bert Saunders. He does the boxing for Crime Illustrated."

"You told me I was like him," Michael reminded her.

"That's right. I remember now. I'm living down off Judd Street in a flat. Why don't you come round and see me there?"

"I will," Michael promised.

"Wasn't Bert Saunders the fellow who was keeping Kitty Metcalfe?" asked Barnes.

"That's right. Only he gave her the push after she hit Maudie Clive over the head with a port-wine glass in the Half Moon upstairs."

"I knew Kitty," said Barnes, shaking his head to imply that acquaintance with Kitty had involved a wider experience than fell to most men. "What's happened to her?"

"Oh, Gard, don't ask me," said Daisy. "She's got in with a fellow who kept a fried-fish place in the Caledonian Road, and I've never even seen her since."

"And what's happened to Dolly?" asked Michael.

"Oh, good job if that love-boy of hers does punch into her. Silly cow! She ought to know better. Fancy going off as soft as you like with that big-mouthed five-to-two, and after I'd just given her six of my new handkerchiefs."

Michael wished he could have an opportunity of explaining to Barnes that on account of Daisy's friendship for Dolly, he and she and the cast-off had spent a night in the police-cells. He thought it would have amused him.

"Where's the Half Moon?" he asked instead.

Daisy said it was a place in Glasshouse Street for which she had no very great affection. However, Michael was anxious to see it; and soon they left the Orange to visit the Half Moon.

It was a public-house with nothing that was demirep in its exterior; but upstairs there was a room frequented after eleven o'clock by ladies of the town. They walked up a narrow twisting staircase carpeted with bright red felt and lit by a red-shaded lamp, and found themselves in a room even more densely fumed with tobacco smoke than downstairs at the Orange. In a corner was an electric organ which was fed with a stream of pennies and blared forth its repertory of ten tunes with maddening persistence. One of these tunes was gay enough to make the girls wish to dance, and always with its recurrence there was a certain amount of cake-walking which was immediately stopped by a commissionaire who stood in the doorway and shouted "Order, please! Quiet, please! No dancing, ladies!" To the nearest couple he always whispered that the police were outside.

Daisy, having stigmatized the Half Moon as the rottenest hole within a mile of the Dilly, proceeded to become more cheerful with every penny dropped into the slot; and finally she invited Michael to come back with her to Judd Street, as her boy had gone down to Margate to see Young Sancy, a prospective lightweight champion, who was training there.

"Anyway, you can see me home," she said. "Even if you don't come in. Besides, my flat's all right. It is, really. You know. Comfortable. He's very good to me, is Bert, though he's a bit soppified. He dresses very nice, and he earns good money. Well, three pound a week. That's not so bad, is it?"

"That's all right," said Barnes. "With what you earn as well."

"There's a nerve," said Daisy. "Well, I can't stay moping indoors all the evening, can I? But he's most shocking jealous is Bert. And he calls me his pussy-cat. Puss, puss! There's a scream. He's really a bit soft, and his eyes is awful. But it's nice, so here's luck." She drained her glass. "'Do you love me, puss?' he says. Silly thing! But they think a lot of him at the office. His governor came down to see him the other morning about something he's been writing. I don't know what it was. I hate the sight of his writing. I carry on at him something dreadful, and then he says, 'My pussy-cat mustn't disturb me.'"

Daisy shrieked with laughter at the recollection, and Michael who was beginning to be rather fearful for her sobriety suggested home as a good move.

"I shan't go if you don't come back with me," she declared.

Since their incarceration Michael had a tender feeling for Daisy, and he promised to accompany her. She would not go in a hansom, however; nor would she allow Barnes to make a third; and in the end she and Michael went wandering off down Shaftesbury Avenue through the warm September night.

Michael enjoyed walking with her, for she rambled on with long tales of her past that seemed the inconsequent threads of a legendary Odyssey. He flattered himself with her companionship, and told himself that here at last was a demonstration of the possibility of a true friendship with a woman of that class with whom mere friendship would be more improbable than with any woman. It was really delightful to stroll with her homeward under this starlit sky of London; to wander on and on while she chattered forth her history. There had been no hint of any other relation between them; she was accepting him as a friend. He was proud as they walked through Russell Square, overshadowed by the benign trees that hung down with truculent green sprays in the lamplight; he felt a thrill in her companionship, as they dawdled along the railings of Brunswick Square in the acrid scent of the privet. It was curious to think that from the glitter and jangle of the Half Moon could rise this friendship that was giving to all the houses they passed a strange peacefulness. He fancied that here and there the windows were blinking at them in drowsy content, when the gas was extinguished by the unknown bedfarer within. Judd Street shone before them in a lane of lamps, and beyond, against the night, the gothic cliff of St. Pancras Station was indistinctly present. They turned down into Little Quondam Street, and presently came to a red brick house with a pretentious portico.

"Our flat's in here. Agnes House, it's called. Come in and have one before you go home," she invited.

Michael entered willingly. He was glad to show so quickly his confidence in their new friendship.

Agnes House was only entitled to the distinction of a name rather than a number, because the rest of the houses in Quondam Street were shabby, small, and old. It was a new building three stories high, and it was already falling to pieces, owing to work which must have been exceptionally dishonest to give so swiftly the effect of caducity. This collapse was more obvious because it was not dignified by the charm of age; and Agnes House in its premature dissolution was not much more admirable than a cardboard box which has been left out in the rain. Upon Michael it made an impression as of something positively corrupt in itself apart from any association with depravity: it was like a young person with a vile disease whose condition nauseated without arousing pity.

"Rather nice, eh?" said Daisy, as she lit the gas in the kitchen of the flat. "Sit down. I'll get some whisky. There's a bathroom, you know. And it's grand being on the ground floor. I should get the hump, if we was upstairs. I always swore I'd never live in a flat. Well, I don't really call them safe, do you? Anything might happen and nothing ever be found out."

Michael as he saw the crude pink sheets of Crime Illustrated strewn about the room was not surprised that Daisy should often get nervous when left alone. These horrors in which fashion-plates with mangled throats lay weltering in pools of blood could scarcely conduce to a placid loneliness, and Michael knew that she probably spent a great deal of every day in solitude. Her life with Crime Illustrated to fright her fancy must always be haunted by presentiments of dread at the sound of a key in the latch. It was curious, this half childlike existence of the underworld always upon the boundaries of fear. Michael could see the villainous paper used for every kind of domestic service—to wrap up a piece of raw meat, to contain the scraps for the cat's dinner, and spread half over the kitchen table as a cloth whereon the disks of grease lay like great thunder-drops. It would be very natural, when the eyes never rested from these views of sordid violence, to expect evil everywhere. Himself, as he sat here, was already half inclined to accept the underworld's preoccupation with crime as a truer judgment of human nature than was held by a sentimental civilization, and he began to wonder whether a good deal of his own privacy had not been spent in a fool's paradise of security. The moated grange and the dark tower were harmless rococo terrors beside the maleficent commonplace of Agnes House.

"The kitchen's in a rare old mess, isn't it?" said Daisy looking round her. "It gives Bert the rats to see it like this."

"Are you fond of him?" Michael asked. He was anxious to display his friendly interest.

"Oh, he's all right. But I wouldn't ever get fond of *any*body. It doesn't pay with men. The more you give them, the more they think they can do as they like with you."

"I don't understand why you live with him, if he's nothing better than all right," said Michael.

"Well, I'm used to him, and he's not always in the way like some fellows are."

Michael would have liked to ask her about the beginning of her life as it was now conducted. Daisy was so essentially of the streets that it was impossible to suppose she had ever known a period of innocence. Her ancestry seemed to go back to the doxies of the eighteenth century, and beyond them to Alsatian queens, and yet farther to the tavern wenches of François Villon and the Chronique Scandaleuse. There was nothing pathetic about her; he could not imagine her ever in a position to be wronged by a man. She was in very fact the gay woman who was bred first from some primordial heedlessness unchronicled. She would be a hard subject for chivalrous treatment, so deeply would she inevitably despise it. Nevertheless, he wanted to try to bring home to her the quality of the feeling she had inspired in him. He was anxious to prove to her the reality of a friendliness untainted by any thought of the relation in which she might justifiably think he would prefer to stand.

"There's something extraordinarily attractive about being friends," he began. "Isn't it a great relief for you to meet someone who wishes to be nothing more than a friend?"

"Friends," Daisy repeated. "I don't know that I think much of friends. You don't get much out of *them*, do you?"

"Is that all anybody is for," Michael asked in disappointment. "To get something out of?"

"Well, naturally. Anyone can't live on nothing, can they?"

"But I don't see why a friend shouldn't be as profitable as an ephemeral ... as a lover ... well, what I mean is, as a man you meet at eleven and say good-bye to next morning. A friend could be quite as generous."

"I never knew anyone in this world give anything unless they wanted twice as much back in return," said Daisy.

"Why do you suppose I gave you money the other day and paid your fine in the police court?" he asked, for, though he did not like it, he was so anxious to persuade her of the feasibleness of friendship, that he could not help making the allusion.

"I suppose you wanted to," she said.

"As a friend," he persisted.

"Oh, all right," she agreed with him lazily. "Have it your own way. I'm too sleepy to argue."

"Then we are friends?" Michael asked gravely.

"Yes. Yes. Yes. Yes. A couple of old talk-you-deads joring over a clothes-line. Get on with it, Roy—or what's your name? Michael, eh? That's right."

"Good! Now, supposing I ask your advice, will you give it to me?"

"Advice is very cheap," said Daisy.

"I used to know a girl," Michael began.

"A straight-cut?"

"Oh, yes. Certainly. Oh, rather. At least in those days she was."

"I see. And now she's got a naughty little twinkle in her eye."

"Look here. Do listen seriously," Michael begged. "She isn't a straight-cut any longer."

"Well, what did I tell you? That's what I said. She's gone gay."

"I want to get her away from this life," Michael announced, with such solemnity that Daisy was insulted.

"Why, what's the matter with it? You're as bad as a German ponce I knew who joined the Salvation Army. Don't you try taking me home to-night to our loving heavenly father. It gives me the sick."

"But this girl was brought up differently. She was what is called a 'lady.'"

"More shame for her then," said Daisy indignantly. "She ought to have known better."

It was curious this sense of intrusion which Lily's fall gave to one so deeply plunged. There was in Daisy's attitude something of the unionist's toward foreign blackleg labor.

"Well, you see," Michael pointed out. "As even you have no pity for her, wouldn't it be right for me to try to get her out of the life altogether?"

"How are you going to do it? If she was walking about with a sunshade all day, before you sprang it on her...."

"I had nothing to do with it," Michael interrupted. "At least not directly."

"Well, what are you pulling your hair out over?" she demanded in surprise.

"I feel a certain responsibility," he explained. "Go on with what you were saying."

"If she left a nice home," Daisy continued, "to live gay, she isn't going to be whistled back to Virginia the same as you would a dog. Now, is she?"

"But I want to marry her," said Michael simply.

Daisy stared at him in commiseration for his folly.

"You must be worse than potty over her," she gasped.

"Why?"

"Why? Why, because it doesn't pay to marry that sort of girl. She'll only do you down with some fancy fellow, and then you'll wish you hadn't been such a grass-eyes."

A blackbeetle ran quickly across the gaudy oilcloth, and Michael sitting in this scrofulous kitchen had a presentiment that Daisy was right. Sitting here, he was susceptible to the rottenness that was coeval with all creation. It called forth in him a sense of futility, so that he felt inclined to surrender his resolve to an universal pessimism. Yet in the same instant he was aware of the need for him to do something, even if his action were to carry within itself the potential destruction of more than he was setting out to accomplish.

"When do you see her?" asked Daisy. "And what does *she* say about being married?"

"Well, as a matter of fact, I haven't seen her for nearly five years," Michael explained rather apologetically. "I'm searching for her now. I've got to find her."

"Strike me, if you aren't the funniest —— I ever met," Daisy exclaimed.

She leaned back in her chair and began to laugh. Her mockery was for Michael intensified by the surroundings through which it was echoing. The kitchen was crowded with untidy accumulations, with half-washed plates and dishes, with odds and ends of attire; but the laughter seemed to be ringing through a desert. Perhaps the illusion of emptiness was due to the pictures nailed without frames to the walls of the room, whose eyes watched him with unnatural fixity; and yet so homely was the behavior of the people in the pictures that by contrast suddenly they made the kitchen seem unreal. Indeed, the whole house, no more substantial than a house in a puppet-show, betrayed its hollowness. It became an interior very much like those glimpses of interiors in Crime Illustrated. The slightest effort of fancy would have shown Daisy Palmer cloven by a hatchet, yet coquettish enough even in sanguinary death to display lisle-thread stockings and the scalloped edge of a white petticoat. There was nothing like this of which to dream in Leppard Street. Death would come as slowly and wearily thither as here he would enter sensationally.

Daisy ceased to rock herself with mirth.

"No, really," she said. "It's a shame to laugh, but you are the limit. Only you did ask my advice, and I tell you straight you'll be sorry if you do marry her. What's she like, Wandering Willie? Have some cocoa if I make it? Go on, do. I'll boil it on the gas-ring."

Michael was touched by her attention, and he accepted the offer of cocoa. Then he began to describe Lily's appearance. He could not, however much she might laugh, keep off the object of his quest. Lily was, after all, the only rational explanation of his present mode of life.

"She sounds a bit washed out according to your description of her," Daisy commented. "Still, everyone to their own fancy, and if you like blue-eyed bottles of peroxide, that's your look-out."

They were drinking the cocoa she had made, and the flame of the gas-ring gave just the barren comfort that the kitchen seemed to demand. Another blackbeetle hurried over the oilcloth. A belated fly buzzed angrily against the shade of the electric light. Daisy yawned and looked up at the metal clock with its husky tick.

Suddenly there was the sound of a latchkey in the outer door. She leaped up.

"Gard, supposing that's Bert come back from Margate!"

She pushed Michael hurriedly across the passage into the front room, commanding him to keep quiet and stay in an empty curtained recess. Then she hurried back to the kitchen, leaving him in a very unpleasant frame of mind. He heard through the closed door Daisy's voice in colloquy with a deeper voice. Evidently Bert had come back; but his return had been so abrupt that he had had no time to prevent himself being placed in this ridiculous position. Would he have to stay in this recess all night? He peered out into the room, which was in a filigree of bleak shadows made by the street lamp shining through the muslin curtains of the window. Through a desolation of undrawn blinds the houses of Little Quondam Street were visible across the road. The unused room smelt moldy, and if Michael had ever pictured himself in the complexity of a clandestine affair, this was not at all the romantic environment he would have chosen for his drama. This was really damned annoying, and he made a step in the direction of the kitchen to put an end to the misunderstanding. Surely Saunders would have realized that his visit to Daisy was harmless: and yet would he? How stupid she had been to hustle him out of the way like this. Naturally the fellow would be suspicious now. Would that hum of conversation never stop? It reminded him of the fly which had been buzzing round the lamp. Supposing Saunders came in here to fetch something? Was he to hide ignominiously behind this confounded curtain, and what on earth would happen if he were discovered? Michael boiled with rage at the prospect of such an indignity. Saunders would probably want to fight him. A man who spent his life helping to produce Crime Illustrated was no doubt deep-dyed himself in the vulgar crudity of his material.

Ten minutes passed. Still that maddening hum of talk rose and fell. Ten more minutes passed; and Michael began to estimate the difficulty of climbing out of the window into the street. It had been delightful, this experience, until he had entered this cursed flat. He should have parted from Daisy on the doorstep, and then he would have carried home with him the memory of a friendship that belonged to the London starlight. The whole relation had been ruined by entering this scabrous building.

He must have been here for more than an hour. It was insufferable. He would go boldly into the kitchen and brave Saunders' violence. Yet he could not do that because Daisy would be involved by such a step. What could they be talking about? It was really unreasonable for people who lived together to sit up chatting half the night. At last he heard the sound of an opening door; there were footsteps in the passage; another door-opened; after a minute or two somebody walked out into the street. Michael had just sighed with relief, when he heard footsteps coming back; and the buzz of conversation began again in a lighter timbre. This was simply intolerable. He was evidently going to stay here until the filigree of shadows faded in the dawn. Saunders must have brought in a friend with him. Another half hour passed and Michael had reached a stage of cynicism which disclaimed any belief in friendship. Not again would he so easily let himself be made ridiculous. Then he became conscious of a keen desire to see this Saunders whom, by the way, he was supposed to resemble. It was tantalizing to miss the opportunity of comparison.

The hum of conversation stopped. Soon afterward Daisy came into the room and whispered that he could creep out now, but that he must not slam the front door. She would see him at the Orange to-morrow.

When they reached the passage, she called back through the kitchen:

"Bert, do you know you left the front door open?"

Idiotically and uxoriously floated from the inner bedroom: "Did I, pussy cat? Puss must shut it then."

Daisy dug Michael violently in the ribs to express her inward hilarity; then suddenly she pulled him to her and kissed him roughly. In another second he was in the lamplight of Little Quondam Street. As in a nightmare it converged before him: a lean dog was routing in some garbage: a drunken man, reeling along the pavement opposite, abused him in queer disjointed obscenities without significance.

Barnes was sitting in Michael's room, when he got back to Leppard Street.

"What ho," he said sleepily. "You've been enjoying yourself with that piece, then?"

Michael regarded him angrily.

"What do you mean?"

"Oh, chuck it, Fane. You needn't look so solemn; she's not a bad bit of goods, either. I've heard of her before."

Michael turned away from him. He knew it would be useless to try to convince Barnes that there was nothing between him and Daisy. Moreover, if he told the true tale of the evening, he would only make himself out utterly absurd. It was a pity that an evening which had promised such a reward for his theories should now be tainted. But when Barnes had slouched upstairs to bed, Michael realized how little his insinuations had mattered. The adventure had been primarily a comic experience; it had displayed him once more grotesquely reflected in the underworld's distorting mirror.

On the following night Michael went to the Café d'Orange, and heard Daisy's account of the wonderful way in which she had fooled Bert Saunders.

"But really, you know," she said. "It did give me a turn. Fancy him coming back all of a sudden like that, and bringing in that fighting fellow. What a terrible thing, if Bert had found out you was in there and put him up to bashing your face. Oh, but Bert's all right with his pussy-cat."

"But why didn't you let me stay where I was?" Michael asked. "And introduce me quite calmly. He couldn't have said anything."

"Couldn't he?" Daisy cried. "I reckon he could then. I reckon he could have said a lot. If he hadn't, I'd have given him the chuck right away. I don't want no fellow hanging around me that hasn't got the pluck to go for anyone he finds messing about with his girl. Couldn't he have said anything?"

Michael was again face to face with topsyturvydom. It really was time to meditate on the absurdity of trying to control these people of the underworld with laws and regulations and penalties which had been devised to control individuals who represented moral declension from the standards of a genteel civilization. Mrs. Murdoch, Poppy, Barnes, Daisy—they all inverted the very fabric of society. They were moral antipodeans to the magistrate or the legislator or the social reformer. They were pursuing and acting up to their own ideals of conduct: they were not fleeing or falling away from a political morality. Was it possible, then, to say that evil was something more than a mere failure to conform to goodness? Was it possible to declare confidently the absolutism of evil? In this topsyturvydom might there not be perceived a great constructive force?

Michael pondered these questions a good deal. He had not enough evidence as yet to provide him with a synthesis; but as he sat through the rapid darkening of the September dusks, it seemed to him that very often he was trembling upon the verge of a discovery. Leppard Street came to stand as a dark antechamber with massive curtains drawn against the light, the light which in the past he had only perceived through the chinks of impenetrable walls. Leppard Street was Dante's obscure wood of the soul; it rustled with a thousand intimations of spiritual events. Leppard Street was dark, but Michael did not fear the gloom, because he knew that he was winning here with each new experience a small advance; at Oxford he had merely contemplated the result of the former pilgrimages of other people. This he promised to do in spite of everything. He was faithful to his search for Lily, and he even went so far as to call upon Drake to ask if he had ever seen of his ambition he told himself that the light would be visible when he married Lily, that through her salvation he would save himself.

Michael did not reënter his own world, whose confusion of minor problems would have destroyed completely his hope to stand unperplexed before the problems of the underworld, the solution of which might help to solve the universe or at any rate his own share in the universe. He did not tell his mother or Stella where he was living, and their letters came to him at his club. They did not worry him, although Stella threatened a terrible punishment if he did not appear in their midst in time to give her away in November. This he promised to do in spite of everything. He was faithful to his search for Lily, and he even went so far as to call upon Drake to ask if he had ever seen her since that night at the Orient. But he had not. Michael did not vex himself over the failure to discover Lily's whereabauts. Having placed himself at the nod of destiny, he was content to believe that if he never found her he must be content to look elsewhere for the expression of himself. September became October. It would be six years this month since first they met, and she was twenty-two now. Could seventeen be captured anew?

One afternoon from his window Michael was pondering the etiolated season whose ghostliness was more apparent in Leppard Street, because no fall of leaves marked material decline. Hurrying along the brindled walls from the direction of Greenarbor Court was a parson whose walk was perfectly familiar, though he could not affix it to any person he knew. Yes, he could. It was Chator's, the dear, the pious and the bubbling Chator's; and how absurdly the same as it used to be along the corridors of St. James'. Michael rushed out to meet him, and had seized and shaken his hand before Chator recognized him. When he did, however, he was twice as much excited as Michael, and spluttered forth a fountain of questions about his progress during these years with a great deal of information about his own. He came in eagerly at Michael's invitation, and so much had he still to ask and tell that it was a long time before he wanted to know what had brought Michael to Leppard Street.

"How extraordinary to find you here, my dear fellow! This isn't my district, you know. But the Senior Curate is ill. Greenarbor Court! I say, what a dreadful slum!" Chator looked very intensely at Michael, as if he expected he would offer to raze it to the ground immediately. "I never realized we had anything quite so bad in the parish. But what really is extraordinary about running across you like this is that a man who's just come to us from Ely was talking about you only yesterday. My goodness, how ..."

"It's no larger than a grain of sand," Michael interrupted quickly.

"What is?" asked Chator, with his familiar expression of perplexity at Michael.

"You were going to comment on the size of the world, weren't you?"

"I suppose you'll rag me just as much as ever, you old brute." Chator was beaming with delight at the prospect. "But seriously, this man Stewart—Nigel Stewart. I think he was at Trinity, Oxford. You do know him?"

"Nigel isn't here, too?" Michael exclaimed.

"He's our deacon."

"Oh, how priceless you'll both be in the pulpit," said Michael. "And to-morrow's Sunday. Which of you will be preaching at Mass?"

"My dear fellow, the Vicar always preaches at Mass. I shall be preaching at Evening Prayer. Why don't you come to supper in the Clergy House afterward?"

"How do you like your Vicar?"

"Oh, very sound, very sound," said Chator, shaking his head.

"Does he take the ablutions at the right moment?" asked Michael, twinkling.

"Oh, yes. Oh, yes. He's very sound. Quite all right. I was afraid at first he was going to be a leetle High Church. But he's not. Not a bit. We had a procession this June on Corpus Christi. The people liked it. And of course we've got the children."

They talked for an hour of old friends, of Viner, of Dom Cuthbert and Clere Abbey and schooldays, until at last Chator had to be going.

"You will come on Sunday?"

"Of course. But what's the name of your church?"

"My dear fellow, that shows you haven't heard your parochial Mass," said Chator, with mock seriousness. "St. Chad's is our church."

"It sounds as if you had a saintly fish for Patron," said Michael.

"I say, steady. Steady. St. Chad, you know, of Lichfield."

Michael laughed loudly.

"My dear old Chator, you are just as inimitable as ever. You haven't changed a bit. Well, Saint Chad's—Sunday."

From the window he watched Chator hurrying along beside the brindled walls. He thought how every excited step he took showed him to be bubbling over with the joy of telling Nigel Stewart of such a coincidence in the district of the Senior Curate.

Michael suggested to Barnes that he should come with him to church on Sunday, and Barnes, who evidently thought his salary demanded deference to Michael's wishes, made no objection. It was an October evening through which a wintry rawness had already penetrated, and the interior of St. Chad's with its smell of people and warm wax and stale incense was significant of comfort and shelter. The church, a dreary Byzantine edifice, was nevertheless a very essential piece of London, being built of the yellow bricks whose texture and color more than that of any other material adapt themselves to the grime of the city. Nothing deliberately beautiful would have had power here. These people who sat thawing in a stupor of waiting felt at home. They were submerged in London streets, and their church was as deeply engulfed as themselves. The Stations of the Cross did not seem much more strange here than the lithographs in their own kitchens, and the raucous drone of Gregorians was familiar music.

As the Office proceeded, Michael glanced from time to time toward his companion. At first Barnes had kept an expression of injured boredom, but with each chant he seemed less able to resist the habits of the past. Michael felt bound to ascribe to habit his compliance with the forms and ceremonies, for it was scarcely conceivable that he could any longer be moved by the appeal of a sensuous worship, still less by the craving of his soul for God.

Chator's discourse was a simple one delivered with all the spluttering simplicity he could bring to it. Michael was not sure of the effect upon the congregation, but himself found it moving in a gently pathetic way. The sermon had the naïve obviousness and the sweet seriousness of a child telling a long tale of imaginary adventure. It was easy to see that Chator had never known from the moment of his Ordination, or indeed from the moment he began to suppose he was thinking for himself, a single doubt of the absolute truth of his religion, still less of its expediency. Michael wondered again what effect the sermon was having upon the congregation, which was sitting all round him woodenly in a sort of browse. Did one sentence reach it, or was the whole business of the sermon merely an excuse to sit here basking in the stuffiness of the homely church? Michael turned a sidelong look at Barnes. Tears were in his eyes, and he was staring into the gloom of the dingy apse with its tesselations of dull gold. This was disconcerting to Michael's opinion of the sermon, for Chator could not be shaking Barnes by his eloquence: these splutterings of dogma were surely not able to rouse one so deep in the quagmire of his own corruption. Must he confess that a positive sanctity abode in this church? He would be glad to believe it did; he would be glad to imagine that an imperishable temple of truth was posited among these perishable streets.

The sermon was over, and as the congregation rose to sing the hymn, Michael was aware, he could not have said how, that these people pouring forth this sacred jingle were all very weary. They had come here to rest from the fatigue of dullness, and in a moment now the chill vapors of the autumn night would wreathe themselves round their journey home. Sunday was a day of pause when the people of the city had leisure to sigh out their weariness: it was no shutting of theaters or shops that made it sad. This congregation was composed of weaklings fit for neither good nor evil, and every Sunday night they were gathered together for a little while in the smell of warm wax and incense. Now already they were trooping out into the frore evening; their footsteps would shuffle for a space over the dark pavements; a few would have pickled cabbage and cheese for supper, a few would not; such was life in this limbo between Hell and Heaven. Barnes, however, was not to be judged with the bulk of the congregation: another reason must be found for the influence of Evening Prayer or of Chator's words upon him.

"Did you like the sermon?" Michael asked in the porch.

"I didn't listen to a word of it," said Barnes emphatically.

"Oh, really? I thought you were interested. You seemed interested," said Michael.

"I was thinking what a mug I'd been not to back The Clown for the Cesarewitch. I had the tip. You know, Fane, I'll tell you what it is. I'm not used to money, and that's a fact. I don't know how to spend it. I'm afraid of it. So bang it all goes on drinks."

"I thought you enjoyed the service," said Michael.

"Oh, I'm used to services. You know. On and off I've done a lot of churchifying, I have. It would take something more than that fellow preaching to curdle me up. I've gone through it. Religion, love, and measles; they're all about the same. I don't reckon anybody gets them more than once properly."

Michael told Barnes he was going on to supper at the Clergy House, and though he had intended to invite him to come as well, he was so much irritated by his unconscious deception that he let him go off, and went back into the empty church to wait for Chator and Nigel Stewart. What puzzled Michael most about Barnes was how himself had ever managed to be impressed by his unusual wickedness. As he beheld him nowadays, a mean and common little squirt of exceptional beastliness really, he was amazed to think that once he had endowed him with almost diabolical powers. He remembered to this day the gleam in Brother Aloysius' blue eyes when he was gathering the blackberries by that hazel-coppice. Perhaps it had been the monkish habit, which by contrast with his expression had made him seem almost supernaturally evil; and yet when he met him again at Earl's Court he had been kindled by those blue eyes. Henry Meats had been very much like Henry Barnes; but where was now that lambent flame in the eyes? He had looked at them many times lately, but they had always been cold and unintelligent as a doll's.

"I really must have been mad when I was young," Michael said to himself. "And yet other people have preserved the influence they used to have over me. Other people haven't changed. Why should he? I wonder whether it was always myself I saw in him: my own evil genius?"

Chator came to fetch him while he was worrying over Barnes' lapse into unimportance, and together they passed through the sacristy into the Clergy House.

Nigel Stewart's room, which they visited in the minutes before supper, had changed very little from his digs in the High. Ely had added a picture or two; that was all. Nor had Nigel changed, except that his clerical attire made him more seraphic than ever. While he and Michael chattered of Oxford friends, Chator stood with his back to the fire beaming at the reunion which he felt he had brought about: his biretta at a military angle gave him a look of knowing benevolence.

The bell sounded for supper, and they went along corridors hung with Arundel prints and faded photographs of cathedrals, until they came to a brightly lit room where it seemed that quite twenty people were going to sit down at the trestle-table. Michael was introduced to the Vicar and two more curates, and also to a dozen church workers who made the same sort of jokes about whatever dish they were helping. Also he met that walrus-like man who, whether as organist or ceremonarius or treasurer of club accounts or vicar's churchwarden, is always to be found attached to the clergy. Michael sat next to him, as it happened, and found he had a deep voice and was unable to get nearer to "th" than "v."

"We're raver finking," he confided to Michael over a high-heaped plate, "of starting Benediction, vis year."

"That will be wonderful," said Michael politely.

"Yes, it ought to annoy ver poor old Bishop raver."

The walrus-like man chuckled and bent over his food with a relish stimulated by such a prospect. After supper the two curates carried off their favorites upstairs to their own rooms; and as Chator, Stewart, and Michael were determined to spend the evening together, the Vicar was left with rather more people than usual to smoke his cigarettes.

"I envy you people," said Michael, as the three of them sank down into deep wicker chairs. "I envy this power you have to bring Oxford—or Cambridge—into London. For it is the same spirit in terms of action, isn't it? And you're free from the thought which must often worry dons that perhaps they are having a very good time without doing very much to deserve it."

"We work hard in this parish," spluttered Chator. "Oh, rather. Very hard."

"That's what I say. You have the true peace that thrives on activity," said Michael. "But at the same time, what I'm rather anxious to know is how nearly you touch the real sinners."

Stewart and Chator looked at one another across his chair.

"How much do we, brother?" asked Stewart.

"No, really," protested Michael. "My dear Nigel, I can't have you being so affected. Brother! You must give up being archaic now that you're a pale young curate."

"What do you call the real sinners?" asked Chator. "You saw our congregation to-night. All poor, of course."

"Shall I say frankly what I think?" Michael asked.

The other two nodded.

"I'm not sure if that congregation is worth a very great deal. I'm not trying to be offensive, so listen to me patiently. That congregation would come whatever you did. They came not because they wanted to worship God or because they desired the forgiveness of their sins, nor even because they think that going to church is a good habit. No, they came in a sort of sad drift of aimlessness; they came in out of the dreariness of their lives to sit for a little while in the glow that a church like yours can always provide. They went out again with a vague memory of comfort, material comfort, I mean; but they took away with them nothing that would kindle a flame to light up the gray week-days. Do you know, I fancy that when these picture-theaters become more common, as they will, most of your people will get from them just the same sensation of warmth and material comfort. Obviously if this is a true observation on my part, your people regard church from a merely negative attitude. That isn't enough, as you'll admit."

"But it's not fair to judge by the evening congregation," Chator burst out. "You must remember that we get quite a different crowd at Mass."

"But do you get the real sinners?" Michael repeated.

"My dear Michael, what does this inquisition forebode?" said Stewart. "You're becoming wrapped in mystery. You're found in Leppard Street for no reason that I've yet heard. And now you attack us in this unkind way."

"I'm not attacking you," Michael said. "I'm trying to extract from you a point of view. Lately it happens that I've found myself in the company of a certain class, well—the company of bullies and prostitutes. You must have lots of them in this parish. Do you get hold of them? I don't believe you do, because the chief thing which has struck me is the utter remoteness of the Church or indeed of any kind of religion from the life of that class. And their standards are upside-down—actually upside-down. They're handed over entirely to the powers of darkness. Now, as far as I can see, the Devil—or whatever you choose to call him—only cares about people who are worth his while. He hands the others over to anybody that likes to deal with them. Equally I would say that God is a little contemptuous of the poor intermediates. The Church, however, in these hard times for religion is glad to get hold even of them, and this miserable spirit of mediocrity runs through the whole organization. The bishops are moderate; the successful parsons are moderate; and the flock is moderate. To come back to the sinners. You know, they *would* be worth getting. You've no idea what a force they would raise. And now, all their industry, all their ingenuity, all their vitality is devoted to the service of evil."

Chator could contain himself no longer.

"My dear fellow, you don't understand how impossible it is to get in touch with the people you're talking about. They elude one. Of course, we should rejoice to get them. But they're impossible."

"Christ moved among sinners," said Michael.

"It's not because we don't long to move among them," Chator spluttered in exasperation. "We would give anything to move among them. But we can't. I don't know why. But they won't relax any of their barriers. They're notoriously difficult."

"Then it all comes down to a 'no' in answer to my question," said Michael. "You don't get the real sinners. That's what's the matter with St. Chad's—until you can compel the sinner to come in, you'll stay in a spiritual backwater."

"If you were a priest," said Chator, "you'd realize our handicap better."

"No doubt," Michael agreed. "But don't forget that the Salvation Army gets hold of sinners. In fact, I'll wager that nine out of ten of the people with whom I've been in contact lately would only understand by religion the Salvation Army. Personally I loathe the Salvation Army. I think it is almost a more disruptive organization than anything else in the world. But at least it is alive; it's not suet like most of the Dissenting Sects or a rather rich and heavy plum-pudding like the greater part of the Church of England. It's a maddening and atrociously bad and cheap alcohol, but it does enflame. I tell you, my dear old Chator and my dear old Nigel, you have the greatest opportunity imaginable for energy, for living and bringing life to others, if only you'll not sit down and be content because you've got the children and can fill the church for Evening Prayer with that colorless, dreary, dreadfully sorrowful crowd I saw to-night."

Michael leaned back in his chair; the fire crackled above the silence; and, outside, the disheartened quiet of the Sabbath was brooding. Chator was the first to speak.

"Some of what you say may be true, but the rest of it is a mere muddle of heresies and misconceptions and misstatements. It's absolute blasphemy to say that God is contemptuous of what you called the intermediates, and you apparently believe that evil is only misdirected good. You apparently think that your harlots and bullies are better for being more actively harmful."

"No, no," Michael corrected. "You didn't follow my argument. As a matter of fact, I believe in the absolutism of evil the more, the more I see of evil men and women. What I meant was that in proportion to the harm they have power to effect would be the inspiration and advantage of turning their abilities toward good. But cut out all theological questions and confess that the Church has failed with the class I speak of."

The argument swayed backward and forward for a long time, without reaching a conclusion.

"You can't have friars nowadays," said Chator in response to Michael's last expression of ambition. "Conditions have changed."

"Conditions had changed when St. Francis of Assisi tried to revive an absolute Christianity," Michael pointed out. "Conditions had changed when the Incarnation took place. Pontius Pilate, Caiaphas, Judas, and a host of contemporaries must have tried to point that out. Materialists are always peculiarly sensitive to the change of external conditions. Do you believe in Christ?"

"Don't try to be objectionable, my dear fellow," said Chator, getting very red.

"Well, if you do," persisted Michael, "if you accept the Gospels, it is utterly absurd for you as a Christian priest to make 'change of conditions' an excuse for having failed to rescue the sinners of your parish."

"Michael," said Stewart, intervening on account of Chator's obviously rising anger. "Why are you living in Leppard Street? What fiery mission are you upon? I believe you're getting too much wrapped up in private fads and fancies. Why don't you come and work for us at St. Chad's?"

"He's one of those clever people who can always criticize with intense fervor," said Chator bitterly. He was still very red and ruffled, and Michael felt rather penitent.

"I wish I *could* work here. Chator, do forgive me for being so offensive. I really have no right to criticize, because my own vice is inability to do anything in company with other people. The very sight of workers in coöperation freezes me into apathy. If I were a priest, I should probably feel like you that the children were the most important. Have neither of you ever heard of anybody whose faith was confirmed by the realization of evil? Usually, it's the other way about, isn't it? I've met many unbelievers who first began to doubt, because the problem of evil upset their notions of divine efficiency. Chator, you have forgiven me, haven't you?"

"I ought to have realized that you didn't mean half you were saying," said Chator.

Michael smiled. Should he start the argument again by insisting that he had meant even twice as much as he had said? In the end, however, he let Chator believe in his exaggeration, and they parted good friends.

Nigel Stewart came often to see him during the next fortnight, and he was very anxious to find out why Michael was living in Leppard Street. Michael would not tell him, however, but instead he introduced him to Barnes who with money in his pocket was very independent and gave up sign of his boasted ability to circumvent parsons financially. No doubt, however, when he was thrown back on his own resources, he would benefit greatly by this acquaintance. Stewart had a theory that Michael had shut himself in Leppard Street to test the personality of Satan, and he used to insist that Michael performed all kinds of magical experiments in his solitude there. Having himself been a Satanist on several occasions at Oxford, he felt less than Chator would have done the daring of discussing Baudelaire and Huysmans. Deacon though he was, Nigel was still an undergraduate, nor did it seem probable that he would ever cease to be one. He tried to thrill Michael with some of his own diabolic experiences, but Michael was a little contemptuous and told him that his devil was merely a figure of academic naughtiness.

"All that kind of subjective wickedness is nothing at all," said Michael. "At the worst, it can only unbalance your judgment. I passed through it at the age of sixteen."

"You must have been horribly precocious," said Nigel disapprovingly.

"Oh, not more so than anyone who has freedom to develop. I should give up subjective encounters with evil, if I were you. You'll be telling me soon that you've been pinched by demons like an Egyptian eremite."

Nigel gave the impression of rather deploring the lack of such an experience, and Michael laughed:

"Go and see Maurice Avery in Grosvenor Road. He's just the person you ought to convert. Nothing could be easier than to turn Mossy into an æsthetic Christian. Would that satisfy your zeal?"

"I really think you *are* growing very offensive," said Nigel.

"No, I'm not. I'm illustrating a point. Your encounters with evil and Maurice's encounters with religion would match each other. Both would have a very wide, but also a very superficial area."

November had arrived, and Michael reappeared in Cheyne Walk to assist at Stella's wedding. He paid no attention to the scorn she flung at his affected mode of life, and he successfully resisted her most carefully planned sallies of curiosity:

"What you have to do at present is to keep your own head, not mine. Think of the responsibilities of marriage and let me alone. I'll tell you quite enough when the moment comes for telling."

"Michael, you're getting dreadfully obstinate," Stella declared. "I remember when I could get a secret out of you in no time."

"It's not I who am obstinate," said Michael. "It's you who are utterly spoiled by the lovelorn Alan."

Michael and Alan went for a long walk in Richmond Park on the day before the wedding. It was a limpid day at the shutting-in of St. Martin's summer, and to Michael it seemed like the ghost of one of those June Saturdays of eight years ago. Time had faded that warmer blue to a wintry turquoise, but there was enough of summer's image in this wraith of a day to render very poignantly to him the past. He wondered if Alan were thinking of the afternoons when they had sent the sun down from Richmond Hill. That evening before the examinations of a summer term recurred to him now more insistently than any of those dead days.

Thick as autumnal leaves that strew the brooks

In Vallombrosa.

Now the leaves were lying brown and dewy in the Richmond thickets. Then it was a summer evening of foliage in the prime. He wished he could remember the lines of Virgil which had matched the Milton. He used to know them so well:

Matres atque viri defunctaque corpora vita

Magnanimum heroum, pueri innuptæque puellæ.

There were two complex hexameters, but all that remained in his memory of the rest were two or three disjointed phrases:

Lapsa cadunt folia ... ubi frigidus annus ... et

... terris apricis.

Even at fourteen he had been able to respond to the melancholy of these lines; really, he had been rather an extraordinary boy. The sensation of other times which was evoked by walking like this in Richmond Park would soon be too strong for him any longer not to speak of it. Yet because those dead summer days seemed now to belong to the mystery of youth, to the still unexpressed and inviolate heart of a period that was forever overpast, Michael could not bring himself to destroy their sanctity with sentimental reminiscence. However, there had been comedy and absurdity also, perhaps rather more fit for exhumation now than those deeper moments.

"Do you remember the wedding of Mrs. Ross?" he asked.

"Rather," said Alan, and they both smiled.

"Do you remember when you first called her Aunt Maud, and we both burst out laughing and had to rush out of the room?"

"Rather," said Alan. "Boys *are* ridiculous, aren't they?"

"Supposing we both laugh like that when Stella is first called Mrs. Merivale?" Michael queried.

"I shall be in much too much of a self-conscious funk to laugh at anything," said Alan.

"And yet do you realize that we're only talking of eight years ago? Nothing at all really. Six years less than we had already lived at the time when that wedding took place."

To Alan upon the verge of the most important action of his life Michael's calculation seemed very profound indeed, and they both walked on in silence, meditating upon the revelation it afforded of a fugitive mortality.

"You'll be writing epitaphs next," said Alan, in rather an aggrieved voice. He had evidently traversed the swift years of the future during the silence.

"At any rate," Michael said. "You can congratulate yourself upon not having wasted time."

"My god," cried Alan, stopping suddenly. "I believe I'm the luckiest man alive."

"I thought you'd found a sovereign," said Michael. He had never heard Alan come so near to emotional expression and, knowing that a moment later Alan would be blushing at his want of reserve, he loyally covered up with a joke the confusion that must ensue.

Very few people came to the wedding, for Stella had insisted that as none of her girl friends were reputable enough to be bridesmaids, she must do without them. Mrs. Ross came, however, and she brought with her Kenneth to be a solemn and freckled and carroty page. She was very anxious that Michael should come back after the wedding to Cobble Place, but he said he would rather wait until after Christmas. Nancy came, and Michael tried to remember if he had once seriously contemplated marrying her. How well he remembered her in short skirts, and here she was a woman of thirty with a brusque jolly manner and gold pince-nez.

"You *are* a brute always to avoid my visits at Cobble Place," grumbled Nancy. "Do you realize we haven't met for years?"

"You're such a woman of affairs," said Michael.

"Well, do let's try to meet next time. I say, don't you think Maud looks terribly ill since she became a Romanist?"

Michael looked across to where Mrs. Ross was standing.

"I think she's looking rather well."

"Absolute destruction of individuality, you know," said Nancy, shaking her head. "I was awfully sick about that business. However, I must admit that she hasn't forced her religion down our throats."

"Did you expect an auto-da-fé in the middle of the lawn?" he asked. She thumped him on the shoulder:

"Silly ass! Don't you try to rag me."

They had a jolly talk, but Michael was glad he had not married her at eight years old. He decided that by now he would probably have regretted the step.

Michael managed to get two or three minutes alone with Stella after the ceremony.

"Well, Mrs. Prescott-Merivale?"

"You've admitted I'm a married woman," she exclaimed. "Now surely you can tell me what you've been doing since August and where you've been."

"I thought very fondly that you were without the curiosity of every woman," said Michael. "Alas, you are not!"

267

"Michael, you're perfectly horrid to me."

"Don't be too much the young wife," he advised, with mocking earnestness.

"I won't listen to anything you say, until I know where you've been. Of course, if I hadn't been so busy, I could easily have found you out."

"Not even can you sting me into the revelation of my hiding-place," Michael laughed.

"You shan't stay with us at Hardingham unless you tell me."

"By the time you come back from your honeymoon, I may have wonderful news," said Michael. "Oh, and by the way, where are you going for your honeymoon? It sounds absurd to ask such a question at this hour, but I've never heard."

"We're going to Compiègne," said Stella. "I wrote to little Castéra-Verduzan, and he's lent us the cottage where you and I stayed."

That choice of Stella's seemed to mark more decisively than anything she had said or done his own second place in her thoughts nowadays.

When the bride and bridegroom were gone, Michael sat with his mother, talking.

"I had arranged to go to the South of France with Mrs. Carruthers," she told him. "But if you're going to be here, I could put her off."

Michael felt rather guilty. He had not considered his mother's loneliness, and he had meant to return at once to Leppard Street.

"No, no, I'm going away again," he told her.

"Just as you like, dearest boy."

"You're glad about Stella?"

"Very glad."

"And you like Alan?"

"Of course. Charming—charming."

The firelight danced in opals on the window-panes, and the macaw who had been brought up to Mrs. Fane's sitting-room out of the way of the wedding guests sharpened his beak on the perch.

"It's really quite chilly this afternoon," said Mrs. Fane.

"Yes, there's a good deal of mist along the river," said Michael. "A pity that the fine weather should have broken up. It may be rather dreary in the forest."

"Why did they go to a forest?" she asked. "So like Stella to choose a forest in November. Most unpractical. Still, when one is young and in love, one doesn't notice the mud."

Next day Mrs. Fane went off to the South of France, and Michael went back to Leppard Street.

CHAPTER V

THE INNERMOST CIRCLE

November fogs began soon after Michael returned to Leppard Street, and these fuliginous days could cast their own peculiar spell. To enter the house at dusk was to stand for a moment choking in blackness; and even when the gas flared and whistled through a sickly nebula, it only made more vast the lightless vapors above, so that the interior seemed at first not a place of shelter, but a mirage of the streets that would presently dissolve in the drifting fog. These nights made Pimlico magical for walking. Distance was obliterated; time was abolished; life was disembodied. He never tired of wandering up and down the Vauxhall Bridge Road where the trams came trafficking like strange ships, so unfamiliar did they seem here beside the dumpy horse omnibuses.

One evening when the fog was not very dense Michael went up to Piccadilly. Here the lamps were strong enough to shine through the murk with a golden softness that made the Circus like a landscape seen in a dying fire. Michael could not bear to withdraw from this glow in which every human countenance was idealized as by amber limes in a theater. At the O.U.D.S. performance of The Merchant of Venice they had been given a sunset like this on the Rialto. It would be jolly to meet somebody from Oxford to-night—Lonsdale, for instance. He looked round half expectant of recognition; but there was only the shifting crowd about him. How were Stella and Alan getting on at Compiègne? Probably they were having clear blue days there, and in the forest would be a smell of woodfires. With such unrelated thoughts Michael strolled round Piccadilly, sometimes in a wider revolution turning up the darker side streets, but always ultimately returning to the Island in the middle. Here he would stand in a dream, watching the omnibuses go east and west and south and north. The crowd grew stronger, for the people were coming out of the theaters. Should he go to the Orange and talk to Daisy? Should he call a hansom and drive home? Bewitched as by the spinning of a polychromatic top, he could not leave the Island.

They were coming out of the Orient now, and he watched the women emerge one by one. Their ankles all looked so white and frail under the opera-cloaks puffed out with swans-down; and they all of them walked to their carriages with the same knock-kneed little steps. Soon he must begin to frequent the Orient again.

Suddenly Michael felt himself seized with the powerless excitement of a nightmare. There in black, strolling nonchalantly across the pavement to a hansom, was Lily! She was with another girl. Then Drake's story had been true. Michael realized that gradually all this time he had been slowly beginning to doubt whether Drake had ever seen her. Lily had become like a princess in a fairy tale. Now she was here! He threw off the stupefaction that was paralyzing him, and started to cross the road. A wave of traffic swept up and he was driven back. When the stream had passed, Lily was gone. In a rage with his silly indecision he set out to walk back to Pimlico. The fog had lifted entirely, and there was frost in the air.

Michael walked very quickly because it seemed the only way to wear out his chagrin. How idiotic it had been to let himself be caught like that. Supposing she did not visit the Orient again for a long time? It would serve him right. Oh, why had he not managed to get in front of those vehicles in time? He and she might have been driving together now; instead of which he was stamping his way along this dull dark pavement. How tall she had seemed, how beautiful in her black frock. At last he knew why all this time women had left him cold. He loved her still. What nonsense it had been for him to think he wanted to marry her in order to rescue her. What priggish insolence! He loved her still; he loved her now: he loved her: he loved her! The railings of Green Park rattled to his stick. He loved her more passionately because the ghost of her whom he had thought of with romantic embellishment all these years was but a caricature of her reality. That image of gossamer which had floated through his dreams was become nothing, now that again he had seen herself with her tall neck and the aureole of her hair and the delicate poise of her as she waited among those knock-kneed women on the pavement. He brought his stick crashing down upon a bin of gravel by the curb that it might clang forth his rage. In what direction had she driven away? Even that he did not know. She might have driven past this very lamp-post a few minutes back.

Here was Hyde Park Corner. In London it was overwhelming to speculate upon a hansom's progress. Here already were main roads branching, and these in their turn would branch, and others after them until the imagination was baffled. Waste of time. Waste of time. He would not picture her in any quarter of London. But never one night should escape without his waiting for her at the Orient. Where was she now? He would put her from his mind until they met. Supposing that round the corner of that wall she were waiting, because the cab horse had slipped. How she would turn toward him in her black dress. "I saw you outside the Orient," he would say. She should know immediately that he was not deceived about her life. So vividly had he conjured the scene that when he rounded the wall on his way down Buckingham Palace Road, he was disappointed to see no cab, no Lily standing perplexed; merely a tabid woman clothed in a cobweb of crape, asleep over her tray of matches and huddled against the wall of the King's garden. He put a sixpence among her match-boxes, and wondered of what were her dark dreams. The stars were blue as steel in the moonless sky above the arc-lamps; and a cold parching wind had sprung up. Michael deviated from the nearest way to Leppard Street, and walked on quickly into the heart of Pimlico. This kind of clear-cut air suited the architecture of the ashen streets. One after another they stretched before him with their dim checkers of doors and windows. Sometimes, where they were intersected by wider thoroughfares, an arc-lamp fizzed above the shape of a solitary policeman, and the corner-houses stood out sharper and more cadaverous. And always in contrast with these necropolitan streets, these masks of human dwellings, were Michael's own thoughts thronged with fancies of himself and Lily.

It was nearly one o'clock when he walked over the arcuated bridge across the lake of railway lines and turned the corner into Leppard Street. From the opposite pavement a woman's figure stepped quickly toward him out of a circle of lamplight. The sudden shadow lanced across the road made him start. Perhaps she noticed him jump, for she stopped at once and stared at him owlishly. He felt sick for a moment, and yet he could not, from an absurd compassion for her, do as he would have liked and run.

"Where are you off to in such a hurry?" he heard her say.

It was too late to avoid her now. He only had two sovereigns in his pocket. It would be ridiculous and cowardly to escape by offering her one of them. He had given his last silver coin to the match-seller. Yet it would have been just as cowardly to have offered her that. He pitied the degradation that prompted her so casual question; the diffidence in her tones marked the fear of answering brutality which must always haunt her. Now that she was close to him, he no longer dreaded her. She was not an ancient drab, a dreadful old woman with black cotton gloves, as at first he had shuddered to suppose her. If those raddled smears and that deathly blanch of coarse powder were cleared from her cheeks, there would be nothing to attract or repel: she would scarcely become even an individual in the multitude of weary London women.

"Where are you off to, dearie, in such a hurry?" she repeated.

"Home. I'm going home," he said.

"Let's walk a bit of the way together."

He could say nothing to her, and if he hurried on, he would hear her voice whining after him like a cat in a yard. He did not wish to let her know where he was living; for every evening he would expect to see her materialize from a quivering circle of lamplight so close to Leppard Street.

"Why don't you come back with me? I live quite near here," she murmured. "Go on. You look as if you wanted someone to make a fuss of you."

Already they were beside the five houses that rose jet-black against the star-incrusted sky.

"Come on, dear. I live in the corner house."

Michael looked at her in astonishment, and she mistaking his scrutiny smiled in pitiable allurement. He felt as if a marionette were blandishing him. The woman evidently thought he was considering the question of money, and she sidled close up to him.

"Go on, dear, you've got some money with you?"

"It's not that," said Michael. "I don't want to come in with you."

Yet he knew that he must enter Number One with her in order to find in what secret room she lived. And to-morrow morning he would leave the house forever, since it would be unimaginable to stay there longer with the consciousness that perhaps they were creatures like this, who slammed the doors in passages far upstairs. He would not sleep comfortably again with the sense that women like this were creeping about the stairs like spiders. He must probe her existence, and he put his foot on the steps of the front door.

"Not that door," she said. "Down here."

She pushed back the gate of the area-steps, and led the way down into the basement. It was incredible that she could live on the same floor as the Cleghornes. Yet obviously she did.

"Don't make a noise," she whispered. "Because the woman who keeps the house sleeps down here."

She opened the back door, and he followed her into the frowsty passage. When the door was dosed behind them, the blackness was absolute.

"Got a vesta with you?" she whispered.

Michael felt her hands pawing him, and he shrank back against the greasy wall.

269

"Here you are. Here you are."

The match flamed, but went out before he could light the nodulous candle she proffered. In the darkness he felt her spongy lips upon his cheek, but disengaging himself from her assiduousness, he managed to light the candle. They went along the corridor past the front room where Cleghorne snored the day away; past the kitchen whose open door exhaled an odorous breath of habitation; and through a stone pantry. Then she led him down three steps and up another, unlocked a rickety door, and welcomed him.

"I'm quite on my own, you see," she said, in a voice of tentative satisfaction.

Michael looked round at the room which was small and smelt very damp. The ceiling sloped to a window closely curtained with the cretonne of black and crimson fruits which Michael recognized as the same stuff he had seen in Barnes' room above. He tried to recall how much of this room he could see from his bedroom window, and he connected it in his mind with a projecting roof of cracked slates which he had often noticed. The action of the rain on the plaster had made it look like a map of the moon in relief. The furniture consisted of a bed, a washstand and a light blue chest. There was also a narrow shelf on which was a lamp with a reflector of corrugated tin, a bald powder-puff, and two boot-buttons. The woman lit the lamp, and as she stooped to look at the jagged flame, Michael saw that her hair was as iridescent as oil on a canal with what remained of henna and peroxide.

"That's more cheerful. Though I must say it's a pity they haven't put the gas in here. Oh, don't sit on that old box. It makes you look such a stranger."

Michael said he had a great fondness for sitting on something that was hard; but he thought how absurd he must appear sitting like this on a pale blue chest next to a washstand.

"Are you looking at my cat?" she asked.

"What cat?"

"He's under the bed, I'll be bound."

She called, and a small black cat came out.

"Isn't he lovely? But, fancy, he's afraid of me. He always gets under the bed like that."

Michael felt he ought to make up to the cat what his cordiality had lacked toward the mistress, and he paid so much attention to it that finally the animal lost all fear and jumped on his knee.

"Well, there!" the woman exclaimed. "Did you ever? I've never seen him do that before. He knows you're a gentleman. Oh, yes, they know. His mother ran away. But she comes to see me sometimes and always looks very well, so she's got a good home. But *he* isn't stinted. Oh, no. He gets his milk every day. What I say is, if you're going to have animals, look after them."

Michael nodded agreement.

"Because to my mind," she went on, "a great many animals are better than human beings."

"Oh, yes, I think they probably are," said Michael.

"Poor Peter!" she crooned. "I wouldn't starve you, would I?"

The cat left Michael and went and sat beside her on the bed.

"Why do you call it Peter?" he asked. The name savored rather of the deliberate novelist.

"After my boy."

"Your boy?" he echoed.

"Oh, he's a fine boy, and a good boy." The mention of her son stiffened the woman into a fleeting dignity.

"I suppose he's about twelve?" Michael asked. Her age had puzzled him.

"Well, thirteen really. Of course, you see, I'm a little older than what I look." As she looked about forty-five, Michael thought that the converse was more probable.

"He's not living with you?"

"Oh, no, certainly not. Why, I wouldn't have him here for anything—not ever. Oh, no, he's at school with the Jesuits. He's to go in the Civil Service. I lived with his father for many years—in fact, from the time I was sixteen. His father was a Frenchman. A silk-merchant he was. He's been dead about six years now."

"I suppose he left money to provide for the boy."

"Oh no! No, he left nothing. Well, you see, silk merchants weren't what they used to be, when he died; and before that his business was always falling off bit by bit. No, the Jesuits took him. Of course I'm a Catholic myself."

As she made her profession of faith, he saw hanging from the knob of the bed a rosary. With whatever repulsion, with whatever curiosity he had entered, Michael now sat here on the pale blue chest in perfect humility of spirit.

"I suppose you don't care for this life?" he asked after a short silence.

"Well, no, I do not. It's not at all what I should call a refined way of living, and often it's really very unpleasant."

Somehow their relation had entirely changed, and Michael found himself discussing her career as if he were talking to an old maid about her health.

"For one thing," she continued, "the police are very rough with one, and if anyone doesn't behave just as they'd like for them to behave, they make it very awkward. They really take it out of anyone. That isn't right, is it? It's really not as it should be, I don't think."

Michael thought of the police in Leicester Square.

"It's damnable!" he growled. "And I suppose you have to put up with a good deal from some of the men?"

270

"Undoubtedly," she said, shaking her head, and becoming every moment more and more like a spinster who kept a stationer's shop in a provincial town. "Undoubtedly. Well, for one thing, I'm at anyone's mercy in here. Of course, if I called out, I might be heard and I might not. Really, if it wasn't for the woman who keeps the house being always so anxious for her rent, I might be murdered any time and stay in here for days without anyone knowing about it. Last Wednesday—or was it Thursday?—time goes by so fast, it seems hardly worth while to count the days, does it? One day last week I did what I've never done before: I accepted six shillings. Well, it was late and what with one thing and another I wanted the money. Will you believe it, I very carefully, as I thought, hid it safe away in my bag, and this man—a very rough sort of a man he was, I'm not surprised poor Peter runs away from them—I heard him walking about the room when I woke up in the middle of the night. And will you believe it, he'd gone to my bag and taken out his six shillings, as well as fourpence-halfpenny of my own which was all I had at the moment. He was really out of the house and gone in a flash, as they say. I wouldn't be surprised if he makes a regular trade of it with women like myself. Well now, you can't say a man like that is any better than my cat. I was very angry about it, but anyone soon forgets. Though I will say it was a warning."

"I suppose you'd be glad to give up the life," said Michael, and as he asked the question, it seemed to him in this room and in the presence of this woman a very futile one.

"Oh, I should be glad to give it up. Yes. You see, as I say, I'm really at anyone's mercy in here. But really what else could I do? You see, in one way, the harm's done."

Michael looked at her tarnished hair; at her baggy cheeks raddled and powdered; at the clumsy black upon her lashes that made so much the more obvious the pleated lids beneath; at her neck already flaccid, and at her dress plumped out like an ill-stuffed pillow to conceal the arid flesh beneath. It certainly seemed as if the harm had been done.

"You see," she went on, "though I have to put up with a great deal, it's only to be expected, after all. Now I was very severely brought up by my father, and my mother being—well, it's no use to mince matters as they say—my mother really was a saint. Then of course after this occurred with the Frenchman I told you about—that really was a downward step, though at the time I was happy and though he was always very good to me from the beginning to the end. Still, I'm used to refinement, and I have a great deal to put up with here in this house. Not that I dislike the woman who keeps it. But having paid my rent regular—eight-and-six, that is...."

"Quite enough, too," said Michael, looking up at the ceiling that was so like the scarred surface of the moon.

"You're right. It is enough. It is quite enough. But still I'm my own mistress. No one interferes with me. At the same time I don't interfere with anybody else. I have the right to use the kitchen for my cooking, but really Mrs. Cleghorne—that is the woman who keeps the house—really she is not a clean cook, and very often my stomach is so turned that I go all day with only a cup of tea."

Michael was grateful to the impulse which had led him to cook his own breakfast on a chafing dish.

"I interrupted you," he said. "You were going to tell me something about Mrs. Cleghorne."

"Well, you must know, I had a friend who was very good to me, and this seemed to annoy her. Perhaps she disliked the independence it gave me. Well, she really caused a row between us by telling me she'd seen him going round drinking with another woman. Now that isn't a nice thing to do, is it? One doesn't want to go round drinking in public-houses. It looks so bad. I spoke to him about it a bit sharp, and we've fallen out over it. In fact, I haven't seen him for some months. Still I shouldn't complain, but just lately what with one thing and another I had some extras to get for my boy which was highly necessary you'll understand—well, as I was saying—what with one thing and another my rent has been a little bit behind. Still, after you've paid regular for close on two years, you expect a little consideration."

"Have you lived in this burrow for two years?" Michael asked in amazement.

"In the week before Christmas it'll be two years. Yes. Not that Mrs. Cleghorne herself has been so nasty, but she lets her mother come round here and abuse me. Her mother's an old woman, you'll understand, and her language—well, really it has sometimes made me feel sick." She put her hand up to her face with a gesture of disgust. "She stands in that doorway and bullies me until I'm ashamed to sit on this bed and stand it. I really am. You'd hardly believe there was such things to say to anyone. I think I have a right to feel aggravated, and I've made up my mind she isn't going to do it again. I'm not going to *have* it." She was nodding at Michael with such energetic affirmation that the springs of the bed creaked.

"The mother doesn't live here?" he asked.

"Oh, no; she simply comes here for the purpose of bullying me. But I'm not going to let it occur again. I don't consider I've been well treated. If I'd spent the money on gin, I shouldn't so much object to what the old woman calls me, for I don't say my life isn't a bit of a struggle. But there's so many things to use up the money, when I've got what's wanted for my boy, and paid the policeman on this beat his half-crown which he expects, and tried to keep myself looking a little bit smart—really I have to buy something occasionally, or where should I be?—and I never waste money on clothes for clothes' sake, as they say—well, after that it's none so easy to find eight-and-six for the week's rent and buy myself a bit of food and the cat's milk."

Michael had nothing to say in commentary. It seemed to him that even by living above this woman he shared in the responsibility for her wretchedness.

"I hope your boy will turn out well," he ventured at last.

"Oh, he's a good boy, he really is. And I have had hopes that perhaps the Fathers will make him a Brother. I should really prefer that to his being in the Civil Service."

"Or even a priest," Michael suggested.

"Well, you see, he wasn't born in wedlock. Would that make a difference?"

"I don't think so," said Michael gently. "Oh, no, I hope that wouldn't make a difference."

He was finding the imagination of this woman's life too poignant, and he rose from the light blue chest to bid her good-bye. He begged inwardly that she would not attempt to remind him of the relation in which she had expected to stand to him. He feared to wound her, but he would have to repulse her or go mad if she came near him. He plunged down into his pocket for the two sovereigns. Half of this money

271

he had thought an exaggerated and cowardly bribe to buy off her importunity when she had stood in the circle of lamplight, owlishly staring. Now he wished he had five times as much. His pocket was empty! He felt quickly and hopelessly in his other pockets. He could not find the gold. She must have robbed him. He looked at her reproachfully. Was that the thief's and liar's film glazing her eyes as they stared straight into his own? Was it impossible to believe that he had pulled the sovereigns out of his pocket, when nervously he had first seen her. But she had pawed him with her hands in the black passage, and if the money had fallen on the road, he must have heard it. He ought to tax her with the unjust theft; he ought to tell her that what she had taken he had meant to give her. And yet supposing she had not taken the money? She had said the cat recognized him as a gentleman. Supposing she had not taken the sovereigns, he would add by his accusation another stone to the weight she bore. And if she had taken them, why not? The cat was not at hand to warn her that he was to be trusted. She had not wanted the money for herself. She had been preyed upon, and had learned to prey upon others in self-defense.

"I find I haven't any money with me," said Michael, looking at her.

"That doesn't matter. I've really quite enjoyed our little talk."

"But I'll send you some more," he promised.

"No, it doesn't matter. I haven't done anything to have you send your money for. I expect when you saw me in the light, you didn't think I was really quite your style. Of course, I've really come down. It's no use denying it. I'm *not* what I was."

If she had robbed him, she wanted nothing more from him. If she had robbed him, it was because in the humility of her degradation she had feared to see him shrink from her in disgust.

"I shall send you some money for your boy," he said, in the darkness by the door.

"No, it doesn't matter."

"What's your name?"

"Well, I'm known here as Mrs. Smith." Doubtfully she whispered as the cold air came in through the open door: "I don't expect you'd care about giving me a kiss."

Michael had never known anything in his life so difficult to do, but he kissed her cold and flaccid cheek and hurried up the area steps.

When he stood again upon the pavement in the menace of the five black houses of Leppard Street, Michael felt that he never again could endure to return to them at night, nor ever again in the day perceive their fifty windows inscrutable as water. Yet he must walk for a while in the stinging northerly air before he went back to his rooms; he must try to rid himself of the oppression which now lay so heavily upon him; he must be braced even by this lugubrious night of Pimlico before he could encounter again the permeating fug of Leppard Street. He walked as far as the corner, and saw in silhouette upon the bridge a solitary policeman thudding his chest for warmth. In this abominable desert of lamps he should have seemed a symbol of comfort, but Michael with the knowledge of the power he wielded over the unfortunates beheld him now as the brutish servant of a dominating class. He was, after all, very much like a dressed-up gorilla, as he stood there thudding his chest in the haggard lamplight.

Michael turned and went back to his rooms.

He stared at the picture of St. Ursula on the white wall, and suddenly in a fit of rage he plucked it from the hook and ground it face downward upon his writing-table. It seemed to him almost monstrous that anything so serene should be allowed any longer to exist. Immediately afterward he thought that his action had been melodramatic, and shamefacedly he put away the broken picture in a drawer.

Lily was in London: and Mrs. Smith was beneath him in this house. In twenty years Lily might be sunk in such a pit, unless he were quick to save her now. All through the night he kept waking up with the fancy that he could hear the rosary rattling in that den beneath; and every time he knew it was only the sound of the broken hasp on his window rattling in the wind.

CHAPTER VI

TINDERBOX LANE

Next morning, when he woke, Michael made up his mind to leave Leppard Street finally in the course of this day. He could not bear the thought that he would only have to lean out of his window to see the actual roof which covered that unforgettable den beneath him. He wondered what would be the best thing to do with the furniture. It might be worth while to install Barnes in these rooms and pay his rent for some months instead of the salary which, now that Lily had been seen, was no longer a justifiable expenditure. He certainly would prefer that Barnes should never meet Lily now, and he regretted he had revealed her name. Still he had a sort of affection for Barnes which precluded the notion of deserting him altogether. These rooms with their simple and unmuffled furniture, the green shelves and narrow white bed, would be good for his character. He would also leave a few chosen books behind, and he would write and ask Nigel Stewart to visit here from time to time. Michael dressed himself and went upstairs to interview Barnes where he lay beneath a heap of bedclothes.

"Oh, I daresay I could make the rooms look all right," said Barnes. "But what about coal?"

"I shall pay for coal and light as well as the rent."

"I thought you'd find it a bit dismal here," said Barnes knowingly. "I wonder you've stuck it out as long as you have."

"After February," Michael said, "I may want to come to some other arrangement; but you can count on being here till then. Of course, you understand that when the three months are up, I shan't be able to allow you five pounds a week any longer."

"No, I never supposed you would," said Barnes, in a tone of resignation.

Michael hesitated whether to speak to him about Mrs. Smith or not: however, probably he was aware of her existence already, and it could do no harm to mention it.

"Did you know that there was a woman living down in the basement here?" he asked.

"I didn't know there was one here; but it's not a very rare occurrence in this part of London, nor any other part of London, if it comes to that."

"If you hear any row going on down there," said Michael, "you had better interfere at once."

"Who with?" Barnes inquired indignantly.

"With the row," said Michael. "If the woman is being badly treated on account of money she owes, you must let me know immediately."

"Well, I'm not in the old tear's secret, am I?" asked Barnes, in an injured tone. "You can't expect me to go routing about after every old fly-by-night stuck in a basement."

"I'm particularly anxious to know that she is all right," Michael insisted.

"Oh well, of course, if she's a friend of yours, Fane, that's another matter. If it's any little thing to oblige you, why certainly I'll do it."

Michael said good-bye and left him in bed. Then he called in to see the Solutionist, who was also in bed.

"I've got a commission for you," said Michael.

The Solutionist's watery eyes brightened faintly.

"You're fond of animals, aren't you?" Michael went on. "I see you feeding your Belgian hares. Well, I'm interested in a cat who appreciated my point of view. I want you to see that this cat has a quart of milk left for her outside Mrs. Smith's door every morning. Mrs. Smith lives in the basement. You must explain to her that you are fond of animals; but you mustn't mention me. Here's a check for five pounds. Spend half this on the cat and the other half on your rabbits."

The Solutionist held the check between his tremulous fingers.

"I couldn't cash this nowadays," he said helplessly. "And get a quart of milk for a cat? Why, the thing would burst."

"All right. I'll send you postal orders," said Michael. "Now I'm going away for a bit. Never mind if a quart is too much. I want that amount left every day. You'll do what I ask? And you'll promise not to say a word about me?"

The Solutionist promised, and Michael left him looking more completely puzzled than he had ever seen him.

Michael could not bring himself to the point either of going down into the basement or of calling to Mrs. Cleghorne from the entrance to her cave; and as the bell-pull in his room had never been mended, he did not know how to reach her. The existence of Mrs. Smith had dreadfully complicated the mechanism of Number One. He ought to have made Barnes get out of bed and fetch her. By good luck Michael saw from his window the landlady standing at the top of the area steps. He ran out and asked her to come and speak to him.

"I see," she said. "Mr. Barnes is to have your rooms, and you're paying in advance up to February. Oh, and his coal and his gas as well? I see. Well, that you can settle month by month. Through me? Oh, yes."

Mrs. Cleghorne was in a very good temper this morning. Michael could not help wondering if Mrs. Smith had paid some arrears of her rent.

"Do you think Mr. Cleghorne would go and fetch me a hansom?" Michael asked.

"He's still in his bed, but I'll go myself."

This cheerfulness was really extraordinary; and Michael was flattered. Already he was beginning to feel some of the deference mixed with hate which throughout the underworld was felt toward landladies. Her condescension struck him with the sense of a peculiar favor, as if it were being bestowed from a superior height.

Michael packed up his kitbags and turned for a last look at the white rooms in Leppard Street. Suddenly it struck him that he would take with him one or two of the pictures and present them to Maurice's studio in Grosvenor Road. Mona Lisa should go there, and the Prince of Orange whom himself was supposed to resemble slightly, and Don Baltazar on his big horse. They should be the contribution which he had been intending for some time to pay to that household. The cab was at the door, and presently Michael drove away from Leppard Street.

As soon as he was in the hansom he felt he could begin to think of Lily again, and though he knew that probably he was going to suffer a good deal when they met, he nevertheless thought of her now with elation. It had not seemed to be so sparkling a morning in Leppard Street; but driving toward Maurice's studio along the banks of the river, Michael thought it was the most crystalline morning he had ever known.

"I've brought you these pictures," he explained to Maurice, and let the gift account for his own long disappearance from communion with his friends. "They're pretty hackneyed, but I think it's rather good for you to have a few hackneyed things amid the riot of originality here. What are you doing, Mossy?"

"Well, I'm rather hoping to get a job as dramatic critic on The Point of View."

"You haven't met your lady-love yet?"

"No, rather not, worse luck. Still, there's plenty of time. What about you?" Maurice asked the question indifferently. He regarded his friend as a stone where women were concerned.

"I've seen her," said Michael. He simply had to give himself the pleasure of announcing so much.

"By Jove, have you really? You've actually found your fate?" Maurice was evidently very much excited by Michael's lapse into humanity; he had been snubbed so often when he had rhapsodized over girls. "What's she like?"

"I haven't spoken to her yet. I've only seen her in the distance."

"And you've really fallen in love? I say, do stay and have lunch with me here. Castleton isn't coming back from the Temple until after tea."

Michael would have liked to sit at the window and talk of Lily, while he stared out over the sea of roofs under one of which at this very moment herself might be looking in his direction. However, he thought if he once began to talk about Lily to Maurice, he would tell him too much, and he might regret that afterward. Yet he could not resist saying that she was tall and fair and slim. Such epithets might be applied to many girls, and it was only for himself that in this case they had all the thrilling significance they did.

"I like fair girls best," Maurice agreed. "But most fair girls are dolls. If I met one who wasn't, I should be hopelessly in love with her."

"Perhaps you will," Michael said. Since he had seen Lily he felt very generous, and even more than generosity he felt that he actually had the power to offer to Maurice dozens of fair girls from whom he could choose his own ideal. Really he must not stay a moment longer in the studio, or he would be blurting out the whole tale of Lily; and were she to be his, he must hold secrets about her that could never be unfolded.

"I really must bolt off," he declared. "I've got a cab waiting."

Michael drove along to Cheyne Walk, and when he reached home, it caused the parlormaid not a flicker to receive him and to take his luggage and inquire what should be obtained for his lunch.

"Life's really too easy in this house," he thought. "It's so impossible to surprise the servants here that one would give up trying ultimately. I suppose that will be the beginning of settling down. At this rate, I shall settle down much too soon. Yes, life is too easy here."

Michael went to the Orient that night certain that he would meet Lily at once, so much since he left Leppard Street had the imagination of her raced backward and forward in his brain. Everything that would have made their meeting painful in such surroundings was forgotten in the joyful prospect at hand. The amount they would have to talk about was really tremendous. Love had destroyed time so completely that Lily was to be exactly the same as when first he had met her in Kensington Gardens. However, her appearance on the pavement outside the theater had made such a vivid new impression that Michael did pay as much attention to lapsing time as to visualize her now in that black dress. Otherwise he was himself again of six years ago, with only the delightful difference that he was now independent and could carry her forthwith into marriage. The knowledge that from a material point of view he could do this filled him with a magnificent consciousness of life's plenitude. So far, all his experiments in living had been bounded by ignorance or credulity on his own side, and on the side of other people by their unsuitableness for experiments. Certainly he had made discoveries, but they might better be called disillusionments. Now here was Lily who would give him herself to discover, who would open for him, not a looking-glass world in which human nature reflected itself in endless reduplications of perversity, but a world such as lovers only know, wherein the greatest deeps are themselves. Michael scarcely bothered to worry himself with the thought that Lily had embarked upon her own discoveries apart from him; she had been bewitched again by his romantic spells into the innocent girl of seventeen. All his hopes, all his quixotry, all his capacity for idealization, all his prejudice and impulsiveness converged upon her. Whatever had lately happened to spoil his theory of behavior was discounted; and even the very theory fell to pieces in this intoxication of happiness.

With so much therefore to make him buoyant, it was depressing to visit the Orient that evening without a glimpse of Lily. The disappointment threw Michael very unpleasantly back into those evenings when he had come here regularly and had always been haunted by the dread that, when he did see her, his resolve would collapse in the presence of a new Lily wrought upon by man and not made more lovable thereby. The vision of her last night (it was only last night) had swept him aloft; the queer adventure with the woman in the basement had exalted him still higher upon his determination; his flight from Leppard Street and his return to Cheyne Walk had helped to strengthen his hopefulness. Now he had returned to this circumambient crowd, looking round as each newcomer came up the steps, and all the while horribly aware that this evening Lily was not coming to the Orient. He had never been upset like this since his resolve was taken. The glimpse of her last night had made him very impatient, and he reviled himself again for having been such a fool as to let her escape. He fell in a rage with his immobility here in London. He demanded why it was not possible to swirl in widening circles round the city until he found her. He was no longer content to remain in this aquarium, stuck like a mollusc to the side of the tank. He wanted to see her again. He was fretful for her slow contemptuous walk and her debonair smile. He wanted to see her again. Already this quest was becoming the true torment of love. Every single other person in sight was a dreary automaton in whom he took no trace of interest. Every movement, every laugh, every shadow made him repine at its uselessness to him. All those years at Oxford of dreams and hesitations had let him store up within himself a very fury of love. He had been living falsely all this time: there had never been one dull hour which could not have been enchanted by her to the most glorious hour imaginable. He had realized that when he saw her last night; he had realized all the waste, all the deadness, all the idiotic philosophy and impotence of these years without her. How the fancy of her vexed him now; how easily could he in his frustration knock down the individuals of this senseless restless crowd, one after another, like the dummies of humanity they were.

The last tableau of the ballet had dissolved behind the falling curtain. Lily was not here to-night, and he hurried out into Piccadilly. She must be somewhere close at hand. It was impossible for her to come casually like that to the Orient and afterward to disappear for weeks. Or was she a man's mistress, the mistress of a man of forty? He could picture him. He would be a stockbroker, the sort of man whom one saw in first-class railway carriages traveling up to town in the morning and reading The Financial Times. He would wear a hideous orchid in his buttonhole and take her to Brighton for week-ends. He knew just the shade of bluish pink that his cheeks were; and the way his neck looked against his collar; the shape of his mustache, the smell of his cigar, and his handicap at golf.

It was impossible that Lily could be the mistress of a man like that. Last night she had come out of the Orient with a girl. Obviously they must at this moment be somewhere near Piccadilly. Michael rushed along as wildly as a cat running after its tail. He entered restaurant after restaurant, café after café, standing in the doorways and staring at the tables one after another. The swinging doors would often hit him, as people came in; the drinkers or the diners would often laugh at his frown and his pale, eager gaze; often the manager would hurry up and ask what he could do for him, evidently suspecting the irruption of a lunatic.

Michael's behavior in the street was even more noticeable. He often ricocheted from the inside to the outside of the pavement to get a nearer view of a passing hansom whose occupant had faintly resembled Lily. He mounted omnibuses going in all sorts of strange directions, because he fancied for an instant that he had caught a glimpse of Lily among the passengers. It was closing-time before he thought he had been searching for five minutes; and when the lights were dimmed, he walked up and down Regent Street, up and down Piccadilly, up and down Coventry Street, hurrying time after time to pursue a walk that might have been hers.

By one o'clock Piccadilly was nearly empty, and it was an insult to suppose that Lily would be found among these furtive women with their waylaying eyes in the gloom. Michael went back tired out to Cheyne Walk. On the following night he visited the Orient again and afterward searched every likely and unlikely place in the neighborhood of the heart of pleasure. He went also to the Empire and to the Alhambra; sometimes hurrying from one to the other twice in the evening, when panics that he was missing Lily overtook him. He met

Lonsdale one night at the Empire, and Lonsdale took him to several night-clubs which gave a great zest to Michael's search; for he became a member of them himself, and so possessed every night another hour or more before he had to give up hope of finding her.

Mrs. Fane wrote to him from Cannes to say she thought that, as she was greatly enjoying herself on the Riviera, she would not come home for Christmas. Michael was relieved by her letter, because he had felt qualms about deserting her, and he would have found it difficult, impossible really, to go away so far from London and Lily.

Guy wrote to him several times, urging him to come and stay at Plashers Mead. Finally he went there for a week-end; and Guy spent the whole time rushing in and out of the house on the chance of meeting Pauline Grey, the girl whom Michael had seen with him in the canoe last summer. Guy explained the complications of his engagement to Pauline; how it seemed he would soon have to choose between love and art; how restrictions were continually being put upon their meeting each other; and how violently difficult life was becoming here at Plashers Mead, where Michael had prophesied such abundant ease. Michael was very sympathetic, and when he met Pauline on a soft December morning, he did think she was beautiful and very much like the wild rose that Guy had taken as the symbol of her. She seemed such a fairy child that he could not imagine problems of conduct in which she could be involved. Nevertheless, it was impossible not to feel that over Plashers Mead brooded a sense of tragedy: and yet it seemed ridiculous to compare Guy's difficulties with his own.

For Christmas Michael went down to Hardingham, where Stella and Alan had by this time settled down in their fat country. He was delighted to see how much the squire Alan was already become; and there was certainly something very attractive in these two young people moving about that grave Georgian house. The house itself was of red brick and stood at the end of an avenue of oaks in a park of about two hundred acres. That it could ever have not been there; that ever those lawns had been defaced by builder's rubbish was now inconceivable. So too within, Michael could not realize that anybody else but Stella and Alan had ever stood in this drawing-room, looking out of the tall windows whose sills scarcely rose above the level of the grass outside; that anyone else but Stella and Alan had ever laughed in this solemn library with its pilasters and calf-bound volumes and terrestrial globe; that anyone else but Stella and Alan had ever sat at dinner under the eyes of those bag-wigged squires, that long-nosed Light Dragoon, or that girl in her chip hat, holding a bunch of cherries.

"No doubt you've got a keen scent for tradition," said Michael to Stella. "But really you have been able to get into the manner surprisingly fast. These cocker-spaniels, for instance, who follow you both round, and the deerhound on the steps of the terrace—Stella, I'm afraid the concert platform has taught you the value of effect; and where do hounds meet to-morrow?"

"We're simply loving it here," Stella said. "But I think the piano is feeling a little bit out of his element. He's stiff with being on his best behavior."

"I'm hoping to get rather a good pitch in Six Ash field," said Alan. "I'll show it to you to-morrow morning."

The butler came in with news of callers:

"The Countess of Stilton and Lady Anne Varley."

"Oh, damn!" Stella exclaimed, when the butler had retired. "I really don't think people ought to call just before Christmas. However, you've both got to come in and be polite."

Michael managed to squeeze himself into a corner of the drawing-room, whence he could watch Lady Stilton and her daughter talking to Mr. and Mrs. Prescott-Merivale.

"We ought not to have bothered you in this busy week before Christmas, but my husband has been so ill in Marienbad, ever since the summer really, that we only got home a fortnight ago. So very trying. And I've been longing to meet you. Poor Dick Prescott was a great friends of ours."

Michael had a sudden intuition that Prescott had bequeathed Stella's interests to Lady Stilton, who probably knew all about her. He wondered if Stella had guessed this.

"And Anne heard you play at King's Hall. Didn't you, Anne dear?"

Lady Anne nodded and blushed.

"That child is going to worship Stella," Michael thought.

"We're hoping you will all be able to come and dine with us for Twelfth Night. My husband is so fond of keeping up old English festivals. Mr. Fane, you'll still be at Hardingham, I hope, so that we may have the pleasure of seeing you as well?"

Michael said he was afraid he would have to be back in town.

"What absolute rot!" Stella cried. "Of course you'll be here."

But Michael insisted that he would be gone.

"They tell us you've been buying Herefords, Mr. Merivale. My husband was so much interested and is so much looking forward to seeing your stock; but at present he must not drive far. I've also heard of you from my youngest boy who went up to Christ Church last October year. He is very much excited to think that Hardingham is going to have such a famous—what is it called, Anne?—some kind of a bowler."

"A googlie bowler, I expect you mean, mother," said Lady Anne.

"Wasn't he in the Eton eleven?" asked Alan.

"Well, no. Something happened to oust him at the last moment," said Lady Stilton. "Possibly a superior player."

"Oh, no, mother!" Lady Anne indignantly declared. "He would have played for certain against Harrow, if he hadn't sprained his ankle at the nets the week before."

"I do hope you'll let him come and see you this vacation," Lady Stilton said.

"Oh, rather. I shall be awfully keen to talk about the cricket round here," Alan replied. "I'm just planning out a new pitch now."

"How delightful all this is," thought Michael, with visions of summer evenings.

Soon Lady Stilton and her daughter went away, having plainly been a great success with Mr. and Mrs. Prescott-Merivale.

"Of course, *you've* got to marry Anne," said Stella to Michael, as soon as they were comfortably round the great fire in the library.

"Alan," Michael appealed. "Is it impossible for you to nip now forever this bud of matchmaking?"

"I think it's rather a good idea," said Alan. "I knew young Varley by sight. He's a very sound bat."

"I shan't come here again," Michael threatened, "until you've dissolved this alliance of mutual admiration. Instead of agreeing with Stella to marry me to every girl you meet, why don't you devote yourself to the task of making Huntingdon a first-class county in cricket? Stella might captain the team."

Time passed very pleasantly with long walks and rides and drives, with long evenings of cut-throat bridge and Schumann; but on New Year's morning Michael said he must go back to London. Nor would he let himself be deterred by Stella's gibes.

"I admit you're as happy as you can be," he said. "Now surely you, after so much generosity on my side, will admit that I may know almost as well as yourselves how to make myself happy, though not yet married."

"Michael, you're having an affair with some girl," Stella said accusingly.

He shook his head.

"Swear?"

"By everything I believe in, I vow I'm not having an affair with any girl. I wish I were."

His luggage was in the hall, and the dogcart was waiting. At King's Cross he found a taxi, which was so difficult to do in those days that it made him hail the achievement as a good omen for the New Year.

Near South Kensington Station he caught sight of a poster advertising a carnival in the neighborhood: he thought it looked rather attractive with the bright colors glowing into the gray January day. Later on in the afternoon, when he went to his tobacconist's in the King's Road, he saw the poster again and read that to-night at Redcliffe Hall, Fulham Road, would take place a Grand Carnival and Masked Ball for the benefit of some orphanage connected with licensed victualing. Tickets were on sale in various public-houses of the neighborhood, at seven and sixpence for gentlemen and five shillings for ladies.

"Ought to be very good," commented the tobacconist. "Well, we want a bit of brightening up nowadays down this way, and that's a fact. Why, I can remember Cremorne Gardens. Tut-tut! Bless my soul. Yes, and the old World's End. That's going back into the seventies, that is. And it seems only yesterday."

"I rather wish I'd got a ticket," said Michael.

"Why not let me get you one, sir, and send it round to Cheyne Walk? I suppose you'd like one for a lady as well?"

"No, I'll have two men's tickets."

Michael had a vague notion of getting Maurice or Lonsdale to accompany him, and he went off immediately to 422 Grosvenor Road; but the studio was deserted. Nor was he successful in finding Lonsdale. Nobody seemed to have finished his holidays yet. It would be rather boring to go alone, he thought; but when he found the tickets waiting for him, they seemed to promise a jolly evening, even if he did no more than watch other people enjoying themselves. No doubt there would be plenty of spectators without masks, like himself, and in ordinary evening dress. So about half-past nine Michael set off alone to the carnival.

Redcliffe Hall, viewed from the outside in the January fog which was deepening over the city, seemed the last place in the world likely to contain a carnival. It was one of those dismal gothic edifices which, having passed through ecclesiastical and municipal hands with equal loss to both, awaits a suitable moment for destruction before it rises again in a phoenix of new flats. However, the awning hung with Japanese lanterns that ran from the edge of the curb up to the entrance made it now not positively forbidding.

Michael went up to the gallery and watched the crowd of dancers. Many of the fancy dresses had a very homely look, but there were also professional equipments from costumiers and a very few really beautiful inventions. The medley of colors, the motion of the dance, the sound of the music, the streamers of bunting and the ribbons fluttering round the Maypole in the middle of the room, all combined to give Michael an illusion of a very jocund assemblage. There were plenty of men dancing without masks, which was rather a pity, as their dull, ordinary faces halted abruptly the play of fancy. On second thoughts he was glad such revelers were allowed upon the floor, since as the scene gradually began to affect him he felt it might be amusing for himself to dance once or twice before the evening ended. With this notion in view, he began to follow more particularly the progress of different girls, balancing their charms one against another, and always deriving a good deal of pleasure from the reflection that, while at this moment they did not know of his existence, in an hour's time he might have entered their lives. This thought did give a romantic zest to an entertainment which would otherwise have been quite cut off from his appreciation.

Suddenly Michael's heart began to quicken: the blood came in rushes and swift recessions that made him feel cold and sick. Two girls walking away from him along the side of the hall—those two pierrettes in black—that one with the pale blue pompons was Lily! Why didn't she turn round? It must be Lily. The figure, the walk, the hair were hers. The pierrettes turned, but as they were masked Michael could still not be sure if one were Lily. They were dancing together now. It must be Lily. He leaned over the rail of the gallery to watch them sweep round below him, so that he might listen if by chance above the noise Lily's languorous voice could reach him. Michael became almost positive that it was she. There could not be another girl to seem so like her. He hurried down from the gallery and stood in the entrance to the ball-room. Where were they now? They were coming toward him: the other pierrette with the rose pompons said something as they passed. It could only be Lily who bowed her head like that in lazy assent. It was Lily! Should he call out to her, when next they passed him? If it were not Lily, what a fool he would look. If it were not Lily, it would not matter what he looked, for the disappointment would outweigh everything else. They were going up the room again. They were turning the corner again. They were sweeping toward him again. They were passing him again. He called "Lily! Lily!" in a voice sharp with eagerness. Neither girl gave a sign of attention. It was not she, after all. Yet his voice might have been drowned in the noise of the dance. He would call again; but again they passed him by unheeding. The dance was over. They had stopped at the other end of the room. He pressed forward against the egress of the dancers. He pressed forward roughly, and once or twice he heard grumbling murmurs because he had deranged a difficult piece of costumery. He was conscious of angry masks regarding him; and then he was free of the crowd, and before him, talking together under a canopy of holly were the two pierrettes. The musicians sat among the palms looking at him as they rested upon their instruments. Michael felt that his voice was going to refuse to utter her name:

"Lily! Lily!"

The pierrette with the pale blue pompons turned at the sound of his voice. Why did she not step forward to greet him, if indeed she were Lily? She was, she was Lily: the other pierrette had turned to see what she was going to do.

"I say, how on earth did you recognize me?" Lily murmured, raising her mask and looking at Michael with her smile that was so debonair and tender, so scornful and so passionate.

"I saw you in November coming out of the Orient. I tried to get across the road to speak to you, but you'd gone before I could manage it. Where have you been all these years? Once I went to Trelawny Road, but the house was empty." He could not tell her that Drake had been the first to bring him news of her.

"It's years since I was there," said Lily. "Years and years." She turned to call her friend, and the pierrette with the rose pompons came closer to be introduced.

"Miss Sylvia Scarlett: Mr. Michael Fane. Aren't I good to remember your name quite correctly?" Michael thought that her mouth for a moment was utterly scornful. "What made you come here? Have you got a friend with you?"

Michael explained that he was alone, and that his visit here was an accident.

"Why did *you* come?" he asked.

"Oh, something to do," said Lily. "We live near here."

"So do I," said Michael hastily.

"Do you?" Her eyebrows went up in what he imagined was an expression of rather cruel interrogation. "This is a silly sort of a show. Still, even Covent Garden is dull now."

Michael thought what a fool he had been not to include Covent Garden in his search. How well he might have known she would go there.

"Where's Doris?" he asked.

Lily shrugged her shoulders.

"I never see anything of her nowadays. She married an actor. I don't often get letters from home, do I, Sylvia?"

The pierrette with rose pompons, who ever since her introduction had still been standing outside the conversation, now raised her mask. Michael liked her face. She had merry eyes, and a wide nose rather Slavonic. Next to Lily she seemed almost dumpy.

"Letters, my dear," she exclaimed, in a very deep voice, "Who wants letters?"

The music of a waltz was beginning, and Michael asked Lily if she would dance with him. She looked at Sylvia.

"I don't think...."

"Oh, what rot, Lily! Of course you can dance."

Michael gave her a grateful smile.

In a moment Lily had lowered her mask, and they were waltzing together.

"My gad, how gloriously you waltz!" he whispered. "Did we ever dance together five years ago?"

She shrugged her shoulders, and he felt the faint movement tremble through the imponderable form he held.

"Lily, I've been looking for you since June," he sighed.

"You're breaking step," she said. Though her mask was down, Michael was sure that she was frowning at him.

"Lily, why are you so cold with me? Have you forgotten?"

"What?"

"Why, everything!" Michael gasped.

"You're absolutely out of time now," she said sternly.

They waltzed for a while in silence, and Michael felt like a midge spinning upon a dazzle.

"Do you remember when we met in Kensington Gardens?" he ventured. "I remember you had black pompons on your shoes then, and now you have pale blue pompons on your dress."

She was not answering him.

"It's funny you should still be living near me," he went on. "I suppose you're angry with me because I suddenly never saw you again. That was partly your mother's fault."

She looked at him in faint perplexity, swaying to the melody of the waltz. Michael thought he had blundered in betraying himself as so obviously lovestruck now. He must be seeming to her like that absurd and sentimental boy of five years ago. Perhaps she was despising him, for she could compare him with other men. Ejaculations of wonder at her beauty would no longer serve, with all the experience she might bring to mock them. She was smiling at him now, and the mask she wore made the smile seem a sneer. He grew so angry with her suddenly that almost he stopped in the swing of the dance to shake her.

"But it was much more your fault," he said savagely. "Do you remember Drake?"

She shook her head; then she corrected herself.

"Oh, yes. Arthur Drake who lived next door to us."

"Well, I saw you in the garden from his window. You were being kissed by some terrible bounder. That was jolly for me. Why did you do that? Couldn't you say 'no'? Were you too lazy?"

Michael thought she moved closer to him as they danced.

"Answer me, will you; answer me, I say. Were you too lazy to resist, or did you enjoy being cheapened by that insufferable brute you were flirting with?"

Michael in his rage of remembrance twisted her hand. But she made no gesture, nor uttered any sound of pain. Instead she sank closer to his arms, and as the dance rolled on, he told himself triumphantly that, while she was with him, she was his again.

What did the past matter?

"Ah, Lily, you love me still! I'll ask no more questions. Am I out of step?"

"No, not now," she whispered, and he saw that her face was pale with the swoon of their dancing.

"Take off that silly mask," he commanded. "Take it off and give it to me. I can hold you with one arm."

She obeyed him, and with a tremendous exultation he swung her round, as if indeed he were carrying her to the edge of the world. The mask no longer veiled her face; her eyelids drooped, clouding her eyes; her lips were parted: she was now dead white. Michael crooked her left arm until he could touch her shoulder.

"Look at me. Look at me. The dance will soon be over."

She opened her eyes, and into their depths of dusky blue he danced and danced until, waking with the end of the music, he found himself and Lily close to Sylvia Scarlett, who was laughing at them where she stood in the corner of the room under a canopy of holly.

Lily was for the rest of the evening herself as Michael had always known her. She had always been superficially indifferent to anything that was happening round her, and she behaved at this carnival as if it were a street full of dull people among whom by chance she was walking. Nor with her companions was she much more alert, though when she danced with Michael her indifference became a passionate languor. Soon after midnight both the girls declared they were tired of the Redcliffe Hall, and they asked Michael to escort them home. He was going to fetch a cab, but they stopped him, saying that Tinderbox Lane, where they lived, was only a little way along on the other side of the Fulham Road. The fog was very dense when they came out, and Michael took the girls' arms with a delicious sense of intimacy, with a feeling, too, of extraordinary freedom from the world, as if they were all three embarked upon an adventure in this eclipse of fog. He had packed their shoes deep down in the pockets of his overcoat, and with the possession of their shoes he had a sensation of possessing the wearers of them. The fog was denser and denser: they paused upon the edge of the curb, listening for oncoming traffic. A distant omnibus was lumbering far down the Fulham Road. Michael caught their arms close, and the three of them seemed to sail across to the opposite pavement. He had nothing to say because he was so happy, and Lily had nothing to say because she talked now no more than she used to talk. So it was Sylvia who had to carry on the conversation, and since most of this consisted of questions to Lily and Michael about their former friendship, which neither Lily nor Michael answered, even Sylvia was discouraged at last; and they walked on silently through the fog, Michael clasping the girls close to him and watching all the time Lily's hand holding up her big black cloak.

"Here we are, you two dreamers," said Sylvia, pulling them to a stop by a narrow turning which led straight from the pavement unexpectedly, without any dip down into a road.

"Through here? How fascinating!" said Michael.

They passed between two posts, and in another three minutes stopped in front of a door set in a wall.

"I've got the key," said Sylvia, and she unlocked the door.

"But this is extraordinary," Michael exclaimed. "Aren't we walking through a garden?"

"Yes, it's quite a long garden," Sylvia informed him. There was a smell of damp earth here that sweetened the harshness of the fog, and Michael thought that he had never imagined anything so romantic as following Lily in single file along the narrow gravel path of a mysterious garden like this. There must have been thirty yards of path, before they walked up the steps of what seemed to be a sort of balcony.

"She's downstairs," said Sylvia, tapping upon a glass door with the key. A woman's figure appeared with an orange-shaded lamp in the passage.

"Open quickly, Mrs. Gainsborough. We're frozen," Sylvia called. As the woman opened the door, Sylvia went on in her deep voice:

"We've brought an old friend of Lily's back from the dance. It wasn't really worth going to. Oh, I oughtn't to have said that, ought I?" she laughed, turning round to Michael. "Come in and get warm. This is Mrs. Gainsborough, who's the queen of cards."

"Get along with you, you great saucy thing," said Mrs. Gainsborough, laughing.

She was a woman of enormous size with a triplication of chins. Her crimson cheeks shone with the same glister as her black dress; and her black hair, so black that it must have been dyed, was parted in the middle and lay in a chignon upon her neck. She seemed all the larger, sitting in this small room full of Victorian finery, and Michael was amused to hear her address Sylvia as "great."

"We want something to eat and something to drink, you lovely old mountain," Sylvia said.

Mrs. Gainsborough doubled herself up and smacked her knees in a tempest of wheezy laughter.

"Sit here, you terrors, while I get the cloth on the dining-room table," and out she went, her laughter dying in sibilations along the diminutive corridor. Lily had flung herself down in an armchair near the fire. Behind her stood a small mahogany table on which was a glass case of humming-birds; by her elbow on the wall was a white china bell coronated with a filigree of gilt, and by chance the antimacassar on the chair was of Berlin wool checkered black and blue. She in her pierrette's dress of black with light blue pompons looked strangely remote from present time in that setting. Michael could not connect this secluded house with anything which had made an impression upon him during his experience of the underworld. Here was nothing that was not cozy and old-fashioned; here was no sign of decay, whether in the fabric of the house or in the attitude of the people living there. This small square room with the heavy furniture that occupied so much of the space had no demirep demeanor. That horsehair sofa with lyre-shaped sides and back of floriated wood; that brass birdcage hanging in the window against the curtains of maroon serge; those cabinets in miniature, some lacquered, some of plain wood with tiny drop-handles of brass; those black chairs with seats of gilded cane; those trays with marquetery in mother-of-pearl of wreaths and rivulets and parrots; that table-cloth like a dish of black Sèvres; those simpering steel engravings—there was nothing that did not bespeak the sobriety of the Victorian prime here miraculously preserved. Lily and Sylvia in such dresses belonged to a period of fantasy; Mrs. Gainsborough was in keeping with her furniture; and Michael, as he looked at himself in the glass overmantel, did not think that he was seeming very intrusive.

"Whose are these rooms?" he asked. Lily was adorable, but he did not believe they were her creation or discovery.

"I found them," said Sylvia. "The old girl who owns the house is bad, but beautiful. Aren't you, you most astonishing but attractive mammoth?" This was addressed to Mrs. Gainsborough, who was at the moment panting into the room for some accessory to the dining-table.

"Get along with you," the landlady chuckled. "Now don't go to sleep, Lily. Your supper is just on ready." She went puffing from the room in busy mirthfulness.

"She's one of the best," said Sylvia. "This house was given to her by an old General who died about two years ago. You can see the painting of him up in her bedroom as a dare-devil hussar with drooping whiskers. She was a gay contemporary of the Albert Memorial. You know. Argyle Rooms and Cremorne. With the Haymarket as the center of naughtiness."

It was funny, Michael thought, that his tobacconist should have mentioned Cremorne only this afternoon. That he had done so affected him more sharply now with a sense of the appropriateness of this house in Tinderbox Lane. Appropriateness to what? Perhaps merely to the mood of this foggy night.

"Supper! Supper!" Mrs. Gainsborough was crying.

It was dismaying for Michael to think that he had not kissed Lily yet, and he wished that Sylvia would hurry ahead into the other room and give him an opportunity. He wanted to pull her gently from that chair, up from that chair into his arms. But Sylvia was the one who did so, and she kissed Lily half fiercely, leaving Michael disconsolately to follow them across the passage.

It was jolly to see Mrs. Gainsborough sitting at the head of the table with the orange-shaded lamp throwing warm rays upon her countenance. That it was near the chilly hour of one, with a cold thick fog outside, was inconceivable when he looked at that cheery great porpoise of a woman unscrewing bottles of India Pale Ale.

Michael did not want the questions about him and Lily to begin again. So he turned the conversation upon a more remote past.

"Oh, my eye, my eye!" laughed Sylvia. "To think that Aunt Enormous was once in the ballet at the Opera."

"How dare you laugh at me? Whoof!" Mrs. Gainsborough gave a sort of muffled bark as her arm pounced out to grab Sylvia. The two of them frisked with each other absurdly, while Lily sat with wide-open blue eyes, so graceful even in that stiff chair close up to the table, that Michael was in an ecstasy of admiration, and marveled gratefully at the New Year's Day which could so change his fortune.

"Were you in the ballet?" he asked.

"Certainly I was, though this great teazing thing beside me would like to make out that when I was eighteen I looked just as I do now."

"Show the kind gentleman your picture," said Sylvia. "She wears it round her neck in a locket, the vain old mountebank."

Mrs. Gainsborough opened a gold locket, and Michael looked at a rosy young woman in a pork-pie hat.

"That's myself," said Mrs. Gainsborough sentimentally. "Well, and I always loved being young better than anything or anybody, so why shouldn't I wear next my own heart myself as I used to be?"

"But show him the others," Sylvia demanded.

Mrs. Gainsborough fetched from a desk two daguerreotypes in stained morocco cases lined with faded piece velvet. By tilting their surfaces against the light could be seen the shadow of a portrait's wraith: a girl appearing in pantalettes and tartan frock; a ballerina glimmering, with points of faint celeste for eyes, and for cheeks the evanescence of a ghostly bloom.

"Oh, look at her," cried Sylvia. "In her beautiful pantalettes!"

"Hold your tongue, you!"

They started again with their sparring and mock encounters, which lasted on and off until supper was over. Then they all went back to the other room and sat round the fire.

"Tell us about the General," said Sylvia.

"Go on, as if you hadn't heard a score of times all I've got to tell about the General—though you know I hate him to be called that. He'll always be the Captain to me."

Soon afterward, notwithstanding her first refusal, Mrs. Gainsborough embarked upon tales of gay days in the 'sixties and 'seventies. It was astonishing to think that this room in which they were sitting could scarcely have changed since then.

"The dear Captain! He bought this house for me in eighteen-sixty-nine before I was twenty, and I've lived in it ever since. Ah, dear! many's the summer daybreak we've walked back here after dancing all night at Cremorne. Such lovely lights and fireworks. Earl's Court is nothing to Cremorne. Fancy their pulling it down as they did. But perhaps it's as well it went, as all the old faces have gone. It would have given me the dismals to be going there now without my Captain."

She went on with old tales of London, tales that had in them the very smoke and grime of the city.

"Who knows what's going to happen when the clock strikes twelve?" she said, shaking her head. "So enjoy yourselves while you can. That's my motto. And if there's a hereafter, which good God forbid, I should be very aggravated to find myself waltzing around as fat and funny as I am now."

279

The old pagan, who had mellowed slowly with her house for company, seemed to sit here hugging the old friend; and as she told her tales it was difficult not to think she was playing hostess to the spirits of her youths to ghostly Dundrearies and spectral belles with oval faces. Michael could have listened all night to her reminiscences of dead singers and dead dancers, of gay women become dust and of rakes reformed, of beauties that were now hags, and of handsome young subalterns grown parched and liverish. Sylvia egged her on from story to story, and Lily lay languidly back in her chair. It must be after two o'clock, and Michael rose to go.

"We'll have one song," cried Sylvia, and she pulled Mrs. Gainsborough to the piano. The top of the instrument was hidden by stacked-up albums, and the front of it was of fretted walnut-wood across a pleating of claret-colored silk.

Mrs. Gainsborough, pounding with her fat fingers the keys that seemed in comparison so frail and old, sang in a wheezy pipe of a voice: *The Captain with his Whiskers took a Sly Glance at Me.*

"But you only get me to do it, so as you can have a good laugh at me behind my back," she declared, swinging round upon the stool to face Sylvia when she had finished.

"Nothing of the sort, you fat old darling. We do it because we like it."

"Bless your heart, my dearie." She laid a hand on Sylvia's for an instant. Michael thanked Mrs. Gainsborough for the entertainment, and asked Sylvia if she thought he might come round to-morrow and take Lily and her out to lunch.

"We can lunch to-morrow, can't we?" Sylvia asked, tugging at Lily's arm, for she was now fast asleep.

"Is Michael going? Yes, we can lunch with him to-morrow," Lily yawned.

He promised to call for them about midday. It seemed ridiculous to shake hands so formally with Lily, and he hoped she would suggest that the outside door was difficult to open. Alas, it was Sylvia who came to speed his departure.

The fog was welcome to Michael for his going home. At this hour of the night there was not a sound of anything, and he could walk on, dreaming undisturbed. He supposed he would arrive ultimately at Cheyne Walk. But he did not care. He would have been content to fill the long winter night with his fancies. Plunging his hands down into the pockets of his overcoat, he discovered that he had forgotten to take out the girls' shoes, and what company they were through the gloom! It was a most fascinating experience, to wander along holding these silky slippers which had twinkled through the evening of this night. Not a cab-horse blew a frosty breath by the curb; not a policeman loomed; nor passer-by nor cat offended his isolation. The London night belonged to him; his only were the footsteps echoing back from the invisible houses on either side; and the golden room in Tinderbox Lane was never more than a few yards in front.

He had found Lily at last, and he held her shoes for a token of his good luck. Let no one tell him again that destiny was a fable. Nothing was ever more deliberately foredoomed than the meeting at that carnival. Michael was so grateful to his tobacconist that he determined to buy all sorts of extravagant pipes and cigarette holders he had fingered vaguely from time to time in the shop. For a while Lily's discovery was colored with such a glamour that Michael did not analyze the situation in which he had found her. Walking back to Chelsea through the fog, he was bemused by the romantic memory of her which was traveling along with his thoughts. He could hold very tightly her shoes: he could almost embrace the phantom of her beauty that curled upon the vapors round each lamp: he was intoxicated merely by the sound of the street where she lived.

"Tinderbox Lane! Tinderbox Lane! Tinderbox Lane!"

He sang it in triumph, remembering how only this morning he had sighed to himself, as he chased the telegraph-wires up and down the window of the railway-carriage: "Where is she? Where is she? Where is she?"

"Tinderbox Lane! Tinderbox Lane! Tinderbox Lane!" he chanted at the fog, and, throwing a slipper into the air, he caught it and ran on ridiculously until he bumped into a policeman standing by the corner.

"I'm awfully sorry, constable."

"Feeling a bit happy, sir, aren't you?"

"Frightfully happy. I say, by the by, happy new year, constable. Drink my health when you're off duty."

He pressed half-a-crown into the policeman's hand, and as he left the stolid form behind him in the fog, he remembered that half-a-crown was the weekly blackmail paid by Mrs. Smith of Leppard Street. He was on the Embankment now, and the fog had lifted so that he saw the black river flowing sullenly through the night. The plane-trees dripped with monotonous beads of dankness. The fog was become a mist here, a frore whitish mist that saturated him with a malignant chill. Michael was glad to find himself looking at the dolphin-headed knocker of 173 Cheyne Walk. The effect of being in his own bedroom again, even though the girls' shoes lay fantastically upon the floor, was at first to make him believe that Tinderbox Lane might have been a dream, and after that, because he knew it was not a dream, to wonder about it.

Yet not even now in this austere and icy bedroom of his own could Michael feel that there was anything really wrong about that small house. It still preserved for him an illusion of sobriety and stability, almost of primness, yet of being rich with a demure gaiety. Mrs. Gainsborough, however, was scarcely a chaperone. Nor was she very demure. And who was Sylvia? And what was Lily doing there? It would have been mysterious, that household, in any case, but was it necessary to assume that there was anything wrong? Sylvia was obviously a girl of high spirits. He had asked her no questions about herself. She might be on the stage. For fun, or perhaps because of their landlady's kindling stories, Sylvia might have persuaded Lily to come once or twice to the Orient. It did not follow that there was anything wrong. There had been nothing wrong in that carnival. Michael's heart leaped with the fancy that he was not too late. That would indeed crown this romantic night; and, picking up Lily's shoe, he held it for a while, wondering about its secrets.

In the morning the fog had turned to a drench of dull January rain; but Michael greeted the outlook as cheerfully as if it had been perfect May weather. He went first to a post office to send off the money he had promised to Mrs. Smith and the Solutionist. After this discharge of business, he felt more cheerful than ever, and, as if to capture the final touch of fantasy necessary to bewitch yesterday night, he suddenly realized, when he was hurrying along Fulham Road in the rain, that he had no idea of the number of Mrs. Gainsborough's house. He also began to wonder if there really could be such a place as Tinderbox Lane, and as he walked on without discovering any indication of its existence, he wondered if Sylvia had invented the name, so that he might never find her and Lily again. It was an uneasy thought, for without a number and without a name—but just as he was planning an elaborate way to discover the real name of the street, he saw in front of him Tinderbox Lane enameled in the ordinary characters of municipal direction. Here were the two posts: here was the narrow entrance. The rumble of the traffic grew fainter. On one side was a high blank wall; on the other a row of two-storied houses. They were naturally dwellings of the poorer classes, but at intervals a painter had acquired one, and had painted it white or affixed green shutters with heart-shaped openings. The width of the pavement varied continually, but generally at the beginning it was very narrow. Later on, however, it became wide enough to allow trees to be planted down the middle. Beyond this part was a block of new flats round which Tinderbox Lane narrowed again to a mere alley looking now rather dank and gloomy in the rain. Michael could not remember from last night in the fog either the trees or the flats. The door of Lily's lodging had been set in a wall: here on one side was certainly a wall, but never a door to relieve the grimy blankness. He began to feel discouraged, and he walked round into the narrow alley behind the flats. Here were doors in the wall at last, and Michael examined each of them in turn. Two were dark blue: one was green: one was brown. 74: 75: 76: 77. He chose 77 because it was farthest away from the flats. After a very long wait, an old woman holding over herself a very large umbrella opened it.

"Mrs. Gainsborough ...?" Michael began.

But the old woman had slammed the door before he could finish his inquiry.

Michael rang the bell of 76, and again he waited a long time. At last the door was opened, and to his relief he saw Mrs. Gainsborough herself under a green and much larger umbrella than the old woman's next door.

"I've come to take the girls out to lunch."

"That's a good boy," she wheezed. "The dearies will be glad to get out and enjoy themselves a bit. Here's a day. This would have suited Noah, wouldn't it?"

She was leading the way up the gravel path, and Michael saw that in the garden-beds there were actually Christmas roses in bloom. The house itself was covered with a mat of Virginia creeper and jasmine, and the astonishing rusticity of it was not at all diminished by the pretentious gray houses of the next road which towered above it behind, nor even in front by the flats with their eruption of windows. These houses with doors in their garden-walls probably all belonged to individuals, and for that reason they had escaped being overwhelmed by the development of the neighborhood twenty years ago. Their four long gardens in a row must be a bower of greenery in summer, and it was sad to think that the flats opposite were no doubt due to the death of someone who had owned a similar house and garden.

Michael remembered the balcony in front with steps on either side. Underneath this he now saw that there was another entrance, evidently to the kitchen. Two fairly large trees were planted in the grass that ran up to the house on either side of the balcony.

"Those are my mulberries," said Mrs. Gainsborough. "This is called Mulberry Cottage. I've been meaning to have the name painted on the outside door for nearly forty years, but I always forget. There's a character to give myself. Ah, dear me! The Captain loved his mulberries. But you ought to see this in the springtime. Well, my flowers are really remarkable. But there, it's not to be wondered at. M' father was a nursery gardener."

She looked round at Michael and winked broadly. He could not think why. Possibly it was a comic association in her mind with the behavior of the Captain in carrying her off from such a home.

"The Duke of Fulham to see you, girls," she wheezed at the door of the sitting-room, and, giving Michael a push, retreated with volleys of bronchial laughter. The girls were sitting in front of the fire. Lily was pretending to trim a hat: Sylvia was reading, but she flung her book down as Michael entered. He had the curiosity to look at the title, and found it was the Contes Drôlatiques of Balzac. An unusual girl, he thought: but his eyes were all for Lily, and because he could not kiss her, he felt shy and stupid. However, the shoes, which he now restored, supplied an immediate topic, and he was soon perfectly at ease again. Presently the girls left him to get ready to go out, and he sat thinking of Lily, while the canary chirped in the brass cage. The silence here was very like the country. London was a thousand miles away, and he could hear Lily and Sylvia moving about overhead. Less and less did he think there could be anything wrong with Mulberry Cottage. Yet the apparent security was going to make it rather difficult to take Lily away. Certainly he could ask her to marry him at once; but she might not want to marry him at once. The discovery of her in this pleasant house with a jolly friend was spoiling the grand swoop of rescue which he had planned. She would not presumably be escaping from a situation she abhorred. It was difficult to approach Lily here. Was it Sylvia who was making it difficult? He must talk to Sylvia and explain that he had no predatory intentions. She would surely be glad he wanted to marry Lily. Or would she not? Michael jumped up and tinkled the lusters on the mantelshelf. "Sweet," said the canary in the brass cage: the rain sizzled without. Faintly pervading this small square room was the malaise of someone's jealousy. The tentative solution that was propounding itself did not come from his own impression of Sylvia, but it seemed positively to be an emanation from the four walls of the room which in the stillness was able to force its reality upon him. "Sweet," said the canary: the lusters stopped their tinkling: the rain sizzled steadily outside.

Lunch at Kettner's was a great success. At least Michael thought it was a great success, because Lily looked exquisite against the bronzy walls, and her hair on this dull day seemed not to lack sunlight, but rather to give to the atmosphere a thought of the sun, the rare and wintry sun. Sylvia talked a great deal in her deep voice, and he was conscious that the other people in the restaurant were turning round to envy their table.

The longer that Michael was in the company of Lily and Sylvia, the less he was able to ask the direct questions that would have been comparatively easy at the beginning. Sylvia, by the capacity she displayed of appreciating worldliness without ever appearing worldly herself, made it impossible for him to risk her contempt by a stupid question. She was not on the stage; so much he had discovered. She and Lily had apparently a number of men friends. That fact would have been disquieting, but that Sylvia talked of them with such a really tomboyish zest as made it impossible to suppose they represented more than what they were superficially, the companions of jolly days on the river and at race-meetings, of jolly evenings at theaters and balls. Quite definitely Michael was able to assure himself that out of the host of allusions there was not one which pointed to any man favored above the rest. He was able to be positive that Lily and Sylvia were independent. Yet Lily had no private allowance or means. It must be Sylvia who was helping her. Perhaps Sylvia was always strict, and perhaps all these friends were by her held at arm's length from Lily, as he felt himself being held now. Her attitude might have nothing to do with jealousy. But Sylvia was not strict in her conversation; she was, indeed, exceptionally free. That might be a good sign. A girl who read the Contes Drôlatiques might easily read Rabelais himself, and a girl who read Rabelais would be inviolable. Michael, when Sylvia had said something particularly broad, used to look away from Lily; and yet he knew he need not have bothered, for Lily was always outside the conversation; always under a spell of silence and remoteness. Of what was she forever thinking? There were looking-glasses upon the bronzy walls.

For a fortnight Michael came every day to Tinderbox Lane and took the girls out; but for the whole of that fortnight he never managed to be alone with Lily. Then one day Sylvia was not there when he called. To find Lily like this after a tantalizing fortnight was like being in a room heavily perfumed with flowers. It seemed to stifle his initiative, so that for a few minutes he sat coldly and awkwardly by the window.

"We're alone," he managed to say at last.

"Sylvia's gone to Brighton. She didn't want to go a bit."

"Bother Sylvia! Lily, we haven't kissed for five years."

He stumbled across to take her in his arms; and as he held her to him, it was a rose falling to pieces, so did she melt upon his passion. He heard her sigh; a coal slipped in the grate; the canary hopped from perch to perch. These small sounds but wrapped him more closely in the trance of silence.

"Lily, you will marry me, won't you? Very soon? At once?"

Michael was kneeling beside her chair, and she was looking down at him from clouded eyes still passionate. Marriage was an intrusion upon the remoteness where they brooded; and he, ravished by their flamy blue relucency, could not care whether she answered him or not. This was such a contentment of desire that the future with the visible shapes of action it tried to display was unheeded, while now she stirred in his arms. She was his, and so for an hour she stayed, immortal, and yet most poignantly the prisoner of time. Michael, with all that he had dreaded at the back of his mind he would have to face in her condition, scarcely knew how to celebrate this reward of his tenacity. This tranquillity of caresses, this slow fondling of her wrist were a lullaby to his fears. It was the very rhapsody of his intention to kneel beside her, murmuring huskily the little words of love. He would have married her wherever and whatever he found her, but the relief was overwhelming. He had thought of a beautiful thing ruined; he had foreshadowed glooms and tragic colloquies; he had desperately hoped his devotion might be granted at least the virtue of a balm. Instead, he found this ivory girl, this loveliness of rose and coral within his arms. So many times she had eluded him in dreams upon the midway of the night, and so often in dreams he had held her for kisses that were robbed from him by the sunlight of the morning, that he scarcely could believe he held her now, now when her hair was thistledown upon his cheeks, when her mouth was a butterfly. He shuddered to think how soon this airy beauty must have perished; and even now what was she? A shred of goldleaf on his open hand, pliant, but fugitive at a breath, and destructible in a moment of adversity.

Always in their youth, when they had sat imparadised, Michael had been aware of the vulgar Haden household in the background. Now, here she was placed in exactly the room where he would have wished to find her, though he would scarcely desire to maintain her in such a setting. He could picture her at not so distant a time in wonderful rooms, about whose slim furniture she would move in delicate and languorous promenades. This room pleased him, because it was the one from which he would have wished to take her into the misty grandeurs he imagined for her lodging. It was a room he would always regard with affection, thinking of the canary in the brass cage and the Christmas roses blowing in the garden and the low sounds of Mrs. Gainsborough busy in her kitchen underneath. Tinderbox Lane! It was an epithalamium in itself; and as for Mulberry Cottage, it had been carried here by the fat pink loves painted on the ceiling of that Cremorne arbor in which the Captain had first imagined his gift.

So with fantastic thoughts and perfect kisses, perfect but yet ineffably vain because they expressed so little of what Michael would have had them express, the hour passed.

"We must talk of practical things," he declared, rising from his knees.

"You always want to talk," Lily pouted.

"I want to marry you. Do you want to marry me?"

"Yes; but it's so difficult to do things quickly."

"We'll be married in a month. We'll be married on Saint Valentine's Day," Michael announced.

"It's so wet now to think of weddings." She looked peevishly out of the window.

"You haven't got to think about it. You've got to do it."

"And it's so dull," she objected. "Sylvia says it's appallingly dull. And she's been married."

"What has Sylvia got to do with it?" he demanded.

"Oh, well, she's been awfully sweet to me. And after all, when mother died, what was I to do? I couldn't bear Doris any more. She always gets on my nerves. Anyway, don't let's talk about marriage now. In the summer I shall feel more cheerful. I hate this weather."

"But look here," he persisted. "Are you in love with me?"

She nodded, yet too doubtfully to please him.

"Well, if you're not in love with me...."

"Oh, I am, I am! Don't shout so, Michael. If I wasn't awfully fond of you, I shouldn't have made Sylvia ask you to come back. She hates men coming here."

"Are you Sylvia's servant?" said Michael, in exasperation.

"Don't be stupid. Of course not."

"It's ridiculous," he grumbled, "to quote her with every sentence."

"Why you couldn't have stayed where you were," said Lily fretfully, "I don't know. It was lovely sitting by the fire and being kissed. If you're so much in love with me, I wonder you wanted to get up."

"So, we're not to talk any more about marriage?"

After all, he told himself, it was unreasonable of him to suppose that Lily was likely to be as impulsive as himself. Her temperament was not the same. She did not mean to discourage him.

"Don't let's talk about anything," said Lily. He could not stand aloof from the arms she held wide open.

Sylvia would not be coming back for at least three days, and Michael spent all his time with Lily. He thought that Mrs. Gainsborough looked approvingly upon their love; at any rate, she never worried them. The weather was steadily unpleasant, and though he took Lily out to lunch, it never seemed worth while to stay away from Tinderbox Lane very long. One night, however, they went to the Palace, and afterward, when he asked her where she would like to go, she suggested Verrey's. Michael had never been there before, and he was rather jealous that Lily should seem to know it so well. However, he liked to see her sitting in what he told himself was the only café in London which had escaped the cheapening of popularity and had kept its old air of the Third Empire.

As Lily was stirring her lemon-squash, her languid forearm looked very white swaying from the somber mufflings of her cloak. Something in her self-possession, a momentary hardness and disdain, made Michael suddenly suspicious.

"Do you enjoy Covent Garden balls?" he asked.

She shrugged her shoulders.

"It depends who we go with. Often I don't care for them much. And the girls you see there are frightfully common."

He could not bring himself to ask her straight out what he feared. If it were so, let it rest unrevealed. The knowledge would make no difference to his resolution. People began to come into the café, shaking the wet from their shoulders; and the noise of the rain was audible above the conversation.

"I wish we could have had one fine day together," said Michael regretfully. "Do you remember when we used to go for long walks in the winter?"

"I must have been very fond of you," Lily laughed. "I don't think you could make me walk like that now."

"Aren't you so fond of me now?" he asked reproachfully.

"You ought to know," she whispered.

All the way home the raindrops were flashing in the road like bayonets, and her cheeks were dabbled with the wet.

"Shall I come in?" Michael asked, as he waited by the door in the wall.

"Yes, come in and have something to drink, of course."

He was stabbed by the ease of her invitation.

"Do you ask all these friends of yours to come in and have a drink after midnight?"

"I told you that Sylvia doesn't like me to," she said.

"But you would, if she didn't mind?" Michael went on, torturing himself.

"How fond you are of 'ifs,'" she answered. "I can't bother to think about 'ifs' myself."

If only he had the pluck to avoid allusions and come at once to grips with truth. Sharply he advised himself to let the truth alone. Already he was feeling the influence of Lily's attitude. He wondered if, when he married her, all his activity would swoon upon Calypso like this. It was as easy to dream life away in the contemplation of a beautiful woman as in the meditation of the Oxford landscape.

"Happiness makes me inactive," said Michael to himself. "So of course I shall never really be happy. What a paradox."

He would not take off his overcoat. He was feeling afraid of a surrender to-night.

"I'm glad I didn't suggest staying late," he thought, as he walked away down the dripping garden path. "I should have been mad with unreasonable suspicions, if she had said 'yes.'"

Sylvia came back next day, and though Michael still liked her very much, he was certain now of her hostility to him. He was conscious of malice in the air, when she said to Lily that Jack wanted them to have dinner with him to-night and go afterward to some dance at Richmond. Michael was furious that Lily should be invited to Richmond, and yet until she had promised to marry him how could he combat Sylvia's influence? And who was Jack? And with whom had Sylvia been to Brighton?

The day after the dance, Michael came round about twelve o'clock as usual, but when he reached the sitting-room only Sylvia was before the fire.

"Lily isn't down yet," she told him.

He was aware of a breathlessness in the atmosphere, and he knew that he and Sylvia were shortly going to clash.

"Jolly dance?" he asked.

She shrugged her shoulders, and there was a long pause.

"Will Lily be dressed soon? I rather want to take her out." Michael flung down his challenge.

"She's been talking to me about what you said yesterday," Sylvia began.

Michael could not help liking her more and more, although her countenance was set against him. He could not help admiring that out-thrust underlip and those wide-set, deep and bitter brown eyes.

"When do you propose to marry her?" Sylvia went on.

"As soon as possible," he said coolly.

"Which of us do you think has the greater influence over her?" she demanded.

"I really don't know. You have rather an advantage over me in that respect."

"I'm glad you admit that," interrupted Sylvia, with sarcastic chill.

"You have personality. You've probably been very kind to Lily. You're cleverer than she is. You're with her all the time. I've only quite suddenly come into her life again."

"I'm glad you think you've managed to do that," she said, glowering.

More and more, Michael thought, with her wide-set eyes was she like a cat crouching by the fire.

"Just because I had to go away for three days and you had an opportunity to be alone with Lily, you now think you've come into her life. My god, you're like some damned fool in a novel!"

"A novel by whom?" Michael asked. Partly he was trying to score off Sylvia, but at the same time he was sincerely curious to know, for he never could resist the amplification of a comparison.

"Oh, any ink-slinger with a brain of pulp," she answered savagely.

He bowed.

"I suppose you're suffering from the virus of sentimental redemption?" she sneered.

Michael was rather startled by her divination.

"What should I redeem her from?"

"I thought you boasted of knowing Lily six years ago?"

"I don't know that I boasted of it," he replied, in rather an injured tone. "But I did know her—very well."

"Couldn't you foresee what she was bound to become? Personally I should have said that Lily's future must have been obvious from the time she was five years old. Certainly at seventeen it must have been. You got out of her life then: what the hell's your object in coming into it again now, as you call it, unless you're a sentimentalist? People don't let passion lapse for six years and pick up the broken thread without the help of sentiment."

Michael in the middle of the increasing tension of the conversation was able to stop for a moment and ask himself if this by chance were true. He was standing by the mantelpiece and tinkling the lusters. Sylvia looked up at him irritably, and he silenced them at once.

"Sentiment about what?" he asked, taking the chair opposite hers.

"You think Lily's a tart, don't you? And you think I am, don't you?"

He frowned at the brutality of the expression.

"I did think so," he said. "But of course I've changed my mind since I've seen something of you."

"Oh, of course you've changed your mind, have you?" she laughed contemptuously. "And what made you do that? My visit to Brighton?"

"Even if *you* are," said Michael hotly, "I needn't believe that Lily is. And even if she is, it makes no difference to my wanting to marry her."

"Sentimentalist," she jeered. "Damned sugar-and-water sentimentalist."

"Your sneers don't particularly affect me, you know," he said politely.

"Oh, for god's sake, be less the well-brought-up little gentleman. Cut out the undergraduate. You fool, I was married to an Oxford man. And I'm sitting here now with the glorious knowledge that I'm a perpetual bugbear to his good form."

"Because you made a hash of marriage," Michael pointed out, "it doesn't follow that I'm not to marry Lily. I can't understand your objections."

"Listen. You couldn't make her happy. You couldn't make her any happier than the dozens of men who want to be fond of her for a short time without accepting the responsibility of marriage. Do you think I let any one of those dozens touch her? Not one, if I can get the money myself. And I usually can. Well, why should I stand aside now and let you carry her off, even though you do want to marry her? I could argue against it on your side by telling you that you have no chance of keeping Lily faithful to you? Can't you see that she has no moral energy? Can't you see that she's vain and empty-headed? Can't you see that? But why should I argue with you for your benefit? I don't care a damn about your side in the matter."

"What exactly do you care about?" Michael asked. "If Lily is what you say, I should have thought you'd be glad to be rid of her. After all, I'm not proposing to do her any wrong."

"Oh, to the devil with your right and wrong!" Sylvia cried. "Man can only wrong woman, when he owns her, and if this marriage is going to be a success, you'll have to own Lily. That's what I rebel against—the ownership of women. It makes me mad."

"Yes, it seems to," Michael put in. He was beginning to be in a rage with Sylvia's unreasonableness. "If it comes to ownership," he went on angrily, "I should have thought that handing her over to the highest bidder time after time would be the real way to make her the pitiable slave of man."

"Why?" challenged Sylvia. "You sentimental ass, can't you understand that she treats them as I treat them, like the swine they are. She's free. I'm free."

"You're not at all free," Michael indignantly contradicted. "You're bound hand and foot by the lust of wealthy brutes. If you read a few less elaborately clever books, and thought a few simpler thoughts, you'd be a good deal happier."

"I don't want to be happier."

"Oh, I think you're merely hysterical," he said disdainfully. "But, after all, your opinions about yourself don't matter to me. Only I can't see what right you have to apply them to Lily; and even if you have the right, I don't grasp your reason for wanting to."

"When I met Lily first," said Sylvia, "she had joined the chorus of a touring company in which I was. Her mother had just died, and I'd just run away from my husband. I thought her the most beautiful thing I'd ever seen. That's three years ago. Is she beautiful still?"

"Of course she is," said Michael.

"Well, it's I who have kept her beautiful. I've kept her free also. If sometimes I've let her have affairs with men, I've taken care that they were with men who could do her no harm, for whom she had no sort of...."

"Look here," Michael burst in. "I'm sick of this conversation. You're talking like a criminal lunatic. I tell you I'm going to marry her, whatever you think."

"I say you won't, and you shan't," Sylvia declared.

The deadlock had been reached, and they sat there on either side of the fire, glaring at each other.

"The extraordinary thing is," said Michael at last, "I thought you had a sense of humor when I first met you. And another extraordinary thing is that I still like you very much. Which probably rather annoys you. But I can't help saying it."

"The opinions of sentimentalists don't interest me one way or the other," Sylvia snapped.

"Will you answer one question? Will you tell me why you were so pleasant on the evening we met?"

"I really can't bother to go back as far as that."

"You weren't jealous *then*," Michael persisted.

"Who says I'm jealous now?" she cried.

"I do. What do you think you are, unless you're jealous? When is Lily coming down?"

"She isn't coming down until you've gone."

"Then I shall go and call her."

"She's not in London."

"I don't believe you."

A second deadlock was reached. Finally Michael decided to give Sylvia the pleasure of supposing that he was beaten for the moment. He congratulated himself upon the cunning of such a move. She was obviously going to be rather difficult to circumvent.

On the steps of the balcony he turned to her:

"You hate me because I love Lily, and you hate me twice as much because Lily loves me."

"It's not true," Sylvia declared. "It's not true. She doesn't love you, and what right have you to love her?"

She tossed back her mane of brown hair, biting her nails.

"What college was your husband at?" Michael suddenly inquired.

"Balliol."

"I wonder if I knew him."

"Oh, no. He was older than you."

It was satisfactory, Michael thought as he walked down Tinderbox Lane, that the conversation had ended normally. At least, he had effected so much. She had really been rather wonderful, that strange Sylvia. He would very much like to pit her against Stella. It was satisfactory to have his doubts allayed: notwithstanding her present opposition, he felt that he did owe Sylvia a good deal. But it would be absurd to let Lily continue in such a life: women always quarreled ultimately, and if Sylvia were to leave her, her fall would be rapid and probably irredeemable. Besides, he wanted her for himself. She was to him no less than to Sylvia the most beautiful thing in the world. He did not want to marry a clever woman: he would be much more content with Lily, from whom there could be no reaction upon his nerves. Somehow all his theories of behavior were being referred back to his own desires. It was useless to pretend any longer that his pursuit had been quixotry. Even if it had seemed so on that night when he first heard the news of Lily from Drake, the impulse at the back of his resolve had been his passion for her. When he looked back at his behavior lately, a good deal of it seemed to have been dictated by self-gratification. He remembered how deeply hurt he had felt by Poppy's treatment of what he had supposed his chivalry. In retrospect his chivalry was seeming uncommonly like self-satisfaction. His friendship for Daisy; for Barnes; for the underworld; it had been nothing but self-satisfaction. Very well, then. If self was to be the touchstone in future, he could face that standard as easily as any other. By the time he had reached the end of Tinderbox Lane Michael was convinced of his profound cynicism. He felt truly obliged to Sylvia for curing him of sentiment. He had so often inveighed against sentiment as the spring of human action, that he was most sincerely grateful for the proof of his own sentimental bias. He would go to Sylvia to-morrow and say frankly that he did not care a bit what Lily had been, was now, or would be; he wanted her. She was something beautiful which he coveted. For the possession of her he was ready to struggle. He would declare war upon Sylvia as upon a rival. She should be rather surprised to-morrow morning, Michael thought, congratulating himself upon this new and ruthless policy.

On the next morning, however, all Michael's plans for his future behavior were knocked askew by being unable to get into Mulberry Cottage. His brutal frankness; his cynical egotism; his cold resolution, were ignominiously repulsed by a fast-closed door. Ringing a bell at intervals of a minute was a very undignified substitute for the position he had imagined himself taking up in that small square room. This errand-boy who stood at his elbow, gazing with such rapt interest at his ringing of the bell, was by no means the audience he had pictured.

"Does it amuse you to watch a bell being rung?" Michael asked.

The errand-boy shook his head.

"Well, why do you do it?"

"I wasn't," said the errand-boy.

"What are you doing, then?"

"Nothing."

Michael could not grapple with the errand-boy, and he retired from Tinderbox Lane until after lunch. He rang again, but he could get no answer to his ringing. At intervals until midnight he came back, but there was never an answer all the time. He went home and wrote to Sylvia:

173 CHEYNE WALK,
S.W.

Dear Sylvia,

If you aren't afraid of being beaten, why are you afraid to let me see Lily?

I dare you to let me see her. Be sporting.

Yours,

M. F.

To Lily he wrote:

Darling,

Meet me outside South Kensington Station any time from twelve to three.

Michael.

Alone, of course.

Next day he waited three hours and a half for Lily, but she did not come. All the time he spent in a second-hand bookshop with one eye on the street. When he got home, he found a note from Sylvia:

Come to-morrow at twelve.

S. S.

Michael crumpled up the note and flung it triumphantly into the waste-paper basket.

"I thought I should sting you into giving way," he exclaimed.

Mrs. Gainsborough opened the door to him, when he arrived.

"They've gone away, the demons!" was what she said.

Michael was conscious of the garden rimmed with hoar-frost stretching behind her in a vista; and as he stared at this silver sparkling desert he realized that Sylvia had inflicted upon him a crushing humiliation.

"Where have they gone?" he asked blankly.

"Oh, they never tell me where they get to. But they took their luggage. There's a note for you from Sylvia. Come in, and I'll give it to you."

Michael followed her drearily along the gravel path.

"We shall be having the snowdrops before we know where we are," Mrs. Gainsborough said.

"Very soon," he agreed. He would have assented if she had foretold begonias to-morrow morning.

In the sitting-room Michael saw Sylvia's note, a bleak little envelope waiting for him on that table-cloth. Mrs. Gainsborough left him to read it alone. The old silence of the room haunted him again now, the silence that was so much intensified by the canary hopping about his cage. Almost he decided to throw the letter unread into the fire.

From every corner of the room the message of Sylvia's hostility was stretching out toward him. "Sweet," said the canary. Michael tore open the envelope and read:

Perhaps you'll admit that my influence is as strong as yours. You'd much better give her up. In a way, I'm rather sorry for you, but not enough to make me hand over Lily to you. Do realize, my dear young thing, that you aren't even beginning to understand women. I admit that there's precious little to understand in Lily. And for that very reason, when even you begin to see through her beauty, you'll hate her. Now I hate to think of this happening. She's a thousand times better off with me than she ever could be with you. Perhaps my maternal instinct has gone off the lines a bit and fixed itself on Lily. And yet I don't think it's anything so sickly as sentimental mothering. No, I believe I just like to sit and look at her. Lily's rather cross with me for taking her away from "such a nice boy." Does that please you? And doesn't it exactly describe you? However, I won't crow. Don't break the lusters, when you read this. They belong to Fatty. What I suggest for you is a walk in Kensington Gardens to the refrain of "Blast the whole bloody world!" Now look shocked, my little Vandyck.

S. S.

Michael tore the letter up. He did not want to read and re-read it for the rest of the day. His eyelids were pricking unpleasantly, and he went out to find Mrs. Gainsborough. He was really sensitive that even a room should witness such a discomfiture. The landlady was downstairs in the kitchen, where he had not yet been. In this room of copper pots and pans, with only the garden in view, she might have been a farmer's wife.

"Sit down," she said. "And make yourself at home."

"Will you sit down?" Michael asked.

"Oh, well, yes, if it's any pleasure to you." She took off her apron and seated herself, smoothing the bombasine skirt over her knees.

A tabby cat purred between them; a kettle was singing; and there was a smell of allspice.

"You really don't know where the girls have gone?" Michael began.

"No more than you do," she assured him. "But that Sylvia is really a Turk."

"I suppose Lily didn't tell you that I used to know her six years ago?" he asked.

"Oh, yes, she talked about you a lot. A good deal more than Miss Sylvia liked, that's a sure thing."

"Well, do you think it's fair for Sylvia to carry her off like this? I want to marry Lily, Mrs. Gainsborough."

"There, only fancy what a daring that Sylvia has. She's a nice girl, and very high-spirited, but she *is* a Miss Dictatorial."

Michael felt encouraged by Mrs. Gainsborough's attitude, and he made up his mind to throw himself upon her mercy. Sentiment would be his only weapon, and he found some irony in the reflection that he had set out this morning to be a brutal cynic in his treatment of the situation.

"Do you think it's fair to try to prevent Lily from marrying me? You know as well as I do that the life she's leading now isn't going to be the best life possible for her. You're a woman of the world, Mrs. Gainsborough——"

"I was once," she corrected. "And a very naughty world it was, too."

"You were glad, weren't you, when the Captain brought you to this house? You were glad to feel secure? You would have married him?"

"No, I wouldn't marry him. I preferred to be as I am. Still that's nothing for Lily to go by. She's more suited for marriage than what I was."

"Don't you think," Michael went on eagerly, "that if after six years I'm longing to marry her, I ought to marry her? I know that she might be much worse off than she is, but equally she might be much better off. Look here, Mrs. Gainsborough, it's up to you. You've got to make it possible for me to see her. You've got to."

"But if I do anything like that," said Mrs. Gainsborough, "it means I have an unpleasantness with Sylvia. That girl's a regular heathen when she turns nasty. I should be left all alone in my little house. And what with Spring coming on and all, and the flowers looking so nice in the garden, I should feel very much the square peg in the round hole."

"Lily and I would come and see you," he promised. "And I don't think Sylvia would leave you. She'd never find another house like Mulberry Cottage or another landlady like you."

"Yes, I daresay; but you can't tell these things. Once she's in her tantrums, there's no saying what will happen. And, besides, I don't know what you want me to do."

"I want you to send me word the first moment that Lily's alone for an hour; and when I ring, do answer the bell."

"Now that wasn't my fault yesterday," said Mrs. Gainsborough. "Really I thought we should have the fire-escape in. The way you nagged at that poor bell! It was really chronic. But would she let me so much as speak to you, even with the door only on the jar? Certainly not! And all the time she was snapping round the house like a young crocodile. And yet I'm really fond of that girl. Well, when the Captain died, she was a daughter to me. Oh, she was, she was really a daughter to me. Well, you see, his sister invited me to the funeral, which I thought was very nice, her being an old maid and very strict. Now, I hardly liked to put on a widow's cap and yet I hardly didn't like to. But Sylvia, she said not on any account, and I was very glad I didn't, because there was a lot of persons there very stand-offish, and I should have been at my wits to know whatever I was going to say."

"Look here," said Michael. "When the Captain gave you this house, he loved you. You were young, weren't you? You were young and beautiful? Well, would you like to think your house was going to be used to separate two people very much in love with each other? You can say I climbed over the wall. You can make any excuse you like to Sylvia. But, Mrs. Gainsborough, do, do let me know when Lily is going to be alone. If she doesn't want to come away with me, it will be my fault, and that will be the end of it. If only you'll help me at the beginning. Will you? Will you promise to help me?"

"I never could resist a man," sighed Mrs. Gainsborough, with resignation. "There's a character! Oh, well, it's my own and no one else's, that's one good job."

Michael had to wait until February was nearly over before he heard from her. It had been very difficult to remain quietly at Cheyne Walk, but he knew that if he were to show any sign of activity, Sylvia would carry Lily off again.

"A person to see you, sir," said the tortoise-mouthed parlormaid.

Michael found Mrs. Gainsborough sitting in the hall. She was wearing a bonnet tied with very bright cerise ribbons.

"They've had a rumpus, the pair of them, this afternoon. And Sylvia's gone off in the sulks. I really was quite aggravated with her. Oh, she's a willful spitfire, that girl, sometimes. She really is."

Michael was coming away without a coat or hat, and Mrs. Gainsborough stopped him.

"Now don't behave like a silly. Dress yourself properly and don't make me run. I'm getting stout, you know," she protested.

"We'll get a hansom."

"What, ride in a hansom? Never! A four-wheeler if you *like*."

It was difficult to find a four-wheeler, and Michael was nearly mad with impatience.

"Now don't upset yourself. Sylvia won't be back to-night, and there's no need to tug at me as if I was a cork in a bottle. People will think we're a walking poppy-show, if you don't act more quiet. They're all turning round to stare at us."

A four-wheeler appeared presently, and very soon they were walking down Tinderbox Lane. Michael felt rather like a little boy out with his nurse, as he kept turning back to exhort Mrs. Gainsborough to come more quickly. She grew more and more red in the face, and so wheezy that he was afraid something would happen to her, and for a few yards made no attempt to hurry her along. At last they reached Mulberry Cottage.

"Supposing Sylvia has come back!" he said.

"I keep on telling you she's gone away for the night. Now get on indoors with you. You've nearly been my death."

"I say, you don't know how grateful I am to you!" Michael exclaimed, turning round and grasping her fat hands.

Mrs. Gainsborough shouted upstairs to Lily as loudly as her breathlessness would permit:

"I've brought you back that surprise packet I promised."

Then she vanished, and Michael waited for Lily at the foot of the stairs. She came down very soon, looking very straight and slim in her philamot frock of Chinese crêpe that so well became her. Soon she was in his arms and glad enough to be petted after Sylvia's rages.

"Lily, how can you bear to let Sylvia manage you like this? It's absolutely intolerable."

"She's been horrid to me to-day," said Lily resentfully.

"Well, why do you put up with it?"

"Oh, I don't know. I hate always squabbling. It's much easier to give way to her, and usually I don't much mind."

"You don't much mind whether we're married!" Michael exclaimed. "How can you let Sylvia persuade you against marriage? Darling girl, if you marry me you shall do just as you like. I simply want you to look beautiful. You'd be happy married to me—you really would."

"Sylvia says marriage is appallingly dull, and my mother and father didn't get on, and Doris doesn't get on with the man she's married to. In fact, everybody seems to hate it."

"Do you hate me?" Michael demanded.

"No, I think you're awfully sweet."

"Well, why don't you marry me? You'll have plenty of money and nothing to bother about. I think you'd thoroughly enjoy being married."

For an instant, as he argued with her, Michael wavered in his resolve. For an instant it seemed, after all, impossible to marry this girl. A chill came over him, but he shook it off, and he saw only her loveliness, the eyes sullen with thoughts of Sylvia, the lips pouting at the remembrance of a tyranny. And again as he watched her beauty, the bitter thought crossed his mind that it would be easier to possess her without marriage. Then he thought of her at seventeen. "*Michael, why do you make me love you so?*" Was that the last protest she ever made against the thralldom of passion? If it was, the blame must primarily be his, since he had not heeded her reproach.

"Lily," he cried, catching her to him. "You're coming away with me now."

He kissed her a hundred times.

"Now! Now! Do you hear me?"

She surrendered to his will, and as he held her Michael thought grimly what an absurd paradox it was, that in order to make her consent to marry him, he like the others must play upon the baser side of her yielding nature. There were difficulties of packing and of choosing frocks and hats, but Michael had his way through them all.

"Quite an elopement," Mrs. Gainsborough proclaimed.

"A very virtuous elopement," said Michael, with a laugh.

"Oh, but shan't I catch it when that Hottentot comes back!"

"Well, it's Sylvia's fault," said Lily fretfully. "She shouldn't worry me all the time to know whether I like her better than anyone else in the world."

The man arrived with a truck for the luggage.

"Where are you going?" Mrs. Gainsborough asked. "I declare, you're like two babes in the wood."

"To my sister's in Huntingdonshire," said Michael, and he wrote out the address.

"Oh, in the country! Well, Summer'll be on us before we know where we are. I declare, my snowdrops are quite finished."

"Is your sister pretty?" Lily asked, as they were driving to King's Cross.

"She's handsome," said Michael. "You'll like her, I think. And her husband was a great friend of mine. By the way, I must send a wire to say we're coming."

CHAPTER VII

THE GATE OF IVORY

It was only when he was sitting opposite to Lily in a first class compartment that Michael began to wonder if their sudden arrival would create a kind of consternation at Hardingham. He managed to reassure himself when he looked at her. The telegram might have puzzled Stella, but in meeting Lily she would understand his action. Nevertheless, he felt a little anxious when he saw the Hardingham brougham waiting outside the little station. The cold drive of four miles through the still, misty evening gave him too long to meditate the consequences of his action. Impulse was very visibly on trial, and he began to fear a little Stella's judgment of it. The carriage-lamps splashed the hedgerows monotonously, and the horses' breath curled round the rigid form of the coachman. Trees, hedges, gates, signposts went past in the blackness and chill. Michael drew Lily close, and asked in a whisper if she were happy.

"It makes me sleepy driving like this," she murmured. Her head was on his shoulder; the astrakan collar was silky to his chin. So she traveled until they reached the gates of the park: then Michael woke her up.

There was not time to do much but dress quickly for dinner when they arrived, though Michael watched Stella's glances rather anxiously.

Lily put on a chiffon frock, of aquamarine, and, though she looked beautiful in it, he wished she had worn black: this frock made her seem a little theatrical, he fancied; or was it the effect of her against the stern dining-room, and nothing whatever to do with the frock? Stella, too, whom he had always considered a personality of some extravagance, seemed to have grown suddenly very stiff and conventional. It used always to be himself who criticized people: Stella had always been rather too lenient. Perhaps it was being married to Alan; or was Lily the reason? Yet superficially everything seemed to be going all right, especially when he consoled himself by remembering the abruptness of Lily's introduction. After dinner Stella took Lily away with her into the drawing-room and left Michael with Alan. Michael tried to feel that this was what he had expected would happen; but he could not drive away the consciousness of a new formality brooding over Hardingham. It was annoying, too, the way in which Alan seemed deliberately to avoid any reference to Lily. He would not even remind Michael of the evening at the Drury Lane pantomime, when he had met her five or six years ago. Perhaps he had forgotten driving home in a cab with her sister on that occasion. Michael grew exasperated by his talk about cricket pitches; and yet he could not bring himself to ask right out what Alan thought of her, because it would have impinged upon his pride to do so. In about ten minutes they heard the sound of the piano, and tacitly they agreed to forego the intimacy of drinking port together any longer.

Stella closed the piano with a slam when they came into the drawing-room, and asked Lily if she would like some bridge.

"Oh, no. I hate playing cards. But you play."

It was for Michael a nervous evening. He was perpetually on guard for hostile criticism; he was terribly anxious that Lily should make a good impression. Everything seemed to go wrong. Games were begun and ended almost in the same breath. Finally he managed to find a song that Lily thought she remembered, and Stella played her accompaniment very aggressively, Michael fancied; for by this time he regarded the slightest movement on her part or Alan's as an implication of disapproval. Lily was tired, luckily, and was ready to go to bed early.

When Stella came down again, Michael felt he ought to supplement the few details of his telegram, and it began to seem almost impossible to explain reasonably his arrival here with Lily. An account of Tinderbox Lane would sound fantastic: a hint of Lily's life would be fatal. He found himself enmeshed in a vague tale of having found her very hard up and of wishing to get her away from the influence of a rather depressing home. It sounded very unconvincing as he told it, but he hoped that the declaration of his intention to marry her at once would smother everything else in a great surprise.

"Of course, that's what I imagined you were thinking of doing," said Stella. "So you've made up your quarrel of five years ago?"

"When are you going to get married?" Alan asked.

"Well, I hoped you'd be able to have us here for a week or so, or at any rate Lily, while I go up to town and find a place for us to live."

"Oh, of course she can stay here," said Stella.

"Oh, rather, of course," Alan echoed.

Next morning it rained hard, and Michael thought he saw Stella making signs of dissent when at breakfast Alan proposed taking him over to a farm a couple of miles away. He was furious to think that Stella was objecting to being left alone with Lily, and he retired to the billiard-room, where he spent half an hour playing a game with himself between spot and plain, a game which produced long breaks that seemed quite unremarkable, so profound was the trance of vexation in which he was plunged.

A fortnight passed, through the whole of which Alan never once referred to Lily; and, as Michael was always too proud to make the first advance toward the topic, he felt that his friendship with Alan was being slowly chipped away. He knew that Stella, on the other hand, was rather anxious to talk to him, but perversely he avoided giving her any opportunity. As for Lily, she seemed perfectly happy doing nothing and saying very little. Obviously, however, this sort of existence under the shadow of disapproval could not continue much longer, and Michael determined to come to grips with the situation. Therefore, one morning of strong easterly wind when Lily wanted to stay indoors, he proposed a walk to Stella.

They crossed three or four fields in complete silence, the dogs scampering to right and left, the gale crimsoning their cheeks.

"I don't think I care much for this country of yours," said Michael at last. "It's flat and cold and damp. Why on earth you ever thought I should care to live here, I don't know."

"There's a wood about a quarter of a mile farther on. We can get out of the wind there."

Michael resented Stella's pleasantness. He wanted her to be angry and so launch him easily upon the grievances he had been storing up for a fortnight.

"I hate badly trained dogs," he grumbled when Stella turned round to whistle vainly for one of the spaniels.

"So do I," she agreed.

It was really unfair of her to effect a deadlock by being perpetually and unexpectedly polite. He would try being gracious himself: it was easier in the shelter of the wood.

"I don't think I've properly thanked you for having us to stay down here," he began.

Stella stopped dead in the middle of the glade:

"Look here, do you want me to talk about this business?" she demanded.

Her use of the word "business" annoyed him: it crystallized all the offensiveness, as he was now calling it to himself, of her sisterly attitude these two weeks.

"I shall be delighted to talk about this 'business.' Though why you should refer to my engagement as if a hot-water pipe had burst, I don't quite know."

"Do you want me to speak out frankly—to say exactly what I think of you and Lily and of your marrying her? You won't like it, and I won't do it unless you ask me."

"Go on," said Michael gloomily. Stella had gathered the dogs round her again, and in this glade she appeared to Michael as a severe Artemis with her short tweed skirt and her golf-coat swinging from her shoulders like a chlamys. These oaks were hers: the starry moss was hers: the anemones flushing and silvering to the ground wind, they were all hers. It suddenly struck him as monstrously unfair that Stella should be able to criticize Lily. Here she stood on her own land forever secure against the smallest ills that could come to the other girl; and, with this consciousness of a strength behind her, already she was conveying that rustic haughtiness of England. Michael loved her, this cool and indomitable mistress of Hardingham; but while he loved her, almost he hated her for the power she had to look down on Lily. Michael wished he had Sylvia with him. That would have been a royal battle in this wood. Stella with her dogs and trees behind her, with her green acres all round her and the very wind fighting for her, might yet have found it difficult to discomfit Sylvia.

"Go on, I'm waiting for you to begin," Michael repeated.

"Straight off, then," she said, "I may as well tell you that this marriage is impossible. I don't know where you found her again, and I don't care. It wouldn't make the slightest difference to me what she had been, if I thought she had a chance of ever being anything else. But, Michael, she's flabby. You'll hate me for saying so, but she is, she really is! In a year you'll admit that; you'll see her growing older and flabbier, more and more vain; emptier and emptier, if that's possible. Even her beauty won't last. These very fair girls fall to pieces like moth-eaten dolls. I've tried to find something in her during this fortnight. I've tried and tried; but there's nothing. You may be in love with her now, though I don't believe you are. I think it's all a piece of sentimentalism. I've often teased you about getting married, but please don't suppose that I haven't realized how almost impossible it would be, ever to find a woman that would stand the wear and tear of your idealism. I'm prepared to bet that behind your determination to marry this girl there's a reason, a lovely, unpractical, idealistic reason. Isn't there? You've been away with her for a week-end, and have tortured yourself into a theory of reparation. Is that it? Or you've fallen in love with the notion of yourself in love at eighteen. Oh, you can't marry her, you foolish old darling."

"Your oratory would be more effective if you wouldn't keep whistling to that infernal dog," said Michael. "If this marriage is so terrible, I should have thought you'd have forgotten there were such animals as cocker-spaniels. It's rubbish for you to say you've tried to find something in Lily. You haven't made the slightest attempt. You've criticized her from the moment she entered the house. You're sunk deep already in the horrible selfishness of being happy. A happy marriage is the most devastating joint egotism in the world. Damn it, Stella, when you were making a fool of yourself with half the men in Europe, I didn't talk as you've been talking to me."

"No, you were always very cautiously fraternal," said Stella. "Ah, no, I won't say bitter things, for, Michael, I adore you; and you'll break my heart if you marry this girl."

"You won't do anything of the kind," he contradicted. "You'll be whistling to spaniels all the time."

"Michael, it's really unkind of you to try and make me laugh, when I'm feeling so wretched about you."

"It's all fine for you to sneer at Lily," said Michael. "But I can remember your coming back from Vienna and crying all day in your room over some man who'd made a fool of you. *You* looked pretty flabby then."

"How dare you remind me of that?" Stella cried, in a fury. "How dare you? How dare you?"

"You brought it on yourself," said Michael coldly.

"You're going to pieces already under the influence of that girl. Marry her, then! But don't come to me for sympathy, when she's forced you to drag yourself through the divorce court."

"No, I shall take care not to come to you for anything ever again," said Michael bitterly. "Unless it's for advice when I want to buy a spaniel."

They had turned again in the direction of the Hall, and over the windy fields they walked silently. Michael was angry with himself for having referred to that Vienna time. After all, it had been the only occasion on which he had seen Stella betray a hint of weakness; besides, she had always treated him generously in the matter of confidences. He looked sidelong at her, but she walked on steadily, and he wondered if she would tell Alan that they had been nearer to quarreling than so far they had ever been. Perhaps this sort of thing was inevitable with marriage. Chains of sympathy and affection forged to last eternally were smashed by marriage in a moment. He had heard nothing said about Stella's music lately. Was that also to vanish on account of marriage? The sooner he and Lily left Hardingham, the better. He supposed he ought to suggest going immediately. But Lily would be a problem until he could find a place for her to live, and someone to chaperone her. They would be married next month, and he would take her abroad. He would be able to see her at last in some of the places where in days gone by he had dreamed of seeing her.

"I suppose you wouldn't object to keeping Lily here two or three days more, while I find a place in town?" said Michael. It only struck him when the request was out how much it sounded like asking for a favor. Stella would despise him more than ever.

"Michael," Stella exclaimed, turning round and stopping in his path. "Once more I beg you to give up this idea of marriage. Surely you can realize how deeply I feel about it, when even after what you said I'm willing actually to plead with you. It's intolerable to think of you tied to her!"

"It's too late," said Michael. "I must marry her. Not for any reasons that the world would consider reasons," he went on. "But because I want to marry her. The least you can do for me is to pretend to support me before the world."

"I won't, I won't, I won't! It's all wrong. She's all wrong. Her people are all wrong. Why, even Alan remembers them as dreadful, and you know how casual he is about people he doesn't like. He usually flings them out of his mind at once."

"Oh, Alan's amazing in every way," said Michael. He longed to say that he and Lily would go by the first train possible, but he dreaded so much the effect of bringing her back to London without any definite place to which she could go, that he was willing to leave her here for a few days, if she would stay. He hated himself for doing this, but the problems of marriage and Lily were growing unwieldy. He wished now that he had asked his mother to come back, so that he could have taken Lily to Cheyne Walk. It was stupid to let himself be caught unprepared like this. After all, perhaps it would be a good thing to leave Lily and Stella together for a bit. As he was going to marry her and as he could not face the possibility of quarreling with Stella finally, it would be better to pocket his pride.

Suddenly Stella caught hold of his arm.

"Look here," she said. "You absurd old Quixote, listen. I'm going to do all in my power to stop your marrying Lily. But meanwhile go up to town and leave her here. I promise to declare a truce of a fortnight, if you'll promise me not to marry her until the middle of April. By a truce I mean that I'll be charming to her and take no steps to influence her to give you up. But after the fortnight it must be war, even if you win in the end and marry her."

"Does that mean we should cease to be on speaking terms?"

"Oh, no, of course; as a matter of fact, if you marry her, I suppose we shall all settle down together and be great friends, until she lands you in the divorce court with half a dozen co-respondents. Then you'll come and live with us at Hardingham, a confirmed cynic and the despair of all the eligible young women in the neighborhood."

290

"I wish you wouldn't talk like that about Lily," said Michael, frowning.

"The truce has begun," Stella declared. "For a fortnight I'll be an angel."

Just before dusk was falling, the gale died away, and Michael persuaded Lily to come for a walk with him. Almost unconsciously he took her to the wood where he and Stella had talked so angrily in the morning. Chaffinches flashed their silver wings about them in the fading light.

"Lily, you look adorable in this glade," he told her. "I believe, if you were a little way off from me, I should think you were a birch tree."

The wood was rosy brown and purple. Every object had taken on rich deeps of quality and color reflected from the March twilight. The body of the missel-thrush flinging his song from the bare oak-bough into the ragged sky, flickered with a magical sublucency. Michael found some primroses and brought them to Lily.

"These are for you, you tall tall primrose of a girl. Listen, will you let me leave you for a very few days so that I can find the house you're going to live in? Will you not be lonely?"

"I like to have you with me always," she murmured.

He was intoxicated by so close an avowal of love from lips that were usually mute.

"We shall be married in a month," he cried. "Can you smell violets?"

"Something sweet I smell."

But it was getting too dusky in the coppice to find these violets themselves twilight-hued, and they turned homeward across the open fields. Birds were flying to the coverts, linnets mostly, in twittering companies.

"These eves of early Spring are like swords," Michael exclaimed.

"Like what?" Lily asked, smiling at his exaggeration.

"Like swords. They seem to cut one through and through with their sharpness and sweetness."

"Oh, you mean it's cold," she said. "Take my arm."

"Well, I meant rather more than that, really," Michael laughed. But because she had offered him her arm he forgot at once how far she had been from following his thoughts.

Michael went up to London after dinner. He left Lily curled up before the fire presumably quite content to stay at Hardingham.

"Not more than a fortnight, mind," were Stella's last words.

He went to see Maurice next morning to get the benefit of his advice about possible places in which to live. Maurice was in his element.

"Of course there really are very few good places. Cheyne Walk and Grosvenor Road, the Albany, parts of Hampstead and Campden Hill, Kensington Square, one or two streets near the Regent's Canal, Adelphi Terrace, the Inns of Court and Westminster. Otherwise, London is impossible. But you're living in Cheyne Walk now. Why do you want to move from there?"

Michael made up his mind to take Maurice into his confidence. He supposed that of all his friends he would be as likely as any to be sympathetic. Maurice was delighted by his description of Lily, so much delighted, that he accepted her as a fact without wanting to know who she was or where Michael had met her.

"By Jove, I must hurry up and find my girl. But I don't think I'm desperately keen to get married yet. I vote for a house near the Canal, if we can find the right one."

That afternoon they set out.

They changed their minds and went to Hampstead first, where Maurice was very anxious to take a large Georgian house with a garden of about fifteen acres. He offered to move himself and Castleton from Grosvenor Road in order to occupy one of the floors, and he was convinced that the stable would be very useful if they wanted to start a printing press.

"Yes, but we don't want to start a printing press," Michael objected. "And really, Mossy, I think twenty-three bedrooms more than one servant can manage."

It was with great reluctance that Maurice gave up the idea of this house, and he was so much depressed by the prospect of considering anything less huge that he declared Hampstead was impossible, and they went off to Regent's Park.

"I don't think you're likely to find anything so good as that house," Maurice said gloomily. "In fact, I know you won't. I wish I could afford to take it myself. I should, like a shot. Castleton could be at the Temple just as soon from there."

"I don't see why he should bother about the Temple," said Michael. "That house was rather bigger."

"You'll never find another house like it," Maurice prophesied. "Look at this neighborhood we're driving through now. Impossible to live here!"

They were in the Hampstead Road.

"I haven't any intention of doing so," Michael laughed. "But there remains the neighborhood of the canal, the neighborhood you originally suggested. Hampstead was an afterthought."

"Wonderful house!" Maurice sighed. "I shall always regret you didn't take it."

However, when they had paid off the cab, he became interested by the new prospect; and they wandered for a while, peering through fantastic railings at houses upon the steep banks of the canal, houses that seemed to have been stained to a sad green by the laurels planted close around them. Nothing feasible for a lodging was discovered near Regent's Park; and they crossed St. John's Wood and Maida Vale, walking on until they reached a point where at the confluence of two branches the canal became a large triangular sheet of water. Occupying the whole length of the base of this triangle and almost level with the water, stood the garden of a very large square house.

"There's a curious place," said Michael. "How on earth does one get at it?"

They followed the road, which was considerably higher than the level of the canal, and found that the front door was reached by an entrance down a flight of steps.

"Ararat House," Michael read.

"Flat to let," Maurice read.

"I think this looks rather promising," said Michael.

It was an extraordinary pile, built in some Palladian nightmare. A portico of dull crimson columns ran round three sides of the house, under a frieze of bearded masks. The windows were all very large, and so irregularly placed as completely to destroy the classic illusion. The stucco had been painted a color that was neither pink nor cream nor buff, but a mixture of all three; and every bit of space left by the windows was filled with banderoles of illegible inscriptions and with plaster garlands, horns, lyres, urns, and Grecian helmets. There must have been half an acre of garden round it, a wilderness of shrubs and rank grass with here and there a dislustered conservatory. The house would have seemed uninhabitable save for the announcement of the flat to be let, which was painted on a board roped to one of the columns.

They descended the steps and pressed a bell marked Housekeeper. Yes, there was a flat to let on the ground floor; in fact, the whole of the ground floor with the exception of this part of the hall and the rooms on either side. The housekeeper threw her apron over her shoulder like a plaid and unlocked a door in a wooden partition that divided the flat called Number One from the rest of Ararat House.

They passed through and examined the two gaunt bedrooms: one of them had an alcove, which pleased Michael very much. He decided that without much difficulty it could be made to resemble a Carpaccio interior. The dining-room was decorated with Spanish leather and must have been very brilliantly lit by the late tenants, for everywhere from the ceiling and walls electric wires protruded like asps. There was also a murky kitchen; and finally the housekeeper led the way through double doors into the drawing-room.

As soon as he had stepped inside, Michael was sure that he and Lily must live here.

It was a room that recalled at the first glance one of those gigantic saloons in ancient Venetian palaces; but as he looked about him he decided that any assignment in known topography was absurd. It was a room at once for Werther, for Taglioni, for the nocturnes of Chopin and the cameos of Théophile Gautier. Beckford might have filled it with orient gewgaws; Barbey d'Aurevilly could have strutted here; and in a corner Villiers de l'Isle Adam might have sat fiercely. The room was a tatterdemalion rococo barbarized more completely by gothic embellishments that nevertheless gave it the atmosphere of the fantasts with whom Michael had identified it.

"But this is like a scene in a pantomime," Maurice exclaimed.

It was indeed like a scene in a pantomime, and a proscenium was wanted to frame suitably the effect of those fluted pillars that supported the ceiling with their groined arches. The traceries of the latter were gilded, and the spaces between were painted with florid groups of nymphs and cornucopias. At either end of the room were large fireplaces fructuated with marble pears and melons, and the floor was a parquet of black and yellow lozenges.

"It's hideous," Maurice exclaimed.

The housekeeper stood aside, watching impersonally.

"Hideous but rather fascinating," Michael said. "Look at the queer melancholy light, and look at the view."

It was, after all, the view which gave the character of romance to the room. Eight French windows, whose shutters one by one the housekeeper had opened while they were talking, admitted a light that was much subdued by the sprays of glossy evergreen outside. Seen through their leaves, the garden appeared to be a green twilight in which the statues and baskets of chipped and discolored stone had an air of overthrown magnificence. The housekeeper opened one of the windows, and they walked out into the wilderness, where ferns were growing on rockeries of slag and old tree-stumps; where the paths were smeared with bright green slime, with moss and sodden vegetation. They came to a wider path running by the bank of the canal, and, pausing here, they pondered the sheet of dead water where two swans were gliding slowly round an islet and where the reflections of the house beyond lay still and deep everywhere along the edge. The distant cries of London floated sharply down the air; smuts were falling perpetually; the bitter March air diffused in a dull sparkle tasted of the city's breath: the circling of the swans round their islet made everything else the more immotionable.

"In summer this will be wonderful," Michael predicted.

"On summer nights those swans will be swimming about among the stars," Maurice said.

"Except that they'll probably have retired to bed," Michael pointed out.

"I wonder if they build their nests on chimney-tops like storks," Maurice laughed.

"Let's ask the housekeeper," Michael said solemnly.

They went back into the drawing-room, and more than ever did it seem exactly the room one would expect to enter after pondering that dead water without.

"Who lives in the other flats?" Michael inquired of the housekeeper.

"There's four others," she began. "Up above there's Colonel and Mrs...."

"I see," Michael interrupted. "Just ordinary people. Do they ever go out? Or do they sit and peer at the water all day from behind strange curtains?"

The housekeeper stared at him.

"They play tennis and croquet a good deal in the summer, sir. The courts is on the other side of the house. Mr. Gartside is the gentleman to see about the flat."

She gave Michael the address, and that afternoon he settled to take Number One, Ararat House.

"It absolutely was made to set her off," he told Maurice. "You wait till I've furnished it as it ought to be furnished."

"And we'll have amazing fêtes aqueuses in the summer," Maurice declared. "We'll buy a barge and—why, of course—the canal flows into the Thames at Grosvenor Road."

"Underground—like the Styx," said Michael, nodding.

"Of course, it's going to be wonderful. We must never visit each other except by water."

"Like splendid dead Venetians," said Michael.

The fortnight of Lily's stay at Hardingham was spent by him and Maurice in a fever of decoration. Michael bought oval mirrors of Venetian glass; oblong mirrors crowned with gilt griffins and scallops; small round mirrors in frames of porcelain garlanded with flowerbuds; so many mirrors that the room became even more mysteriously vast. The walls were hung with brocades of gold and philamot and pomona green. There were slim settees the color of ivory, with cushions of primrose and lemon satin, of cinnamon and canary citron and worn russet silks. Over the parquet was a great gray Aubusson carpet with a design of monstrous roses as deep as damsons or burgundy; and from the ceiling hung two chandeliers of cut glass.

"You know," said Maurice seriously, "she'll have to be very beautiful to carry this off."

"She is very beautiful," said Michael. "And there's room for her to walk about here. She'll move about this room as wonderfully as those swans upon the canal."

"Michael, what's happened to you? You're becoming as eccentric as me." Maurice looked at him rather jealously. "And, I say, do you really want me to come with you to King's Cross to-morrow afternoon?"

Michael nodded.

"After you've helped to gather together this room, you deserve to see the person we've done it for."

"Yes, but look here. Who's going to stay in the flat with her? You can't leave her alone until you're married. As you told me the story, it sounded very romantic; but if she's going to be your wife, you've got to guard her reputation."

Michael had never given Maurice more than a slight elaboration of the tale which had served for Stella; and he thought how much more romantic Maurice would consider the affair if he knew the whole truth. He felt inclined to tell him, but he doubted his ability to keep it to himself.

"I thought of getting hold of some elderly woman," he said.

"That's all very well, but you ought to have been doing it all this time."

"You don't know anybody?"

"I? Great scott, no!"

They were walking toward Chelsea, and presently Maurice had to leave him for an appointment.

"To-morrow afternoon then at King's Cross," he said, and jumped on an omnibus.

Michael walked along in a quandary. Whom on earth could he get to stay with Lily? Would it not be better to marry at once? But that would involve breaking his promise to Stella. If he asked Mrs. Gainsborough, it would mean Sylvia knowing where Lily was. If, on the other hand, he should employ a strange woman, Lily might dislike her. Could he ask Mrs. Ross to come up to town? No, of course, that was absurd. It looked as if he would have to ask Mrs. Gainsborough. Or why not ask Sylvia herself? In that case, why establish Lily at Ararat House before they were married? This marriage had seemed so very easy an achievement; but slowly it was turning into an insoluble complex. He might sound Sylvia upon her attitude. It would enormously simplify everything if she would consent; and if she consented she would, he believed, play fair with him. The longer Michael thought about it, the more it seemed the safest course to call in Sylvia's aid. He was almost hailing a hansom to go to Tinderbox Lane, when he realized how foolish it would be not to try to sever Lily completely from the life she had been leading in Sylvia's company. Not even ought he to expose her to the beaming laxity of Mrs. Gainsborough.

Michael had reached Notting Hill Gate, and, still pondering the problem which had destroyed half the pleasure of the enterprise, he caught sight of a Registry for servants. Why not employ two servants, two of the automatons who simplified life as it was simplified in Cheyne Walk? Then he remembered that he had forgotten to make any attempt to equip the kitchen. Surely Lily would be able to help with that. He entered the Registry and interviewed a severe woman wearing glasses, who read in a sing-song the virtues of a procession of various automatons seeking situations as cooks and housemaids.

"What wages do you wish to give?"

"Oh, the usual wages," Michael said. "But I rather want these servants to-day."

He made an appointment to interview half a dozen after lunch. He chose the first two that presented themselves, and told them to come round to Ararat House. Here he threw himself on their mercy and begged them to make a list of what was wanted in the kitchen. They gave notice on the spot, and Michael rushed off to the Registry again. To the severe woman in glasses he explained the outlines of the situation and made her promise to suit him by to-morrow at midday. She suggested a capable housekeeper; and next morning a hard-featured, handsome woman very well dressed in the fashion of about 1892 arrived at Ararat House. She undertook to find someone to help, and also to procure at once the absolute necessities for the kitchen. Miss Harper was a great relief to Michael, though he did not think he liked her very much; and he made up his mind to get rid of her, as soon as some sort of domestic comfort was perceptible. Lily would arrive about four o'clock, and he drove off to King's Cross to meet her. He felt greatly excited by the prospect of introducing her to Maurice, who for a wonder was punctually waiting for him on the platform.

Lily evidently liked Maurice, and Michael was rather disappointed when he said he could not come back with them to assist at the first entry into Ararat House. Maurice had certainly given him to understand that he was free this afternoon.

"Look in at Grosvenor Road on your way home to-night," said Maurice. "Or will you be very late?"

"Oh, no, I shan't be late," Michael answering, flushing. He had a notion that Maurice was implying a suspicion of him by his invitation. It seemed as if he were testing his behavior.

Lily liked the rooms; and, although she thought the Carpaccio bedroom was a little bare, it was soon strewn with her clothes, and made thereby inhabitable.

"And of course," said Michael, "you've got to buy lots and lots of clothes this fortnight. How much do you want to spend? Two hundred—three hundred pounds?"

The idea of buying clothes on such a scale of extravagance seemed to delight her, and she kissed him, he thought almost for the first time, in mere affection without a trace of passion. Michael felt happy that he had so much money for her to spend, and he was glad that no one had been given authority to interfere with his capital. There flashed through his mind a comparison of himself with the Chevalier des Grieux, and, remembering how soon that money had come to an end, he was glad that Lily would not be exposed to the temptation which had ruined Manon.

"And do you like Miss Harper?" he inquired.

"Yes, she seems all right."

They went out to dine in town, and came back about eleven to find the flat looking wonderfully settled. Michael confessed how much he had forgotten to order, but Lily talked of her dresses and took no interest in household affairs.

"I think I ought to go now," said Michael.

"Oh, no, stay a little longer."

But he would not, feeling the violent necessity to impress upon her as much as possible, during this fortnight before they were married, how important were the conventions of life, even when it was going to be lived in so strange a place as Ararat House.

"Oh, you're going now?" said Miss Harper, looking at him rather curiously.

"I shall be round in the morning. You'll finish making the lists of what you still want?"

Michael felt very deeply plunged into domestic arrangements, as he drove to Grosvenor Road.

Maurice was sitting up for him, but Castleton had gone to bed.

"Look here, old chap," Maurice began at once, "you can't possibly marry that girl."

Michael frowned.

"You too?"

"I know all about her," Maurice went on. "I've never actually met her, but I recognized her at once. Even if you did know her people five years ago, you ought to have taken care to find out what had happened in between. As a matter of fact, I happen to know a man who's had an affair with her—a painter called Walker. Ronnie Walker. He's often up here. You're bound to meet him some time."

"Not at all, if I never come here again," said Michael, in a cold rage.

"It's no use for you to be angry with me," said Maurice. "I should be a rotten friend, if I didn't warn you."

"Oh, go to hell!" said Michael, and he marched out of the studio.

"I'll die first," retorted Maurice, grinning.

Maurice came on the landing and called, begging him to come up and not to be so hasty, but Michael paid no attention.

"So much for 422 Grosvenor Road," he said, slamming the big front door behind him. He heard Maurice calling to him from the window, but he walked on without turning his head.

It was a miserable coincidence that one of his friends should know about her. It was a disappointment, but it could not be helped. If Maurice chattered about a disastrous marriage, why, other friends would have to be dropped in the same way. After all, he had been aware from the first moment of his resolve that this sort of thing was bound to happen. It left him curiously indifferent.

A week passed. There were hundreds of daffodils blooming in the garden round Ararat House; and April bringing an unexpected halcyon was the very April of the poets whose verses haunted that great rococo room. Every day Michael went with Lily to dressmakers and worshiped her taste. Every day he bought her old pieces of jewelry, old fans, or old silver, or pots of purple hyacinths. He was just conscious that it was London and the prime of the Spring; but mostly he lived in the enchantment of her presence. Often they walked up and down the still deserted garden, by the edge of the canal. The swans used to glide nearer to them, waiting for bread to be thrown; and Lily would stand with her hair in a stream of sunlight and her arms moving languidly like the necks of the birds she was feeding. Nor was she less graceful in the long luminous dusks under the young moon and the yellow evening star that were shining upon them as they walked by the edge of the water.

For a week Michael lived in a city that was become a mere background to the swoons and fevers of love. He knew that round him houses blinked in the night and that chimney-smoke curled upward in the morning; that people paced the streets; that there was a thunder of far-off traffic; that London was possessed by April. But the heart of life was in this room, when the candles were lit in the chandeliers and he could see a hundred Lilies in the mirrors. It seemed wrong to leave her at midnight, to leave that room so perilously golden with the golden stuffs and candle-flames. It seemed unfair to surprise Miss Harper by going away at midnight, when so easily he could have stayed. Yet every night he went away, however hard it was to leave Lily in her black dress, to leave in the mirrors those hundred Lilies that drowsily were not forbidding him to stay. Or when she stood under the portico sleepily resting in his arms, it was difficult to let her turn back alone. How close were their kisses wrapped in that velvet moonlessness! This was no London that he knew, this scented city of Spring, this tropic gloom, this mad innominate cavern that engorged them. The very stars were melting in the water of the canal: the earth bedewed with fevers of the Spring was warm as blood: why should he forsake her each night of this week? Yet every midnight when the heavy clocks buzzed and clamored, Michael left her, saying that May would come, and June, and another April, when she would have been his a year.

The weather veered back in the second week of the fortnight to rawness and wet. Yet it made no difference to Michael; for he was finding these days spent with Lily so full of romance that weather was forgotten. They could not walk in the garden and watch the swans: of nothing else did the weather deprive him.

Two days before the marriage was to take place, Mrs. Fane arrived back from the South of France. Michael was glad to see her, for he was so deeply infatuated with Lily that his first emotion was of pleasure in the thought of being able now to bring her to see his mother, and of taking his mother to see her in Ararat House among those chandeliers and mirrors.

"Why didn't you wire me to say you were coming?" he asked.

"I came because Stella wrote to me."

Michael frowned, and his mother went on:

"It wasn't very thoughtful of you to let me know about your marriage through her. I think you might have managed to write to me about it yourself."

Michael had been so much wrapped up in his arrangements, and apart from them so utterly engrossed in his secluded life with Lily during the past ten days, that it came upon him with a shock to realize that his mother might be justified in thinking that he had treated her very inconsiderately.

"I'm sorry. It was wrong of me," he admitted. "But life has been such a whirl lately that I've somehow taken for granted the obvious courtesies. Besides, Stella was so very unfair to Lily that it rather choked me off taking anybody else into my confidence. And, mother, why do you begin on the subject at once, before you've even taken your things off?"

She flung back her furs and regarded him tragically.

"Michael, how can you dare to think of such trivialities when you are standing at the edge of this terrible step?"

"Oh, I think I'm perfectly level-headed," he said, "even on the brink of disaster."

"Such a dreadful journey from Cannes! I wish I'd come back in March as I meant to. But Mrs. Carruthers was ill, and I couldn't very well leave her. She's always nervous in lifts, and hates the central-heating. I did not sleep a moment, and a most objectionable couple of Germans in the next compartment of the wagons-lits used all the water in the washing-place. So very annoying, for one never expects foreigners to think about washing. Oh, yes, a dreadful night and all because of you, and now you ask most cruelly why I don't take my things off."

"There wasn't any need for you to worry yourself," he said hotly. "Stella had no business to scare you with her prejudices."

"Prejudices!" his mother repeated. "Prejudice is a very mild word for what she feels about this dreadful girl you want to marry."

"But it is prejudice," Michael insisted. "She knows nothing against her."

"She knows a great deal."

"How?" he demanded incredulously.

"You'd better read her letter to me. And I really must go and take off these furs. It's stifling in London. So very much hotter than the Riviera."

Mrs. Fane left him with Stella's letter.

LONG'S HOTEL,
April 9.

Darling Mother,

When you get this you must come at once *to London. You are the only person who can save Michael from marrying the most impossible creature imaginable. He had a stupid love-affair with her, when he was eighteen, and I think she treated him badly even then—I remember his being very upset about it in the summer before my first concert. Apparently he rediscovered her this winter, and for some reason or other wants to* marry *her now. He brought her down to Hardingham, and I saw then that she was a minx. Alan remembers her mother as a dreadful woman who tried to make love to him. Imagine Alan at eighteen being pursued!*

Of course, I tackled Michael about her, and we had rather a row about it. We kept her at Hardingham for a month (a fortnight by herself), and we were bored to death by her. She had nothing to say, and nothing to do except look at herself in the glass. I had declared war on the marriage from the moment she left, but I had only a fortnight to stop it. I was rather in a difficulty because I knew nothing definite against her, though I was sure that if she wasn't a bad lot already, she would be later on. I wrote first of all to Maurice Avery, who told me that she'd had a not at all reputable affair with a painter friend of his. It seems, however, that he had already spoken to Michael about this and that Michael walked out of the house in a rage. Then I came up to town with Alan and saw Wedderburn, who knew nothing about her and hadn't seen Michael for months. Then we got hold of Lonsdale. He has apparently met her at Covent Garden, and I'm perfectly sure that he has actually been away with her himself. Though, of course, he was much too polite to tell me so. He was absolutely horrified when he heard about her and Michael. I asked him to tell Michael anything he knew against her, but he didn't see how he could. He said he wouldn't have the heart. I told him it was his duty, but he said he wouldn't be able to bear the sight of Michael's face when he told him. Of course, the poor darling knows nothing about her. You must come at once to London and talk to him yourself. You've no time to lose. I'll meet you if you send me a wire. I've no influence over Michael any more. You're the only person who can stop it. He's so sweet about her. She's rather lovely to look at, I must say. Lots of love from Alan and from me.

Your loving
Stella.

Michael was touched by Lonsdale's attitude. It showed, he thought, an exquisite sensitiveness, and he was grateful for it. Stella had certainly been very active: but he had foreseen all of this. Nothing was going to alter his determination. He waited gloomily for his mother to come down. Of all antagonists she would be the hardest to combat in argument, because he was debarred from referring to so much that had weighed heavily with him in his decision. His mother was upstairs such a very short time that Michael realized with a smile how deeply she must have been moved. Nothing but this marriage of his had ever brought her downstairs so rapidly from taking off her things.

"Have you read Stella's letter?" she asked.

He nodded.

"Well, of course you see that the whole business must be stopped at once. It's dreadful for you to hear all these things, and I know you must be suffering, dearest boy; but you ought to be obliged to Stella and not resent her interference."

"I see that you feel bound to apologize for her," Michael observed.

"Now, that is so bitter."

He shrugged his shoulders.

"I feel rather bitter that she should come charging up to town to find out things I know already."

"Michael! You knew about Lonsdale?"

"I didn't know about him in particular, but I knew that there had been people. That's one of the reasons I'm going to marry her."

"But you'll lose all your friends. It would be impossible for you to go on knowing Lonsdale, for instance."

"Marriage seems to destroy friendships in any case," Michael said. "You couldn't have a better example of that than Stella and Alan. I daresay I shall be able to make new friends."

"But, darling boy," she said pleadingly, "your position will be so terribly ambiguous. Here you are with everything that you can possibly want, with any career you choose open to you. And you let yourself be dragged down by this horrible creature!"

"Mother, believe me, you're getting a very distorted idea of Lily. She's beautiful, you know; and if she's not so clever as Stella, I'm rather glad of it. I don't think I want a clever wife. At any rate, she hasn't committed the sin of being common. She won't disgrace you outwardly, and if Stella hadn't gone round raking up all this abominable information about her you would have liked her very much."

"My dearest boy, you are very young, but you surely aren't too young to know that it's impossible to marry a woman whose past is not without reproach."

"But, mother, you ..." he stopped himself abruptly, and looked out of the window in embarrassment. Yet his mother seemed quite unconscious that she was using a weapon which could be turned against herself.

"Will nothing persuade you? Oh, why did Dick Prescott kill himself? I knew at the time that something like this would happen. You won't marry her, you won't, will you?"

"Yes, mother. I'm going to," he said coldly.

"But why so impetuously?" she asked. "Why won't you wait a little time?"

"There's no object in waiting while Stella rakes up a few more facts."

"If only your father were alive!" she exclaimed. "It would have shocked him so inexpressibly."

"He felt so strongly the unwisdom of marriage, didn't he?" Michael said, and wished he could have bitten his tongue out.

She had risen from her chair, and seemed to tower above him in tragical and heroic dignity of reproach:

"I could never have believed you would say such a thing to me."

"I'm awfully sorry," he murmured. "It was inexcusable."

"Michael," she pleaded, coming to him sorrowfully, "won't you give up this marriage?"

He was touched by her manner so gently despairing after his sneer.

"Mother, I must keep faith with myself."

"Only with yourself? Then she doesn't care for you? And you're not thinking of *her?*"

"Of course she cares for me."

"But she'd get over it almost at once?"

"Perhaps," he admitted.

"Do you trust her? Do you believe she will be able to be a good woman?"

"That will be my look-out," he said impatiently. "If she fails, it will be my fault. It's always the man's fault. Always."

"Very well," said his mother resignedly. "I can say no more, can I? You must do as you like."

The sudden withdrawal of her opposition softened him as nothing else would have done. He compared the sweetness of her resignation with his own sneer of a minute ago. He felt anxious to do something that would show his penitence.

"Mother, I hate to wound you. But I must be true to what I have worked out for myself. I must marry Lily. Apart from a mad love I have for her, there is a deeper cause, a reason that's bound up with my whole theory of behavior, my whole attitude toward existence. I could not back out of this marriage."

"Is all your chivalry to be devoted to the service of Lily?" she asked.

He felt grateful to her for the name. When his mother no longer called her "this girl," half his resentment fled. The situation concerned the happiness of human beings again; there were no longer prejudices or abstractions of morality to obscure it.

"Not at all, mother. I would do anything for you."

"Except not marry her."

"That wouldn't be a sacrifice worth making," he argued. "Because if I did that I should destroy myself to myself, and what was left of me wouldn't be a complete Michael. It wouldn't be your son."

"Will you postpone your marriage, say for three months?"

He hesitated. How could he refuse her this?

"Not merely for your own sake," she urged; "but for all our sakes. We shall all see things more clearly and pleasantly, perhaps, in three months' time."

He was conquered by the implication of justice for Lily.

"I won't marry her for three months," he promised.

"And you know, darling boy, the dreadful thing is that I very nearly missed the train owing to the idiocy of the head porter at the hotel."

She was smiling through her tears, and very soon she became her stately self again.

Michael went at once to Ararat House, and told Lily that he had promised his mother to put off their marriage for three months. She pouted over her frocks.

"I wish you'd settled that before. What good will all these dresses be now?"

"You shall have as many more as you want. But will you be happy here without me?"

"Without you? Why are you going away?"

"Because I must, Lily. Because ... oh, dearest girl, can't you see that I'm too passionately in love with you to be able to see you every day and every night as I have been all this fortnight?"

"If you want to go away, of course you must; but I shall be rather dull, shan't I?"

"And shan't I?" he asked.

She looked at him.

"Perhaps."

"I shall write every day to you, and you must write to me."

He held her close and kissed her. Then he hurried away.

Now that he had made the sacrifice to please his mother, he was angry with himself for having done so. He felt that during this coming time of trial he could not bear to see either his mother or Stella. He must be married and fulfill his destiny, and, after that, all would be well. He was enraged with his weakness, wondering where he could go to avoid the people who had brought it about.

Suddenly Michael thought he would like to see Clere Abbey again, and he turned into Paddington Station to find out if there were a train that would take him down into Berkshire at once.

CHAPTER VIII

SEEDS OF POMEGRANATE

It was almost dark when Michael reached the little station at the foot of the Downs. He was half inclined to put up at the village inn and arrive at the Abbey in the morning; but he was feeling depressed by the alteration of his plans, and longed to withdraw immediately into the monastic peace. He had bought what he needed for the couple of nights before any luggage could reach him, and he thought that with so little to carry he might as well walk the six miles to the Abbey. He asked when the moon would be up.

"Oh, not much before half-past nine, sir," the porter said.

Michael suddenly remembered that to-morrow was Easter Sunday, and, thinking it would be as well not to arrive too late, in case there should be a number of guests, he managed to get hold of a cart. The wind blew very freshly as they slowly climbed the Downs, and the man who was driving him was very voluble on the subject of the large additions which had been made to the Abbey buildings during the last few years.

"They've put up a grand sort of a lodge—Gatehouse, so some do call it. A bit after the style of the Tower of London, I've heard some say."

Michael was glad to think that Dom Cuthbert's plans seemed to be coming to perfection in their course. How long was it since he and Chator were here? Eight or nine years; now Chator was a priest, and himself had done nothing.

The Abbey Gatehouse was majestic in the darkness, and the driver pealed the great bell with a portentous clangor. Michael recognized the pock-marked brother who opened the door; but he could not remember his name. He felt it would be rather absurd to ask the monk if he recognized him by this wavering lanthorn-light.

"Is the Reverend—is Dom Cuthbert at the Abbey now?" he asked. "You don't remember me, I expect? Michael Fane. I stayed here one Autumn eight or nine years ago."

The monk held up the lanthorn and stared at him.

"The Reverend Father is in the Guest Room now," said Brother Ambrose. Michael had suddenly recalled his name.

"Do you think I shall be able to stay here to-night? Or have you a lot of guests for Easter?"

"We can always find room," said Brother Ambrose. Michael dismissed his driver and followed the monk along the drive.

Dom Cuthbert knew him at once, and seemed very glad that he had come to the Abbey.

"You can have a cell in the Gatehouse. Our new Gatehouse. It's copied from the one at Cerne Abbas in Dorsetshire. Very beautiful. Very beautiful."

Michael was introduced to the three or four guests, all types of ecclesiastical laymen, who had been talking with the Abbot. The Compline bell rang almost at once, and the Office was still held in the little chapel of mud and laths built by the hands of the monks.

Keep me as the apple of an eye.

Hide me in the shadow of thy
wing.

Here was worship unhampered by problems of social behavior: here was peace.

Lying awake that night in his cell; watching the lattices very luminous in the moonlight; hearing the April wind in the hazel coppice, Michael tried to reach a perspective of his life these nine months since Oxford, but sleep came to him and pacified all confusions. He went to Mass next morning, but did not make his Communion, because he had a feeling that he could only have done so under false pretenses. There was no reason why he should have felt thus, he assured himself; but this morning there had fallen upon him at the moment a dismaying chill. He went for a walk on the Downs, over the great green spaces that marked no season save in the change of the small flowers blowing in their turf. He wondered if he would be able to find the stones he had erected that July day when he first came here with Chator. He found what, as far as he could remember, was the place; and he also found a group of stones that might have been the ruins of his little monument. More remarkable than old stones now seemed to him a Pasque anemone colored a sharp cold violet. It curiously reminded him of the evening in March when he had walked with Lily in the wood at Hardingham.

The peace of last night vanished in a dread of the future: Michael's partial surrender to his mother cut at his destiny with ominous stroke. He was in a turmoil of uncertainty, and afraid to find himself out here on these Downs with so little achieved behind him in the city. He hurried back to the Abbey and wrote a wild letter to Lily, declaring his sorrow for leaving her, urging her to be patient, protesting a feverish adoration. He wrote also to Miss Harper a hundred directions for Lily's entertainment while he was away. He wrote to Nigel Stewart, begging him to look after Barnes. All the time he had a sense of being pursued and haunted; an intolerable idea that he was the quarry of an evil chase. He could not stay at the Abbey any longer: he was being rejected by the spirit of the place.

Dom Cuthbert was disappointed when he said he must go.

"Stay at least to-night," he urged, and Michael gave way.

He did not sleep at all that night. The alabaster image of the Blessed Virgin kept turning to a paper thing, kept nodding at him like a zany. He seemed to hear the Gatehouse bell clanging hour after hour. He felt more deeply sunk in darkness than ever in Leppard Street. At daybreak he dressed and fled through the woods, trampling under foot the primroses limp with dew. He hurried faster and faster across the Downs; and when the sun was up, he was standing on the platform of the railway station. To-day he ought to have married Lily.

At Paddington, notwithstanding all that he had suffered in the parting, unaccountably to himself he did not want to turn in the direction of Ararat House. It puzzled him that he should drive so calmly to Cheyne Walk.

"I think my temperature must have been a point or two up last night," was the explanation he gave himself of what already seemed mere sleeplessness.

Michael found his mother very much worried by his disappearance; she had assumed that he had broken his promise. He consoled her, but excused himself from staying with her in town.

"You mustn't ask too much of me," he said.

"No, no, dearest boy; I'm glad for you to go away, but where will you go?"

He thought he would pay an overdue visit to Cobble Place.

Mrs. Ross and Mrs. Carthew were delighted to see him, and he felt as he always felt at Cobble Place the persistent tranquillity which not the greatest inquietude of spirit could long withstand. It was now nearly three years since he had been there, and he was surprised to see how very old Mrs. Carthew had grown in that time. This and the active presence of Kenneth, now a jolly boy of nine, were the only changes in the aspect of the household. Michael enjoyed himself in firing Kenneth with a passion for birds' eggs and butterflies, and they went long walks together and made expeditions in the canoe.

Yet every day when Michael sat down to write to Lily, he almost wrote to say he was coming to London as soon as his letter. Her letters to him, written in a sprawling girlish hand, were always very much alike.

1 ARARAT HOUSE,
ISLAND ROAD, W.

My dear,

Come back soon. I'm getting bored. Miss Harper isn't bad. Can't write a long letter because this nib is awful. Kisses.

Your loving

Lily.

This would stand for any of them.

May month had come in: Michael and Kenneth were finding whitethroats' nests in the nettle-beds of the paddock, before a word to Mrs. Ross was said about the marriage.

"Stella has written to me about it," she told him.

They were sitting in the straggling wind-frayed orchard beyond the stream: lamps were leaping: apple-blossom stippled the grass: Kenneth was chasing Orange Tips up the slope toward Grogg's Folly.

"Stella has been very busy all round," said Michael. "I suppose according to her I'm going to marry an impossible creature. Creature is as far as she usually gets in particular description of Lily."

"She certainly wasn't very complimentary about your choice," Mrs. Ross admitted.

"I wish somebody could understand that it doesn't necessarily mean that I'm mad because I'm going to marry a beautiful girl who isn't very clever."

"But I gathered from Stella," Mrs. Ross said, "that her past ... Michael, you must be very tolerant of me if I upset you, because we happen to be sitting just where I was stupid and unsympathetic once before. You see what an impression that made on me. I actually remember the very place."

"She probably has done things in the past," said Michael. "But she's scarcely twenty-three yet, and I love her. Her past becomes a trifle. Besides, I was in love with her six years ago, and I—well, six years ago I was rather thoughtless very often. I don't want you to think that

I'm going to marry her now from any sense of duty. I love her. At the same time when people argue that she's not the correct young Miss they apparently expect me to marry, I'm left unmoved. Pasts belong to men as well as to women."

Mrs. Ross nodded slowly. Kenneth came rushing up, shouting that he had caught a frightfully rare butterfly. Michael looked at it.

"A female Orange Tip," was the verdict.

"But isn't that frightfully rare?"

Michael shook his head.

"No rarer than the males; but you don't notice them, that's all."

Kenneth retired to find some more.

"And you're sure you'll be happy with her?" Mrs. Ross asked.

"As sure as I am that I shall be happy with anybody. I ought to be married to her by now. This delay that I've so weakly allowed isn't going to effect much."

Michael sighed. He had meant to be in Provence this month of May.

"But the delay can't do any harm," Mrs. Ross pointed out. "At any rate, it will enable you to feel more sure of yourself, and more sure of her, too."

"I don't know," said Michael doubtfully. "My theory has always been that if a thing's worth doing at all, it's worth doing at once."

"And after you're married," she asked, "what are you going to do? Just lead a lazy life?"

"Oh, no; I suppose I shall find some occupation that will keep me out of mischief."

"That sounds a little cynical. Ah, well, I suppose it is a disappointment to me."

"What's a disappointment?"

"I've hoped and prayed so much lately that you would have a vocation...."

"A priest," he interrupted quickly, "It's no good, Mrs. Ross. I have thought of being one, but I'm always put off by the professional side of it. And there are ways of doing what a priest does without being one."

"Of course, I can't agree with you there," she said.

"Well, apart from the sacraments, I mean. Lately I've seen something of the underworld, and I shall think of some way of being useful down there. Already I believe I've done a bit."

They talked of the problems of the underworld and Michael was encouraged by what he fancied was a much greater breadth in her point of view nowadays to speak of things that formerly would have made her gray eyes harden in fastidious disapproval.

"I feel happier about you since this talk," she said. "As long as you won't be content to let your great gift of humanity be wasted, as long as you won't be content to think that in marrying your Lily you have done with all your obligations."

"Oh, no, I shan't feel that. In fact, I shall be all the more anxious to justify myself."

Kenneth came back to importune Michael for a walk as far as Grogg's Folly.

"It's such fun for Kenneth to have you here!" Mrs. Ross exclaimed. "I've never seen him so boisterously happy."

"I used to enjoy myself here just as much as he does," said Michael. "Though perhaps I didn't show it. I always think of myself as rather a dreary little beast when I was a kid."

"On the contrary, you were a most attractive boy; such a wide-eyed little boy," said Mrs. Ross softly, looking back into time. "I've seldom seen you so happy as just before I blew out your candle the first night of your first stay here."

"I say, do come up the hill," interrupted Kenneth despairingly.

"A thousand apologies, my lord," said Michael. "We'll go now."

They did not stop until they reached the tower on the summit.

"When I was your age," Michael told him, "I used to think that I could see the whole of England from here."

"Could you really?" said Kenneth, in admiration. "Could you see any of France, too?"

"I expect so," Michael answered. "I expect really I thought I could see the whole world. Kenneth, what are you going to be when you grow up? A soldier?"

"Yes, if I can—or what is a philosopher?"

"A philosopher philosophizes."

"Does he really? Is that a difficult thing to do, to philosopherize?"

"Yes; it's almost harder to do than to pronounce."

Soon they were tearing down the hill, frightening the larks to right and left of their progress.

The weather grew warmer every day, and at last Mrs. Carthew came out in a wheel-chair to see the long-spurred columbines, claret and gold, watchet, rose and white.

"Really quite a display," she said to Michael. "And so you're to get married?"

He nodded.

"What for?" the old lady demanded, looking at him over her spectacles.

"Well, principally because I want to," Michael answered, after a short pause.

"The best reason," she agreed. "But in your case insufficient, and I'll tell you why—you aren't old enough yet to know what you do want."

"Twenty-three," Michael reminded her.

"Twenty-fiddlesticks!" she snapped. "And isn't there a good deal of opposition?"

"A good deal."

"And no doubt you feel a fine romantical heroical young fellow?"

"Not particularly."

"Well, I'm not going to argue against your marrying her," said Mrs. Carthew. "Because I know quite well that the more I proved you to be wrong, the more you'd be determined to prove *I* was. But I can give you advice about marriage, because I've been married and you haven't. Is she dark? If she's dark, be very cold for a year, and if she doesn't leave you in that time, she'll adore you for the rest of her life."

"But she's fair," said Michael. "Very fair indeed."

"Then beat her. Not actually, of course; but beat her figuratively for a year. If you don't, she'll either be a shrew or a whiner. Both impossible to live with."

"Which did Captain Carthew do to you?" asked Michael, twinkling.

"Neither; I ruled him with a rod of iron."

"But do you think I'm wise to wait like this before marrying her?" Michael asked.

"There's no wisdom in waiting to do an unwise thing."

"You're so sure it is unwise?"

"All marriages are unwise," said Mrs. Carthew sharply. "That's why everybody gets married. For most people it is the only imprudence they have an opportunity of committing. After that, they're permanently cured of rashness, and settle down. There are exceptions, of course: they take to drink. I must say I'm greatly pleased with these long-spurred columbines."

Michael thought she had finished the discussion of his marriage, but suddenly she said:

"I thought I told you to come and see me when you went down from Oxford."

"I ought to have come," Michael agreed rather humbly. He always felt inclined to propitiate the old lady.

"Here we have the lamentable result. Marriage at twenty-three."

"Alan married at twenty-three," he pointed out.

"Two fools don't make a wise-man," said Mrs. Carthew.

"He's very happy."

"He would be satisfied with much less than you, and he has married a delightful girl."

"I'm going to marry a delightful girl."

The old lady made no reply. Nor did she comment again upon his prospect of happiness.

In mid-May, after a visit of nearly a month, Michael left Cobble Place and went to stay at Plashers Mead. Guy Hazlewood was the only friend he still had who could not possibly have come into contact with Lily or her former surroundings. Moreover, Guy was deep in love himself, and he had been very sympathetic when he wrote to Michael about his engagement.

"Do I intrude upon your May idyll?" Michael asked.

"My dear chap, don't be so absurd. But why aren't you married? You're as bad as me."

"Why aren't *you* married?"

"Oh, I don't know," Guy sighed. "Everybody seems to be conspiring to put it off."

They were sitting in Guy's green library. The windows wide open let in across the sound of the burbling stream the warm air of the lucid May night, where bats and owls and evejars flew across the face of the decrescent moon.

"It's this dreamy country in which you live," said Michael.

"What about you? You've let people put off your marriage."

"Only for another two months," Michael explained.

"You see I'm down to one hundred and fifty pounds a year now," Guy muttered. "I can't marry on that, and I can't leave this place, and her people can't afford to make her an allowance. They think I ought to go away and work at journalism. However, I'm not going to worry you with my troubles."

Guy was a good deal with Pauline every day: Michael wrote long letters to Lily and read poetry.

"Browning?" asked Guy one afternoon, looking over Michael's shoulder.

"Yes; The Statue and The Bust."

"Oh, don't remind me of that poem. It haunts me," Guy declared.

A week passed. There was no moon now, and the nights grew warmer. It was weather to make lovers happy, but Guy seemed worried. He would not come for walks with Michael through the dark and scented water-meadows, and Michael used to think that often at night he was meeting Pauline. It made him jealous to imagine them lost in this amaranthine profundity. They were happy now, if through all their lives they should never be happy again. Yet Guy was obviously fretted: he was getting spoiled by good fortune. "And I have had about a fortnight of incomplete happiness," Michael said to himself. Supposing that a calamity fell upon him during this delay. He would never cease to regret his weakness in granting his mother's request: he would hate Stella for having interfered: his life would be miserable forever. Yet what calamity did he fear? In a sudden apprehension, he struck a match and read her last letter:

1 ARARAT HOUSE,
ISLAND ROAD, W.

My dear,

It's getting awfully dull in London. Miss Harper asked me to call her "Mabel." Rather cheek, I thought, don't you think so? But she's really awfully decent. I can't write a long letter because we're going to the Palace. I say, do buck up and come back to London, I'm getting bored. Love and kisses.

Lily.

What's the good of *writing* "kisses"?

What indeed was the good of writing "kisses"? Michael thought, as the match fizzed out in the dewy grass at his feet. It was not fair to treat Lily like this. He had captured her from life with Sylvia, because he had meant to marry her at once. Now he had left her alone in that flat with a woman he did not know at all. Whatever people might say against Lily, she was very patient and trustful. "She must love me a good deal," Michael said. "Or she wouldn't stand this casual treatment."

Pauline came to tea next day with her sisters Margaret and Monica. Michael had an idea that she did not like him very much. She talked shyly and breathlessly to him; and he, embarrassed by her shyness, answered in monosyllables.

"Pauline is rather jealous of you," said Guy that evening, as they sat in the library.

"Jealous of me?" Michael was amazed.

"She has some fantastic idea that you don't approve of our engagement. Of course, I told her what nonsense she was thinking; but she vowed that this afternoon you showed quite plainly your disapproval of her. She insists that you are very cold and severe."

"I'm afraid I was very dull," Michael confessed apologetically. "But I was really envying you and her for being together in May."

"Together!" Guy repeated. "It's the object of everyone in Wychford to keep us apart!"

"Do tell her I'm not cold," Michael begged. "And say how lovely I think her; for really, Guy, she is very lovely and strange. She is a fairy's child."

"She is, she is," Guy said. "Sometimes I'm nearly off my head with the sense of responsibility I have for her happiness. I wonder and wonder until I'm nearly crazed."

"I'm feeling responsible just now about Lily. I've never told you, Guy, but you may hear from other people that I've made what is called a mésalliance. Of course, Lily has been...." He stumbled. He could find no words that would not humiliate himself and her. "Guy, come up with me to-morrow and meet her. It's not fair to leave her like this," he suddenly proclaimed.

"I don't think I can come away."

"Oh, yes, you can. Of course. You must," Michael urged.

"Pauline will be more jealous of you than ever, if I do."

"For one night," Michael pleaded. "I must see her. And you must meet her. Everyone has been so rotten about her, and, Guy, you'll appreciate her. I won't bore you by describing her. You must meet her to-morrow. And the rooms in Ararat House. By Jove, you'll think them wonderful. You should see her in candlelight among the mirrors. Pauline won't mind your coming away with me for a night. We'll stay at Cheyne Walk."

"Well, as a matter of fact, I'm rather hard up just now...."

"Oh, what rot! This is my expedition. And when you've seen her, you must talk to my mother about her. She's so prejudiced against Lily. You will come, won't you?"

Guy nodded a promise, and Michael went off to bed on the excitement of to-morrow's joy.

Guy would not start before the afternoon, and Michael spent the morning under a willow beside the river. It was good to lie staring up at the boughs, and know that every fleecy cloud going by was a cloud nearer to his seeing Lily again.

Michael and Guy arrived at Paddington about five o'clock.

"We'll go straight round from here and surprise her," Michael said, laughing with excitement, as they got into a taxi. "She'll have had a letter from me this morning, in which I was lamenting not seeing her for six weeks. My gad, supposing she isn't in! Oh, well, we can wait. You'll love the room, and we'll all three sit out in the garden to-night, and you'll tell me as we walk home to Chelsea what you think of her. Guy you've absolutely got to like her. And if you don't ... oh, but you will. It isn't everybody who can appreciate beauty like hers. And there's an extraordinary subtlety about her. Of course, she isn't at all subtle. She's simple. In fact, that's one of the things Stella has got against her. What I call simplicity and absence of training for effect Stella calls stupidity. My own belief is that you'll be quite content to look at her and not care whether she talks or not. I tell you, she's like a Piero della Francesca angel. Cheer up, Guy. Why are you looking so depressed?"

"Oh, I don't know," said Guy. "I'm thinking what a lucky chap you are. What's a little family opposition when you know you're going to be able to do what you want? Who can stop you? You're independent, and you're in love."

"Of course they can't stop me!" Michael cried, jumping up and down on the cushions of the taxi in his excitement. "Guy, you're great! You really are. You're the only person who's seen the advantage of going right ahead. But don't look so sad yourself. You'll marry your Pauline."

"Yes, in about four years," Guy sighed.

"Oh, no, no; in about four months. Will Pauline like Lily? She won't be jealous of me when I'm married will she?"

"No, but I think I shall be," Guy laughed.

301

"Laugh, you old devil, laugh!" Michael shouted. "Here we are. Did you ever see such a house? It hasn't quite the austerity of Plashers Mead, has it?"

"It looks rather fun," Guy commented.

"You know," Michael said solemnly, pausing for a moment at the head of the steps going down to the front door. "You know, Guy, I believe that you'll be able to persuade my mother to withdraw all her opposition to-night. I believe I'm going to marry Lily this week. And I shall be so glad—Guy, you don't know how glad I shall be."

He ran hurriedly down the steps and had pressed the bell of Number One before Guy had entered the main door.

"I say, you know, it will be really terrible if she's out after all my boasting," said Michael. "And Miss Harper, too—that's the housekeeper—my housekeeper, you know. If they're both out, we'll have to go round and wait in the garden until they come in. Hark, there's somebody coming."

The door opened, and Michael hurried in.

"Hullo, good afternoon, Miss Harper. You didn't expect to see me, eh? I've brought a friend. Is Miss Haden in the big room?"

"Miss Haden is out, Mr. Fane," said the housekeeper.

"What's the matter? You're looking rather upset."

"Am I, Mr. Fane?" she asked blankly. "Am I? Oh, no, I'm very well. Oh, yes, very well. It's the funny light, I expect, Mr. Fane."

She seemed to be choking out all her words, and Michael looked at her sharply.

"Well, we'll wait in the big room."

"It's rather untidy. You see, we—I wasn't expecting you, Mr. Fane."

"That's all right," said Michael. "Hulloa ...I say, Guy, go on into that room ahead. I'll be with you in a minute."

Guy mistook the direction and turned the handle of Lily's bedroom door.

"No, no," Michael called. "The double doors opposite."

"My mistake," said Guy cheerfully. "But don't worry: the other door was locked. So if you've got a Bluebeard's Closet, I've done no harm."

He disappeared into the big room, and the moment he was inside Michael turned fiercely to Miss Harper.

"Who's is this hat?" he demanded, snatching it up.

"Hat? What hat?" she choked out.

"Why is the door of her bedroom locked? Why is it locked—locked?"

The stillness of the crepuscular hall seemed to palpitate with the woman's breath.

"Miss Haden must have locked it when she went out," she stammered.

"Is that the truth?" Michael demanded. "It's not the truth. It's a lie. You wouldn't be panting like a fish in a basket, unless there was something wrong. I'll break the door in."

"No, Mr. Fane, don't do that!" the woman groaned out, in a cracked expostulation. "This is the first time since you've been away. And it was an old friend."

"How dare you tell me anything about him? Guy! Guy!"

Michael rushed into the big room and dragged Guy out.

"Come away, come away, come away! I've been sold!"

"If you'd only listen a moment. I could——" Miss Harper began.

Michael pushed her out of their path.

"What on earth is it?" Guy asked.

"Come on, don't hang about in this hell of a house. Come on, Guy."

Michael had flung the door back to slam into Miss Harper's face, and, seizing Guy by the wrist, he dragged him up the steps, and had started to run down the road, when Guy shouted:

"Michael, the taxi! The taxi's waiting with our bags."

"Oh, very well, in a taxi then, a taxi if you like," Michael chattered, and he plunged into it.

"Where to?" the driver asked.

"Cheyne Walk. But drive quickly. Don't hang about up and down this road."

The driver looked round with an expression of injured dignity, shook his head in exclamation, and drove off.

"What on earth has happened?" Guy asked. "And why on earth are you holding a top-hat?"

Michael burst into laughter.

"So I am. Look at it. A top-hat. I say, Guy, did you ever hear of anyone being cut out by a top-hat, cuckolded by a top-hat? We'll present it to the driver. Driver! Do you want a top-hat?"

"Here, who are you having a game with?" demanded the driver, pulling up the car.

"I'm not having a game with anybody," Michael said. "But two people and this top-hat have just been having a hell of a game with me. You'd much better take it as a present. I shall only throw it away. He refuses," Michael went on. "He refuses a perfectly good top-hat. Who's the maker? My god, his dirty greasy head has obliterated the name of the maker. Good-bye, hat! Drive on, drive on!" he shouted to the driver, and hurled the hat spinning under an omnibus. Then he turned to Guy.

"I've been sold by the girl I was going to marry," he said. "I say, Guy, I've got some jolly good advice for you. Don't you marry a whore. Sorry, old chap!—I forgot you were engaged already. Besides, people don't marry whores, unless they're fools like me. Didn't you say just now that I was very lucky? Do you know—I think I am lucky. I think it was a great piece of luck bringing you to see that girl to-day. Don't you? Oh, Guy, I could go mad with disappointment. Will nothing in all the world ever be what it seems?"

"Look here, Michael, are you sure you weren't too hasty? You didn't wait to see if there was any explanation, did you?"

"She was only going back to her old habits," said Michael bitterly. "I was a fool to think she wouldn't. And yet I adored her. Fancy, you've never seen her, after all. Lovely, lovely animal!"

"Oh, you knew what she was?" exclaimed Guy.

"Knew? Yes, of course I knew; but I thought she loved me. I didn't care about anything when I was sure she loved me. She could only have gone such a little way down, I thought. She seemed so easy to bring out. Seeds of pomegranate. Seeds of pomegranate! She's only eaten seeds of pomegranate, but they were enough to keep her behind. Where are we going? Oh, yes, Cheyne Walk. My mother will be delighted when she hears my news, and so will everybody. That's what's amusing me. Everybody will clap their hands, and I'm wretched. But you are sorry for me, Guy? You don't think I'm just a fool being shown his folly? And at eighteen I was nearly off my head only because I saw someone kiss her! There's one thing over which I score—the only person who can appreciate all the humor of this situation is myself."

Nearly all the way to Cheyne Walk Michael was laughing very loudly.

CHAPTER IX

THE GATE OF HORN

Guy thought it would be better if he went straight back to Plashers Mead; but Michael asked him to stay until the next day. He was in no mood, he said, for a solitary evening, and he could not bear the notion of visiting friends, or of talking to his mother without the restriction that somebody else's presence would produce.

So Guy agreed to spend the night in London, and they dined with Mrs. Fane. Michael in the sun-colored Summer room felt smothered by a complete listlessness; and talking very little, he sat wondering at the swiftness with which a strong fabric of the imagination had tumbled down. The quiet of Cheyne Walk became a consciousness of boredom and futility, and he suggested on a sudden impulse that he and Guy should go and visit Maurice in the studio. It would be pleasant walking along the Embankment, he said.

"But I thought you wanted to keep quiet," Guy exclaimed.

"No, I've grown restless during dinner; and, besides, I want to make a few arrangements about the flat, and then be done with that business—forever."

They started off without waiting for coffee. It was a calm Summer evening of shadows blue and amethyst, of footfalls and murmurs, an evening plumy as a moth, warm and gentle as the throat of a pigeon. Nobody on any pavement was hurrying; and maidservants loitered in area gates, looking up and down the roads.

The big room at the top of 422 Grosvenor Road had never seemed so romantic. There were half a dozen people sitting at the open windows; and Cunningham was playing a sonata of Brahms, a sonata with a melody that was drawing the London night into this big room where the cigarettes dimmed and brightened like stars. The player sat at the piano for an hour, and Maurice unexpectedly made no attempt to disturb the occasion. Michael thought that perhaps he was wondering what had brought himself and Guy here, and for that reason did not rush to show Guy his studio by gaslight: Maurice was probably thinking how strange it was for Michael to revisit him suddenly like this after their quarrel.

When the room was lighted up, Michael and Guy were introduced to the men they did not know. Among them was Ronnie Walker, the painter whom Maurice had mentioned to Michael as an old lover of Lily. Michael knew now why Maurice had allowed the music to go on so long, and he was careful to talk as much as possible to Walker in order to embarrass Maurice, who could scarcely pay any attention to Guy, so nervously was he watching over his shoulder the progress of the conversation.

Later on Michael called Maurice aside, and they withdrew to the window-seat which looked out over the housetops. A cat was yauling on a distant roof, and in the studio Cunningham had seated himself at the piano again.

"I say, I'm awfully sorry that Ronnie Walker should happen to be here to-night," Maurice began. "I have been rather cursing myself for telling you about him and...."

"It doesn't matter at all," Michael interrupted. "I'm not going to marry her."

"Oh, that's splendid!" Maurice exclaimed. "I've been tremendously worried about you."

Michael looked at him; he was wondering if it were possible that Maurice could be "tremendously worried" by anything.

"I want you to arrange matters," said Michael. "I can't go near the place again. She will probably prefer to go away from Ararat House. The rent is paid up to the June quarter. The furniture you can do what you like with. Bring some of it here. Sell the rest, and give her the money. Get rid of the woman who's there—Miss Harper her name is."

"But I shall feel rather awkward...."

"Oh, don't do it. Don't do it, then!" Michael broke in fretfully. "I'll ask Guy."

"You're getting awfully irascible," Maurice complained. "Of course I'll do anything you want, if you won't always jump down my throat at the first word I utter. What has happened, though?"

"What do you expect to happen when you're engaged to a girl like that?" Michael asked.

Maurice shrugged his shoulders.

"Oh, well, of course I should expect to be badly let down. But then, you see, I'm not a very great believer in women. What are you going to do yourself?"

"I haven't settled yet. I've got to arrange one or two things in town, and then I shall go abroad. Would you be able to come with me in about a week?"

"I daresay I might," Maurice answered, looking vaguely round the room. Already, Michael thought, the subject was floating away from his facile comprehension.

The piano had stopped, and conversation became general again.

"This is where you ought to be, if you want to write," Maurice proclaimed to Guy. "It's ridiculous for you to bury yourself in the country. You'll expire of stagnation."

"Just at present I recommend you to stay where you are," said Castleton. "I'm almost expiring from the violence with which I am being precipitated from one to another of Maurice's energies."

Soon afterward Michael and Guy left the studio and walked home; and next morning Guy went back to Wychford.

Michael was astonished at his own calmness. After the first shock of the betrayal he had gone and talked to a lot of people; he had coldly made financial arrangements; he had even met and rather liked a man whom only yesterday morning he could not have regarded without hatred for the part he had played in Lily's life. Perhaps he had lost the power to feel anything deeply for long; perhaps he was become a sort of Maurice; already Lily seemed a shade of the underworld, merely more clearly remembered than the others. Yet in the moment that he was calling her a shade his present emotion proved that she was much more than that, for the conjured image of her was an icy pang to his heart. Then the indifference returned, but always underneath it the chill remained.

Mrs. Fane asked if he would care to go to the Opera in the evening: and they went to Bohême. Michael used to be wrung by the music, but he sat unmoved to-night. Afterward, at supper, he looked at his mother as if she were a person in a picture; he was saddened by the uselessness of all beauty, and by the number of times he would have to undress at night and dress again in the morning. He had no objection to life itself, but he felt an overwhelming despair at the thought of any activity in the conduct of it. He was sorry for the people sitting here at supper and for their footmen waiting outside. He felt that he was spiritually withered, because he was aware that he was surrendering to the notion of a debased material comfort as the only condition worth achieving for a body that remained perfectly well; grossly well, it almost seemed.

"Michael, have you been bored to-night?" his mother asked, when they had come home and were sitting by the window in the drawing-room, while Michael finished a cigar.

He shook his head.

"You seemed to take no interest in the opera, and you usually enjoy Puccini, don't you? Or was it Wagner you enjoy so much?"

"I think summer in London is always tiring," he said.

She was in that rosy mist of clothes with which his earliest pictures of her were vivid. Suddenly he began to cry.

"Dear child, what is it?" she whispered, with fluttering arms outstretched to comfort him.

"Oh, I've finished with all that! I've finished with all that! You'll be delighted—you mustn't be worried because I seem upset for the moment. I found out that Lily did not care anything about me. I'm not going to marry her or even see her again."

"Michael! My dearest boy! What is it?"

"Finished! Finished! Finished!" he sobbed.

"Nothing is finished at twenty-three," she murmured, leaning over to pet him.

"I do hate myself for having hurt your feelings the other day."

It was as if he seized upon a justification for grief so manifest. It seemed to him exquisitely sad that he should have wounded his mother on account of that broken toy of a girl. Soon he could control himself again; and he went off to bed.

Next day Michael's depression was profound because he could perceive no reaction from himself on Lily. The sense of personal loss was merged in the reproach of failure; he had simply been unable to influence her. She was the consummation of many minor failures. And what was to happen to her now? What was to happen to all the people with whose lives he had lately been involved? Must he withdraw entirely and confess defeat? No doubt a cynic would argue that Lily was hopeless, and indeed he knew that from any point of view where marriage was concerned she was hopeless. He must leave her where he had found her, in that pretty paradise of evil which now she well adorned. If her destiny was to whirl downward through the labyrinths of the underworld, he could do no more. That himself had issued with the false dreams through the ivory gate was her fault, and she must pay the penalty of her misdirection. He would revisit Leppard Street, and from the innermost circle where he had beheld Mrs. Smith he would seek a way out through the gate of true dreams. He would be glad to see if the amount of security he had been able to guarantee to Barnes had helped him at all. He had money and he could leave money behind in Leppard Street, money that might preserve the people in the house where he had lived. Was this a quixotic notion, to leave one set of people free from the necessity to hand themselves over to evil? Michael's spirits began to rise as he looked forward to what he could still effect in Leppard Street. And for Lily what could he still do? He would visit Sylvia and consult with her. She was strong, and if she had chosen harlotry, she was still strong. She was not lazy nor languid. Lazy, laughing, languid Lily! Lily did not laugh much; she was too lazy even for that. How beautiful she had been! Her beauty stabbed him with the poignancy of what was past. How beautiful she had been! When Maurice went to tell her of the final ending of it all, she would pout and shrug her shoulders. That was all she would do; and she would be faintly resentful at having been disturbed in her lazy life. Perhaps Maurice would fall in love with her, and it would be ironical and just that she should fall violently in love with Maurice and be cast off by him. Maurice would never suffer; as soon as a woman showed a sign of upsetting his theories about feminine behavior he would be done with her. He would jilt her as easily as he jilted one Muse for another. Why was he being so hard on Maurice?

"I believe that down in my heart I still don't really like him," Michael said to himself. "Right back from the time I met him in Macrae's form at Randell's I've never really liked him."

It was curious how one could grow more and more intimate with a person, and all the time never really like him; so intimate with him as to intrust him with the disposal of a wrecked love-affair, and all the while never really like him. Why, then, had he invited Maurice to go abroad? Perhaps he wanted the company of someone he could faintly despise. Even friendship must pay tribute to human vanity. Life became a merciless business when one ceased to stand alone. The herding instinct of man was responsible for the corruption of civilization, and Michael thought of the bestiality of a crowd. How loathsome humanity was in the aggregate, but individually how rare, how wonderful.

Michael walked boldly enough toward Tinderbox Lane; and when he rang the bell of Mulberry Cottage not a qualm of sentiment assailed him. He was definitely pleased with himself, as he stood outside the door in the wall, to think with what a serenity of indifference he was able to visit a place so much endeared to him a little time ago.

Mrs. Gainsborough answered the door and nearly fell upon Michael's neck.

"Good Land! Here's a surprise."

"It's almost more of a surprise for me to see you, Mrs. Gainsborough."

"Why, who else should you see?"

"I was beginning to think you never existed. Can I come in?"

"Sylvia's indoors," she said warningly.

"I rather wanted to see her."

"She's been carrying on alarming about you ever since you stole her Lily. And she didn't take me on her knee and cuddle me, when she found you were gone off. How do you like me new frock?"

Michael thought that in her checkered black and green gingham she looked like an old Summer number of an illustrated magazine, and he told her so.

"Well, there! Did you ever? I never did. There's a bouquet to hand a lady! Back number! Whatever next? I wonder you hadn't the liberty to say I'd rose from the grave."

"Aren't I to see Sylvia?" Michael asked, laughing.

"Well, don't blame me if she packs you off with a flea in your ear, as they say—well, she is a Miss Temper, and no mistake. How do you like me garden?"

Mulberry Cottage was just the bower of greenery that Michael had supposed he would find in early June.

"Actually roses," he exclaimed. "Or at least there will be very soon."

"Oh, yes. Glory de Die-Johns. That was always Pa's favorite. That and a good snooze of a Sunday afternoon was about what he cared most for in this world. But my Captain he used to like camellias, and gardenias of course—oh, he had a very soft corner in his heart for a nice gardenia. Ah dear, what a masher he was to be sure!"

Sylvia had evidently seen them walking up the garden path, for leaning over the railings of the balcony she was waiting for them.

"Here's quite a stranger come to see you," said Mrs. Gainsborough, with a propitiatory glance in Sylvia's direction.

"I rather want to have a talk with you," said Michael, and he, too, found himself rather annoyingly adopting a deprecating manner.

Sylvia came slowly down the balcony steps.

"I suppose you want my help," she said, and her underlip had a warning out-thrust.

"I'll get on with my fal-lals," Mrs. Gainsborough muttered, and she bundled herself quickly indoors.

Sylvia and Michael sat down on the garden-seat under the mulberry tree whose leaves were scarcely yet uncurling. Michael found a great charm in sitting close to Sylvia like this: she and Stella both possessed a capacity for bracing him that he did not find in anyone else. Sylvia was really worth quarreling with; but it would be very delightful to be friends with her. He had never liked a person so much whom he had so little reason to like. He could not help thinking that in her heart Sylvia must like him. It was a strangely provocative fancy.

"Lily and I have parted," he began at once.

"And why do you suppose that piece of information will interest me?" Sylvia asked.

Michael was rather taken aback. When he came to consider it, there did seem no good reason why Sylvia should any longer be interested after the way in which Lily had been snatched away from her. He was silent for a moment.

"But it would have interested you a short time ago," he said.

"No doubt," Sylvia agreed. "But luckily for me one of the benefits conferred by my temperament is an ability to throw aside things that have disappointed me, things that have ceased to be useful—and what applies to things applies even more strongly to people."

"You mean to say you've put Lily right out of your life?" Michael exclaimed.

He was shocked by the notion, for he did not realize until this moment how much he had been depending upon Sylvia for peace of mind.

"Haven't you put her out of *your* life?" she asked, looking round at him sharply. Until this question she had been staring sullenly down at the grass.

"Well, I had to," said Michael.

"You're bearing up very well under the sad necessity," she sneered.

"I don't know that I am bearing up very well. I don't think that coming to you to talk about it is a special sign of fortitude."

"What do you want me to do?" Sylvia demanded. "Get her back into your life again? Isn't that the phrase you like?"

"Oh, no, that's unimaginable," said Michael. "You see, it was really the second time. Once six years ago, and again now, very much more—more utterly. You said that your temperament enables you to throw off things and people. Mine makes me bow to what I fancy are irremediable strokes of fate."

"Unimaginable! Irremediable! We're turning this interview into a Rossetti sonnet," Sylvia scoffed.

"I was thinking about that poem Jenny to-day. It's funny you should mention Rossetti."

"Impervious youth!" she exclaimed.

"It's hopeless for you to try to wound me with words," Michael assured her, with grave earnestness. "I was wounded the day before yesterday into complete immunity from small pains."

"I suppose you found her ..."

Michael flushed and gripped her by the wrist.

"No, no, don't say something brutal and beastly!" he stammered. "You know what happened. You prophesied it. Well, I thought you were wrong, and you were right. That's a victory for you. You couldn't wish for me to be more humbled than I am by having to admit that I wasn't strong enough to keep her faithful for six weeks. But we did agree, I think, about one thing." He smiled sadly. "We did agree that she was beautiful. You were as proud of that as I was, and of course you had a great deal more reason to be proud. You did own her. I never owned her, and isn't that your great objection to the relation between man and woman?"

"What are you trying to make me do?" Sylvia asked.

"I want you to have Lily to live with you again."

"To relieve yourself of all responsibility, I suppose," she said bitterly.

"No, no; why will you persist in ascribing the worst motive to everything I say? Isn't your jealousy fed full enough even yet?"

Sylvia made the garden-seat quiver with an irritable movement.

"You will persist in thinking that jealousy solved all problems," she cried.

"Oh, don't let us turn aside into what isn't very important. You can't care whether I think you're jealous or not."

"I don't care in so far as it is your opinion," Sylvia admitted. "But I object to inaccurate thinking. If your life was spent in a confusion of all moral values as mine is, you would be anxious for a little straightforward computation for a change."

"Perhaps you are right," Michael admitted, "in thinking that I'm asking you to look after Lily to relieve myself of a responsibility. But it's only because I see no chance of doing it in any other way. I mean—it's not laziness on my part. It's a confession of absolute failure."

"In fact, you're throwing yourself on my mercy," Sylvia said.

"Yes; and also her," he added gently.

"Am I such a moral companion—such an ennobling influence?"

"I would sooner think of her under your influence than think of her drifting. What I want you to understand is that I'm not consigning her to you for sentimental reasons. I would sooner that Lily were dragged down by you at a gallop than that she should sink slowly and lazily of her own accord. You have a strong personality. You are well-read. You are quite out of the common, and in the life you have chosen, so far as I have had experience, you are unique."

Sylvia stared in front of her, and Michael waited anxiously for the reply.

"Have you ever read Petronius?" she asked suddenly.

"Yes, but what an extraordinary girl you are—have you ever read Petronius?"

"It's the only book in which anyone in my position with my brains could behold herself. Oh, it is such a nightmare. And life is a nightmare, too. After all, what is life for me? Strange doors in strange houses. Strange men and strange intimacies. Scenes incredibly grotesque and incredibly beastly. The secret vileness of human nature flung at me. Man revealing himself through individual after individual as utterly contemptible. What can I worship? Not my own body soiled by my traffic in it. Not any religion I've ever heard of, for in all religions man is set up to be respected. I tell you, my dear eager fool, it is beyond my conception ever, ever, ever to regard a man as higher than a frog, as less repulsive than—ugh! it makes me shudder—but oh, my son, doesn't it make me laugh...." She rocked herself with extravagant mirth for a moment. Then she began again, staring out in front of her intensely, fiercely, speaking with the monotonous voice of a visionary. "So I worship woman, and in this nightmare city, in this nightmare life, Lily was always beautiful; only beautiful, mind you. I don't want to worship anything but beauty. I don't care about purity or uprightness, but I must have beauty. And you came blundering along and kidnapped my lovely girl. You came along, thinking you were going to regenerate her, and you can't understand that I'm only able to see you in the shape of a frog. It does amuse me to hear you talking to me so solemnly and so earnestly and so nobly ... and all the time I can only see a clumsy frog."

"But what has all this to do with Petronius? There's nothing in that romance particularly complimentary to women," Michael argued.

"It's the nightmare effect of it that I adore," Sylvia exclaimed. "It's the sensation of being hopelessly plunged into a maze of streets from which there's no escape. I was plunged just like that into London. It is gloriously and sometimes horribly mad, and that's all I want in my reading now. I want to be given the sensation of other people having been mad before me ... years ago in a nightmare. Besides, think of the truth, the truth of a work of art that seems ignorant of goodness. Not one moderately decent person all through."

"And you will take Lily back?" Michael asked.

"Yes, yes, of course I will. But not because you ask me, mind. Don't for heaven's sake, puff yourself up with the idea that I'm doing anything except gratify myself in this matter."

"I don't want you to do it for any other reason," he said. "I shall feel more secure with that pledge than with any you could think of. By the way, tell me about a man called Walker. Ronald Walker—a painter. He had an affair with Lily, didn't he?"

"Ronnie Walker? He painted her; that was all. There was never anything more."

"And Lonsdale? Arthur Lonsdale?"

"Who? The Honorable Arthur?"

Michael nodded.

"Yes, we met him first at Covent Garden, and went to Brighton with him and another boy—Clarehaven—Lord Clarehaven."

"Oh, I remember him at the House," said Michael.

"Money is necessary sometimes, you know," Sylvia laughed.

"Of course it is. Look here. Will you in future, whenever you feel you're in a nightmare—will you write to me and let me send money?" he asked. "I know you despise me and of course ... I understand; but I can't bear to think of anyone being haunted as you must be haunted sometimes. Don't be proud about this, because *I've* got no pride left. I'm only terribly anxious to be of service to somebody. There's really no reason for you to be proud. You see, I should always be so very much more anxious to help than you would to be helped. And it really isn't only because of Lily that I say this. I've got a good many books you'd enjoy, and I think I'll send them to you. Good-bye."

"Good-bye," she said, looking at him curiously.

Michael turned away from her down the gravel-path, and a moment later slammed the door. He had only gone a few steps away, when he heard Sylvia calling after him.

"You stupid!" she said. "You never told me Lily's address."

"I'll give you a card."

"Mr. Michael Fane," she read, "1 Ararat House, Island Road." She looked at him and raised her eyebrows.

"You see, I expected to live there myself," Michael explained. "I told a friend of mine, Maurice Avery, to clear up everything. The furniture can all be sold. If you want anything for here, take it of course; but I think most of the things will be too large for Mulberry Cottage."

"And what shall I say to Lily?" she asked.

"Oh, I don't think I should say anything about me."

"Who was the man?"

"I never saw him," said Michael. "I only saw his hat."

She pulled him to her and kissed him.

"How many women have done that suddenly like that?" she demanded.

"One—well, perhaps two." He was wondering if Mrs. Smith's kiss ought to count in the comparison.

"I never have to any man," she said, and vanished through the door in the wall.

Michael hoped that Sylvia intended to imply by that kiss that his offer of help was accepted. Fancy her having read Petronius! He could send her his Adlington's Apuleius. She would enjoy reading that, and he would write in it: *I've eaten rose-leaves and I am no longer a golden ass.* Perhaps he would also send her his Shelton's Don Quixote.

When Michael turned out of Tinderbox Lane into the Fulham Road, each person of humanity he passed upon the pavement seemed to him strange with unrevealed secrets. The people of London were somehow transfigured, and he longed to see their souls, if it were only in the lucid flashes of a nightmare. Yet for nearly a year he had been peering into the souls of people. Had he, indeed. Had he not rather been peering to see in their souls the reflection of his own? He was moved by the thought of Sylvia in London, and suddenly he was swept from his feet by the surging against him of the thoughts of all the passers-by and, struggling in the trough of these thoughts, he was more and more conscious that unless he fought for himself he would be lost. The illusion fled on the instant of its creation; and the people were themselves again—dull, quick, slow, ordinary, depressed, gay; political busy-bodies, political fools, political slaves, political animals. How they huddled together, each one of them afraid to stand for himself. It was political passion that made them animals, each dependent in turn on the mimicry of his neighbor. Each was solicitous or jealous or fond or envious of his neighbor's opinion. God was meaningless to the political state: this herd cared only for idols. Michael began to make a catalogue of the Golden Calves that the Golden Asses of green England worshiped. They were bowing down and braying to their Golden Calves, these Golden Asses, and they could not see that there were rose-trees growing everywhere, most prodigally of all in the gutter, any one petal of which (what did the thorns matter?) would have given back to them their humanity. Yet even then, Michael dismally concluded, they would continue to bow down to the Golden Calves, because they would fancy that it was the Calves who had planted and cultivated the rose-trees. Then out of all the thronging thoughts made visible he began to pursue the fancy of Sylvia in London, and, as he did so, she faded farther and farther from his vision like a butterfly seen from a train, that keeps pace, it seems for a moment, and is lost upon the flowery embankment behind.

Meanwhile, Michael was feeling sharpened for conflict by that talk under the mulberry tree: he realized what an amount of determination he had stored up for the persuasion of Sylvia. Now there only remained Leppard Street, and then he would go away from London. He walked on through the Chelsea slums.

Leppard Street was more melancholy in the sunshine than it had ever seemed in Winter, not so much because the sun made more evident the corrosion and the foulness as because of the stillness it shed. Not a breath of air twitched the torn paper-bag on the doorstep of Number One; and the five tall houses with their fifty windows stared at the blank wall opposite.

Michael wondered if Barnes would be out of bed: it was not yet one o'clock. He rang the front-door bell, or rather he hoped that the creaking of the broken wire along the basement passage would attract Mrs. Cleghorne's attention. When he had tugged many times, she came out into the area, and peered up to see who it was. The sudden sunlight must have dazzled her eyes, for she was shading them with her hand. With her fibrous neck working and with an old cap of her husband's pinned on a skimpy bun at the back of her head, she was

307

horrible after Mrs. Gainsborough in the black and green gingham. Michael looked down at her over the railings; and she, recognizing him at last, pounced back to come up and open the door.

"I couldn't think who it was. We had a man round selling pots of musk this morning, and I didn't want to come trapesing upstairs for nothing."

Mrs. Cleghorne was receiving him so pleasantly that Michael scarcely knew what to say. No doubt his regular payment of rent had a good deal to do with it.

"Is Mr. Barnes up?" he asked.

"I don't know, I'm sure. I never go inside his door now. No."

"Oh, really? Why not?"

"I'm the last person to make mischief, Mr. Fane, but I don't consider he has treated us fair."

"Oh, really?"

"He's got a woman here living with him. Now of course that's a thing I should never allow, but seeing as you weren't here and was paying the rent regular I thought to myself that I'll just shut my eyes until you came back. It's really disgusting, and we has to be so particular with the other lodgers. It's quite upset me, it has; and *Mis*-ter Cleghorne has been intending to speak to him about it. Only his asthma's been so bad lately—it really seems to have knocked all the heart out of him."

This pity for her husband was very ominous, Michael thought. Evidently the landlady was defending herself against an abrupt forfeiture of rent for the ground floor. Michael tapped at the door of his old room: it was locked.

"I'll get on down again to my oven," said Mrs. Cleghorne with a ratlike glance at the closed door. "I'm just cooking a bit of fish for my old man's dinner."

She fixed him with her eyes that were beady like the head of the hatpin in her cap, and sweeping her hand upward over her nose, she vanished.

Michael rapped again and, as there was no answer, he went along the passage and tried the bedroom door. Barnes' voice called out to know who was there. Michael shouted his name, and heard Barnes whispering to somebody inside. Presently he opened the sitting-room door and invited Michael to come in.

It was extraordinary to see how with a few additions the character of the room had changed since Michael left it. The furniture was still there; but what had seemed ascetic was now mean. Spangled picture-postcards were standing along the mantelpiece. The autotypes of St. George and the Knight in Armor were both askew: the shelves had novelettes interspersed among the books; a soiled petticoat of yellow moirette lay over Michael's narrow bed, which he was surprised to see in the sitting-room: a gas-stove had been fixed in the fireplace, and the old steel grate had been turned into a deposit for dirty plates and dishes: but what struck Michael most were the heavy curtains over the folding-doors between the two rooms. He looked at Barnes, waiting for him to explain the alterations.

"Looks a bit more homelike than it did, doesn't it?" said Barnes, blinking round him.

A deterioration was visible even in Barnes himself. This was not merely the result of being without a collar or a shave, Michael decided: it was as hard to define as the evidence of death in a man's eyes; but there clung to him an aura of corruption, and it seemed as if at a touch he would dissolve into a vile deliquescence.

"You look pretty pasty," said Michael severely.

"Worry, old man, worry," said Barnes. "Well, to put it straight, I fell in with a girl who was down on her luck, and I knew you'd be the very one to encourage a bit of charity. So I brought her here."

"Why are you sleeping in this room?" Michael asked.

"You're getting a Mr. Smart, aren't you?" said Barnes. "Fancy you're noticing that. Oh, well, I suppose you've come to ask for your rooms back?"

Michael with the consciousness of the woman behind those curtained doors knew that he could discuss nothing at present. He felt that all the time her ear was at the keyhole, and he went out suddenly, telling Barnes to meet him at the Orange that night.

Again the beerhall impressed him with its eternal sameness. It was as if a cinema film had broken when he last went out of the Café d'Orange, and had been set in action again at the moment of his return. He looked round to see if Daisy was there, and she was. Her hat which had formerly been black and trimmed with white daisies was now, to mark the season, white and trimmed with black daisies.

"Hulloa!, little stranger!" she exclaimed. "Where have you been?"

So exactly the same was the Orange that Michael was almost surprised that she should have observed a passage of time.

"You never seem to come here now," she said reproachfully. "Come on. Sit down. Don't stand about like a man selling matches on the curb."

"How's Bert?" Michael asked.

"Who?"

"Bert Saunders. The man you were living with in Little Quondam Street."

"Oh, him! Oh, I had to get rid of him double quick. What? Yes, when it came to asking me to go to Paris with a fighting fellow. Only fancy the cheek of it! It would help him, he said, with his business. Dirty Ecnop! I soon shoved him down the Apples-and-pears."

"I haven't understood a word of that last sentence," said Michael.

"Don't you know back-slang and rhyming-slang? Oh, it's grand! Here, I forgot, there's something I wanted to tell you. Do you remember you was in here with a fellow who you said his name was Burns?"

"Barnes, you mean, I expect. Yes, he's supposed to be meeting me here to-night, as a matter of fact."

"Well, you be careful of him. He'll get you into trouble."

Michael looked incredulous.

"It's true as I sit here," said Daisy earnestly. "Come over in the corner and let's have our drink there. I can't talk here with that blue-nosed —— behind me, squinting at us across his lager." She looked round indignantly at the man in question.

They moved across to one of the alcoves, and Daisy leaned over and spoke quietly and rather tensely, so differently from the usual rollick of her voice that Michael began to feel a presentiment of dread.

"I was out on the Dilly one night soon after you'd been round to my place, and I was with a girl called Janie Filson. 'Oo-er,' she said to me. 'Did you see who that was passed?' I looked round and saw this fellow Burns."

"Barnes," Michael corrected.

"Oh, well, Barnes. His name doesn't matter, because it isn't his own, anyway. 'That's Harry Meats,' she said. And she called out after him. 'Hulloa, Harry, where's Cissie?' He went as white as ... oh, he did go shocking white. He just turned to see who it was had called out after him, and then he slid up Swallow Street like a bit of paper. 'Who's Cissie?' I said. 'Don't you remember Cissie Cummings?' she said. 'That fair girl who always wore a big purple hat and used to be in the Leicester Lounge and always carried a box of chocolates for swank?' I did remember the girl when Janie spoke about her. Only I never knew her, see? 'He wasn't very pleased when you mentioned her,' I said. 'Didn't he look awful?' said Janie, and just then she got off with a fellow and I couldn't ask her any more."

"I don't think that's enough to make me very much afraid of Barnes," Michael commented.

"Wait a minute, I haven't finished yet. Don't be in such a hurry. The other day I saw Janie Filson again. She's been away to Italy—is there a place called Italy? Of course there is. Well, as I was saying, she'd been to Italy with her fellow who's a commercial traveler and that's why I hadn't seen her. And Janie said to me, 'Do you know what they're saying?' I said, 'No, what?' And she said, 'Did you read nearly a year ago about a woman who was found murdered in the Euston Road? A gay woman it was,' she said. So I said, 'Lots of women is found murdered, my dear. I can't remember every one I see the picture of.' Well, anyone can't, can they?" Daisy broke off to ask Michael in an injured voice. Then she resumed her tale. "When I was with that fellow Bert I used to read nothing else but murders all the time. Give anyone the rats, it would. 'Lots of women, my dear,' I said. And she said, 'Well, there was one in particular who the police never found out the name of, because there wasn't any clothing or nothing found.' So I did remember about it, and she said, 'Well, they're saying now it was Cissie Cummings.' And I said, 'Well, what of it, if it was?' And she said, 'What of it?' she said. 'Well, if it was her,' she said, 'I know who done it.' 'Who done it?' I asked—because, you see, I'd forgotten about this fellow Burns. 'Why, Harry Meats,' she said. 'That fellow I saw on the Dilly the night when I was along with you.'"

"I don't think you have enough evidence for the police," Michael decided, with half a smile. Yet nevertheless a malaise chilled him, and he looked over his shoulder at the mob in the beer hall.

"—— the police!" Daisy exclaimed. "I don't care about them when I'm positive certain of something. I tell you, I know that fellow Burns, or Meats, or whatever his name is, done it."

"But what am I to do about it?" Michael asked.

"Well, you'll get into trouble, that's all," Daisy prophesied. "You'd look very funny if he was pinched for murder while you was out walking with him. Ugh! It gives me the creeps. Order me a gin, there's a good boy."

Michael obtained for Daisy her drink, and sat waiting for Barnes to appear.

"He won't come," Daisy scoffed. "If he's feeling funny about the neck, he won't come down here. He's never been down since that night he came down with you. Fancy, to go and do a poor girl in like that! I'd spit in his face, if I saw him."

"Daisy, you really mustn't assume such horrible things about a man. He's as innocent as you or me."

"Is he?" Daisy retorted. "I don't think so then. You never saw how shocking white his face went when Janie asked him about Cissie."

"But if there were any suspicion of him," Michael pointed out, "the police would have tackled him long ago."

"Oh, they aren't half artful, the police aren't," said Daisy. "Nothing they'd like better than get waiting about and seeing if he didn't go and murder another poor girl, so as they could have him for the two, and be all the more pleased about it."

"That's talking nonsense," Michael protested. "The police don't do that sort of thing."

"I don't know," Daisy argued. "One or two poor girls more or less wouldn't worry them. After all, that's what we're for—to get pinched when they've got nothing better to do. Of course, I know it's part of the game, but there it is. If you steal my purse and I follow you round and tell a copper, what would he do? Why, pinch me for soliciting. No, my motto is, 'Keep out of the way of the police.' And if you take my advice, you'll do the same. If this fellow didn't do the girl in," Daisy asked earnestly, leaning forward over the table, "why doesn't he come down here and keep his appointment with you to-night? Don't you worry. He knows the word has gone round, and he's going to lie very low for a bit. I wouldn't say the tecs aren't watching out for him even now."

"My dear Daisy, you're getting absolutely fanciful," Michael declared.

"Oh, well, good luck to fanciful," said Daisy, draining her glass. "Here, why don't you come home with me to-night?"

"What, and spend another three hours hiding in a cupboard?"

"No, properly, I mean, this time. Only we should have to go to a hotel, because the woman I'm living with's got her son come home from being a soldier and she wouldn't like for him to know anything. Well, it's better not. You're much more comfortable when you aren't in gay rooms, because they haven't got a hold over you. Are you coming?"

For a moment Michael was inclined to invite Daisy to go away with him. For a moment it seemed desirable to bury himself in a corner of the underworld: to pass his life there for as long as he could stand it. He could easily make this girl fond of him, and he might be happy with her. No doubt, it would be ultimately a degrading happiness, but yet not much more degrading than the prosperity of many of his friends. He had always escaped so far and hidden himself successfully. Why not again more completely? What, after all, did he know of this underworld without having lived of it as well as in it? Hitherto he had been a spectator, intervening sometimes in the sudden tragedies and comedies, but never intervening except as very essentially a spectator. He thought, as he sat opposite to Daisy with her white dress and candid roguery, that it would be amusing to become a rogue himself. There would be no strain in living with Daisy. Love in the way that he had loved Lily would be a joke to her. Why should not he take her for what she was—shrewd, mirthful, kind, honest, the natural light of love? He would do her no wrong by accepting her as such. She was immemorial in the scheme of the universe.

Michael was on the point of offering to Daisy his alliance, when he remembered what Sylvia had said about men and, though he knew that Daisy could not possibly think in that way about men, he had no courage to plunge with her into deeper labyrinths not yet explored. He thought of the contempt with which Sylvia would hail him, were they in this nightmare of London to meet in such circumstances. A few weeks ago—yesterday, indeed—he might have joined himself to Daisy under the pretext of helping her and improving her. Now he must help himself: he must aim at perfecting himself. Experiments, when at any moment passion might enter, were too dangerous.

"No, I won't come home with you, dear Daisy," he said, taking her hand over the puddly table. "You know, you didn't kiss me that night in Quondam Street because you thought I might one day come home with you, did you?"

She shrugged her shoulders.

"What's the good of asking me why I kissed you?" she said, embarrassed and almost made angry by his reminder. "Perhaps I was twopence on the can. I can get very loving on a quartern of gin, I can. Oh, well, if you aren't coming home, you aren't, and I must get along. Sitting talking to you isn't paying my rent, is it?"

He longed to offer her money, but he could not, because it was seeming to him now indissolubly linked with hiring. However genuinely it was a token of exchange, money was eluding his capacity for idealization, and he was at a loss to find a symbol service.

"Is there nothing I can do for you?"

"Yes, you can give me two quid in case I don't get off to-night."

He offered them to her eagerly.

"Go on, you silly thing," she said, pushing the money away. "As if I meant it."

"If you didn't, I did," said Michael.

"Oh, all right," she replied, with a wink, putting the money in her purse. "Well, chin-chin, Clive, don't be so long coming down here next time."

"Michael is my name," he said, for he was rather distressed to think that she would pass forever from his life supposing him to be called Clive.

"As if I didn't know that," she said. "I remember, because it's a Jew name."

"But it isn't," Michael contradicted.

"Jews are called that."

"Very likely," he admitted.

"Oh, well, it'll be all the same in a hundred years."

She picked up her white gloves, and swaggered across the crowded beerhall. At the foot of the stairs she turned and waved them to him. Then she disappeared.

Michael sat on in the Café d'Orange, waiting for Barnes, but he did not arrive before closing-time; and when Michael was walking home, the tale of Daisy gathered import, and he had a dreary feeling that her suspicions were true. He did not feel depressed so much because he was shocked by the notion of Barnes as a murderer (he thought that probably murder was by no means the greatest evil he had done), as because he feared the fancy of him in the hands of the police. It appalled him to imagine that material hell of the trial. The bandage dropped from the eyes of justice, and he saw her pig's-eyes mean, cowardly, revengeful; and her scales were like a grocer's. He pitied Barnes in the clutches of anthropocracy. What a ridiculous word: it probably did not exist. After all, Daisy's story was ridiculous, too. Barnes had objected to himself's hailing him as Meats: and there were plenty of reasons to account for his dislike of Janie Filson's salute without supposing murder. Nevertheless, back again, as softly and coaxingly as the thought used to come to Michael when he was a small boy lying in bed, the thought of murder maintained an innuendo of probability. Yet it was absurd to think of murder on this summer night, with all these jingling hansoms and all that fountainous sky of stars. Why, then, had Barnes not met him at the Orange to-night? It was not like him to break an appointment when his pocket might be hurt. What rumor of Cissie Cummings had traveled even to Leppard Street?

Michael had reached Buckingham Palace Road, and he took the direction for Pimlico; it was not too late to get into the house. He changed his mind again and drove back to Cheyne Walk. Up in his bedroom, the curiosity to know why Barnes had not kept the appointment recurred with double force, and Michael after a search found the key of the house in Leppard Street and went out again. It was getting on for two o'clock, and without the lights of vehicles the night was more than ever brilliant. Under the plane-trees Michael was stabbed with one pang for Lily, and he repined at the waste of this warm June.

The clocks had struck two when he reached Leppard Street, and the houses confronted him, their roofs and chimneys prinked with stars. Several windows glimmered with a turbid orange light; but these signals of habitation only emphasized the unconsciousness of the sleepers behind, and made the desolation of the rest more positive. The windows of his old rooms were black, and Michael unlocked the front door quietly and stood listening for a moment in the passage. He could hear a low snarling in the bedroom, but from where he was standing not a word was distinct, and he could not bring himself to point of listening close to the keyhole. He shut the front door and waited in the blackness, fascinated by the rise and fall of the low snarl that was seeming so sinister in this house. It was incredible that a brief movement would open the front door again and let in the starlight; for, as he stood here, Leppard Street was under the earth deep down. He moved a little farther into the hall, and, putting out his hand to feel for the balusters, drew back with a start, for he might have clapped it down upon a cold bald head, so much like that was the newel's wooden knob. Still the snarling rose and fell: the darkness grew thicker and every instant more atramental, beating upon him from the steeps of the house like the filthy wings of a great bat: and still the snarling rose and fell. It rose and fell like the bubbling of a kettle, and then without warning the kettle overflowed with spit and hiss and commotion. Every word spoken by Barnes and the woman was now audible.

"I say he gave you thirty shillings. Now then!" Barnes yapped.

"And I tell you he only gave me a sovereign, which you've had."

"Don't I hear through the door what you get?"

Michael knew why Barnes had not been able to keep his appointment to-night, and though he was outraged at the use to which his rooms had been put, he was glad to be relieved of the fear that this snarling was the prelude to the revelation of Barnes as a murderer. The recriminations with their details of vileness were not worth hearing longer, and Michael went quickly and quietly out into the Summer night, which smelled so sweet after that passage.

He turned round by the lamp-post at the corner and looked back at the five stark houses; he could not abandon their contemplation; and he pored upon them as intensely as he might have pored upon a tomb of black basalt rising out of desert sand. He was immured in the speculation of their blackness: he pondered hopelessly their meaning and brooded upon the builders that built them and the sphinx that commanded them to be built.

In his present mood Michael would have thought Stonehenge rather prosaic; and he leaned against the wall in the silence, thinking of brick upon brick, or brick upon brick slabbed with mortar and chipped and tapped in the past, of brick upon brick as the houses grew higher and higher ... a railway engine shrieked suddenly: the door of Number One slammed: and a woman came hurrying down the steps. She looked for a moment to right and left of her, and then she moved swiftly with a wild, irregular walk in Michael's direction. He had a sensation that she had known he was standing here against this wall, that she had watched him all the while and was hurrying now to ask why he had been standing here against this wall. He could not turn and walk away: he could not advance to meet her: so he stood still leaning against the wall. Michael saw her very plainly as she passed him in the lamplight. Her hat was askew, and a black ostrich plume hung down over her big chalky face: her lips were glistening as if they had been smeared with jam. She was wearing a black satin cloak, and she seemed, as her skirts swept past him, like an overblown grotesque of tragedy being dragged by a wire from the scene.

Michael shuddered at the monstrousness of her femininity; he seemed to have been given a glimpse of a mere mass of woman, a soft obscene primeval thing that demanded blows from a club, nothing else. He realized how in a moment men could become haters of femininity, could hate its animalism and wish to stamp upon it. The physical repulsion he had felt vanished when the sound of her footsteps had died away. In the reaction Michael pitied her, and he went back quietly to Number One with the intention of turning Barnes into the street. He was rather startled as he walked up the steps to see Barnes' face pressed against the window-pane, for it seemed to him ludicrous that he should wave reassuringly to a mask like that.

Barnes hurried to open the front door before Michael had taken the key from his pocket, and was not at all surprised to see him.

"Here, I couldn't get down to the Orange to-night. I've had a bit of trouble with this girl."

The gas was flaring in the sitting-room by now, and the night, which outside had been lightening for dawn, was black as ink upon the panes.

"Sit on the bed. The chairs are all full of her dirty clothes. I'll pull the blinds down. I'm going to leave here to-morrow, Fane. Did you see her going down the road? She must have passed you by. I tell you straight, Fane, half an hour back I was in two minds to do her in. I was, straight. And I would have, if ... Oh, well, I kept my temper and threw her out instead. Gratitude! It's my belief gratitude doesn't exist in this world. You sit down and have a smoke. He left some cigarettes behind."

"Who did?" Michael asked sharply.

"Who did what?"

"Left these cigarettes."

"Oh, they're some I bought yesterday," said Barnes.

"I think it's just as well for you that you are going to-morrow morning. I hope you quite realize that otherwise I should have turned you out."

"Well, don't look at me in that tone of voice," Barnes protested. "I've had quite enough to worry me without any nastiness between old friends to make it worse."

"You can't expect me to be pleased at the way you've treated my rooms," Michael said.

"Oh, the gas-stove, you mean?"

"It's not a question of gas-stoves. It's a question of living on a woman."

"Who did?"

"You."

"If I'd had to live on her earnings, I should be very poorly off now," grumbled Barnes, in an injured voice.

Under Michael's attack he was regaining his old perkiness.

"At any rate, you must go to-morrow morning," Michael insisted.

"Don't I keep on telling you that I'm going? It's no good for you to nag at me, Fane."

"And what about the woman?"

"Her? Let her go to ——," said Barnes contemptuously. "She can't do me any harm. What if she does tell the coppers I've been living on her? They won't worry me unless they've nothing better to do, and I'll have hooked it by then."

"You're sure she can't do you any harm?" Michael asked gravely. "There's nothing else she could tell the police?"

311

"Here, what are you talking about?" asked Barnes, coming close to Michael and staring at him fixedly. Michael debated whether he should mention Cissie Cummings, but he lacked the courage either to frighten Barnes with the suggestion of his guilt or to preserve a superior attitude in the face of his enraged innocence.

"I shall come round to-morrow morning, or rather this morning, at nine," said Michael. "And I shall expect to find you ready to clear out of here for good."

"You're very short with a fellow, aren't you?" said Barnes. "What do you want to go away for? Why don't you stay so as you can see me off the premises?"

Michael thought that he could observe underneath all the assurance a sharp anxiety on Barnes' part not to be left alone.

"You can lay down and have a sleep in here. I'll get on into the bedroom."

Michael consented to stay, and Barnes was obviously relieved. He put out the gas and retired into the bedroom. The dawn was graying the room, and the sun would be up in less than an hour. Early sparrows were beginning to chirp. The woman who had burst out of the door and fled up the street seemed now a chimera of the night. Half-dozing, Michael lay on the bed, half dozing and faintly oppressed by the odor of patchouli coming from the clothes heaped upon the chairs. St. George was visible already, and even the outlines of The Knight in Armor were tremulously apparent. Michael wondered why he did not feel a greater resentment at the profanation of these rooms. And why did Barnes keep fidgeting on the other side of the folding doors? The sparrows were cheeping more loudly: the trains were more frequent. Michael woke from sleep with a start and saw that Barnes was throwing the clothes from the chairs on the floor: stirred up thus in this clear light the scent of patchouli was even more noticeable. What on earth was Barnes doing? He was turning the whole room upside-down.

"What the deuce are you looking for?" Michael yawned.

"That's all right, old man, you get on with your sleep. I'm just putting my things together," Barnes told him.

Michael turned over and was beginning to doze again when Barnes woke him by the noise he made in taking the dirty dishes out of the old grate.

"How on earth can I sleep, when you're continually fidgeting?" Michael demanded fretfully. "What's the time?"

"Just gone half-past five."

Barnes paid no more attention to Michael's rest, but began more feverishly than ever to rummage among all the things in the room.

Michael could not stand his activity any longer, and dry-mouthed from an uncomfortable sleep, he sat up.

"What *are* you looking for?"

"Well, if you want to know, I'm looking for a watch-bracelet."

"It's not likely to be under the carpet," said Michael severely.

Barnes was wrenching out the tacks to Michael's annoyance.

"Perhaps it isn't," Barnes agreed. "But I've got to find this watch-bracelet. It's gold. I don't want to lose it."

"Was it a woman's?"

Barnes looked round at him like a small animal alarmed.

"Yes, it was a woman's. What makes you ask?"

"What's it like?"

"Gold. Gold, I keep telling you."

"When did you have it last?"

"Last night."

"Well, it can't have gone far."

"No, blast it, of course it can't," said Barnes, searching with renewed impatience. He was throwing the clothes about the room again, and the odor of staleness became nauseating.

"I'm going to wash," Michael announced, moving across to the bedroom.

"You'll excuse the untidiness," Barnes called out after him, in a tone of rather strained jocularity.

Of Michael's old room no vestige remained. A very large double-bed took up almost all the space, and all the furniture was new and tawdry. The walls were hung with studies of cocottes pretending to be naiads and dryads, horrible women posed in the silvanity of a photographer's studio. The room was littered with clothes, and Michael could not move a step without entangling his feet in a petticoat or treading upon hidden shoes. He tried to splash his face, but the very washstand was sickly.

"Well, you've managed to debauch my bedroom quite successfully," he said to Barnes, when he came back to the sitting-room.

"That's all right. I'll get rid of all the new furniture. I can pop the lot. Well, it's mine. If I could find this bloody watch-bracelet, I could begin to make some arrangements."

"What about breakfast?" Michael began to look for something to eat. Every plate and knife was dirty, and there were three or four half-finished tins of condensed milk which had turned pistachio green and stank abominably.

"There's a couple of herrings somewhere," said Barnes. "Or there was. But everything seems upside-down this morning. Where the hell is that watch? It can't have walked away on its own. If that mare took it! I've a very particular reason for not wanting to lose that watch. Oh, —— ——! wherever can it have got to?"

"Well, anyway shut up using such filthy language. When does the milkman come round?"

"I don't know when he comes round. Here, Fane, have you ever heard of anyone talking in their sleep?"

"Of course I've heard of people talking in their sleep," Michael answered. "It's not very unusual."

"Ah, hollering out, yes—but talking in a sensible sort of a way, so that if you came in and listened to what they said, you'd think it was the truth? Have you ever heard of that?"

"I don't suppose I can give you an instance, but obviously it must often happen."

"Must it?" said Barnes, in a depressed voice. "You see, I set particular value by this watch-bracelet; and I thought perhaps I might have talked about it in my sleep, and that mare just to spite me have gone and taken it. I wonder where it is now."

Michael also began to wonder where it was now, and Barnes' anxiety was transferred to him, so that he began to fancy the whole of this fine morning was tremendously bound up with exactly where the watch-bracelet now was. Barnes had begun to turn over everything for about the sixth time.

"If the watch is here," said Michael irritably, "it will be found when you move your things out, and if it's not here, it's useless to go on worrying about it."

"Ah, it's all very nice for you to be so calm! But what price it's being my watch that's lost, not yours, old sport?"

"I'm not going to talk about it any more," Michael declared. "I want to know what you're going to do when you leave here."

"Ah, that's it! What am I?"

"Would you like to go to the Colonies?"

"What, say good-bye to dear old Leicester Square and pop off for good and all? I wouldn't mind."

"I don't mind telling you," said Michael, "that if I'd discovered you here a week ago living like this, I should have had nothing more to do with you. As it is, I've a good mind to sling you out to look after yourself. However, I'm willing to get you a ticket for wherever you think you'd like to go, and when I hear you've arrived, I'll send you enough money to keep you going for a time."

"Fane, I don't mind saying it. You've been a good pal to me."

"Hark, there's the milkman at last!" Michael exclaimed. He went out into the sparkling air of the fine Summer morning and came back with plenty of milk for breakfast. After they had made a sort of meal, he suggested that Barnes ought to come with him and visit some of the Colonial Agencies. They walked down Victoria Street and across St. James' Park, and in the Strand he made Barnes have a shave. The visit to the barber took away some of his nocturnal raffishness, and Michael found him very amusing during the various discussions that took place in the Agencies.

"I think the walk has done you good."

"Yes," Barnes doubtfully admitted. "I don't think it has done me much harm."

They had lunch at Romano's, where Barnes drank a good deal of Chianti and became full of confidence in his future.

"That's where it is, Fane. A fellow like you is lucky. But that's no reason why I shouldn't be lucky in my turn. My life has been a failure so far. Yes, I'm not going to attempt to deny it. There are lots of things in my life that might have been different. You'll understand when I say different I mean pleasanter for everybody all round, myself included. But that's all finished. With this fruit-farm—well, of course it's no good grumbling and running down good things—those apples we saw were big enough to make anybody's fortune. Cawdashit, Fane, I can see myself sitting under one of those apple-trees and counting the bloody fruit falling down at my feet and me popping them into baskets and selling them—where was it he said we sold them?" Barnes poured out more Chianti. "Really, it seems a sin on a fine day like this to be hanging about in London. Well, I've had some sprees in old London, and that's a fact; so I'm not going to start running it down now. If I hadn't lost that watch-bracelet, I wouldn't give a damn for anybody. Good old London," he went on meditatively. "Yes, I've had some times—good times and bad times—and here I am."

He gradually became incoherent, and Michael thought it would be as well to escort him back to Leppard Street and impress on him once again that he must remove all his things immediately.

"You'll have to be quick with your packing-up. You ought to sail next week. I shall go and see about your passage to-morrow."

They drove back to Leppard Street in a taxi, and as they got out Barnes said emphatically:

"You know what it is, Fane? Cawdashit! I feel like a marquis when I'm out with you, and it I hadn't have lost that watch-bracelet I'd feel like the bloody German Emperor. That's me. All up in the air one minute, and yet worry myself barmy over a little thing like a watch the next."

"Hullo!" he exclaimed, looking up the road as their taxi drove off. "Somebody else is playing at being a millionaire."

Another taxi was driving into Leppard Street.

Michael had already opened the front door, and he told Barnes not to hang about on the steps. Barnes turned reluctantly from his inspection of the new taxi's approach. It pulled up at Number One, and three men jumped out.

"That's your man," Michael heard one of them say, and in another moment he heard, "Henry Meats ... I hold a warrant ... murder of Cissie ... anything you say ... used against you," all in the mumbo-jumbo of a nightmare.

Michael came down the steps again very quickly; and Barnes, now handcuffed, turned to him despairingly.

"Tell 'em my name isn't Meats, Fane. Tell 'em they've made a mistake. Oh, my God, I never done it! I never done it!"

The two men were pushing him, dead white, crumpled, sobbing, into the taxi; he seemed very small beside the big men with their square shoulders and bristly mustaches. Michael heard him still moaning as the taxi jangled and whirred abruptly forward. The third man watched it disappear between the two walls; then he strolled up the steps to enter the house. Mrs. Cleghorne was already in the hall, and over the balusters of each landing faces could be seen peering down. As if the word were uttered by the house itself, "murder" floated in a whisper upon the air. The faces shifted; doors opened and shut far above; footsteps hurried to and fro; and still of all these sounds "murder" was the most audible.

"This is the gentleman who rents the rooms," Mrs. Cleghorne was saying.

"But I've not been near them till yesterday evening for six months," Michael hurriedly explained.

"That's quite right," Mrs. Cleghorne echoed.

"Well, I'm afraid we must go through them," said the officer.

"Oh, of course."

"Let me see, is this your address?"

"Well, no—Cheyne Walk—173."

"We might want to have a little talk with you about this here Meats."

Michael was enraged with himself for not asseverating "Barnes! Barnes! Barnes!" as he had been begged to do. He despised himself for not trying to save that white crumpled thing huddled between those big men with their bristly mustaches; yet all the while he felt violently afraid that the police officer would think him involved in these disgraceful rooms, that he would suppose the pictures and the tawdry furniture belonged to him, that he would imagine the petticoats and underlinen strewn about the floor had something to do with him.

"If you want me," he found himself saying, "you have my address."

Quickly he hurried away from Leppard Street, and traveled in a trance of shame to Hardingham. Alan was just going in to bat, when Michael walked across from the Hall to the cricket-field.

Stella came from her big basket chair to greet him, and for a while he sat with her in the buttercups, watching Alan at the wicket. Nothing had ever seemed so easy as the bowling of the opposite side on this fine June evening, and Michael tried to banish the thought of Barnes in the spaciousness of these level fields. Stella was evidently being very careful not to convey the impression that she had lately won a victory over him. It was really ridiculous, Michael thought, as he plucked idly the buttercups and made desultory observations to Stella about the merit of a stroke by Alan, it was more than ridiculous, it was deliberate folly to enmesh himself with such horrors as he had beheld at Leppard Street. There were doubtless very unpleasant events continually happening in this world, but willfully to drag one's self into misery on account of them was merely to show an incapacity to appreciate the more fortunate surroundings of one's allotted niche. The avoidance of even the sight of evil was as justifiable as the avoidance of evil itself, and the moral economy of the world might suffer a dangerous displacement, if everyone were to involve themselves in such events as those in which himself had lately been involved. Duty was owing all the time to people nearer at hand than Barnes. No doubt the world would be better for being rid of him; diseases of the body must be fought, and the corruption of human society must be cleansed. Any pity for Barnes was a base sentimentalism; it was merely a reaction of personal discomfort at having seen an unpleasant operation. The sentimentalism of that cry "Don't hurt him!" was really contemptible, and since it seemed that he was likely to be too weak to bear the sight of the cleansing knife, he must in future avoid the occasion of its use. Otherwise his intellectual outlook was going to be sapped, and he would find himself in the ranks of the faddists.

"I think I shall stay down here the rest of the summer, if I may," he said to Stella.

"My dear, of course you can. We'll have a wonderful time. Hullo, Alan is retiring."

Alan came up and sat beside them in the buttercups.

"I thought I saw you just as I was going in," he said. "Anything going on in town?"

"No, nothing much," said Michael. "I saw a man arrested for murder this afternoon."

"Did you really? How beastly! Our team's just beginning to get into shape. I say, Stella. That youth working on old Rundle's farm is going to be pret-ty good. Did you see him lift their fast bowlers twice running over the pond?"

Michael strolled away to take a solitary walk. It seemed incredible now to think that he had brought Lily down here, that he had wandered with her over this field. What an infringement it must have seemed to Stella and Alan of their already immemorial peace. They had really been very good about his invasion. And here was the wood where he and Stella had fought. Michael sat down in the glade and listened to the busy flutterings of the birds. Why had Stella objected to his marriage with Lily? All the superficial answers were ready at once; but was not her real objection only another facet of the diamond of selfishness? Selfishness was a diamond. Precious, hard, and very often beautiful—when seen by itself.

Michael spent a week at Hardingham, during which he managed to put out of his mind the thought of Barnes in prison awaiting his trial. Then one day the butler informed him of a person wishing to speak to him. In the library he found the detective who had asked for his address at Leppard Street.

"Sorry to have to trouble you, sir, but there was one or two little questions we wanted to ask."

Michael feared he would have to appear at the trial, and asked at once if that was going to be necessary.

"Oh, no, I don't think so. We've got it all marked out fair and square against Mr. Meats. He doesn't stand a chance of getting off. How did you come to be mixed up with him?"

Michael explained the circumstances which had led up to his knowing Meats.

"I see; and you just wanted to give him a bit of a helping hand. Oh, well, the feeling does you credit, I'm bound to say; but another time, sir, I should make a few inquiries first. We should probably have had him before, if he hadn't been helped by you. Of course, I quite understand you knew nothing about this murder, but anyone can often do a lot of harm by helping undeserving people. We mightn't have nabbed him even now, if some woman hadn't brought us a nice little bit of evidence, and I found some more things myself after a search. Oh, yes, he doesn't stand an earthly. We knew for a moral cert who did it, straightaway; but the police don't get a fair chance in England. We let all these blooming Radicals interfere too much. That's my opinion. Anyone would think the police was a lot of criminals by the way some people talk about them."

"Is anybody defending him?" Michael asked.

"Oh, he'll be awarded a counsel," said the detective indignantly. "For which you and me has to pay. That's a nice thing, isn't it? But he doesn't stand an earthly."

"Where will he be hanged?"

"Pentonville."

Michael thought how Mrs. Murdoch in Neptune Crescent would shudder some Tuesday morning in the near future.

"I'm sorry you should have had to come all this way to find me," Michael said. He hated himself for being polite to the inspector, but he could not help it. He rang the bell.

"Oh, Dawkins, will you give Inspector—what is your name, by the bye?"

"Dawkins," said the inspector.

"How curious!" Michael laughed.

"Yes, sir," the inspector laughed.

"Lunch in the gun room, Dawkins. You must be hungry."

"Well, sir, I could do with a snack, I daresay." He followed his namesake from the room, and outside Michael could hear them begin to chatter of the coincidence.

"But supposing I'd been in the same state of life as Meats," Michael said to himself. "What devil's web wouldn't they be trying to spin round me?"

He was seized with fury at himself for his cowardice. He had thought of nothing but his own reputation ever since Meats had been arrested. He had worried over the opinion of a police inspector; had been ashamed of the appearance of the rooms; had actually been afraid that he would be implicated in the disgraceful affair. So long as it had been easy to flatter himself with the pleasure he was giving or the good he was doing to Meats, he had kept him with money. Now when Meats had been dragged away, he was anxious to disclaim the whole acquaintanceship for fear of the criticism of a big man with a bristly mustache. The despair in Meats' last cry to him echoed round this library. He had seen society in action: not all the devils and fiends imagined by mediæval monks were so horrible as those big men with bristly mustaches. What did they know of Meats and his life? What did they care, but that they were paid by society to remove rubbish? Justice had decreed that Meats should be arrested, and like a dead rat in the gutter he was swept up by these scavengers. What compact had he broken that men should freeze to stones and crush him? He had broken the laws of men and the laws of God; he had committed murder. And were not murders as foul being committed every moment? Murdered ambition, murdered love, murdered pity, murdered gratitude, murdered faith, did none of these cry out for vengeance?

Society had seized the murderer, and it was useless to cry out. Himself was as impotent as the prisoner. Meats had sinned against the hive: this infernal hive, herd, pack, swarm, whichever word expressed what he felt to be the degradation of an interdependent existence. Mankind was become a great complication of machinery fed by gold and directed by fear. Something was needed to destroy this gregarious organism. War and pestilence must come; but in the past these two had come often enough, and mankind was the same afterward. This ant-hill of a globe had been ravaged often enough, but the ants were all busy again carrying their mean little burdens of food hither and thither in affright for the comfort of their mean little lives.

"And I'm as bad as any of them," said Michael to himself. "I know I have obligations in Leppard Street, and I've run away from them because I'm afraid of what people will think. Of course, I always fail. I'm a coward."

He could not stay any longer at Hardingham. He must go and see about Mrs. Smith now. Society would be seizing her soon and bringing her miserable life to an end in whitewashed prison corridors. He must do something for Meats. Perhaps he would not be able to save him from death, but he must not sit here ringing bells for butlers called Dawkins to feed inspectors called Dawkins.

Stella came in with the first roses of the year.

"Aren't they beauties?"

"Yes, splendid. I'm going up to town this afternoon."

"But not for long?"

"I don't know. It depends. Do you know, Stella, it's an extraordinary thing, but ever since you've practically given up playing, I feel very much more alive. How do you account for that?"

"Well, I haven't given up playing for one thing," Stella contradicted.

"Stella do you ever feel inspired nowadays?"

"Not so much as I did," she admitted.

"I feel now as if I were on the verge of an inspiration."

"Not another Lily," she said quickly, with half a laugh.

"You've no right to sneer at me about that," he said fiercely. "You must be very careful, you know. *You'll* become flabby, if you aren't careful, here at Hardingham."

"Oh, Michael!" she laughed. "Don't look at me as if you were a Major Prophet. I won't become flabby. I shall start composing at once."

"There you are!" he cried triumphantly. "Never say again that I can't wake you up."

"You did not wake me up."

"I did. I did. And do you know I believe I've discovered that I'm an anarchist?"

"Is that your inspiration?"

"Who knows? It may be."

"Well, don't come and be anarchical down here, because Alan is going to stand at the next election."

"What on earth good would Alan be in Parliament?" Michael asked derisively. "He's much too happy."

"Michael, why are you so horrid about Alan nowadays?"

He was penitent in a moment at the suggestion, but when he said good-bye to Stella he had a curious feeling that from henceforth he was going to be stronger than her.

On reaching London, Michael went to see Castleton at the Temple, and he found him in chambers at the top of dusty stairs in King's Beach Walk.

"Lucky to get these, wasn't I?" said Castleton. By craning out of the window, the river was visible.

"I suppose you've never had a murder case yet?" Michael asked.

"Not yet," said Castleton. "In fact, I'm going in for Chancery work. And I shall get my first brief in about five years, with luck."

Michael inquired how one went to work to retain the greatest criminal advocate of the day, and Castleton said he would have to be approached through a solicitor.

"Well, will you get hold of him for me?"

Castleton looked rather blank.

"If you can't get him, get the next best, and so on. Tell him the man I want to defend hasn't a chance, and that's why I'm particularly anxious he should get off."

They discussed details for some time, and Castleton was astonished at Michael's wish to aid Meats.

"It seems very perverse," he said.

"Perverse!" Michael echoed. "And what about your profession? That is really the most perverse factor in modern life."

"But in this case," Castleton argued, "the victim seems so utterly worthless."

"Exactly," said Michael. "But as society never interfered when he was passively offensive, why, the moment he becomes actively offensive, should society have the right to put him out of the way? They never tried to cure him for his own good. Why should they kill him for their own?"

"You want to strike at the foundations of the legal system," said the barrister.

"Exactly," Michael agreed; and the argument came to an end because there was obviously nothing more to be said.

Castleton promises to do all he could for Meats, and also to keep Michael's name out of the business. As Michael walked down the stairs, it gave him a splendid satisfaction to think how already the law was being set in motion against the law. A blow for Inspector Dawkins. And what about the murdered girl? "She won't be helped by Meats' death," said Michael to himself. "Society is not considering her protection now any more than it did when she was alive." *No slops must be emptied here*: and as Michael read the ascetic command above the tap on the stairs he wondered for a moment if he were, after all, a sentimentalist.

Mrs. Cleghorne was very voluble when he reached Leppard Street.

"A nice set-out and no mistake!" she declared. "Half of the neighborhood have been peeping over my area railings as if the murder had been done in here. Mr. Cleghorne's quite hoarse with hollering out to them to keep off. And it never rains but what it pours. There's a poor woman gone and died here now. However, a funeral's a little more lively than the police nosing round, though her not having a blessed halfpenny and owing me three weeks on the rent it certainly won't be anything better than a pauper's funeral."

"What woman?" Michael asked.

"Oh, a invalid dressmaker which I've been very good to—a Mrs. Smith."

"Dead?" he echoed.

"Yes, dead, and laid out, and got a clergyman sitting with her body. What clergyman? Roman Catholic, I *should* say. It quite worried Mr. Cleghorne. He said it gave him the rats to have a priest hanging around so close at hand. You see, being asthmatic, he's read a lot about these Roman Catholics, and he doesn't hold with them. They're that underhand, he says, it makes him nervous."

"Can I see this priest?" Michael asked.

"Well, it's hardly the room you're accustomed to. I've really looked at her more as a charity than an actual lodger. In fact, my poor old mother has gone on at me something cruel for being so good to her."

"I think I should like to see this priest," Michael persisted.

Mrs. Cleghorne was with difficulty persuaded to show him the way, and she was evidently a little suspicious of the motive of his visit. They descended into the gloom of the basement, and the landlady pointed out to him the room that was down three steps and up another. She excused herself from coming too. The priest, a monkey-faced Irishman, was sitting on the pale blue chest, and as Michael entered, he did not look up from his Office.

"Is that you, Sister?" he asked. Then he perceived Michael and waited for him to explain his business.

"I wanted to ask about this poor woman."

Mrs. Smith lay under a sheet with candles winking at her head. Nothing was visible except her face still faintly rouged in the daylight.

"I was interested in her," Michael exclaimed.

"Indeed!" said the priest dryly. "I wouldn't have thought so."

"Is her cat here?"

"There was some sort of an animal, but the woman of the house took it off."

A silence followed, and Michael was aware of the priest's hostility.

"I suppose she didn't see her son before she died?" Michael went on. "Her son is with the Jesuits."

"You seem to know a great deal about the poor soul?"

"I thought I had managed to help her," said Michael, in a sad voice.

"Indeed?" commented the priest, even more dryly.

"And there is nothing I can do now?"

"Almighty God has taken her," said the priest. "There is nothing you can do."

"I could have some Masses said for her."

"Are you a Catholic?" the priest asked.

"No; but I fancy I shall be a Catholic," Michael said; and as he spoke it was like a rushing wind. He hurried out into the passage where a nun passed him in the gloom. "She will be praying," Michael thought, and, looking back over his shoulder, he said:

"Pray for me, Sister."

The nun was evidently startled by the voice, and went on quickly down the three steps and up the other into Mrs. Smith's den.

Michael climbed upstairs to interview the Solutionist. He found him lying in bed.

"Why wasn't that money paid regularly?" he asked severely.

"Who is it?" the Solutionist muttered, in fuddled accents. "Wanted the money myself. Had a glorious time. The cat's all right, and the poor old rabbits are dead. Can't give everybody a good time. Somebody's got to suffer in this world."

Michael left him, and without entering his old rooms again went away from Leppard Street.

The moment had come to visit Rome, and remembering how he had once dissuaded Maurice from going there, he felt some compunction now in telling him that he wanted to travel alone. However, it would be impossible to visit Rome for the first time with Maurice. In the studio he led up to his backing out of the engagement.

"About this going abroad," he began.

"I say, Michael, I don't think I can come just now. The editor of The Point of View wants a series of articles on the ballet, and I'm going to start on them at once."

It was a relief to Michael, and he wished Maurice good luck.

"Yes, I think they're going to be rather good," he said confidently. "I'm going to begin with the Opera: then the Empire and the Alhambra: and in September there will be the new ballet at the Orient. Of course, I've got a theory about English ballet."

"Is there anything about which you haven't got a theory?" Michael asked. "Hullo, you've got the Venetian mirror from Ararat House. I'm so glad!"

"I've arranged all that," Maurice said. "Lily Haden has gone to live with a girl called Sylvia Scarlett. Rather a terror, I thought."

"Yes, I had an idea you'd find her a bit difficult."

"Oh, but I scored off her in the end," said Maurice quickly.

"Congratulations," said Michael. "Well, I'm going to Rome."

"I say, rather hot."

"So much the better."

"I used to be rather keen on Rome, but I've a theory it's generally a disappointment. However, I suppose I shall have to go one day."

"Yes, I don't think Rome ought to miss your patronage, Maurice."

They parted as intimate friends, but while Michael was going downstairs from the studio he thought that it might very easily be for the last time.

His mother was at home for tea; lots of women and a bishop were having a committee about something. When they had all rustled away into the mellow June evening, Michael asked what had been accomplished.

"It's this terrible state of the London streets," said Mrs. Fane. "Something has got to be done about these miserable women. The Bishop of Chelsea has promised to bring in some kind of a bill in Parliament. He feels so strongly about it."

"What does he feel?" Michael asked.

"Why, of course, that they shouldn't be allowed."

"The remedy lies with him," Michael said. "He must take them the Sacraments."

"My dearest boy, what are you talking about? He does his best. He's always picking them up and driving them home in his brougham. He can't do more than that. Really he quite thrilled us with some of his experiences."

Michael laughed and took hold of her hand.

"What would you say if I told you that I was thinking very seriously of being a priest?"

"Oh, my dear Michael, and you look so particularly nice in tweeds!"

Michael laughed and went upstairs to pack. He would leave London to-morrow morning.

CHAPTER X

THE OLD WORLD

The train crashed southward from Paris through the night; and when dawn was quivering upon the meadows near Chambéry Michael was sure with an almost violent elation that he had left behind him the worst hardships of thought. Waterfalls swayed from the mountains, and the gray torrents they fed plunged along beside the train. Down through Italy they traveled all day, past the cypresses, and the olive-trees wise and graceful in the sunlight. It was already dusk when they reached the Campagna, and through the ghostly light the ghostly flowers and grasses shimmered for a while and faded out. It was hot traveling after sunset; but when the lights of Rome broke in a sudden blaze and the train reached the station it was cool upon the platform. Michael let a porter carry his luggage to a hotel close at hand. Then he walked quickly down the Esquiline Hill. He wandered on past the restaurants and the barber shops, caring for nothing but the sensation of walking down a wide street in Rome.

"There has been nothing like this," he said, "since I walked down the High. There will be nothing like this ever again."

Suddenly in a deserted square he was looking over a parapet at groups of ruined columns, and immediately afterward he was gazing up at one mighty column jet black against the starshine. He saw that it was figured with innumerable horses and warriors.

"We must seek for truth in the past," he said.

How this great column affected him with the secrets of the past! It was only by that made so much mightier than the bars of his cot in Carlington Road, which had once seemed to hold passions, intrigues, rumors, ambitions, and revenges. All that he had once dimly perceived as shadowed forth by them was here set forth absolutely. What was this column called? He looked round vaguely for an indication of the name. What did the name matter? There would be time to find a name in the morning. There would be time in the morning to begin again the conduct of his life. The old world held the secret; and he would accept this solitary and perdurable column as the symbol of that secret.

"All that I have done and experienced so far," Michael thought, "would not scratch this stone. I have been concerned for the happiness of other people without gratitude for the privilege of service. I have been given knowledge and I fancied I was given disillusion. If now I offer myself to God very humbly, I give myself to the service of man. Man for man standing in his own might is a blind and arrogant leader. The reason why the modern world is so critical of the fruits of Christianity after nineteen hundred years is because they have expected it from the beginning to be a social panacea. God has only offered to the individual the chance to perfect himself, but the individual is much more anxious about his neighbor. How in a moment our little herds are destroyed, whether in ships on the sea or in towns by earthquake, or by the great illusions of political experiment! Soon will come a great war, and everybody will discover it has come either because people are Christians or because they are not Christians. Nobody will think it is because each man wants to interfere with the conduct of his neighbor. That woman in Leppard Street who died in the peace of God, how much more was she a Christian than me, who, without perceiving the beam in my own eye, have trotted round operating on the motes of other people. And once I had to make an effort to kiss her in fellowship. Rome! Rome! How parochial you make my youth!"

The last exclamation was uttered aloud.

"Meditating upon the decline and fall of the Roman Empire?" said a voice.

A man in a black cloak was speaking.

"No; I was thinking of the pettiness of youthful tragedies," said Michael.

"There is only one tragedy for youth."

"And that is?"

"Age," said the stranger.

"And what is the tragedy of age?"

"There is no tragedy of age," said the stranger.

THE END

CPSIA information can be obtained at www.ICGtesting.com
Printed in the USA
BVOW05s1647120115

382922BV00016B/155/P